Robert Main, Manuel John Johnson

The Radcliffe Catalogue of 6317 stars

chiefly circumpolar, reduced to the epoch of 1845.0

Robert Main, Manuel John Johnson

The Radcliffe Catalogue of 6317 stars
chiefly circumpolar, reduced to the epoch of 1845.0

ISBN/EAN: 9783337423230

Printed in Europe, USA, Canada, Australia, Japan

Cover: Foto ©Andreas Hilbeck / pixelio.de

More available books at **www.hansebooks.com**

THE
RADCLIFFE CATALOGUE

OF

6317 STARS,

CHIEFLY CIRCUMPOLAR,

REDUCED TO

THE EPOCH 1845.0;

FORMED FROM THE OBSERVATIONS MADE AT

THE RADCLIFFE OBSERVATORY,

UNDER THE SUPERINTENDENCE OF

MANUEL JOHN JOHNSON, M.A.

LATE RADCLIFFE OBSERVER.

WITH INTRODUCTION BY

THE REV. ROBERT MAIN, M.A.

RADCLIFFE OBSERVER.

PUBLISHED BY ORDER OF THE RADCLIFFE TRUSTEES.

OXFORD,
J. H. AND JAS. PARKER.
1860.

ERRATA IN THE RADCLIFFE CATALOGUE.

Page.	No.	Column.				
2	4	Precession	*for*	3ˢ.100	*read*	3ˢ.097
...	21	Mag.		7.3		7.6
3	10	Mean year R.		44.3		44.8
5	31	Mean N.P.D. R.		48′		50′
25	394	,,		35″.8		35″.0
41	675	Mean N.P.D. R.		97° 17′ 58″.9		40° 34′ 28″.8
...	...	Sec. Var.		0″.26		0″.30
...	...	No. of Obs. R.		1		2
...	...	Mean year R.		52.0		49.0
...	676	Mean N.P.D. R.		40° 34′ 28″.8		38° 9′ 27″.8
...	...	,, G.	*insert* 28″.0			
...	...	Precession	*for*	− 16″.96	*read*	− 16″.94
...	...	Sec. Var.		+ 0″.30		+ 0″.32
...	...	No. of Obs. R.		2		3
...	...	Mean year R.		49.0		49.6
...	...	,, G.	*insert* 12.9			
...	677	Mean N.P.D. R.	*for*	38° 9′ 27″.8	*read*	97° 17′ 58″.9
...	...	,, G.	*dele* 28″.0			
...	...	Precession	*for*	− 16″.94	*read*	− 16″.96
...	...	Sec. Var.		+ 0″.32		+ 0″.26
...	...	No. of Obs. R.		3		1
...	...	Mean year R.		49.6		52.0
...	...	,, G.	*dele* 12.9			
...	680	Mean N.P.D. R.	*for*	9″.2	*read*	9″.0
43	715	,, R.		52″.0		51″.7
60	1013 & 1014	The Right Ascensions belong to the same Star; *dele* the latter, and make the following corrections :				
...	1013	Estimates of Mag.	*for*	3	*read*	4
...	...	Mean R.A.		3ʰ 26ᵐ 24ˢ.71		3ʰ 26ᵐ 24ˢ.80
...	...	Number of Obs.		1		2
65	1111	Mean N.P.D. R.		42° 16′		42° 19′
113	1942	,,		33° 8′		33° 10′
124	2148	Mag.	*insert* 6.4			
...	...	Estimates of Mag.	*insert* 3			
135	2337	Mean N.P.D. R.	*for*	22° 27′	*read*	22° 28′
142	2462	Sec. Var. in R.A.		− 1ˢ.834		− 1ˢ.749
...	2463	,,		− 4ˢ.044		− 4ˢ.063
143	2462	Sec. Var. in N.P.D.		+ 0″.75		+ 0″.72
...	2463	,,		+ 0″.92		+ 1″.02
177	3055	Mean N.P.D. R.		36° 33′		36° 35′
202	3499	Mean R.A. G.		49ˢ.25		9ˢ.25
216	3748	Sec. Var. in R.A.		+ 0ˢ.003		+ 0ˢ.001
...	3749	,,		+ 0ˢ.258		+ 0ˢ.251
246	4287	Mag.	*insert* 5.6			
...	...	Estimates of Mag.	*insert* 4			
257	4446	Mean N.P.D. G.	*for*	4″.7	*read*	4″.6
326	5681	Sec. Var. in R.A.		− 0ˢ.069		− 0ˢ.073
...	5689	,,		− 0ˢ.029		− 0ˢ.034
361	6277	Adopted P. M. in N.P.D.		− 0″.02		+ 0″.02

Page.	No. in Gr.	Column.		
6	144	Bessel's Bradley	insert 65	
...	166	Precession in R.A.	for $3^s.321$	read $3^s.315$
...	...	Precession in N.P.D.	$19''.676$	$19''.693$
7	177	Bessel's Bradley	insert 92	
...	195	Bessel's Bradley	insert 95	
9	257	Precession in R.A.	for $3^s.551$	read $3^s.543$
...	280	N.P.D. Jan. 1, 1810.	$4'.30$	$43'.0$
11	338	Precession in R.A.	$5^s.314$	$5^s.133$
13	420	Bessel's Bradley	insert 261	
14	421 to 455	Precession in N.P.D.	for $+$	read $-$
15	459	Hevelius	insert 2 Persei	
...	462 & 463	Flamsteed's No.	insert 59 Andromedæ	
19	620	Bessel's Bradley	insert 443	
20	644	Precession in R.A.	for $4^s.134$	read $4^s.116$
21	684	Bessel's Bradley	insert 473	
23	745	R.A.	for 36^m	read 37^m
24	790	Precession in R.A.	$4^s.620$	$4^s.617$
24 & 25	805 & 806	Hevelius	dele 14?	
25	808	Hevelius	insert 14	
...	811	Precession in N.P.D.	for $9''.751$	read $9''.571$
...	817	N.P.D.	$59'$	$58'$
29	946	Precession in R.A.	$4^s.369$	$4^s.399$
32	1056	Bessel's Bradley	insert 861	
33	1119	Precession in R.A.	for $85^s.043$	read $85^s.057$
35	1172	Flamsteed's No.	insert 7 Lyncis	
...	1184	N.P.D.	for $23°$	read $33°$
37	1255	Piazzi	insert 285	
...	1259	Precession in R.A.	for $13^s.300$	read $13^s.297$
39	1297 & 1298	Flamsteed's No.	insert 20 Lyncis	
40	1339	Hevelius	insert 28	
43	1456	Flamsteed's No.	insert B F 1190	
44	1478	Flamsteed's No.	dele 7 Ursæ Maj.	
45	1534	Precession in R.A.	for $4^s.509$	read $4^s.500$
49	1658	"	$3^s.560$	$3^s.556$
51	1737.	"	$3^s.579$	$3^s.565$
55	1863	Flamsteed's No.	insert B F 1693	
...	1867	R.A.	for $9^s.26$	read $44^s.24$
...	...	Precession in R.A.	$3^s.020$	$3^s.017$
...	...	Precession in N.P.D.	$20''.028$	$20''.026$
56	1923	Precession in R.A.	$0^s.775$	$0^s.779$
57	1937	Pond	insert 520	
58	1984	Flamsteed's No.	dele 22 Can. Ven.	
62	2128	Precession in N.P.D.	for $16''.061$	read $16''.029$
64	2185	Flamsteed's No.	insert 8 Urs. Min.	

Page.	No. in Gr.	Column.			
65	2226	Bessel's Bradley	*insert* 1950		
...	...	Piazzi	*insert* 73		
...	...	Flamsteed's No.	*insert* 51 Boötis μ.		
...	2227	Piazzi	*insert* 74		
66	2270	N.P.D.	*for* 1′	*read*	2′
67	2309	R.A.	*for* 13ˢ.78	*read*	33ˢ.78
...	...	Precession in N.P.D.	9″.929		9″.904
68	2332	N.P.D.	45′		46′
70	2410	No. of Obs. in N.P.D.	4		3
...	2413	No. of Obs. (R.A. & N.P.D.)	5		6
...	2414	Piazzi	*insert* 4		
71	2416	Precession in R.A.	*for* 0ˢ.690	*read*	0ˢ.692
...	...	N.P.D.	23′		33′
...	2437	Precession in N.P.D	3ˢ.585		3ˢ.549
...	2445	R.A.	29ᵐ		28ᵐ
...	...	Precession in R.A.	1ˢ.154		1ˢ.156
...	...	Precession in N.P.D.	2″.665		2″.752
...	2446	R.A.	29ᵐ		28ᵐ
...	...	Precession in R.A.	1ˢ.155		1ˢ.157
...	...	Precession in N.P.D.	2″.657		2″.744
72	2479	Bessel's Bradley	2248		2245
...	...	Piazzi	295		289
...	...	Flamsteed's No.	*dele* 90 Herculis ƒ		
...	2484	Bessel's Bradley	*insert* 2248		
...	...	Piazzi	*insert* 295		
...	...	Flamsteed's No.	*insert* 90 Herculis ƒ		
75	2562	No. of Obs. (R.A. & N.P.D.)	*for* 4	*read*	5
81	2780	Flamsteed's No.	*dele* 19 Lyræ		
82	2816	Precession in R.A.	*for* 1ˢ.340	*read*	1ˢ.380
86	2943	Bessel's Bradley	2534		2529
...	...	Flamsteed's No.	*dele* 19 Cygni		
...	2949	Bessel's Bradley	*insert* 2534		
...	...	Flamsteed's No.	*insert* 19 Cygni		
89	3052	Precession in R.A.	*for* 0ˢ.952	*read*	0ˢ.955
93	3196	Flamsteed's No.	*dele* 44 Cygni		
...	3210	"	*insert* 46 Cygni ω^3		
96	3292	Precession in R.A.	*for* 2ˢ.271	*read*	2ˢ.269
98	3377	Bessel's Bradley	*insert* 2748		
99	3412	"	*dele* 2775		
...	...	Flamsteed's No.	*dele* 68 Cygni A		
...	3426	Precession in R.A.	*for* 0ˢ.173	*read*	0ˢ.169
...	...	N.P.D.	32′		33′
...	3427	Bessel's Bradley	*insert* 2775		
...	...	Flamsteed's No.	*insert* 68 Cygni A		
100	*for* 3838		*read* 3438		
103	3545	Piazzi	*insert* 256		

Page.	No. in Gr.	Column.				
103	3550	Precession in R.A.	*for*	1ˢ.743	*read*	1ˢ.758
110	3810	Precession in N.P.D.		11″.355		18″.355
111	3844	Bessel's Bradley	*insert* 2990			
116	4024	Bessel's Bradley	*insert* 3086			
118	4080	,,	*insert* 3131			
123	4240	,,	*for*	3215	*read*	3216
...	4241	,,		3216		3217

DISCORDANCES IN GROOMBRIDGE'S CATALOGUE.

Page.	No. in Rad.		
15	215	Groombridge has	52′ in N.P.D.
35	558	....	23′ ......
71	1207	....	27′ ......
...	1217	....	32′ ......
81	1390	....	15′ ......
121	2076	....	7′ ......
145	2493	....	22′ ......
151	2593	....	46′ ......
...	2598	....	43′ ......
175	3036	....	6′ ......
177	3073	....	32′ ......
188	3251	....	37ᵐ in R.A.
237	4113	....	6′ in N.P.D.
243	4225	....	26′ ......
244	4238	....	10ᵐ in R.A.
245	,,	....	49′ in N.P.D.
255	4425	....	30′ ......
279	4849	....	39′ ......
284	4944	....	42ᵐ in R.A.
285	,,	....	38′ in N.P.D.
291	5039	....	52′ ......
307	5342	....	23′ ......
345	5998	....	49′ ......
...	6007	....	10′ ......
353	6127	....	35′ ......
361	6288	....	41° 7′ ......

INTRODUCTION.

The Radcliffe Catalogue of Stars contains the result of *all* the Star-observing at the Radcliffe Observatory from 1840 to the end of the year 1853. For the year 1854, only Fundamental Stars are included and those which were necessary to make more complete the reobservation of Groombridge's Catalogue of Circumpolar Stars; and, for the following years as far as 1859, in general such observations only were used as were necessary to complete the results of former years for the Stars already included in the Catalogue.

The compilation of the Catalogue was commenced as early as the year 1850; and, at the time of the death of Mr. Johnson, the whole of the work was in the hands of the printer, and a few sheets were actually printed off under his superintendence. After his decease, the printing of the remainder of the Catalogue went on without serious interruption till its completion, under the superintendence of Mr. Quirling, the First Assistant of the Observatory.

The chief labour of the comparison of the proofs with the manuscript was performed by Mr. Luff, of whose most valuable and almost gratuitous labours mention was so frequently made by Mr. Johnson in the Introductions to separate volumes of the Radcliffe Observations. While treating of the matters relating to the history of the Catalogue, it is right to mention, that the greater portion of the calculations was performed by Mr. Luff, in the intervals of leisure snatched from his business occupations, sometimes with considerable difficulty; and I may be allowed to say, that I believe there are very few instances on record of services so disinterested and so important to science performed by a private individual, as are those of this Gentleman.

The MSS. used in the compilation of the Catalogue have been with few exceptions bound up and labelled, and they admit of very easy reference. The largest portion of them consists of two sets of folio books, of which one, labelled "*Materials for the Catalogue*," contains the results of the reduction of all the Stars in each yearly Catalogue from 1840 to 1853 to the epoch of the Radcliffe Catalogue, namely, 1845.0; and the other, labelled "*Great Catalogue*," contains the combination of the results of the separate years to produce the result printed in the Catalogue. These latter volumes are four in number, three containing only Groombridge's Stars, and the fourth the Stars not found in that Catalogue. There are two other bound volumes containing the computations of Precessions, one for the Stars in Groombridge, and the other for the remaining Stars. There is also a series of ten other volumes at present unbound, which appear to contain only a transcript of the results for each year when reduced to 1845, as computed in the series labelled "*Materials for the Catalogue*." The remaining MS. books unbound are three in number, containing the "*Reduction of Groombridge's Places to* 1845," and "*Reductions of Stars within* 10° *of the Pole*."

I will proceed now to explain the processes of reduction which have been used in the compilation of the Catalogue, and it will conduce to clearness if I take the columns in order.

Columns 1 and 2 require no explanation, being simply the ordinal numbers of the Stars in the Radcliffe Catalogue and in Groombridge's Catalogue respectively.

Column 3 gives the final estimation of the magnitude of each Star as determined by the results of all the observations; weights in some respect arbitrary being given by the observers to the separate estimations, depending upon the state of the sky and other circumstances.

Column 4 gives the number of estimations of magnitude for each Star, on which the estimation in column 3 depends.

Column 5 gives the final result for Right Ascension, as deduced from the combination of the results for different years reduced to 1845, by application of the Precession, and, in some cases, of the Proper Motion.

The separate results for Right Ascension are taken without alteration from the yearly Catalogues of Stars-places given in the observations of each year, and the Annual Variations which have been employed to reduce them to the epoch of the Radcliffe Catalogue, namely 1845, are those given in the Catalogues for the different years. The Annual

Variations, for Stars included in the Nautical Almanac, are taken from that work; the others were rigorously computed; in earlier years, from the elements given in the Astronomical Society's Catalogue, which are those of Bessel's *Fundamenta* for the epoch 1830; and in later years from the elements given in the British Association Catalogue, which are those of Bessel's *Tabulæ Regiomontanæ* for the epoch 1850. The trifling difference in the values of the constants used is of scarcely any importance; but an error having its origin in the use of the Annual Variations of the Nautical Almanac has arisen, which affects the places of a few of the Fundamental Stars. The error is of the following nature. For several of these Stars, including *a* Andromedæ, *a* Arietis, Aldebaran, Castor, *e* Hydræ, Regulus, *δ* Leonis, *β* Leonis, and *a* Serpentis, the Geometrical Precessions are given in the Nautical Almanac as far as the year 1847 inclusive, but afterwards Proper Motions are included in the Annual Variations; for others, including Procyon, Pollux, and *a* Aquilæ, the Proper Motions are introduced after the year 1840. The use of the Annual Variations of the Nautical Almanac has therefore introduced errors which became sensible in the Right Ascensions of the Stars above mentioned, and the corrections to be applied are given in the following Table.

Stars.	Correction to Mean R.A. 1845, Jan. 1.
	s.
a Andromedæ	+ 0.03
a Arietis.............	+ 0.04
Aldebaran	+ 0.02
Castor................	− 0.02
Procyon	− 0.04
Pollux	− 0.07
e Hydræ	− 0.03
Regulus	− 0.02
δ Leonis.............	+ 0.04
β Leonis	− 0.02
a Serpentis	+ 0.02
a Aquilæ	+ 0.03

None of the other Stars are sensibly affected by these errors.

In combining the results for R.A. for different years when reduced to 1845, half weight is given to each observation made with the old Transit

Instrument, that is, to the observations of the years from 1840 to 1843 inclusive; otherwise weights are given strictly proportional to the number of observations.

The equinox to which the Right Ascensions are referred is fundamentally that of the Nautical Almanac of 1840, the times of transit of the Stars employed for Clock Error in that year being compared with the Right Ascensions given in the Nautical Almanac. In 1841 and succeeding years the same equinox was fundamentally used, that is, the assumed Right Ascensions of the Clock Stars are deduced generally from the results of 1840, and so on for all the succeeding years. In the later years of Mr. Johnson's Directorship, however, it was his practice not to confine himself to the Stars of the Nautical Almanac, nor even to those whose places were settled by a great number of his own observations, but to use for Clock Errors any Stars of a magnitude higher than the 8th, whose Right Ascensions had been determined by more than one observation in the previous years. On the whole, therefore, the equinox employed is based on that of the Nautical Almanac of 1840, without any attempt at independent determination by observations of the Sun. This is stated explicitly in the Introduction to the " Provisional Catalogue of Stars" given in the volume for 1856, and in that Introduction Mr. Johnson compares the Right Ascensions of 62 Stars used for Clock Errors, with the Right Ascensions given in the Nautical Almanac for 1860, as determined in a great measure by Mr. Adams, and communicated by him to the Superintendent of that work. The result is as follows:

The Right Ascensions of the N.A. for 1840 are in excess of those of the N.A. for 1860 by $0^s.039$, while those deduced from the Radcliffe Observations are in excess of the N.A. for 1840 by $0^s.043$. Hence the Radcliffe Observations are in excess of the N.A. for 1860 by $0^s.08$. This statement with respect to the equinox might probably be sufficient, but a very easy and satisfactory way existing for comparing with the Greenwich Right Ascensions, I have thought it desirable to make the comparison. One of the epochs, namely, of the Greenwich Twelve-year Catalogue being 1845, it was only necessary to compare directly the Right Ascensions of the Stars employed for Clock Error by Mr. Johnson as given in the Radcliffe Catalogue, with their Right Ascensions as given in the Greenwich Catalogue, and the mean difference would be very accurately the difference of the equinoxes used in the two Catalogues.

The following Table gives an abstract of the results of this comparison for all Stars whose N.P.D. is not smaller than 40°. The only explanation required is, that the weights are determined as usual by the formula $\dfrac{nn'}{n+n'}$, where n and n' are the numbers of the observations in the Greenwich and Radcliffe Catalogues.

Hour of R.A.	Extent of Group.	Least Number of Obs.	Diff. of R.A. (Green. 12-year C. —Rad.)	Weights.
			s.	
0ʰ to iʰ	α Andromedæ to ε Piscium	166	0.00	109
i to ii	e Piscium to α Arietis	164	0.00	95
ii to iii	ξ¹ Ceti to κ Persei.....................	126	— 0.06	72
iii to iv	δ Arietis to A¹ Tauri	78	— 0.04	44
iv to v	μ Persei to 11 Orionis	116	+ 0.01	68
v to vi	Capella to 2 Geminorum	192	0.00	131
vi to vii	η Geminorum to ζ Geminorum.....	132	— 0.02	86
vii to viii	63 Aurigæ to φ Geminorum	300	— 0.03	187
viii to ix	ζ¹ Cancri to κ Cancri	158	— 0.05	92
ix to x	36 Lyncis to η Leonis	168	— 0.05	97
x to xi	Regulus to χ Leonis	132	— 0.09	77
xi to xii	ψ Ursæ Maj. to o Virginis	181	— 0.09	112
xii to xiii	2 Canum Venat. to g Virginis	93	— 0.10	59
xiii to xiv	θ Virginis to η Boötis	178	— 0.08	110
xiv to xv	κ Virginis to 44 Boötis	192	— 0.07	125
xv to xvi	47 Boötis to υ Herculis	157	— 0.03	114
xvi to xvii	ν Scorpii to ε Herculis	74	— 0.05	54
xvii to xviii	η Ophiuchi to ν Ophiuchi	156	— 0.03	92
xviii to xix	μ Sagittarii to ζ Aquilæ..............	213	— 0.03	145
xix to xx	π Sagittarii to 26 Cygni	288	— 0.02	193
xx to xxi	a² Capricorni to ξ Cygni	54	— 0.03	37
xxi to xxii	ν Aquarii to ι Aquarii	261	— 0.02	168
xxii to xxiii	θ Aquarii to α Pegasi	175	— 0.01	103
xxiii to 0	4 Andromedæ to 33 Piscium.........	95	— 0.02	59

The result of this comparison is so far satisfactory, as shewing that, on the whole, the equinox to which the Right Ascensions of the Radcliffe Catalogue have been referred does not differ materially from that of the Greenwich Twelve-year Catalogue; but there is a variation in the differences of Right Ascension for different hours, which is too well marked to be accidental, and of which I am unable to give any account. From xʰ to xvʰ, namely, the mean of the differences is — 0ˢ.09, while the mean for the remaining hours is only 0ˢ.025.

There is no doubt that this anomaly depends on something which has affected the Radcliffe observations, or their process of reduction, because similar differences are found to exist in the mean Right Ascensions of the Fundamental Stars as deduced by *Wolfers* for the year 1860, when compared with Johnson's results from the observations of 1854 and 1855 reduced to 1860 as given in the sixteenth volume of the Radcliffe Observations. (*Tabulæ Reductionum Observationum Astronomicarum Annis 1860 usque ad 1880 respondentes, auctore J. Ph. Wolfers, Præfatio*, p. lxii.) Still the origin of it is very obscure, and, after thinking of many possible causes, I do not find one which is altogether adequate. It may be however remarked, that the hours of Right Ascension for which the differences are greatest, are those which correspond to the Spring and early Summer months for evening observations of the stars in those hours.

Column 6 contains the seconds of R.A. of Groombridge, brought up to 1845 by the precessional motion in the interval between 1810 and 1845. For all Stars whose N.P.D.'s are greater than 10°, this is done by taking the mean of the geometrical precessions given in Groombridge for 1810, and in the Radcliffe Catalogue for 1845, (after multiplying the former by 1.0007, to reduce them to the precessions of the *Tabulæ Regiomontanæ*,) and multiplying this mean by 35, to produce the whole precessional motion. For Stars closer to the pole than 10°, the reduction is made rigorously by Bessel's method, the value of $z + \lambda$ which is employed being $+ 13' 22''5$, that of $z' - \lambda'$, $+ 13' 29''4$, and that of θ, $+ 11' 42''0$.

Mr. Quirling has made a very diligent and useful examination of the differences between the results of the Radcliffe Catalogue and those of Groombridge, which will be given in connexion with the lists of errata.

The precessions given in the 7th column are simply geometrical, and are computed rigorously from the elements of the *Tabulæ*, as I have satisfied myself by comparison of several given for the same Stars in the British Association Catalogue, the differences being almost always insignificant, when those of the B.A.C. are reduced to 1845.

The Secular Variations given in the 8th column are, for the Stars of Groombridge's Catalogue, found by simply comparing the precessions given in Groombridge (multiplied by 1.0007) with those given in the Radcliffe Catalogue, and multiplying the difference by $\frac{100}{35}$. This is sufficiently accurate for all practical purposes. For Stars not in Groombridge they are taken generally from a table of double entry computed by Mr. Luff for intervals of 15^m of Right Ascension and of 10° of North Polar Distance; but, for stars very close to the pole, they have been computed accurately from the formulæ. The variations of the constants *m* and *n* are not taken into account.

The *Adopted Proper Motions* in column 9, are those assumed by Mr. Johnson for application to the mean of the Right Ascensions as deduced from the various years, by the help of the numbers in column 11, which gives the mean year and fraction of the year for the observations of each Star at the Radcliffe Observatory.

Column 10 gives the number of observations of R.A. of each Star made at the Radcliffe Observatory.

Column 11 has been already explained.

Column 12 gives the mean year and fraction of the year for the observations used in compiling Groombridge's Catalogue. For the purpose of obtaining these numbers, Mr. Johnson borrowed the Groombridge MSS. from the Royal Astronomical Society, and they form a very valuable addition to the Catalogue.

The remaining columns of the Catalogue on the right hand page require very little explanation, with the exception of columns 2 and 10, the explanation which has been given for the Right Ascensions applying generally to the North Polar Distances.

The numbers in column 2 (right hand page) are deduced by combination of the mean N.P.D's for the different years precisely as in the case of Right Ascensions, excepting that certain corrections are applied to the mean result (in addition to that for proper motion). These corrections are for refraction, latitude, and polar-point, and are taken from the Table at pages xxvi and xxvii of the Introduction to the volume for 1854, which is the result of an elaborate discussion of all the observations of preceding years capable of determining these quantities.

There is an error in the places of all the Stars observed in 1840, arising from the introduction in that year of a constant correction of $+$ 0″6 to direct results, and of $-$ 0″6 to reflexion results, for discordance of direct and reflexion results.

This correction was not continued beyond the year 1840; and as the results of 1840, as well as of succeeding years, were included in the general discussion given in the volume for 1854, the results of 1840 should first have been cleared of this correction before proceeding farther.

The corrections due on account of this error are for the most part small, but, being the result of an oversight in the compilation of the Catalogue, I have thought it worth while to compute them for each Star observed in N.P.D. in the year 1840, and they are contained in the following Table.

No. in Cat.	Name of Star.	Corr. to N.P.D.	No. in Cat.	Name of Star.	Corr. to N.P.D.	No. in Cat.	Name of Star.	Corr. to N.P.D.
		′			′			′
5	β Cassiop.	− 0.3	540	ε Cassiop.	− 0.2	1316	α Camelop.	− 0.1
13	6 Gr.	− 0.1	578	47 Cassiop.......	− 0.2	1366	*	− 0.1
35	23 Gr...........	− 0.4	580	50 Cassiop.......	− 0.4	1367	β Camelop.	− 0.2
39	35 Piscium......	− 0.6	584	49 Cassiop.......	− 0.3	1396	η Aurigæ	− 0.2
42	29 Gr...........	− 0.3	609	54 Cassiop.......	− 0.3	1433	Capella	+ 0.1
46	31 Gr...........	− 0.4	615	α Arietis.........	− 0.3	1511	986 Gr.	− 0.3
57	26 Andromedæ.	− 0.3	625	h Persei	− 0.3	1627	37 Camelop.....	− 0.3
68	48 Gr...........	− 0.2	658	8 Persei	− 0.4	1668	*	− 0.2
75	53 Gr...........	− 0.2	659	χ Persei	− 0.3	1816	Sirius	− 0.1
84	58 Gr...........	− 0.2	689	i Persei	− 0.3	1870	ε Canis Maj. ...	− 0.1
88	12 Cassiop......	− 0.3	704	506 Gr.	− 0.1	1982	Castor	− 0.2
90	62 Gr...........	− 0.3	706	511 Gr.	− 0.3	2013	Procyon	− 0.2
110	13 Cassiop.	− 0.3	763	537 Gr.	− 0.4	2058	53 Camelop. ...	− 0.2
116	λ Cassiop.	− 0.5	777	θ Persei	− 0.3	2087	55 Camelop. ...	− 0.3
126	κ Cassiop.	− 0.4	784	γ Ceti...........	− 0.3	2111	29 Lyncis	− 0.3
157	ζ Cassiop.	− 0.3	800	η Persei	− 0.5	2242	ι Ursæ Maj.	− 0.3
181	120 Gr.	− 0.2	816	τ Persei..........	− 0.3	2272	σ² Ursæ Maj. ...	− 0.1
184	ξ Cassiop.	− 0.3	834	581 Gr.	− 0.2	2292	17 Ursæ Maj....	− 0.2
192	21 Cassiop.	− 0.1	858	γ Persei	− 0.2	2293	e Ursæ Maj.	− 0.1
217	ν Cassiop.	− 0.2	860	601 Gr.	− 0.3	2340	α Hydræ	− 0.3
224	ν Andromedæ..	− 0.1	914	634 Gr.	− 0.2	2345	d Ursæ Maj. ...	− 0.1
433	ω Andromedæ..	− 0.2	937	a Persei	− 0.3	2370	27 Ursæ Maj....	− 0.2
442	A Cassiop.	− 0.1	969	678 Gr.	− 0.3	2398	υ Ursæ Maj.....	− 0.3
447	325 Gr.	− 0.3	973	*	− 0.2	2401	φ Ursæ Maj....	− 0.1
453	329 Gr.	− 0.2	981	σ Persei.........	− 0.4	2411	31 Ursæ Maj....	− 0.3
459	χ Cassiop.	− 0.3	990	684 Gr.	− 0.4	2418	19 Leo. Min. ...	− 0.2
470	40 Cassiop.	− 0.5	1011	ψ Persei.........	− 0.4	2431	1601 Gr..........	− 0.3
483	51 Andromedæ.	− 0.2	1029	716 Gr.	− 0.3	2468	λ Ursæ Maj. ...	− 0.4
489	χ Andromedæ..	− 0.2	1039	723 Gr.	− 0.4	2487	μ Ursæ Maj. ...	− 0.2
492	351 Gr.	− 0.4	1044	γ Camelop.......	− 0.1	2501	36 Ursæ Maj....	− 0.4
493	354 Gr.	− 0.3	1088	753 Gr.	− 0.2	2514	37 Ursæ Maj....	− 0.1
498	362 Gr.	− 0.3	1152	779 Gr.	− 0.3	2533	38 Ursæ Maj....	− 0.4
501	44 Cassiop.	− 0.4	1189	808 Gr.	− 0.5	2539	1673 Gr..........	− 0.3
513	54 Andromedæ.	− 0.3	1206	818 Gr.	− 0.2	2542	39 Ursæ Maj....	− 0.2
518	376 Gr.	− 0.5	1240	1 Camelop. (1st)	− 0.3	2573	44 Ursæ Maj....	− 0.3
532	385 Gr.	− 0.3	1241	1 Camelop. (2d)	− 0.2	2578	ω Ursæ Maj. ...	− 0.3
533	386 Gr.	− 0.2	1243	836 Gr.	− 0.2	2596	47 Ursæ Maj....	− 0.2
535	1 Persei	− 0.3	1301	4 Camelop.	− 0.2	2606	β Ursæ Maj....	− 0.1

No. in Cat.	Name of Star.	Corr. to N.P.D.	No. in Cat.	Name of Star.	Corr. to N.P.D.	No. in Cat.	Name of Star.	Corr. to N P.D.
		″			″			″
2616	51 Ursæ Maj....	− 0.3	2902	76 Ursæ Maj....	− 0.3	3219	2121 Gr...........	− 0.1
2626	ψ Ursæ Maj. ...	− 0.2	2905	1923 Gr..........	− 0.3	3225	5 Ursæ Min. ...	− 0.3
2634	1746 Gr...........	− 0.3	2912	1927 Gr..........	− 0.2	3232	2132 Gr..........	− 0.1
2640	δ Leonis.........	− 0.3	2913	1926 Gr..........	− 0.3	3238	2135 Gr..........	− 0.3
2661	55 Ursæ Maj....	− 0.3	3008	Spica	− 0.5	3255	2145 Gr..........	− 0.3
2669	σ Leonis.........	− 0.1	3009	ζ¹ Ursæ Maj....	− 0.2	3258	ε Boötis	− 0.2
2674	56 Ursæ Maj....	− 0.2	3010	ζ² Ursæ Maj....	− 0.1	3264	a² Libræ	− 0.3
2679	1776 Gr...........	− 0.3	3029	2002 Gr..........	− 0.4	3292	β Ursæ Min. ...	− 0.1
2701	λ Draconis......	− 0.2	3050	24 Canum Ven.	− 0.3	3308	β Boötis.........	− 0.2
2707	1797 Gr...........	− 0.3	3051	81 Ursæ Maj....	− 0.4	3325	2196 Gr..........	− 0.3
2712	2 Draconis......	− 0.2	3052	2017 Gr..........	− 0.3	3327	2192 Gr..........	− 0.2
2730	1816 Gr..........	− 0.2	3070	82 Ursæ Maj....	− 0.4	3336	2201 Gr..........	− 0.2
2733	3 Draconis......	− 0.2	3073	83 Ursæ Maj....	− 0.3	3343	2206 Gr..........	− 0.3
2741	χ Ursæ Maj. ...	− 0.3	3074	2032 Gr..........	− 0.3	3352	2214 Gr..........	− 0.2
2744	1825 Gr..........	− 0.1	3091	2044 Gr..........	− 0.3	3373	11 Ursæ Min....	− 0.4
2748	β Leonis	− 0.6	3094	84 Ursæ Maj....	− 0.4	3377	μ Boötis	− 0.4
2757	γ Ursæ Maj. ...	− 0.3	3095	η Ursæ Maj. ...	− 0.1	3386	γ Ursæ Min. ...	− 0.3
2761	65 Ursæ Maj....	− 0.1	3097	2051 Gr..........	− 0.3	3389	ι Draconis	− 0.3
2763	66 Ursæ Maj....	− 0.3	3104	2056 Gr..........	− 0.2	3400	ν¹ Boötis........	− 0.2
2767	1838 Gr.	− 0.2	3107	i Draconis	− 0.3	3412	μ Coronæ Bor..	− 0.4
2792	1850 Gr..........	− 0.1	3108	2063 Gr..........	− 0.1	3413	2253 Gr..........	− 0.4
2799	1853 Gr..........	− 0.3	3112	86 Ursæ Maj....	− 0.3	3421	φ Boötis	− 0.1
2809	68 Ursæ Maj....	− 0.4	3117	2066 Gr..........	− 0.3	3427	θ Ursæ Min. ...	− 0.2
2817	1 Canum Ven...	− 0.3	3134	2075 Gr..........	− 0.3	3438	a Serpentis	+ 0.3
2819	δ Ursæ Maj. ...	− 0.4	3138	a Draconis......	− 0.3	3458	2280 Gr..........	− 0.4
2822	2 Can. Ven. (2d)	− 0.3	3140	2078 Gr.....	− 0.3	3468	2288 Gr..........	− 0.2
2835	3 Canum Ven...	− 0.3	3142	13 Boötis	− 0.4	3473	4 Herculis	− 0.2
2842	70 Ursæ Maj....	− 0.5	3152	3 Ursæ Min. ...	− 0.3	3489	υ Herculis	− 0.2
2854	5 Canum Ven...	− 0.3	3165	κ² Boötis	− 0.3	3490	2302 Gr..........	− 0.2
2858	71 Ursæ Maj....	− 0.3	3170	2091 Gr..........	− 0.5	3493	θ Draconis......	− 0.2
2861	6 Canum Ven...	− 0.3	3172	4 Ursæ Min. ...	− 0.2	3504	φ Herculis......	− 0.1
2867	73 Ursæ Maj....	− 0.1	3176	λ Boötis.........	− 0.4	3511	2320 Gr..........	− 0.3
2872	74 Ursæ Maj....	− 0.3	3177	ι Boötis	− 0.4	3515	δ Ophiuchi......	− 0.6
2875	4 Draconis......	− 0.1	3198	2108 Gr..........	− 0.1	3533	2328 Gr..........	− ˋ0.3
2883	β Canum Ven..	− 0.2	3202	θ Boötis	− 0.3	3539	19 Ursæ Min. ...	− 0.2
2884	κ Draconis......	− 0.3	3209	g Boötis	− 0.2	3545	Antares	− 0.1
2888	1909 Gr..........	− 0.2	3211	2116 Gr..........	− 0.3	3556	2345 Gr..........	− 0.1
2893	9 Canum Ven...	− 0.1	3216	γ Boötis.........	− 0.4	3558	η Ursæ Min.....	− 0.1

No. in Cat.	Name of Star.	Corr. to N.P.D.	No. in Cat.	Name of Star.	Corr. to N.P.D.	No. in Cat.	Name of Star.	Corr. to N.P.D.
		´			´			´
3568	34 Herculis......	— 0.1	3983	2612 Gr..........	— 0.3	4341	ι^2 Cygni	— 0.2
3578	σ Herculis	— 0.3	4021	2638 Gr..........	— 0.3	4363	2875 Gr..........	— 0.3
3580	2361 Gr..........	— 0.1	4043	c Draconis	— 0.3	4370	2878 Gr..........	— 0.1
3592	2370 Gr..........	— 0.2	4051	2659 Gr..........	— 0.4	4373	2881 Gr..........	— 0.4
3595	η Herculis	— 0.2	4058	2664 Gr..........	— 0.2	4391	2891 Gr..........	— 0.2
3598	g Draconis	— 0.2	4070	2671 Gr..........	— 0.3	4396	θ Cygni	— 0.3
3602	2377 Gr..........	— 0.1	4071	2672 Gr..........	— 0.2	4413	2907 Gr..........	— 0.2
3609	52 Herculis	— 0.3	4082	β Lyræ	— 0.1	4428	c Cygni	— 0.3
3624	2389 Gr..........	— 0.1	4096	2685 Gr..........	— 0.3	4430	2924 Gr..........	— 0.2
3639	h^1 Draconis	— 0.3	4109	2699 Gr..........	— 0.2	4441	2928 Gr..........	— 0.2
3640	h^2 Draconis	— 0.2	4119	47 Draconis (2d)	— 0.3	4445	δ Cygni	— 0.4
3661	μ^1 Draconis	— 0.2	4121	2709 Gr..........	— 0.1	4446	2935 Gr..........	— 0.3
3683	ζ Draconis	— 0.1	4124	2719 Gr..........	— 0.2	4449	2933 Gr..........	— 0.1
3699	74 Herculis	— 0.2	4129	13 Lyræ..........	— 0.3	4456	α Aquilæ	— 0.1
3704	2437 Gr..........	— 0.2	4133	2720 Gr..........	— 0.3	4469	2950 Gr..........	— 0.4
3713	x Herculis	— 0.3	4146	48 Draconis	— 0.1	4481	d Cygni	— 0.4
3718	β Draconis	— 0.3	4160	2742 Gr..........	— 0.3	4490	2968 Gr..........	— 0.3
3723	ν^1 Draconis	— 0.2	4164	υ Draconis	— 0.2	4498	ϵ Draconis	— 0.1
3724	ν^2 Draconis	— 0.3	4167	2743 Gr..........	— 0.3	4505	23 Cygni	— 0.2
3731	f Draconis	— 0.1	4171	16 Lyræ..........	— 0.3	4513	ψ Cygni	— 0.3
3739	ι Herculis.......	— 0.3	4186	2759 Gr..........	— 0.3	4528	2990 Gr..........	— 0.1
3747	ω Draconis......	— 0.2	4199	2775 Gr..........	— 0.3	4535	2996 Gr..........	— 0.5
3757	2476 Gr..........	— 0.2	4201	2772 Gr..........	— 0.2	4544	3001 Gr..........	— 0.2
3768	ψ^1 Draconis	— 0.2	4205	2784 Gr..........	— 0.2	4548	3004 Gr..........	— 0.3
3771	30 Draconis	— 0.2	4219	2782 Gr..........	— 0.3	4556	3011 Gr..........	— 0.3
3784	f Herculis.......	— 0.2	4225	2789 Gr..........	— 0.3	4574	3026 Gr..........	— 0.2
3793	ξ Draconis	— 0.3	4231	53 Draconis	— 0.2	4582	e Draconis	— 0.2
3799	γ Draconis......	— 0.1	4233	55 Draconis	— 0.2	4596	3041 Gr..........	— 0.3
3800	2493 Gr..........	— 0.3	4248	54 Draconis	— 0.2	4597	ρ Draconis	— 0.4
3803	2494 Gr..........	— 0.3	4271	κ Cygni	— 0.3	4598	3042 Gr..........	— 0.2
3814	2496 Gr..........	— 0.2	4272	2812 Gr..........	— 0.4	4607	3049 Gr..........	— 0.1
3816	35 Draconis.....	— 0.1	4289	2822 Gr..........	— 0.3	4611	69 Draconis	— 0.2
3828	2502 Gr..........	— 0.3	4293	2827 Gr..........	— 0.1	4654	3087 Gr..........	— 0.1
3848	2517 Gr..........	— 0.3	4307	2832 Gr..........	— 0.3	4745	γ Cygni..........	— 0.1
3849	2518 Gr..........	— 0.2	4315	π Draconis	— 0.2	4882	3241 Gr..........	— 0.3
3851	2520 Gr..........	— 0.2	4327	2850 Gr..........	— 0.3	4918	α Cygni	— 0.1
3864	2527 Gr..........	— 0.3	4329	2852 Gr..........	— 0.1	4925	51 Cygni	— 0.2
3885	2538 Gr..........	— 0.1	4332	ι^1 Cygni	— 0.3	4931	3265 Gr..........	— 0.3

No. in Cat.	Name of Star.	Corr. to N.P.D.	No. in Cat.	Name of Star.	Corr. to N.P.D.	No. in Cat.	Name of Star.	Corr. to N.P.D.
		″			″			″
4949	3402 Gr............	− 0.1	5391	ν Cephei...........	− 0.3	5974	3994 Gr...........	− 0.3
4959	η Cephei..........	− 0.3	5392	π² Cygni	− 0.3	5980	π Cephei	− 0.1
5006	3319 Gr...........	− 0.3	5394	78 Draconis	− 0.1	5981	2 Cassiopeiæ ...	− 0.3
5012	3324 Gr...........	− 0.3	5430	3591 Gr...........	− 0.4	5995	7 Andromedæ ..	− 0.1
5020	*..............	− 0.2	5450	3606 Gr...........	− 0.4	6013	4022 Gr...........	− 0.4
5032	3337 Gr...........	− 0.4	5453	3609 Gr.,........	− 0.2	6018	4024 Gr...........	− 0.3
5035	ν Cygni	− 0.3	5475	79 Draconis	− 0.4	6019	4025 Gr...........	− 0.3
5056	3352 Gr...........	− 0.2	5489	3633 Gr...........	− 0.3	6022	8 Andromedæ ..	− 0.4
5067	ƒ¹ Cygni	− 0.2	5519	3660 Gr...........	− 0.4	6023	4027 Gr...........	− 0.2
5083	3377 Gr...........	− 0.3	5524	3655 Gr...........	− 0.3	6027	4029 Gr...........	− 0.3
5102	ξ Cygni	− 0.2	5545	18 Cephei........	− 0.3	6058	4050 Gr...........	− 0.2
5113	ƒ² Cygni.........	− 0.1	5578	3707 Gr...........	− 0.4	6055	4056 Gr...........	− 0.3
5134	3409 Gr...........	− 0.4	5580	3709 Gr...........	− 0.5	6059	4 Cassiopeiæ....	− 0.3
5151	3415 Gr...........	− 0.3	5594	ζ Cephei	− 0.3	6080	4068 Gr...........	− 0.3
5154	77 Draconis.....	− 0.2	5611	3723 Gr...........	− 0.2	6084	4071 Gr...........	− 0.3
5178	3428 Gr...........	− 0.3	5643	3739 Gr...........	− 0.3	6092	4078 Gr...........	− 0.3
5191	α Cephei	− 0.3	5654	3746 Gr...........	− 0.3	6109	4089 Gr...........	− 0.2
5200	6 Cephei.........	− 0.3	5675	β Lacertæ........	− 0.2	6147	4117 Gr...........	− 0.3
5212	3452 Gr...........	− 0.3	5678	4 Lacertæ	− 0.2	6149	κ Andromedæ ..	− 0.2
5227	3458 Gr...........	− 0.2	5692	3777 Gr...........	− 0.3	6166	4133 Gr...........	− 0.1
5238	3467 Gr...........	− 0.3	5716	δ² Cephei	− 0.4	6173	ψ Andromedæ..	− 0.3
5245	*..............	− 0.3	5718	6 Lacertæ	− 0.3	6179	τ Cassiopeiæ....	− 0.3
5276	β¹ Cephei	− 0.3	5730	28 Cephei	− 0.2	6184	4141 Gr...........	− 0.3
5277	β² Cephei	− 0.1	5750	ρ Cephei	− 0.1	6190	6 Cassiopeiæ ...	− 0.2
5280	3489 Gr...........	− 0.2	5787	11 Lacertæ......	− 0.3	6206	4156 Gr...........	− 0.2
5307	3519 Gr...........	− 0.5	5790	3857 Gr...........	− 0.2	6213	ρ Cassiopeiæ ...	− 0.4
5334	3528 Gr...........	− 0.4	5809	13 Lacertæ......	− 0.1	6215	4163 Gr...........	− 0.2
5336	3530 Gr...........	− 0.3	5837	3893 Gr...........	− 0.2	6244	σ Cassiopeiæ ...	− 0.4
5367	π¹ Cygni	− 0.4	5855	ι Cephei	− 0.3	6290	9 Cassiopeiæ ...	− 0.4
5386	11 Cephei	− 0.1	5881	3928 Gr...........	− 0.2			

In the application of the Annual Variations for the reduction of the Mean N.P.D.'s in different years to the year 1845, an error has occurred similar to that which has been explained and corrected in the case of Right Ascensions. I have investigated the corrections due to this cause, and I find that very few Stars are sensibly affected by it.

The Stars which require correction on this account are Aldebaran, μ Geminorum, and α Aquilæ; and, taking into account the correction for the errors previously explained, the whole corrections to be applied to the N.P.D.'s given in the Catalogue for these Stars, will be

$$
\begin{array}{ll}
\text{For Aldebaran} & +\ 0.4 \\
\mu\ \text{Geminorum} & +\ 0.9 \\
\alpha\ \text{Aquilæ} & -\ 0.5
\end{array}
$$

The numbers in column 3 on the right hand pages are computed by methods precisely similar to those for Right Ascension, and the remaining columns evidently need no additional explanation. It may however be mentioned, that the Stars in the last column but one are as usual designated by Bayer's Letters and Flamsteed's Numbers; and that the work referred to in the last column is Oeltzen's Catalogue of the Stars in Argelander's Northern Zones, (from 45° to 80° North Declination,) which was published in 1852 as the First Volume of the Third Series of the Annals of the Imperial Observatory of Vienna.

As the principal object which Mr. Johnson had in view in star-observing was the complete reobservation of the stars in Groombridge's Catalogue, all in that Catalogue were looked for with great care, and, with very few exceptions, all have been reobserved. The following is a list of those which have not been found, in consequence probably of errors either in the original observations or the reductions: Nos. 214, 584, 805, 812, 2940, 3164, 3170, 3202, 3647, 3745, 3932, and 4018.

On account of the lamented death of Mr. Johnson, the publication of the Radcliffe Catalogue has been delayed considerably beyond the time which would have been necessary, if he had been spared to see the printing of the work completed. In fact, the printing was completed about the middle of last year, and has waited only for the Introduction and general revision, which could be performed only by a person authorized to assume the direction of the Observatory. On my appointment to the office of Director in June last, the study of the details of the computations was one of my earliest cares, and I did not rest satisfied till I had convinced myself by a searching scrutiny of the accuracy of all the elements and of all the processes employed, and had put myself into a condition enabling me to hold myself responsible for the general accuracy of the work. I found, however, that it would not be prudent to proceed to the publication of it till I had come into residence, and, since that time, or from October 1, I have been employed upon it as incessantly as my other duties permitted; and I now confidently offer it to the world as a work well sustaining the reputation of the late Director, and as one of the most important and accurate of modern Star Catalogues.

ROBERT MAIN.

Radcliffe Observatory, Oxford,
1860, October 31.

THE

RADCLIFFE CATALOGUE OF STARS

REDUCED TO THE EPOCH

1845.0.

Ordinal Number.		Magnitude.	Estimates of Magnitude.	Mean Right Ascension 1845.0.			Precession 1845.0.	Secular Variation	Adopted Proper Motion.	Observations of R.A.		
R.	G.	R.	R.	R.		G.				No. R.	Mean year. R.	G.
				h. m. s.		s.	s.	s.	s.		1800 +	
1	...	2.0	A	0 0 23.10		...	+ 3.071	+ 0.016	+ 0.009	73	46.2	...
2	4239	7.7	6	0 0 31.63		31.78	+ 3.080	+ 0.097	......	3	51.5	14.8
3	4238	7.9	5	0 0 32.29		31.89	+ 3.074	+ 0.037	......	3	49.5	12.8
4	4241	6.2	3	0 0 53.85		53.75	+ 3.100	+ 0.155	......	2	51.3	14.9
5	4240	2.9	4	0 0 56.35		56.08	+ 3.079	+ 0.049	+ 0.067	5	45.8	6.9
6	4242	8.3	3	0 0 58.66		58.81	+ 3.077	+ 0.034	......	3	51.5	12.9
7	4243	7.0	4	0 1 26.09		26.19	+ 3.079	+ 0.031	......	4	47.4	13.8
8	1	7.6	5	0 2 1.20		1.15	+ 3.082	+ 0.031	......	3	48.9	13.8
9	2	7.3	6	0 2 12.96		12.73	+ 3.086	+ 0.037	......	4	47.6	10.6
10	3	5.4	4	0 2 17.02		16.91	+ 3.084	+ 0.031	......	3	44.9	8.5
11	4	7.6	5	0 2 30.52		30.27	+ 3.088	+ 0.037	......	5	47.3	10.8
12	5	8.7	5	0 2 54.20		54.47	+ 3.106	+ 0.063	......	2	48.8	15.0
13	6	7.0	5	0 3 0.41		0.52	+ 3.129	+ 0.103	......	3	46.8	14.8
14	7	7.1	9	0 3 38.31		38.77	+ 3.116	+ 0.063	......	7	48.6	14.9
15	8	8.7	5	0 3 48.20		48.09	+ 3.097	+ 0.037	......	2	48.9	11.0
16	9	6.7	6	0 3 53.97		53.58	+ 3.094	+ 0.031	......	4	48.4	11.9
17	10	8.8	5	0 3 58.69		58.67	+ 3.120	+ 0.066	......	3	50.8	15.0
18	11	7.7	7	0 4 4.12		3.76	+ 3.095	+ 0.031	......	4	49.3	11.9
19	12	8.4	4	0 4 22.45		22.26	+ 3.095	+ 0.031	......	4	49.1	13.8
20	13	6.6	5	0 4 29.04		28.67	+ 3.095	+ 0.029	......	5	48.8	12.0
21	14	7.3	3	0 4 29.88		29.91	+ 3.095	+ 0.029	......	3	46.8	12.0
22	15	7.2	5	0 4 31.50		31.24	+ 3.095	+ 0.029	......	4	49.4	13.9
23	16	6.9	3	0 4 42.35		41.96	+ 3.097	+ 0.029	......	2	47.9	13.8
24	17	7.6	3	0 4 46.01		45.55	+ 3.104	+ 0.037	......	3	48.2	11.0
25	18	7.5	3	0 4 56.00		55.87	+ 3.104	+ 0.037	......	2	50.3	12.9
26	19	7.4	4	0 5 13.80		13.72	+ 3.106	+ 0.037	......	2	49.8	12.9
27	...	2.7	A	0 5 15.58		...	+ 3.078	+ 0.008	......	58	45.7	...
28	...	8.5	10	0 5 16.65		...	+ 3.495	+ 0.527	......	7	53.5	...
29	20	5.5	4	0 5 28.86		28.86	+ 3.097	+ 0.026	......	4	46.7	9.9
30	...	7.2	4	0 5 30.95		...	+ 3.191	+ 0.117	......	3	52.5	...

REDUCED TO THE EPOCH 1845.0.

Ordinal Number.	Mean North Polar Distance 1845.0.		Precession 1845.0.	Secular Variation.	Adopted Proper Motion.	Observations of N.P.D.			Names.	Oeltzen-Argelander Number.
R.	R.	G.				No. R.	Mean year R.	G.		
	° ′ ″	″	″	″	″		1800 +			
1	61 45 56.5	...	− 20.06	0.00	+ 0.15	12	40.8	...	21 Androm. α	......
2	16 38 57.1	59.6	− 20.06	0.00	...	4	46.9	14.3	....	10
3	37 36 31.3	30.0	− 20.06	0.00	...	3	46.5	12.3	....	......
4	11 8 49.9	50.1	− 20.06	0.00	...	4	46.1	14.9	....	19
5	31 42 19.7	18.7	− 20.06	0.00	+ 0.17	5	44.5	6.9	11 Cassiop. β	......
6	41 0 19.3	17.5	− 20.06	0.00	...	3	46.8	12.9	....	20
7	44 28 27.3	28.4	− 20.06	0.00	...	4	46.6	13.8	....	26
8	44 28 18.5	19.0	− 20.06	0.00	...	4	46.6	13.8	....	......
9	38 36 27.0	28.7	− 20.06	0.00	...	3	46.6	10.6	....	42
10	44 47 25.3	27.2	− 20.05	0.00	...	3	44.3	8.5	22 Andromedæ	44
11	38 32 41.9	43.4	− 20.05	0.00	...	3	44.5	10.8	....	48
12	24 46 59.5	56.9	− 20.05	0.00	...	3	49.8	15.0	....	......
13	16 22 39.6	39.3	− 20.05	0.00	...	5	45.6	14.8	....	63
14	24 44 11.5	12.4	− 20.05	0.00	...	4	44.6	14.9	....	......
15	39 22 57.2	60.6	− 20.05	0.00	...	5	50.0	11.0	....	......
16	42 42 39.1	39.5	− 20.05	0.00	...	4	49.1	11.9	....	......
17	24 51 38.8	43.0	− 20.05	0.00	...	3	50.6	15.0	....	......
18	42 40 49.1	47.1	− 20.05	0.00	...	4	49.1	11.9	....	......
19	44 54 8.4	11.2	− 20.05	0.00	...	2	49.4	13.8	....	......
20	46 9 15.6	13.8	− 20.05	0.00	...	3	46.5	12.0	....	......
21	46 16 16.9	16.1	− 20.05	0.00	...	1	50.8	12.0	....	......
22	46 32 47.4	47.7	− 20.05	0.00	...	3	48.2	13.9	....	......
23	44 45 59.1	60.5	− 20.05	0.00	...	3	47.4	13.8	....	......
24	39 22 39.0	40.8	− 20.05	0.00	...	3	50.5	11.0	....	......
25	40 56 11.8	10.8	− 20.05	0.00	...	2	46.8	12.9	....	98
26	41 8 20.1	19.0	− 20.05	0.00	...	3	50.8	12.9	....	......
27	75 40 41.4	...	− 20.05	0.00	+ 0.02	10	53.8	...	88 Pegasi γ ...	......
28	4 8 10.7	...	− 20.05	+ 0.01	...	4	52.1	...	....	......
29	49 49 14.0	11.6	− 20.05	0.00	+ 0.08	3	44.4	9.9	23 Andromedæ	......
30	14 50 7.9	...	− 20.05	+ 0.01	...	3	51.5	...	....	108

Ordinal Number.		Magnitude.	Estimates of Magnitude.	Mean Right Ascension 1845.0.		Precession 1845.0.	Secular Variation	Adopted Proper Motion.	Observations of R.A.		
R.	G.	R.		R.	G.				No. R.	Mean year. R.	G.
				h. m. s.	s.	s.	s.	s.		1800 +	
31	...	7.6	3	0 5 50.75	...	+ 3.199	+ 0.117	......	3	52.5	...
32	21	8.3	5	0 5 58.11	57.71	+ 3.146	+ 0.069	......	3	51.8	15.0
33	...	8.6	6	0 5 58.86	...	+ 3.546	+ 0.534	......	5	53.2	...
34	22	7.7	5	0 6 3.21	3.09	+ 3.146	+ 0.066	......	4	50.6	15.0
35	23	8.6	3	0 6 26.77	26.82	+ 3.147	+ 0.066	......	3	51.5	12.8
36	24	7.0	5	0 6 28.55	28.24	+ 3.102	+ 0.026	......	3	44.5	9.9
37	25	8.0	4	0 6 33.13	32.81	+ 3.116	+ 0.034	......	4	52.3	11.0
38	26	8.0	2	0 6 43.13	43.28	+ 3.154	+ 0.066	......	2	50.9	15.0
39	...	6.0	A	0 7 0.13	...	+ 3.076	+ 0.005	+ 0.004	5	41.3	...
40	27	7.4	3	0 7 11.80	12.00	+ 3.109	+ 0.023	......	2	49.9	13.8
41	28	7.6	6	0 7 25.31	25.23	+ 3.121	+ 0.040	......	3	51.5	12.9
42	29	6.3	4	0 7 32.12	32.43	+ 3.247	+ 0.131	......	3	49.2	14.9
43	...	8.8	3	0 8 1.23	...	+ 3.120	+ 0.034	......	2	49.3	...
44	30	6.9	6	0 8 14.24	13.91	+ 3.114	+ 0.029	......	3	46.4	14.0
45	...	9.0	5	0 8 27.85	...	+ 3.120	+ 0.034	......	3	54.3	...
46	31	5.0	4	0 8 39.82	39.39	+ 3.160	+ 0.057	......	5	46.1	10.5
47	32	7.1	5	0 8 43.56	43.40	+ 3.122	+ 0.031	......	3	44.9	11.9
48	33	6.1	6	0 8 59.76	59.44	+ 3.126	+ 0.031	......	5	45.1	12.0
49	...	4.8	2	0 9 0.52	...	+ 3.111	+ 0.024	......	4	40.9	...
50	35	6.2	4	0 9 31.62	31.35	+ 3.137	+ 0.037	......	3	44.8	10.9
51	34	7.9	6	0 9 34.15	25.45	+ 3.122	+ 0.031	......	3	47.5	9.9
52	37	7.4	6	0 9 38.53	38.78	+ 3.244	+ 0.103	......	3	45.9	14.8
53	36	7.2	6	0 9 40.12	39.71	+ 3.287	+ 0.131	......	4	46.4	12.9
54	38	7.8	6	0 9 52.43	52.63	+ 3.118	+ 0.020	......	4	47.3	13.9
55	39	7.7	6	0 9 58.20	57.76	+ 3.175	+ 0.060	......	4	44.3	10.8
56	...	8.4	6	0 10 6.50	...	+ 5.467	+ 3.087	......	6	50.8	...
57	40	6.2	5	0 10 33.07	32.68	+ 3.127	+ 0.029	......	4	45.9	9.9
58	41	7.3	3	0 10 38.88	39.29	+ 3.264	+ 0.103	......	3	45.2	14.8
59	...	8.5	4	0 11 3.34	...	+ 3.142	+ 0.035	......	3	51.4	...
60	42	8.6	5	0 11 21.70	21.68	+ 3.131	+ 0.029	......	3	46.5	13.9
61	...	4.7	1	0 11 32.09	...	+ 3.059	− 0.004	− 0.006	1	54.9	...
62	43	6.7	4	0 11 33.63	33.71	+ 3.126	+ 0.026	......	4	48.3	13.9
63	44	6.9	5	0 11 52.53	52.42	+ 3.146	+ 0.031	.....	4	47.2	12.0
64	45	8.0	5	0 11 57.37	57.47	+ 3.135	+ 0.029	......	3	47.1	13.9
65	47	8.6	4	0 12 17.37	17.28	+ 3.140	+ 0.031	....	3	48.4	11.9

Ordinal Number.	Mean North Polar Distance 1845.0.			Precession 1845.0.	Secular Variation.	Adopted Proper Motion.	Observations of N.P.D.				Names.	Oeltzen-Argelander Number.
R.	R.		G.				No. R.	Mean year. R.	G.			
	o ′ ″		″	″	″	″		1800 +				
31	14 48 ...		...	......	...	...	...	...	...		....	115
32	24 31 12.8		11.6	— 20.05	0.00	...	3	45.5	15.0		....	119
33	4 11 24.0		...	— 20.05	+ 0.01	...	3	51.7	...		....	....
34	24 39 26.6		25.6	— 20.05	0.00	...	4	47.4	15.0		....	120
35	26 17 45.3		45.0	— 20.05	0.00	...	3	42.9	12.8		....	122
36	49 49 50.2		50.4	— 20.05	0.00	...	3	46.2	9.9		....	....
37	39 14 41.3		42.2	— 20.04	0.00	...	3	47.5	11.0		....	126
38	24 44 53.6		49.6	— 20.04	0.00	...	3	48.9	15.0		....	131
39	82 2 25.4		...	— 20.04	+ 0.01	+ 0.05	2	40.8	...		35 Piscium (1)	....
40	46 39 31.0		31.8	— 20.04	0.00	...	4	50.1	13.8		....	....
41	40 48 41.8		42.0	— 20.04	0.00	...	3	48.9	12.9		....	149
42	13 54 41.1		41.6	— 20.04	0.00	...	4	44.3	14.9		....	150
43	42 58 9.6		...	— 20.04	+ 0.01	...	3	54.2	...		....	159
44	47 15 56.8		55.5	— 20.04	0.00	...	4	49.9	14.0		....	....
45	42 56 36.4		...	— 20.04	+ 0.01	...	3	52.2	...		....	163
46	29 19 43.3		42.8	— 20.04	+ 0.02	...	3	43.8	10.5		....	164
47	44 14 48.4		47.1	— 20.04	+ 0.02	...	3	44.5	11.9		....	165
48	42 54 52.4		49.5	— 20.04	+ 0.02	...	3	43.8	12.0		....	169
49	52 10 45.0		...	— 20.04	+ 0.02	...	3	54.8	...		24 Androm. θ	....
50	39 25 41.7		43.3	— 20.04	+ 0.02	...	4	45.8	10.9		....	180
51	46 51 23.2		34.6	— 20.04	+ 0.02	...	3	47.2	9.9		....	....
52	17 54 52.7		52.5	— 20.04	+ 0.02	...	3	49.5	14.8		....	184
53	14 35 5.3		7.1	— 20.04	+ 0.02	...	4	46.9	12.9		....	....
54	50 6 49.6		49.7	— 20.04	+ 0.02	...	4	51.9	13.9		....	....
55	29 8 3.2		4.6	— 20.04	+ 0.02	...	4	48.6	10.8		....	186
56	1 24 53.3		...	— 20.04	+ 0.04	...	3	46.9	...		....	....
57	47 4 12.1		11.4	— 20.03	+ 0.02	...	4	44.9	5.9		26 Andromedæ	....
58	17 44 16.8		17.8	— 20.03	+ 0.02	...	3	44.6	14.8		....	203
59	41 55 46.0		...	— 20.03	+ 0.02	...	2	52.3	...		....	....
60	47 10 57.1		56.3	— 20.03	+ 0.02	...	2	50.4	13.9		....	....
61	99 41 1.0		...	— 20.03	+ 0.02	+ 0.06	4	53.9	...		8 Ceti ι	....
62	50 7 51.1		51.9	— 20.03	+ 0.02	...	3	47.9	13.9		....	....
63	41 59 42.2		41.2	— 20.03	+ 0.02	...	4	46.4	12.0		....	230
64	46 56 3.4		3.7	— 20.03	+ 0.02	...	3	48.9	13.9		....	....
65	45 55 18.3		16.8	— 20.03	+ 0.02	...	3	45.4	11.9		....	....

Ordinal Number		Magnitude.	Estimates of Magnitude.	Mean Right Ascension 1845.0.		Precession 1845.0.	Secular Variation	Adopted Proper Motion.	Observations of R.A.		
R.	G.	R.		R.	G.				No. R.	Mean year. R.	Mean year. G.
				h. m. s.	s.	s.	s.	s.		1800 +	
66	46	6.8	3	0 12 17.73	17.60	+ 3.150	+ 0.037	......	4	47.3	12.0
67	49	8.2	6	0 12 19.87	19.96	+ 3.130	+ 0.026	......	5	50.9	13.8
68	48	6.3	4	0 12 19.88	19.44	+ 3.200	+ 0.060	......	5	46.6	10.6
69	50	8.2	3	0 12 21.59	22.00	+ 3.137	+ 0.026	......	2	49.8	13.9
70	...	6.0	6	0 12 37.66	...	+ 3.079	+ 0.005	− 0.002	6	45.3	...
71	...	7.4	4	0 12 49.62	...	+ 3.239	+ 0.076	......	2	51.3	...
72	51	8.6	3	0 12 50.50	50.18	+ 3.139	+ 0.029	......	3	47.6	14.0
73	52	7.5	4	0 12 59.14	59.01	+ 3.143	+ 0.029	......	4	46.4	11.9
74	...	8.2	6	0 13 10.52	...	+ 3.244	+ 0.074	......	4	53.4	...
75	53	7.2	7	0 13 13.71	12.39	+ 3.209	+ 0.068	......	5	47.1	10.9
76	...	8.7	5	0 13 18.71	...	+ 3.244	+ 0.074	......	4	53.4	...
77	54	7.6	5	0 13 30.48	30.27	+ 3.294	+ 0.097	......	3	49.2	12.9
78	...	7.8	5	0 13 35.26	...	+ 3.244	+ 0.074	......	4	52.5	...
79	...	9.0	5	0 14 19.90	...	+ 3.151	+ 0.033	......	3	48.2	...
80	55	7.4	7	0 14 28.34	28.13	+ 3.185	+ 0.043	......	4	46.3	11.0
81	...	7.2	4	0 14 50.29	...	+ 3.155	+ 0.032	......	3	45.3	...
82	56	7.6	7	0 15 28.94	28.56	+ 3.158	+ 0.031	......	5	48.5	11.9
83	57	6.6	3	0 15 51.79	51.65	+ 3.157	+ 0.029	......	5	42.6	10.7
84	58	5.5	3	0 15 56.16	55.93	+ 3.186	+ 0.043	......	4	45.8	10.0
85	59	8.4	6	0 15 58.30	58.15	+ 3.163	+ 0.029	......	4	46.4	12.0
86	...	8.6	3	0 15 59.20	...	+ 3.209	+ 0.052	......	4	53.4	...
87	...	8.4	4	0 16 8.87	...	+ 3.209	+ 0.052	......	4	53.4	...
88	60	5.2	6	0 16 16.89	16.42	+ 3.241	+ 0.060	......	6	45.6	8.9
89	61	6.0	7	0 16 45.00	44.78	+ 3.196	+ 0.031	......	5	44.7	10.9
90	62	7.1	4	0 16 57.66	57.19	+ 3.357	+ 0.106	......	4	46.0	12.8
91	63	8.9	5	0 17 9.52	9.86	+ 3.165	+ 0.031	......	3	45.5	11.9
92	...	7.3	5	0 17 17.22	...	+ 3.226	+ 0.054	......	4	51.4	...
93	...	6.7	8	0 17 46.80	...	+ 3.223	+ 0.049	......	4	51.4	...
94	...	8.2	3	0 17 56.59	...	+ 3.227	+ 0.053	......	2	52.4	...
95	...	7.1	9	0 18 2.77	...	+ 3.187	+ 0.039	......	4	46.4	...
96	...	6.7	3	0 18 12.55	...	+ 3.226	+ 0.049	......	2	51.4	...
97	...	9.7	3	0 18 49.83	...	+ 3.197	+ 0.037	......	2	50.3	...
98	64	7.0	6	0 18 51.60	51.32	+ 3.197	+ 0.037	......	4	45.5	10.0
99	65	5.5	9	0 19 55.14	54.69	+ 3.181	+ 0.034	+ 0.003	9	47.9	11.9
100	66	7.2	6	0 20 35.88	35.58	+ 3.202	+ 0.040	......	4	45.9	11.0

Ordinal Number.	Mean North Polar Distance 1845.0.		Precession 1845.0.	Secular Variation.	Adopted Proper Motion.	Observations of N.P.D.			Names.	Oeltzen-Argelander Number.
						No.	Mean year.			
R.	R.	G.				R.	R.	G.		
	° ′ ″	″	″	″	″		1800 +			
66	41 53 31.3	31.1	− 20.03	+ 0.02	...	3	46.9	12.0	....	237
67	49 56 18.5	15.4	− 20.03	+ 0.02	...	2	53.3	13.8	....	......
68	28 58 53.0	52.9	− 20.03	+ 0.02	...	3	43.5	10.6	....	239
69	47 9 57.3	53.9	− 20.03	+ 0.02	...	3	48.2	13.9	....	......
70	82 40 15.6	...	− 20.02	+ 0.02	− 0.01	5	45.8	...	41 Piscium *d* .	......
71	23 51 20.0	...	− 20.02	+ 0.02	...	3	52.2	...	....	......
72	47 8 50.2	44.4	− 20.02	+ 0.02	...	3	48.9	14.0	....	......
73	45 55 23.9	24.0	− 20.02	+ 0.03	...	5	48.7	11.9	....	......
74	24 23 47.2	...	− 20.02	+ 0.03	...	3	51.8	...	....	......
75	29 10 2.7	1.4	− 20.02	+ 0.03	...	3	44.9	10.9	....	253
76	24 23 34.3	...	− 20.02	+ 0.03	...	2	52.4	...	....	......
77	19 21 9.6	11.4	− 20.02	+ 0.03	...	4	50.8	12.9	....	......
78	24 23 57.9	...	− 20.02	+ 0.03	...	3	53.6	...	....	......
79	45 55 56.7	...	− 20.02	+ 0.03	...	2	47.5	...	....	......
80	36 12 53.2	53.0	− 20.02	+ 0.03	...	4	43.3	11.0	....	......
81	46 20 4.9	...	− 20.01	+ 0.03	...	4	46.7	...	....	......
82	45 46 16.8	17.9	− 20.01	+ 0.03	...	3	44.5	11.9	....	......
83	46 35 41.6	40.2	− 20.01	+ 0.03	...	4	44.3	10.7	....	......
84	38 50 22.4	23.2	− 20.01	+ 0.03	...	4	45.4	10.0	....	305
85	44 59 12.6	13.6	− 20.00	+ 0.03	...	3	47.0	12.0	....	307
86	33 54 14.2	...	− 20.00	+ 0.03	...	3	53.5	...	....	......
87	33 53 31.8	...	− 20.00	+ 0.03	...	3	52.6	...	....	......
88	29 1 42.8	43.5	− 20.00	+ 0.03	...	6	44.0	8.9	12 Cassiopeiæ	311
89	37 48 45.1	46.2	− 20.00	+ 0.03	...	5	47.7	10.9	....	......
90	19 3 9.7	9.8	− 20.00	+ 0.03	...	4	44.0	12.8	....	322
91	46 32 4.2	6.8	− 20.00	+ 0.03	...	4	47.9	11.9	....	......
92	32 53 42.2	...	− 20.00	+ 0.03	...	3	51.6	...	....	......
93	34 4 41.5	...	− 19.99	+ 0.03	...	5	51.7	...	....	......
94	32 53 3.8	...	− 19.99	+ 0.04	...	4	52.3	...	....	......
95	41 48 36.3	...	− 19.99	+ 0.04	...	5	47.0	...	....	......
96	34 13 4.6	...	− 19.99	+ 0.04	− 0.04	4	51.9	...	....	......
97	40 52 12.3	...	− 19.98	+ 0.03	...	2	49.4	...	....	......
98	40 52 21.8	23.0	− 19.98	+ 0.03	...	4	46.5	10.0	....	362
99	46 27 47.5	47.5	− 19.97	+ 0.03	+ 0.01	4	44.4	11.9	....	......
100	42 26 39.9	39.9	− 19.97	+ 0.03	...	4	46.6	11.0	....	387

Ordinal Number.		Magnitude.	Estimates of Magnitude.	Mean Right Ascension 1845.0.		Precession 1845.0.	Secular Variation	Adopted Proper Motion.	Observations of R.A.		
R.	G.	R.	R.	R.	G.				No. R.	Mean year. R.	G.
				h. m. s.	s.	s.	s.	s.		1800 +	
101	68	6.8	4	0 20 56.47	56.02	+ 3.293	+ 0.066	......	5	45.3	10.9
102	67	7.9	20	0 21 41.13	38.76	+ 4.660	+ 0.717	......	25	49.6	8.9
103	...	9.9	6	0 21 57.59	...	+ 3.188	+ 0.031	......	4	53.4	...
104	...	8.6	9	0 21 57.81	...	+ 4.835	+ 0.782	......	8	54.1	...
105	70	9.2	5	0 22 0.14	0.22	+ 3.188	+ 0.031	......	2	47.3	13.8
106	69	7.7	4	0 22 0.62	0.27	+ 3.306	+ 0.063	......	3	44.8	10.8
107	...	5.7	1	0 22 7.83	...	+ 3.060	− 0.001	− 0.002	2	53.3	...
108	...	9.2	3	0 22 21.03	...	+ 3.222	+ 0.040	......	2	48.9	...
109	...	8.9	5	0 22 32.40	...	+ 4.347	+ 0.525	......	4	51.9	...
110	71	6.2	4	0 22 33.54	32.96	+ 3.360	+ 0.077	......	5	45.8	8.9
111	72	7.0	4	0 22 37.44	37.06	+ 3.224	+ 0.040	......	3	44.9	10.0
112	73	8.6	6	0 22 43.80	43.90	+ 3.191	+ 0.029	......	3	45.9	13.8
113	74	6.8	9	0 22 53.41	53.09	+ 3.194	+ 0.031	......	7	49.0	12.0
114	75	5.9	6	0 23 13.61	13.87	+ 3.243	+ 0.043	......	4	46.8	14.0
115	77	7.9	3	0 23 14.51	14.52	+ 3.251	+ 0.049	......	3	49.4	12.9
116	76	4.9	3	0 23 14.98	14.69	+ 3.255	+ 0.049	+ 0.006	5	45.6	7.6
117	78	7.4	5	0 23 25.26	25.05	+ 3.207	+ 0.034	......	3	45.4	11.9
118	79	7.9	6	0 23 38.14	38.05	+ 3.247	+ 0.043	......	3	48.9	13.9
119	80	7.3	6	0 23 41.35	41.63	+ 3.253	+ 0.046	......	3	48.1	13.0
120	...	9.1	4	0 23 49.20	...	+ 3.199	+ 0.032	......	2	50.4	...
121	...	7.1	5	0 24 1.99	...	+ 3.242	+ 0.042	......	3	52.6	...
122	82	8.6	5	0 24 5.12	4.70	+ 3.201	+ 0.031	......	4	50.1	13.9
123	84	6.8	3	0 24 6.51	6.31	+ 3.200	+ 0.034	......	2	48.4	13.8
124	83	8.6	4	0 24 6.75	6.64	+ 3.239	+ 0.040	......	2	50.4	14.8
125	81	6.7	6	0 24 8.70	8.20	+ 3.459	+ 0.103	......	3	49.2	12.9
126	85	3.7	4	0 24 13.88	13.68	+ 3.337	+ 0.069	......	5	45.6	7.2
127	86	7.2	4	0 24 15.02	14.39	+ 3.260	+ 0.049	......	3	51.6	13.0
128	87	8.0	4	0 24 23.89	23.82	+ 3.201	+ 0.034	......	2	51.3	13.9
129	...	8.1	7	0 24 32.72	...	+ 4.486	+ 0.573	......	4	51.8	...
130	88	7.7	3	0 24 52.14	51.73	+ 3.317	+ 0.057	......	3	48.6	11.0
131	89	6.0	3	0 25 26.57	26.41	+ 3.402	+ 0.086	+ 0.010	5	46.9	9.3
132	90	7.6	5	0 25 27.23	27.96	+ 3.207	+ 0.031	......	3	50.5	13.9
133	...	9.1	4	0 25 30.91	...	+ 3.207	+ 0.031	......	2	50.4	...
134	...	7.2	5	0 25 34.72	...	+ 4.445	+ 0.512	......	4	52.4	...
135	91	7.9	3	0 25 39.83	39.86	+ 3.270	+ 0.046	......	2	50.8	13.0

Ordinal Number.	Mean North Polar Distance 1845.0.		Preces-sion 1845.0.	Secular Variation.	Adopted Proper Motion.	Observations of N.P.D.			Names.	Oeltzen-Argelander Number.
R.	R.	G.				No.	Mean year.			
						R.	R.	G.		
	° ′ ″	″	″	″	″		1800 +			
101	28 47 36.3	36.1	− 19.97	+ 0.04	...	4	44.1	10.9	....	393
102	4 32 16.5	15.0	− 19.96	+ 0.08	...	10	48.0	8.9	....	....
103	47 28 18.0	...	− 19.96	+ 0.06	...	2	51.9	...	....	....
104	4 8 51.0	...	− 19.96	+ 0.08	...	3	52.7	...	....	....
105	47 27 51.8	49.5	− 19.96	+ 0.06	...	3	49.9	13.8	....	....
106	28 30 13.4	11.5	− 19.96	+ 0.06	...	4	44.1	10.8	....	417
107	94 48 52.2	...	− 19.96	+ 0.04	+ 0.01	1	52.8	...	12 Ceti.........	....
108	40 35 46.4	...	− 19.95	+ 0.05	...	3	53.5	...	....	425
109	5 52 3.3	...	− 19.95	+ 0.08	...	2	53.4	...	....	....
110	24 20 14.9	14.6	− 19.95	+ 0.06	...	4	43.8	8.9	13 Cassiopeiæ	431
111	40 36 13.1	14.0	− 19.95	+ 0.06	...	4	46.1	10.0	....	432
112	47 28 44.1	41.0	− 19.95	+ 0.06	...	4	45.3	13.8	....	....
113	46 54 36.5	36.5	− 19.95	+ 0.06	...	4	44.9	12.0	....	....
114	38 0 59.8	59.5	− 19.95	+ 0.06	...	4	44.2	14.0	....	448
115	36 53 42.3	41.4	− 19.95	+ 0.06	...	2	50.4	12.9	....	....
116	36 20 3.5	2.1	− 19.95	+ 0.06	...	4	42.4	7.6	14 Cassiop. λ .	....
117	44 55 44.8	44.3	− 19.95	+ 0.06	...	3	46.2	11.9	....	449
118	37 51 16.0	16.6	− 19.95	+ 0.06	...	3	51.6	13.9	....	452
119	37 2 30.0	28.8	− 19.95	+ 0.06	...	4	47.6	13.0	....	....
120	47 8 41.0	...	− 19.95	+ 0.05	...	2	53.4	...	....	....
121	39 7 39.7	...	− 19.95	+ 0.05	...	4	52.3	...	....	456
122	47 1 13.1	11.7	− 19.95	+ 0.06	...	3	45.5	13.9	....	....
123	47 21 39.4	40.2	− 19.95	+ 0.06	...	3	48.3	13.8	....	....
124	39 45 9.8	9.6	− 19.94	+ 0.06	...	2	54.4	14.8	....	....
125	19 52 28.4	28.5	− 19.94	+ 0.06	− 0.02	3	46.8	12.9	....	457
126	27 55 29.0	28.8	− 19.94	+ 0.06	...	5	44.5	7.2	15 Cassiop. κ .	459
127	36 44 6.0	2.7	− 19.94	+ 0.06	...	2	46.4	13.0	....	....
128	47 38 6.0	7.0	− 19.94	+ 0.06	...	3	54.4	13.9	....	....
129	5 45 46.4	...	− 19.94	+ 0.08	...	4	52.0	...	....	....
130	30 18 26.7	26.2	− 19.94	+ 0.06	...	2	49.4	11.0	....	475
131	24 6 20.1	19.3	− 19.93	+ 0.06	...	3	44.9	9.3	16 Cassiopeiæ	....
132	47 11 18.1	16.2	− 19.93	+ 0.06	...	3	49.9	13.9	....	....
133	47 23 36.9	...	− 19.93	+ 0.06	...	2	53.3	...	....	....
134	6 10 44.7	...	− 19.93	+ 0.08	...	3	51.0	...	....	....
135	36 47 19.0	18.5	− 19.93	+ 0.06	...	2	52.4	13.0	....	....

Magnitude.	Estimates of Magnitude.	Mean Right Ascension 1845.0		Precession 1845.0.	Secular Variation	Adopted Proper Motion.	Observations of R.A.		
R.	R.	R.	G.				No. R.	Mean year. R.	G.
		h. m. s.	s.	s.	s.	s.		1800 +	
8.4	4	0 25 40.71	40.74	+ 3.249	+ 0.043	......	2	52.3	14.8
8.2	4	0 25 40.95	...	+ 3.205	+ 0.032	......	2	52.8	...
8.3	5	0 25 44.67	...	+ 3.210	+ 0.033	......	2	51.5	...
8.6	3	0 25 51.81	...	+ 3.208	+ 0.031	......	2	52.4	...
7.4	5	0 25 57.57	56.16	+ 3.233	+ 0.040	......	3	44.8	10.0
9.0	4	0 26 27.08	...	+ 3.342	+ 0.065	......	3	53.9	...
7.8	4	0 26 34.37	...	+ 4.515	+ 0.522	......	4	52.4	...
7.9	5	0 26 34.63	34.40	+ 3.350	+ 0.066	......	5	47.1	14.0
7.3	3	0 26 53.33	53.16	+ 3.280	+ 0.046	......	3	44.3	12.0
8.4	5	0 26 53.68	52.79	+ 3.334	+ 0.057	......	3	48.3	12.0
8.3	4	0 26 55.54	...	+ 4.536	+ 0.544	......	3	52.9	...
7.4	5	0 27 1.69	...	+ 3.276	+ 0.044	......	3	47.6	...
6.0	2	0 27 16.30	...	+ 3.058	− 0.001	+ 0.027	5	54.2	...
6.9	4	0 27 20.07	...	+ 3.248	+ 0.040	......	3	51.6	...
8.6	3	0 27 25.21	24.88	+ 3.503	+ 0.107	......	2	48.9	12.9
6.0	5	0 27 32.38	32.34	+ 3.285	+ 0.046	......	3	44.7	12.0
5.7	6	0 27 41.12	41.04	+ 3.343	+ 0.060	......	4	46.9	11.0
8.7	5	0 27 53.26	...	+ 3.327	+ 0.056	......	4	54.2	...
7.4	6	0 27 55.45	55.16	+ 3.226	+ 0.034	......	4	47.7	11.9
8.0	4	0 28 3.32	...	+ 3.283	+ 0.046	......	2	48.8	...
6.3	6	0 28 19.37	18.64	+ 4.191	+ 0.331	− 0.049	5	46.0	7.9
4.0	4	0 28 21.85	21.67	+ 3.289	+ 0.046	+ 0.003	5	45.2	9.6
4.7	5	0 28 22.25	22.14	+ 3.227	+ 0.031	......	5	45.3	11.9
7.4	4	0 28 33.44	...	+ 3.327	+ 0.056	......	3	45.5	...
8.5	13	0 28 41.90	41.24	+ 3.353	+ 0.063	......	6	45.7	11.0
8.4	5	0 28 54.79	54.29	+ 3.542	+ 0.113	......	4	49.4	12.9
8.7	5	0 29 11.52	11.17	+ 3.544	+ 0.106	......	3	48.6	12.9
7.7	5	0 29 22.53	...	+ 3.251	+ 0.038	......	4	49.4	...
7.5	4	0 29 26.52	25.93	+ 3.251	+ 0.037	......	3	47.6	10.0
6.5	6	0 29 44.18	43.73	+ 3.363	+ 0.060	......	5	44.4	10.9
7.6	6	0 29 50.18	49.89	+ 3.280	+ 0.043	......	4	46.9	10.8
6.9	6	0 29 52.35	...	+ 3.768	+ 0.170	......	4	51.4	...
7.9	4	0 30 9.54	9.09	+ 3.283	+ 0.043	......	3	48.9	10.9
8.8	5	0 30 10.80	...	+ 3.776	+ 0.170	......	3	52.9	...
6.6	6	0 30 13.23	13.12	+ 3.252	+ 0.034	......	6	49.9	11.0

Ordinal Number.	Mean North Polar Distance 1845.0.		Precession 1845.0.	Secular Variation.	Adopted Proper Motion.	Observations of N.P.D.			Names.	Oeltzen-Argelander Number.
R.	R.	G.				No. R.	Mean year. R.	G.		
	° ′ ″	″	″	″	″		1800 +			
136	39 51 31.1	32.5	− 19.93	+ 0.06	...	2	52.9	14.3	....	....
137	47 49 55.9	...	− 19.93	+ 0.05	...	2	51.5	...	....	....
138	47 0 56.3	...	− 19.93	+ 0.05	...	3	53.4	...	....	....
139	47 29 44.2	...	− 19.93	+ 0.05	...	2	53.3	...	....	....
140	42 56 33.4	35.2	− 19.93	+ 0.06	...	2	45.9	10.0	....	....
141	29 4 51.7	...	− 19.93	+ 0.05	...	2	50.4	...	....	....
142	6 6 25.6	...	− 19.92	+ 0.08	...	2	50.9	...	....	....
143	28 59 26.2	26.5	− 19.92	+ 0.06	...	2	51.8	14.0	....	504
144	36 39 6.7	5.7	− 19.92	+ 0.06	...	3	48.5	12.0	....	....
145	30 33 33.8	32.2	− 19.92	+ 0.06	...	3	44.2	12.0	....	513
146	6 6 3.8	...	− 19.92	+ 0.08	...	1	54.9	...	....	....
147	37 21 58.5	...	− 19.92	+ 0.05	...	2	44.3	...	....	....
148	94 26 49.9	...	− 19.91	+ 0.05	+ 0.03	1	52.8	...	13 Ceti..........	....
149	41 50 0.1	...	− 19.91	+ 0.06	...	3	51.8	...	....	522
150	20 16 53.4	54.2	− 19.91	+ 0.06	...	2	50.9	12.9	....	526
151	36 41 11.5	9.5	− 19.91	+ 0.06	...	3	45.3	12.0	....	....
152	30 31 42.2	41.6	− 19.91	+ 0.06	...	4	44.3	11.0	....	530
153	32 20 19.3	...	− 19.91	+ 0.06	...	2	52.4	...	....	535
154	46 12 56.2	56.1	− 19.90	+ 0.06	...	3	46.6	11.9	....	....
155	37 22 56.2	...	− 19.90	+ 0.06	...	2	44.9	...	....	....
156	8 21 48.4	50.1	− 19.90	+ 0.08	− 0.08	3	43.5	7.9	....	....
157	36 57 25.7	23.9	− 19.90	+ 0.06	+ 0.01	5	47.2	9.6	17 Cassiop. ζ .	....
158	46 22 1.4	2.5	− 19.90	+ 0.06	− 0.01	3	44.6	11.9	....	....
159	32 50 16.3	...	− 19.90	+ 0.06	...	2	46.4	...	....	....
160	30 32 37.7	36.9	− 19.90	+ 0.06	...	8	50.7	11.0	....	544
161	19 41 9.8	12.3	− 19.89	+ 0.07	...	2	49.4	12.9	....	548
162	19 40 13.2	16.2	− 19.89	+ 0.07	...	2	50.4	12.9	....	552
163	43 20 53.1	...	− 19.89	+ 0.06	...	2	47.4	...	....	556
164	43 26 32.9	29.8	− 19.89	+ 0.06	...	2	47.9	10.0	....	558
165	30 31 43.5	43.3	− 19.88	+ 0.07	...	4	45.1	10.9	....	....
166	39 35 1.5	3.6	− 19.88	+ 0.07	...	3	44.5	10.8	....	562
167	13 58 55.7	...	− 19.88	+ 0.07	...	3	51.8	...	....	....
168	39 27 43.1	44.7	− 19.88	+ 0.06	...	3	45.2	10.9	....	564
169	14 0 28.0	...	− 19.88	+ 0.07	...	2	54.9	...	....	....
170	43 53 50.7	48.7	− 19.88	+ 0.06	...	3	43.8	11.0	....	566

Estimates of Magnitude.	Mean Right Ascension 1845.0.		Precession 1845.0.	Secular Variation	Adopted Proper Motion.	Observations of R.A.		
	R.	G.				No. R.	Mean year R.	G.
	h. m. s.	s.	s.	s.	s.		1800 +	
7	0 30 31.38	31.27	+ 3.240	+ 0.031	.....	5	49.7	13.8
6	0 30 37.45	37.26	+ 3.271	+ 0.038	......	7	49.8	12.0
5	0 30 59.68	59.48	+ 3.561	+ 0.108	......	2	49.4	12.8
4	0 31 1.50	1.48	+ 3.275	+ 0.040	......	3	46.8	11.9
3	0 31 20.08	19.54	+ 3.377	+ 0.060	......	2	49.3	11.0
2	0 31 44.71	44.29	+ 3.340	+ 0.053	+ 0.006	54	42.2	6.8
6	0 31 50.12	...	+ 3.384	+ 0.063	......	4	47.3	...
5	0 32 23.73	23.20	+ 3.474	+ 0.083	......	3	46.9	11.9
6	0 32 34.93	34.80	+ 3.306	+ 0.043	......	5	45.9	10.9
7	0 32 44.08	44.07	+ 3.222	+ 0.029	......	5	48.4	9.4
4	0 32 52.64	52.41	+ 3.485	+ 0.082	......	3	45.5	11.9
4	0 33 3.82	...	+ 3.612	+ 0.110	......	3	54.8	...
7	0 33 4.61	3.87	+ 3.612	+ 0.110	......	5	50.5	12.9
7	0 33 26.59	26.54	+ 3.299	+ 0.042	......	4	45.8	8.9
6	0 33 36.50	36.60	+ 3.233	+ 0.029	......	4	47.4	13.9
8	0 33 57.80	57.70	+ 3.318	+ 0.045	......	4	46.3	10.9
5	0 34 11.73	...	+ 3.320	+ 0.043	......	3	51.5	...
4	0 34 27.73	27.52	+ 3.620	+ 0.113	......	2	48.4	12.9
7	0 34 33.93	30.42	+ 3.823	+ 0.164	......	4	48.3	13.0
13	0 34 54.79	54.74	+ 3.281	+ 0.037	......	10	48.2	10.7
6	0 35 28.72	28.55	+ 3.284	+ 0.037	......	4	48.3	10.9
6	0 35 31.15	30.95	+ 3.796	+ 0.155	......	3	45.2	10.0
5	0 35 38.40	...	+ 3.348	+ 0.051	......	3	49.4	...
A	0 35 48.34	...	+ 2.999	− 0.008	+ 0.013	2	40.8	...
5	0 35 49.91	49.91	+ 3.244	+ 0.031	......	3	48.2	13.9
5	0 35 51.19	...	+ 3.293	+ 0.040	......	3	47.2	...
5	0 36 6.76	6.61	+ 3.299	+ 0.039	......	3	44.9	9.3
6	0 36 10.02	10.01	+ 3.245	+ 0.029	......	3	48.0	13.9
4	0 36 29.27	29.17	+ 3.366	+ 0.051	......	3	44.7	12.0
2	0 37 0.59	0.28	+ 3.367	+ 0.048	......	2	49.3	12.0
3	0 37 25.14	24.72	+ 3.375	+ 0.053	......	3	46.9	12.0
5	0 37 31.60	30.89	+ 3.829	+ 0.156	......	6	48.8	10.0
4	0 37 33.85	33.49	+ 3.252	+ 0.029	......	4	47.9	13.9
4	0 37 37.32	37.05	+ 3.281	+ 0.034	......	3	47.9	14.0
5	0 37 49.45	38.81	+ 3.376	+ 0.057	......	2	49.4	12.0

Ordinal Number. R.	Mean North Polar Distance 1845.0. R.	G.	Precession 1845.0.	Secular Variation.	Adopted Proper Motion.	Observations of N.P.D. No. R.	Mean year. R. (1800 +)	G.	Names.	Oeltzen-Argelander Number.
171	46 11 23.5	24.7	− 19.87	+ 0.06	...	3	44.5	13.8	....	......
172	41 29 55.0	53.1	− 19.87	+ 0.06	...	3	44.2	12.0	....	576
173	20 8 38.8	37.9	− 19.87	+ 0.07	...	4	47.9	12.8	....	585
174	41 16 45.2	46.4	− 19.87	+ 0.06	...	4	50.9	11.9	....	587
175	30 39 7.6	7.8	− 19.86	+ 0.07	...	3	47.2	11.0	....	593
176	34 18 50.1	49.3	− 19.86	+ 0.07	+ 0.04	25	45.9	6.8	18 Cassiop. α .	602
177	30 31 40.9	...	− 19.86	+ 0.07	...	2	49.9	...	....	603
178	24 58 52.0	49.1	− 19.86	+ 0.07	...	4	48.1	11.9	....	......
179	38 39 11.2	10.5	− 19.86	+ 0.06	...	4	46.8	10.9	....	......
180	51 23 34.8	34.6	− 19.85	+ 0.06	...	5	49.3	9.4	32 Andromedæ	......
181	24 42 13.6	12.2	− 19.85	+ 0.07	...	5	47.3	11.9	....	......
182	19 29 2.5	...	− 19.85	+ 0.07	...	3	50.4	...	....	619
183	19 29 6.7	6.2	− 19.85	+ 0.07	...	3	47.6	12.9	....	......
184	40 20 19.7	19.6	− 19.84	+ 0.07	...	5	46.9	8.9	19 Cassiop. ξ .	628
185	50 9 37.5	36.5	− 19.84	+ 0.07	...	3	49.9	13.9	....	......
186	38 30 49.3	48.1	− 19.84	+ 0.07	...	5	44.9	10.9	....	......
187	38 25 7.9	...	− 19.83	+ 0.07	...	3	44.2	...	....	......
188	20 1 35.5	33.7	− 19.83	+ 0.07	...	3	46.2	12.9	....	648
189	14 54 31.3	27.4	− 19.83	+ 0.07	...	4	47.9	13.0	....	650
190	43 49 28.2	27.4	− 19.83	+ 0.07	+ 0.01	5	44.5	10.7	20 Cassiop. π .	......
191	43 53 8.2	8.5	− 19.82	+ 0.07	...	4	49.8	10.5	....	......
192	15 51 39.4	40.2	− 19.82	+ 0.08	+ 0.07	4	43.1	10.0	21 Cassiopeiæ	666
193	36 41 50.5	...	− 19.81	+ 0.08	...	3	47.9	...	....	673
194	108 50 18.5	...	− 19.81	+ 0.07	− 0.02	2	54.9	...	16 Ceti β	......
195	50 9 49.3	50.2	− 19.81	+ 0.07	...	3	50.5	13.9	....	......
196	42 59 12.0	...	− 19.81	+ 0.08	...	5	45.3	...	....	680
197	42 33 55.3	53.2	− 19.81	+ 0.08	...	4	45.4	9.3	22 Cassiop. o .	......
198	50 10 9.8	12.2	− 19.81	+ 0.07	...	4	50.4	13.9	....	......
199	35 37 41.0	39.8	− 19.80	+ 0.08	...	5	47.1	12.0	....	688
200	35 52 5.8	2.1	− 19.79	+ 0.08	...	3	50.9	12.0	....	694
201	35 32 36.4	33.5	− 19.79	+ 0.08	...	4	46.9	12.0	....	707
202	16 0 2.2	1.9	− 19.79	+ 0.09	...	4	45.8	10.0	23 Cassiopeiæ	711
203	50 2 14.5	12.6	− 19.79	+ 0.08	...	3	47.5	13.9	....	......
204	45 59 13.1	12.1	− 19.78	+ 0.08	...	3	45.2	14.0	....	......
205	35 42 11.3	9.1	− 19.78	+ 0.08	...	3	50.6	12.0	....	721

Ordinal Number.		Magnitude.	Estimates of Magnitude.	Mean Right Ascension 1845.0.		Precession 1845.0.	Secular Variation	Adopted Proper Motion.	Observations of R.A.		
R.	G.	R.		R.	G.				No. R.	Mean year. R.	G.
				h. m. s.	s.	s.	s.	s.		1800 +	
206	141	7.0	6	0 38 0.84	0.42	+ 3.299	+ 0.037	......	4	50.1	11.0
207	...	7.7	5	0 38 41.54	...	+ 3.340	+ 0.043	......	3	51.2	...
208	...	7.7	4	0 38 46.42	...	+ 3.341	+ 0.043	......	2	51.3	...
209	142	7.0	3	0 39 14.40	14.23	+ 3.348	+ 0.045	......	3	44.8	10.9
210	...	7.8	5	0 39 42.40	...	+ 3.334	+ 0.042	......	4	51.3	...
211	146	4.3	5	0 39 45.57	44.92	+ 3.426	+ 0.060	+ 0.132	3	44.6	6.8
212	...	8.3	4	0 39 46.93	...	+ 3.426	+ 0.060	......	3	46.1	...
213	145	7.8	4	0 39 48.65	45.64	+ 3.691	+ 0.112	......	2	48.5	12.9
214	143	7.1	6	0 39 51.92	51.84	+ 4.071	+ 0.180	......	3	46.5	14.8
215	149	7.2	7	0 39 58.32	58.13	+ 3.295	+ 0.034	......	4	49.5	14.0
216	147	7.5	5	0 40 3.92	4.05	+ 3.722	+ 0.121	......	4	48.9	13.0
217	150	5.4	3	0 40 4.68	4.53	+ 3.349	+ 0.044	+ 0.008	3	46.7	7.4
218	148	6.9	6	0 40 11.88	11.42	+ 3.707	+ 0.110	......	3	45.2	12.8
219	...	6.0	1	0 40 14.37	...	+ 3.097	+ 0.006	......	2	56.9	...
220	...	7.4	5	0 40 30.80	...	+ 3.269	+ 0.030	......	4	48.3	...
221	...	4.9	9	0 40 38.76	...	+ 3.098	+ 0.006	+ 0.003	17	49.5	...
222	...	7.0	9	0 40 45.35	...	+ 3.270	+ 0.030	......	7	50.5	...
223	151	6.8	7	0 40 57.59	57.48	+ 3.324	+ 0.039	......	6	48.2	9.9
224	152	4.8	5	0 41 17.05	16.98	+ 3.273	+ 0.031	......	4	45.2	7.5
225	153	6.4	5	0 41 40.33	39.98	+ 3.305	+ 0.036	......	4	46.4	14.0
226	154	6.4	7	0 42 7.25	6.99	+ 3.368	+ 0.045	+ 0.018	5	44.2	10.9
227	155	6.2	7	0 42 45.00	44.87	+ 3.374	+ 0.046	......	4	45.7	10.9
228	156	8.1	6	0 43 16.95	16.65	+ 3.434	+ 0.053	......	3	47.1	12.0
229	144	6.4	54	0 43 35.14	29.87	+11.061	+ 6.022	......	68	49.6	7.9
230	157	8.5	4	0 43 44.21	44.05	+ 3.324	+ 0.039	......	4	46.4	15.8
231	158	4.8	7	0 43 51.97	51.88	+ 3.515	+ 0.069	......	4	44.9	9.9
232	159	7.7	4	0 43 58.71	58.56	+ 3.319	+ 0.036	......	3	47.2	14.0
233	160	8.4	5	0 44 12.56	12.30	+ 3.360	+ 0.040	......	3	48.3	11.9
234	162	7.0	5	0 44 20.28	20.64	+ 3.281	+ 0.029	......	4	47.9	14.8
235	161	6.9	4	0 44 29.02	28.09	+ 3.638	+ 0.090	......	3	44.9	11.0
236	163	7.2	4	0 44 32.01	31.79	+ 3.365	+ 0.042	......	3	48.8	11.9
237	164	7.6	3	0 44 48.14	47.44	+ 3.355	+ 0.040	......	3	48.6	9.8
238	165	6.4	5	0 44 52.88	52.52	+ 3.401	+ 0.048	......	3	47.5	13.5
239	166	8.5	5	0 44 56.45	56.17	+ 3.331	+ 0.039	......	4	46.9	15.8
240	...	5.3	4	0 45 5.37	...	+ 3.062	+ 0.001	− 0.004	5	51.8	...

Ordinal Number. R.	Mean North Polar Distance 1845.0 R.		G.	Precession 1845.0.	Secular Variation.	Adopted Proper Motion.	Observations of N.P.D. No. R.	Mean year. R.	G.	Names.	Oeltzen-Argelander Number.
	° ′ ″		″	″	″	″		1800 +			
206	43 57 17.1		18.2	− 19.78	+ 0.08	...	4	48.9	11.0	....	......
207	39 45 4.9		...	− 19.77	+ 0.08	...	2	50.8	...	....	......
208	39 44 53.7		...	− 19.77	+ 0.08	...	3	52.2	...	....	......
209	39 24 7.3		11.2	− 19.76	+ 0.08	...	4	45.9	10.5	....	......
210	41 7 52.4		...	− 19.75	+ 0.08	...	3	47.6	...	....	761
211	33 0 29.9		32.3	− 19.75	+ 0.09	+ 0.49	5	44.7	6.8	24 Cassiop. η .	......
212	33 0 32.3		...	− 19.75	+ 0.09	...	3	46.5	...	....	......
213	20 24 21.2		29.9	− 19.75	+ 0.09	...	4	49.4	12.5	....	......
214	12 53 32.9		33.1	− 19.75	+ 0.10	...	4	47.4	14.8	....	767
215	45 51 26.5		25.1	− 19.75	+ 0.09	...	3	47.5	14.0	....	......
216	19 40 14.9		15.1	− 19.74	+ 0.10	...	3	45.6	13.0	....	......
217	39 52 42.6		42.3	− 19.74	+ 0.09	...	8	45.7	7.4	25 Cassiop. ν .	......
218	20 4 20.0		20.2	− 19.74	+ 0.10	...	4	46.4	12.8	....	......
219	83 32 50.7		...	− 19.74	+ 0.08	...	1	46.9	...	62 Piscium	......
220	49 42 49.0		...	− 19.74	+ 0.08	...	3	44.6	...	....	......
221	83 15 36.0		...	− 19.74	+ 0.08	+ 0.05	9	50.4	...	63 Piscium δ .	......
222	49 45 49.9		...	− 19.73	+ 0.08	...	4	45.6	...	....	......
223	43 4 53.5		51.7	− 19.73	+ 0.09	...	4	46.4	9.5	....	......
224	49 45 58.8		58.6	− 19.72	+ 0.09	...	6	46.9	7.5	35 Androm. ν .	......
225	45 50 36.4		37.8	− 19.72	+ 0.09	...	4	46.9	14.0	....	......
226	39 20 12.9		16.0	− 19.71	+ 0.09	...	6	47.7	10.5	....	......
227	39 16 22.4		23.2	− 19.70	+ 0.09	...	5	46.5	10.5	....	......
228	34 34 48.1		45.9	− 19.70	+ 0.09	...	4	48.4	12.0	....	......
229	1 48 40.8		41.5	− 19.69	+ 0.32	...	60	45.3	7.9	....	......
230	45 2 18.5		19.3	− 19.69	+ 0.09	...	3	43.9	15.8	....	......
231	29 43 38.4		44.3	− 19.69	+ 0.10	...	5	46.4	9.9	....	820
232	45 42 33.9		32.6	− 19.68	+ 0.09	...	3	46.5	14.0	....	......
233	41 23 59.2		60.9	− 19.68	+ 0.09	...	3	50.2	11.5	....	829
234	50 36 0.9		3.3	− 19.68	+ 0.09	...	3	49.6	14.8	....	......
235	24 24 29.9		28.5	− 19.68	+ 0.10	...	3	43.5	11.0	....	836
236	41 11 15.9		14.7	− 19.68	+ 0.10	...	3	44.2	11.5	....	837
237	42 19 25.2		23.5	− 19.67	+ 0.10	...	3	47.2	9.8	....	......
238	38 9 10.7		10.6	− 19.67	+ 0.10	...	3	46.6	13.5	....	......
239	45 1 28.2		27.8	− 19.67	+ 0.10	...	3	48.0	15.8	....	......
240	91 59 13.5		...	− 19.66	+ 0.09	+ 0.01	1	53.7	...	20 Ceti..........	......

Ordinal Number.		Magnitude.	Estimates of Magnitude.	Mean Right Ascension 1845.0			Precession 1845.0	Secular Variation	Adopted Proper Motion.	Observations of R.A.		
R.	G.		R.	R.		G.				No. R.	Mean year. R.	G.
				h. m. s.		s.	s.	s.	s.		1800 +	
241	167	7.4	6	0 45 26.28		25.83	+ 3.442	+ 0.056	......	3	45.5	12.0
242	168	4.8	7	0 45 50.66		50.37	+ 3.497	+ 0.063	......	5	45.2	9.9
243	...	8.7	5	0 45 57.60		...	+ 3.458	+ 0.056	......	2	48.9	...
244	169	8.0	4	0 46 5.32		5.02	+ 3.373	+ 0.043	......	3	45.0	11.9
245	170	8.9	5	0 46 6.15		5.76	+ 3.393	+ 0.045	......	3	48.9	11.9
246	...	8.2	4	0 46 8.51		...	+ 3.461	+ 0.057	......	2	48.4	...
247	171	6.2	2	0 46 18.39		18.16	+ 3.366	+ 0.041	......	3	45.1	9.0
248	174	8.2	5	0 46 24.99		25.17	+ 3.349	+ 0.040	......	2	46.4	15.0
249	172	8.8	5	0 46 33.94		33.58	+ 3.796	+ 0.118	......	3	51.6	12.8
250	173	8.4	4	0 46 35.24		34.63	+ 3.666	+ 0.096	......	3	49.2	11.0
251	176	7.5	5	0 46 44.70		44.55	+ 3.334	+ 0.037	......	3	51.5	15.0
252	178	8.1	2	0 46 51.86		51.67	+ 3.294	+ 0.040	......	2	49.4	14.8
253	...	9.2	16	0 47 5.21		...	+11.556	+ 5.934	......	14	50.1	...
254	179	7.8	3	0 47 5.62		5.66	+ 3.353	+ 0.037	......	2	50.0	15.0
255	...	9.0	4	0 47 9.94		...	+ 3.528	+ 0.066	......	2	52.4	...
256	180	8.0	6	0 47 13.10		13.22	+ 3.342	+ 0.037	......	4	47.4	15.8
257	181	2.8	6	0 47 23.85		23.47	+ 3.544	+ 0.069	......	5	45.6	6.8
258	...	8.4	6	0 47 27.12		...	+ 3.528	+ 0.066	......	3	54.3	...
259	185	7.7	3	0 47 28.46		28.40	+ 3.353	+ 0.037	......	2	46.4	14.9
260	183	5.1	4	0 47 28.47		28.56	+ 3.516	+ 0.061	......	3	49.2	9.9
261	182	7.9	5	0 47 29.43		28.94	+ 3.531	+ 0.066	......	3	53.6	13.6
262	184	6.0	6	0 47 29.45		29.34	+ 3.537	+ 0.067	......	4	49.6	13.5
263	...	8.7	4	0 47 30.46		...	+ 3.526	+ 0.065	......	2	51.5	...
264	188	7.0	4	0 47 51.50		51.70	+ 3.321	+ 0.034	......	3	47.6	14.8
265	187	8.2	5	0 47 59.46		59.12	+ 3.542	+ 0.067	......	3	52.2	13.9
266	186	7.3	7	0 48 4.82		4.52	+ 3.822	+ 0.121	......	3	50.2	12.8
267	190	8.7	6	0 48 18.42		18.39	+ 3.348	+ 0.040	......	4	49.0	15.9
268	189	8.9	6	0 48 22.79		22.64	+ 3.543	+ 0.065	......	3	51.5	13.9
269	191	7.0	4	0 48 23.66		23.47	+ 3.421	+ 0.048	......	3	47.1	10.9
270	177	4.4	22	0 48 35.77		35.24	+ 6.589	+ 1.222	+ 0.065	24	50.6	7.2
271	...	9.1	4	0 48 39.40		...	+ 3.545	+ 0.067	......	2	51.9	...
272	192	5.6	5	0 48 46.26		45.52	+ 3.690	+ 0.093	......	4	46.4	11.0
273	193	6.2	6	0 48 54.78		55.10	+ 3.353	+ 0.037	......	4	47.0	15.8
274	194	7.5	6	0 48 58.41		58.06	+ 3.424	+ 0.048	......	3	48.3	10.9
275	...	8.4	7	0 49 21.26		...	+ 3.336	+ 0.035	......	5	48.3	...

Ordinal Number.	Mean North Polar Distance 1845.0.		Precession 1845.0.	Secular Variation.	Adopted Proper Motion.	Observations of N.P.D.			Names.	Oeltzen-Argelander Number.
						No.	Mean year.			
R.	R.	G.				R.	R.	G.		
	° ′ ″	″	″	″	″		1800 +			
241	34 31 21.9	18.9	− 19.66	+ 0.10	...	4	46.9	12.0	....	......
242	31 52 4.9	4.8	− 19.65	+ 0.10	+ 0.09	4	45.3	9.9	26 Cassiop. υ¹	......
243	34 27 46.4	...	− 19.65	+ 0.10	...	3	47.3	...	....	......
244	41 26 12.9	13.8	− 19.64	+ 0.10	...	`2	44.9	11.9	....	861
245	39 38 17.3	19.7	− 19.64	+ 0.10	...	2	51.4	11.9	....	862
246	34 21 34.5	...	− 19.64	+ 0.10	...	2	49.9	...	....	......
247	42 9 47.8	46.2	− 19.64	+ 0.10	...	3	44.9	9.0	....	863
248	43 57 29.9	29.1	− 19.64	+ 0.10	...	3	47.2	15.0	....	......
249	20 23 18.1	18.6	− 19.64	+ 0.10	...	2	50.4	12.8	....	867
250	24 25 43.7	44.6	− 19.63	+ 0.10	...	3	47.5	11.0	....	869
251	45 44 55.4	55.1	− 19.63	+ 0.10	...	3	48.9	15.0	....	......
252	50 27 30.1	30.5	− 19.63	+ 0.10	...	3	51.8	14.8	....	......
253	1 50 24.9	...	− 19.63	+ 0.34	...	3	50.6	...	....	......
254	43 57 55.9	55.3	− 19.63	+ 0.10	...	2	50.4	15.0	....	882
255	30 50 5.7	...	− 19.63	+ 0.10	...	3	52.5	...	....	......
256	45 9 28.1	29.9	− 19.63	+ 0.10	...	2	51.8	15.8	....	......
257	30 7 27.1	26.0	− 19.63	+ 0.11	...	4	46.4	6.8	27 Cassiop. γ .	889
258	30 44 32.7	...	− 19.63	+ 0.10	...	2	51.9	...	....	891
259	44 11 12.1	10.1	− 19.63	+ 0.11	...	2	49.4	14.9	....	892
260	31 39 28.5	26.6	− 19.63	+ 0.11	...	4	49.4	9.9	28 Cassiop. υ²	......
261	30 48 28.1	26.1	− 19.63	+ 0.11	...	3	51.9	13.6	....	894
262	30 28 40.4	40.4	− 19.63	+ 0.11	...	4	48.9	13.5	....	893
263	31 6 11.1	...	− 19.63	+ 0.10	...	2	51.9	...	....	......
264	47 51 40.9	41.9	− 19.62	+ 0.10	...	3	47.9	14.8	....	......
265	30 30 5.3	5.5	− 19.62	+ 0.11	...	2	51.9	13.9	....	902
266	20 20 37.3	38.4	− 19.61	+ 0.12	...	7	50.3	12.8	....	907
267	45 13 46.2	47.5	− 19.61	+ 0.10	...	3	51.2	15.9	....	909
268	30 36 8.2	8.2	− 19.61	+ 0.11	...	3	50.2	13.9	....	912
269	38 36 0.0	2.8	− 19.61	+ 0.11	...	3	47.2	10.9	....	......
270	4 34 40.4	40.3	− 19.60	+ 0.21	...	12	49.1	7.2	2 Urs. Min. ...	......
271	30 44 8.4	...	− 19.60	+ 0.11	...	2	53.4	...	....	917
272	24 29 15.1	14.6	− 19.60	+ 0.11	...	4	45.9	11.0	....	919
273	44 59 59.5	61.6	− 19.60	+ 0.11	...	3	44.6	15.8	....	924
274	38 42 9.4	9.2	− 19.60	+ 0.11	...	3	47.2	10.9	....	926
275	46 58 48.2	...	− 19.59	+ 0.11	...	2	51.0	...	....	......

Ordinal Number		Magnitude	Estimates of Magnitude	Mean Right Ascension 1845.0		Precession 1845.0	Secular Variation	Adopted Proper Motion	Observations of R.A.		
R.	G.	R.		R.	G.				No. R.	Mean year R.	G.
				h. m. s.	s.	s.	s.	s.		1800 +	
276	196	7.1	5	0 49 31.92	32.12	+ 3.353	+ 0.037	......	4	44.8	15.8
277	175	9.4	8	0 49 53.79	52.25	+ 9.518	+ 3.040	......	6	50.3	8.0
278	198	7.3	4	0 49 55.25	55.18	+ 3.372	+ 0.042	......	3	46.9	14.9
279	199	7.2	5	0 49 57.46	57.51	+ 3.350	+ 0.034	......	4	49.9	15.2
280	197	6.8	4	0 50 11.95	11.27	+ 3.874	+ 0.121	......	4	45.0	12.9
281	200	8.7	2	0 50 29.12	29.16	+ 3.422	+ 0.045	......	3	48.5	12.0
282	...	8.7	3	0 50 39.56	...	+ 3.374	+ 0.039	......	2	49.9	...
283	201	7.4	6	0 50 39.97	39.69	+ 3.571	+ 0.067	......	3	46.2	13.9
284	202	7.7	3	0 50 48.54	48.42	+ 3.311	+ 0.032	......	3	47.2	14.8
285	...	8.5	8	0 51 10.67	...	+ 3.575	+ 0.070	......	6	46.7	...
286	204	6.8	6	0 51 16.56	16.30	+ 3.537	+ 0.065	......	4	46.8	9.6
287	...	8.1	4	0 51 18.36	...	+ 3.355	+ 0.033	......	3	48.9	...
288	205	7.0	4	0 51 18.44	18.44	+ 3.355	+ 0.033	......	3	47.7	15.9
289	203	8.0	7	0 51 21.59	20.92	+ 3.872	+ 0.117	......	4	49.4	12.8
290	...	8.3	5	0 51 23.76	...	+ 3.378	+ 0.040	......	4	46.9	...
291	195	6.6 6.2	16	0 51 30.10	28.75	+ 7.697	+ 1.848	......	15	49.8	7.7
292	206	8.3	4	0 51 42.45	41.93	+ 3.578	+ 0.068	......	2	48.9	13.9
293	207	7.9	6	0 51 58.80	58.07	+ 3.429	+ 0.045	......	3	48.5	12.0
294	208	8.5	5	0 52 1.69	1.95	+ 3.383	+ 0.039	......	2	50.4	15.0
295	209	8.3	5	0 52 24.63	24.59	+ 3.911	+ 0.126	......	2	50.5	12.9
296	211	7.0	3	0 52 30.29	29.84	+ 3.369	+ 0.036	......	3	45.2	13.4
297	210	8.7	6	0 52 31.90	31.79	+ 4.086	+ 0.162	......	3	52.2	13.0
298	212	8.4	5	0 52 49.54	49.25	+ 3.883	+ 0.113	......	3	51.5	12.8
299	213	7.9	5	0 52 52.43	51.92	+ 3.396	+ 0.039	......	3	51.5	15.9
300	...	7.8	3	0 53 15.13	...	+ 3.572	+ 0.067	......	2	48.9	...
301	...	8.9	7	0 53 26.19	...	+ 3.591	+ 0.070	......	3	51.5	...
302	216	8.2	3	0 53 32.73	32.17	+ 3.627	+ 0.073	. ..	3	51.6	11.9
303	...	8.5	4	0 53 35.38	...	+ 3.582	+ 0.069	......	2	49.9	...
304	215	7.1	2	0 53 48.42	48.14	+ 4.122	+ 0.169	......	2	50.4	13.6
305	217	8.7	4	0 53 54.05	54.04	+ 3.402	+ 0.039	......	3	51.9	15.9
306	218	8.4	4	0 53 57.53	57.61	+ 3.377	+ 0.036	......	2	51.3	15.9
307	219	6.1	4	0 54 7.24	6.72	+ 3.617	+ 0.072	......	4	48.4	10.9
308	220	7.0	4	0 54 7.95	7.25	+ 3.400	+ 0.039	......	3	52.1	16.1
309	222	6.7	1	0 54 12.73	12.62	+ 3.338	+ 0.033	......	2	49.8	8.9
310	221	6.4	3	0 54 14.17	13.79	+ 3.573	+ 0.064	......	3	49.6	11.0

Ordinal Number.	Mean North Polar Distance 1845.0.		Precession 1845.0.	Secular Variation.	Adopted Proper Motion.	Observations of N.P.D.			Names.	Oeltzen-Argelander Number.
						No.	Mean year.			
R.	R.	G.				R.	R.	G.		
	o ′ ″	″	″	″			1800 +			
276	45 14 29.3	27.0	− 19.59	+ 0.11	...	3	44.2	15.8	....	936
277	2 33 55.1	56.7	− 19.58	+ 0.30	...	2	47.9	8.0	....	......
278	43 48 8.2	7.7	− 19.58	+ 0.11	...	3	48.5	14.9	....	......
279	45 52 56.4	57.0	− 19.58	+ 0.11	...	2	52.3	15.2	....	......
280	19 51 18.3	19.0	− 19.57	+ 0.13	...	3	44.6	12.9	....	943
281	39 43 40.7	41.0	− 19.57	+ 0.11	...	3	48.2	12.0	....	951
282	43 59 50.3	...	− 19.56	+ 0.12	...	1	47.0	...	....	955
283	30 19 38.1	38.6	− 19.56	+ 0.12	...	3	46.8	13.9	....	......
284	50 40 55.9	55.7	− 19.56	+ 0.11	...	3	49.3	14.8	....	......
285	30 23 34.6	...	− 19.55	+ 0.12	...	2	51.5	...	....	......
286	32 28 22.5	21.7	− 19.55	+ 0.11	...	3	44.6	9.6	....	......
287	46 7 31.9	...	− 19.55	+ 0.11	...	2	46.4	...	....	......
288	46 7 25.0	24.0	− 19.55	+ 0.11	...	2	46.0	15.9	....	......
289	20 18 56.5	57.1	− 19.55	+ 0.13	...	3	49.6	12.8	... .	965
290	43 57 40.6	...	− 19.55	+ 0.12	...	2	49.5	...	....	966
291	3 41 1.9	1.8	− 19.54	+ 0.25	...	7	47.8	7.7	....	......
292	30 28 39.9	39.5	− 19.54	+ 0.12	...	2	50.9	13.9	....	......
293	39 57 27.9	28.5	− 19.54	+ 0.11	...	3	48.6	12.0	....	......
294	43 54 41.3	41.1	− 19.54	+ 0.11	...	3	49.6	15.0	....	978
295	19 49 19.4	22.0	− 19.53	+ 0.13	...	3	51.6	12.9	....	985
296	45 23 1.5	0.0	− 19.53	+ 0.11	...	4	47.9	13.4	....	......
297	16 38 46.6	45.8	− 19.53	+ 0.14	...	3	52.9	13.0	....	......
298	20 30 52.8	52.5	− 19.53	+ 0.13	...	4	50.9	12.8	....	993
299	43 7 42.8	42.4	− 19.52	+ 0.11	...	1	52.3	15.9	....	......
300	31 32 52.8	...	− 19.51	+ 0.12	...	3	48.6	...	....	997
301	30 42 31.0	...	− 19.51	+ 0.12	...	4	49.2	...	....	1002
302	29 3 37.8	39.1	− 19.51	+ 0.12	...	3	51.2	11.5	....	1005
303	31 10 44.9	...	− 19.51	+ 0.12	...	2	51.5	...	....	1006
304	16 27 43.2	45.4	− 19.50	+ 0.14	...	3	47.0	13.6	....	1010
305	43 8 10.4	11.4	− 19.50	+ 0.12	...	1	52.4	15.5	....	1011
306	45 24 34.2	39.7	− 19.50	+ 0.12	...	2	52.9	15.9	....	......
307	29 45 36.5	36.6	− 19.50	+ 0.12	...	3	47.9	10.9	....	1018
308	43 27 30.4	28.6	− 19.50	+ 0.12	...	3	48.5	16.1	....	1019
309	49 29 21.5	21.9	− 19.49	+ 0.12	...	4	48.3	8.9	39 Andromedæ	......
310	31 55 30.6	30.0	− 19.49	+ 0.12	...	3	47.8	11.0	....	1020

Mean Right Ascension 1845.0.		Precession 1845.0.	Secular Variation	Adopted Proper Motion.	Observations of R.A.		
					No.	Mean year.	
R.	G.				R.	R.	G.
h. m. s.	s.	s.	s.	s.		1800 +	
0 54 16.45	16.13	+ 3.407	+ 0.042	......	2	51.3	16.0
0 54 30.26	29.87	+ 3.637	+ 0.072	......	2	49.9	11.9
0 54 48.11	48.33	+ 3.635	+ 0.070	......	3	50.1	11.9
0 54 54.24	...	+ 3.109	+ 0.007	......	14	48.0	...
0 54 59.74	59.77	+ 3.408	+ 0.039	......	2	51.3	16.0
0 55 4.29	4.27	+ 3.563	+ 0.062	......	2	51.4	13.9
0 55 7.12	...	+ 3.563	+ 0.064	......	3	51.9	...
0 55 13.18	12.73	+ 3.923	+ 0.123	......	2	51.4	12.8
0 55 13.34	12.96	+ 3.565	+ 0.062	......	3	52.3	13.9
0 55 44.80	44.50	+ 3.456	+ 0.044	......	3	50.3	12.0
0 55 54.57	54.17	+ 3.333	+ 0.028	......	2	47.4	11.0
0 55 56.88	...	+ 3.768	+ 0.094	+ 0.005	2	50.8	...
0 56 12.62	13.88	+ 4.769	+ 0.323	......	2	50.3	14.8
0 56 21.03	20.33	+ 3.969	+ 0.127	......	3	49.9	12.9
0 56 39.48	38.72	+ 3.684	+ 0.080	......	3	47.9	10.9
0 56 42.12	...	+ 3.573	+ 0.064	......	2	52.0	...
0 56 51.40	50.88	+ 3.683	+ 0.076	......	3	48.6	11.0
0 57 58.51	58.44	+ 3.509	+ 0.054	......	3	47.5	11.9
0 58 0.04	59.55	+ 3.533	+ 0.056	+ 0.386	6	47.6	7.9
0 58 6.63	6.93	+ 3.984	+ 0.126	......	3	45.0	12.9
0 58 9.43	9.05	+ 3.696	+ 0.076	......	3	45.3	11.0
0 58 12.52	12.15	+ 3.453	+ 0.044	......	5	48.4	12.0
0 58 42.21	42.00	+ 3.358	+ 0.030	......	5	46.0	14.5
0 58 55.65	...	+ 3.544	+ 0.058	......	4	47.0	...
0 59 1.13	1.44	+ 3.363	+ 0.033	......	5	48.3	14.5
0 59 6.33	6.33	+ 3.604	+ 0.064	......	3	44.8	13.5
0 59 6.49	6.49	+ 4.800	+ 0.315	+ 0.034	3	44.9	12.2
0 59 8.28	8.38	+ 3.389	+ 0.034	+ 0.018	9	49.4	10.5
0 59 46.68	46.54	+ 3.613	+ 0.062	......	4	48.8	13.8
1 0 14.81	14.41	+ 3.928	+ 0.115	+ 0.008	4	43.9	9.9
1 0 23.42	...	+ 3.099	+ 0.006	+ 0.021	8	50.8	...
1 0 24.78	24.43	+ 3.496	+ 0.047	......	4	48.8	11.9
1 0 26.00	...	+ 3.723	+ 0.085	......	3	46.2	...
1 0 28.09	27.20	+ 3.546	+ 0.053	......	4	48.9	14.0
1 0 31.91	31.70	+ 3.437	+ 0.041	......	4	47.8	10.2

Ordinal Number.	Mean North Polar Distance 1845.0.		Precession 1845.0.	Secular Variation.	Adopted Proper Motion.	Observations of N.P.D.				Names.	Oeltzen-Argelander Number.
R.	R.	G.				No. R.	Mean year. R.	G.			
	° ′ ″	″	″	″	″		1800 +				
311	42 58 47.9	49.3	— 19.49	+ 0.12	...	2	52.5	16.0	....	1021
312	29 1 26.0	24.6	— 19.49	+ 0.13	...	2	48.9	11.9	....	1026
313	29 15 11.3	9.1	— 19.48	+ 0.13	...	2	44.8	11.9	....	1031
314	82 56 44.7	...	— 19.48	+ 0.11	...	10	48.5	...	71 Piscium ε..	......
315	43 11 30.6	30.7	— 19.48	+ 0.12	...	2	45.9	16.0	....	1038
316	32 51 9.6	8.6	— 19.47	+ 0.12	...	2	51.9	13.9	....	1041
317	32 53 36.1	...	— 19.47	+ 0.12	...	2	54.0	...	....	1043
318	20 30 50.2	53.7	— 19.47	+ 0.13	...	5	51.2	12.3	....	1045
319	32 47 41.1	41.5	— 19.47	+ 0.12	...	2	51.9	13.3	....	1046
320	39 49 24.6	24.2	— 19.46	+ 0.12	...	3	47.9	12.0	....	......
321	50 50 29.4	30.4	— 19.45	+ 0.12	...	2	48.9	11.0	....	......
322	24 51 41.0	...	— 19.45	+ 0.13	...	3	47.3	..	....	......
323	10 49 4.2	4.1	— 19.45	+ 0.17	...	4	46.2	14.8	....	1060
324	19 54 1.6	2.0	— 19.45	+ 0.14	...	3	43.9	12.3	....	1065
325	28 4 10.8	10.1	— 19.45	+ 0.13	...	4	45.9	10.3	....	1071
326	33 4 32.0	...	— 19.45	+ 0.13	...	4	51.9	...	....	1073
327	28 9 39.6	39.5	— 19.44	+ 0.13	...	4	48.4	11.0	....	1080
328	37 19 57.6	57.9	— 19.41	+ 0.13	...	4	48.4	11.9	....	......
329	35 50 33.2	33.0	— 19.41	+ 0.14	+ 1.56	8	50.1	7.9	30 Cassiop. μ.	......
330	20 8 54.3	55.4	— 19.41	+ 0.15	...	4	47.4	12.9	....	1100
331	28 10 39.8	39.5	— 19.41	+ 0.14	...	3	46.9	11.0	....	1106
332	41 16 31.3	31.0	— 19.41	+ 0.13	...	4	49.4	12.0	....	1110
333	49 34 10.4	8.6	— 19.40	+ 0.13	...	5	48.7	14.5	....	......
334	35 40 23.3	...	— 19.39	+ 0.13	...	4	48.9	...	....	1118
335	49 18 59.4	59.7	— 19.39	+ 0.13	...	4	47.6	14.5	....	......
336	32 33 57.4	57.9	— 19.39	+ 0.13	...	5	48.4	13.5	....	1122
337	11 9 14.0	14.3	— 19.39	+ 0.18	...	5	45.1	12.2	[illegible]	1120
338	46 53 8.2	7.6	— 19.39	+ 0.13	+ 0.04	3	46.9	10.5	41 Andromedæ	......
339	32 24 54.0	51.7	— 19.37	+ 0.13	...	2	48.5	13.8	....	1130
340	22 2 53.5	53.4	— 19.36	+ 0.15	+ 0.01	5	48.5	9.9	31 Cassiopeiæ	1141
341	85 10 17.9	...	— 19.36	+ 0.12	+ 0.19	6	50.7	...	80 Piscium e .	......
342	39 15 4.3	5.8	— 19.36	+ 0.13	...	3	50.6	11.9	....	......
343	28 6 46.9	...	— 19.36	+ 0.14	...	3	47.2	...	....	1144
344	36 11 58.5	56.9	— 19.36	+ 0.13	...	3	50.3	14.0	....	......
345	43 35 11.3	10.6	— 19.36	+ 0.13	+ 0.01	4	49.2	10.2	42 Androm. φ	1150

| Ordinal Number. | | Magnitude. | Estimates of Magnitudes. | Mean Right Ascension 1845.0. | | Precession 1845.0. | Secular Variation | Adopted Proper Motion. |
R.	G.	R.		R.	G.			
				h. m. s.	s.	s.	s.	s.
346	251	7.2	5	1 0 34.61	34.24	+ 3.549	+ 0.053	......
347	253	7.3	6	1 0 49.48	49.24	+ 3.462	+ 0.042	......
348	...	8.2	7	1 0 59.08	...	+ 3.503	+ 0.047	......
349	254	7.9	4	1 0 59.39	59.42	+ 3.503	+ 0.047	......
350	...,	3.7	2	1 1 4.23	...	+ 3.317	+ 0.027	+ 0.015
351	...	7.1	7	1 1 26.39	...	+ 3.495	+ 0.048	......
352	256	6.0	6	1 1 32.03	31.94	+ 3.381	+ 0.034	− 0.007
353	255	5.9	6	1 1 39.34	38.87	+ 3.805	+ 0.091	......
354	257	4.1	5	1 1 42.03	41.62	+ 3.565	+ 0.056	+ 0.023
355	258	7.7	5	1 1 47.78	47.73	+ 3.755	+ 0.082	......
356	260	7.7	5	1 1 48.64	48.35	+ 3.470	+ 0.042	......
357	259	8.0	4	1 2 5.30	4.94	+ 4.247	+ 0.163	......
358	262	7.4	4	1 2 16.41	16.19	+ 3.439	+ 0.039	......
359	...	6.3	2	1 2 35.08	...	+ 3.080	+ 0.004	......
360	...	7.7	4	1 2 38.26	...	+ 3.816	+ 0.100	......
361	...	8.4	10	1 2 38.67	...	+ 8.379	+ 1.891	......
362	261	6.6	6	1 3 2.22	3.49	+ 4.952	+ 0.334	− 0.014
363	263	8.8	2	1 3 7.64	7.73	+ 3.514	+ 0.047	......
364	...	8.9	18	1 3 12.12	...	+16.779	+11.410	......
365	...	7.0	5	1 3 24.57	...	+ 3.758	+ 0.086	......
366	235	2.0	A	1 3 35.72	31.42	+16.876	+11.427	+ 0.065
367	264	6.3	4	1 3 36.95	36.61	+ 3.430	+ 0.036	......
368	265	7.7	3	1 3 41.40	40.95	+ 3.519	+ 0.047	......
369	...	7.3	6	1 3 56.77	...	+ 3.457	+ 0.044	......
370	268	7.9	4	1 4 38.22	37.88	+ 3.453	+ 0.039	.....
371	270	8.3	4	1 4 42.79	42.33	+ 3.483	+ 0.042	......
372	...	7.1	6	1 4 47.54	...	+ 5.194	+ 0.392	......
373	...	7.9	9	1 4 56.54	...	+12.591	+ 5.253	......
374	266	8.1	4	1 4 59.80	58.81	+ 4.308	+ 0.171	......
375	269	7.8	4	1 5 1.45	1.44	+ 4.142	+ 0.141	......
376	267	7.1	4	1 5 5.50	5.06	+ 4.311	+ 0.171	......
377	271	6.3	4	1 5 9.49	9.39	+ 4.154	+ 0.145	......
378	...	6.5	5	1 5 10.52	...	+ 5.208	+ 0.397	......
379	...	7.4	4	1 5 27.21	...	+ 3.498	+ 0.046	......
380	...	6.0	1	1 5 38.43	...	+ 3.115	+ 0.007	+ 0.008

Ordinal Number. R.	Mean North Polar Distance 1845.0.		Precession 1845.0.	Secular Variation.	Adopted Proper Motion.	Observations of N.P.D.			Names.	Oeltzen-Argelander Number.
	R.	G.				No. R.	Mean year R.	Mean year G.		
	o ' "	"	"	"	"		1800 +			
346	36 5 27.5	29.4	— 19.36	+ 0.13	...	3	46.2	12.0	....	1151
347	41 46 25.7	28.2	— 19.35	+ 0.13	...	3	46.0	11.0	....	1155
348	39 5 3.6	...	— 19.35	+ 0.13	...	4	49.9	...	....	....
349	39 4 49.7	51.0	— 19.35	+ 0.13	...	3	47.9	11.9	....	1159
350	55 12 10.6	...	— 19.34	+ 0.13	+ 0.09	11	54.4	...	43 Androm. β	......
351	39 48 55.4	...	— 19.34	+ 0.13	...	3	48.9	...	....	1166
352	48 44 39.5	39.1	— 19.34	+ 0.13	...	3	49.3	10.9	44 Andromedæ	....
353	25 48 26.8	26.5	— 19.33	+ 0.15	...	5	49.7	8.9	32 Cassiopeiæ	......
354	35 40 36.2	34.0	— 19.33	+ 0.14	+ 0.02	3	44.9	7.1	33 Cassiop. θ .	1175
355	27 27 48.9	50.9	— 19.33	+ 0.15	...	3	48.2	15.9	....	1178
356	41 39 46.2	47.9	— 19.33	+ 0.13	...	2	48.0	11.0	....	1181
357	16 54 18.0	18.8	— 19.32	+ 0.16	...	3	49.9	12.5	....	1184
358	44 11 47.9	47.9	— 19.32	+ 0.13	...	2	51.8	14.4	....	....
359	88 22 51.8	...	— 19.32	+ 0.12	...	1	51.8	...	33 Ceti..........	....
360	25 48 56.6	...	— 19.32	+ 0.15	...	3	50.9	...	....	....
361	3 53 4.0	...	— 19.32	+ 0.33	...	3	52.7	...	....	....
362	10 54 58.2	60.9	— 19.31	+ 0.20	— 0.03	5	47.3	14.8	....	....
363	39 18 0.2	2.1	— 19.30	+ 0.15	...	3	52.6	11.9	....	1205
364	1 31 18.1	...	— 19.30	+ 0.70	...	7	44.1	...	....	....
365	27 59 42.5	...	— 19.29	+ 0.15	...	3	44.7	...	....	1213
366	1 31 1.6	1.9	— 19.29	+ 0.71	...	550	42.6	7.1	1 Urs. Min. α.	....
367	45 29 19.4	20.5	— 19.29	+ 0.15	...	3	44.6	10.9	....	....
368	39 13 11.3	9.0	— 19.29	+ 0.15	...	3	46.6	11.9	....	1221
369	43 37 46.6	...	— 19.28	+ 0.14	...	3	49.6	...	....	1228
370	44 9 56.3	54.1	— 19.26	+ 0.15	...	2	47.0	15.0	....	1246
371	42 2 9.6	11.1	— 19.26	+ 0.14	...	2	51.4	13.9	....	....
372	9 57 33.4	...	— 19.25	+ 0.20	...	3	52.2	...	....	....
373	2 14 59.1	...	— 19.25	+ 0.51	...	4	51.4	...	....	......
374	16 48 37.9	40.7	— 19.25	+ 0.18	...	3	50.6	12.9	....	1259
375	19 14 52.8	53.9	— 19.25	+ 0.17	...	2	51.3	12.9	....	1261
376	16 47 42.4	45.1	— 19.25	+ 0.18	...	3	47.6	12.9	....	....
377	19 4 43.9	44.1	— 19.25	+ 0.17	...	3	44.5	13.0	....	1265
378	9 55 35.0	...	— 19.25	+ 0.21	...	3	51.5	...	....	....
379	41 23 35.0	...	— 19.24	+ 0.14	...	2	51.5	...	....	....
380	83 14 45.7	...	— 19.23	+ 0.13	+ 0.07	2	49.0	...	86 Piscium ζ^1.	....

Magnitude.	Estimated Magnitude.	Mean Right Ascension 1845.0		Precession 1845.0.	Secular Variation	Adopted Proper Motion.
R.		R.	G.			
		h. m. s.	s.	s.	s.	s.
8.7	6	1 5 49.68	49.81	+ 3.490	+ 0.046	......
7.8	5	1 5 58.88	58.35	+ 3.460	+ 0.040	......
8.0	4	1 6 12.45	12.30	+ 3.539	+ 0.051	......
8.2	4	1 6 12.52	12.26	+ 3.420	+ 0.037	......
7.1	5	1 7 17.99	17.57	+ 3.489	+ 0.042	......
6.7	6	1 7 35.47	36.08	+ 4.720	+ 0.257	......
7.0	7	1 7 35.89	35.81	+ 3.421	+ 0.035	......
6.7	5	1 7 46.52	...	+ 3.988	+ 0.112	......
6.6	5	1 8 5.17	5.16	+ 3.449	+ 0.039	......
8.5	5	1 8 18.09	18.13	+ 3.832	+ 0.087	......
8.2	6	1 8 20.37	21.12	+ 5.151	+ 0.344	......
7.2	4	1 8 42.09	42.17	+ 3.449	+ 0.036	......
6.1	2	1 8 44.34	...	+ 3.048	+ 0.002	− 0.005
6.7	1	1 9 3.15	...	+ 3.049	+ 0.002	+ 0.014
6.6	7	1 9 3.54	3.41	+ 3.490	+ 0.042	......
6.7	7	1 9 33.61	32.67	+ 4.607	+ 0.224	......
7.3	8	1 9 38.97	38.78	+ 4.444	+ 0.186	......
7.2	6	1 10 2.33	1.76	+ 3.397	+ 0.031	......
7.3	11	1 10 9.73	9.90	+ 3.700	+ 0.067	......
8.7	2	1 10 11.24	...	+ 3.700	+ 0.068	......
6.7	6	1 10 20.04	20.69	+ 4.956	+ 0.300	......
5.1	7	1 10 22.45	21.82	+ 3.702	+ 0.066	......
9.0	5	1 10 24.12	...	+ 4.459	+ 0.196	......
8.1	5	1 10 46.65	...	+ 3.897	+ 0.093	......
6.4	4	1 10 47.77	47.11	+ 3.897	+ 0.093	......
8.1	5	1 11 4.03	3.80	+ 3.574	+ 0.051	......
7.2	5	1 11 8.89	8.62	+ 3.427	+ 0.034	......
7.0	7	1 11 18.74	19.98	+ 3.448	+ 0.039	......
7.1	5	1 11 20.26	20.21	+ 3.572	+ 0.050	......
7.7	1	1 11 37.17	36.07	+ 3.581	+ 0.050	......
7.2	4	1 12 7.19	...	+ 3.448	+ 0.037	......
7.9	6	1 12 25.99	...	+ 3.722	+ 0.069	......
6.6	6	1 12 34.81	34.88	+ 3.554	+ 0.045	......
7.7	7	1 13 6.61	6.44	+ 3.587	+ 0.053	......
6.7	8	1 13 11.68	11.30	+ 3.458	+ 0.036	......

Ordinal Number. R.	Mean North Polar Distance 1845.0. R.		G.	Precession 1845.0.	Secular Variation.	Adopted Proper Motion.	Observations of N.P.D. No R.	Mean year 1800 + R.	G.	Names.	Oeltzen-Argelander Number.
	° ′ ″		″	″	″	″					
381	42 4 20.8		19.9	− 19.23	+ 0.14	...	4	52.4	13.9	....	1273
382	44 11 32.9		32.0	− 19.23	+ 0.14	...	3	43.3	14.9	....	......
383	39 4 49.6		49.3	− 19.23	+ 0.14	...	3	47.6	11.9	....	1280
384	47 26 4.7		3.7	− 19.23	+ 0.14	...	3	49.2	14.0	....	......
385	42 44 19.4		20.0	− 19.20	+ 0.15	...	3	45.2	10.9	....	1301
386	13 15 7.3		9.0	− 19.19	+ 0.20	...	5	49.1	12.0	....	......
387	47 52 46.5		46.9	− 19.19	+ 0.14	...	4	45.9	11.0	....	......
388	23 0 11.5		...	− 19.18	+ 0.17	...	3	47.6	...	....	1307
389	45 54 58.8		58.7	− 19.17	+ 0.15	...	3	45.7	13.9	....	......
390	27 16 29.4		31.0	− 19.17	+ 0.17	...	3	47.3	15.8	....	......
391	10 41 14.7		16.1	− 19.17	+ 0.20	...	4	45.4	14.8	....	......
392	46 11 14.6		13.9	− 19.16	+ 0.15	...	3	43.3	13.9	....	......
393	93 19 5.7		...	− 19.15	+ 0.13	+ 0.01	1	51.8	...	39 Ceti.........	......
394	93 5 35.8		...	− 19.15	+ 0.13	+ 0.14	2	57.4	...	40 Ceti.........	......
395	43 23 56.5		57.1	− 19.15	+ 0.15	...	5	49.3	14.4	....	1345
396	14 34 35.6		35.0	− 19.14	+ 0.20	...	3	45.7	12.9	....	1356
397	16 14 7.8		9.5	− 19.14	+ 0.19	...	4	43.4	12.9	....	1357
398	50 51 11.6		10.7	− 19.13	+ 0.14	...	4	51.4	11.0	....	......
399	32 36 33.0		32.7	− 19.12	+ 0.16	...	7	47.1	19.0	....	1371
400	32 30 28.9		...	− 19.12	+ 0.16	...	3	54.6	...	....	1372
401	12 5 21.8		20.2	− 19.12	+ 0.21	...	3	48.3	11.9	....	1375
402	32 35 8.1		7.1	− 19.12	+ 0.16	+ 0.01	4	44.1	8.9	34 Cassiop. φ.	1379
403	16 14 56.4		...	− 19.11	+ 0.20	...	3	49.0	...	....	1377
404	26 8 34.2		...	− 19.10	+ 0.17	...	2	50.0	...	....	1386
405	26 9 25.0		24.3	− 19.10	+ 0.17	...	4	45.9	10.0	35 Cassiopeiæ	1387
406	38 58 58.4		57.3	− 19.10	+ 0.15	...	3	43.6	13.5	....	1397
407	48 50 36.0		35.6	− 19.10	+ 0.15	...	4	49.0	10.9	....	......
408	47 18 23.0		24.1	− 19.10	+ 0.15	...	4	43.1	11.0	....	......
409	39 13 15.2		14.4	− 19.09	+ 0.15	...	3	49.3	13.5	....	1400
410	38 49 40.2		36.2	− 19.08	+ 0.16	...	3	49.6	14.7	....	1405
411	47 34 51.0		...	− 19.06	+ 0.15	...	4	51.6	...	....	......
412	32 31 28.9		...	− 19.05	+ 0.17	...	3	47.0	...	....	1421
413	40 41 32.4		33.3	− 19.05	+ 0.16	...	4	43.9	14.9	....	1430
414	39 2 11.2		11.6	− 19.04	+ 0.16	...	4	49.9	14.0	....	1436
415	47 13 45.7		46.3	− 19.04	+ 0.15	...	4	47.8	10.9	....	......

Ordinal Number.		Magnitude.	Estimates of Magnitude.	Mean Right Ascension 1845.0.		Precession 1845.0.	Secular Variation	Adopted Proper Motion.	Observations of R.A.		
R.	G.	R.		R.	G.				No.	Mean year.	
									R.	R.	G.
				h. m. s.	s.	s.	s.	s.		1800 +	
416	300	5.2	5	1 13 14.30	14.30	+ 3.486	+ 0.040	+ 0.005	11	49.8	7.7
417	296	7.9	3	1 13 18.56	18.91	+ 4.872	+ 0.261	......	3	48.9	12.0
418	...	6.1	6	1 13 32.45	...	+ 3.727	+ 0.070	......	4	46.8	...
419	...	7.4	5	1 14 12.37	...	+ 3.488	+ 0.041	......	3	50.6	...
420	302	8.2	4	1 14 17.40	17.34	+ 3.425	+ 0.034	......	2	50.3	13.9
421	301	7.0	5	1 14 27.64	28.20	+ 4.253	+ 0.138	......	3	49.6	12.0
422	304	7.3	5	1 14 48.42	48.19	+ 3.587	+ 0.047	. ....	3	48.6	12.9
423	303	4.9	5	1 15 3.63	3.14	+ 4.099	+ 0.116	+ 0.005	3	46.9	8.0
424	305	2.9	9	1 15 43.49	43.25	+ 3.804	+ 0.075	+ 0.042	4	47.7	6.9
425	306	8.3	6	1 15 53.90	54.14	+ 3.605	+ 0.051	......	4	49.9	12.9
426	...	4.6	3	1 16 16.61	...	+ 3.001	0.000	− 0.007	35	46.9	...
427	308	8.6	5	1 16 18.53	18.85	+ 3.430	+ 0.031	......	3	50.5	13.9
428	307	7.5	6	1 16 46.48	44.10	+ 4.544	+ 0.185	......	3	49.2	12.0
429	309	6.2	6	1 17 13.30	12.91	+ 3.477	+ 0.037	+ 0.004	4	46.7	9.9
430	...	8.0	5	1 17 24.36	...	+ 3.822	+ 0.076	......	2	47.4	...
431	310	7.0	5	1 17 36.48	35.81	+ 3.482	+ 0.037	......	4	45.6	9.9
432	311	8.1	7	1 18 8.80	8.46	+ 3.622	+ 0.050	......	3	48.6	12.9
433	312	5.2	8	1 18 24.55	24.10	+ 3.512	+ 0.040	+ 0.031	8	48.8	8.0
434	313	6.9	4	1 18 48.88	48.71	+ 3.442	+ 0.034	......	3	46.8	13.9
435	314	8.1	5	1 18 59.43	59.12	+ 3.492	+ 0.037	......	3	48.6	12.6
436	317	7.0	4	1 19 5.53	5.38	+ 3.495	+ 0.037	......	3	46.9	14.0
437	316	8.9	7	1 19 9.41	9.28	+ 3.626	+ 0.050	......	3	49.5	12.9
438	315	7.1	7	1 19 12.09	11.49	+ 3.831	+ 0.075	......	5	46.1	10.9
439	...	8.5	5	1 19 14.74	...	+ 3.632	+ 0.053	......	3	51.6	...
440	319	7.2	8	1 19 31.56	31.60	+ 3.629	+ 0.050	......	3	46.4	12.9
441	320	7.3	6	1 19 46.16	45.57	+ 3.842	+ 0.075	......	5	47.3	10.9
442	318	6.3	3	1 19 47.49	46.95	+ 4.287	+ 0.139	+ 0.029	5	45.9	8.9
443	321	7.0	3	1 20 14.54	14.26	+ 3.832	+ 0.073	......	3	49.2	10.9
444	324	5.5	5	1 20 49.92	49.74	+ 3.552	+ 0.043	......	4	46.9	7.7
445	322	7.6	5	1 20 52.93	52.59	+ 3.965	+ 0.104	......	3	48.9	11.9
446	323	7.0	6	1 21 9.90	9.55	+ 4.292	+ 0.137	......	4	47.0	12.0
447	325	6.3	3	1 21 15.55	15.28	+ 4.197	+ 0.122	+ 0.032	5	46.5	10.0
448	...	8.4	5	1 21 27.56	...	+ 4.175	+ 0.117	......	2	48.9	...
449	327	7.1	6	1 21 35.90	36.05	+ 3.597	+ 0.042	......	4	48.4	12.9
450	326	7.6	6	1 21 46.51	46.01	+ 3.979	+ 0.090	......	3	50.2	11.0

Ordinal Number.	Mean North Polar Distance 1845.0.		Precession 1845.0.	Secular Variation.	Adopted Proper Motion.	Observations of N.P.D.			Names.	Oeltzen-Argelander Number.
R.	R.	G.				No. R.	Mean year. R.	G.		
	° ′ ″	″	″	″	″		1800 +			
416	45 17 7.8	8.7	− 19.04	+ 0.16	...	4	44.1	7.7	46 Androm. ξ .	1438
417	13 7 56.8	54.6	− 19.04	+ 0.21	...	4	51.1	12.0	....	1437
418	32 39 58.0	...	− 19.03	+ 0.17	...	4	45.7	...	....	1445
419	45 28 45.3	...	− 19.01	+ 0.16	...	3	48.9	...	....	......
420	50 12 8.0	10.3	− 19.01	+ 0.16	...	4	51.9	13.9	....	......
421	19 49 50.1	48.7	− 19.00	+ 0.20	...	4	47.9	12.0	....	1455
422	39 38 16.0	12.6	− 18.99	+ 0.17	...	3	45.3	12.9	....	......
423	22 40 54.0	55.2	− 18.99	+ 0.19	...	4	44.4	8.0	36 Cassiop. ψ .	1470
424	30 34 22.2	21.4	− 18.97	+ 0.18	+ 0.05	6	44.9	6.5	37 Cassiop. δ .	1481
425	39 7 35.0	34.8	− 18.96	+ 0.17	...	3	45.7	12.5	....	......
426	98 59 6.6	...	− 18.95	+ 0.14	+ 0.22	1	46.9	...	45 Ceti θ^1	......
427	50 29 45.5	47.5	− 18.95	+ 0.16	...	2	51.5	13.9	....	......
428	16 35 51.0	41.3	− 18.94	+ 0.23	...	3	48.3	12.0	....	1504
429	47 20 54.9	53.0	− 18.92	+ 0.17	+ 0.04	4	45.4	9.9	....	......
430	30 31 24.1	...	− 18.92	+ 0.18	...	3	47.6	...	....	1510
431	47 6 52.4	50.6	− 18.91	+ 0.17	...	5	46.9	9.9	....	......
432	38 59 52.4	53.4	− 18.90	+ 0.18	...	4	47.0	12.9	....	1525
433	45 23 45.2	46.1	− 18.89	+ 0.17	+ 0.11	4	43.1	8.0	48 Androm. ω	......
434	50 28 12.1	13.2	− 18.88	+ 0.17	...	4	48.0	13.9	....	......
435	46 55 42.1	41.8	− 18.88	+ 0.17	...	3	51.6	12.6	....	......
436	46 45 24.1	23.4	− 18.87	+ 0.17	...	4	48.9	14.0	....	......
437	39 7 34.2	34.6	− 18.87	+ 0.18	...	4	50.9	12.9	....	1540
438	30 46 11.0	12.8	− 18.87	+ 0.20	...	5	47.4	10.9	....	1543
439	38 55 16.0	...	− 18.87	+ 0.18	...	3	49.9	...	....	1545
440	39 7 11.8	12.7	− 18.86	+ 0.18	...	5	44.3	12.9	....	1554
441	30 33 11.7	11.0	− 18.85	+ 0.20	...	4	47.2	10.9	....	1560
442	20 32 9.8	10.4	− 18.85	+ 0.21	+ 0.08	8	48.6	8.9	38 Cassiop. A .	1558
443	31 1 19.9	20.7	− 18.84	+ 0.20	...	4	47.6	10.9	....	......
444	43 47 41.2	40.4	− 18.82	+ 0.18	+ 0.03	5	47.7	7.7	49 Androm. A	1579
445	27 27 19.2	19.6	− 18.82	+ 0.21	...	3	47.9	11.9	....	1580
446	20 46 55.5	53.5	− 18.81	+ 0.22	+ 0.02	3	45.0	12.0	....	1583
447	22 23 25.7	26.9	− 18.80	+ 0.21	+ 0.08	4	43.1	10.0	....	......
448	22 50 26.2	...	− 18.79	+ 0.22	...	3	48.9	...	....	......
449	41 27 25.9	24.3	− 18.79	+ 0.20	...	4	45.7	12.9	....	1594
450	27 10 51.6	51.5	− 18.79	+ 0.21	...	4	47.4	11.0	....	......

Ordinal Number.		Magnitude.	Estimates of Magnitude.	Mean Right Ascension 1845.0.		Precession 1845.0.	Secular Variation	Adopted Proper Motion.	Observations of R.A.		
R.	G.	R.		R.	G.				No. R.	Mean year. R.	G.
				h. m. s.	s.	s.	s.	s.		1800 +	
451	328	7.9	4	1 21 56.56	56.29	+ 3.504	+ 0.040	......	3	50.6	13.9
452	...	5.0	5	1 22 4.20	...	+ 3.114	+ 0.007	+ 0.019	5	51.9	...
453	329	7.6	2	1 22 14.27	13.83	+ 3.983	+ 0.091	......	2	48.4	11.0
454	330	7.9	4	1 23 1.44	0.73	+ 4.235	+ 0.121	......	4	49.6	9.9
455	...	4.7	3	1 23 11.80	...	+ 3.193	+ 0.012	......	17	43.7	...
456	...	8.7	5	1 23 14.16	...	+ 4.227	+ 0.129	......	4	48.4	...
457	...	7.3	5	1 23 31.96	...	+ 3.750	+ 0.064	......	2	51.4	...
458	331	7.1	7	1 23 34.16	34.09	+ 4.506	+ 0.161	......	4	50.7	15.8
459	332	5.3	5	1 23 50.86	50.63	+ 3.848	+ 0.073	......	3	47.5	8.9
460	333	8.3	5	1 24 16.42	16.03	+ 4.006	+ 0.090	......	3	48.3	11.0
461	...	7.6	5	1 24 38.26	...	+ 4.359	+ 0.146	......	4	47.3	...
462	334	7.0	5	1 24 47.45	46.99	+ 4.702	+ 0.184	......	2	48.3	12.0
463	...	9.1	4	1 24 49.28	...	+ 4.488	+ 0.170	......	3	50.6	...
464	...	7.0	5	1 24 54.43	...	+ 3.992	+ 0.096	......	2	50.8	...
465	336	7.3	4	1 25 42.04	42.02	+ 3.707	+ 0.053	......	2	45.5	13.1
466	340	7.5	8	1 25 58.99	58.93	+ 3.683	+ 0.054	......	4	46.2	12.9
467	...	8.0	7	1 26 5.88	...	+ 8.099	+ 1.245	......	7	51.3	...
468	335	8.2	4	1 26 9.97	10.41	+ 4.562	+ 0.170	......	3	49.0	15.8
469	341	7.5	7	1 26 12.29	11.79	+ 4.018	+ 0.090	......	3	49.2	11.0
470	337	4.7	3	1 26 15.07	14.83	+ 4.605	+ 0.178	......	5	45.6	10.9
471	342	7.1	6	1 26 41.09	40.96	+ 3.587	+ 0.043	......	3	47.2	13.9
472	338	7.1	4	1 26 42.03	41.97	+ 5.239	+ 0.300	+ 0.007	3	50.5	11.9
473	...	6.4	4	1 26 45.36	...	+ 3.489	+ 0.034	......	4	52.6	...
474	344	7.3	3	1 27 0.44	0.29	+ 3.593	+ 0.045	......	2	46.4	13.9
475	343	6.3	6	1 27 0.53	0.44	+ 3.619	+ 0.047	......	5	47.3	13.0
476	...	7.3	3	1 27 15.44	...	+ 3.860	+ 0.073	......	4	51.9	...
477	...	9.1	4	1 27 18.08	...	+ 3.858	+ 0.073	......	2	55.0	...
478	345	6.7	4	1 27 43.07	42.96	+ 3.992	+ 0.083	......	3	49.5	11.9
479	...	5.0	5	1 27 43.24	...	+ 3.499	+ 0.035	......	4	47.9	...
480	346	7.7	4	1 27 54.45	54.32	+ 3.591	+ 0.044	......	2	49.4	13.9
481	...	5.8	4	1 28 2.36	...	+ 3.847	+ 0.069	......	2	46.5	...
482	347	7.2	4	1 28 15.08	14.04	+ 3.620	+ 0.047	......	4	45.8	8.9
483	348	4.1	7	1 28 30.42	30.22	+ 3.626	+ 0.047	+ 0.006	7	47.7	6.7
484	349	7.8	4	1 29 23.97	23.81	+ 3.550	+ 0.040	......	3	51.5	10.9
485	339	8.3	15	1 29 48.62	48.17	+10.677	+ 2.498	+ 0.068	28	50.4	9.4

Ordinal Number. R.	Mean North Polar Distance 1845.0.		Precession 1845.0.	Secular Variation.	Adopted Proper Motion.	Observations of N.P.D.			Names.	Oeltzen-Argelander Number.
	R.	G.				No. R.	Mean year. R.	Mean year. G.		
	° ′ ″	″	″	″	″		1800 +			
451	47 10 51.6	51.0	− 18.78	+ 0.20	...	3	50.3	13.9	....	......
452	84 39 25.6	...	− 18.78	+ 0.16	+ 0.18	9	51.6	...	98 Piscium μ .	......
453	27 12 27.5	26.4	− 18.78	+ 0.21	...	5	41.5	11.0	....	......
454	22 7 0.4	1.7	− 18.75	+ 0.20	...	3	43.9	9.9	....	1626
455	75 27 18.8	...	− 18.75	+ 0.17	...	2	45.9	...	99 Piscium η .	......
456	22 20 16.8	...	− 18.74	+ 0.22	...	3	43.9	...	....	1632
457	34 58 56.9	...	− 18.74	+ 0.20	...	4	49.2	...	....	1644
458	18 21 22.5	24.0	− 18.74	+ 0.22	...	4	47.4	15.8	....	1645
459	31 33 58.7	58.4	− 18.73	+ 0.20	+ 0.05	6	45.2	8.9	39 Cassiop. χ .	......
460	27 10 16.4	16.9	− 18.72	+ 0.20	...	3	44.7	11.0	....	......
461	20 31 32.4	...	− 18.70	+ 0.24	...	4	45.9	...	....	......
462	16 29 42.5	40.6	− 18.69	+ 0.25	...	4	46.2	12.0	....	1666
463	18 50 15.4	...	− 18.69	+ 0.24	...	2	50.4	...	....	1672
464	27 42 53.7	...	− 18.69	+ 0.21	...	4	48.8	...	....	......
465	37 27 3.4	2.4	− 18.66	+ 0.20	...	3	46.2	13.1	....	1690
466	38 37 54.5	53.7	− 18.66	+ 0.20	...	5	48.6	12.9	....	1694
467	5 34 11.8	...	− 18.65	+ 0.42	...	4	51.5	...	....	......
468	18 12 42.8	46.1	− 18.65	+ 0.25	...	3	49.6	15.8	....	1701
469	27 22 50.2	52.4	− 18.65	+ 0.22	...	5	48.5	11.0	....	......
470	17 45 13.3	12.6	− 18.65	+ 0.25	...	4	41.5	10.9	40 Cassiopeiæ	1702
471	43 40 50.1	48.4	− 18.64	+ 0.19	...	3	48.6	13.9	....	......
472	12 49 22.5	21.6	− 18.63	+ 0.28	...	3	47.6	11.9	....	1711
473	49 43 8.1	...	− 18.63	+ 0.19	...	3	50.3	...	....	......
474	43 28 6.2	6.4	− 18.62	+ 0.19	...	4	50.4	13.9	....	......
475	42 4 17.3	17.3	− 18.62	+ 0.20	...	4	43.4	13.0	....	1718
476	32 9 22.9	...	− 18.62	+ 0.21	...	2	50.9	...	....	......
477	32 9 16.0	...	− 18.62	+ 0.21	...	2	52.5	...	....	......
478	28 26 29.5	30.1	− 18.61	+ 0.21	...	3	48.0	11.9	....	1737
479	49 22 20.4	...	− 18.60	+ 0.19	...	4	47.7	...	50 Andromedæ	......
480	43 50 40.5	39.6	− 18.60	+ 0.20	...	3	52.3	13.9	....	......
481	32 48 53.5	...	− 18.59	+ 0.21	...	3	47.9	...	....	......
482	42 22 49.9	52.1	− 18.59	+ 0.20	...	4	48.9	8.9	....	......
483	42 9 34.0	35.3	− 18.58	+ 0.20	+ 0.14	6	46.1	6.7	51 Andromedæ	1753
484	46 38 47.5	50.5	− 18.55	+ 0.20	...	3	45.6	10.9	....	......
485	3 50 24.4	24.0	− 18.54	+ 0.60	...	14	49.1	9.4	....	......

Magnitude.	Estimates of Magnitude.	Mean Right Ascension 1845.0.		Precession 1845.0.	Secular Variation.	Adopted Proper Motion.
	R.	R.	G.			
		h. m. s.	s.	s.	s.	s.
7.9	3	1 29 48.67	48.63	+ 3.711	+ 0.051	......
8.0	5	1 30 1.32	1.12	+ 3.628	+ 0.047	......
8.7	5	1 30 4.03	3.94	+ 3.583	+ 0.043	......
5.7	4	1 30 4.64	4.44	+ 3.557	+ 0.037	......
6.7	5	1 30 11.81	11.01	+ 3.584	+ 0.039	......
7.0	5	1 30 24.15	24.02	+ 3.754	+ 0.060	......
7.4	4	1 30 29.79	29.61	+ 4.858	+ 0.208	......
7.2	4	1 30 48.03	47.64	+ 4.848	+ 0.202	......
6.0	6	1 30 56.53	55.99	+ 4.302	+ 0.121	+ 0.006
5.4	7	1 31 0.66	0.80	+ 4.478	+ 0.148	......
6.4	5	1 31 23.56	22.98	+ 3.546	+ 0.038	......
5.5	5	1 31 27.06	27.23	+ 3.503	+ 0.034	+ 0.011
6.9	5	1 32 11.62	11.29	+ 3.968	+ 0.078	......
5.2	4	1 32 22.27	22.40	+ 3.539	+ 0.037	+ 0.080
8.1	7	1 32 45.37	...	+16.346	+ 6.697	......
5.6	5	1 32 53.27	52.80	+ 3.974	+ 0.080	......
7.7	6	1 32 53.72	53.04	+ 4.298	+ 0.119	......
8.6	7	1 33 2.73	3.53	+ 4.916	+ 0.213	......
7.5	2	1 33 5.00	4.91	+ 3.649	+ 0.045	......
6.8	6	1 33 7.17	...	+ 6.096	+ 0.476	......
4.6	4	1 33 22.08	...	+ 3.114	+ 0.007	− 0.004
7.6	7	1 33 28.71	...	+ 3.976	+ 0.080	......
7.1	3	1 33 29.12	29.10	+ 3.508	+ 0.032	......
7.1	5	1 33 38.70	38.59	+ 3.654	+ 0.045	......
7.2	4	1 33 45.43	...	+ 3.832	+ 0.065	......
7.0	8	1 33 49.76	49.74	+ 3.754	+ 0.057	
7.0	6	1 33 52.03	51.50	+ 3.594	+ 0.043	
4.2	3	1 33 58.57	58.28	+ 3.703	+ 0.051	
8.5	4	1 34 21.36	21.41	+ 3.598	+ 0.040	
6.4	7	1 35 0.75	0.47	+ 3.615	+ 0.043	
7.8	6	1 36 15.77	15.19	+ 4.134	+ 0.093	......
8.3	3	1 36 29.66	29.57	+ 3.749	+ 0.051	......
5.6	5	1 36 36.15	32.83	+ 4.147	+ 0.096	+ 0.007
8.3	4	1 36 59.55	59.38	+ 4.139	+ 0.096	......
4.7	10	1 37 12.94	...	+ 3.151	+ 0.009	+ 0.006

Ordinal Number. R.	Mean North Polar Distance 1845.0. R.	G.	Precession 1845.0.	Secular Variation.	Adopted Proper Motion.	Observations of N.P.D. No. R.	Mean year. R.	G.	Names.	Oeltzen-Argelander Number.
							1800 +			
486	38 31 21.7	21.4	− 18.54	+ 0.20	...	3	48.9	12.9	....	1785
487	42 32 10.8	8.6	− 18.52	+ 0.20	...	2	50.9	12.9	....	......
488	44 57 40.4	42.5	− 18.52	+ 0.20	...	2	52.4	13.9	....	......
489	46 24 17.8	18.2	− 18.52	+ 0.20	...	5	44.7	10.8	52 Androm. χ	......
490	44 54 9.3	3.2	− 18.52	+ 0.20	...	3	45.3	13.9	....	......
491	36 55 15.9	16.0	− 18.51	+ 0.21	...	4	46.0	13.0	....	......
492	16 2 41.9	40.1	− 18.51	+ 0.28	...	3	42.9	12.0	....	1801
493	16 10 52.9	50.9	− 18.50	+ 0.28	...	4	44.0	12.0	....	1809
494	22 44 40.0	38.0	− 18.49	+ 0.25	...	3	43.7	10.0	43 Cassiop. ω	1812
495	20 9 51.7	49.2	− 18.49	+ 0.25	+ 0.02	4	46.1	9.0	42 Cassiopeiæ	1815
496	47 29 20.3	19.4	− 18.48	− 0.20	...	3	45.0	14.5	....	......
497	50 12 37.0	37.3	− 18.48	+ 0.20	...	3	45.3	8.0	53 Androm. τ	......
498	30 14 16.6	15.6	− 18.45	+ 0.23	+ 0.02	4	45.7	10.0	....	1842
499	48 10 1.3	58.3	− 18.45	+ 0.20	+ 0.06	3	45.2	10.9	....	......
500	2 16 22.0	...	− 18.43	+ 0.94	...	5	50.5	...	....	......
501	30 14 0.1	58.6	− 18.43	+ 0.23	+ 0.04	5	44.5	10.0	44 Cassiopeiæ	1860
502	23 13 13.8	14.0	− 18.43	+ 0.24	...	5	48.4	11.9	....	1858
503	15 57 37.1	32.6	− 18.43	+ 0.26	...	4	50.4	12.0	....	1866
504	42 22 6.2	7.8	− 18.42	+ 0.22	...	4	50.4	12.9	....	1871
505	9 53 35.5	...	− 18.42	+ 0.35	...	3	51.2	...	....	1869
506	85 17 55.1	...	− 18.41	+ 0.18	+ 0.04	6	53.1	...	106 Piscium ν	......
507	30 20 49.7	...	− 18.41	+ 0.22	...	3	45.0	...	....	......
508	50 24 27.7	28.8	− 18.41	+ 0.20	...	2	51.6	14.0	....	......
509	42 16 2.3	3.2	− 18.41	+ 0.22	...	2	48.5	12.9	....	1884
510	34 54 21.4	...	− 18.40	+ 0.22	...	3	51.6	...	....	1886
511	37 53 53.4	54.2	− 18.40	+ 0.22	...	4	48.2	13.0	....	......
512	45 27 43.6	43.1	− 18.40	+ 0.21	...	4	47.5	13.5	....	......
513	40 5 41.4	40.5	− 18.40	+ 0.22	+ 0.03	4	46.2	6.5	54 Andromedæ	1892
514	45 21 2.4	59.7	− 18.38	+ 0.21	...	3	46.5	13.8	....	......
515	44 38 29.6	29.6	− 18.35	+ 0.21	...	4	45.7	11.0	....	1920
516	27 7 31.3	32.9	− 18.31	+ 0.23	...	3	51.0	12.9	....	1941
517	38 45 31.6	31.8	− 18.30	+ 0.22	...	3	47.0	12.9	....	1948
518	26 54 58.2	54.0	− 18.30	+ 0.25	+ 0.14	4	42.4	10.0	....	1954
519	27 11 52.1	53.4	− 18.28	+ 0.25	...	2	51.4	13.9	....	1965
520	81 37 27.9	...	− 18.28	+ 0.19	− 0.01	9	50.5	...	110 Piscium o	......

| Magnitude. | Estimates of Magnitude. | Mean Right Ascension 1845.0. | | Precession 1845.0. | Secular Variation | Adopted Proper Motion. |
R.	R.	R.	G.			
		h. m. s.	s.	s.	s.	s.
6.7	5	1 37 16.92	...	+ 6.622	+ 0.586	......
7.4	7	1 37 44.09	43.74	+ 3.810	+ 0.061	......
6.9	7	1 38 2.67	1.70	+ 5.114	+ 0.236	......
8.7	4	1 38 4.71	4.46	+ 3.809	+ 0.060	......
6.5	7	1 38 18.88	18.63	+ 3.635	+ 0.043	......
7.1	8	1 38 38.97	...	+ 6.280	+ 0.492	......
6.8	6	1 39 30.34	29.71	+ 5.592	+ 0.327	......
6.2	3	1 39 39.97	...	+ 3.677	+ 0.046	......
8.1	6	1 40 24.13	...	+ 3.864	+ 0.065	......
6.6	10	1 41 3.70	3.56	+ 3.779	+ 0.057	......
8.3	6	1 41 8.01	...	+ 3.875	+ 0.066	......
7.2	8	1 41 20.03	19.58	+ 3.862	+ 0.063	......
8.0	5	1 41 33.24	32.84	+ 3.864	+ 0.063	......
8.4	7	1 41 42.92	42.89	+ 3.780	+ 0.056	......
5.8	5	1 41 50.94	50.48	+ 3.872	+ 0.062	......
8.2	4	1 42 16.66	...	+ 3.881	+ 0.066	......
6.0	7	1 42 19.79	19.30	+ 3.758	+ 0.052	......
6.4	5	1 42 58.19	...	+ 3.780	+ 0.053	− 0.006
8.4	3	1 43 0.71	0.66	+ 3.555	+ 0.036	......
3.3	4	1 43 18.32	17.99	+ 4.209	+ 0.097	+ 0.006
8.8	5	1 43 25.71	25.52	+ 3.578	+ 0.037	......
6.5	5	1 43 35.21	...	+ 3.899	+ 0.067	......
7.2	5	1 43 44.10	44.01	+ 3.735	+ 0.047	......
6.8	8	1 43 58.93	59.77	+ 5.193	+ 0.233	......
6.1	5	1 44 0.92	0.64	+ 3.561	+ 0.035	......
5.1	5	1 44 2.89	2.15	+ 4.515	+ 0.134	......
8.1	3	1 44 25.03	24.96	+ 3.736	+ 0.051	......
4.7	1	1 45 2.10	...	+ 3.270	+ 0.015	......
5.0	1	1 45 2.17	...	+ 3.270	+ 0.015	......
9.5	6	1 45 18.10	17.70	+ 5.238	+ 0.236	......
7.2	3	1 45 20.65	20.40	+ 3.566	+ 0.036	......
6.5	5	1 45 35.55	35.21	+ 3.568	+ 0.036	......
7.1	5	1 45 41.49	42.02	+ 4.945	+ 0.187	......
7.5	5	1 45 48.93	48.43	+ 3.803	+ 0.053	......
2.9	3	1 46 5.32	...	+ 3.288	+ 0.016	+ 0.002

Ordinal Number.	Mean North Polar Distance 1845.0.		Precession 1845.0.	Secular Variation.	Adopted Proper Motion.	Observations of N.P.D.			Names.	Oeltzen-Argelander Number.
						No.	Mean year.			
R.	R.	G.				R.	R.	G.		
	° ′ ″	″	″	″	″		1800 +			
521	8 48 45.6	...	− 18.27	+ 0.40	...	4	45.7	...	....	......
522	36 46 23.4	22.6	− 18.26	+ 0.22	...	5	46.7	11.0	....	1979
523	15 10 59.9	56.9	− 18.25	+ 0.29	...	4	45.2	11.9	....	......
524	36 53 14.1	17.1	− 18.24	+ 0.23	...	4	47.2	10.9	....	1990
525	44 32 42.7	44.4	− 18.24	+ 0.22	+ 0.12	4	43.9	9.0	....	1999
526	9 51 30.6	...	− 18.23	+ 0.38	...	5	51.3	...	....	2003
527	12 34 22.1	20.8	− 18.20	+ 0.34	+ 0.01	4	46.2	12.0	....	2018
528	42 52 40.6	...	− 18.19	+ 0.23	...	4	46.4	...	....	......
529	35 33 21.4	...	− 18.16	+ 0.24	...	4	46.9	...	....	......
530	38 50 2.3	1.3	− 18.13	+ 0.23	+ 0.07	7	49.7	12.9	....	2043
531	35 21 56.3	...	− 18.13	+ 0.24	...	4	48.0	...	....	......
532	35 50 50.0	48.3	− 18.12	+ 0.24	...	4	42.7	10.5	....	......
533	35 49 39.3	38.8	− 18.12	+ 0.24	...	4	44.3	10.9	....	......
534	38 58 15.1	16.5	− 18.11	+ 0.24	...	3	47.3	12.8	....	2052
535	35 37 24.4	22.9	− 18.10	+ 0.24	+ 0.06	6	45.3	10.0	1 Persei.........	......
536	35 26 20.0	...	− 18.09	+ 0.25	...	3	45.3	...	....	......
537	39 58 35.5	34.3	− 18.09	+ 0.24	...	6	45.6	10.4	2 Persei *g*......	2064
538	39 17 37.8	...	− 18.06	+ 0.24	...	3	49.3	...	....	2076
539	50 8 46.0	48.5	− 18.06	+ 0.23	...	3	47.6	11.0	....	......
540	27 5 48.3	47.3	− 18.05	+ 0.27	+ 0.02	7	46.4	7.1	45 Cassiop. ε...	2082
541	48 55 35.0	38.8	− 18.05	+ 0.23	...	4	51.4	14.9	....	......
542	35 10 11.7	...	− 18.04	+ 0.25	...	3	44.9	...	....	......
543	41 19 25.0	23.7	− 18.03	+ 0.24	...	5	49.3	10.9	....	2090
544	15 25 37.0	36.1	− 18.03	+ 0.31	...	4	47.9	11.9	....	2091
545	50 2 16.6	17.7	− 18.02	+ 0.23	...	3	45.6	11.0	55 Andromedæ	......
546	22 4 47.3	46.8	− 18.02	+ 0.29	...	5	46.4	8.9	46 Cassiopeiæ.	2092
547	41 27 39.1	37.6	− 18.01	+ 0.24	...	3	44.6	11.0	....	2101
548	71 27 58.1	...	− 17.97	+ 0.21	+ 0.11	3	54.0	...	5 Arietis γ (n.)	......
549	71 28 5.9	...	− 17.97	+ 0.21	+ 0.11	2	55.0	...	5 Arietis γ (s.)	......
550	15 17 46.5	46.0	− 17.97	+ 0.31	...	3	51.5	11.9	....	2119
551	50 6 33.0	35.2	− 17.97	+ 0.23	...	2	49.4	11.0	....	......
552	50 3 36.2	35.6	− 17.97	+ 0.23	+ 0.03	3	46.3	13.0	....	......
553	17 36 25.5	21.9	− 17.96	+ 0.30	...	3	47.3	14.0	....	2131
554	39 4 29.1	28.4	− 17.96	+ 0.24	...	2	45.0	12.9	....	......
555	69 57 7.0	...	− 17.94	+ 0.21	+ 0.11	1	45.9	...	6 Arietis β	......

Magnitude.	Estimates of Magnitude.	Mean Right Ascension 1845.0.		Precession 1845.0.	Secular Variation	Adopted Proper Motion.
	R.	R.	G.			
		h. m. s.	s.	s.	s.	s.
8.4	4	1 46 17.38	16.93	+ 4.297	+ 0.101	......
7.3	7	1 46 33.04	32.81	+ 3.852	+ 0.056	......
8.6	7	1 46 37.46	36.99	+ 3.826	+ 0.054	......
8.1	11	1 46 50.39	...	+25.079	+15.008	......
7.0	7	1 46 50.88	50.76	+ 3.831	+ 0.054	......
7.7	4	1 46 51.94	51.77	+ 4.474	+ 0.122	......
7.1	5	1 47 9.97	9.89	+ 3.596	+ 0.037	......
6.2	4	1 47 29.12	29.03	+ 5.721	+ 0.324	......
7.2	4	1 47 29.63	29.46	+ 4.446	+ 0.121	......
8.4	5	1 47 46.64	46.65	+ 3.857	+ 0.058	......
8.1	3	1 47 50.96	50.94	+ 3.597	+ 0.037	......
6.5	7	1 47 57.07	56.86	+ 5.294	+ 0.236	......
9.5	7	1 47 58.39	55.77	+ 5.290	+ 0.240	......
5.9	5	1 48 16.07	...	+ 4.311	+ 0.103	......
6.6	5	1 48 18.62	18.33	+ 3.708	+ 0.045	......
7.8	6	1 48 23.74	23.85	+ 3.858	+ 0.056	......
8.0	4	1 48 24.72	24.34	+ 4.479	+ 0.121	......
6.9	3	1 48 33.70	33.64	+ 3.599	+ 0.037	......
5.6	4	1 48 44.53	44.06	+ 3.759	+ 0.048	+ 0.003
7.7	3	1 48 54.84	54.61	+ 3.710	+ 0.045	......
4.7	3	1 49 19.83	19.85	+ 4.770	+ 0.160	......
6.7	5	1 49 35.48	36.18	+ 5.094	+ 0.202	......
5.4	5	1 49 48.58	47.65	+ 5.643	+ 0.301	+ 0.027
7.2	2	1 49 51.24	51.48	+ 4.816	+ 0.167	......
4.0	6	1 50 19.13	19.03	+ 4.938	+ 0.183	......
7.0	3	1 50 41.69	41.80	+ 3.663	+ 0.043	......
6.2	5	1 50 42.64	42.35	+ 6.800	+ 0.551	......
8.9	5	1 50 48.37	47.64	+ 4.338	+ 0.105	......
5.5	3	1 50 53.81	54.84	+ 5.451	+ 0.264	− 0.009
7.8	5	1 50 58.29	57.99	+ 3.889	+ 0.060	......
6.3	6	1 51 23.80	23.63	+ 4.359	+ 0.106	......
7.0	4	1 51 24.40	22.62	+ 6.899	+ 0.558	......
7.6	5	1 51 30.60	31.42	+ 4.832	+ 0.163	......
6.2	9	1 51 35.73	35.86	+ 4.333	+ 0.103	......
6.0	6	1 52 1.14	0.85	+ 3.925	+ 0.061	......

Ordinal Number.	Mean North Polar Distance 1845.0.		Precession 1845.0.	Secular Variation.	Adopted Proper Motion.	Observations of N.P.D.			Names.	Oeltzen-Argelander Number.
R.	R.	G.				No. R.	Mean year. R.	Mean year. G.		
	° ′ ″	″	″	″	″		1800 +			
556	25 58 46.8	45.4	− 17.94	+ 0.28	...	2	48.9	13.9	....	2145
557	37 27 28.2	27.7	− 17.93	+ 0.25	...	3	45.7	13.0	....	2149
558	38 25 52.0	16.3	− 17.93	+ 0.24	...	4	50.4	14.0	....	2151
559	1 33 45.9	...	− 17.92	+ 1.65	...	5	51.1	...	....	......
560	38 16 22.3	23.0	− 17.92	+ 0.24	...	4	47.2	14.0	....	2154
561	23 10 53.0	51.4	− 17.92	+ 0.28	...	3	50.9	12.0	....	2153
562	48 52 10.8	13.5	− 17.90	+ 0.23	...	4	51.4	14.9	....	......
563	12 50 24.9	24.3	− 17.88	+ 0.38	...	4	46.3	12.0	....	2164
564	23 42 56.3	55.2	− 17.88	+ 0.29	...	4	50.2	12.4	....	2165
565	37 35 55.8	54.4	− 17.87	+ 0.26	...	2	52.5	13.0	....	2174
566	48 59 39.7	42.6	− 17.87	+ 0.25	...	2	52.4	14.0	....	......
567	15 15 17.3	14.4	− 17.86	+ 0.36	...	4	45.4	11.0	....	2180
568	15 17 11.4	9.5	− 17.86	+ 0.36	...	4	46.9	11.0	....	2181
569	26 8 11.0	...	− 17.85	+ 0.29	...	5	49.1	...	....	2189
570	43 39 51.8	51.9	− 17.85	+ 0.25	...	3	45.2	11.0	....	......
571	37 40 53.8	53.2	− 17.85	+ 0.26	...	3	43.6	13.0	....	2191
572	23 22 32.2	31.2	− 17.85	+ 0.29	...	3	50.3	12.0	....	2190
573	49 3 53.0	54.9	− 17.84	+ 0.25	...	3	49.9	14.9	....	......
574	41 33 24.0	25.5	− 17.84	+ 0.25	...	6	48.6	10.5	3 Persei	......
575	43 43 7.7	8.2	− 17.83	+ 0.25	...	3	51.0	11.0	....	......
576	19 50 55.9	54.9	− 17.81	+ 0.32	...	5	44.9	8.0	48 Cassiopeiæ.	2204
577	16 54 12.9	12.6	− 17.80	+ 0.35	...	3	48.6	15.1	....	2208
578	13 28 8.2	5.6	− 17.79	+ 0.38	+ 0.02	7	47.5	8.9	47 Cassiopeiæ.	2213
579	19 27 26.2	26.0	− 17.79	+ 0.32	...	2	46.5	15.0	....	2214
580	18 19 59.7	60.5	− 17.78	+ 0.33	− 0.02	3	41.8	7.0	50 Cassiopeiæ.	2222
581	46 20 3.6	2.5	− 17.76	+ 0.25	...	2	49.9	14.5	....	......
582	9 27 6.7	7.4	− 17.76	+ 0.46	...	3	48.3	8.0	....	......
583	26 6 55.8	55.1	− 17.75	+ 0.30	...	4	50.4	13.9	....	2231
584	14 38 7.4	4.8	− 17.75	+ 0.37	...	4	45.5	9.5	49 Cassiopeiæ.	2232
585	37 13 52.5	51.0	− 17.75	+ 0.27	...	3	46.3	11.0	....	2238
586	25 51 2.2	2.5	− 17.73	+ 0.30	...	3	43.9	13.4	52 Cassiopeiæ.	2245
587	9 15 48.9	48.1	− 17.73	+ 0.46	...	3	47.0	8.0	....	......
588	19 32 23.7	21.3	− 17.72	+ 0.33	...	3	48.6	15.0	....	2247
589	26 21 44.3	43.7	− 17.72	+ 0.30	...	5	45.4	12.4	53 Cassiopeiæ.	2251
590	36 15 54.7	54.2	− 17.70	+ 0.27	...	3	46.7	10.3	4 Persei	......

Ordinal Number.		Magnitude.	Estimates of Magnitude.	Mean Right Ascension 1845.0.			Precession 1845.0.	Secular Variation	Adopted Proper Motion.	Observations of R.A.		
R.	G.	R.		R.		G.				No. R.	Mean year. R.	G.
				h. m. s.		s.	s.	s.	s.		1800 +	
591	435	7.5	5	1 52 2.58		2.12	+ 5.236	+ 0.225	......	3	50.5	10.0
592	430	7.3	6	1 52 6.23		6.61	+ 6.185	+ 0.394	......	3	49.7	11.9
593	438	7.9	4	1 52 10.07		9.87	+ 3.900	+ 0.060	......	3	46.6	11.0
594	439	7.1	5	1 52 36.53		36.70	+ 3.725	+ 0.043	......	4	48.4	15.0
595	440	6.7	5	1 53 4.99		4.87	+ 4.389	+ 0.107	......	3	47.9	13.9
596	441	7.6	4	1 53 7.48		7.14	+ 3.940	+ 0.063	......	4	45.8	10.9
597	442	7.3	6	1 53 33.95		33.75	+ 4.352	+ 0.102	......	2	49.5	13.9
598	...	6.7	5	1 53 42.25		...	+ 8.125	+ 0.909	......	3	48.9	...
599	...	5.0	1	1 54 1.88		...	+ 3.092	+ 0.006	+ 0.009	4	46.6	...
600	444	8.1	5	1 54 4.32		4.01	+ 4.352	+ 0.102	......	2	48.4	13.9
601	...	8.4	3	1 54 19.55		...	+ 3.951	+ 0.066	......	3	49.1	...
602	447	2.7	7	1 54 24.44		24.26	+ 3.638	+ 0.037	......	8	48.8	6.9
603	...	5.8	5	1 54 25.35		...	+ 3.638	+ 0.037	......	5	46.9	...
604	446	8.2	4	1 54 47.92		47.65	+ 4.378	+ 0.103	......	2	49.5	14.0
605	443	7.4	5	1 55 8.82		8.87	+ 6.367	+ 0.417	......	4	48.9	11.9
606	...	8.7	9	1 55 10.00		...	+21.478	+ 9.733	......	5	52.2	...
607	449	6.9	4	1 55 25.64		25.15	+ 3.836	+ 0.051	......	4	48.4	11.0
608	445	6.7	6	1 55 28.10		28.38	+ 6.376	+ 0.419	......	4	48.9	14.9
609	448	6.4	5	1 55 52.24		51.64	+ 4.931	+ 0.172	+ 0.067	5	45.9	8.9
610	450	9.2	3	1 56 24.48		24.68	+ 3.951	+ 0.063	......	3	45.4	14.9
611	451	8.4	5	1 57 19.29		19.47	+ 3.890	+ 0.057	......	4	49.4	12.9
612	...	5.9	5	1 57 54.14		...	+ 4.111	+ 0.075	......	3	46.6	...
613	...	5.8	2	1 57 54.18		...	+ 3.336	+ 0.018	+ 0.005	2	55.0	...
614	453	7.4	4	1 58 11.35		1.26	+ 3.698	+ 0.043	......	2	46.9	13.9
615	...	2.0	A	1 58 26.79		...	+ 3.347	+ 0.018	+ 0.012	70	45.2	...
616	452	7.2	6	1 58 48.28		48.61	+ 6.310	+ 0.391	......	4	48.9	11.9
617	456	6.6	4	1 58 53.95		53.73	+ 3.704	+ 0.041	......	2	45.4	13.9
618	455	9.3	5	1 58 54.82		55.17	+ 3.969	+ 0.063	......	2	49.5	15.0
619	457	7.7	5	1 59 8.10		8.36	+ 3.936	+ 0.060	......	3	48.9	13.0
620	454	6.3	5	1 59 13.13		12.39	+ 5.284	+ 0.217	......	4	47.4	12.0
621	458	8.4	5	1 59 41.35		41.33	+ 3.974	+ 0.060	......	5	47.7	14.9
622	459	6.7	7	1 59 46.03		46.01	+ 3.959	+ 0.061	+ 0.005	3	45.6	12.9
623	...	7.3	6	1 59 47.87		...	+ 4.043	+ 0.070	......	3	51.6	...
624	460	8.1	3	2 0 20.03		19.99	+ 3.943	+ 0.059	......	2	47.4	13.0
625	461	6.3	5	2 0 44.37		43.96	+ 4.101	+ 0.069	......	4	46.5	10.1

Ordinal Number. R.	Mean North Polar Distance 1845.0. R.	G.	Precession 1845.0.	Secular Variation.	Adopted Proper Motion.	Observations of N.P.D. No. R.	Mean year. R. 1800 +	G.	Names.	Oeltzen-Argelander Number.
	° ′ ″	″	″	″	″					
591	16 9 56.2	55.7	− 17.70	+ 0.36	...	3	50.3	10.0	51 Cassiopeiæ.	2256
592	11 24 2.8	4.0	− 17.70	+ 0.41	...	2	51.5	11.9	....	2255
593	37 7 23.4	22.3	− 17.70	+ 0.27	...	2	45.8	11.0	....	2262
594	43 54 33.0	31.4	− 17.68	+ 0.26	...	3	43.6	15.0	....	2275
595	25 38 43.1	43.5	− 17.66	+ 0.30	+ 0.09	3	47.0	13.9	....	2283
596	36 3 24.3	19.6	− 17.66	+ 0.27	...	2	45.3	10.9	....	......
597	26 21 45.8	47.4	− 17.64	+ 0.30	...	4	50.7	13.9	....	2299
598	7 10 29.6	...	− 17.64	+ 0.57	...	5	47.5	...	....	......
599	87 59 14.9	...	− 17.62	+ 0.22	...	4	53.4	...	113 Pisc. α (2)	......
600	26 27 38.9	37.9	− 17.62	+ 0.30	...	5	50.5	13.9	....	2309
601	35 59 29.4	...	− 17.61	+ 0.29	...	2	46.0	...	....	......
602	48 25 2.1	1.7	− 17.60	+ 0.25	+ 0.06	5	44.3	6.9	57 Androm. γ (1)	......
603	48 24 57.6	...	− 17.60	+ 0.25	...	3	47.2	...	57 Audrom. γ (2)	......
604	26 8 13.1	11.6	− 17.59	+ 0.30	...	3	43.3	14.0	....	2323
605	11 2 54.4	57.1	− 17.58	+ 0.43	...	3	43.6	11.9	....	2329
606	2 0 12.3	...	− 17.58	+ 1.51	...	7	51.7	...	....	......
607	40 6 9.0	8.5	− 17.56	+ 0.27	...	3	43.2	11.0	....	......
608	11 2 56.5	59.5	− 17.56	+ 0.44	...	3	49.6	14.9	....	2333
609	19 10 51.0	50.6	− 17.55	+ 0.35	+ 0.24	6	45.1	8.9	54 Cassiopeiæ.	2340
610	36 26 8.6	7.4	− 17.52	+ 0.27	...	3	45.3	14.9	....	......
611	38 36 49.2	49.7	− 17.48	+ 0.27	...	3	43.2	12.9	....	2369
612	32 19 3.9	...	− 17.46	+ 0.30	...	3	45.2	...	....	......
613	68 5 34.9	...	− 17.46	+ 0.24	− 0.04	1	52.0	...	12 Arietis κ ...	......
614	46 22 44.7	44.4	− 17.45	+ 0.27	...	4	45.2	13.9	....	......
615	67 16 24.2	...	− 17.43	+ 0.24	+ 0.15	16	40.8	...	13 Arietis α ...	......
616	11 33 18.0	12.8	− 17.42	+ 0.46	...	4	44.9	11.9	....	2388
617	46 16 42.9	41.1	− 17.42	+ 0.27	...	3	44.6	13.9	....	......
618	36 25 10.5	10.1	− 17.42	+ 0.28	...	3	49.9	15.0	....	......
619	37 29 48.2	47.7	− 17.41	+ 0.28	...	4	43.2	13.0	....	......
620	16 42 23.2	20.1	− 17.40	+ 0.38	...	6	43.1	12.0	....	2401
621	36 24 24.4	23.5	− 17.38	+ 0.29	...	3	44.9	14.9	....	......
622	36 53 34.6	34.3	− 17.38	+ 0.29	+ 0.02	4	43.8	12.9	....	......
623	34 26 20.1	...	− 17.38	+ 0.30	...	4	51.4	...	....	2410
624	37 31 18.7	16.1	− 17.36	+ 0.29	...	3	45.6	13.0	....	2421
625	33 5 24.7	23.6	− 17.34	+ 0.30	...	4	45.4	10.1	5 Persei h......	2427

Ordinal Number		Magnitude	Estimates of Magnitude	Mean Right Ascension 1845.0		Precession 1845.0	Secular Variation	Adopted Proper Motion	Observations of R.A.		
R.	G.	R.	R.	R.	G.				No. R.	Mean year R.	Mean year G.
				h. m. s.	s.	s.	s.	s.		1800 +	
626	...	7.9	5	2 0 53.77	...	+ 4.045	+ 0.070	......	3	51.6	...
627	...	7.8	2	2 0 53.94	...	+ 4.046	+ 0.070	......	3	51.6	...
628	462	7.1	4	2 1 29.96	29.98	+ 3.604	+ 0.034	......	2	48.0	13.9
629	463	7.3	5	2 1 30.82	30.85	+ 3.604	+ 0.034	......	3	50.6	13.9
630	...	8.9	5	2 2 4.74	...	+ 4.097	+ 0.070	......	3	52.9	...
631	...	7.3	5	2 2 6.91	...	+ 4.596	+ 0.131	......	3	52.6	...
632	...	7.2	5	2 2 7.54	...	+ 4.095	+ 0.070	......	3	53.3	...
633	464	5.5	3	2 2 23.92	23.16	+ 4.584	+ 0.120	......	4	48.7	9.0
634	465	8.1	4	2 2 45.43	45.50	+ 3.992	+ 0.061	......	3	47.7	14.9
635	...	8.6	4	2 2 47.58	...	+ 4.587	+ 0.131	......	2	51.9	...
636	...	7.2	7	2 2 52.19	...	+ 4.574	+ 0.131	......	4	46.2	...
637	466	6.9	6	2 3 12.77	13.08	+ 3.957	+ 0.060	......	3	45.0	13.0
638	467	6.0	6	2 3 19.86	19.63	+ 3.897	+ 0.054	+ 0.035	7	49.4	10.0
639	...	5.7	A	2 3 23.36	...	+ 3.460	+ 0.024	− 0.002	4	40.9	...
640	468	5.0	4	2 3 31.48	31.38	+ 3.721	+ 0.040	......	6	47.4	10.9
641	470	6.5	5	2 4 8.19	8.27	+ 3.803	+ 0.048	......	3	47.9	14.0
642	472	8.9	5	2 4 25.32	25.03	+ 3.799	+ 0.044	......	3	47.9	14.0
643	...	4.7	8	2 4 47.46	...	+ 3.169	+ 0.010	− 0.004	8	51.3	...
644	473	7.4	6	2 4 53.37	53.27	+ 3.787	+ 0.046	......	3	48.9	13.9
645	469	7.2	5	2 4 59.20	59.46	+ 6.206	+ 0.350	......	3	46.9	11.9
646	474	7.0	7	2 5 9.12	9.14	+ 3.952	+ 0.056	......	3	48.3	12.9
647	475	7.7	5	2 5 59.40	59.17	+ 4.117	+ 0.066	......	4	47.3	13.6
648	477	8.3	4	2 6 0.18	59.69	+ 3.959	+ 0.066	......	3	49.9	9.1
649	471	8.0	7	2 6 1.63	1.50	+ 6.683	+ 0.440	......	5	49.7	12.0
650	476	7.1	5	2 6 4.38	4.20	+ 4.119	+ 0.070	......	3	46.1	13.7
651	481	7.6	4	2 6 7.97	7.71	+ 3.694	+ 0.040	......	3	45.5	11.0
652	480	7.4	5	2 6 15.57	15.35	+ 3.966	+ 0.059	......	3	51.9	12.9
653	482	8.2	4	2 6 18.08	18.13	+ 3.793	+ 0.043	......	3	51.6	13.9
654	483	7.9	3	2 6 23.41	23.41	+ 3.700	+ 0.039	......	3	51.6	11.0
655	...	8.2	3	2 6 37.69	...	+ 4.136	+ 0.070	......	2	52.5	...
656	484	7.6	6	2 6 39.52	39.50	+ 4.162	+ 0.069	......	3	51.9	14.9
657	...	7.1	6	2 6 55.02	...	+ 4.493	+ 0.105	......	3	49.3	...
658	485	5.5	3	2 7 4.50	4.46	+ 4.161	+ 0.073	+ 0.008	3	48.8	14.9
659	486	5.6	4	2 7 13.03	12.61	+ 4.146	+ 0.071	......	4	47.9	9.0
660	...	8.0	5	2 7 38.09	...	+ 4.138	+ 0.074	......	3	45.6	...

Ordinal Number. R.	Mean North Polar Distance 1845.0.		Precession 1845.0.	Secular Variation.	Adopted Proper Motion.	Observations of N.P.D.			Names.	Oeltzen Argelander Number.
	R.	G.				No. R.	Mean year R.	Mean year G.		
	° ′ ″	″	″	″	″		1800 +			
626	34 36 22.7	...	− 17.33	+ 0.30	...	4	51.7	...	....	......
627	34 34 37.6	...	− 17.33	+ 0.30	...	4	51.9	...	....	......
628	51 41 42.5	43.1	− 17.30	+ 0.27	...	4	50.2	13.5	59 Andromedæ	......
629	51 41 29.2	25.1	− 17.30	+ 0.27	...	4	49.2	13.9	....	......
630	33 30 25.3	...	− 17.28	+ 0.30	...	2	54.9	...	....	2449
631	24 0 7.9	...	− 17.27	+ 0.35	...	4	46.7	...	....	2451
632	33 31 10.2	...	− 17.27	+ 0.30	...	4	52.0	...	....	2453
633	24 12 25.2	23.3	− 17.26	+ 0.34	...	4	45.4	9.0	55 Cassiopeiæ	2458
634	36 30 46.4	46.9	− 17.25	+ 0.29	...	3	49.0	14.9	....	......
635	24 13 53.6	...	− 17.24	+ 0.35	...	3	49.6	...	....	2464
636	24 24 32.3	...	− 17.24	+ 0.35	...	3	49.0	...	....	2470
637	37 40 20.4	20.9	− 17.22	+ 0.29	...	4	47.2	13.0	....	2477
638	39 39 29.1	28.9	− 17.22	+ 0.29	+ 0.16	4	44.5	10.0	6 Persei	......
639	60 25 31.1	...	− 17.22	+ 0.26	+ 0.05	1	55.0	...	6 Trianguli (1)	......
640	46 29 55.8	56.2	− 17.21	+ 0.28	...	4	45.9	10.5	60 Androm. b	......
641	43 14 35.0	33.1	− 17.18	+ 0.28	...	5	50.6	14.0	....	2497
642	43 26 26.2	28.4	− 17.17	+ 0.28	...	2	50.9	14.0	....	2512
643	81 53 0.4	...	− 17.16	+ 0.24	+ 0.04	6	49.6	...	65 Ceti ξ¹......	......
644	44 2 23.7	22.8	− 17.15	+ 0.28	...	3	47.9	13.5	....	2522
645	12 28 2.3	2.3	− 17.14	+ 0.48	...	3	43.6	11.5	....	2520
646	38 12 56.3	56.9	− 17.14	+ 0.29	...	4	48.0	12.5	....	......
647	33 41 43.5	45.2	− 17.10	+ 0.31	...	2	48.5	13.6	....	......
648	38 9 57.4	60.4	− 17.10	+ 0.30	...	2	50.5	9.1	....	......
649	10 56 47.3	44.0	− 17.10	+ 0.50	...	2	48.9	12.0	....	2549
650	33 40 12.2	8.4	− 17.10	+ 0.31	...	3	46.3	13.7	....	......
651	48 15 26.6	27.9	− 17.10	+ 0.28	...	3	49.6	11.0	....	......
652	38 0 10.4	10.1	− 17.09	+ 0.31	...	3	52.6	12.9	....	......
653	44 3 44.7	44.0	− 17.08	+ 0.30	...	2	52.5	13.9	....	2555
654	48 1 41.6	42.6	− 17.08	+ 0.28	...	3	48.7	11.0	....	......
655	33 21 27.4	...	− 17.07	+ 0.32	...	2	52.0	...	....	......
656	32 42 8.2	8.6	− 17.07	+ 0.31	...	3	48.9	14.9	....	2566
657	26 17 49.2	...	− 17.05	+ 0.35	...	3	53.6	...	....	2570
658	32 49 24.4	24.9	− 17.03	+ 0.31	...	3	44.9	14.9	8 Persei	2574
659	33 12 22.9	21.9	− 17.03	+ 0.32	...	4	43.4	9.0	7 Persei χ	......
660	33 30 47.2	...	− 17.02	+ 0.32	...	3	43.6	...	....	......

Ordinal Number.		Magnitude.	Estimates of Magnitude.	Mean Right Ascension 1845.0.		Precession 1845.0.	Secular Variation	Adopted Proper Motion.	Observations of R.A.		
R.	G.	R.		R.	G.				No. R.	Mean year. R.	G.
				h. m. s.	s.	s.	s.	s.		1800 +	
661	479	8.2	4	2 7 47.06	47.30	+ 6.663	+ 0.422	......	3	48.3	12.0
662	478	8.0	6	2 7 47.39	46.48	+ 6.686	+ 0.430	......	3	50.2	12.0
663	487	7.6	5	2 7 52.28	52.28	+ 4.028	+ 0.060	......	3	46.9	15.0
664	489	8.1	5	2 8 2.92	2.52	+ 3.705	+ 0.037	......	4	47.1	11.0
665	488	6.0	6	2 8 14.21	14.20	+ 4.139	+ 0.071	+ 0.014	5	47.1	11.0
666	...	9.1	6	2 8 19.91	...	+ 4.139	+ 0.071	......	4	51.5	...
667	...	8.8	4	2 8 20.04	...	+ 4.139	+ 0.071	+ 0.009	2	50.9	...
668	492	7.2	5	2 8 20.23	19.71	+ 3.713	+ 0.037	......	3	49.1	11.0
669	...	6.6	2	2 8 22.38	...	+ 4.502	+ 0.105	+ 0.001	2	51.5	...
670	490	6.2	5	2 8 23.11	23.02	+ 4.142	+ 0.071	......	3	47.3	13.1
671	491	8.9	2	2 8 24.12	24.13	+ 4.026	+ 0.060	......	2	49.9	15.1
672	...	7.1	3	2 8 30.03	...	+ 4.267	+ 0.082	......	2	52.9	...
673	...	6.9	2	2 8 32.87	...	+ 4.267	+ 0.082	......	1	55.0	...
674	...	9.2	7	2 8 51.94	...	+25.181	+11.956	......	4	54.1	...
675	...	7.2	2	2 9 1.88	...	+ 3.903	+ 0.052	......	2	51.4	...
676	493	7.3	4	2 9 13.57	13.57	+ 3.979	+ 0.056	......	2	47.0	12.9
677	...	7.5	1	2 9 14.90	...	+ 2.980	+ 0.003	......	2	56.9	...
678	494	6.8	4	2 9 18.03	17.96	+ 3.870	+ 0.049	— 0.006	3	45.6	11.0
679	495	5.8	5	2 9 18.49	18.40	+ 3.827	+ 0.046	— 0.005	4	43.4	10.0
680	...	5.9	3	2 9 30.91	...	+ 3.319	+ 0.016	......	7	46.1	...
681	...	6.9	3	2 9 52.12	...	+ 3.933	+ 0.053	......	2	49.9	...
682	496	6.8	3	2 10 6.10	5.52	+ 3.654	+ 0.031	......	3	48.3	11.9
683	497	7.2	5	2 10 35.68	35.87	+ 4.055	+ 0.061	......	3	48.3	14.9
684	499	6.5	7	2 10 41.29	41.40	+ 3.833	+ 0.046	......	5	46.4	10.0
685	498	5.4	5	2 10 44.40	44.10	+ 3.913	+ 0.051	+ 0.003	5	45.8	9.5
686	...	6.2	9	2 11 1.05	...	+ 4.164	+ 0.071	......	7	46.5	...
687	500	8.7	4	2 11 10.54	10.72	+ 4.050	+ 0.061	......	2	49.4	15.0
688	...	8.9	6	2 11 22.15	...	+ 4.165	+ 0.070	......	3	54.0	...
689	501	5.7	3	2 11 35.47	35.19	+ 4.112	+ 0.066	......	4	47.7	9.0
690	...	7.5	7	2 11 57.93	...	+ 4.171	+ 0.074	......	6	50.0	...
691	...	7.0	5	2 12 3.77	...	+ 4.178	+ 0.074	......	5	50.7	...
692	...	8.3	4	2 12 15.38	...	+ 4.171	+ 0.074	......	2	52.9	...
693	...	8.8	10	2 12 17.92	...	+27.998	+14.753	......	6	52.0	...
694	...	8.3	5	2 12 28.23	...	+ 4.174	+ 0.074	......	2	52.9	...
695	502	6.8	6	2 12 54.38	53.84	+ 3.987	+ 0.061	......	3	47.3	10.9

Original Number.	Mean North Polar Distance 1845.0.			Precession 1845.0.	Secular Variation.	Adopted Proper Motion.	Observations of N.P.D.				Names.	Oeltzen-Argelander Number.
R.	R.		G.				No. R.	Mean year. R.		G.		
	° ′ ″		″	″	″	″		1800 +				
661	11 8 16.1		14.2	− 17.02	+ 0.50	...	3	49.9	12.0		....	2587
662	11 4 18.3		13.6	− 17.02	+ 0.50	...	3	48.9	12.0		....	2588
663	36 26 29.8		27.8	− 17.01	+ 0.31	...	3	51.3	15.0		....	....
664	48 7 51.4		53.3	− 17.00	+ 0.28	...	3	51.0	11.0		....	....
665	33 35 5.8		4.1	− 16.99	+ 0.32	...	4	42.2	11.0		....	....
666	33 35 34.0		...	− 16.99	+ 0.32	...	3	46.3	...		....	....
667	33 35 22.0		...	− 16.99	+ 0.32	− 0.07	5	42.3	...		....	....
668	47 49 12.3		15.7	− 16.99	+ 0.29	...	3	49.3	11.0		....	....
669	26 22 58.0		...	− 16.99	+ 0.35	...	2	49.0	...		....	....
670	33 33 3.1		0.1	− 16.99	+ 0.32	...	4	42.1	13.1		....	....
671	36 37 27.7		27.4	− 16.98	+ 0.32	...	2	52.0	15.1		....	....
672	30 42 20.2		...	− 16.98	+ 0.33	...	1	51.0	...		....	....
673	30 41 22.6		...	− 16.98	+ 0.33	...	1	53.9	...		....	....
674	1 50 43.6		...	− 16.96	+ 1.95	...	3	51.8	...		....	....
675	97 17 58.9		...	− 16.96	+ 0.26	...	1	52.0	...		....	....
676	40 34 28.8		...	− 16.96	+ 0.30	...	2	49.0	...		....	....
677	38 9 27.8		28.0	− 16.94	+ 0.32	...	3	49.6	12.9		....	....
678	41 46 0.6		59.9	− 16.94	+ 0.30	− 0.08	4	47.7	11.0		....	2621
679	43 20 19.4		19.5	− 16.94	+ 0.30	...	3	44.6	10.0		62 Androm. c .	....
680	70 49 9.2		...	− 16.93	+ 0.26	+ 0.01	1	56.9	...		22 Arietis θ ...	....
681	39 45 29.8		...	− 16.92	+ 0.30	...	2	49.0	...		....	2632
682	50 52 56.7		55.8	− 16.90	+ 0.30	...	3	51.0	11.9		....	....
683	36 12 20.0		19.0	− 16.89	+ 0.31	...	3	45.7	14.9		....	2646
684	43 24 18.4		17.2	− 16.89	+ 0.30	...	3	44.3	10.0		....	....
685	40 33 47.2		47.1	− 16.88	+ 0.31	...	3	43.9	9.5		63 Andromedæ	2651
686	33 28 17.7		...	− 16.87	+ 0.33	...	4	48.2	...		....	....
687	36 27 54.5		51.3	− 16.86	+ 0.31	...	3	50.9	15.0		....	2659
688	36 26 30.7		...	− 16.86	+ 0.31	...	3	52.3	...		....	....
689	34 52 5.2		4.0	− 16.84	+ 0.32	+ 0.01	4	45.6	9.0		9 Persei i	....
690	33 28 3.1		...	− 16.82	+ 0.33	...	3	47.6	...		....	....
691	33 19 31.1		...	− 16.82	+ 0.33	...	3	47.6	...		....	....
692	33 30 43.9		...	− 16.81	+ 0.33	...	3	47.6	...		....	....
693	1 40 35.7		...	− 16.80	+ 2.23	...	6	52.0	...		....	....
694	33 29 57.8		...	− 16.80	+ 0.33	...	4	52.4	...		....	....
695	38 37 38.6		37.8	− 16.78	+ 0.31	...	4	45.9	10.9		....	....

Ordinal Number.		Magnitude.	Estimates of Magnitude.	Mean Right Ascension 1845.0.		Precession 1845.0.	Secular Variation	Adopted Proper Motion.
R.	G.	R.		R.	G.	s.	s.	s.
				h. m. s.	s.			
696	503	6.0	7	2 13 12.86	12.96	+ 3.701	+ 0.037	......
697	504	7.4	5	2 13 15.47	15.22	+ 3.703	+ 0.037	......
698	...	9.4	5	2 13 28.55	...	+ 3.985	+ 0.064	......
699	505	8.1	5	2 13 35.58	35.64	+ 4.064	+ 0.063	......
700	507	5.3	7	2 14 8.96	8.78	+ 3.929	+ 0.051	+ 0.003
701	508	6.5	7	2 14 22.20	21.61	+ 4.162	+ 0.069	......
702	509	5.0	7	2 15 19.05	18.77	+ 3.944	+ 0.053	......
703	...	7.6	7	2 15 19.29	...	+ 4.181	+ 0.074	......
704	506	7.7	5	2 15 45.71	45.34	+ 7.756	+ 0.640	......
705	...	7.3	1	2 16 14.05	...	+ 3.190	+ 0.010	......
706	511	4.7	5	2 16 22.66	22.46	+ 4.810	+ 0.129	......
707	...	9.0	8	2 16 52.82	...	+ 4.818	+ 0.130	......
708	...	8.2	4	2 17 8.86	...	+ 4.211	+ 0.074	......
709	510	7.6	3	2 17 10.28	10.04	+ 6.959	+ 0.450	......
710	...	9.2	6	2 17 25.30	...	+ 4.823	+ 0.134	......
711	513	8.0	4	2 17 27.81	27.44	+ 4.031	+ 0.060	......
712	514	6.3	6	2 17 29.93	29.46	+ 3.965	+ 0.052	+ 0.003
713	...	8.0	15	2 17 37.79	...	+14.958	+ 3.397	......
714	512	6.5	7	2 18 2.18	1.53	+ 6.114	+ 0.286	......
715	...	5.7	1	2 18 17.83	...	+ 3.530	+ 0.025	− 0.007
716	...	6.7	2	2 18 27.27	...	+ 3.203	+ 0.011	+ 0.004
717	...	7.0	4	2 18 33.00	...	+ 4.148	+ 0.069	......
718	...	6.7	1	2 19 8.93	...	+ 3.199	+ 0.011	......
719	...	7.3	1	2 19 20.80	...	+ 4.146	+ 0.069	......
720	515	7.8	6	2 19 39.23	39.35	+ 5.202	+ 0.162	......
721	...	4.4	5	2 19 55.47	...	+ 3.174	+ 0.010	......
722	516	6.6	5	2 20 1.28	0.67	+ 5.248	+ 0.171	......
723	517	8.4	4	2 20 14.52	14.03	+ 4.070	+ 0.061	......
724	518	7.0	3	2 20 21.16	21.04	+ 3.680	+ 0.034	......
725	520	7.6	4	2 20 38.25	37.95	+ 3.677	+ 0.033	......
726	519	8.1	4	2 21 20.00	19.27	+ 5.192	+ 0.170	......
727	521	8.0	4	2 21 25.58	25.37	+ 4.869	+ 0.129	......
728	522	8.4	5	2 21 50.80	50.34	+ 5.228	+ 0.168	......
729	523	9.5	5	2 22 3.25	2.94	+ 5.213	+ 0.161	......
730	...	6.7	1	2 22 19.09	...	+ 3.309	+ 0.015	......

Ordinal Number.	Mean North Polar Distance 1845.0.		Precession 1845.0.	Secular Variation.	Adopted Proper Motion.	Observations of N.P.D.		
R.	R.	G.				No. R.	Mean year R.	G.
	° ′ ″	″	″	″	″		1800 +	
696	49 18 37.1	37.1	− 16.76	+ 0.30	...	4	44.2	11.0
697	49 13 50.5	51.8	− 16.76	+ 0.30	...	4	50.0	11.0
698	36 30 41.7	...	− 16.74	+ 0.32	...	3	51.9	...
699	36 31 7.0	3.9	− 16.74	+ 0.32	...	4	48.5	15.0
700	40 42 1.2	1.0	− 16.71	+ 0.32	...	3	48.0	10.0
701	34 5 51.5	51.1	− 16.70	+ 0.34	...	4	48.5	9.0
702	40 25 35.8	36.9	− 16.65	+ 0.33	...	5	46.1	10.0
703	33 28 36.2	...	− 16.65	+ 0.34	...	3	46.9	...
704	9 2 59.7	59.3	− 16.63	+ 0.63	...	4	45.4	8.0
705	80 59 24.1	...	− 16.61	+ 0.26	...	1	52.0	...
706	23 17 57.7	57.4	− 16.61	+ 0.39	...	5	45.5	11.1
707	23 16 6.3	...	− 16.58	+ 0.40	...	4	50.9	...
708	33 25 35.2	...	− 16.57	+ 0.34	...	3	44.9	...
709	10 57 46.2	44.7	− 16.57	+ 0.56	...	3	47.3	12.0
710	23 16 57.1	...	− 16.55	+ 0.40	...	3	51.0	...
711	38 9 5.3	6.7	− 16.55	+ 0.34	...	4	46.5	10.9
712	40 7 38.2	38.7	− 16.55	+ 0.33	+ 0.10	5	48.0	9.7
713	3 38 8.0	...	− 16.55	+ 1.23	...	6	51.7	...
714	13 58 24.3	22.4	− 16.52	+ 0.52	...	3	43.9	11.9
715	58 53 52.0	...	− 16.50	+ 0.29	+ 0.02	1	57.0	...
716	80 8 6.0	...	− 16.50	+ 0.27	+ 0.13	2	58.9	...
717	35 9 43.1	...	− 16.50	+ 0.35	...	3	48.3	...
718	80 29 38.0	...	− 16.49	+ 0.27	...	1	58.9	...
719	35 21 8.6	...	− 16.46	+ 0.36	...	3	50.0	...
720	19 44 9.4	8.1	− 16.44	+ 0.45	...	4	46.7	11.1
721	82 14 16.6	...	− 16.43	+ 0.27	...	3	52.3	...
722	19 23 42.1	37.5	− 16.43	+ 0.43	...	3	47.0	11.1
723	37 31 25.0	23.5	− 16.42	+ 0.33	...	3	47.0	9.0
724	51 33 29.0	28.1	− 16.41	+ 0.31	...	3	48.0	11.0
725	51 44 25.1	22.5	− 16.40	+ 0.30	...	3	48.3	11.0
726	20 2 43.5	43.0	− 16.36	+ 0.43	...	3	43.6	14.0
727	23 16 23.9	24.6	− 16.35	+ 0.41	...	3	45.0	11.9
728	19 46 10.0	9.7	− 16.33	+ 0.45	...	3	48.3	13.9
729	19 55 1.6	1.7	− 16.32	+ 0.45	...	3	52.2	13.9
730	72 59 5.2	...	− 16.31	+ 0.28	+ 0.09	3	54.9	...

Magnitude. R.	Estimates of Magnitude.	Mean Right Ascension 1845.0.		Precession 1845.0.	Secular Variation	Adopted Proper Motion.	Observations of R.A.		
		R.	G.				No. R.	Mean year. R.	G.
		h. m. s.	s.	s.	s.	s.		1800 +	
7.5	3	2 22 23.19	...	+ 4.261	+ 0.073	......	3	54.6	...
6.6	6	2 22 43.55	43.03	+ 4.054	+ 0.055	......	4	47.4	10.5
8.7	5	2 23 12.75	...	+ 4.418	+ 0.085	......	3	51.3	...
6.9	7	2 23 21.28	20.90	+ 4.898	+ 0.126	......	4	48.7	11.9
5.2	7	2 23 25.62	25.31	+ 5.500	+ 0.200	......	5	46.1	7.5
5.6	3	2 24 16.40	...	+ 3.047	+ 0.005	......	2	53.5	...
7.4	2	2 24 20.24	...	+ 4.321	+ 0.077	......	2	48.5	...
8.8	5	2 24 26.81	25.87	+ 5.261	+ 0.170	......	3	47.8	14.0
6.0	1	2 24 44.59	...	+ 2.845	0.000	......	2	56.9	...
7.5	3	2 25 16.39	...	+ 4.970	+ 0.122	......	3	50.2	...
7.6	5	2 25 46.99	47.01	+ 5.318	+ 0.171	......	2	46.4	11.1
6.8	7	2 25 47.70	47.28	+ 3.713	+ 0.033	......	3	47.6	10.9
6.1	5	2 25 52.85	51.97	+ 7.968	+ 0.628	+ 0.016	3	44.0	7.3
7.1	4	2 26 11.34	11.07	+ 4.063	+ 0.055	......	6	45.4	9.0
8.4	12	2 26 20.29	...	+24.882	+ 9.988	......	10	52.7	...
7.0	4	2 26 57.62	...	+ 4.569	+ 0.093	......	4	51.4	...
7.9	6	2 27 2.98	...	+ 4.568	+ 0.093	......	3	51.6	...
...	...	2 27 4.00	...	+ 2.951	+ 0.030	......	1	56.9	...
8.4	4	2 27 6.07	5.65	+ 4.099	+ 0.057	......	4	44.2	11.0
7.2	7	2 27 12.38	12.32	+ 3.775	+ 0.037	......	6	47.3	10.0
8.7	9	2 27 19.14	...	+12.623	+ 2.300	......	5	54.6	...
7.0	6	2 27 37.83	37.77	+ 5.395	+ 0.180	......	3	45.7	12.9
4.7	1	2 27 44.78	...	+ 3.139	+ 0.008	− 0.008	11	48.3	...
9.1	6	2 28 13.93	...	+ 5.397	+ 0.174	......	3	49.0	...
8.0	4	2 28 24.64	...	+ 4.352	+ 0.077	......	3	50.2	...
8.9	7	2 28 45.36	...	+12.733	+ 2.200	......	5	54.6	...
7.3	7	2 29 8.74	8.29	+ 5.015	+ 0.136	......	5	46.0	11.1
7.4	4	2 29 36.62	36.34	+ 4.115	+ 0.058	+ 0.007	5	46.4	11.0
6.0	1	2 30 1.64	...	+ 3.387	+ 0.017	− 0.002	2	41.4	...
7.0	3	2 30 10.03	...	+ 4.389	+ 0.077	......	2	51.4	...
8.3	4	2 30 49.72	...	+ 5.190	+ 0.156	......	2	49.9	...
7.8	3	2 31 0.73	...	+ 5.094	+ 0.148	......	2	51.0	...
5.5	4	2 31 34.75	34.26	+ 5.019	+ 0.133	......	5	47.4	11.1
5.5	4	2 31 59.84	59.49	+ 4.222	+ 0.064	+ 0.007	4	46.4	8.9
8.4	3	2 32 0.50	...	+ 3.813	+ 0.039	......	2	53.4	...

Distance	Precession 1845.0.	Secular Variation.	Adopted Proper Motion.	Observations of N.P.D.		
G.				No.	Mean year.	
				R.	R.	G.
					1800 +	
...	− 16.31	+ 0.34	...	2	54.0	...
47.7	− 16.29	+ 0.34	...	4	42.9	10.5
...	− 16.27	+ 0.38	...	3	44.6	...
28.6	− 16.26	+ 0.41	...	5	46.2	11.9
57.6	− 16.25	+ 0.47	...	5	44.0	7.5
...	− 16.21	+ 0.26	+ 0.06	1	54.9	...
...	− 16.21	+ 0.37	...	3	48.3	...
50.9	− 16.20	+ 0.45	...	3	46.3	14.0
...	− 16.18	+ 0.25	...	1	52.0	...
...	− 16.15	+ 0.44	...	3	49.3	...
11.8	− 16.14	+ 0.45	...	4	46.2	11.1
3.4	− 16.14	+ 0.31	...	3	47.0	10.9
59.7	− 16.13	+ 0.69	...	5	45.6	7.3
11.1	− 16.11	+ 0.35	...	3	43.2	9.0
...	− 16.10	+ 2.17	...	5	51.7	...
...	− 16.07	+ 0.40	...	3	52.3	...
...	− 16.06	+ 0.40	...	3	52.3	...
...	− 16.06	+ 0.26	...	1	52.0	...
58.2	− 16.06	+ 0.36	...	3	44.3	11.0
52.4	− 16.06	+ 0.32	...	3	43.3	10.0
...	− 16.05	+ 1.16	...	4	53.6	...
52.3	− 16.03	+ 0.48	...	4	45.7	12.9
...	− 16.03	+ 0.28	+ 0.03	2	51.0	...
...	− 16.01	+ 0.50	...	3	47.6	...
...	− 15.99	+ 0.38	...	3	48.3	...
...	− 15.96	+ 1.17	...	3	54.3	...
22.2	− 15.95	+ 0.45	...	3	45.3	11.1
6.3	− 15.93	+ 0.37	...	3	43.5	11.0
...	− 15.91	+ 0.30	+ 0.02	1	52.0	...
...	− 15.90	+ 0.39	...	2	51.5	...
...	− 15.86	+ 0.46	...	3	49.3	...
...	− 15.86	+ 0.46	...	4	51.5	...
22.7	− 15.82	+ 0.45	+ 0.04	3	41.6	11.1
37.6	− 15.81	+ 0.38	+ 0.03	4	44.4	8.9
...	− 15.81	+ 0.35	...	2	55.0	...

Ordinal Number.		Magnitude.	Estimates of Magnitude.	Mean Right Ascension 1845.0.		Precession 1845.0.	Secular Variation	Adopted Proper Motion.	Observations of R.A.		
R.	G.		R.	R.	G.				No. R.	Mean year. R.	G.
				h. m. s.	s.	s.	s.	s.		1800 +	
766	540	6.1	4	2 32 6.54	5.99	+ 4.157	+ 0.059	......	3	44.4	10.9
767	...	8.0	4	2 32 9.86	...	+ 3.813	+ 0.039	......	2	51.9	...
768	...	7.9	4	2 32 17.18	...	+ 3.813	+ 0.039	......	2	46.9	...
769	541	8.3	5	2 32 19.11	19.13	+ 3.976	+ 0.047	......	3	47.4	13.0
770	542	5.6	7	2 32 29.14	29.03	+ 3.751	+ 0.034	......	8	50.5	10.0
771	538	8.0	6	2 32 35.30	35.74	+ 5.476	+ 0.176	......	5	47.3	13.0
772	...	7.2	7	2 32 39.40	...	+ 3.811	+ 0.039	......	6	47.0	...
773	543	6.7	2	2 32 39.78	39.60	+ 3.975	+ 0.047	......	2	44.6	13.0
774	...	8.9	5	2 32 43.40	...	+ 5.031	+ 0.142	......	3	53.0	...
775	...	7.0	3	2 33 33.91	...	+ 3.841	+ 0.040	......	2	50.0	...
776	...	5.7	A	2 33 38.13	...	+ 3.363	+ 0.016	......	1	52.0	...
777	545	4.3	5	2 33 38.68	38.20	+ 4.011	+ 0.049	+ 0.033	5	45.9	8.1
778	546	6.0	5	2 34 1.01	0.65	+ 3.864	+ 0.042	......	4	44.7	9.7
779	544	7.7	5	2 34 44.10	45.40	+ 7.560	+ 0.491	......	3	46.3	15.0
780	...	9.0	8	2 34 49.44	...	+11.022	+ 1.350	......	6	54.5	...
781	...	6.4	6	2 35 2.92	...	+ 5.247	+ 0.153	......	3	48.6	...
782	547	7.9	4	2 35 4.12	3.55	+ 5.515	+ 0.181	......	2	47.5	12.6
783	548	8.9	6	2 35 7.86	7.29	+ 5.351	+ 0.165	......	3	50.3	14.9
784	...	4.0	1	2 35 16.54	...	+ 3.108	+ 0.007	— 0.011	33	44.0	...
785	...	7.0	1	2 35 40.58	...	+ 3.330	+ 0.015	......	1	56.9	...
786	551	7.9	6	2 35 49.40	49.38	+ 4.037	+ 0.049	......	4	48.2	15.0
787	550	8.1	5	2 36 12.95	13.22	+ 5.365	+ 0.165	......	2	50.4	14.9
788	...	4.5	2	2 36 34.21	...	+ 3.212	+ 0.010	+ 0.020	6	54.2	...
789	549	7.4	2	2 36 36.02	35.53	+ 6.031	+ 0.235	......	3	49.1	11.9
790	553	6.7	8	2 37 24.94	24.88	+ 3.878	+ 0.043	......	7	47.6	10.9
791	552	7.0	6	2 37 29.90	28.83	+ 5.781	+ 0.210	......	4	47.3	11.1
792	...	8.0	4	2 37 30.36	...	+ 5.188	+ 0.144	......	2	51.4	...
793	555	7.5	7	2 37 48.56	48.10	+ 3.878	+ 0.043	......	5	49.5	10.9
794	554	7.0	5	2 37 51.30	50.86	+ 4.348	+ 0.071	......	3	45.3	11.0
795	...	5.0	1	2 37 52.09	...	+ 2.774	0.000	+ 0.026	1	52.0	...
796	556	6.5	4	2 38 7.37	6.83	+ 4.352	+ 0.071	......	3	49.1	11.0
797	...	6.2	4	2 38 14.25	...	+ 5.203	+ 0.144	+ 0.002	2	50.4	...
798	557	7.6	6	2 39 12.57	12.33	+ 4.904	+ 0.115	......	4	47.8	11.9
799	560	7.8	4	2 39 18.03	17.97	+ 3.822	+ 0.037	......	3	44.5	15.1
800	559	4.0	5	2 39 25.78	25.54	+ 4.305	+ 0.066	+ 0.003	6	45.9	8.1

Ordinal Number.	Mean North Polar Distance 1845.0.			Precession 1845.0.	Secular Variation.	Adopted Proper Motion.	Observations of N.P.D.			Names.	Oeltzen-Argelander Number.
	R.	R.	G.				No. R.	Mean year. R.	Mean year. G.		
	° ′ ″		″	″	″	″		1800 +			
766	37 8 24.4		21.7	− 15.80	+ 0.37	...	3	44.9	10.9	....	......
767	47 57 36.2		...	− 15.80	+ 0.35	...	2	49.0	...	....	......
768	47 58 5.2		...	− 15.79	+ 0.35	...	2	48.0	...	....	......
769	42 18 15.1		13.3	− 15.79	+ 0.35	...	2	48.0	13.0	....	3059
770	50 27 54.4		55.8	− 15.78	+ 0.34	+ 0.18	3	47.0	10.0	12 Persei	......
771	18 56 18.5		19.7	− 15.77	+ 0.50	...	3	45.0	13.0	....	3063
772	48 4 30.3		...	− 15.77	+ 0.35	...	4	47.2	...	....	......
773	42 24 3.1		3.9	− 15.77	+ 0.36	...	3	43.3	13.0	....	3070
774	22 51 13.9		...	− 15.77	+ 0.47	...	3	46.3	...	....	......
775	47 7 32.0		...	− 15.71	+ 0.35	...	2	48.5	...	....	......
776	70 39 10.4		...	− 15.71	+ 0.31	...	1	57.9	....	34 Arietis μ...	......
777	41 25 55.0		55.8	− 15.71	+ 0.36	+ 0.14	4	44.7	8.1	13 Persei θ....	3089
778	46 21 57.6		59.1	− 15.70	+ 0.35	...	3	43.3	9.7	14 Persei	......
779	10 32 33.8		33.5	− 15.65	+ 0.68	...	3	48.0	15.0	....	3108
780	6 0 5.9		...	− 15.65	+ 1.06	...	4	53.2	...	....	......
781	21 1 26.0		...	− 15.63	+ 0.48	...	3	50.6	...	....	3115
782	18 54 4.4		2.2	− 15.63	+ 0.52	...	4	47.2	12.6	....	3116
783	20 9 27.8		23.5	− 15.63	+ 0.50	...	3	52.2	14.9	....	3120
784	87 25 15.1		...	− 15.62	+ 0.28	+ 0.19	8	43.8	...	86 Ceti γ	......
785	72 53 43.3		...	− 15.60	+ 0.31	...	1	52.0	...	36 Arietis......	......
786	41 0 18.5		17.0	− 15.60	+ 0.36	...	2	49.5	15.0	....	3137
787	20 9 37.9		39.1	− 15.57	+ 0.50	...	3	52.3	14.9	....	3142
788	80 32 36.2		...	− 15.55	+ 0.30	+ 0.05	3	53.9	...	μ Ceti	......
789	15 54 36.7		34.7	− 15.55	+ 0.56	...	3	43.9	11.9	....	3147
790	46 22 58.0		58.4	− 15.51	+ 0.36	...	3	45.6	10.9	....	......
791	17 22 17.2		16.8	− 15.50	+ 0.53	...	5	48.0	11.1	....	3161
792	21 49 9.4		...	− 15.50	+ 0.48	...	3	51.6	...	....	3162
793	46 26 51.4		52.0	− 15.49	+ 0.35	...	4	46.4	10.9	....	......
794	33 37 7.2		7.3	− 15.48	+ 0.41	...	4	45.5	11.0	....	......
795	109 13 54.4		...	− 15.48	+ 0.26	− 0.03	1	55.0	...	1 Eridani τ¹...	......
796	33 34 2.7		2.9	− 15.46	+ 0.41	...	3	44.9	11.0	....	......
797	21 45 35.6		...	− 15.46	+ 0.48	...	3	47.6	...	....	3175
798	25 0 44.1		44.0	− 15.40	+ 0.47	...	3	46.0	11.9	....	......
799	48 42 54.2		53.1	− 15.40	+ 0.34	...	3	45.3	15.1	....	......
800	34 45 10.9		7.9	− 15.39	+ 0.40	...	4	42.4	8.1	15 Persei η....	3197

Ordinal Number.		Magnitude.	Estimates of Magnitude.	Mean Right Ascension 1845.0.		Precession 1845.0.	Secular Variation	Adopted Proper Motion.	Observations of R.A.		
R.	G.	R.		R.	G.				No. R.	Mean year. R.	G.
				h. m. s.	s.	s.	s.	s.		1800 +	
801	561	7.4	5	2 39 42.20	41.87	+ 4.154	+ 0.056	......	3	49.9	14.0
802	558	6.5	8	2 39 57.05	56.62	+ 5.834	+ 0.213	......	5	46.4	11.1
803	563	8.9	5	2 40 36.12	36.35	+ 3.827	+ 0.036	......	3	47.6	15.1
804	...	5.7	5	2 40 39.11	...	+ 3.331	+ 0.014	− 0.002	20	49.2	...
805	...	4.7	A	2 40 49.11	...	+ 3.737	+ 0.032	+ 0.020	4	40.9	...
806	564	6.7	5	2 40 50.01	49.44	+ 4.190	+ 0.057	......	4	47.2	10.4
807	562	7.9	4	2 40 51.23	50.68	+ 5.767	+ 0.205	......	3	44.6	12.5
808	565	8.1	6	2 41 9.32	8.98	+ 4.159	+ 0.056	......	4	48.4	14.0
809	566	7.7	6	2 41 30.48	29.75	+ 3.918	+ 0.039	......	4	48.9	13.0
810	567	6.7	8	2 41 40.83	40.79	+ 3.914	+ 0.039	......	4	46.5	13.0
811	568	6.1	4	2 41 54.44	54.11	+ 4.195	+ 0.057	......	4	44.0	10.4
812	571	6.9	4	2 42 23.02	23.02	+ 3.836	+ 0.037	......	3	47.7	15.0
813	...	6.3	3	2 42 49.29	...	+ 4.036	+ 0.047	......	3	51.3	...
814	570	7.7	4	2 42 59.46	59.15	+ 4.955	+ 0.114	......	3	49.7	11.9
815	569	7.8	4	2 43 4.35	3.97	+ 5.763	+ 0.199	......	3	45.1	11.5
816	573	4.3	6	2 43 18.18	18.15	+ 4.194	+ 0.058	......	5	46.9	11.3
817	576	7.1	6	2 43 36.14	35.90	+ 3.993	+ 0.045	......	4	49.8	11.0
818	574	7.0	5	2 43 36.53	36.55	+ 4.133	+ 0.052	......	3	44.5	13.1
819	572	8.8	5	2 43 45.35	45.67	+ 5.474	+ 0.162	......	3	49.6	14.9
820	...	5.0	1	2 44 0.65	...	+ 2.723	0.000	......	2	56.9	...
821	...	6.7	6	2 44 8.37	...	+ 3.859	+ 0.037	......	4	52.4	...
822	...	9.4	6	2 44 23.84	...	+ 4.002	+ 0.046	......	3	54.6	...
823	...	9.0	1	2 44 26.38	...	+ 4.006	+ 0.046	......	1	45.0	...
824	...	6.3	1	2 44 34.51	...	+ 3.321	+ 0.014	......	1	52.0	...
825	...	7.2	4	2 44 35.85	...	+ 3.864	+ 0.037	......	4	52.4	...
826	578	8.2	4	2 44 41.98	40.91	+ 4.135	+ 0.052	......	3	49.9	13.1
827	...	7.7	6	2 44 43.51	...	+11.786	+ 1.740	......	4	54.8	...
828	...	8.0	3	2 45 0.36	...	+ 3.866	+ 0.037	......	2	51.4	...
829	...	8.8	7	2 45 4.59	...	+ 4.007	+ 0.046	......	7	49.1	...
830	579	7.1	11	2 45 7.39	7.14	+ 4.005	+ 0.044	......	8	46.3	11.0
831	575	8.5	5	2 45 18.22	17.73	+ 7.040	+ 0.360	......	3	50.7	12.1
832	577	5.5	4	2 45 45.84	45.20	+ 7.537	+ 0.449	......	4	46.9	11.9
833	583	7.9	5	2 45 54.52	54.47	+ 3.844	+ 0.037	......	4	48.2	15.0
834	581	6.3	6	2 46 0.77	0.84	+ 4.150	+ 0.052	......	4	47.3	13.1
835	585	6.0	9	2 46 6.82	6.58	+ 4.005	+ 0.044	......	6	46.9	11.0

Ordinal Number.	Mean North Polar Distance 1845.0.		Precession 1845.0.	Secular Variation.	Adopted Proper Motion.	Observations of N.P.D.			Names.	Oeltzen-Argelander Number.
R.	R.	G.				No.	Mean year.			
						R.	R.	G.		
	° ′ ″	″	″	″	″		1800 +			
801	38 21 55.8	55.7	− 15.38	+ 0.38	...	3	44.9	14.0	....	....
802	17 16 15.3	14.1	− 15.37	+ 0.53	...	5	45.5	11.1	....	3207
803	48 42 7.5	8.3	− 15.33	+ 0.35	...	3	52.3	15.1	....	....
804	73 11 2.1	...	− 15.32	+ 0.31	− 0.02	2	53.0	...	42 Arietis π...	....
805	52 19 26.3	...	− 15.31	+ 0.35	+ 0.08	1	48.0	...	16 Persei	....
806	37 36 48.6	49.1	− 15.31	+ 0.41	...	4	44.4	10.4	....	3221
807	17 45 8.1	5.5	− 15.31	+ 0.56	...	4	45.4	12.5	....	3218
808	38 26 39.1	39.6	− 15.30	+ 0.39	...	3	47.6	14.0	....	....
809	45 35 7.0	6.2	− 15.28	+ 0.36	...	2	44.0	13.0	....	....
810	45 44 58.1	57.6	− 15.26	+ 0.36	...	5	44.0	13.0	....	....
811	37 38 42.0	40.6	− 15.25	+ 0.41	...	4	44.4	10.4	....	3238
812	48 37 18.2	16.4	− 15.23	+ 0.35	...	3	50.3	15.0	....	....
813	42 4 13.9	...	− 15.20	+ 0.38	...	2	51.0	...	....	3247
814	24 49 45.9	46.9	− 15.19	+ 0.48	...	3	50.9	11.9	....	....
815	17 57 39.5	38.4	− 15.19	+ 0.54	...	3	47.3	11.5	....	3250
816	37 52 36.6	36.0	− 15.17	+ 0.40	...	7	43.2	11.3	18 Persei τ	3255
817	43 28 40.2	40.6	− 15.16	+ 0.37	...	2	48.0	11.0	....	3260
818	39 28 14.6	14.8	− 15.16	+ 0.39	...	3	44.6	13.1	....	3259
819	20 1 5.6	3.8	− 15.15	+ 0.50	...	2	51.4	14.9	....	3262
820	111 38 45.2	...	− 15.13	+ 0.26	...	1	52.0	...	2 Eridani τ² ..	....
821	48 2 44.7	...	− 15.13	+ 0.37	...	2	52.5	...	....	....
822	43 18 47.0	...	− 15.11	+ 0.39	...	3	54.0	...	....	....
823	43 12 ...	...	......	...	...	...	...	...	....	....
824	74 9 9.6	...	− 15.10	+ 0.31	...	1	57.0	...	....	....
825	47 56 22.0	...	− 15.10	+ 0.37	...	3	53.3	...	....	....
826	39 33 24.7	27.8	− 15.10	+ 0.39	...	2	50.9	13.1	....	3276
827	5 45 59.3	...	− 15.09	+ 1.19	...	3	51.4	...	....	....
828	47 54 35.6	...	− 15.08	+ 0.37	...	2	52.5	...	....	....
829	43 15 32.3	...	− 15.08	+ 0.39	...	2	49.5	...	....	....
830	43 19 51.6	50.8	− 15.07	+ 0.37	...	6	44.2	11.0	....	....
831	12 32 9.1	0.9	− 15.06	+ 0.66	...	3	45.7	12.1	....	3283
832	11 12 11.5	11.6	− 15.03	+ 0.73	...	3	43.6	11.9	47 Cephei	3289
833	48 49 33.7	33.9	− 15.03	+ 0.36	...	2	50.0	15.0	....	....
834	39 22 12.4	11.3	− 15.02	+ 0.40	...	4	43.9	13.1	....	3295
835	43 28 8.4	8.7	− 15.01	+ 0.39	...	6	43.9	11.0	....	....

Ordinal Number.		Magnitude.	Estimates of Magnitude.	Mean Right Ascension 1845.0.		Precession 1845.0.	Secular Variation	Adopted Proper Motion.	Observations of R.A.		
R.	G.	R.		R.	G.				No.	Mean year.	
									R.	R.	G.
				h. m. s.	s.	s.	s.	s.		1800 +	
836	...	7.9	5	2 46 10.43	...	+12.215	+ 1.600	......	5	53.6	...
837	586	8.2	4	2 46 23.01	22.80	+ 4.201	+ 0.059	......	3	47.5	13.9
838	587	7.7	6	2 48 5.81	5.86	+ 3.861	+ 0.037	......	4	46.0	15.0
839	580	6.2	6	2 48 7.22	6.99	+ 8.632	+ 0.646	......	4	45.3	8.0
840	...	6.0	6	2 48 13.98	...	+ 3.769	+ 0.031	......	4	47.4	...
841	582	8.4	3	2 48 14.82	16.38	+ 7.990	+ 0.510	......	2	48.0	14.9
842	588	6.8	5	2 48 39.54	39.36	+ 3.899	+ 0.037	......	4	48.2	12.9
843	...	7.8	4	2 48 48.50	...	+ 4.566	+ 0.079	......	2	53.4	...
844	589	5.0	7	2 48 52.23	51.87	+ 3.798	+ 0.033	......	7	47.5	8.0
845	...	7.1	5	2 48 55.70	...	+ 4.567	+ 0.079	......	4	52.1	...
846	...	8.4	5	2 49 6.20	...	+ 4.023	+ 0.046	......	6	48.9	...
847	590	4.8	3	2 49 20.51	20.19	+ 4.022	+ 0.044	......	5	46.3	10.7
848	592	6.0	8	2 49 40.27	40.04	+ 3.838	+ 0.035	......	5	48.7	13.0
849	591	5.8	5	2 49 51.51	51.57	+ 4.214	+ 0.056	+ 0.012	4	43.7	13.9
850	...	7.6	5	2 49 52.93	...	+ 4.214	+ 0.056	......	3	46.3	...
851	593	8.3	7	2 50 14.47	14.66	+ 3.870	+ 0.035	......	6	49.5	15.0
852	...	5.3	1	2 50 21.57	...	+ 3.412	+ 0.017	......	3	42.8	...
853	...	...	...	2 51 12.58	...	+ 2.662	— 0.001	......	2	57.9	...
854	...	4.7	A	2 51 24.77	...	+ 3.204	+ 0.010	+ 0.009	2	53.5	...
855	598	6.9	7	2 52 1.91	1.73	+ 3.789	+ 0.032	......	5	48.9	10.0
856	...	6.9	3	2 52 20.72	...	+ 4.032	+ 0.047	......	3	48.3	...
857	596	8.2	4	2 52 59.12	59.83	+ 5.535	+ 0.158	......	2	47.0	15.0
858	600	3.3	5	2 53 36.31	35.87	+ 4.284	+ 0.058	......	4	45.9	8.0
859	594	6.7	10	2 53 56.06	57.15	+ 8.050	+ 0.490	......	6	48.3	14.9
860	601	5.0	5	2 53 56.23	55.97	+ 4.439	+ 0.068	......	4	48.1	8.0
861	599	7.6	4	2 54 1.97	2.15	+ 7.253	+ 0.368	......	3	49.6	11.9
862	...	2.3	A	2 54 10.99	...	+ 3.126	+ 0.008	......	38	46.9	...
863	597	9.7	5	2 54 26.82	26.46	+ 8.045	+ 0.491	......	2	49.5	14.9
864	...	6.0	A	2 55 6.07	...	+ 2.936	+ 0.004	......	4	40.9	...
865	607	4.1	7	2 55 15.79	15.91	+ 3.799	+ 0.032	+ 0.013	6	48.3	10.0
866	602	4.9	7	2 55 17.22	16.47	+ 6.255	+ 0.234	......	4	45.9	10.0
867	...	3.7	A	2 55 33.26	...	+ 2.653	— 0.001	......	1	55.9	...
868	604	7.9	6	2 56 6.46	5.64	+ 6.227	+ 0.231	......	4	48.0	11.0
869	610	8.0	5	2 56 40.36	39.89	+ 4.244	+ 0.051	......	2	51.5	10.9
870	595	5.7	16	2 56 42.02	37.38	+12.476	+ 1.557	......	21	51.5	7.8

Ordinal Number.	Mean North Polar Distance 1845.0. R. (° ′ ″)	Mean North Polar Distance 1845.0. G.	Precession 1845.0.	Secular Variation.	Adopted Proper Motion.	Observations of N.P.D. No. R.	Observations of N.P.D. Mean year. R. (1800 +)	Observations of N.P.D. Mean year. G. (1800 +)	Names.	Oeltzen Argelander Number.
836	5 37 29.1	...	− 15.01	+ 1.22	...	1	55.0	...	....	......
837	38 7 46.7	47.4	− 15.00	+ 0.40	...	2	45.0	13.9	....	3302
838	48 30 59.6	58.7	− 14.89	+ 0.38	...	4	47.7	15.0	....	......
839	9 8 24.6	23.6	− 14.89	+ 0.85	...	4	45.5	8.0	....	......
840	52 0 44.6	...	− 14.89	+ 0.36	...	3	48.0	...	....	......
841	10 18 57.0	57.4	− 14.88	+ 0.79	...	3	44.6	14.9	....	3326
842	47 15 37.7	36.6	− 14.86	+ 0.39	...	3	45.6	12.9	....	......
843	30 58 11.3	...	− 14.86	+ 0.44	...	2	51.0	...	....	3336
844	50 57 43.7	42.7	− 14.86	+ 0.36	+ 0.03	5	47.4	8.0	22 Persei π....	......
845	30 57 24.0	...	− 14.85	+ 0.44	...	1	54.9	...	....	3337
846	43 20 16.0	...	− 14.84	+ 0.41	...	2	47.0	...	....	......
847	43 24 18.6	18.0	− 14.83	+ 0.39	...	4	46.6	10.7	....	......
848	49 35 22.2	20.5	− 14.80	+ 0.38	...	4	45.9	13.0	....	......
849	38 16 11.4	10.2	− 14.79	+ 0.42	...	4	46.7	13.5	....	3344
850	38 16 10.8	...	− 14.79	+ 0.42	...	4	49.2	...	....	3345
851	48 28 47.3	44.8	− 14.77	+ 0.38	...	3	47.6	15.0	....	......
852	69 16 59.1	...	− 14.77	+ 0.34	+ 0.02	2	56.5	...	48 Arietis ϵ ...	......
853	114 13 58.4	...	− 14.71	+ 0.26	...	2	52.0	...	6 Eridani	......
854	81 42 48.0	...	− 14.70	+ 0.32	− 0.01	1	52.0	...	91 Ceti λ......	......
855	51 44 23.9	24.7	− 14.67	+ 0.37	...	3	48.3	10.0	....	......
856	43 30 12.9	...	− 14.64	+ 0.41	...	4	44.7	...	....	3373
857	20 23 9.2	8.1	− 14.61	+ 0.55	...	4	47.0	15.0	....	3384
858	37 6 20.6	18.7	− 14.57	+ 0.43	...	4	43.7	8.0	23 Persei γ....	3394
859	10 27 53.4	51.2	− 14.55	+ 0.80	...	5	48.7	14.9	....	3395
860	33 54 31.5	30.3	− 14.55	+ 0.45	− 0.08	4	45.4	8.0	....	3400
861	12 24 37.0	36.0	− 14.54	+ 0.74	...	3	46.3	11.9	....	3399
862	86 31 19.0	...	− 14.53	+ 0.31	+ 0.11	5	51.8	...	92 Ceti a......	......
863	10 30 6.9	6.8	− 14.52	+ 0.80	...	5	45.4	14.9	....	3407
864	98 17 54.2	...	− 14.48	+ 0.30	...	1	54.0	...	9 Eridani ρ^2....	......
865	51 45 52.7	52.8	− 14.47	+ 0.38	+ 0.08	4	47.5	10.0	25 Persei ρ....	......
866	16 12 12.4	11.9	− 14.47	+ 0.63	+ 0.07	5	44.0	10.0	....	......
867	114 14 7.3	...	− 14.45	+ 0.27	...	1	52.0	...	11 Eridani τ^3 .	......
868	16 24 1.1	0.2	− 14.42	+ 0.63	...	3	44.7	11.0	....	3426
869	38 25 11.6	12.5	− 14.38	+ 0.45	...	3	48.0	10.9	....	3441
870	5 39 18.0	18.0	− 14.38	+ 1.26	+ 0.12	6	47.9	7.8	....	....

Ordinal Number		Magnitude.	Estimates of Magnitude.	Mean Right Ascension 1845.0		Precession 1845.0	Secular Variation	Adopted Proper Motion.	Observations of R.A.		
R.	G.	R.		R.	G.				No. R.	Mean year R.	G.
				h. m. s.	s.	s.	s.	s.		1800 +	
871	608	7.3	6	2 56 48.82	47.89	+ 6.257	+ 0.231	......	3	49.3	11.0
872	605	7.8	3	2 56 49.71	49.64	+ 7.421	+ 0.382	......	3	48.6	12.1
873	606	7.1	6	2 56 58.10	58.76	+ 7.566	+ 0.404	......	3	47.9	11.9
874	611	6.9	5	2 56 58.23	57.82	+ 4.247	+ 0.053	......	4	47.0	10.5
875	603	8.2	6	2 57 5.06	5.99	+ 8.229	+ 0.517	......	4	50.5	14.9
876	...	7.5	3	2 57 21.46	...	+ 5.777	+ 0.187	......	2	52.5	...
877	609	7.1	7	2 57 38.74	38.00	+ 6.258	+ 0.218	......	4	48.2	11.0
878	...	7.3	8	2 57 43.02	...	+ 9.384	+ 0.775	......	4	53.3	...
879	613	4.4	3	2 57 54.73	54.54	+ 4.147	+ 0.048	+ 0.129	3	44.6	7.5
880	...	7.7	4	2 58 4.03	...	+10.652	+ 1.034	......	2	51.4	...
881	615	2.7	4	2 58 6.22	6.28	+ 3.866	+ 0.034	......	5	45.2	7.2
882	612	6.6	7	2 58 40.19	39.61	+ 6.198	+ 0.221	......	5	46.4	11.1
883	...	6.5	2	2 58 42.62	...	+ 3.364	+ 0.014	− 0.005	1	54.9	...
884	617	4.1	7	2 59 3.86	3.66	+ 3.998	+ 0.041	+ 0.016	5	46.6	7.9
885	614	9.4	4	3 0 24.84	25.61	+ 8.368	+ 0.527	......	3	49.9	15.0
886	...	6.7	2	3 0 27.56	...	+ 3.419	+ 0.016	+ 0.005	1	52.1	...
887	618	6.9	4	3 0 34.75	34.45	+ 4.265	+ 0.056	......	4	45.5	10.7
888	616	5.5	5	3 0 53.07	51.29	+ 7.231	+ 0.349	......	4	46.9	9.4
889	619	8.9	5	3 0 58.75	58.76	+ 4.105	+ 0.044	......	3	45.1	12.0
890	620	4.9	7	3 1 18.25	17.90	+ 3.840	+ 0.032	......	6	48.0	7.0
891	621	6.5	6	3 1 56.71	56.32	+ 3.922	+ 0.036	......	4	46.9	10.1
892	...	7.6	5	3 2 29.27	...	+ 6.553	+ 0.256	......	2	47.0	...
893	...	8.0	4	3 2 30.19	...	+ 5.058	+ 0.119	......	4	48.4	...
894	...	7.9	4	3 2 33.37	...	+ 3.983	+ 0.039	......	3	51.6	...
895	623	8.1	8	3 2 38.19	37.42	+ 4.155	+ 0.046	......	4	47.9	11.9
896	624	6.4	5	3 2 39.75	39.29	+ 4.177	+ 0.045	......	5	48.0	12.0
897	622	7.1	7	3 2 43.87	43.34	+ 5.198	+ 0.119	......	3	45.0	11.0
898	...	4.1	4	3 2 46.60	...	+ 3.402	+ 0.015	+ 0.010	15	45.5	...
899	625	7.8	6	3 3 6.94	6.87	+ 4.110	+ 0.047	......	3	47.6	12.0
900	626	8.2	6	3 3 21.75	21.58	+ 4.106	+ 0.041	......	3	48.5	12.0
901	627	5.7	7	3 3 58.07	58.28	+ 4.526	+ 0.066	......	4	47.4	13.0
902	...	6.7	7	3 4 1.36	...	+ 5.140	+ 0.111	......	3	47.7	...
903	...	7.2	7	3 4 28.42	...	+ 6.247	+ 0.270	......	4	46.9	...
904	630	6.2	6	3 4 40.97	40.91	+ 3.936	+ 0.036	+ 0.011	6	48.7	10.7
905	629	6.6	4	3 4 45.40	45.19	+ 4.235	+ 0.050	......	3	47.0	13.0

Ordinal Number.	Mean North Polar Distance 1845.0.		Precession 1845.0.	Secular Variation.	Adopted Proper Motion.	Observations of N.P.D.			Names.	Oeltzen-Argelander Number.
R.	R.	G.				No. R.	Mean year. R.	G.		
	° ′ ″	″	″	″	″		1800 +			
871	16 17 57.8	55.8	− 14.37	+ 0.64	...	5	42.3	11.0	....	3442
872	12 5 26.9	24.6	− 14.37	+ 0.77	...	2	48.0	12.1	....	3439
873	11 42 59.0	59.8	− 14.36	+ 0.78	...	4	48.7	11.9	....	3443
874	38 23 21.2	20.1	− 14.36	+ 0.46	...	3	46.9	10.5	....	3447
875	10 15 13.6	14.7	− 14.35	+ 0.85	...	2	52.0	14.9	....	......
876	19 2 31.2	...	− 14.34	+ 0.57	...	3	52.3	...	....	3452
877	16 21 3.1	1.6	− 14.32	+ 0.66	...	5	47.2	11.0	....	3460
878	8 25 52.5	...	− 14.32	+ 0.98	...	4	54.2	...	....	......
879	40 59 3.8	1.4	− 14.31	+ 0.43	...	3	45.0	7.5	Persei ι.........	3463
880	7 2 49.5	...	− 14.30	+ 1.10	...	3	48.3	...	....	......
881	49 38 46.2	45.7	− 14.30	+ 0.40	...	4	45.5	7.2	26 Persei β ...	......
882	16 43 20.5	18.7	− 14.27	+ 0.61	...	3	47.0	11.2	....	3474
883	72 43 18.7	...	− 14.26	+ 0.34	...	3	53.0	...	53 Arietis......	......
884	45 44 4.6	6.0	− 14.23	+ 0.41	+ 0.15	4	45.0	7.9	27 Persei κ....	......
885	10 8 11.8	6.1	− 14.16	+ 0.84	...	2	51.0	15.0	....	......
886	69 50 3.3	...	− 14.16	+ 0.35	+ 0.25	2	55.0	...	....	......
887	38 25 46.1	45.9	− 14.15	+ 0.43	...	3	45.5	10.7	....	3514
888	12 50 40.6	38.1	− 14.13	+ 0.74	+ 0.04	10	44.8	9.4	....	3515
889	42 32 15.8	17.4	− 14.12	+ 0.42	...	2	51.9	12.0	....	3521
890	50 58 54.9	55.1	− 14.10	+ 0.40	...	3	46.7	7.0	28 Persei ω ...	......
891	48 12 52.1	51.6	− 14.06	+ 0.41	...	3	43.6	10.1	....	......
892	15 20 29.2	...	− 14.03	+ 0.69	− 0.05	3	49.0	...	....	3545
893	25 40 28.8	...	− 14.03	+ 0.54	...	3	48.6	...	....	3547
894	46 18 2.3	...	− 14.03	+ 0.41	...	2	51.0	...	....	......
895	42 28 37.6	36.9	− 14.02	+ 0.43	...	4	48.7	11.3	....	3548
896	42 24 38.8	37.5	− 14.02	+ 0.42	...	5	46.8	12.0	....	3551
897	24 12 11.5	12.2	− 14.01	+ 0.55	+ 0.06	4	45.5	11.0	....	3552
898	70 51 49.5	...	− 14.01	+ 0.36	...	6	50.8	...	57 Arietis δ ...	......
899	42 40 8.7	7.6	− 13.98	+ 0.43	...	3	46.4	12.0	....	3562
900	42 47 1.3	59.8	− 13.97	+ 0.43	...	3	48.0	12.0	....	3573
901	33 26 34.5	34.6	− 13.93	+ 0.49	...	4	45.9	13.0	....	3581
902	24 55 21.4	...	− 13.93	+ 0.54	+ 0.07	4	49.3	...	....	3584
903	16 52 33.6	...	− 13.90	+ 0.67	...	4	45.2	...	....	3593
904	48 4 48.4	49.2	− 13.89	+ 0.41	− 0.02	3	45.3	10.7	....	......
905	39 37 30.1	30.4	− 13.89	+ 0.45	...	3	45.6	13.0	....	3600

Ordinal Number		Magnitude	Estimates of Magnitude	Mean Right Ascension 1845.0			Precession 1845.0	Secular Variation	Adopted Proper Motion	Observations of R.A.		
R.	G.	R.		R.		G.				No. R.	R.	G.
				h. m. s.		s.	s.	s.	s.		1800 +	
906	...	6.0	1	3 4 52.10		...	+ 3.042	+ 0.006	......	2	55.9	...
907	631	5.5	8	3 5 9.11		9.25	+ 4.236	+ 0.050	......	5	46.9	13.0
908	632	8.1	6	3 5 16.92		16.65	+ 4.123	+ 0.043	......	4	49.2	12.0
909	628	6.6	3	3 5 18.53		17.92	+ 5.610	+ 0.151	......	3	46.6	11.0
910	...	3.3	A	3 5 29.38		...	+ 2.521	− 0.001	+ 0.025	4	40.9	...
911	633	6.5	6	3 5 34.18		33.72	+ 4.030	+ 0.043	......	4	47.9	13.9
912	635	8.1	6	3 5 49.74		49.63	+ 4.135	+ 0.045	......	3	48.3	12.0
913	...	5.3	2	3 6 0.12		...	+ 3.432	+ 0.016	− 0.006	2	50.4	...
914	634	5.0	5	3 6 25.36		24.88	+ 5.160	+ 0.110	......	3	45.6	8.0
915	636	6.2	6	3 7 23.04		22.76	+ 3.994	+ 0.038	......	5	48.0	9.5
916	637	5.5	5	3 7 37.23		37.28	+ 4.219	+ 0.048	+ 0.008	4	45.4	9.0
917	639	6.5	4	3 7 44.11		43.95	+ 3.853	+ 0.031	......	4	46.0	10.9
918	638	8.2	5	3 7 47.13		47.09	+ 4.202	+ 0.051	......	3	46.3	15.0
919	...	7.2	7	3 8 4.07		...	+ 4.019	+ 0.039	......	4	51.3	...
920	640	5.0	4	3 8 7.60		7.55	+ 4.217	+ 0.049	+ 0.004	2	44.2	8.4
921	...	5.7	1	3 8 18.54		...	+ 2.909	+ 0.003	......	1	52.0	...
922	644	8.7	6	3 8 55.15		54.92	+ 4.134	+ 0.045	......	4	47.2	12.0
923	...	5.8	1	3 9 5.07		...	+ 2.902	+ 0.003	......	2	52.0	...
924	...	7.5	6	3 9 8.61		...	+ 4.931	+ 0.096	......	4	49.2	...
925	641	7.0	4	3 9 19.82		18.68	+ 6.217	+ 0.204	......	3	45.6	11.1
926	...	7.4	5	3 9 24.46		...	+ 4.932	+ 0.096	......	4	49.2	...
927	643	7.8	6	3 9 42.92		42.54	+ 5.949	+ 0.177	......	3	44.3	13.9
928	...	7.4	5	3 9 45.62		...	+ 4.065	+ 0.041	......	4	50.4	...
929	...	8.1	7	3 10 21.23		...	+ 4.176	+ 0.046	......	4	47.4	...
930	646	6.2	7	3 10 54.76		54.19	+ 4.189	+ 0.047	+ 0.021	5	46.2	10.6
931	...	7.7	7	3 10 56.50		...	+ 4.053	+ 0.040	......	4	51.2	...
932	647	5.8	6	3 11 4.97		4.82	+ 3.986	+ 0.037	......	3	47.2	9.5
933	648	8.6	4	3 11 15.04		14.63	+ 4.146	+ 0.045	......	3	45.0	12.0
934	645	5.3	4	3 11 17.01		16.91	+ 5.104	+ 0.103	+ 0.007	3	45.3	11.1
935	649	5.6	7	3 12 15.93		16.10	+ 4.200	+ 0.046	+ 0.017	5	43.4	10.6
936	...	5.5	1	3 12 17.17		...	+ 3.445	+ 0.016	......	2	53.9	...
937	650	2.6	3	3 13 17.07		16.87	+ 4.231	+ 0.047	......	35	43.7	6.8
938	652	7.9	5	3 13 17.37		17.17	+ 3.927	+ 0.034	......	5	46.2	11.0
939	...	9.0	4	3 13 21.08		...	+ 4.206	+ 0.047	......	3	54.3	...
940	653	8.2	10	3 13 32.54		32.11	+ 4.203	+ 0.046	......	5	46.7	12.0

Ordinal Number.	Mean North Polar Distance 1845.0.		Precession 1845.0.	Secular Variation.	Adopted Proper Motion.	Observations of N.P.D.			Names.
R.	R.	G.				No. R.	Mean year. R.	Mean year. G.	
	° ′ ″	″	″	″	″		1800 +		
906	91 46 20.0	...	− 13.87	+ 0.32	...	1	52.0	...	94 Ceti.........
907	39 38 34.4	34.5	− 13.86	+ 0.45	...	5	44.2	13.0	....
908	42 33 10.1	12.9	− 13.85	+ 0.43	...	4	49.8	12.0	....
909	20 50 39.0	38.0	− 13.85	+ 0.59	...	4	42.4	11.0	....
910	119 36 3.6	...	− 13.83	+ 0.27	− 0.62	1	54.0	...	12 Eridani ....
911	45 14 0.1	58.2	− 13.83	+ 0.42	...	3	49.3	13.9	....
912	42 17 51.3	51.4	− 13.81	+ 0.43	...	4	50.5	12.0	....
913	69 32 3.1	...	− 13.80	+ 0.36	+ 0.07	2	46.0	...	58 Arietis ζ ...
914	24 55 16.7	16.9	− 13.78	+ 0.55	...	5	45.8	8.0	....
915	46 32 58.2	58.6	− 13.72	+ 0.42	...	5	47.9	9.5	30 Persei ......
916	40 21 3.5	3.6	− 13.70	+ 0.45	...	3	43.3	9.0	29 Persei ......
917	51 17 28.7	29.0	− 13.70	+ 0.41	...	4	48.5	10.9	....
918	40 48 10.5	9.9	− 13.69	+ 0.46	...	3	47.3	15.0	....
919	45 51 11.1	...	− 13.68	+ 0.43	...	4	51.0	...	....
920	40 28 35.7	35.9	− 13.67	+ 0.45	...	3	42.3	8.4	31 Persei ......
921	99 23 59.3	...	− 13.66	+ 0.31	...	1	56.9	...	13 Eridani ζ ..
922	42 41 59.5	59.1	− 13.61	+ 0.44	...	4	48.7	12.0	....
923	99 43 55.0	...	− 13.60	+ 0.31	...	1	57.9	...	14 Eridani.....
924	27 49 29.9	...	− 13.60	+ 0.54	...	2	49.5	...	....
925	17 21 7.2	7.9	− 13.59	+ 0.67	+ 0.09	3	44.3	11.1	....
926	27 50 9.3	...	− 13.58	+ 0.54	...	2	48.9	...	....
927	18 52 35.9	31.6	− 13.57	+ 0.64	...	3	47.7	13.9	....
928	44 41 40.7	...	− 13.56	+ 0.44	...	3	50.3	...	....
929	41 44 12.5	...	− 13.53	+ 0.46	...	3	49.0	...	....
930	41 29 29.1	28.1	− 13.49	+ 0.45	...	3	44.0	10.6	....
931	45 10 42.8	...	− 13.49	+ 0.44	...	4	51.2	...	....
932	47 14 8.4	8.5	− 13.48	+ 0.43	...	4	47.0	9.5	32 Persei l ....
933	42 37 43.6	43.6	− 13.47	+ 0.44	...	3	46.7	12.0	....
934	25 58 29.8	29.7	− 13.47	+ 0.55	...	4	45.2	11.1	....
935	41 20 49.5	49.6	− 13.40	+ 0.46	...	3	44.3	10.6	....
936	69 24 56.5	...	− 13.40	+ 0.37	...	3	54.3	...	61 Arietis τ¹ .
937	40 41 45.4	45.0	− 13.34	+ 0.46	...	22	42.5	6.8	33 Persei λ ....
938	49 21 4.7	5.1	− 13.34	+ 0.42	...	4	45.9	11.0	....
939	41 20 9.3	...	− 13.33	+ 0.46	...	4	54.5	...	....
940	41 25 0.6	58.7	− 13.31	+ 0.46	...	5	50.2	12.0	....

Ordinal Number		Magnitude	Estimates of Magnitude	Mean Right Ascension 1845.0		Precession 1845.0	Secular Variation	Adopted Proper Motion	Observations of R.A.		
R.	G.	R.		R.	G.				No. R.	Mean year R.	G.
				h. m. s.	s.	s.	s.	s.		1800 +	
941	654	8.1	5	3 13 41.73	41.26	+ 3.933	+ 0.034	......	4	48.2	11.0
942	655	8.3	7	3 14 11.42	10.86	+ 4.210	+ 0.046	......	4	50.0	11.1
943	651	6.2	7	3 14 22.06	21.65	+ 6.036	+ 0.178	......	6	45.5	13.9
944	658	8.3	4	3 14 33.39	33.79	+ 3.955	+ 0.034	......	3	48.7	13.1
945	661	6.7	5	3 14 55.41	55.15	+ 3.934	+ 0.034	......	3	49.0	10.6
946	659	6.3	7	3 14 58.96	58.59	+ 4.209	+ 0.046	......	4	44.4	11.5
947	660	7.5	4	3 15 2.23	2.35	+ 4.234	+ 0.048	......	3	48.0	15.0
948	...	7.3	5	3 15 6.81	...	+ 3.926	+ 0.032	......	2	47.0	...
949	...	6.0	1	3 15 9.92	...	+ 3.521	+ 0.018	......	3	43.3	...
950	657	8.0	7	3 15 29.50	29.05	+ 6.047	+ 0.177	......	6	47.0	13.9
951	656	8.1	4	3 15 29.57	28.54	+ 6.070	+ 0.178	......	3	51.6	13.9
952	...	7.5	4	3 15 59.59	...	+ 4.773	+ 0.077	......	2	49.0	...
953	) 642	5.9	36	3 16 25.27	19.03	+18.053	+ 3.147	......	50	49.9	7.5
954	663	7.4	6	3 16 27.00	27.02	+ 4.016	+ 0.037	......	2	48.4	16.0
955	...	4.7	1	3 16 28.80	...	+ 3.222	+ 0.010	......	1	50.8	...
956	662	4.2	4	3 16 33.91	33.71	+ 4.779	+ 0.075	+ 0.005	4	47.0	7.6
957	664	7.5	5	3 16 36.23	36.48	+ 4.235	+ 0.044	......	2	49.9	15.0
958	668	5.4	6	3 17 3.65	3.57	+ 4.216	+ 0.044	+ 0.007	4	47.2	13.0
959	670	8.1	4	3 17 13.14	13.23	+ 4.253	+ 0.046	......	2	48.9	15.0
960	672	8.1	3	3 17 30.85	30.73	+ 4.045	+ 0.039	......	2	48.5	15.1
961	673	8.7	4	3 17 31.45	31.49	+ 4.043	+ 0.038	......	2	48.9	15.1
962	671	4.4	5	3 17 34.87	34.86	+ 4.716	+ 0.072	+ 0.005	7	46.5	7.4
963	666	7.7	2	3 17 37.25	37.10	+ 5.448	+ 0.121	......	2	48.5	11.9
964	667	7.8	4	3 17 38.25	37.79	+ 5.466	+ 0.122	......	2	47.0	11.9
965	675	7.0	5	3 17 46.75	46.56	+ 4.045	+ 0.038	......	2	48.6	15.1
966	674	6.0	5	3 17 47.06	47.22	+ 4.251	+ 0.047	......	7	50.3	15.0
967	676	7.9	6	3 17 53.67	53.17	+ 4.220	+ 0.045	......	4	49.3	13.0
968	680	7.2	4	3 18 4.54	4.69	+ 4.025	+ 0.037	......	2	51.4	16.0
969	678	5.5	3	3 18 13.24	12.83	+ 4.518	+ 0.060	......	4	47.0	8.0
970	665	8.4	5	3 18 16.46	16.47	+ 6.924	+ 0.261	......	3	50.6	12.0
971	681	5.6	3	3 18 18.72	18.64	+ 4.239	+ 0.046	......	2	49.0	12.0
972	669	7.0	4	3 18 21.18	20.77	+ 6.361	+ 0.203	......	2	50.9	13.9
973	...	7.1	3	3 18 25.68	...	+ 4.515	+ 0.064	......	2	51.4	...
974	...	6.3	4	3 18 39.03	...	+ 4.141	+ 0.042	......	3	53.0	...
975	682	8.8	3	3 18 45.70	43.48	+ 4.228	+ 0.046	......	2	52.0	13.0

Ordinal Number.	Mean North Polar Distance 1845.0.		Precession 1845.0.	Secular Variation.	Adopted Proper Motion.	Observations of N.P.D.			Names.	Oeltzen-Argelander Number.
R.	R.	G.				No. R.	Mean year R.	G.		
	° ′ ″	″	″	″	″		1800 +			
941	49 13 15.2	18.1	− 13.30	+ 0.43	...	4	48.2	11.0	....	....
942	41 18 11.6	12.0	− 13.27	+ 0.47	...	3	50.7	11.1	....	....
943	18 41 5.5	5.3	− 13.26	+ 0.66	+ 0.02	3	43.6	13.9	....	3741
944	48 34 35.6	34.9	− 13.25	+ 0.43	...	2	51.0	13.1	....	....
945	49 17 50.8	51.7	− 13.23	+ 0.43	...	3	44.7	10.6	....	....
946	41 25 53.8	54.2	− 13.22	+ 0.47	...	4	45.8	11.5	....	3753
947	40 48 27.7	26.1	− 13.21	+ 0.49	...	3	47.7	15.0	....	....
948	49 36 1.0	...	− 13.21	+ 0.43	...	3	47.7	...	....	....
949	65 49 43.3	...	− 13.21	+ 0.39	...	2	55.5	...	64 Arietis	....
950	18 41 7.3	4.9	− 13.19	+ 0.66	...	3	45.6	13.9	....	3758
951	18 31 35.4	36.6	− 13.19	+ 0.67	...	3	51.6	13.9	....	3757
952	30 38 28.3	...	− 13.15	+ 0.52	...	2	52.0	...	....	....
953	3 51 29.9	28.2	− 13.13	+ 2.00	...	14	45.2	7.5	....	....
954	46 53 35.1	32.0	− 13.12	+ 0.46	...	4	51.0	16.0	....	....
955	81 31 13.9	...	− 13.13	+ 0.36	+ 0.10	1	53.1	...	1 Tauri o	....
956	30 36 22.1	22.7	− 13.12	+ 0.53	...	3	45.9	7.6	....	....
957	40 56 51.5	50.8	− 13.11	+ 0.50	...	3	48.0	15.0	....	3782
958	41 29 0.6	0.0	− 13.08	+ 0.47	...	3	46.0	13.0	....	3786
959	40 35 33.1	34.2	− 13.08	+ 0.47	...	2	51.5	15.0	....	3787
960	46 9 16.0	15.2	− 13.05	+ 0.46	...	2	53.0	15.1	....	....
961	46 12 18.4	19.1	− 13.05	+ 0.46	...	3	52.7	15.1	....	....
962	31 39 54.4	54.4	− 13.05	+ 0.52	− 0.03	3	43.3	7.4	....	....
963	23 6 48.0	47.0	− 13.05	+ 0.61	...	2	45.6	11.9	....	....
964	22 57 15.9	13.8	− 13.05	+ 0.61	...	3	49.6	11.9	....	3795
965	46 10 6.7	4.8	− 13.04	+ 0.45	...	3	49.3	15.1	....	....
966	40 41 44.8	43.6	− 13.04	+ 0.47	...	3	47.9	15.0	....	3800
967	41 28 22.9	23.0	− 13.03	+ 0.47	...	2	50.6	13.0	....	3803
968	46 47 28.2	29.7	− 13.02	+ 0.44	...	2	51.0	16.0	....	....
969	35 5 25.6	26.5	− 13.01	+ 0.50	...	2	41.5	8.0	....	3808
970	14 47 24.4	21.6	− 13.01	+ 0.76	...	2	52.5	12.0	....	3807
971	41 2 1.2	1.7	− 13 00	+ 0.47	+ 0.06	3	43.6	12.0	34 Persei	3811
972	17 11 15.3	15.2	− 13.00	+ 0.71	+ 0.08	3	45.9	13.9	....	3809
973	35 9 59.5	...	− 12.99	+ 0.50	...	2	41.5	...	....	3812
974	43 36 13.7	...	− 12.98	+ 0.47	...	2	53.0	...	....	3815
975	41 23 13.4	10.1	− 12.97	+ 0.47	...	2	52.4	13.0	....	....

Ordinal Number.		Magnitude.	Estimates of Magnitude.	Mean Right Ascension 1845.0.		Precession 1845.0.	Secular Variation	Adopted Proper Motion.	Observations of R.A.		
R.	G.	R.		R.	G.				No. R.	Mean year. R.	G.
				h. m. s.	s.	s.	s.	s.		1800 +	
976	...	4.3	3	3 18 46.51	...	+ 3.235	+ 0.010	+ 0.002	3	50.0	...
977	683	7.8	4	3 18 50.20	50.12	+ 4.230	+ 0.046	......	3	47.6	13.0
978	677	9.0	4	3 19 18.08	18.41	+ 6.654	+ 0.230	......	2	45.5	11.1
979	...	6.3	1	3 19 23.43	...	+ 3.490	+ 0.016	......	1	52.0	...
980	679	8.9	4	3 19 23.59	22.02	+ 6.374	+ 0.204	......	2	51.9	13.9
981	686	4.4	5	3 19 40.44	40.32	+ 4.184	+ 0.043	+ 0.002	5	46.9	10.0
982	687	6.8	3	3 19 41.84	41.91	+ 4.189	+ 0.043	+ 0.009	3	47.7	10.1
983	688	7.8	4	3 19 59.93	60.26	+ 4.006	+ 0.034	......	2	47.0	15.0
984	689	8.1	3	3 20 16.43	16.04	+ 4.246	+ 0.045	......	2	52.0	14.1
985	690	7.1	5	3 20 27.16	27.12	+ 4.236	+ 0.045	......	3	45.1	13.0
986	691	7.2	5	3 20 38.96	38.80	+ 4.184	+ 0.043	+ 0.005	4	48.0	10.9
987	692	8.4	4	3 20 43.97	43.46	+ 4.227	+ 0.044	......	2	52.0	13.0
988	693	6.7	4	3 20 45.24	44.98	+ 4.246	+ 0.046	......	2	49.9	13.6
989	685	7.4	3	3 20 49.00	48.11	+ 6.701	+ 0.231	......	2	52.4	11.1
990	684	6.7	4	3 20 54.29	54.51	+ 6.963	+ 0.263	......	3	50.0	12.0
991	694	6.1	8	3 21 13.08	12.74	+ 4.192	+ 0.043	......	5	46.9	10.0
992	695	6.8	5	3 21 15.18	14.72	+ 3.940	+ 0.034	......	3	47.0	11.0
993	696	7.1	5	3 21 39.89	39.58	+ 4.076	+ 0.037	......	3	49.6	14.0
994	697	6.0	5	3 21 43.46	43.56	+ 4.120	+ 0.039	− 0.003	3	47.7	13.0
995	698	7.5	4	3 21 44.22	44.45	+ 4.005	+ 0.035	......	2	49.4	15.0
996	...	7.4	6	3 21 45.99	...	+ 4.799	+ 0.076	......	4	53.8	...
997	701	7.0	2	3 22 1.24	0.96	+ 3.948	+ 0.034	.....	2	49.5	11.0
998	699	6.9	6	3 22 2.16	1.91	+ 4.078	+ 0.039	......	3	51.6	14.0
999	...	4.7	1	3 22 19.28	...	+ 3.298	+ 0.011	+ 0.002	1	52.9	...
1000	702	6.9	6	3 22 23.77	23.74	+ 4.194	+ 0.042	+ 0.021	5	46.7	10.9
1001	...	6.4	4	3 22 24.43	...	+ 4.825	+ 0.076	......	2	52.5	...
1002	...	7.1	4	3 22 45.29	...	+ 5.079	+ 0.098	......	3	51.0	...
1003	...	7.3	2	3 23 12.36	...	+ 4.224	+ 0.044	......	3	51.5	...
1004	703	6.4	7	3 23 23.14	23.05	+ 3.921	+ 0.033	......	4	48.0	13.1
1005	704	8.4	4	3 24 2.30	2.31	+ 4.249	+ 0.045	......	3	44.4	13.0
1006	705	7.7	6	3 24 4.74	4.47	+ 4.084	+ 0.040	......	3	48.0	14.0
1007	700	8.3	4	3 24 10.03	11.30	+ 7.779	+ 0.348	......	2	51.4	12.0
1008	...	6.3	1	3 24 13.12	...	+ 3.234	+ 0.010	......	3	56.9	...
1009	706	7.2	5	3 25 6.07	5.34	+ 4.021	+ 0.038	......	4	45.8	15.0
1010	708	8.0	5	3 25 24.42	24.06	+ 4.022	+ 0.038	......	3	44.4	15.0

Ordinal Number.	Mean North Polar Distance 1845.0.		Precession 1845.0.	Secular Variation.	Adopted Proper Motion	Observations of N.P.D.		
R.	R.	G.				No. R.	Mean year. R.	G.
	° ′ ″	″	″	″	″		1800 +	
976	80 48 42.4	...	− 12.97	+ 0.36	+ 0.05	3	49.1	...
977	41 19 40.2	35.3	− 12.97	+ 0.47	...	2	50.0	13.0
978	15 54 13.9	14.4	− 12.93	+ 0.75	...	3	48.9	11.1
979	67 44 6.9	...	− 12.93	+ 0.39	...	1	57.9	...
980	17 11 22.3	17.2	− 12.93	+ 0.72	...	2	53.1	13.9
981	42 32 45.9	45.8	− 12.91	+ 0.47	...	4	43.9	10.0
982	42 26 7.7	6.2	− 12.91	+ 0.47	− 0.05	3	45.7	10.1
983	47 33 34.0	34.8	− 12.89	+ 0.45	...	2	51.0	15.0
984	41 4 52.3	64.0	− 12.87	+ 0.47	...	2	47.5	14.1
985	41 19 39.7	39.9	− 12.86	+ 0.47	...	3	46.4	13.0
986	42 40 25.6	26.0	− 12.85	+ 0.47	+ 0.05	3	45.0	10.9
987	41 35 0.3	58.8	− 12.84	+ 0.48	...	3	53.0	13.0
988	41 8 7.8	6.9	− 12.84	+ 0.48	...	3	46.7	13.6
989	15 47 27.6	27.4	− 12.84	+ 0.75	...	3	52.3	11.1
990	14 47 9.8	9.8	− 12.83	+ 0.78	...	3	42.9	12.0
991	42 30 39.5	36.7	− 12.80	+ 0.47	...	3	45.4	10.0
992	49 46 28.6	28.6	− 12.80	+ 0.45	...	3	49.6	11.0
993	45 41 36.3	38.2	− 12.77	+ 0.46	...	2	44.6	14.0
994	44 28 26.4	26.5	− 12.77	+ 0.46	+ 0.08	2	44.4	13.0
995	47 47 2.8	5.1	− 12.77	+ 0.46	...	3	50.6	15.0
996	30 47 46.7	...	− 12.77	+ 0.54	...	3	53.6	...
997	49 36 45.4	46.2	− 12.76	+ 0.45	...	2	47.5	11.0
998	45 40 38.3	36.8	− 12.76	+ 0.46	...	4	48.0	14.0
999	77 35 54.3	...	− 12.74	+ 0.37	+ 0.03	1	53.0	...
1000	42 34 50.4	50.4	− 12.73	+ 0.47	...	4	45.7	10.9
1001	30 29 18.3	...	− 12.73	+ 0.54	...	3	51.7	...
1002	27 14 21.3	...	− 12.71	+ 0.58	...	3	45.3	...
1003	41 54 38.2	...	− 12.68	+ 0.47	...	2	51.5	...
1004	50 37 41.5	42.2	− 12.66	+ 0.45	...	4	49.3	13.1
1005	41 24 24.6	28.1	− 12.62	+ 0.48	...	2	45.0	13.0
1006	45 43 25.4	26.6	− 12.62	+ 0.46	...	4	48.7	14.0
1007	12 27 2.1	57.4	− 12.61	+ 0.87	...	2	52.5	12.0
1008	81 9 14.2	...	− 12.60	+ 0.37	...	1	52.0	...
1009	47 37 48.8	43.8	− 12.54	+ 0.46	...	3	43.6	15.0
1010	47 38 9.9	8.4	− 12.52	+ 0.46	...	3	43.3	15.0

Estimates of Magnitude.	Mean Right Ascension 1845.0.		Precession 1845.0.	Secular Variation	Adopted Proper Motion.
R.	R.	G.			
	h. m. s.	s.	s.	s.	s.
5	3 25 30.00	29.79	+ 4.217	+ 0.042	......
2	3 25 37.94	...	+ 2.887	+ 0.003	— 0.061
3	3 26 24.71	...	+ 5.158	+ 0.098	......
1	3 26 24.89	...	+ 5.159	+ 0.098	......
5	3 26 49.23	...	+ 4.800	+ 0.069	......
A	3 26 56.66	...	+ 2.643	+ 0.001	......
3	3 26 58.02	...	+ 4.812	+ 0.069	......
6	3 27 3.40	...	+ 4.809	+ 0.069	......
4	3 27 7.43	...	+ 4.260	+ 0.045	......
6	3 27 14.21	13.95	+ 6.743	+ 0.222	......
6	3 27 19.24	...	+ 4.199	+ 0.043	......
5	3 27 19.45	19.18	+ 5.857	+ 0.142	......
3	3 27 19.92	...	+ 4.266	+ 0.045	......
5	3 27 32.63	32.15	+ 4.019	+ 0.033	......
6	3 27 38.50	39.13	+ 7.863	+ 0.346	......
6	3 27 38.84	38.48	+ 4.097	+ 0.038	......
7	3 27 42.69	42.21	+ 4.097	+ 0.038	......
6	3 28 32.29	32.57	+ 4.021	+ 0.034	......
6	3 28 45.63	45.41	+ 5.116	+ 0.088	......
5	3 29 22.48	22.67	+ 7.979	+ 0.359	......
1	3 29 52.60	...	+ 4.149	+ 0.040	......
5	3 29 57.41	57.30	+ 6.170	+ 0.174	......
6	3 29 59.19	59.05	+ 4.868	+ 0.073	......
4	3 30 2.93	...	+ 4.100	+ 0.038	......
4	3 30 3.25	3.10	+ 4.869	+ 0.075	......
2	3 31 22.15	...	+ 2.956	+ 0.004	......
5	3 31 25.26	25.33	+ 5.545	+ 0.116	+ 0.033
7	3 31 54.79	54.42	+ 4.226	+ 0.040	......
3	3 32 32.40	32.12	+ 5.155	+ 0.089	......
2	3 32 58.02	...	+ 2.962	+ 0.005	......
5	3 33 0.67	...	+ 4.261	+ 0.043	......
4	3 33 12.48	...	+ 6.078	+ 0.168	......
6	3 33 12.49	...	+ 4.039	+ 0.034	......
6	3 34 5.92	4.90	+ 6.164	+ 0.160	......
6	3 34 26.45	...	+ 4.231	+ 0.041	......

Ordinal Number.	Mean North Polar Distance 1845.0.			Precession 1845.0.	Secular Variation.	Adopted Proper Motion.	Observations of N.P.D.				Names.	Oeltzen-Argelander Number.
R.	R.		G.				No. R.	Mean year. R.	G.		Names.	
	o ′ ″		″	″	″	″		1800 +				
1011	42 19 45.0		45.1	− 12.51	+ 0.48	+ 0.06	5	43.6	7.2		37 Persei ψ ...	3928
1012	99 59 10.0		...	− 12.51	+ 0.33	+ 0.03	2	55.0	...		18 Eridani ε...	......
1013	26 38 21.3		...	− 12.46	+ 0.59	...	3	52.0	...		....	......
1014	26 38 ...		...	....	...	...	...	...	...		....	......
1015	31 15 3.6		...	− 12.43	+ 0.55	...	4	52.5	...		....	3947
1016	112 9 21.6		...	− 12.42	+ 0.30	+ 0.03	4	52.2	...		19 Eridani τ⁵ .	......
1017	31 4 13.6		...	− 12.42	+ 0.55	...	3	52.3	...		....	3952
1018	31 8 39.5		...	− 12.41	+ 0.55	...	3	52.7	...		....	3953
1019	41 26 4.0		...	− 12.41	+ 0.49	...	3	48.3	...		....	3956
1020	15 57 54.9		55.3	− 12.40	+ 0.77	...	4	44.3	11.1		....	3955
1021	42 56 20.4		...	− 12.40	+ 0.48	...	3	45.4	...		....	3960
1022	20 39 48.8		47.4	− 12.40	+ 0.65	...	3	47.7	11.0		....	3958
1023	41 18 38.7		...	− 12.40	+ 0.49	...	4	50.0	...		....	3961
1024	47 55 59.0		58.2	− 12.38	+ 0.46	...	4	44.7	10.1		....	......
1025	12 22 51.5		51.1	− 12.37	+ 0.90	...	4	45.7	12.0		....	3963
1026	45 42 47.0		46.7	− 12.37	+ 0.47	...	4	47.5	14.0		....	......
1027	45 42 51.2		49.6	− 12.37	+ 0.46	...	3	46.4	14.0		....	......
1028	47 58 12.1		9.3	− 12.31	+ 0.45	...	4	44.0	10.1		....	......
1029	27 17 36.1		35.9	− 12.29	+ 0.59	− 0.08	4	43.7	11.0		....	3979
1030	12 9 57.1		58.4	− 12.26	+ 0.88	...	2	51.4	12.0		....	3986
1031	44 29 9.6		...	− 12.22	+ 0.48	...	3	51.6	...		....	......
1032	18 53 1.1		0.5	− 12.21	+ 0.71	...	4	48.8	12.0		....	3997
1033	30 32 13.4		13.9	− 12.21	+ 0.56	...	3	46.0	13.0		....	3999
1034	45 49 14.7		...	− 12.20	+ 0.47	...	2	50.0	...		....	......
1035	30 31 27.4		28.3	− 12.20	+ 0.57	...	3	50.7	13.1		....	4002
1036	96 7 40.9		...	− 12.12	+ 0.34	...	2	56.9	...		21 Eridani	......
1037	23 17 34.5		30.2	− 12.11	+ 0.65	...	4	46.5	11.0		....	4018
1038	42 42 51.3		50.3	− 12.07	+ 0.49	+ 0.05	4	44.5	8.0		39 Persei δ....	4031
1039	27 9 8.0		7.0	− 12.03	+ 0.60	...	3	43.2	7.9		....	4036
1040	95 42 54.0		...	− 12.00	+ 0.35	...	2	53.5	...		22 Eridani.....	......
1041	41 58 31.7		...	− 12.00	+ 0.50	...	4	49.5	...		....	......
1042	19 37 2.3		...	− 11.98	+ 0.71	...	3	51.0	...		....	4050
1043	47 53 6.7		...	− 11.98	+ 0.47	...	4	45.0	...		....	......
1044	19 9 15.1		14.2	− 11.92	+ 0.72	+ 0.03	4	43.7	8.1		Camelopardi γ	4065
1045	42 50 2.7		...	− 11.90	+ 0.50	...	3	47.6	...		....	4079

Ordinal Number.		Magnitude.	Estimates of Magnitude.	Mean Right Ascension 1845.0		Precession 1845.0	Secular Variation	Adopted Proper Motion.	Observations of R.A.		
R.	G.	R.		R.	G.				No. R.	Mean year R.	G.
				h. m. s.	s.	s.	s.	s.		1800 +	
1046	728	4.1	6	3 34 40.92	40.63	+ 4.042	+ 0.032	......	5	46.1	7.6
1047	...	7.7	6	3 34 46.08	...	+ 4.142	+ 0.038	......	3	51.6	...
1048	725	7.3	5	3 35 0.54	0.10	+ 5.571	+ 0.115	......	3	44.4	11.0
1049	...	7.5	4	3 35 2.01	...	+ 5.307	+ 0.102	......	3	53.4	...
1050	729	7.0	6	3 35 2.85	2.54	+ 4.024	+ 0.032	......	4	49.0	13.0
1051	730	7.8	5	3 35 4.58	7.08	+ 4.152	+ 0.036	......	3	49.0	12.0
1052	731	6.0	6	3 35 10.11	9.71	+ 4.156	+ 0.036	......	4	48.0	12.1
1053	726	5.2	4	3 35 23.60	23.32	+ 5.389	+ 0.101	......	4	45.5	8.1
1054	733	7.0	3	3 35 26.40	26.53	+ 3.919	+ 0.027	......	4	47.7	13.0
1055	732	7.0	5	3 35 39.43	39.15	+ 4.415	+ 0.047	......	3	45.0	13.9
1056	727	7.4	6	3 35 48.93	49.16	+ 6.044	+ 0.148	......	3	49.0	15.1
1057	...	8.2	4	3 35 50.49	...	+ 7.267	+ 0.320	......	3	53.5	...
1058	...	4.8	2	3 35 59.52	...	+ 3.553	+ 0.016	......	5	54.2	...
1059	...	5.9	5	3 36 4.08	...	+ 5.176	+ 0.096	......	4	47.1	...
1060	734	7.6	4	3 36 10.61	10.32	+ 4.409	+ 0.048	......	3	48.0	13.9
1061	...	8.1	3	3 36 23.00	...	+ 4.709	+ 0.063	......	2	52.5	...
1062	...	7.9	4	3 36 28.84	...	+10.000	+ 0.623	......	4	53.3	...
1063	735	7.5	3	3 36 35.70	35.44	+ 4.101	+ 0.033	......	3	49.1	10.9
1064	...	6.5	3	3 36 54.41	...	+ 4.374	+ 0.046	......	3	51.7	...
1065	...	6.6	6	3 37 0.51	...	+ 4.717	+ 0.057	......	4	53.3	...
1066	...	7.3	3	3 37 6.71	...	+ 4.427	+ 0.048	......	3	49.7	...
1067	...	7.3	5	3 37 7.39	...	+ 4.718	+ 0.057	......	4	53.3	...
1068	736	7.2	5	3 37 10.62	10.44	+ 4.406	+ 0.046	......	2	50.0	13.9
1069	738	6.8	4	3 37 48.54	48.39	+ 4.471	+ 0.048	......	2	46.5	14.5
1070	...	3.7	2	3 38 16.85	...	+ 3.546	+ 0.016	......	53	44.9	...
1071	740	6.4	6	3 38 27.82	27.50	+ 4.104	+ 0.035	......	3	47.4	10.4
1072	737	6.9	4	3 38 41.22	41.20	+ 6.778	+ 0.208	......	3	47.6	11.1
1073	741	7.0	7	3 38 46.73	46.56	+ 4.466	+ 0.047	......	6	48.5	14.5
1074	...	4.5	1	3 38 49.02	...	+ 2.827	+ 0.003	......	1	56.0	...
1075	739	7.6	5	3 38 52.93	53.04	+ 6.024	+ 0.143	......	2	48.5	15.1
1076	743	5.8	5	3 39 18.21	18.06	+ 4.144	+ 0.035	......	4	46.3	11.0
1077	...	9.2	2	3 39 30.79	...	+ 4.525	+ 0.052	......	2	51.5	...
1078	744	9.0	3	3 39 42.69	42.56	+ 4.472	+ 0.048	......	2	52.0	15.0
1079	742	6.8	6	3 39 53.43	54.16	+ 6.313	+ 0.157	......	3	50.3	15.1
1080	...	5.3	3	3 39 58.47	...	+ 3.551	+ 0.016	Adopted..	2	53.4	...

stance	Precession 1845.0.	Secular Variation.	Adopted Proper Motion.	Observations of N.P.D.		
				No.	Mean year.	
G.				R.	R.	G.
"	"	"	"		1800 +	
61.0	— 11.88	+ 0.48	...	4	43.0	7.6
...	— 11.88	+ 0.49	...	3	51.7	...
16.0	— 11.86	+ 0.65	...	3	44.7	11.0
...	— 11.86	+ 0.65	...	3	53.3	...
8.3	— 11.85	+ 0.49	...	4	47.7	13.0
32.9	— 11.85	+ 0.50	...	2	46.5	12.0
37.4	— 11.85	+ 0.49	...	3	45.0	12.1
39.8	— 11.83	+ 0.64	...	4	44.2	8.1
5.5	— 11.82	+ 0.48	...	3	48.3	13.0
48.9	— 11.81	+ 0.53	...	3	47.7	13.9
26.4	— 11.80	+ 0.71	...	3	48.7	15.1
...	— 11.80	+ 0.88	...	2	54.0	...
...	— 11.79	+ 0.42	...	1	57.9	...
...	— 11.79	+ 0.62	...	3	45.0	...
31.1	— 11.78	+ 0.52	...	2	47.6	13.9
...	— 11.76	+ 0.56	...	3	52.3	...
...	— 11.75	+ 1.20	...	3	44.7	...
51.2	— 11.74	+ 0.49	...	3	49.0	10.9
...	— 11.72	+ 0.52	...	3	52.3	...
...	— 11.71	+ 0.55	...	2	53.0	...
...	— 11.70	+ 0.52	...	2	48.0	...
...	— 11.70	+ 0.55	...	2	53.0	...
30.4	— 11.70	+ 0.52	...	3	47.0	13.9
42.2	— 11.66	+ 0.53	...	4	44.8	14.5
...	— 11.63	+ 0.42	+ 0.06	7	52.0	...
17.3	— 11.61	+ 0.50	...	4	47.8	10.4
31.1	— 11.60	+ 0.79	...	2	46.0	11.1
57.3	— 11.59	+ 0.54	...	3	44.0	14.5
...	— 11.59	+ 0.34	...	1	52.0	...
37.8	— 11.58	+ 0.72	...	3	47.7	15.1
40.4	— 11.55	+ 0.50	...	4	44.2	11.0
...	— 11.53	+ 0.54	...	1	54.9	...
19.4	— 11.52	+ 0.56	...	2	49.5	15.0
51.5	— 11.51	+ 0.75	...	4	47.5	15.1
...	— 11.50	+ 0.43	...	2	58.1	...

Ordinal Number.		Magnitude.	Estimates of Magnitude.	Mean Right Ascension 1845.0.		Precession 1845.0.	Secular Variation	Adopted Proper Motion.	Observations of R.A.		
R.	G.	R.	R.	R.	G.	s.	s.	s.	No. R.	Mean year. R.	Mean year. G.
				h. m. s.	s.					1800 +	
1081	...	5.0	1	3 40 10.74	...	+ 2.589	+ 0.001	......	3	54.0	...
1082	745	8.3	3	3 41 28.17	24.81	+ 7.392	+ 0.252	......	2	45.6	12.0
1083	...	7.2	8	3 41 29.63	...	+ 8.135	+ 0.360	......	3	51.3	...
1084	...	7.6	6	3 41 40.30	...	+ 4.004	+ 0.029	......	3	51.6	...
1085	747	8.7	5	3 41 54.54	54.16	+ 4.485	+ 0.049	......	3	47.9	15.0
1086	...	6.1	5	3 42 26.07	...	+ 4.303	+ 0.041	......	2	49.0	...
1087	752	8.1	7	3 43 8.54	8.34	+ 4.484	+ 0.049	......	3	48.0	15.0
1088	...	6.0	1	3 43 44.71	...	+ 3.189	+ 0.008	......	2	56.1	...
1089	753	5.3	6	3 43 47.91	47.30	+ 5.208	+ 0.083	......	4	44.6	8.1
1090	749	8.5	6	3 43 50.51	50.69	+ 6.112	+ 0.138	......	4	47.8	15.1
1091	755	7.1	4	3 43 55.29	55.42	+ 4.498	+ 0.049	......	2	46.0	15.0
1092	754	5.3	9	3 43 58.03	57.70	+ 5.041	+ 0.074	......	3	44.4	9.0
1093	...	8.6	4	3 43 58.58	...	+ 4.478	+ 0.049	......	3	53.0	...
1094	757	7.0	5	3 43 59.34	59.41	+ 4.476	+ 0.047	......	3	46.7	11.0
1095	748	8.4	6	3 44 11.23	11.55	+ 7.425	+ 0.257	......	3	48.0	12.0
1096	746	5.1	5	3 44 25.33	25.12	+ 9.535	+ 0.512	......	3	44.4	7.2
1097	751	7.9	8	3 44 45.07	45.50	+ 7.426	+ 0.256	......	4	47.7	12.0
1098	759	5.4	6	3 44 49.80	49.27	+ 4.279	+ 0.041	......	5	45.5	9.4
1099	...	5.7	1	3 45 2.35	...	+ 2.957	+ 0.004	......	2	53.5	...
1100	760	5.1	6	3 45 6.54	5.98	+ 4.407	+ 0.043	+ 0.013	7	50.0	8.1
1101	758	7.7	5	3 46 9.24	8.52	+ 7.535	+ 0.263	......	3	48.6	12.5
1102	756	7.8	9	3 46 19.02	17.78	+ 8.563	+ 0.376	......	6	50.0	13.9
1103	...	7.5	3	3 46 30.58	...	+ 3.004	+ 0.005	......	3	57.0	...
1104	764	7.1	7	3 46 44.02	43.69	+ 4.056	+ 0.030	......	4	46.5	11.0
1105	...	5.5	2	3 47 7.16	...	+ 2.547	+ 0.001	......	2	57.5	...
1106	765	3.7	5	3 47 28.11	27.82	+ 3.995	+ 0.028	......	7	49.4	7.0
1107	761	9.4	6	3 47 28.65	28.19	+ 8.519	+ 0.366	......	3	52.3	14.1
1108	767	6.5	7	3 48 11.51	11.25	+ 3.959	+ 0.027	......	4	47.0	10.2
1109	762	7.4	9	3 48 17.03	14.80	+ 7.185	+ 0.218	......	4	47.5	13.0
1110	...	7.8	5	3 48 32.46	...	+ 4.304	+ 0.038	......	3	53.0	...
1111	...	9.8	3	3 48 32.91	...	+ 4.304	+ 0.038	......	3	54.1	...
1112	763	7.0	8	3 49 6.21	5.29	+ 8.647	+ 0.374	......	6	48.0	14.0
1113	...	7.0	1	3 49 14.73	...	+ 2.789	+ 0.003	......	1	52.0	...
1114	769	6.6	5	3 49 22.60	22.70	+ 3.961	+ 0.026	......	3	47.0	10.2
1115	750	6.8	39	3 49 40.20	41.82	+16.304	+ 1.818	+ 0.057	43	51.6	7.8

Ordinal Number.	Mean North Polar Distance 1845.0.			Precession 1845.0.	Secular Variation.	Adopted Proper Motion.	Observations of N.P.D.				Names.	Oeltzen-Argelander Number.
							No.	Mean year.				
R.	R.		G.				R.	R.	G.			
	° ′ ″		″	″	″	″		1800 +				
1081	113 42 50.2		...	− 11.49	+ 0.31	+ 0.51	1	57.0	...		27 Eridani τ^6.	......
1082	14 16 38.6		18.6	− 11.40	+ 0.86	...	3	44.0	12.0		....	......
1083	12 15 10.4		...	− 11.40	+ 0.98	...	6	51.9	...		....	4209
1084	49 40 32.0		...	− 11.39	+ 0.48	...	4	51.5	...		....	......
1085	37 54 11.8		8.0	− 11.36	+ 0.56	...	2	47.0	15.0		....	4219
1086	41 49 5.9		...	− 11.32	+ 0.51	...	4	49.7	...		....	......
1087	38 2 26.1		21.9	− 11.27	+ 0.56	...	5	48.0	15.0		....	4236
1088	83 56 6.4		...	− 11.23	+ 0.39	...	3	54.0	...		31 Tauri u^2 ...	......
1089	27 23 23.9		24.8	− 11.23	+ 0.63	...	6	46.2	8.1		....	4250
1090	20 0 28.6		27.8	− 11.23	+ 0.72	...	3	48.0	15.1		....	......
1091	37 49 22.3		21.1	− 11.22	+ 0.54	...	3	44.4	15.0		....	4254
1092	29 21 9.2		9.3	− 11.21	+ 0.62	...	9	50.3	9.0		....	4256
1093	38 12 10.6		...	− 11.21	+ 0.54	...	3	47.6	...		....	4257
1094	38 14 32.8		35.4	− 11.21	+ 0.53	...	4	44.5	11.0		....	4259
1095	14 17 10.1		6.8	− 11.20	+ 0.88	...	4	50.8	12.0		....	......
1096	9 44 31.7		32.1	− 11.19	+ 1.16	...	4	45.0	7.2		....	......
1097	14 18 12.5		11.0	− 11.16	+ 0.89	...	5	49.1	12.0		....	......
1098	42 35 26.1		23.4	− 11.15	+ 0.52	...	4	44.4	9.4		....	4268
1099	95 49 40.9		...	− 11.14	+ 0.36	...	1	55.9	...		30 Eridani.....	......
1100	39 45 36.7		39.2	− 11.14	+ 0.53	+ 0.16	6	47.7	8.1		43 Persei A ...	4270
1101	14 1 33.9		31.5	− 11.06	+ 0.92	...	3	44.7	12.5		....	......
1102	11 28 58.9		57.1	− 11.05	+ 1.03	...	3	49.3	13.9		....	4281
1103	93 25 2.3		...	− 11.03	+ 0.37	...	1	52.0	...		32 Eridani.....	......
1104	48 34 33.0		33.9	− 11.02	+ 0.49	...	4	49.3	11.0		....	......
1105	115 4 24.9		...	− 10.98	+ 0.31	...	1	52.0	...		33 Eridani τ^8.	......
1106	50 26 37.4		37.9	− 10.96	+ 0.49	...	3	48.0	7.0		45 Persei ϵ....	......
1107	11 36 38.8		40.3	− 10.96	+ 1.04	...	3	51.4	14.1		....	4299
1108	51 36 38.3		38.3	− 10.91	+ 0.48	...	3	47.6	10.2		....	......
1109	15 15 4.5		54.6	− 10.90	+ 0.89	...	5	48.4	13.0		....	......
1110	42 17 53.6		...	− 10.88	+ 0.53	...	3	51.3	...		....	......
1111	42 16 ...		...	....	...	...	...	...	...		....	......
1112	11 23 59.8		60.5	− 10.84	+ 1.06	...	4	45.8	14.0		....	4325
1113	104 3 9.0		...	− 10.82	+ 0.34	...	2	57.1	...		....	......
1114	51 37 42.2		44.1	− 10.81	+ 0.50	...	3	47.4	10.2		....	......
1115	4 51 54.8		55.2	− 10.80	+ 1.99	− 0.05	11	48.1	7.8		....	......

Ordinal Number.		Magnitude.	Estimates of Magnitude.	Mean Right Ascension 1845.0		Precession 1845.0	Secular Variation	Adopted Proper Motion.	Observations of R.A.		
R.	G.	R.		R.	G.				No. R.	Mean year. R.	G.
				h. m. s.	s.	s.	s.	s.		1800 +	
1116	768	7.7	4	3 49 55.02	54.69	+ 4.910	+ 0.064	......	2	48.0	11.1
1117	770	8.3	6	3 50 4.27	3.70	+ 4.910	+ 0.065	......	3	50.0	11.1
1118	...	3.5	1	3 50 47.98	...	+ 2.790	+ 0.003	......	1	52.0	...
1119	771	6.8	6	3 51 27.19	27.26	+ 6.806	+ 0.186	......	3	45.0	11.1
1120	772	5.3	6	3 51 34.76	34.25	+ 4.934	+ 0.065	......	5	46.7	9.1
1121	...	6.9	4	3 52 3.48	...	+ 4.347	+ 0.040	......	2	51.9	...
1122	...	4.5	1	3 52 5.93	...	+ 3.312	+ 0.010	......	1	47.1	...
1123	...	6.1	4	3 52 10.72	...	+ 9.583	+ 0.488	......	3	49.2	...
1124	773	6.4	5	3 52 12.45	12.23	+ 5.513	+ 0.096	......	3	45.7	13.0
1125	766	5.7	6	3 52 53.97	53.80	+12.907	+ 1.013	......	4	47.3	7.8
1126	...	7.9	6	3 53 7.77	...	+ 5.201	+ 0.080	......	4	53.6	...
1127	...	5.0	1	3 53 19.16	...	+ 2.553	+ 0.001	......	3	56.3	...
1128	775	7.8	5	3 53 38.83	37.83	+ 6.056	+ 0.126	......	3	45.0	10.9
1129	...	8.0	4	3 53 48.17	...	+ 5.209	+ 0.079	......	3	54.0	...
1130	...	7.0	6	3 54 13.02	...	+ 5.205	+ 0.078	......	5	53.3	...
1131	...	7.2	7	3 54 15.42	...	+ 5.205	+ 0.078	......	5	53.2	...
1132	...	6.7	6	3 54 34.00	...	+ 4.617	+ 0.050	......	4	49.0	...
1133	776	6.6	8	3 54 54.61	54.41	+ 4.274	+ 0.035	+ 0.005	5	47.0	10.1
1134	...	5.0	1	3 54 54.89	...	+ 3.182	+ 0.007	+ 0.007	1	52.0	...
1135	777	4.4	6	3 55 3.61	3.30	+ 4.428	+ 0.040	......	7	48.0	7.3
1136	...	8.0	5	3 55 21.41	...	+ 9.562	+ 0.465	......	3	49.2	...
1137	...	4.7	3	3 55 32.43	...	+ 3.524	+ 0.014	+ 0.004	4	44.5	...
1138	...	7.6	6	3 56 4.42	...	+ 4.487	+ 0.043	......	3	48.1	...
1139	778	6.2	6	3 56 22.30	21.71	+ 5.016	+ 0.065	......	3	44.7	9.1
1140	...	8.8	4	3 56 24.28	...	+ 4.428	+ 0.040	......	3	50.3	...
1141	774	5.7	7	3 56 28.95	29.05	+12.344	+ 0.874	......	4	45.3	7.9
1142	...	7.5	4	3 56 41.46	...	+ 4.590	+ 0.048	......	2	52.0	...
1143	...	5.5	1	3 57 6.46	...	+ 3.662	+ 0.016	......	1	52.0	...
1144	...	8.1	6	3 57 10.25	...	+ 4.432	+ 0.040	......	3	51.6	...
1145	...	8.6	5	3 57 15.50	...	+ 4.254	+ 0.035	......	3	53.0	...
1146	...	7.3	6	3 57 15.92	...	+ 4.429	+ 0.040	......	3	50.6	...
1147	781	4.6	5	3 57 25.85	25.27	+ 4.317	+ 0.036	......	5	46.3	8.1
1148	...	7.2	5	3 57 50.66	...	+ 4.254	+ 0.035	......	3	52.4	...
1149	780	7.3	8	3 58 21.81	21.39	+ 6.088	+ 0.120	......	4	44.6	10.9
1150	...	6.3	2	3 59 14.55	...	+ 2.455	+ 0.001	......	3	57.0	...

Distance	Precession 1845.0.	Secular Variation.	Adopted Proper Motion.	Observations of N.P.D. No.	Mean year.		Names.	Oeltzen-Argelander Number.
G.				R.	R.	G.		
′	′	′	′		1800 +			
36.5	− 10.78	+ 0.61	...	3	45.7	11.1	....	......
7.3	− 10.77	+ 0.63	...	3	44.8	11.1	....	......
...	− 10.72	+ 0.34	+ 0.12	1	52.0	...	34 Eridani γ ..	......
42.3	− 10.67	+ 0.83	...	5	45.0	11.1	....	4369
57.4	− 10.66	+ 0.61	...	4	45.8	9.1	....	......
...	− 10.62	+ 0.54	...	3	49.3	...	....	......
...	− 10.62	+ 0.41	...	2	48.6	...	35 Tauri λ	......
...	− 10.61	+ 1.22	...	4	44.3	...	....	4379
42.4	− 10.61	+ 0.69	...	5	47.8	13.0	....	4386
24.1	− 10.56	+ 1.60	− 0.02	7	48.4	7.8	....	......
...	− 10.54	+ 0.65	...	3	53.7	...	....	4409
...	− 10.53	+ 0.32	...	2	52.0	...	36 Eridani τ⁹ .	......
10.4	− 10.51	+ 0.74	...	3	44.3	10.9	....	4416
...	− 10.49	+ 0.65	...	3	54.3	...	....	4420
...	− 10.48	+ 0.64	...	3	51.7	...	....	4425
...	− 10.48	+ 0.64	...	3	52.1	...	....	4427
...	− 10.43	+ 0.58	...	4	47.5	...	....	......
5.8	− 10.41	+ 0.53	...	5	47.7	10.1	....	4442
...	− 10.41	+ 0.40	...	2	57.0	...	38 Tauri ν	......
34.7	− 10.40	+ 0.55	+ 0.05	7	46.0	7.3	47 Persei λ ...	4444
...	− 10.38	+ 1.19	...	3	46.7	...	....	4446
...	− 10.36	+ 0.44	+ 0.09	2	54.0	...	37 Tauri A¹ ...	......
...	− 10.32	+ 0.56	...	4	48.6	...	....	......
49.7	− 10.30	+ 0.63	...	4	45.5	9.1	....	4454
...	− 10.30	+ 0.55	...	2	51.0	...	....	4457
11.7	− 10.29	+ 1.53	...	4	44.7	7.9	....	......
...	− 10.28	+ 0.57	...	3	48.3	...	....	4462
...	− 10.25	+ 0.46	...	2	57.5	...	41 Tauri	......
...	− 10.24	+ 0.55	...	4	50.8	...	....	4473
...	− 10.23	+ 0.54	...	2	54.0	...	....	4476
...	− 10.23	+ 0.55	...	4	49.3	...	....	4478
28.2	− 10.22	+ 0.54	...	4	44.5	8.1	48 Persei c	4481
...	− 10.19	+ 0.54	...	3	51.3	...	....	4484
14.6	− 10.15	+ 0.77	...	4	47.0	10.9	....	4498
...	− 10.08	+ 0.31	...	2	52.0	...	....	......

Magnitude.	Estimates of Magnitude.	Mean Right Ascension 1845.0		Precession 1845.0.	Secular Variation	Adopted Proper Motion.
R.	R.	R.	G.			
		h. m. s.	s.	s.	s.	s.
7.6	7	3 59 55.79	54.70	+ 7.172	+ 0.208	.....
5.1	6	4 0 22.78	22.25	+ 9.950	+ 0.486	......
9.0	5	4 0 25.35	...	+ 6.304	+ 0.132	......
7.4	8	4 0 31.45	30.45	+ 7.178	+ 0.200	......
7.4	4	4 0 36.61	36.28	+ 6.265	+ 0.132	......
6.8	6	4 1 8.51	8.17	+ 7.632	+ 0.236	......
8.0	6	4 1 20.97	20.24	+ 7.194	+ 0.200	......
6.5	3	4 2 15.08	...	+ 4.395	+ 0.037	......
7.9	6	4 2 18.27	18.16	+ 4.461	+ 0.040	......
7.3	8	4 2 38.99	37.73	+10.074	+ 0.475	......
8.3	6	4 3 11.15	10.64	+ 4.635	+ 0.044	......
10.5	6	4 3 11.25	...	+ 3.339	+ 0.010	......
5.8	7	4 3 16.50	16.18	+ 5.216	+ 0.078	......
7.5	5	4 3 22.99	22.91	+ 4.476	+ 0.043	......
4.4	6	4 3 32.25	31.83	+ 4.367	+ 0.036	......
7.8	6	4 3 43.82	43.38	+ 5.213	+ 0.072	
7.8	6	4 4 17.35	16.68	+ 5.563	+ 0.089	
4.6	2	4 4 18.06	...	+ 2.922	+ 0.004	
5.9	4	4 4 20.65	20.20	+ 4.904	+ 0.056	
5.0	4	4 4 21.31	20.87	+ 4.055	+ 0.025	
7.9	4	4 4 32.30	31.97	+ 5.228	+ 0.072	......
5.5	5	4 4 39.27	38.86	+ 4.636	+ 0.044	......
7.1	5	4 4 57.97	...	+ 4.974	+ 0.060	......
7.5	4	4 5 1.39	...	+ 4.272	+ 0.033	......
7.3	7	4 5 15.43	...	+ 5.109	+ 0.065	......
6.8	7	4 5 31.08	31.02	+ 4.493	+ 0.042	
7.4	6	4 6 6.29	...	+ 4.299	+ 0.034	
5.5	7	4 6 8.69	8.42	+ 5.562	+ 0.084	
7.1	6	4 6 12.35	...	+ 4.279	+ 0.033	
7.8	4	4 6 35.65	35.40	+ 4.639	+ 0.047	
5.1	4	4 6 36.73	36.55	+ 4.467	+ 0.038	+ 0.011
7.3	3	4 6 40.98	...	+ 4.557	+ 0.042	......
8.6	5	4 7 2.75	...	+10.058	+ 0.463	......
6.2	5	4 7 25.36	25.01	+ 4.122	+ 0.027	......
6.0	5	4 7 36.44	36.04	+ 4.459	+ 0.037	......

Ordinal Number.	Mean North Polar Distance 1845.0.			Preces-sion 1845.0.	Secular Variation.	Adopted Proper Motion.	Observations of N.P.D.			Names.	Oeltzen-Argelander Number.
	R.		G.				No.	Mean year.			
R.	R.		G.				R.	R.	G.		
	° ′ ″		″	″	″	″		1800 +			
1151	15 45 49.5		47.6	− 10.03	+ 0.91	...	5	47.4	11.1	....	....
1152	9 33 41.4		40.9	− 10.00	+ 1.26	...	4	43.7	7.8	....	4522
1153	19 43 4.8		...	− 10.00	+ 0.80	...	3	49.3	...	....	4528
1154	15 45 43.2		40.2	− 9.99	+ 0.90	...	6	46.3	11.1	....	....
1155	19 57 0.9		0.9	− 9.98	+ 0.79	...	3	44.3	10.9	....	4531
1156	14 17 16.3		15.0	− 9.94	+ 0.97	...	6	43.9	11.1	....	....
1157	15 44 0.8		56.6	− 9.92	+ 0.93	...	4	45.0	11.0	....	....
1158	41 18 41.8		...	− 9.86	+ 0.56	...	4	43.0	...	....	4566
1159	39 55 35.6		33.3	− 9.85	+ 0.57	...	4	45.8	13.1	....	4569
1160	9 26 49.3		50.6	− 9.82	+ 1.30	...	4	46.3	8.0	....	....
1161	36 41 52.7		51.0	− 9.78	+ 0.61	...	4	50.3	13.9	....	4583
1162	77 6 7.9		...	− 9.78	+ 0.43	...	1	46.0	...	....	....
1163	28 32 52.0		51.7	− 9.78	+ 0.66	+ 0.01	5	46.5	10.1	....	4585
1164	39 42 49.6		49.5	− 9.77	+ 0.57	...	3	50.0	13.1	....	4590
1165	41 59 28.5		28.5	− 9.76	+ 0.55	+ 0.05	4	43.5	8.4	51 Persei μ ...	4594
1166	28 35 59.5		59.9	− 9.74	+ 0.67	...	4	43.8	11.1	....	4598
1167	25 8 24.0		22.1	− 9.70	+ 0.71	...	3	46.7	14.2	....	....
1168	97 13 43.9		...	− 9.70	+ 0.37	− 0.06	1	52.0	...	38 Eridani o¹.	....
1169	32 32 3.2		1.6	− 9.70	+ 0.63	...	3	43.7	13.0	....	4609
1170	49 54 53.6		53.6	− 9.70	+ 0.52	...	4	43.6	8.1	52 Persei f.....	....
1171	28 28 53.4		55.2	− 9.68	+ 0.67	...	3	46.7	11.1	....	4614
1172	36 47 4.9		3.8	− 9.67	+ 0.60	...	4	45.0	12.0	....	4616
1173	31 36 10.3		...	− 9.64	+ 0.63	...	4	52.0	...	....	4624
1174	44 15 52.0		...	− 9.64	+ 0.55	...	4	52.0	...	....	4626
1175	29 53 51.1		...	− 9.62	+ 0.65	...	3	52.1	...	....	4629
1176	39 31 40.5		41.5	− 9.60	+ 0.59	...	4	46.3	13.1	....	4630
1177	43 41 45.5		...	− 9.57	+ 0.55	...	3	47.4	...	....	....
1178	25 14 46.9		47.1	− 9.56	+ 0.71	...	6	46.5	11.6	....	4642
1179	44 10 29.9		...	− 9.56	+ 0.55	...	3	51.7	...	....	4646
1180	36 52 25.1		22.9	− 9.52	+ 0.60	...	3	46.0	13.9	....	....
1181	40 5 33.2		34.0	− 9.52	+ 0.58	+ 0.05	3	44.0	8.1	Persei b¹........	4651
1182	38 21 50.4		...	− 9.52	+ 0.59	...	3	49.0	...	....	4652
1183	9 34 3.2		...	− 9.49	+ 1.34	...	2	49.1	...	....	....
1184	48 14 47.3		46.8	− 9.46	+ 0.53	...	4	44.8	11.0	....	....
1185	40 20 10.1		8.1	− 9.44	+ 0.58	...	4	45.0	12.2	....	4671

Ordinal Number.		Magnitude.	Estimates of Magnitude.	Mean Right Ascension 1845.0.		Precession 1845.0.	Secular Variation	Adopted Proper Motion.	Observations of R.A.		
R.	G.	R.		R.	G.				No.	Mean year.	
									R.	R.	G.
				h. m. s.	s.	s.	s.	s.		1800 +	
1186	...	8.6	6	4 8 3.21	...	+ 5.075	+ 0.061	......	3	54.6	...
1187	806	8.2	8	4 8 5.70	5.16	+ 5.149	+ 0.062	......	5	45.2	11.1
1188	...	5.3	1	4 8 11.27	...	+ 3.504	+ 0.012	− 0.004	1	44.0	...
1189	808	5.2	6	4 8 21.13	21.62	+ 5.146	+ 0.063	+ 0.029	5	47.3	10.6
1190	809	6.0	6	4 8 28.31	28.02	+ 4.505	+ 0.038	......	3	46.4	12.9
1191	...	7.5	5	4 8 38.40	...	+ 4.772	+ 0.050	......	2	52.0	...
1192	...	7.6	5	4 8 42.59	...	+ 4.772	+ 0.050	......	3	54.7	...
1193	813	8.3	6	4 8 59.33	59.65	+ 4.517	+ 0.038	......	4	51.2	13.1
1194	811	8.3	4	4 9 11.40	10.86	+ 5.593	+ 0.082	......	2	43.5	14.1
1195	...	6.0	3	4 9 16.75	...	+ 4.834	+ 0.050	......	2	50.5	...
1196	...	7.2	4	4 9 19.36	...	+ 4.476	+ 0.037	......	3	51.8	...
1197	814	6.3	5	4 9 33.06	32.81	+ 4.116	+ 0.026	......	4	46.8	11.0
1198	...	7.1	5	4 9 43.07	...	+10.169	+ 0.459	......	3	49.2	...
1199	810	7.9	4	4 9 44.30	44.31	+ 6.595	+ 0.144	......	3	47.1	13.0
1200	807	7.9	5	4 10 3.59	1.39	+ 8.319	+ 0.281	......	4	48.0	12.0
1201	816	8.8	6	4 10 20.83	20.81	+ 4.517	+ 0.038	......	3	51.6	13.1
1202	817	5.2	4	4 10 21.71	21.53	+ 4.304	+ 0.031	......	5	46.5	9.1
1203	819	7.7	7	4 10 42.40	41.47	+ 4.567	+ 0.045	......	3	47.0	11.1
1204	815	8.3	5	4 10 53.07	52.93	+ 5.815	+ 0.096	......	3	46.8	14.1
1205	...	4.1	3	4 10 58.69	...	+ 3.394	+ 0.010	+ 0.009	13	49.5	...
1206	818	8.7	4	4 11 43.76	44.01	+ 6.588	+ 0.142	......	2	50.4	15.0
1207	821	7.2	6	4 12 20.72	20.45	+ 4.572	+ 0.045	......	3	44.1	11.1
1208	822	7.3	6	4 12 47.83	47.58	+ 4.516	+ 0.043	......	3	44.7	13.1
1209	824	6.3	5	4 12 49.47	69.13	+ 4.147	+ 0.026	......	4	45.7	11.0
1210	823	8.5	5	4 13 7.29	6.98	+ 4.517	+ 0.036	......	3	46.7	13.0
1211	826	7.5	5	4 13 45.15	44.81	+ 4.123	+ 0.025	......	4	44.4	10.1
1212	820	7.1	3	4 13 47.29	47.87	+ 9.024	+ 0.336	......	3	49.3	12.0
1213	...	4.0	2	4 14 0.14	...	+ 3.440	+ 0.010	+ 0.004	3	47.9	...
1214	...	7.3	5	4 14 17.14	...	+ 4.798	+ 0.046	......	3	51.7	...
1215	825	7.6	5	4 14 28.21	28.12	+ 6.361	+ 0.134	......	2	47.0	14.1
1216	...	7.6	5	4 14 36.31	...	+ 4.342	+ 0.031	......	3	51.7	...
1217	830	7.3	6	4 15 4.91	4.65	+ 4.586	+ 0.069	......	5	45.4	11.1
1218	829	8.0	4	4 15 5.13	4.50	+ 5.737	+ 0.085	......	3	47.4	11.1
1219	827	7.6	4	4 15 8.91	8.45	+ 6.406	+ 0.120	......	3	48.7	14.1
1220	...	4.9	3	4 15 9.94	...	+ 3.440	+ 0.010	+ 0.007	2	53.4	...

Ordinal Number.	Mean North Polar Distance 1845.0.		Precession 1845.0.	Secular Variation.	Adopted Proper Motion.	Observations of N.P.D.			Names.	Oeltzen-Argelander Number.
						No.	Mean year.			
R.	R.	G.				R.	R.	G.		
	° ′ ″	″	″	″	″		1800 +			
1186	30 28 48.5	...	− 9.41	+ 0.66	...	3	49.0	...	....	......
1187	29 35 21.3	21.4	− 9.41	+ 0.66	...	3	46.1	11.1	....	......
1188	69 48 30.1	...	− 9.40	+ 0.45	+ 0.05	1	54.0	...	50 Tauri ω² ...	......
1189	29 38 29.2	26.4	− 9.39	+ 0.66	+ 0.07	4	42.4	10.6	....	......
1190	39 27 45.8	47.0	− 9.38	+ 0.58	...	3	45.1	12.9	Persei b^2	4680
1191	34 51 3.3	...	− 9.36	+ 0.61	...	3	53.0	...	....	......
1192	34 52 36.5	...	− 9.36	+ 0.61	...	3	53.3	...	....	......
1193	39 15 55.6	58.3	− 9.34	+ 0.58	...	3	49.0	13.1	....	4687
1194	25 8 12.4	12.7	− 9.32	+ 0.74	...	2	48.1	14.1	....	4688
1195	33 52 25.4	...	− 9.32	+ 0.62	...	3	52.3	...	....	4693
1196	40 7 35.5	...	− 9.31	+ 0.58	...	2	53.0	...	....	......
1197	48 34 21.9	22.3	− 9.29	+ 0.53	...	3	45.0	11.0	....	......
1198	9 28 23.6	...	− 9.28	+ 1.36	...	2	44.5	...	....	......
1199	18 35 18.4	17.4	− 9.28	+ 0.86	...	3	47.7	13.0	....	4699
1200	12 43 53.2	49.6	− 9.25	+ 1.09	...	5	49.7	12.0	....	4706
1201	39 21 32.2	32.9	− 9.23	+ 0.59	...	3	50.6	13.1	....	4712
1202	43 52 42.1	42.9	− 9.23	+ 0.56	+ 0.07	4	43.8	9.1	53 Persei d	......
1203	38 25 50.5	54.7	− 9.20	+ 0.61	...	5	47.2	11.1	....	4720
1204	23 24 30.6	27.3	− 9.19	+ 0.76	...	3	49.9	14.1	....	4723
1205	74 45 6.5	...	− 9.18	+ 0.44	+ 0.03	5	51.0	...	54 Tauri γ	......
1206	18 41 56.6	57.7	− 9.12	+ 0.87	...	4	46.0	15.0	....	4734
1207	38 25 59.0	51.9	− 9.08	+ 0.60	...	4	44.3	11.1	....	4746
1208	39 31 16.5	15.9	− 9.04	+ 0.60	...	3	45.0	13.1	....	4758
1209	47 56 28.5	28.2	− 9.04	+ 0.52	...	4	44.5	11.0	....	......
1210	39 31 20.5	19.0	− 9.02	+ 0.59	...	2	46.5	13.0	....	4761
1211	48 38 11.0	9.5	− 8.97	+ 0.53	...	3	43.3	10.1	....	......
1212	11 21 25.0	23.7	− 8.96	+ 1.18	...	4	45.3	12.0	....	4771
1213	72 49 34.0	...	− 8.95	+ 0.45	+ 0.03	2	54.1	...	61 Tauri δ^1	......
1214	34 43 8.5	...	− 8.93	+ 0.63	...	3	51.7	...	....	4779
1215	20 0 59.4	59.9	− 8.91	+ 0.84	...	4	45.5	14.1	....	......
1216	43 18 18.4	...	− 8.90	+ 0.57	...	4	52.0	...	....	4785
1217	38 21 30.9	35.3	− 8.86	+ 0.61	...	3	43.7	11.1	....	4791
1218	24 12 45.6	44.0	− 8.86	+ 0.77	...	3	44.4	11.1	....	4788
1219	19 46 31.5	30.2	− 8.86	+ 0.83	...	3	45.0	14.1	....	4790
1220	72 55 12.6	...	− 8.85	+ 0.45	+ 0.04	3	53.0	...	64 Tauri δ^2	......

Magnitude.	Estimates of Magnitude.	Mean Right Ascension 1845.0.		Precession 1845.0.	Secular Variation	Adopted Proper Motion.
R.		R.	G.			
		h. m. s.	s.	s.	s.	s.
6.5	7	4 15 37.93	38.08	+ 6.806	+ 0.144	......
9.3	5	4 15 41.76	...	+ 4.520	+ 0.035	......
8.4	2	4 15 51.98	...	+ 3.263	+ 0.007	......
5.0	1	4 16 31.71	...	+ 3.452	+ 0.010	......
6.9	7	4 16 7.45	...	+ 4.337	+ 0.031	......
9.4	4	4 16 39.16	...	+ 6.399	+ 0.119	......
7.3	1	4 16 46.90	...	+ 3.407	+ 0.010	......
4.2	2	4 17 2.44	...	+ 3.568	+ 0.012	+ 0.007
7.3	2	4 17 7.77	...	+ 3.538	+ 0.012	......
5.5	1	4 17 31.29	...	+ 3.400	+ 0.009	+ 0.005
7.1	4	4 17 33.52	33.09	+ 5.949	+ 0.091	......
8.1	7	4 17 33.78	33.51	+ 8.145	+ 0.241	......
8.0	5	4 17 41.19	...	+10.298	+ 0.431	......
8.0	11	4 17 55.02	54.58	+ 6.385	+ 0.116	......
8.8	5	4 18 12.51	12.69	+ 8.144	+ 0.239	......
8.9	4	4 18 52.48	52.07	+ 7.233	+ 0.175	......
7.7	5	4 19 9.76	...	+10.090	+ 0.414	− 0.022
7.9	4	4 19 21.18	...	+ 8.009	+ 0.292	......
3.7	2	4 19 34.39	...	+ 3.483	+ 0.010	+ 0.005
7.4	5	4 19 45.73	...	+ 4.711	+ 0.041	......
5.6	4	4 19 46.68	46.43	+ 4.711	+ 0.041	......
8.2	6	4 19 52.25	...	+ 7.335	+ 0.244	......
7.9	3	4 20 7.08	6.70	+ 6.705	+ 0.132	......
8.8	6	4 20 24.56	...	+ 6.620	+ 0.143	......
7.6	5	4 20 47.50	...	+ 6.623	+ 0.143	......
8.1	7	4 21 8.43	...	+ 4.295	+ 0.029	......
9.0	6	4 21 25.30	25.24	+ 4.555	+ 0.036	......
7.6	5	4 21 28.01	...	+ 4.267	+ 0.027	......
6.5	1	4 21 39.15	...	+ 3.967	+ 0.020	......
7.3	7	4 21 58.38	...	+ 4.269	+ 0.029	......
7.7	3	4 22 5.38	...	+10.220	+ 0.414	− 0.030
7.0	8	4 22 28.15	27.76	+ 4.193	+ 0.025	......
6.3	5	4 22 31.43	31.31	+ 4.195	+ 0.025	+ 0.004
7.9	5	4 22 48.44	48.22	+ 4.557	+ 0.036	......
7.1	5	4 23 2.24	2.02	+ 4.512	+ 0.033	......

Ordinal Number.	Mean North Polar Distance 1845.0.		Precession 1845.0.	Secular Variation.	Adopted Proper Motion.	Observations of N.P.D.				Names.	Oeltzen-Argelander Number.
	R.	G.				No.	Mean year.				
R.	R.	G.				R.	R.	G.			
	° ′ ″	″	″	″	″		1800 +				
1221	17 49 1.5	57.0	− 8.82	+ 0.88	...	4	45.0	15.0		....	4796
1222	39 38 27.9	...	− 8.81	+ 0.59	...	3	51.7	...		....	4798
1223	81 0 50.6	...	− 8.80	+ 0.43	...	1	57.1	...		....	....
1224	72 25 55.6	...	− 8.75	+ 0.45	...	3	51.7	...		68 Tauri δ^3....	....
1225	43 29 34.5	...	− 8.78	+ 0.57	...	5	52.5	...		....	4806
1226	19 52 37.0	...	− 8.74	+ 0.83	...	3	51.7	...		....	4818
1227	74 25 6.6	...	− 8.73	+ 0.45	...	1	52.0	...		70 Tauri	....
1228	67 32 36.2	...	− 8.71	+ 0.46	+ 0.05	1	57.0	...		69 Tauri υ^1....	....
1229	68 53 10.8	...	− 8.71	+ 0.45	...	2	52.0	...		71 Tauri	....
1230	74 44 20.7	...	− 8.67	+ 0.45	+ 0.04	1	55.0	...		71 Tauri	....
1231	22 42 52.1	51.8	− 8.67	+ 0.77	...	5	47.4	11.0		....	4828
1232	13 21 44.8	45.2	− 8.67	+ 1.06	...	8	49.3	12.1		....	....
1233	9 28 20.3	...	− 8.66	+ 1.36	...	3	52.1	...		....	....
1234	19 59 50.5	49.4	− 8.64	+ 0.85	...	4	47.1	14.1		....	4837
1235	13 23 2.7	0.2	− 8.62	+ 1.06	...	4	49.1	12.0		....	....
1236	16 11 36.9	36.7	− 8.56	+ 0.97	...	3	44.4	13.0		....	....
1237	9 46 35.8	...	− 8.54	+ 1.34	+ 0.09	3	44.4	...		....	4855
1238	13 45 57.5	...	− 8.53	+ 1.08	...	4	47.6	...		....	....
1239	71 10 6.6	...	− 8.51	+ 0.46	+ 0.03	2	53.0	...		74 Tauri ϵ.....	....
1240	36 25 55.1	...	− 8.49	+ 0.62	...	4	44.0	...		1 Camelop. (1)	....
1241	36 26 0.7	0.9	− 8.49	+ 0.62	...	5	43.4	9.1		1 Camelop. (2)	4868
1242	15 51 33.8	...	− 8.49	+ 1.00	...	4	50.8	...		....	....
1243	18 26 22.5	20.3	− 8.47	+ 0.87	...	4	44.7	11.0		....	4871
1244	18 51 28.4	...	− 8.44	+ 0.90	...	3	50.4	...		....	4874
1245	18 51 42.3	...	− 8.41	+ 0.90	...	3	47.4	...		....	4879
1246	44 45 39.2	...	− 8.39	+ 0.57	...	3	52.7	...		....	4882
1247	39 17 21.1	21.8	− 8.36	+ 0.61	...	4	46.7	13.1		....	4887
1248	45 26 15.5	...	− 8.36	+ 0.56	...	3	51.7	...		....	4890
1249	53 35 47.6	...	− 8.34	+ 0.52	...	2	57.0	...		....	....
1250	45 24 40.6	...	− 8.32	+ 0.56	...	3	50.1	...		....	4898
1251	9 39 27.3	...	− 8.31	+ 1.36	+ 0.12	5	47.4	...		....	4897
1252	47 18 9.9	9.2	− 8.28	+ 0.56	+ 0.04	5	43.6	10.0		....	....
1253	47 16 24.4	24.8	− 8.28	+ 0.56	...	4	44.5	10.1		57 Persei m ...	....
1254	39 19 46.0	46.4	− 8.25	+ 0.61	...	3	44.7	13.1		....	4910
1255	40 12 33.9	32.7	− 8.23	+ 0.60	...	4	43.0	12.0		....	4915

Magnitude.	Estimates of Magnitude.	Mean Right Ascension 1845.0.		Precession 1845.0.	Secular Variation	Adopted Proper Motion.
R.	R.	R.	G.			
		h. m. s.	s.	s.	s.	s.
7.3	6	4 23 10.57	10.14	+ 4.197	+ 0.025	......
7.7	5	4 23 34.84	34.33	+ 5.928	+ 0.091	......
5.0	1	4 23 57.16	...	+ 3.063	+ 0.005	......
7.5	3	4 24 36.55	...	+ 4.287	+ 0.027	......
6.7	9	4 24 38.78	...	+ 8.089	+ 0.228	......
7.7	5	4 24 50.00	...	+ 4.383	+ 0.029	......
7.4	4	4 24 51.76	...	+ 4.383	+ 0.029	......
6.5	1	4 24 56.84	...	+ 3.739	+ 0.014	......
8.0	4	4 25 37.10	...	+ 4.434	+ 0.030	......
8.4	6	4 25 56.62	56.56	+ 4.126	+ 0.023	......
8.1	3	4 25 57.52	57.01	+ 6.369	+ 0.111	......
4.0	6	4 25 57.84	57.58	+ 4.134	+ 0.023	......
8.3	5	4 26 11.53	11.57	+ 4.911	+ 0.044	......
7.3	1	4 26 34.76	...	+ 3.509	+ 0.010	......
7.0	2	4 26 37.43	...	+ 3.507	+ 0.010	......
7.7	6	4 26 37.90	37.49	+ 5.959	+ 0.088	.....
8.0	11	4 26 38.98	...	+20.845	+ 2.158	......
1.0	A	4 27 1.91	...	+ 3.427	+ 0.009	+ 0.004
7.2	6	4 27 17.27	16.73	+ 4.168	+ 0.022	......
5.5	8	4 27 42.41	41.54	+ 4.712	+ 0.037	......
5.6	5	4 27 43.54	43.17	+ 4.688	+ 0.036	......
8.0	5	4 27 48.31	...	+ 4.673	+ 0.037	......
8.4	6	4 27 58.72	58.70	+ 4.655	+ 0.037	......
6.7	4	4 28 3.24	3.16	+ 4.175	+ 0.023	......
6.3	10	4 28 5.49	4.68	+ 7.879	+ 0.192	......
7.8	4	4 28 58.09	57.83	+ 6.371	+ 0.114	......
7.0	4	4 29 30.06	30.15	+ 4.123	+ 0.022	......
6.5	5	4 29 51.42	50.88	+ 4.441	+ 0.029	......
5.4	2	4 30 24.95	...	+ 3.416	+ 0.008	......
7.9	7	4 30 25.38	25.24	+ 4.523	+ 0.032	......
8.6	7	4 30 34.26	34.23	+ 5.972	+ 0.080	......
7.4	4	4 30 38.72	36.70	+ 4.177	+ 0.022	......
4.0	1	4 31 4.62	...	+ 2.748	+ 0.002	......
6.2	8	4 31 35.82	35.49	+ 4.529	+ 0.032	......
5.5	5	4 31 36.00	35.07	+10.820	+ 0.451	......

Ordinal Number.	Mean North Polar Distance 1845.0.			Precession 1845.0.	Secular Variation.	Adopted Proper Motion.	Observations of N.P.D.				Names.	Oeltzen-Argelander Number.
	R.	R.	G.				No. R.	Mean year. R.	G.			
	° ′ ″		″	″	″	″		1800 +				
1256	47 14 47.4		44.8	− 8.22	+ 0.56	...	4	45.0	10.1	....	....
1257	23 7 26.9		25.2	− 8.19	+ 0.79	...	3	44.3	14.1	....	4924
1258	90 22 53.4		...	− 8.16	+ 0.41	...	1	52.0	...	45 Eridani	....
1259	45 6 52.5		...	− 8.11	+ 0.57	...	4	50.1	...	....	4943
1260	13 41 42.4		...	− 8.10	+ 1.10	...	9	49.5	...	....	4941
1261	42 58 18.0		...	− 8.09	+ 0.58	...	3	52.7	...	....	4951
1262	42 57 20.8		...	− 8.09	+ 0.58	...	2	53.0	...	....	4952
1263	61 22 5.9		...	− 8.08	+ 0.50	...	1	55.9	...	....	....
1264	41 55 32.8		...	− 8.03	+ 0.59	...	4	52.0	...	....	....
1265	49 14 54.4		54.6	− 8.00	+ 0.56	...	3	43.8	13.0	....	....
1266	20 23 10.7		9.8	− 8.00	+ 0.86	...	3	44.4	11.0	....	....
1267	49 3 35.3		37.0	− 8.00	+ 0.55	...	4	44.0	8.1	58 Persei e	....
1268	33 40 58.2		57.2	− 7.98	+ 0.66	...	3	45.1	15.0	....	4971
1269	70 21 17.9		...	− 7.95	+ 0.47	...	1	52.0	...	....	....
1270	70 26 37.6		...	− 7.94	+ 0.47	...	1	58.1	...	....	....
1271	23 1 17.7		17.8	− 7.94	+ 0.81	...	4	45.3	14.1	....	4977
1272	3 57 1.1		...	− 7.94	+ 2.79	...	7	52.4	...	....	....
1273	73 48 28.4		...	− 7.91	+ 0.46	+ 0.17	22	44.7	...	87 Tauri α	....
1274	48 12 3.5		2.3	− 7.89	+ 0.57	...	5	48.1	12.0	....	....
1275	36 50 24.1		24.2	− 7.86	+ 0.63	+ 0.11	5	47.1	8.4	2 Camelop.	4984
1276	37 14 12.6		12.5	− 7.86	+ 0.63	+ 0.03	4	46.3	8.9	3 Camelop.	4987
1277	37 29 48.5		...	− 7.85	+ 0.62	...	3	47.1	...	....	4993
1278	37 49 47.4		47.5	− 7.84	+ 0.62	...	3	49.4	13.2	....	4996
1279	48 4 34.5		34.9	− 7.83	+ 0.56	...	4	47.3	12.0	....	....
1280	14 21 14.1		11.4	− 7.83	+ 1.06	+ 0.10	10	45.5	11.1	....	4995
1281	20 28 52.2		50.2	− 7.76	+ 0.86	...	4	45.8	11.0	....	5010
1282	49 31 25.1		23.4	− 7.71	+ 0.58	...	3	44.8	13.0	....	....
1283	42 0 28.6		27.1	− 7.69	+ 0.59	...	4	46.3	12.1	....	5023
1284	74 23 39.1		...	− 7.64	+ 0.46	...	2	57.5	...	92 Tauri σ² ...	....
1285	40 23 14.0		12.0	− 7.64	+ 0.62	...	4	49.6	10.1	....	5031
1286	23 4 20.7		20.5	− 7.63	+ 0.81	...	4	51.6	14.1	....	....
1287	48 10 20.7		17.7	− 7.62	+ 0.58	...	3	45.7	12.0	....	....
1288	104 36 42.6		...	− 7.59	+ 0.37	...	3	53.4	...	53 Eridani	....
1289	40 19 47.3		45.7	− 7.54	+ 0.62	...	5	45.0	10.1	....	5056
1290	9 4 53.1		54.6	− 7.54	+ 1.47	...	5	45.8	7.0	*50. ⨍...*	....

Magnitude.	Estimates of Magnitude.	Mean Right Ascension 1845.0.		Precession 1845.0.	Secular Variation	Adopted Proper Motion.	Observations of R.A.		
R.		R.	G.				No. R.	Mean year R.	G.
		h. m. s.		s.	s.	s.		1800 +	
7.3	6	4 31 37.95	37.33	+ 6.517	+ 0.110	......	3	45.1	11.0
5.7	6	4 31 55.42	55.43	+ 4.228	+ 0.023	+ 0.007	8	46.8	11.0
7.1	6	4 32 16.92	15.07	+ 7.842	+ 0.188	......	5	46.7	11.1
8.3	5	4 32 25.24	25.12	+ 6.512	+ 0.108	......	3	48.8	11.1
7.3	8	4 32 48.61	48.61	+ 4.662	+ 0.034	......	3	44.8	13.1
7.7	2	4 32 54.31	...	+ 3.589	+ 0.011	+ 0.003	1	52.0	...
4.6	2	4 32 56.86	...	+ 3.589	+ 0.011	......	6	48.2	...
7.3	7	4 33 10.21	...	+ 4.193	+ 0.028	......	4	49.5	...
6.6	5	4 33 19.26	18.82	+ 6.609	+ 0.110	......	3	46.4	14.1
6.3	1	4 33 40.10	...	+ 2.497	+ 0.001	......	2	56.5	...
5.4	6	4 35 6.93	6.41	+ 4.951	+ 0.040	......	5	47.5	11.2
6.4	4	4 35 12.36	11.81	+ 6.138	+ 0.086	......	4	45.0	11.1
6.6	5	4 35 25.72	...	+ 4.872	+ 0.038	......	3	48.4	...
6.8	5	4 35 32.37	32.40	+ 4.726	+ 0.036	......	3	47.1	13.0
7.2	6	4 35 33.89	...	+ 4.196	+ 0.022	......	5	49.6	...
7.9	5	4 35 46.74	46.52	+ 4.716	+ 0.036	......	3	49.7	13.0
7.4	8	4 36 15.25	14.86	+ 4.156	+ 0.022	......	5	46.2	12.0
7.9	5	4 36 39.29	38.90	+ 4.328	+ 0.023	......	3	44.8	10.1
9.0	5	4 37 4.60	4.54	+ 4.994	+ 0.039	......	3	48.0	13.1
5.3	6	4 37 36.97	36.23	+ 5.551	+ 0.060	......	4	45.8	9.1
6.8	9	4 37 40.81	...	+19.850	+ 1.682	......	8	52.7	...
7.5	6	4 37 45.25	44.38	+ 6.160	+ 0.084	1	4	45.3	11.1
4.2	2	4 37 45.34	...	+ 2.993	+ 0.004	......	2	55.5	...
8.1	7	4 37 56.68	56.40	+ 4.944	+ 0.039	......	4	45.2	13.1
9.0	4	4 38 1.74	...	+ 6.582	+ 0.100	......	3	51.3	...
4.7	7	4 38 41.01	41.03	+ 5.895	+ 0.070	+ 0.007	6	44.3	7.1
9.0	6	4 38 57.97	...	+ 4.683	+ 0.033	......	4	51.5	...
7.0	2	4 39 2.14	...	+ 3.190	+ 0.005	......	2	53.5	...
9.0	3	4 39 2.79	...	+ 4.698	+ 0.033	......	3	49.4	...
7.4	3	4 39 3.50	...	+ 5.910	+ 0.074	. ..	2	46.6	...
8.0	3	4 39 13.84	13.62	+ 4.941	+ 0.038	......	2	49.1	13.1
6.0	6	4 39 31.11	31.01	+ 4.487	+ 0.026	+ 0.003	3	48.9	12.0
8.5	5	4 39 59.49	59.29	+ 4.706	+ 0.031	......	2	47.2	13.0
7.0	10	4 40 20.37	18.72	+ 4.353	+ 0.024	......	7	47.6	10.1
6.0	2	4 40 38.93	...	+ 2.681	+ 0.002	......	3	56.3	...

Ordinal Number.	Mean North Polar Distance 1845.0.			Preces-sion 1845.0.	Secular Variation.	Adopted Proper Motion.	Observations of N.P.D.				Names.	Oeltzen-Argelander Number.
R.	R.		G.				No.	Mean year.				
							R.	B.		G.		
	° ′ ″		″	″	″	″		1800 +				
291	19 46	2.5	2.8	− 7.54	+ 0.89	...	5	47.9		11.0	....	5052
292	46 56	11.9	11.9	− 7.52	+ 0.57	...	4	44.0		11.0	59 Persei	....
293	14 34	8.1	1.7	− 7.49	+ 1.07	...	5	47.0		11.1	....	5063
294	19 49	10.6	8.8	− 7.48	+ 0.88	...	6	48.5		11.1	....	5070
295	37 57	33.2	33.7	− 7.44	+ 0.66	...	5	47.3		13.1	....	5078
296	67 21	36.7	...	− 7.43	+ 0.49	...	1	52.0		...	94 Tauri τ (1st)	....
297	67 20	45.6	...	− 7.43	+ 0.49	...	1	56.9		...	94 Tauri τ (2d)	....
298	47 52	50.4	...	− 7.42	+ 0.57	...	4	48.3		...	....	......
299	19 20	45.2	44.5	− 7.40	+ 0.92	...	4	47.1		14.1	....	5086
300	114 47	23.7	...	− 7.37	...	...	2	52.1		...	....	....
1301	33 31	34.5	34.2	− 7.26	+ 0.67	+ 0.17	4	42.8		11.2	4 Camelopardi	5128
1302	22 6	53.3	53.5	− 7.25	+ 0.84	...	4	44.3		11.1	....	5129
1303	34 40	56.5	...	− 7.23	+ 0.66	+ 0.07	3	47.4		...	....	5137
1304	36 59	5.5	2.4	− 7.22	+ 0.65	...	4	46.0		13.0	....	....
1305	47 56	44.5	...	− 7.22	+ 0.57	...	4	47.8		...	....	....
1306	37 9	59.5	56.1	− 7.20	+ 0.65	...	4	44.8		13.0	....	....
1307	48 59	1.0	0.5	− 7.17	+ 0.56	...	5	48.1		12.0	....	....
1308	44 47	47.4	45.1	− 7.13	+ 0.60	...	4	46.8		10.1	....	5159
1309	33 42	34.4	34.7	− 7.10	+ 0.68	...	3	48.4		13.1	....	5164
1310	26 46	5.7	5.2	− 7.05	+ 0.76	+ 0.07	4	44.1		9.1	....	5170
1311	4 15	55.7	...	− 7.05	+ 2.71	...	7	51.9		...	....	....
1312	22 3	10.7	8.3	− 7.04	+ 0.85	...	5	47.1		11.1	....	....
1313	93 32	37.1	...	− 7.03	+ 0.41	...	2	52.0		...	57 Eridani μ..	....
1314	33 44	56.0	56.0	− 7.03	+ 0.68	...	6	47.7		13.1	....	5174
1315	19 37	37.0	...	− 7.02	+ 0.90	...	2	48.6		...	....	5173
1316	23 55	48.9	49.1	− 6.97	+ 0.81	− 0.02	14	47.1		7.1	9 Camelop. α .	5184
1317	37 52	38.9	...	− 6.94	+ 0.64	...	3	50.8		...	....	....
1318	84 29	39.2	...	− 6.94	+ 0.45	...	2	55.5		...	....	....
1319	37 37	7.9	...	− 6.94	+ 0.65	...	2	49.0		...	....	5195
1320	23 49	57.2	...	− 6.94	+ 0.83	...	4	45.5		...	....	5192
1321	33 50	57.0	54.2	− 6.92	+ 0.69	...	2	44.1		13.1	....	....
1322	41 32	2.7	0.1	− 6.90	+ 0.61	...	3	43.3		12.0	....	5201
1323	37 30	45.5	43.7	− 6.86	+ 0.65	...	3	48.8		13.0	....	5211
1324	44 24	57.2	36.3	− 6.83	+ 0.60	...	4	47.0		10.1	....	5219
1325	107 13	18.0	...	− 6.81	+ 0.37	...	1	52.0		...	58 Eridani.....	....

Magnitude.	Estimates of Magnitudes.	Mean Right Ascension 1845.0.		Precession 1845.0.	Secular Variation	Adopted Proper Motion.
R.	R.	R.	G.			
		h. m. s.	s.	s.	s.	s.
6.9	5	4 40 55.45	55.33	+ 4.714	+ 0.032	......
7.0	6	4 41 2.28	1.78	+ 4.358	+ 0.024	......
6.1	5	4 41 51.60	51.37	+ 4.218	+ 0.022	......
8.3	5	4 41 55.45	...	+19.191	+ 1.502	......
8.8	4	4 42 21.54	...	+ 6.383	+ 0.084	......
5.8	4	4 42 24.14	...	+ 4.871	+ 0.035	......
8.3	5	4 42 27.26	26.83	+ 6.330	+ 0.084	......
6.2	7	4 42 45.13	44.36	+ 7.474	+ 0.138	......
8.3	4	4 42 54.13	...	+ 6.571	+ 0.096	......
8.8	3	4 42 59.60	...	+ 6.500	+ 0.090	......
5.0	1	4 43 12.54	...	+ 2.697	+ 0.002	......
6.6	5	4 43 13.26	...	+ 5.394	+ 0.050	......
7.6	5	4 43 13.77	...	+ 6.483	+ 0.089	......
6.8	5	4 43 44.48	44.10	+ 4.282	+ 0.023	......
9.3	6	4 43 45.74	...	+ 6.391	+ 0.085	......
4.6	4	4 43 46.11	...	+ 3.384	+ 0.007	......
6.2	8	4 43 51.18	51.11	+ 4.724	+ 0.031	......
6.2	5	4 44 3.74	3.33	+ 4.914	+ 0.035	......
5.1	5	4 44 52.82	52.58	+ 4.780	+ 0.031	......
5.9	5	4 44 58.74	58.32	+ 7.350	+ 0.126	.....
7.2	8	4 45 11.31	10.73	+ 4.561	+ 0.024	......
5.7	6	4 45 12.01	11.50	+ 7.435	+ 0.130	......
7.3	5	4 45 28.46	27.52	+ 6.356	+ 0.080	......
8.5	6	4 46 7.15	6.46	+ 8.312	+ 0.175	......
4.0	1	4 46 54.42	...	+ 3.892	+ 0.013	......
8.1	4	4 47 1.65	0.83	+ 7.457	+ 0.135	......
6.2	5	4 47 10.27	...	+ 6.004	+ 0.066	+ 0.017
6.2	7	4 47 26.53	26.29	+ 4.751	+ 0.029	......
8.3	5	4 47 42.19	...	+ 4.293	+ 0.022	......
8.0	4	4 47 48.02	47.11	+ 8.323	+ 0.176	......
8.0	5	4 48 32.17	31.66	+ 6.409	+ 0.080	......
8.9	5	4 48 37.39	36.66	+ 6.406	+ 0.082	......
6.3	1	4 48 46.32	...	+ 2.950	+ 0.003	......
8.0	6	4 48 54.56	...	+ 4.288	+ 0.022	......
7.1	2	4 48 58.14	...	+ 4.911	+ 0.033	......

Ordinal Number.	Mean North Polar Distance 1845.0.			Precession 1845.0.	Secular Variation.	Adopted Proper Motion.	Observations of N.P.D.			Names.	Oeltzen-Argelander Number.
R.	R.		G.				No.	Mean year.			
							R.	R.	G.		
	° ′ ″		″	″	″	″		1800 +			
1326	37 25 42.2		41.0	− 6.78	+ 0.66	...	3	44.7	13.0	....	5233
1327	44 19 45.2		41.9	− 6.77	+ 0.60	...	5	46.5	10.1	....	5235
1328	47 40 56.5		56.2	− 6.70	+ 0.61	...	3	44.7	12.0	....	....
1329	4 28 50.9		...	− 6.70	+ 2.68	...	5	52.3	...	....	....
1330	20 56 49.6		...	− 6.66	+ 0.88	...	4	53.0	...	....	....
1331	35 0 17.9		...	− 6.66	+ 0.67	+ 0.09	3	47.4	...	5 Camelopardi	5249
1332	21 8 44.1		43.7	− 6.66	+ 0.86	...	6	51.1	13.1	....	5248
1333	15 58 58.9		59.5	− 6.63	+ 1.03	...	3	44.8	11.0	....	....
1334	19 49 14.1		...	− 6.62	+ 0.91	...	2	48.6	...	....	....
1335	20 11 55.6		...	− 6.61	+ 0.90	...	3	51.4	...	....	....
1336	106 29 27.5		...	− 6.59	+ 0.37	...	1	59.1	...	60 Eridani.....	....
1337	28 30 20.1		...	− 6.59	+ 0.75	...	4	51.6	...	....	....
1338	20 17 41.1		...	− 6.59	+ 0.90	...	3	51.4	...	....	....
1339	46 11 56.0		53.5	− 6.55	+ 0.60	...	3	44.8	12.1	....	....
1340	20 49 57.2		...	− 6.55	+ 0.89	...	3	51.8	...	....	5277
1341	76 0 45.9		...	− 6.55	+ 0.47	+ 0.08	3	52.0	...	4 Orionis o¹....	....
1342	37 23 24.9		24.7	− 6.54	+ 0.66	...	5	46.9	13.0	....	5281
1343	34 25 58.0		57.4	− 6.52	+ 0.68	+ 0.02	3	43.3	9.1	6 Camelopardi	5283
1344	36 30 14.5		13.3	− 6.46	+ 0.66	...	4	44.6	8.1	7 Camelopardi	5298
1345	16 28 41.7		42.1	− 6.45	+ 1.01	...	4	43.6	11.1	....	5297
1346	40 19 43.0		37.3	− 6.43	+ 0.64	...	4	47.8	12.0	....	5304
1347	16 10 27.2		26.1	− 6.43	+ 1.03	...	3	44.1	11.0	....	5300
1348	21 4 55.7		52.4	− 6.40	+ 0.91	...	3	44.4	13.1	....	5307
1349	13 35 48.8		46.3	− 6.35	+ 1.16	...	3	47.4	13.2	....	5315
1350	57 5 7.8		...	− 6.29	+ 0.54	...	2	51.0	...	3 Aurigæ ι.....	....
1351	16 8 34.0		31.6	− 6.28	+ 1.03	...	3	48.4	11.0	....	5324
1352	23 24 14.8		...	− 6.27	+ 0.83	+ 0.52	3	48.4	...	....	5328
1353	37 5 26.9		26.9	− 6.24	+ 0.66	+ 0.06	3	43.7	10.1	8 Camelopardi	5332
1354	46 6 24.0		...	− 6.22	+ 0.59	...	4	52.8	...	....	....
1355	13 36 13.1		8.7	− 6.21	+ 1.17	...	2	44.1	13.2	....	5337
1356	20 51 18.2		18.2	− 6.15	+ 0.91	...	2	45.6	13.1	....	5346
1357	20 53 3.0		58.9	− 6.15	+ 0.90	...	2	48.6	13.1	....	5348
1358	95 25 18.1		...	− 6.12	+ 0.41	...	1	52.0	...	62 Eridani b...	....
1359	46 15 26.6		...	− 6.12	+ 0.59	...	4	51.8	...	....	....
1360	34 39 52.0		...	− 6.12	+ 0.68	...	3	51.3	...	....	5353

Magnitude.	Estimates of Magnitude.	Mean Right Ascension 1845.0.		Precession 1845.0	Secular Variation	Adopted Proper Motion.
R.	R.	R.	G.			
		h. m. s.	s.	s.	s.	s.
7.6	5	4 49 2.32	...	+ 5.553	+ 0.051	......
7.3	3	4 49 4.70	...	+ 5.553	+ 0.051	......
7.5	7	4 49 6.94	...	+ 7.910	+ 0.176	......
7.3	5	4 49 7.48	...	+ 7.979	+ 0.178	......
6.9	5	4 49 33.94	33.90	+ 6.345	+ 0.076	......
7.8	6	4 49 34.37	...	+ 5.294	+ 0.042	......
4.1	5	4 49 39.39	39.21	+ 5.296	+ 0.042	+ 0.004
6.2	7	4 49 39.60	39.57	+ 4.108	+ 0.016	......
6.0	7	4 49 42.84	42.68	+ 4.117	+ 0.016	......
8.3	1	4 50 3.88	...	+ 3.104	+ 0.004	......
8.8	6	4 50 15.58	...	+ 4.287	+ 0.021	......
3.5	7	4 50 51.44	51.22	+ 4.285	+ 0.019	......
8.3	7	4 51 8.01	7.36	+ 5.164	+ 0.038	......
9.0	5	4 51 20.02	...	+ 4.283	+ 0.020	......
4.4	5	4 51 39.17	39.13	+ 4.175	+ 0.018	......
8.9	6	4 51 48.09	...	+ 6.472	+ 0.080	......
7. { 7.0 7.2 }	20	4 51 50.36	...	+19.344	+ 1.296	......
6.6	7	4 52 26.88	26.66	+ 4.190	+ 0.016	......
5.4	5	4 52 41.38	41.31	+ 5.179	+ 0.037	+ 0.003
6.4	7	4 52 41.88	...	+ 6.479	+ 0.080	......
5.5	1	4 52 43.85	...	+ 2.782	+ 0.002	......
6.3	4	4 52 44.29	44.15	+ 5.183	+ 0.037	+ 0.004
6.9	5	4 52 50.93	50.32	+ 8.306	+ 0.162	......
5.9	8	4 52 53.39	52.77	+ 7.456	+ 0.118	.....
6.9	5	4 52 55.21	54.53	+ 4.375	+ 0.022	......
7.4	5	4 53 25.90	...	+ 4.285	+ 0.019	......
4.9	7	4 53 50.14	...	+ 3.571	+ 0.008	+ 0.004
7.2	5	4 53 58.15	57.96	+ 4.429	+ 0.020	......
7.2	6	4 54 0.63	0.69	+ 4.588	+ 0.023	......
7.7	4	4 54 21.57	21.33	+ 4.585	+ 0.024	......
5.5	4	4 54 33.27	33.14	+ 4.676	+ 0.026	......
7.5	3	4 54 53.27	53.21	+ 4.683	+ 0.026	......
8.2	5	4 54 53.70	53.88	+ 4.585	+ 0.024	......
6.7	4	4 55 20.96	...	+ 5.512	+ 0.045	......
7.6	5	4 55 25.47	...	+ 4.605	+ 0.024	......

Ordinal Number. R.	Mean North Polar Distance 1845.0. R.	G.	Precession 1845.0.	Secular Variation.	Adopted Proper Motion.	Observations of N.P.D. No. R.	Mean year. R.	G.	Names.	Oeltzen-Argelander Number.
	° ′ ″	″	″	″			1800 +			
1361	27 10 17.9	...	− 6.11	+ 0.76	...	2	52.1	...	....	5357
1362	27 9 48.9	...	− 6.11	+ 0.76	...	2	52.6	...	....	5358
1363	14 44 31.6	...	− 6.10	+ 1.12	...	3	48.4	...	....	5354
1364	14 32 29.3	...	− 6.10	+ 1.12	...	3	51.4	...	....	5355
1365	21 15 29.2	29.0	− 6.07	+ 0.87	...	4	46.6	13.1	....	......
1366	29 48 47.0	...	− 6.07	+ 0.74	...	7	48.0	...	....	......
1367	29 47 35.7	34.8	− 6.06	+ 0.74	...	6	46.8	8.4	10 Camelop. β	......
1368	50 50 49.0	48.9	− 6.06	+ 0.57	...	3	45.1	11.1	5 Aurigæ	......
1369	50 35 11.6	12.5	− 6.05	+ 0.57	...	5	47.1	11.1	6 Aurigæ	......
1370	88 34 11.9	...	− 6.03	+ 0.43	...	1	52.0	...	....	......
1371	46 20 10.6	...	− 6.03	+ 0.60	...	2	52.1	...	....	......
1372	46 24 46.9	46.5	− 5.96	+ 0.60	...	4	44.5	6.7	7 Aurigæ ε	......
1373	31 22 10.0	7.7	− 5.94	+ 0.71	...	4	47.1	11.1	....	5400
1374	46 28 13.6	...	− 5.92	+ 0.60	...	3	44.7	...	....	......
1375	49 9 25.3	25.3	− 5.89	+ 0.58	...	3	43.7	8.1	8 Aurigæ ζ	......
1376	20 34 19.4	...	− 5.88	+ 0.91	...	3	46.7	...	....	5409
1377	4 29 27.0	...	− 5.88	+ 2.70	...	5	51.8	...	....	......
1378	48 47 20.6	20.2	− 5.82	+ 0.60	...	4	44.3	12.0	....	......
1379	31 15 10.6	10.0	− 5.80	+ 0.72	+ 0.01	5	43.3	9.9	11 Camelopardi	5425
1380	20 34 38.7	...	− 5.80	+ 0.91	...	6	48.4	...	....	5424
1381	102 46 13.1	...	− 5.79	+ 0.39	...	1	52.0	...	64 Eridani	......
1382	31 12 10.2	8.0	− 5.80	+ 0.72	+ 0.03	4	44.3	10.5	12 Camelopardi	5428
1383	13 44 14.1	13.7	− 5.79	+ 1.16	...	3	45.4	13.0	....	5426
1384	16 15 57.5	57.3	− 5.79	+ 1.04	+ 0.03	7	44.8	10.2	....	5434
1385	44 26 46.7	45.3	− 5.79	+ 0.60	...	3	45.7	12.2	....	5439
1386	46 29 54.6	...	− 5.75	+ 0.60	...	3	49.8	...	....	......
1387	68 38 11.8	...	− 5.71	+ 0.50	+ 0.06	3	51.5	...	102 Tauri ι ...	......
1388	43 18 28.4	28.8	− 5.70	+ 0.61	...	3	45.0	12.9	....	......
1389	40 10 36.4	36.6	− 5.69	+ 0.66	...	3	47.1	13.0	....	5455
1390	40 14 37.7	34.4	− 5.66	+ 0.66	...	3	49.1	13.1	....	5467
1391	38 36 57.4	56.0	− 5.65	+ 0.66	+ 0.15	4	45.3	11.1	9 Aurigæ	......
1392	38 30 47.1	49.5	− 5.62	+ 0.66	...	2	48.6	11.1	....	......
1393	40 16 44.9	41.6	− 5.62	+ 0.65	...	2	49.1	13.1	....	5479
1394	27 43 57.2	...	− 5.58	+ 0.77	...	3	51.7	...	....	5492
1395	39 54 46.0	...	− 5.58	+ 0.65	...	4	52.8	...	....	5495

M

Magnitude.	Estimates of Magnitude.	Mean Right Ascension 1845.0.		Precession 1845.0.	Secular Variation	Adopted Proper Motion.
R.		R.	G.			
		h. m. s.	s.	s.	s.	s.
3.8	4	4 55 39.18	38.73	+ 4.187	+ 0.016	+ 0.003
4.5	1	4 55 43.05	...	+ 3.419	+ 0.006	......
6.4	4	4 55 46.04	45.78	+ 4.266	+ 0.017	......
6.9	6	4 56 2.87	...	+ 5.635	+ 0.047	......
6.0	1	4 56 12.69	...	+ 2.524	+ 0.001	......
7.7	4	4 56 42.14	...	+ 9.218	+ 0.220	......
4.9	4	4 57 8.26	8.46	+ 9.713	+ 0.224	......
7.6	4	4 57 14.40	...	+ 8.139	+ 0.140	......
6.9	5	4 57 17.31	...	+ 4.546	+ 0.022	......
7.5	7	4 57 30.72	30.31	+ 7.663	+ 0.110	......
9.2	9	4 57 38.88	38.88	+ 4.724	+ 0.026	......
7.6	7	4 57 39.01	38.57	+ 4.810	+ 0.026	......
4.0	1	4 58 54.12	...	+ 2.534	+ 0.001	......
7.8	6	4 59 5.25	...	+ 4.784	+ 0.026	......
6.4	5	4 59 7.13	6.91	+ 5.547	+ 0.042	......
6.3	6	4 59 9.27	8.83	+ 7.310	+ 0.100	......
6.1	9	4 59 10.94	10.95	+ 4.442	+ 0.020	+ 0.010
7.3	7	4 59 28.87	28.39	+ 4.798	+ 0.024	......
8.1	6	5 0 11.13	10.87	+ 4.443	+ 0.020	......
8.7	6	5 0 33.56	...	+12.554	+ 0.407	......
6.0	1	5 0 49.90	...	+ 3.427	+ 0.006	......
8.2	4	5 1 3.88	3.73	+ 4.242	+ 0.013	......
7.6	5	5 1 18.05	...	+ 4.594	+ 0.021	......
8.8	5	5 1 25.45	...	+ 4.583	+ 0.021	......
8.4	3	5 1 37.71	37.63	+ 4.441	+ 0.018	......
4.0	A	5 1 44.05	...	+ 2.867	+ 0.002	......
6.5	6	5 1 51.30	50.64	+ 9.288	+ 0.183	......
7.9	7	5 2 17.82	17.63	+ 4.448	+ 0.018	......
6.3	6	5 2 18.95	18.52	+ 4.790	+ 0.024	......
6.7	4	5 2 33.13	...	+ 6.952	+ 0.087	......
5.4	7	5 2 49.77	49.55	+ 4.093	+ 0.013	......
8.6	10	5 3 40.55	40.30	+ 4.247	+ 0.015	......
8.6	6	5 4 1.24	1.24	+ 4.250	+ 0.014	......
8.4	6	5 4 31.10	30.90	+ 4.253	+ 0.015	......
6.6	5	5 4 35.06	34.72	+ 9.251	+ 0.172	+ 0.017

stance G.	Precession 1845.0.	Secular Variation.	Adopted Proper Motion.	Observations of N.P.D. No. R.	Mean year. R. 1800 +	Mean year. G.
54.8	− 5.56	+ 0.59	+ 0.09	3	43.7	7.0
...	− 5.55	+ 0.48	+ 0.03	2	53.0	...
37.0	− 5.55	+ 0.59	...	3	44.7	12.0
...	− 5.52	+ 0.80	...	4	51.6	...
...	− 5.51	+ 0.35	...	1	52.0	...
...	− 5.47	+ 1.32	...	4	51.0	...
52.0	− 5.43	+ 1.37	− 0.05	5	46.4	8.4
...	− 5.42	+ 1.14	...	2	50.1	...
...	− 5.42	+ 0.64	...	4	52.1	...
29.5	− 5.40	+ 1.09	...	4	50.7	14.1
39.8	− 5.39	+ 0.65	...	5	46.9	14.1
56.9	− 5.39	+ 0.66	...	3	44.1	12.0
...	− 5.29	+ 0.36	...	3	52.1	...
...	− 5.27	+ 0.68	...	4	47.1	...
34.4	− 5.26	+ 0.79	...	3	44.7	8.4
18.5	− 5.26	+ 1.03	...	6	47.3	11.0
10.5	− 5.26	+ 0.63	+ 0.10	4	47.1	12.5
2.2	− 5.23	+ 0.69	...	3	44.8	12.1
34.4	− 5.17	+ 0.64	...	3	44.7	13.0
...	− 5.15	+ 1.77	...	3	52.4	...
...	......	...	...	...	...	...
58.9	− 5.10	+ 0.60	...	3	45.0	13.2
...	− 5.08	+ 0.65	...	4	49.4	...
...	− 5.07	+ 0.64	...	3	51.7	...
17.2	− 5.05	+ 0.64	...	2	46.0	13.1
......	− 5.03	+ 0.40	...	1	52.0	...
29.4	− 5.03	+ 1.32	...	5	45.7	11.0
1.0	− 5.00	+ 0.62	...	5	45.1	13.0
41.3	− 5.00	+ 0.66	...	4	44.0	12.1
...	− 4.97	+ 0.98	...	4	51.8	...
20.2	− 4.95	+ 0.58	+ 0.06	4	47.6	11.1
15.5	− 4.88	+ 0.60	...	3	49.8	13.2
42.7	− 4.85	+ 0.60	...	3	47.8	13.1
23.5	− 4.81	+ 0.60	...	4	46.1	13.1
26.9	− 4.80	+ 1.31	...	4	44.8	11.0

Ordinal Number		Magnitude	Estimates of Magnitude	Mean Right Ascension 1845.0			Precession 1845.0	Secular Variation	Adopted Proper Motion	Observations of R.A.		
R.	G.	R.		R.		G.				No.	Mean year	
				h. m. s.		s.	s.	s.	s.	R.	R. (1800 +)	G. (1800 +)
1431	945	7.0	7	5 4 58.97		59.04	+ 4.426	+ 0.017	+ 0.010	6	45.0	9.1
1432	947	8.1	7	5 5 9.98		9.91	+ 4.263	+ 0.013	......	3	47.7	13.1
1433	946	1.0	A	5 5 14.77		14.66	+ 4.407	+ 0.016	+ 0.008	23	48.8	6.6
1434	949	8.1	5	5 5 31.00		31.13	+ 4.260	+ 0.013	......	3	49.8	13.1
1435	...	6.8	5	5 5 39.10		...	+ 9.090	+ 0.161	+ 0.008	3	47.4	...
1436	951	8.1	7	5 5 50.76		50.83	+ 4.261	+ 0.013	......	5	49.9	13.1
1437	...	3.7	2	5 5 58.31		...	+ 2.688	+ 0.001	......	3	55.1	...
1438	950	6.3	5	5 6 6.74		6.14	+ 5.146	+ 0.029	......	4	47.1	10.1
1439	...	8.2	2	5 6 58.93		...	+ 5.166	+ 0.030	......	2	47.2	...
1440	...	1.0	A	5 7 5.43		...	+ 2.878	+ 0.002	......	8	49.5	...
1441	953	6.0	5	5 7 12.05		11.71	+ 4.268	+ 0.014	......	3	45.8	12.7
1442	948	7.2	7	5 7 30.17		29.72	+ 7.732	+ 0.104	......	5	46.7	14.1
1443	...	6.4	5	5 7 51.48		...	+ 4.174	+ 0.013	......	3	47.0	...
1444	...	8.9	4	5 8 1.56		...	+ 4.173	+ 0.013	......	2	47.6	...
1445	954	5.1	8	5 8 14.61		14.27	+ 4.161	+ 0.012	+ 0.043	8	49.9	8.1
1446	952	7.1	6	5 8 31.62		30.95	+ 7.662	+ 0.098	......	4	48.1	14.1
1447	955	6.6	7	5 8 47.62		47.34	+ 4.341	+ 0.016	......	3	47.1	12.5
1448	957	6.6	5	5 9 6.13		5.81	+ 4.459	+ 0.017	......	4	44.2	11.1
1449	...	5.0	1	5 9 58.09		...	+ 3.595	+ 0.006	......	2	43.7	...
1450	...	4.0	1	5 10 4.95		...	+ 2.910	+ 0.002	......	1	56.0	...
1451	958	5.6	7	5 10 12.41		11.76	+ 5.110	+ 0.027	......	4	49.4	9.1
1452	...	8.2	4	5 10 18.17		...	+ 4.448	+ 0.017	......	3	51.1	...
1453	...	8.1	6	5 10 33.31		...	+ 4.448	+ 0.017	......	4	51.5	...
1454	...	6.5	5	5 10 45.00		...	+ 5.002	+ 0.025	......	3	48.5	...
1455	959	5.5	7	5 10 50.52		50.55	+ 4.231	+ 0.012	+ 0.007	6	47.1	10.2
1456	...	6.7	4	5 11 38.39		...	+ 4.465	+ 0.016	......	3	44.7	...
1457	...	7.7	6	5 11 49.78		...	+ 4.455	+ 0.016	......	3	52.4	...
1458	...	5.8	7	5 11 57.63		...	+ 4.202	+ 0.012	......	6	45.9	...
1459	944	6.2	37	5 12 55.62		55.07	+18.325	+ 0.756	......	33	48.5	7.3
1460	...	9.1	6	5 13 31.35		...	+ 4.239	+ 0.013	......	3	51.4	...
1461	...	8.0	6	5 13 32.33		...	+ 4.236	+ 0.013	......	4	48.7	...
1462	...	7.8	7	5 14 41.16		...	+ 4.455	+ 0.014	......	4	52.3	...
1463	960	8.9	5	5 14 52.00		51.99	+ 4.838	+ 0.020	.....	3	44.8	13.1
1464	961	5.3	9	5 15 32.79		32.46	+ 5.636	+ 0.032	......	4	45.4	10.1
1465	...	6.6	3	5 15 58.06		...	+ 5.354	+ 0.028	......	3	49.4	...

Ordinal Number.	Mean North Polar Distance 1845.0.		Preces- sion 1845.0.	Secular Variation.	Adopted Proper Motion.	Observations of N.P.D.			Names.	Oeltzen- Argelander Number.
R.	R.	G.				No. R.	Mean year. R.	G.		
	o ′ ″	″	″	″	″		1800 +			
1431	43 46 5.4	5.5	− 4.77	+ 0.62	...	5	47.7	9.1	12 Aurigæ......	5667
1432	47 25 38.8	39.5	− 4.75	+ 0.61	...	4	47.1	13.1	....	....
1433	44 10 1.4	1.5	− 4.74	+ 0.63	+ 0.43	17	46.2	6.6	13 Aurigæ a...	5670
1434	47 30 54.6	58.5	− 4.72	+ 0.61	...	3	49.1	13.1	....	....
1435	12 10 51.5	...	− 4.71	+ 1.29	+ 0.02	4	48.1	...	....	5672
1436	47 30 13.1	12.3	− 4.69	+ 0.61	...	4	51.8	13.1	....	....
1437	106 23 33.5	...	− 4.69	+ 0.38	...	2	52.1	...	5 Leporis μ ...	....
1438	32 3 29.8	28.4	− 4.67	+ 0.73	+ 0.03	4	46.1	10.1	15 Camelopardi	5690
1439	31 49 33.4	...	− 4.60	+ 0.74	...	3	47.1	...	....	5705
1440	98 23 7.2	...	− 4.59	+ 0.41	...	5	51.7	...	19 Orionis β..	....
1441	47 23 0.5	58.4	− 4.58	+ 0.61	...	3	43.7	12.7	....	....
1442	15 36 11.6	14.2	− 4.55	+ 1.11	...	3	44.4	14.1	....	5712
1443	49 42 32.5	...	− 4.52	+ 0.59	...	5	49.2	...	....	....
1444	49 45 42.1	...	− 4.51	+ 0.59	...	2	48.5	...	....	....
1445	50 2 43.7	47.1	− 4.49	+ 0.60	+ 0.70	4	45.5	8.1	15 Aurigæ λ...	....
1446	15 50 49.2	49.3	− 4.47	+ 1.08	...	3	49.8	14.1	....	5721
1447	45 44 38.6	40.2	− 4.44	+ 0.62	...	4	47.1	12.5	....	....
1448	43 12 17.3	16.1	− 4.42	+ 0.63	...	3	43.7	11.1	....	....
1449	68 4 10.5	...	− 4.34	+ 0.51	...	1	54.1	...	109 Tauri n ...	....
1450	97 0 58.5	...	− 4.33	+ 0.41	...	1	52.0	...	20 Orionis τ...	....
1451	32 36 53.5	53.9	− 4.32	+ 0.73	+ 0.08	5	45.5	9.1	16 Camelopardi	5754
1452	43 27 9.1	...	− 4.31	+ 0.63	...	3	50.4	...	....	....
1453	43 27 20.4	...	− 4.29	+ 0.63	...	4	51.6	...	....	....
1454	34 4 17.8	...	− 4.28	+ 0.72	...	4	48.6	...	....	....
1455	48 21 25.6	25.9	− 4.27	+ 0.60	+ 0.03	4	46.1	10.2	20 Aurigæ ρ...	....
1456	43 8 14.0	...	− 4.20	+ 0.64	...	5	48.1	...	....	....
1457	43 21 54.3	...	− 4.18	+ 0.64	...	4	52.5	...	....	....
1458	49 7 48.3	...	− 4.17	+ 0.60	...	4	47.1	...	....	....
1459	4 54 15.2	15.4	− 4.09	+ 2.60	...	18	46.5	7.3	64 Cam.	....
1460	48 14 57.1	...	− 4.04	+ 0.61	...	3	50.4	...	....	....
1461	48 19 34.0	...	− 4.04	+ 0.61	...	4	47.6	...	....	....
1462	43 19 39.9	...	− 3.94	+ 0.64	...	5	52.9	...	....	5819
1463	36 33 15.9	14.8	− 3.92	+ 0.71	...	3	45.7	13.1	....	5821
1464	27 4 19.8	18.1	− 3.87	+ 0.80	...	7	44.7	10.1	17 Camelopardi	5833
1465	29 52 12.4	...	− 3.83	+ 0.77	...	4	48.6	...	....	....

Ordinal Number.		Magnitude.	Estimates of Magnitude.	Mean Right Ascension 1845.0.		Precession 1845.0.	Secular Variation	Adopted Proper Motion.	Observations of R.A.		
R.	G.	R.		R.	G.				No. R.	Mean year. R.	G.
				h. m. s.	s.	s.	s.	s.		1800 +	
1466	963	6.8	6	5 16 10.25	10.03	+ 4.532	+ 0.014	......	4	48.1	11.0
1467	964	7.2	6	5 16 12.89	12.65	+ 4.540	+ 0.014	......	3	44.8	11.0
1468	...	5.0	1	5 16 28.91	...	+ 2.887	+ 0.002	+ 0.008	1	52.0	...
1469	...	2.0	A	5 16 29.84	...	+ 3.782	+ 0.007	+ 0.003	65	43.2	...
1470	965	7.0	6	5 16 30.49	30.14	+ 4.304	+ 0.012	......	3	47.4	12.0
1471	...	7.6	5	5 16 38.60	...	+ 4.372	+ 0.013	......	2	51.0	...
1472	...	3.3	A	5 16 41.10	...	+ 3.012	+ 0.002	......	1	57.1	...
1473	962	7.2	8	5 16 50.52	49.79	+ 7.710	+ 0.079	......	6	45.4	14.1
1474	...	7.9	11	5 16 55.17	...	+30.803	+ 2.243	......	6	53.3	...
1475	...	7.4	6	5 17 9.61	...	+ 5.632	+ 0.035	......	3	48.1	...
1476	...	8.2	6	5 17 11.97	...	+ 7.831	+ 0.108	......	3	49.5	...
1477	956	7.6	31	5 17 16.26	13.38	+18.770	+ 0.781	......	26	50.0	9.6
1478	967	7.0	4	5 17 22.41	22.36	+ 4.832	+ 0.019	......	3	46.5	13.1
1479	969	6.9	5	5 17 58.79	58.41	+ 4.260	+ 0.011	......	3	47.1	12.1
1480	968	8.7	5	5 18 16.36	16.41	+ 4.817	+ 0.018	......	3	50.1	13.1
1481	...	5.5	2	5 18 19.68	...	+ 3.596	+ 0.005	+ 0.005	3	51.4	...
1482	971	8.6	5	5 18 41.34	41.09	+ 4.829	+ 0.015	......	2	51.0	13.1
1483	...	4.9	2	5 18 43.25	...	+ 3.138	+ 0.003	......	2	58.1	...
1484	972	7.5	6	5 18 57.92	57.61	+ 4.703	+ 0.016	......	4	50.1	11.1
1485	966	6.0	7	5 19 2.27	2.60	+ 7.955	+ 0.086	+ 0.041	5	47.0	9.1
1486	973	6.2	3	5 19 17.80	17.73	+ 5.104	+ 0.021	+ 0.020	2	47.7	10.1
1487	974	7.5	4	5 19 44.03	43.84	+ 4.690	+ 0.015	......	3	46.5	11.1
1488	975	7.8	5	5 19 46.05	45.82	+ 4.702	+ 0.016	......	2	48.5	11.1
1489	976	8.0	5	5 19 51.62	51.29	+ 4.162	+ 0.008	......	3	47.4	13.1
1490	...	7.6	5	5 19 56.86	...	+ 4.574	+ 0.014	......	3	51.7	...
1491	977	6.9	7	5 19 58.12	58.10	+ 4.162	+ 0.007	......	3	47.4	13.1
1492	970	8.4	4	5 20 2.76	2.00	+ 7.706	+ 0.081	......	2	51.0	14.1
1493	979	7.7	4	5 20 14.83	14.75	+ 4.171	+ 0.008	......	3	50.0	13.1
1494	...	7.7	5	5 20 25.68	...	+ 4.600	+ 0.013	......	3	45.1	...
1495	978	7.6	4	5 20 26.58	25.79	+ 4.600	+ 0.013	......	3	48.1	12.1
1496	980	7.1	5	5 20 49.03	48.54	+ 4.106	+ 0.007	......	4	48.1	11.0
1497	982	6.3	8	5 22 15.95	15.30	+ 5.780	+ 0.030	......	5	44.4	9.1
1498	983	6.7	5	5 22 27.55	27.28	+ 4.257	+ 0.009	......	3	44.7	12.7
1499	...	7.7	5	5 22 31.44	...	+ 4.374	+ 0.011	......	3	51.7	...
1500	...	7.1	6	5 22 54.00	...	+ 6.670	+ 0.046	......	3	49.8	...

Ordinal Number	Mean North Polar Distance 1845.0 R.	G.	Precession 1845.0	Secular Variation	Adopted Proper Motion	No. R.	Mean year R. (1800 +)	Mean year G.	Names	Oeltzen-Argelander Number
1466	41 54 50.1	49.5	− 3.81	+ 0.66	...	4	45.1	11.0	....	5847
1467	41 45 37.0	38.1	− 3.81	+ 0.65	...	5	46.7	11.0	....	5848
1468	97 57 20.6	...	− 3.78	+ 0.41	...	2	57.1	...	29 Orionis e...	——
1469	61 31 47.2	...	− 3.78	+ 0.54	+ 0.20	6	40.8	...	112 Tauri β...	......
1470	46 46 27.2	25.8	− 3.78	+ 0.63	...	4	46.8	12.0	....	......
1471	45 13 45.0	...	− 3.77	+ 0.64	...	3	50.4	...	....	5857
1472	92 32 40.3	...	− 3.77	+ 0.43	...	1	52.0	...	28 Orionis η...	......
1473	15 48 3.8	0.0	− 3.75	+ 1.12	...	4	46.3	14.1	....	......
1474	2 42 41.8	...	− 3.75	+ 4.41	...	5	52.5	...	....	......
1475	27 8 51.6	...	− 3.73	+ 0.82	...	4	44.5	...	....	5863
1476	15 25 34.0	...	− 3.72	+ 1.13	...	4	48.9	...	....	......
1477	4 47 0.4	0.1	− 3.72	+ 2.67	...	10	47.9	9.6	....	......
1478	36 42 16.7	18.0	− 3.71	+ 0.69	...	4	45.8	13.1	....	5864
1479	47 51 53.3	52.4	− 3.66	+ 0.61	...	4	46.8	12.1	....	......
1480	36 58 12.0	13.0	− 3.63	+ 0.70	...	2	47.6	13.1	....	5876
1481	68 12 3.9	...	− 3.62	+ 0.52	+ 0.10	2	54.1	...	114 Tauri o...	......
1482	36 46 50.9	52.5	− 3.59	+ 0.70	...	3	51.4	13.1	....	5883
1483	87 1 45.8	...	− 3.59	+ 0.45	...	1	52.0	...	30 Orionis ψ^2.	......
1484	38 50 48.5	47.7	− 3.57	+ 0.68	...	4	45.6	11.1	....	5890
1485	15 4 20.5	20.1	− 3.57	+ 1.14	...	6	44.6	9.1	....	5888
1486	32 53 50.5	47.7	− 3.54	+ 0.74	+ 0.18	5	45.5	10.1	18 Camelopardi	5897
1487	39 5 57.5	58.0	− 3.51	+ 0.67	...	3	48.4	11.1	....	5907
1488	38 53 23.5	24.3	− 3.50	+ 0.69	...	3	47.4	11.1	....	5910
1489	50 18 2.9	2.7	− 3.49	+ 0.62	...	2	49.6	13.1	....	....
1490	41 11 35.2	...	− 3.49	+ 0.65	...	3	48.8	...	....	5914
1491	50 18 6.8	7.6	− 3.48	+ 0.62	...	4	51.6	13.1	....	....
1492	15 51 11.3	12.2	− 3.48	+ 1.11	...	3	51.8	14.1	....	5913
1493	50 5 47.9	47.9	− 3.46	+ 0.61	...	2	50.6	13.1	....	......
1494	40 43 53.1	...	− 3.44	+ 0.67	...	2	44.6	...	....	......
1495	40 43 51.4	51.8	− 3.44	+ 0.67	...	3	47.7	12.1	....	......
1496	51 48 19.1	18.0	− 3.41	+ 0.60	...	3	47.1	11.0	....	......
1497	25 57 21.6	20.1	− 3.29	+ 0.83	+ 0.05	6	44.1	9.1	19 Camelopardi	5946
1498	48 0 38.7	39.7	− 3.27	+ 0.62	...	6	47.1	12.7	....	......
1499	45 20 0.7	...	− 3.26	+ 0.64	...	4	51.1	...	....	....
1500	20 7 31.3	...	− 3.23	+ 0.96	...	3	48.7	...	....	5954

Ordinal Number		Magnitude.	Estimates of Magnitude.	Mean Right Ascension 1845.0		Precession 1845.0	Secular Variation	Adopted Proper Motion.	Observations of R.A.		
R.	G.	R.		R.	G.				No. R.	Mean year R.	Mean year G.
				h. m. s.	s.	s.	s.	s.		1800 +	
1501	981	7.0	6	5 23 10.20	8.81	+ 7.637	+ 0.069	......	3	45.8	14.1
1502	...	8.3	7	5 23 46.60	...	+ 7.026	+ 0.055	......	3	51.4	...
1503	984	6.1	5	5 23 52.46	52.01	+ 4.909	+ 0.016	......	3	43.8	12.1
1504	...	7.6	6	5 23 53.47	...	+ 4.535	+ 0.012	......	4	46.2	...
1505	...	2.0	A	5 24 5.43	...	+ 3.060	+ 0.002	......	24	46.4	...
1506	985	7.4	4	5 24 21.20	20.52	+ 5.056	+ 0.018	......	5	46.7	9.1
1507	...	5.5	1	5 24 26.15	...	+ 2.900	+ 0.001	......	3	55.1	...
1508	987	6.2	5	5 24 34.13	33.80	+ 4.516	+ 0.011	......	4	45.1	11.1
1509	...	7.4	5	5 25 36.81	...	+ 4.530	+ 0.012	......	4	49.4	...
1510	989	7.0	5	5 26 0.42	59.57	+ 5.050	+ 0.018	......	4	48.1	9.1
1511	986	7.5	6	5 26 0.80	58.98	+ 7.847	+ 0.071	......	4	44.5	14.1
1512	991	6.3	6	5 26 2.93	2.80	+ 4.183	+ 0.008	......	4	47.1	12.7
1513	990	7.8	4	5 26 7.24	8.87	+ 4.722	+ 0.012	......	3	44.7	11.0
1514	988	7.0	8	5 26 7.64	7.27	+ 5.541	+ 0.023	......	4	46.8	10.1
1515	992	7.4	5	5 26 15.09	15.24	+ 4.112	+ 0.006	......	3	47.1	13.1
1516	...	5.6	9	5 26 55.25	...	+ 5.987	+ 0.029	......	3	48.7	...
1517	994	7.2	5	5 27 0.52	0.06	+ 4.609	+ 0.009	......	3	48.1	12.1
1518	...	8.4	5	5 27 35.71	...	+ 4.123	+ 0.008	......	2	47.0	...
1519	...	7.3	9	5 27 57.33	...	+13.395	+ 0.253	......	4	50.5	...
1520	...	2.0	A	5 28 21.07	...	+ 3.040	+ 0.002	......	19	44.0	...
1521	...	4.0	3	5 28 23.05	...	+ 3.579	+ 0.004	......	7	50.1	...
1522	996	8.6	4	5 28 34.85	34.92	+ 4.122	+ 0.006	......	3	47.5	13.1
1523	997	8.5	5	5 28 45.55	45.67	+ 4.121	+ 0.007	......	2	47.2	13.1
1524	995	5.9	3	5 28 46.32	46.24	+ 4.854	+ 0.013	+ 0.007	4	46.9	11.1
1525	998	7.0	5	5 28 53.12	52.79	+ 4.316	+ 0.010	......	3	45.8	12.7
1526	993	7.9	6	5 29 2.89	2.46	+ 8.244	+ 0.072	......	3	47.1	14.1
1527	1000	8.3	5	5 29 13.55	13.31	+ 4.318	+ 0.006	......	3	49.8	13.0
1528	1002	8.7	4	5 29 48.06	47.68	+ 4.945	+ 0.014	......	2	45.6	11.1
1529	1003	6.3	4	5 29 53.46	53.01	+ 5.072	+ 0.016	+ 0.003	3	47.1	10.1
1530	999	6.3	4	5 29 53.91	53.45	+ 5.500	+ 0.020	......	4	47.3	9.2
1531	...	7.9	5	5 29 57.79	...	+ 4.561	+ 0.011	......	3	52.1	...
1532	...	8.2	5	5 30 19.85	...	+ 4.122	+ 0.007	......	3	47.8	...
1533	1006	8.3	4	5 30 53.09	53.14	+ 4.110	+ 0.006	......	3	46.1	13.2
1534	1005	7.2	7	5 31 10.01	9.86	+ 4.948	+ 0.013	+ 0.005	4	46.1	10.8
1535	...	8.1	4	5 31 21.64	...	+ 4.071	+ 0.006	......	3	52.7	...

Ordinal Number.	Mean North Polar Distance 1845.0. R.	G.	Precession 1845.0.	Secular Variation.	Adopted Proper Motion.	No. R.	Mean year. R.	G.	Names.	Oeltzen-Argelander Number.
	° ′ ″	″	″	″	″		1800 +			
1501	16 6 56.8	57.6	− 3.21	+ 1.10	...	4	45.8	14.1	....	5959
1502	18 27 22.5	...	− 3.16	+ 1.01	...	4	52.6	...	....	......
1503	35 40 58.9	57.7	− 3.15	+ 0.71	...	4	45.6	12.1	....	5973
1504	42 2 3.2	...	− 3.15	+ 0.66	...	4	47.1	...	....	......
1505	90 25 8.6	...	− 3.13	+ 0.44	+ 0.04	9	53.6	...	34 Orionis δ...	......
1506	33 37 15.7	15.7	− 3.11	+ 0.73	...	2	43.1	9.1	20 Camelopardi	5977
1507	97 25 14.1	...	− 3.09	+ 0.42	...	1	52.0	...	36 Orionis υ...	......
1508	42 23 41.4	41.0	− 3.09	+ 0.65	...	4	44.3	11.1	....	......
1509	42 10 1.2	...	− 3.00	+ 0.66	...	3	46.1	...	....	......
1510	33 44 14.0	13.6	− 2.96	+ 0.74	+ 0.12	4	46.1	9.1	22 Camelopardi	6002
1511	15 28 17.0	13.7	− 2.96	+ 1.15	...	5	46.1	14.1	....	5999
1512	49 55 28.0	27.3	− 2.96	+ 0.61	...	3	44.8	12.7	....	......
1513	38 39 47.0	51.1	− 2.95	+ 0.69	...	4	46.8	11.0	....	6006
1514	28 9 6.0	6.3	− 2.95	+ 0.80	...	5	47.3	10.1	21 Camelopardi	6003
1515	51 45 46.7	47.1	− 2.94	+ 0.61	...	4	49.9	13.1	....	......
1516	24 23 47.9	...	− 2.88	+ 0.86	...	8	47.4	...	....	......
1517	40 41 6.5	6.4	− 2.88	+ 0.66	...	3	45.7	12.2	....	......
1518	51 29 40.2	...	− 2.83	+ 0.60	...	3	49.5	...	....	......
1519	7 18 17.7	...	− 2.80	+ 1.93	...	6	49.1	...	....	......
1520	91 18 22.6	...	− 2.76	+ 0.44	...	8	53.8	...	46 Orionis ε...	......
1521	68 57 26.5	...	− 2.76	+ 0.52	+ 0.05	3	52.8	...	123 Tauri ζ...	......
1522	51 32 53.6	56.0	− 2.74	+ 0.60	...	3	49.4	13.1	....	......
1523	51 35 23.5	25.1	− 2.72	+ 0.61	...	3	51.4	13.1	....	......
1524	36 35 25.0	6.0	− 2.72	+ 0.71	...	4	44.8	11.1	....	6054
1525	46 46 11.7	9.7	− 2.71	+ 0.64	...	4	46.6	12.7	....	......
1526	14 21 39.1	37.7	− 2.70	+ 1.19	...	4	47.1	14.1	....	6056
1527	46 41 39.6	38.2	− 2.68	+ 0.63	...	2	46.5	13.0	....	......
1528	35 15 23.4	25.4	− 2.63	+ 0.73	...	4	50.1	11.1	....	......
1529	33 30 29.2	30.1	− 2.63	+ 0.73	...	3	44.4	10.1	24 Camelopardi	6079
1530	28 36 36.4	36.2	− 2.63	+ 0.79	...	3	43.7	9.2	23 Camelopardi	6078
1531	41 37 30.9	...	− 2.62	+ 0.66	...	3	52.4	...	....	6083
1532	51 34 30.6	...	− 2.59	+ 0.60	...	3	53.0	...	....	......
1533	51 54 3.1	2.8	− 2.54	+ 0.60	...	3	48.8	13.2	....	......
1534	35 13 8.3	5.4	− 2.52	+ 0.71	...	5	45.5	10.8	25 Camelopardi	6102
1535	52 58 15.4	...	− 2.50	+ 0.59	...	1	54.2	...	....	......

Magnitude.	Estimates of Magnitude.	Mean Right Ascension 1845.0.		Precession 1845.0.	Secular Variation	Adopted Proper Motion.	Observations of R.A.		
R.	R.	R.	G.		'		No. R.	Mean year. R.	G.
		h. m. s.	s.	s.	s.	s.		1800 +	
8.4	3	5 31 33.59	33.70	+ 8.313	+ 0.067	......	2	49.0	14.1
7.8	7	5 31 39.12	38.79	+ 4.386	+ 0.008	......	4	48.6	12.0
7.9	5	5 31 40.78	40.77	+ 4.111	+ 0.006	......	3	48.4	13.2
9.8	4	5 31 58.40	...	+ 4.077	+ 0.006	......	3	54.1	...
7.3	6	5 32 7.45	7.23	+ 4.525	+ 0.008	......	5	48.9	11.1
7.4	5	5 32 9.28	9.00	+ 4.111	+ 0.006	......	3	47.4	13.1
7.1	5	5 32 13.29	12.72	+ 4.249	+ 0.006	......	3	47.4	11.1
9.0	3	5 32 13.60	...	+ 4.073	+ 0.006	......	2	51.7	...
8.8	5	5 32 52.06	52.29	+ 4.107	+ 0.006	......	3	48.7	13.2
7.9	6	5 33 4.86	4.04	+ 4.329	+ 0.006	......	3	47.0	13.1
5.8	5	5 33 26.92	26.46	+ 5.042	+ 0.013	......	4	45.6	7.9
6.8	7	5 33 41.83	41.55	+ 5.103	+ 0.013	+ 0.007	5	46.7	10.1
6.1	8	5 33 53.90	53.96	+ 4.639	+ 0.009	+ 0.010	5	46.5	9.1
6.9	5	5 34 44.52	44.46	+ 4.737	+ 0.009	......	4	46.2	11.2
7.5	1	5 35 57.59	...	+ 3.452	+ 0.002	......	3	55.1	...
7.8	4	5 35 58.37	...	+ 5.109	+ 0.014	......	4	44.7	...
6.3	8	5 36 9.14	8.82	+ 4.287	+ 0.006	......	4	46.1	11.1
6.1	5	5 36 15.81	...	+ 6.432	+ 0.026	......	3	47.4	...
7.1	10	5 36 39.17	38.91	+ 4.479	+ 0.006	......	5	47.9	11.1
6.2	6	5 37 21.21	20.80	+ 5.108	+ 0.012	......	4	44.2	10.1
7.7	3	5 37 35.01	34.99	+ 4.732	+ 0.010	......	3	44.8	11.2
7.7	6	5 37 52.77	...	+ 4.643	+ 0.007	......	4	49.6	...
6.8	9	5 38 5.17	5.18	+ 4.166	+ 0.005	+ 0.003	6	49.1	10.1
5.0	10	5 38 26.34	26.12	+ 4.152	+ 0.005	......	7	48.0	7.6
6.2	7	5 38 37.51	36.90	+ 4.740	+ 0.007	......	4	44.6	11.1
6.1	7	5 38 37.85	37.41	+ 5.278	+ 0.012	+ 0.003	6	45.9	9.1
7.4	8	5 39 21.77	21.43	+ 4.353	+ 0.005	......	3	46.4	11.0
7.6	6	5 40 22.00	...	+ 4.699	+ 0.013	......	4	52.3	...
4.5	11	5 40 45.01	44.85	+ 4.152	+ 0.004	+ 0.003	9	48.8	7.7
5.5	8	5 41 5.20	4.70	+ 5.363	+ 0.011	......	4	43.6	8.1
7.8	5	5 41 42.85	...	+ 4.698	+ 0.012	......	3	50.1	...
5.2	5	5 41 51.71	51.20	+ 5.021	+ 0.009	......	3	44.5	9.1
7.3	5	5 43 2.14	...	+ 4.867	+ 0.008	......	3	51.1	...
8.9	5	5 43 5.87	...	+ 4.867	+ 0.008	......	3	54.1	...
6.5	1	5 43 34.07	...	+ 3.406	+ 0.002	......	3	55.1	...

Ordinal Number.	Mean North Polar Distance 1845.0. R.	G.	Precession 1845.0.	Secular Variation.	Adopted Proper Motion	Observations of N.P.D. No. R.	Mean year. R. (1800 +)	Mean year. G. (1800 +)	Names.	Oeltzen Argelander Number.
1536	14 11 49.2	47.2	− 2.48	+ 1.20	...	2	47.6	14.1	....	6106
1537	45 14 0.8	0.4	− 2.47	+ 0.64	...	3	47.1	12.0	....	6112
1538	51 53 17.7	19.1	− 2.47	+ 0.60	...	3	48.8	13.2	....	....
1539	52 48 34.0	...	− 2.45	+ 0.59	...	1	53.0	...	....	....
1540	42 22 6.2	4.3	− 2.43	+ 0.66	...	5	46.9	11.1	....	6124
1541	51 53 10.2	11.4	− 2.43	+ 0.60	...	3	49.8	13.1	....	....
1542	48 22 58.1	55.6	− 2.42	+ 0.63	...	3	45.5	11.1	....	....
1543	52 5 59.6	...	− 2.42	+ 0.59	...	1	54.2	...	....	....
1544	51 59 54.3	51.0	− 2.37	+ 0.60	...	2	50.1	13.2	....	....
1545	46 31 22.0	23.5	− 2.35	+ 0.63	...	3	46.5	13.1	....	....
1546	33 57 27.0	25.7	− 2.32	+ 0.73	+ 0.03	6	45.5	7.9	26 Camelopardi	......
1547	33 8 56.3	56.3	− 2.30	+ 0.74	+ 0.03	4	46.8	10.1	28 Camelopardi	6150
1548	40 14 58.0	58.1	− 2.28	+ 0.67	...	5	48.1	9.1	27 Aurigæ o...	6156
1549	38 32 57.3	55.3	− 2.20	+ 0.70	...	4	47.1	11.2	....	....
1550	73 59 17.7	...	− 2.10	+ 0.50	...	1	52.0	...	128 Tauri......	....
1551	33 6 37.6	...	− 2.10	+ 0.74	...	3	44.4	...	....	6188
1552	47 32 16.9	14.6	− 2.08	+ 0.63	...	5	47.7	11.1	....	....
1553	21 35 4.3	...	− 2.07	+ 0.93	...	5	48.7	...	....	....
1554	43 20 35.8	36.3	− 2.04	+ 0.65	...	5	47.5	11.1	....	6201
1555	33 8 27.4	27.8	− 1.98	+ 0.74	...	5	44.6	10.1	29 Camelopardi	6209
1556	38 41 15.4	17.8	− 1.96	+ 0.68	...	4	45.6	11.2	....	6213
1557	40 13 5.0	...	− 1.93	+ 0.68	...	4	48.6	...	....	....
1558	50 31 38.0	33.2	− 1.91	+ 0.61	...	4	47.1	10.1	28 Aurigæ	......
1559	50 52 43.9	43.6	− 1.88	+ 0.61	...	4	46.9	7.6	29 Aurigæ τ...	......
1560	38 32 27.7	26.0	− 1.87	+ 0.68	...	3	43.7	11.1	....	6228
1561	31 5 23.1	20.9	− 1.87	+ 0.76	...	4	44.3	9.1	30 Camelopardi	6226
1562	46 2 42.1	41.4	− 1.80	+ 0.64	...	5	46.5	11.0	....	......
1563	39 16 21.6	...	− 1.72	+ 0.69	...	4	52.6	...	....	6247
1564	50 54 14.6	14.8	− 1.68	+ 0.61	− 0.03	4	46.6	7.7	32 Aurigæ ν...	......
1565	30 9 22.0	21.8	− 1.65	+ 0.79	...	5	45.0	8.1	31 Camelopardi	6264
1566	39 18 35.4	...	− 1.60	+ 0.69	...	3	49.1	...	....	6275
1567	34 20 15.1	15.6	− 1.58	+ 0.75	...	4	43.8	9.1	30 Aurigæ ξ...	6277
1568	36 34 48.2	...	− 1.48	+ 0.71	...	3	51.8	...	....	6288
1569	36 35 18.9	...	− 1.48	+ 0.71	...	2	52.0	...	....	6289
1570	75 52 22.7	...	− 1.43	+ 0.55	...	1	52.0	...	137 Tauri......	......

Ordinal Number.		Magnitude.	Estimates of Magnitude.	Mean Right Ascension 1845.0.		Precession 1845.0	Secular Variation	Adopted Proper Motion.	Observations of R.A.		
R.	G.	R.		R.	G.				No. R.	Mean year. R.	G.
				h. m. s.	s.	s.	s.	s.		1800 +	
1571	1004	6.6	49	5 43 34.44	32.12	+26.593	+ 0.660	......	66	50.8	7.6
1572	...	5.7	1	5 43 35.24	...	+ 3.766	+ 0.002	......	4	41.9	...
1573	...	7.6	6	5 43 44.12	...	+ 4.873	+ 0.009	......	3	51.4	...
1574	1030	6.2	6	5 43 47.38	46.90	+ 8.251	+ 0.037	......	4	45.6	11.2
1575	1034	6.6	5	5 43 55.51	55.30	+ 4.762	+ 0.006	......	4	44.7	10.1
1576	1033	7.2	6	5 44 4.76	4.42	+ 5.042	+ 0.010	......	4	48.1	12.1
1577	...	8.3	5	5 44 34.77	...	+ 4.760	+ 0.011	......	3	48.4	...
1578	1035	7.4	6	5 44 41.69	41.23	+ 5.020	+ 0.008	+ 0.007	3	47.1	9.9
1579	1032	6.8	6	5 44 44.61	44.05	+ 6.211	+ 0.015	......	6	49.7	11.1
1580	1037	7.0	3	5 44 58.90	58.65	+ 4.242	+ 0.004	......	3	44.8	11.1
1581	1036	8.3	5	5 45 10.71	10.47	+ 5.039	+ 0.007	......	2	47.6	12.0
1582	1031	7.6	7	5 45 19.06	19.00	+ 7.717	+ 0.025	......	4	46.1	12.1
1583	1039	6.8	5	5 46 7.64	7.53	+ 4.446	+ 0.005	......	3	47.5	13.1
1584	1038	6.3	4	5 46 14.83	14.74	+ 6.195	+ 0.013	......	4	47.3	11.1
1585	...	7.5	4	5 46 19.06	...	+ 4.485	+ 0.005	......	2	48.1	...
1586	1042	8.1	5	5 46 34.69	34.51	+ 4.409	+ 0.005	......	3	50.1	13.0
1587	1040	4.0	5	5 46 46.00	45.98	+ 4.925	+ 0.005	+ 0.004	4	48.1	7.1
1588	...	1.0	A	5 46 46.95	...	+ 3.243	+ 0.001	......	36	44.2	...
1589	1041	6.3	5	5 46 50.61	50.04	+ 4.998	+ 0.007	......	4	47.7	9.1
1590	1043	6.3	4	5 47 1.04	0.57	+ 4.943	+ 0.006	......	3	47.5	10.1
1591	1044	8.0	3	5 47 16.17	16.14	+ 4.932	+ 0.006	......	2	49.6	16.1
1592	1046	6.3	5	5 47 19.52	19.29	+ 4.655	+ 0.004	......	2	50.1	14.1
1593	1045	7.6	3	5 47 22.55	22.33	+ 5.117	+ 0.004	......	2	50.0	11.2
1594	1047	7.8	5	5 47 30.88	29.65	+ 4.445	+ 0.004	......	3	48.1	13.2
1595	1048	6.8	4	5 47 57.06	56.76	+ 4.722	+ 0.003	......	2	49.1	14.1
1596	1050	2.4	6	5 48 9.59	9.89	+ 4.401	+ 0.003	......	6	49.3	6.7
1597	1051	5.0	6	5 48 25.93	25.80	+ 4.448	+ 0.003	......	4	46.9	10.2
1598	1052	7.9	3	5 48 35.31	34.97	+ 4.659	+ 0.003	......	2	50.1	14.0
1599	1053	8.0	4	5 48 40.95	40.80	+ 4.723	+ 0.004	......	2	49.0	14.1
1600	1054	8.2	4	5 48 42.65	42.46	+ 4.404	+ 0.003	......	2	51.0	13.0
1601	1049	8.0	6	5 48 51.76	51.01	+ 6.205	+ 0.005	......	3	48.5	11.2
1602	1055	6.8	6	5 48 58.96	59.05	+ 4.385	+ 0.003	......	3	48.1	13.1
1603	1056	6.1	4	5 49 13.11	12.82	+ 4.547	+ 0.003	......	3	50.5	10.5
1604	...	8.4	3	5 49 32.12	...	+ 4.412	+ 0.004	......	3	51.8	...
1605	1057	6.7	5	5 49 48.82	48.53	+ 5.127	+ 0.004	......	2	48.1	11.2

Ordinal Number. R.	Mean North Polar Distance 1845.0.		Precession 1845.0.	Secular Variation.	Adopted Proper Motion.	Observations of N.P.D.			Names.	Oeltzen-Argelander Number.
	R.	G.				No. R.	Mean year. R.	Mean year. G.		
	° ′ ″	″	″	″	″		1800 +			
1571	3 14 38.8	39.4	− 1.44	+ 3.85	+ 0.10	23	46.4	7.6	....	......
1572	62 25 49.9	...	− 1.43	+ 0.55	+ 0.07	2	52.5	...	136 Tauri......	......
1573	36 29 0.4	...	− 1.42	+ 0.71	...	4	51.5	...	....	6298
1574	14 26 5.1	1.8	− 1.42	+ 1.20	...	4	44.5	11.2	....	6294
1575	38 13 58.8	57.6	− 1.41	+ 0.69	...	4	45.6	10.1	....	......
1576	34 5 0.0	57.3	− 1.39	+ 0.74	...	3	44.8	12.1	....	6304
1577	38 15 56.6	...	− 1.35	+ 0.69	...	4	44.1	...	....	......
1578	34 22 36.1	36.3	− 1.34	+ 0.73	...	4	45.9	9.9	....	......
1579	23 0 43.2	39.7	− 1.33	+ 0.91	...	4	44.3	11.1	....	......
1580	48 42 39.7	40.1	− 1.31	+ 0.62	...	4	46.1	11.1	....	......
1581	34 7 17.4	14.4	− 1.30	+ 0.72	...	3	47.5	12.0	....	6324
1582	16 1 0.4	58.0	− 1.28	+ 1.13	...	3	44.4	12.1	....	6325
1583	44 7 44.6	42.1	− 1.21	+ 0.65	...	3	45.4	13.1	....	6335
1584	23 7 17.7	17.8	− 1.20	+ 0.91	+ 0.04	3	45.1	11.1	....	......
1585	43 19 24.0	...	− 1.20	+ 0.66	...	3	46.1	...	....	6337
1586	44 55 6.9	7.6	− 1.17	+ 0.65	...	3	45.8	13.0	....	......
1587	35 44 8.5	7.2	− 1.16	+ 0.72	+ 0.13	5	44.9	7.1	33 Aurigæ δ...	6345
1588	82 37 37.9	...	− 1.16	+ 0.47	...	19	45.0	...	58 Orionis α...	......
1589	34 42 2.2	59.8	− 1.15	+ 0.73	+ 0.06	5	47.3	9.1	....	6347
1590	35 28 34.5	34.1	− 1.14	+ 0.72	+ 0.08	3	48.7	10.1	....	6354
1591	35 37 52.0	50.6	− 1.11	+ 0.72	...	3	49.1	16.1	....	6357
1592	40 6 0.9	1.0	− 1.11	+ 0.67	...	3	47.1	14.1	....	6359
1593	33 5 55.9	55.3	− 1.10	+ 0.75	...	3	45.8	11.2	....	......
1594	44 9 41.5	41.2	− 1.09	+ 0.66	...	3	50.8	13.2	....	6360
1595	38 56 22.8	23.3	− 1.05	+ 0.70	...	3	47.8	14.1	....	6366
1596	45 4 30.6	32.7	− 1.03	+ 0.65	...	5	48.7	6.7	34 Aurigæ β..	......
1597	44 5 6.2	5.4	− 1.01	+ 0.65	+ 0.02	3	47.4	10.2	35 Aurigæ π..	6373
1598	40 2 25.5	25.8	− 1.00	+ 0.67	...	1	50.1	14.0	....	6374
1599	38 55 45.7	48.5	− 0.99	+ 0.69	...	2	49.1	14.1	....	6378
1600	45 1 56.9	52.0	− 0.98	+ 0.66	...	2	51.1	13.0	....	......
1601	23 4 8.7	1.7	− 0.97	+ 0.92	...	4	50.1	11.2	....	6380
1602	45 25 35.0	35.1	− 0.96	+ 0.65	+ 0.04	3	44.8	13.1	....	......
1603	42 6 55.6	56.4	− 0.94	+ 0.66	...	4	45.6	10.5	36 Aurigæ......	......
1604	44 51 18.8	...	− 0.92	+ 0.64	...	1	51.2	...	....	......
1605	32 59 35.2	32.9	− 0.89	+ 0.75	...	4	44.6	11.2	....	6395

Ordinal Number.		Magnitude.	Estimates of Magnitude.	Mean Right Ascension 1845.0.		Precession 1845.0.	Secular Variation	Adopted Proper Motion.	Observations of R.A.		
R.	G.	R.		R.	G.				No. R.	Mean year. R.	G.
				h. m. s.	s.	s.	s.	s.		1800 +	
1606	1058	8.0	6	5 49 53.27	52.98	+ 4.413	+ 0.003	......	3	50.8	13.0
1607	1060	6.6	5	5 50 46.05	45.70	+ 4.656	+ 0.003	......	3	45.8	11.1
1608	1061	7.0	8	5 51 0.10	59.91	+ 4.543	+ 0.003	......	4	44.6	11.0
1609	...	7.7	3	5 51 19.88	...	+ 4.133	+ 0.001	......	2	52.2	...
1610	1064	7.2	4	5 51 22.02	21.84	+ 4.553	+ 0.003	......	3	46.4	11.2
1611	...	7.2	2	5 51 23.07	...	+ 4.140	+ 0.001	......	2	52.2	...
1612	1065	6.8	5	5 51 41.46	41.41	+ 4.332	+ 0.002	+ 0.007	4	46.1	11.1
1613	1062	6.3	4	5 51 49.13	48.87	+ 5.744	+ 0.006	......	3	44.7	14.1
1614	1063	8.8	6	5 51 53.52	53.08	+ 5.736	+ 0.006	......	3	49.7	14.1
1615	1067	6.3	8	5 52 7.60	7.46	+ 4.312	+ 0.002	+ 0.015	8	49.0	9.1
1616	1066	6.1	4	5 52 11.78	11.39	+ 4.754	+ 0.003	+ 0.003	5	46.3	8.1
1617	1059	8.0	5	5 52 41.83	41.61	+ 8.645	+ 0.013	......	3	47.8	12.1
1618	1068	7.3	8	5 53 5.94	5.78	+ 4.433	+ 0.002	......	6	47.9	13.1
1619	1069	7.0	7	5 53 10.42	10.11	+ 4.372	+ 0.002	......	5	47.2	13.0
1620	1070	7.7	6	5 53 37.81	37.57	+ 4.429	+ 0.002	......	3	48.1	13.1
1621	1071	6.1	7	5 53 54.67	54.30	+ 4.316	+ 0.002	......	5	44.7	9.1
1622	...	6.9	5	5 53 58.35	...	+ 4.136	+ 0.001	......	4	49.4	...
1623	1072	7.5	8	5 54 4.16	4.07	+ 4.567	+ 0.002	......	4	47.1	13.2
1624	...	6.4	5	5 54 24.76	...	+ 4.113	+ 0.001	− 0.003	4	50.1	...
1625	1075	5.9	6	5 55 54.04	53.84	+ 4.133	+ 0.001	......	4	46.9	10.2
1626	1073	8.2	6	5 55 55.33	55.09	+ 4.698	+ 0.002	......	4	48.1	14.1
1627	1074	5.4	6	5 56 18.50	18.32	+ 5.290	+ 0.002	+ 0.007	6	45.9	8.7
1628	1078	8.5	5	5 56 25.00	24.96	+ 4.240	+ 0.001	......	2	46.1	13.2
1629	1077	6.5	5	5 56 25.01	24.79	+ 4.268	+ 0.001	......	4	47.6	14.1
1630	...	7.1	7	5 56 43.41	...	+ 4.302	+ 0.001	......	3	51.4	...
1631	...	8.6	3	5 56 45.45	...	+ 4.410	+ 0.001	......	3	52.4	...
1632	...	6.5	1	5 56 47.02	...	+ 3.168	0.000	......	2	56.1	...
1633	1081	7.4	5	5 56 51.51	51.48	+ 4.433	+ 0.001	......	4	47.3	13.1
1634	...	6.8	4	5 56 52.88	...	+ 4.118	+ 0.001	+ 0.004	3	49.5	...
1635	1080	7.1	6	5 57 10.24	10.15	+ 5.312	+ 0.001	......	4	48.1	11.1
1636	1079	6.2	4	5 57 12.47	12.61	+ 5.430	+ 0.001	......	4	44.8	15.0
1637	1076	5.5	9	5 57 15.48	15.17	+ 6.036	+ 0.002	......	8	49.2	13.3
1638	...	7.0	1	5 57 21.77	...	+ 3.656	0.000	......	1	52.0	...
1639	1083	7.0	5	5 57 26.42	26.65	+ 4.235	0.000	......	3	46.4	13.2
1640	1084	8.7	4	5 58 16.26	16.25	+ 5.133	0.000	......	2	48.1	15.2

Ordinal Number. R.	Mean North Polar Distance 1845.0.		Precession 1845.0.	Secular Variation.	Adopted Proper Motion.	Observations of N.P.D.			Names.	Oeltzen-Argelander Number.
	R.	G.				No. R.	Mean year. R.	G.		
	° ′ ″	″	″	″	″		1800 +			
1606	44 51 19.5	19.3	− 0.88	+ 0.65	...	3	47.5	13.0	....	......
1607	40 6 16.8	14.2	− 0.81	+ 0.67	...	3	45.1	11.1	....	6409
1608	42 12 21.6	25.2	− 0.79	+ 0.65	...	4	47.1	11.0	....	6416
1609	51 33 9.3	...	− 0.76	+ 0.60	...	1	53.1	...	....	......
1610	42 1 7.0	4.9	− 0.76	+ 0.65	...	3	45.1	11.2	....	6420
1611	51 17 29.5	...	− 0.75	+ 0.60	...	1	51.1	...	....	......
1612	46 37 49.8	48.8	− 0.73	+ 0.63	...	3	45.8	11.1	....	......
1613	26 32 57.8	58.1	− 0.72	+ 0.82	...	3	42.4	14.1	....	6432
1614	26 37 9.7	52.8	− 0.71	+ 0.83	...	3	50.1	14.1	....	6434
1615	47 5 26.5	27.5	− 0.69	+ 0.63	+ 0.15	3	45.4	9.1	38 Aurigæ	......
1616	38 25 51.8	52.2	− 0.68	+ 0.69	+ 0.04	4	44.6	8.1	....	6437
1617	13 28 47.0	48.6	− 0.64	+ 1.25	...	3	48.5	12.1	....	......
1618	44 24 57.2	55.7	− 0.60	+ 0.66	...	5	48.5	13.1	....	6451
1619	45 44 14.1	10.4	− 0.60	+ 0.63	...	3	44.4	13.0	....	......
1620	44 30 50.9	50.3	− 0.56	+ 0.64	...	4	47.1	13.1	....	6461
1621	47 0 50.2	47.6	− 0.53	+ 0.63	+ 0.07	4	44.5	9.1	39 Aurigæ	......
1622	51 25 37.6	...	− 0.53	+ 0.60	...	3	47.8	...	....	......
1623	41 45 3.2	1.8	− 0.52	+ 0.66	...	4	44.4	13.2	....	6466
1624	52 2 9.1	...	− 0.49	+ 0.60	+ 0.08	4	49.6	...	....	......
1625	51 30 37.0	35.6	− 0.36	+ 0.60	...	4	45.6	10.2	40 Aurigæ	......
1626	39 24 21.7	20.5	− 0.36	+ 0.68	...	4	45.1	14.1	....	......
1627	31 3 12.0	13.2	− 0.32	+ 0.78	− 0.03	4	42.8	8.7	37 Camelopardi	6492
1628	48 47 29.6	25.3	− 0.31	+ 0.63	...	4	46.6	13.2	....	......
1629	48 8 14.9	13.2	− 0.31	+ 0.63	...	5	44.6	14.1	....	......
1630	47 19 30.4	...	− 0.29	+ 0.63	...	4	51.6	...	....	......
1631	44 56 16.7	...	− 0.28	+ 0.65	...	1	52.2	...	....	6501
1632	85 50 14.1	...	− 0.28	+ 0.46	...	1	52.0	...	66 Orionis	......
1633	44 26 7.9	7.0	− 0.27	+ 0.66	...	4	46.6	13.1	....	6502
1634	51 54 30.6	...	− 0.27	+ 0.60	+ 0.06	4	49.1	...	....	......
1635	30 48 53.9	53.0	− 0.25	+ 0.77	+ 0.02	3	43.8	11.2	38 Camelopardi	6513
1636	29 31 47.9	46.4	− 0.24	+ 0.80	+ 0.01	5	44.4	15.0	39 Camelopardi	......
1637	24 15 40.6	41.7	− 0.24	+ 0.88	+ 0.07	7	46.2	13.3	36 Camelopardi	6514
1638	66 21 10.8	...	− 0.23	+ 0.53	...	3	55.1	...	2 Geminorum .	......
1639	48 55 51.8	48.7	− 0.22	+ 0.63	...	3	44.4	13.2	....	......
1640	32 57 7.8	7.0	− 0.15	+ 0.75	...	2	47.6	15.2	....	6533

Ordinal Number.		Magnitude.	Estimates of Magnitude.	Mean Right Ascension 1845.0.			Precession 1845.0.	Secular Variation	Adopted Proper Motion.	Observations of R.A.		
R.	G.	R.	R.	R.		G.				No. R.	Mean year R.	G.
				h. m. s.		s.	s.	s.	s.		1800 +	
1641	1089	7.9	4	5 58 32.85		32.74	+ 4.243	0.000	......	2	50.1	13.2
1642	1036	7.4	6	5 58 35.14		34.67	+ 4.492	0.000	......	3	47.4	14.1
1643	1087	7.8	6	5 58 37.00		36.80	+ 4.542	0.000	......	3	46.7	14.1
1644	1088	9.6	3	5 58 38.92		39.29	+ 4.535	0.000	'......	2	49.1	15.1
1645	1082	7.7	5	5 59 8.95		8.01	+ 7.440	0.000	......	3	47.1	12.1
1646	1092	8.0	6	5 59 13.77		14.16	+ 4.530	0.000	......	3	46.8	15.1
1647	1085	9.1	5	5 59 26.79		26.70	+ 6.102	0.000	......	3	49.8	15.1
1648	1093	7.4	4	5 59 30.56		30.48	+ 4.551	0.000	......	3	44.4	14.1
1649	...	7.5	7	5 59 44.10		...	+ 4.594	0.000	+ 0.012	7	49.7	...
1650	1094	6.4	3	5 59 44.30		43.87	+ 4.594	0.000	......	7	49.7	10.1
1651	1096	7.5	6	5 59 50.13		50.08	+ 4.406	0.000	......	3	50.4	13.0
1652	1090	7.1	4	5 59 51.01		50.93	+ 6.098	0.000	......	5	46.3	15.0
1653	1091	9.5	7	6 0 0.42		0.12	+ 6.096	0.000	......	4	50.6	15.0
1654	1097	7.7	5	6 0 6.01		5.59	+ 4.242	0.000	......	2	51.0	13.2
1655	1095	8.9	5	6 0 17.39		17.02	+ 5.318	0.000	......	2	45.6	11.2
1656	1099	8.5	4	6 0 26.28		26.40	+ 4.410	0.000	......	2	51.0	13.1
1657	1101	8.4	5	6 0 53.21		52.98	+ 4.411	0.000	......	3	49.1	13.1
1658	...	7.6	5	6 0 53.94		...	+ 4.526	0.000	......	3	51.8	...
1659	...	8.9	3	6 1 15.21		...	+ 4.782	0.000	......	2	50.1	...
1660	1103	6.4	5	6 1 31.70		31.54	+ 4.733	0.000	......	3	47.4	14.1
1661	...	7.4	6	6 1 34.42		...	+ 6.039	— 0.001	......	4	47.6	...
1662	1104	7.4	4	6 1 37.39		37.29	+ 4.784	0.000	......	2	47.1	15.3
1663	1102	5.9	6	6 1 44.93		44.34	+ 5.388	— 0.001	+ 0.004	3	43.9	9.2
1664	1100	5.2	2	6 1 45.49		44.88	+ 6.620	— 0.003	+ 0.003	4	44.9	8.2
1665	1106	8.8	4	6 2 8.79		8.61	+ 4.733	— 0.001	......	2	50.0	14.0
1666	1105	6.8	5	6 2 19.95		19.71	+ 5.317	— 0.002	......	3	47.4	11.1
1667	1098	7.9	6	6 2 22.62		21.87	+ 8.024	— 0.002	......	3	47.5	11.1
1668	...	6.5	3	6 2 24.48		...	+ 6.667	— 0.004	— 0.007	3	48.5	...
1669	1107	8.0	4	6 2 27.79		27.62	+ 4.396	— 0.003	......	3	47.8	13.1
1670	1110	7.2	6	6 2 42.46		42.37	+ 4.262	— 0.003	......	3	47.5	13.0
1671	1112	8.7	5	6 2 56.43		56.28	+ 4.252	— 0.003	......	2	50.5	13.1
1672	1108	7.6	4	6 3 1.95		2.66	+ 5.128	— 0.003	......	3	49.2	15.8
1673	1109	7.7	4	6 3 9.96		9.98	+ 5.111	— 0.003	......	2	48.1	15.8
1674	1113	8.3	3	6 3 19.38		19.21	+ 4.389	— 0.002	......	2	49.2	13.2
1675	...	7.8	5	6 3 24.90		...	+ 4.476	— 0.001	....	2	52.2	...

Ordinal Number.	Mean North Polar Distance 1845.0.			Precession 1845.0.	Secular Variation.	Adopted Proper Motion.	Observations of N.P.D.				Names.	Oeltzen-Argelander Number.
R.	R.		G.				No. R.	Mean year. R.		G.		
	° ′ ″		″	″	″	″		1800 +				
1641	48 44 24.6		24.7	− 0.13	+ 0.61	...	3	49.8	13.2		....	....
1642	43 13 25.3		26.5	− 0.12	+ 0.67	...	3	44.8	14.1		....	6541
1643	42 14 36.0		37.0	− 0.12	+ 0.67	...	3	47.1	14.1		....	....
1644	42 22 41.8		42.5	− 0.12	+ 0.65	...	3	47.8	15.1.		....	....
1645	17 0 43.9		41.1	− 0.07	+ 1.10	...	3	45.1	12.1		....	6543
1646	42 28 28.4		26.5	− 0.07	+ 0.65	...	3	46.1	15.1		....	....
1647	23 47 36.6		36.7	− 0.05	+ 0.89	...	3	49.8	15.1		....	6553
1648	42 4 18.4		17.5	− 0.04	+ 0.67	...	5	47.7	14.1		....	....
1649	41 15 46.2		...	− 0.02	+ 0.68	+ 0.12	3	48.3	...		....	....
1650	41 15 55.7		57.1	− 0.02	+ 0.68	+ 0.12	6	47.4	10.1		41 Aurigæ	6562
1651	45 1 35.5		37.0	− 0.01	+ 0.65	...	3	47.7	13.0		....	6566
1652	23 49 21.7		21.6	− 0.01	+ 0.90	...	4	45.6	15.0		....	6554
1653	23 50 0.5		2.2	0.00	+ 0.84	...	4	47.6	15.0		....	6557
1654	48 44 45.4		43.7	+ 0.01	+ 0.65	...	3	49.8	13.2		....	....
1655	30 44 17.5		13.7	+ 0.02	+ 0.76	...	3	46.4	11.2		....	6572
1656	44 56 24.7		23.1	+ 0.04	+ 0.65	...	2	50.6	13.1		....	6576
1657	44 55 35.7		34.2	+ 0.08	+ 0.65	...	2	50.1	13.1		....	6583
1658	42 33 15.6		...	+ 0.08	+ 0.66	...	2	49.2	...		....	6584
1659	37 58 43.1		...	+ 0.11	+ 0.70	...	2	51.7	...		....	6590
1660	38 47 44.7		43.3	+ 0.13	+ 0.68	...	3	44.5	14.1		....	6596
1661	24 14 38.2		...	+ 0.14	+ 0.88	...	3	46.1	...		....	6594
1662	37 57 19.7		16.1	+ 0.14	+ 0.69	...	3	46.3	15.3		....	6599
1663	29 58 2.2		2.0	+ 0.15	+ 0.78	+ 0.04	5	46.9	9.2		40 Camelopardi	6602
1664	20 38 12.5		12.3	+ 0.15	+ 0.96	+ 0.09	5	47.0	8.2		....	....
1665	38 48 7.7		10.9	+ 0.19	+ 0.70	...	2	44.5	14.0		....	6611
1666	30 44 58.2		54.9	+ 0.20	+ 0.76	...	3	43.8	11.1		....	6613
1667	15 6 18.1		18.1	+ 0.21	+ 1.18	...	3	46.5	11.1		....	....
1668	20 23 16.5		...	+ 0.21	+ 0.97	+ 0.08	4	43.6	...		....	6615
1669	45 12 55.3		54.7	+ 0.22	+ 0.66	...	3	47.8	13.1		....	6618
1670	48 16 16.9		18.7	+ 0.24	+ 0.63	...	5	45.7	13.0		....	....
1671	48 29 59.9		59.7	+ 0.26	+ 0.63	...	3	48.8	13.1		....	....
1672	33 1 15.7		11.0	+ 0.27	+ 0.76	...	3	44.4	15.8		....	6623
1673	33 13 40.5		40.4	+ 0.28	+ 0.76	...	3	44.8	15.8		....	6626
1674	45 22 53.6		53.3	+ 0.29	+ 0.64	...	2	50.6	13.2		....	....
1675	43 34 8.6		...	+ 0.30	+ 0.66	...	4	51.6	...		....	6631

Ordinal Number.		Magnitude.	Estimates of Magnitude.	Mean Right Ascension 1845.0.		Precession 1845.0.	Secular Variation	Adopted Proper Motion.	Observations of R.A.		
R.	G.	R.		R.	G.	s.	s.	s.	No. R.	Mean year. R.	G.
				h. m. s.	s.					1800 +	
1676	1116	7.7	4	6 3 32.34	32.09	+ 4.180	− 0.003	......	2	47.2	13.1
1677	1111	4.6	2	6 3 37.05	36.62	+ 5.538	− 0.003	......	5	46.3	9.1
1678	1115	7.4	4	6 3 42.02	41.77	+ 4.795	− 0.002	......	2	47.7	14.1
1679	...	7.3	3	6 3 48.38	...	+ 5.283	− 0.002	......	2	51.2	...
1680	1117	8.6	3	6 3 48.54	48.51	+ 4.265	− 0.002	......	2	50.1	13.1
1681	1120	8.7	5	6 4 49.28	49.38	+ 5.102	− 0.006	......	3	48.8	15.2
1682	1121	7.4	5	6 5 14.10	14.20	+ 5.349	− 0.006	......	4	48.6	15.0
1683	...	4.2	4	6 5 30.10	...	+ 3.828	− 0.001	− 0.005	5	49.5	...
1684	1122	7.9	7	6 5 30.11	30.26	+ 4.891	− 0.003	......	3	45.8	15.1
1685	...	3.5	7	6 5 31.33	...	+ 3.625	− 0.001	− 0.007	18	51.6	...
1686	...	7.7	4	6 5 43.91	...	+ 4.458	− 0.002	......	2	50.0	...
1687	1114	8.1	6	6 5 44.38	44.09	+ 8.464	− 0.011	......	3	49.7	12.1
1688	1123	4.4	6	6 5 56.60	56.56	+ 5.299	− 0.006	......	5	46.0	6.5
1689	1124	6.7	8	6 6 1.52	1.53	+ 5.095	− 0.006	......	5	46.1	15.2
1690	1125	6.8	6	6 6 1.54	1.27	+ 4.477	− 0.003	......	4	46.1	10.1
1691	1127	8.1	8	6 6 24.76	24.73	+ 5.074	− 0.006	......	3	47.4	16.2
1692	...	5.7	1	6 6 28.78	...	+ 3.459	− 0.001	+ 0.007	1	52.0	...
1693	1128	6.6	4	6 6 43.36	43.08	+ 4.474	− 0.002	......	6	49.4	10.0
1694	1130	6.9	7	6 6 58.20	58.16	+ 4.173	− 0.001	......	3	46.1	13.1
1695	1131	6.9	7	6 7 23.88	23.53	+ 4.525	− 0.003	......	4	46.1	12.1
1996	1118	6.6	4	6 7 24.26	23.89	+ 9.981	− 0.023	......	4	47.9	11.1
1697	1129	7.0	5	6 7 46.63	45.68	+ 5.564	− 0.006	......	7	43.9	9.2
1698	...	7.6	7	6 7 59.90	...	+ 4.124	− 0.002	......	3	49.4	...
1699	1132	6.1	3	6 8 18.05	18.04	+ 5.331	− 0.006	......	3	45.1	15.0
1700	1133	7.6	7	6 8 27.90	27.89	+ 4.793	− 0.005	......	3	45.4	15.1
1701	1126	7.3	7	6 8 59.78	59.14	+ 9.492	− 0.026	......	4	47.1	11.1
1702	1135	7.2	7	6 9 2.80	2.59	+ 4.133	0.000	......	3	46.7	13.0
1703	1134	5.6	3	6 9 10.34	10.39	+ 4.876	− 0.006	......	7	42.8	14.6
1704	1136	6.6	6	6 9 51.88	51.93	+ 5.130	− 0.009	......	3	44.8	15.1
1705	1140	6.9	4	6 10 13.21	13.02	+ 4.290	− 0.003	......	3	48.1	13.1
1706	1139	7.4	3	6 10 17.67	17.29	+ 4.438	− 0.003	......	4	47.2	12.1
1707	...	6.4	7	6 10 33.03	...	+ 6.862	− 0.014	......	3	51.4	...
1708	...	7.4	6	6 10 43.25	...	+ 5.362	− 0.006	......	4	52.6	...
1709	1142	6.8	3	6 10 44.82	44.72	+ 4.365	− 0.003	......	2	50.0	16.1
1710	...	7.5	3	6 10 53.59	...	+ 4.465	− 0.004	......	2	48.6	...

Ordinal Number.	Mean North Polar Distance 1845.0.			Precession 1845.0.	Secular Variation.	Adopted Proper Motion.	Observations of N.P.D.			Names.
							No.	Mean year.		
R.	R.		G.				R.	R.	G.	
	o ′ ″		″	″	″	″		1800 +		
1676	50 17 28.9		27.3	+ 0.31	+ 0.61	...	3	50.8	13.1	....
1677	28 26 38.6		39.2	+ 0.32	+ 0.82	...	4	44.8	9.1	1 Lyncis ....
1678	37 46 38.4		37.2	+ 0.32	+ 0.69	...	3	44.1	14.1	....
1679	31 7 59.8		...	+ 0.33	+ 0.77	...	3	49.4	...	....
1680	48 12 39.7		41.0	+ 0.33	+ 0.61	...	2	49.7	13.1	....
1681	33 19 51.5		48.2	+ 0.42	+ 0.75	...	5	47.5	15.2	....
1682	30 23 34.0		32.3	+ 0.46	+ 0.79	...	5	46.1	15.0	....
1683	60 27 3.8		...	+ 0.48	+ 0.56	+ 0.29	8	52.4	...	44 Aurigæ κ...
1684	36 17 2.7		2.1	+ 0.48	+ 0.71	...	4	50.6	15.1	....
1685	67 27 12.7		...	+ 0.48	+ 0.53	+ 0.02	1	47.2	...	7 Geminorum η
1686	43 55 32.7		...	+ 0.50	+ 0.65	...	3	50.8	...	....
1687	13 55 4.7		4.7	+ 0.50	+ 1.23	...	4	48.7	12.1	....
1688	30 56 30.5		30.4	+ 0.52	+ 0.73	− 0.03	4	43.6	6.5	2 Lyncis ....
1689	33 25 28.5		26.5	+ 0.53	+ 0.75	...	4	45.6	15.2	....
1690	43 31 55.8		55.5	+ 0.53	+ 0.66	...	3	44.8	10.1	42 Aurigæ .....
1691	33 41 35.7		34.4	+ 0.56	+ 0.74	...	5	48.6	16.2	....
1692	73 48 53.6		...	+ 0.57	+ 0.50	− 0.05	2	55.1	...	72 Orionis f^2..
1693	43 35 12.1		11.9	+ 0.59	+ 0.66	+ 0.11	4	45.4	10.1	43 Aurigæ .....
1694	50 28 44.4		45.5	+ 0.61	+ 0.61	...	4	48.6	13.1	....
1695	42 33 17.7		15.2	+ 0.65	+ 0.67	...	3	46.1	12.1	....
1696	10 56 36.4		34.4	+ 0.65	+ 1.75	...	4	44.6	11.1	....
1697	28 10 43.4		44.8	+ 0.68	+ 0.81	+ 0.12	4	44.4	9.2	3 Lyncis ....
1698	51 42 46.6		...	+ 0.70	+ 0.60	...	4	50.6	...	....
1699	30 34 15.1		14.1	+ 0.73	+ 0.78	+ 0.02	5	47.9	15.0	4 Lyncis ....
1700	37 47 45.2		44.0	+ 0.74	+ 0.70	...	5	47.6	15.1	....
1701	11 45 5.0		6.3	+ 0.79	+ 1.40	...	3	46.5	11.1	....
1702	51 30 33.9		34.6	+ 0.79	+ 0.60	...	4	47.9	13.0	....
1703	36 29 8.7		7.6	+ 0.80	+ 0.70	...	4	45.6	14.6	45 Aurigæ .....
1704	32 57 30.8		28.7	+ 0.86	+ 0.74	...	4	45.4	15.1	....
1705	47 35 55.4		54.7	+ 0.89	+ 0.61	...	3	44.8	13.1	....
1706	44 19 40.8		40.6	+ 0.90	+ 0.65	...	3	48.1	12.1	....
1707	19 23 31.8		...	+ 0.92	+ 1.00	...	4	51.6	...	....
1708	30 13 56.4		...	+ 0.94	+ 0.77	...	3	52.4	...	....
1709	45 52 42.8		42.4	+ 0.94	+ 0.64	...	3	49.8	16.1	....
1710	43 44 33.4		...	+ 0.95	+ 0.65	...	3	47.1	...	....

Magnitude.	Estimates of Magnitude.	Mean Right Ascension 1845.0.		Precession 1845.0.	Secular Variation	Adopted Proper Motion.
R.		R.	G.			
		h. m. s.	s.	s.	s.	s.
7.4	6	6 10 54.45	...	+ 5.359	− 0.006	......
7.7	4	6 10 59.56	...	+ 4.381	− 0.003	......
7.2	6	6 12 5.56	5.42	+ 5.249	− 0.009	......
7.1	6	6 12 24.01	24.12	+ 5.264	− 0.009	− 0.004
7.5	6	6 12 32.45	31.55	+ 9.361	− 0.043	......
7.1	5	6 12 45.48	45.33	+ 4.214	− 0.003	......
5.1	4	6 12 57.46	57.07	+ 4.625	− 0.006	......
7.0	4	6 12 59.21	59.15	+ 4.225	− 0.006	......
7.9	4	6 13 4.48	4.16	+ 5.248	− 0.009	......
9.0	6	6 13 16.40	...	+ 4.210	− 0.003	......
4.8	6	6 13 16.60	16.58	+ 5.248	− 0.009	......
6.1	7	6 13 20.38	20.66	+ 5.075	− 0.009	......
6.9	6	6 13 33.72	33.02	+10.413	− 0.051	......
7.2	6	6 13 34.02	33.55	+ 4.342	− 0.003	......
3.4	14	6 13 34.97	...	+ 3.625	− 0.002	+ 0.005
8.0	6	6 13 52.08	52.07	+ 4.481	− 0.006	......
8.4	4	6 14 0.18	0.33	+ 4.227	− 0.006	......
8.2	6	6 14 4.86	...	+10.088	− 0.057	......
8.7	3	6 14 54.85	54.46	+ 4.817	− 0.006	......
7.1	5	6 15 19.66	19.59	+ 4.272	− 0.006	......
8.4	5	6 15 31.54	31.24	+ 4.207	− 0.003	......
6.9	4	6 16 10.39	10.12	+ 4.524	− 0.009	......
8.3	4	6 16 19.05	19.13	+ 4.201	− 0.003	......
5.8	4	6 16 21.06	19.91	+ 9.398	− 0.054	......
7.4	4	6 16 25.45	25.34	+ 4.810	− 0.006	......
7.5	7	6 16 34.32	34.43	+ 4.790	− 0.006	......
7.3	2	6 16 59.39	...	+ 3.337	− 0.002	......
8.8	6	6 17 10.41	10.44	+ 4.472	− 0.006	......
6.1	3	6 17 18.89	18.85	+ 5.226	− 0.011	......
8.3	4	6 18 3.69	3.65	+ 4.197	− 0.006	......
7.5	6	6 18 6.25	...	+ 4.832	− 0.009	......
6.1	4	6 18 18.66	...	+ 7.658	− 0.035	......
6.5	4	6 18 28.12	28.10	+ 4.488	− 0.006	......
8.3	6	6 19 13.68	13.31	+ 4.358	− 0.006	......
7.6	7	6 19 14.74	...	+ 6.855	− 0.026	......

Ordinal Number. R.	Mean North Polar Distance 1845.0. R.	G.	Precession 1845.0.	Secular Variation.	Adopted Proper Motion.	Observations of N.P.D. No. R.	Mean year. 1800 + R.	G.	Names.	Oeltzen-Argelander Number.
	° ′ ″	″	″	″	″					
1711	30 15 41.1	...	+ 0.95	+ 0.77	...	3	52.5	...	....	....
1712	45 31 30.4	...	+ 0.96	+ 0.64	...	3	50.5	...	....	......
1713	31 29 58.7	56.0	+ 1.06	+ 0.75	+ 0.07	4	45.6	13.2	....	5781
1714	31 19 32.3	33.1	+ 1.08	+ 0.75	− 0.04	3	45.1	13.5	....	5787
1715	11 58 51.9	51.3	+ 1.10	+ 1.38	...	3	44.5	11.1	....	....
1716	49 24 34.3	34.8	+ 1.11	+ 0.60	...	5	48.5	13.1	....	....
1717	40 38 26.7	28.5	+ 1.13	+ 0.67	...	4	44.6	8.6	46 Aurigæ	6797
1718	49 7 17.3	17.7	+ 1.14	+ 0.63	...	4	49.1	13.1	....	....
1719	31 30 22.0	17.5	+ 1.14	+ 0.76	...	4	45.2	10.2	....	6799
1720	49 30 32.1	...	+ 1.16	+ 0.61	...	2	48.1	...	....	....
1721	31 30 25.6	24.4	+ 1.16	+ 0.76	+ 0.03	6	43.8	10.2	5 Lyncis	6807
1722	33 38 27.3	27.9	+ 1.17	+ 0.75	...	4	47.4	15.0	....	6809
1723	10 17 59.3	60.3	+ 1.19	+ 1.54	...	5	49.6	10.2	....	6808
1724	46 22 40.9	40.7	+ 1.19	+ 0.65	...	4	50.1	12.2	....	....
1725	67 24 44.7	...	+ 1.19	+ 0.53	+ 0.14	9	50.1	...	13 Geminor. μ	....
1726	43 23 31.4	32.5	+ 1.21	+ 0.65	...	3	46.4	15.1	....	6819
1727	49 4 22.3	21.1	+ 1.22	+ 0.60	...	3	50.8	13.1	....	....
1728	10 46 5.3	...	+ 1.22	+ 1.49	...	3	47.1	...	....	....
1729	37 22 6.8	6.2	+ 1.30	+ 0.69	...	2	49.7	14.1	....	6817
1730	47 57 41.3	42.0	+ 1.34	+ 0.62	...	4	49.1	14.1	....	6831
1731	49 33 44.7	44.8	+ 1.36	+ 0.62	...	3	47.5	13.1	....	....
1732	42 30 45.5	45.8	+ 1.41	+ 0.65	...	4	46.6	12.1	....	....
1733	49 42 17.0	14.0	+ 1.43	+ 0.62	...	3	50.1	13.2	....	6859
1734	11 53 50.8	50.5	+ 1.43	+ 1.38	...	3	44.1	11.1	....	....
1735	37 28 1.7	5.4	+ 1.43	+ 0.69	...	3	44.8	13.7	....	6858
1736	37 47 14.9	15.8	+ 1.45	+ 0.70	...	4	47.3	13.7	....	6872
1737	78 41 51.5	...	+ 1.50	+ 0.48	...	2	52.2	...	....	....
1738	43 33 37.7	38.0	+ 1.50	+ 0.65	...	3	48.8	15.1	....	6887
1739	31 43 56.1	56.2	+ 1.51	+ 0.75	+ 0.36	3	44.5	10.2	6 Lyncis	6891
1740	49 47 28.3	25.6	+ 1.58	+ 0.62	...	4	48.6	13.2	....	....
1741	37 5 53.1	...	+ 1.58	+ 0.70	...	4	48.7	...	....	6896
1742	16 11 52.3	...	+ 1.60	+ 1.11	...	4	49.9	...	....	....
1743	43 13 25.0	25.0	+ 1.61	+ 0.65	...	3	44.4	11.8	47 Aurigæ	6900
1744	45 58 2.0	2.5	+ 1.68	+ 0.64	...	4	47.1	12.1	....	....
1745	19 23 18.5	...	+ 1.68	+ 1.01	...	4	50.1	...	....	6920

| Magnitude. | Estimates of Magnitude. | Mean Right Ascension 1845.0. | | Precession 1845.0. | Secular Variation | Adopted Proper Motion. |
	R.	R.	G.			
		h. m. s.	s.	s.	s.	s.
7.0	7	6 19 27.34	27.26	+ 4.249	− 0.006	......
7.5	6	6 19 30.59	30.20	+ 4.355	− 0.007	......
5.8	4	6 19 40.46	40.39	+10.410	− 0.089	......
8.3	6	6 20 28.48	28.01	+ 4.347	− 0.009	. ...
8.2	6	6 21 8.71	8.65	+ 4.379	− 0.006	......
7.7	6	6 21 33.30	33.05	+ 4.809	− 0.009	......
7.2	5	6 21 36.51	36.64	+ 4.477	− 0.006	......
6.5	7	6 21 38.44	38.20	+ 5.004	− 0.011	......
8.5	6	6 21 38.85	38.85	+ 4.481	− 0.009	......
8.4	5	6 22 8.59	8.33	+ 5.014	− 0.014	......
8.1	6	6 22 9.42	9.22	+ 5.208	− 0.017	......
6.9	4	6 22 45.58	44.93	+ 5.218	− 0.017	......
7.1	3	6 22 56.02	55.64	+ 4.168	− 0.009	......
6.2	3	6 22 57.16	56.99	+ 5.080	− 0.014	......
6.1	6	6 23 30.73	31.09	+ 5.530	− 0.020	......
6.8	4	6 23 41.73	41.52	+ 4.116	− 0.006	......
8.9	3	6 24 1.44	...	+ 4.133	− 0.009	......
7.9	5	6 24 1.53	1.36	+ 4.133	− 0.009	......
7.0	8	6 24 21.38	20.81	+ 5.528	− 0.017	......
6.2	6	6 24 27.14	27.10	+ 5.115	− 0.017	......
7.1	4	6 24 42.02	41.71	+ 4.346	− 0.006	......
7.4	5	6 24 47.03	46.76	+ 5.002	− 0.014	......
5.7	5	6 25 53.22	53.16	+ 4.129	− 0.009	......
5.3	92	6 25 59.55	62.96	+30.822	− 1.476	− 0.027
8.2	7	6 26 6.72	...	+ 6.196	− 0.027	......
6.9	5	6 26 10.48	10.31	+ 5.573	− 0.020	......
7.2	5	6 26 17.41	17.17	+ 5.213	− 0.017	......
9.1	5	6 26 37.24	36.97	+ 4.128	− 0.009	......
8.2	6	6 27 9.51	9.51	+ 4.372	− 0.009	......
7.4	6	6 27 36.47	36.01	+ 5.115	− 0.017	......
7.1	6	6 27 42.29	42.02	+ 4.252	− 0.011	......
5.9	7	6 27 54.87	54.72	+ 4.165	− 0.006	......
7.1	6	6 27 57.62	57.37	+ 5.055	− 0.017	......
7.5	5	6 28 0.96	0.58	+ 4.249	− 0.009	......
5.6	3	6 28 1.24	0.94	+ 4.184	− 0.009	......

Ordinal Number. R.	Mean North Polar Distance 1845.0. R.	G.	Precession 1845.0.	Secular Variation.	Adopted Proper Motion.	Observations of N.P.D. No. R.	Mean year. R.	G.	Names.	Oeltzen-Argelander Number.
	o ' "	"	"	"	"		1800 +			
1746	48 30 13.2	12.1	+ 1.70	+ 0.62	...	5	48.1	13.1	....	......
1747	46 1 25.0	26.3	+ 1.71	+ 0.65	...	4	47.7	12.1	....	......
1748	10 17 6.4	6.5	+ 1.72	+ 1.52	+ 0.61	6	48.1	10.2	....	6932
1749	46 11 13.6	10.7	+ 1.79	+ 0.64	...	3	49.2	12.2	....	......
1750	45 29 6.1	4.4	+ 1.85	+ 0.65	...	5	49.5	13.2	....	......
1751	37 25 51.2	48.1	+ 1.88	+ 0.69	...	4	47.3	13.0	....	......
1752	43 25 14.5	15.5	+ 1.89	+ 0.66	...	3	44.8	14.8	....	......
1753	34 32 30.1	29.0	+ 1.89	+ 0.73	+ 0.03	6	48.3	11.2	7 Lyncis	6966
1754	43 19 16.6	15.7	+ 1.89	+ 0.65	...	4	48.4	14.8	....	......
1755	34 23 31.0	28.2	+ 1.93	+ 0.72	...	4	48.6	11.2	....	6980
1756	31 54 13.1	11.0	+ 1.93	+ 0.74	...	4	47.1	11.2	....	......
1757	31 46 26.9	18.5	+ 1.99	+ 0.77	...	4	46.6	11.2	....	......
1758	50 26 43.9	43.2	+ 2.00	+ 0.60	...	3	47.5	14.1	....	......
1759	33 30 1.3	0.7	+ 2.00	+ 0.73	+ 0.05	4	44.9	10.2	9 Lyncis	6994
1760	28 23 31.6	30.0	+ 2.05	+ 0.79	+ 0.25	5	48.1	9.1	8 Lyncis	7005
1761	51 48 51.2	53.1	+ 2.07	+ 0.60	...	3	46.8	13.1	....	......
1762	51 21 ...	...	......	...	...	...	...	...	....	......
1763	51 20 56.3	57.1	+ 2.10	+ 0.61	...	3	49.8	13.1	....	......
1764	28 24 11.9	11.3	+ 2.13	+ 0.82	+ 0.01	6	43.5	9.1	10 Lyncis	7015
1765	33 1 33.2	34.0	+ 2.13	+ 0.73	− 0.01	5	47.6	11.1	11 Lyncis	7019
1766	46 10 45.9	44.0	+ 2.16	+ 0.64	...	4	48.2	12.1	....	......
1767	34 31 26.2	23.9	+ 2.16	+ 0.72	...	3	45.5	11.2	....	7026
1768	51 26 9.5	10.1	+ 2.26	+ 0.60	...	4	51.1	13.1	....	......
1769	2 44 25.7	24.6	+ 2.27	+ 4.49	...	122	46.5	7.1	_[handwritten]_	......
1770	23 1 15.5	...	+ 2.28	+ 0.91	...	4	49.1	...	....	7038
1771	27 57 11.3	10.7	+ 2.28	+ 0.80	...	4	47.4	10.2	41 Camelopardi	7040
1772	31 46 46.7	45.4	+ 2.29	+ 0.75	...	4	45.9	11.2	....	7045
1773	51 27 0.0	0.5	+ 2.32	+ 0.59	...	3	51.5	13.1	....	......
1774	45 33 48.5	47.0	+ 2.37	+ 0.63	...	5	50.8	13.2	....	......
1775	32 59 12.6	12.3	+ 2.41	+ 0.75	...	4	45.7	11.1	....	7064
1776	48 17 37.6	40.0	+ 2.42	+ 0.63	...	3	48.5	12.1	....	......
1777	50 28 44.8	42.7	+ 2.44	+ 0.62	...	3	45.7	8.8	51 Aurigæ	......
1778	33 46 14.7	12.6	+ 2.44	+ 0.74	...	5	48.7	11.2	....	7066
1779	48 22 42.8	44.4	+ 2.44	+ 0.61	...	3	45.8	12.1	....	......
1780	49 58 17.1	16.6	+ 2.45	+ 0.59	...	3	45.8	8.8	52 Aurigæ	......

Magnitude.	Estimates of Magnitude.	Mean Right Ascension 1845.0.		Precession 1845.0.	Secular Variation	Adopted Proper Motion.
	R.	R.	G.			
		h. m. s.	s.	s.	s.	s.
5.2	2	6 28 15.44	15.17	+ 4.291	− 0.009	+ 0.003
7.6	5	6 28 19.22	...	+ 4.270	− 0.007	......
6.6	5	6 28 43.00	42.87	+ 4.557	− 0.011	......
2.6	2	6 28 45.42	...	+ 3.464	− 0.003	......
8.6	6	6 28 49.88	...	+ 4.281	− 0.008	......
6.7	5	6 28 55.95	55.72	+ 4.372	− 0.009	......
6.6	5	6 29 27.16	26.79	+ 5.683	− 0.026	......
7.6	7	6 29 44.10	43.90	+ 5.098	− 0.017	......
7.5	6	6 31 8.32	8.10	+ 5.327	− 0.020	......
8.3	6	6 31 9.02	...	+ 5.131	− 0.017	......
7.0	6	6 31 13.71	13.35	+ 5.116	− 0.017	......
8.5	6	6 31 44.84	44.50	+ 4.149	− 0.009	......
5.2	9	6 31 47.85	47.68	+ 4.379	− 0.009	......
7.1	8	6 31 53.04	53.01	+ 4.144	− 0.009	......
8.4	5	6 32 20.54	19.78	+ 4.374	− 0.011	......
8.0	5	6 32 30.70	...	+ 5.325	− 0.020	......
5.8	5	6 32 31.83	31.63	+ 5.325	− 0.020	......
7.6	5	6 32 49.15	48.87	+ 5.690	− 0.026	......
7.0	9	6 33 25.91	25.58	+ 4.211	− 0.009	......
7.0	6	6 33 29.21	28.90	+ 4.376	− 0.011	......
5.5	8	6 33 35.98	35.59	+ 5.132	− 0.020	......
7.5	6	6 34 11.51	10.65	+ 4.364	− 0.011	......
3.6	4	6 34 23.67	...	+ 3.694	− 0.005	......
4.8	6	6 34 45.74	45.43	+ 6.298	− 0.034	+ 0.006
7.2	7	6 35 15.42	...	+ 5.018	− 0.019	......
6.7	3	6 35 16.16	...	+ 5.018	− 0.019	......
5.7	5	6 35 33.73	33.51	+ 4.333	− 0.011	+ 0.003
8.8	8	6 35 35.39	...	+ 4.333	− 0.011	......
5.5	5	6 35 50.04	49.99	+ 4.587	− 0.012	+ 0.003
4.1	5	6 36 35.33	...	+ 3.376	− 0.003	− 0.007
5.5	17	6 36 57.40	57.04	+ 6.517	− 0.049	+ 0.005
7.9	5	6 37 11.84	...	+ 4.833	− 0.016	......
4.4	14	6 37 22.71	21.09	+ 8.858	− 0.100	+ 0.014
8.3	6	6 37 37.78	37.94	+ 5.165	− 0.026	......
7.9	6	6 38 1.07	...	+ 5.307	− 0.023	......

Ordinal Number. R.	Mean North Polar Distance 1845.0.		Precession 1845.0.	Secular Variation.	Adopted Proper Motion.	Observations of N.P.D.			Names.	Oeltzen-Argelander Number.
	R.	G.				No. R.	Mean year R.	Mean year G.		
	° ′ ″	″	″	″	″		1800 +			
1781	47 22 53.3	53.0	+ 2.47	+ 0.61	...	3	46.8	8.8	50 Aurigæ	......
1782	47 52 1.2	...	+ 2.47	+ 0.62	...	3	51.1	...	....	......
1783	45 51 25.3	25.2	+ 2.51	+ 0.64	...	3	46.8	14.1	....	......
1784	73 28 27.5	...	+ 2.51	+ 0.50	+ 0.04	3	52.8	...	24 Geminor. γ	......
1785	47 37 24.3	...	+ 2.52	+ 0.62	...	2	53.2	...	....	......
1786	45 32 11.0	9.3	+ 2.52	+ 0.62	...	4	47.2	13.2	....	......
1787	26 53 53.2	52.5	+ 2.57	+ 0.83	...	4	44.7	11.2	....	7092
1788	33 10 14.7	13.8	+ 2.59	+ 0.72	...	4	45.7	11.1	....	7099
1789	30 24 31.4	31.4	+ 2.72	+ 0.78	...	5	47.7	10.1	....	7126
1790	32 44 10.3	...	+ 2.72	+ 0.75	...	4	48.2	...	....	7128
1791	32 55 27.0	23.2	+ 2.72	+ 0.73	...	3	44.8	11.1	....	7131
1792	50 49 34.5	35.5	+ 2.77	+ 0.60	...	3	51.2	13.1	......	......
1793	45 20 2.5	2.2	+ 2.77	+ 0.62	+ 0.02	4	44.7	9.5	55 Aurigæ	7145
1794	50 57 53.2	49.6	+ 2.78	+ 0.59	...	3	50.1	13.1	......	......
1795	45 26 7.1	5.8	+ 2.82	+ 0.63	...	3	49.4	12.2	....	......
1796	30 24 32.0	...	+ 2.84	+ 0.78	...	3	43.8	...	12 Lyncis (1st)	......
1797	30 24 37.0	36.6	+ 2.84	+ 0.78	...	7	48.4	10.2	12 Lyncis (2d)	7156
1798	26 47 35.1	36.0	+ 2.86	+ 0.82	...	3	47.5	11.2	....	7163
1799	49 13 28.0	23.2	+ 2.91	+ 0.59	...	5	48.5	13.1	......	......
1800	45 20 50.2	51.3	+ 2.92	+ 0.63	...	4	46.1	12.1	......	......
1801	32 40 42.9	42.3	+ 2.93	+ 0.74	+ 0.06	4	44.9	11.1	13 Lyncis	7172
1802	45 36 34.1	25.1	+ 2.98	+ 0.63	...	4	48.7	12.2	....	......
1803	64 43 16.2	...	+ 3.00	+ 0.53	+ 0.02	3	51.8	...	27 Geminor. ε	......
1804	22 16 3.4	2.8	+ 3.03	+ 0.91	...	5	46.8	8.2	42 Camelopardi	7199
1805	34 8 6.2	...	+ 3.07	+ 0.73	...	4	47.1	...	....	7206
1806	34 8 5.5	...	+ 3.07	+ 0.73	...	3	46.8	...	....	......
1807	46 16 30.8	33.4	+ 3.10	+ 0.63	− 0.14	5	46.5	8.8	56 Aurigæ (1st)	......
1808	46 15 40.3	...	+ 3.10	+ 0.63	...	4	48.1	...	56 Aurigæ (2d)	......
1809	41 3 15.3	16.1	+ 3.12	+ 0.65	...	4	43.7	11.2	57 Aurigæ	7218
1810	76 56 33.1	...	+ 3.19	+ 0.49	+ 0.22	4	48.7	...	31 Geminor. ξ	......
1811	20 56 33.2	32.0	+ 3.22	+ 0.94	...	8	44.9	7.8	43 Camelopardi	......
1812	36 48 13.1	...	+ 3.24	+ 0.70	...	4	50.1	...	....	7233
1813	12 50 24.9	24.6	+ 3.26	+ 1.30	...	11	46.3	8.7	44 Camel.	7231
1814	32 11 3.3	4.0	+ 3.28	+ 0.75	...	4	46.9	15.0	....	......
1815	30 31 28.8	...	+ 3.31	+ 0.76	...	4	45.6	...	....	7245

Ordinal Number.		Magnitude.	Estimates of Magnitude.	Mean Right Ascension 1845.0.		Precession 1845.0.	Secular Variation	Adopted Proper Motion.	Observations of R.A.		
R.	G.	R.	R.	R.	G.				No. R.	Mean year R.	G.
				h. m. s.	s.	s.	s.	s.		1800 +	
1816	...	1.0	A	6 38 19.20	...	+ 2.679	− 0.001	− 0.035	24	45.5	...
1817	1222	5.2	6	6 39 24.04	23.74	+ 5.317	− 0.026	....	5	45.4	10.2
1818	...	8.2	2	6 39 25.20	...	+ 4.175	− 0.010	....	3	53.4	...
1819	1223	8.5	5	6 39 26.73	26.73	+ 4.136	− 0.011	....	3	47.5	11.1
1820	1224	4.7	6	6 39 47.99	47.73	+ 4.254	− 0.011	....	5	46.9	8.4
1821	1225	7.9	8	6 39 58.28	58.22	+ 4.351	− 0.014	....	4	48.6	15.1
1822	...	8.2	6	6 40 0.83	...	+ 5.011	− 0.021	....	2	51.1	...
1823	1226	6.8	7	6 41 14.33	14.08	+ 4.735	− 0.017	....	5	46.9	11.2
1824	1227	8.2	4	6 41 17.70	17.49	+ 4.743	− 0.014	....	4	46.6	11.2
1825	...	8.5	7	6 41 41.10	...	+ 4.733	− 0.017	....	3	46.3	...
1826	...	6.7	8	6 41 49.07	...	+ 4.385	− 0.013	....	4	51.6	...
1827	1229	6.4	9	6 42 21.25	21.40	+ 4.136	− 0.010	+ 0.011	7	50.4	11.1
1828	1230	6.4	8	6 42 35.35	35.09	+ 4.120	− 0.011	....	6	50.3	10.2
1829	1233	7.9	8	6 43 18.02	17.50	+ 4.215	− 0.011	....	3	45.5	12.1
1830	1234	6.5	4	6 43 19.15	19.08	+ 4.122	− 0.009	....	4	45.4	10.2
1831	1236	7.4	4	6 43 41.72	41.55	+ 4.300	− 0.011	....	3	44.4	14.1
1832	1228	5.8	7	6 43 42.13	41.57	+ 6.885	− 0.057	....	5	44.3	13.2
1833	1231	4.7	4	6 43 50.31	50.15	+ 5.222	− 0.029	+ 0.004	5	45.5	8.2
1834	...	6.8	6	6 43 50.52	...	+ 4.430	− 0.014	....	3	51.5	...
1835	1235	5.6	7	6 43 57.44	57.41	+ 5.150	− 0.029	+ 0.006	4	43.7	11.6
1836	1237	6.7	6	6 44 2.99	2.97	+ 4.342	− 0.011	....	3	46.8	15.2
1837	1232	6.7	7	6 44 42.84	42.17	+ 6.644	− 0.054	....	5	46.8	13.1
1838	...	8.4	4	6 44 45.32	...	+ 5.236	− 0.026	....	2	51.7	...
1839	...	8.1	4	6 44 53.26	...	+ 5.246	− 0.026	....	3	53.2	...
1840	1241	6.9	5	6 44 58.00	57.90	+ 4.098	− 0.011	....	3	44.8	12.1
1841	...	6.6	5	6 45 3.84	...	+ 4.450	− 0.014	....	2	51.7	...
1842	1240	8.3	6	6 45 22.81	22.43	+ 5.150	− 0.029	....	4	47.4	14.2
1843	...	6.5	4	6 45 26.09	...	+ 4.471	− 0.015	....	2	51.7	...
1844	1242	8.2	6	6 45 35.65	35.41	+ 5.153	− 0.026	....	4	48.6	11.2
1845	1238	8.0	6	6 45 35.73	35.55	+ 6.608	− 0.057	....	3	47.1	13.1
1846	1239	7.7	5	6 45 51.48	51.27	+ 6.557	− 0.057	....	2	48.2	13.2
1847	...	5.0	1	6 45 53.95	...	+ 3.382	− 0.004	....	1	52.0	...
1848	1243	5.0	5	6 46 17.97	17.77	+ 4.393	− 0.014	....	4	46.3	9.1
1849	1246	7.0	7	6 46 56.80	56.67	+ 4.244	− 0.014	....	3	47.1	14.1
1850	1244	6.8	5	6 47 11.88	12.15	+ 5.739	− 0.037	....	2	44.7	15.2

Ordinal Number.	Mean North Polar Distance 1845.0.		Precession 1845.0.	Secular Variation.	Adopted Proper Motion.	Observations of N.P.D.				Names.	Oeltzen-Argelander Number.
						No.	Mean year.				
R.	R.	G.				R.	R.	G.			
	o ′ ″	″	″	″	″		1800 +				
1816	106 30 28.2	...	+ 3.34	+ 0.38	+ 1.24	23	47.8	...	9 Can. Maj. α	......
1817	30 22 35.5	35.3	+ 3.43	+ 0.76	+ 0.04	6	45.5	10.2	14 Lyncis......	7270
1818	49 52 19.7	...	+ 3.43	+ 0.60	...	1	57.1	...	....	......
1819	51 0 15.0	15.5	+ 3.43	+ 0.58	...	3	46.8	11.1	....	......
1820	48 2 35.7	37.5	+ 3.46	+ 0.60	+ 0.13	4	44.1	8.4	58 Aurigæ	......
1821	45 46 6.3	4.8	+ 3.48	+ 0.63	...	5	47.0	15.1	....	......
1822	34 8 45.1	...	+ 3.48	+ 0.73	...	4	49.2	...	....	7279
1823	38 18 14.2	11.3	+ 3.59	+ 0.68	...	4	44.7	11.2	....	7298
1824	38 10 37.1	35.4	+ 3.59	+ 0.67	...	4	46.9	11.2	....	7299
1825	38 19 34.1	...	+ 3.63	+ 0.68	...	6	48.3	...	....	7308
1826	44 58 46.7	...	+ 3.64	+ 0.63	...	5	51.5	...	....	......
1827	50 57 10.5	10.3	+ 3.68	+ 0.58	...	4	47.3	11.1	59 Aurigæ	......
1828	51 22 31.2	29.2	+ 3.70	+ 0.58	+ 0.15	4	46.7	10.2	60 Aurigæ	......
1829	48 55 26.8	26.0	+ 3.77	+ 0.62	...	5	46.4	12.1	....	......
1830	51 18 43.0	42.3	+ 3.77	+ 0.60	+ 0.01	4	47.6	10.2	61 Aurigæ	......
1831	46 52 5.9	5.2	+ 3.80	+ 0.61	...	3	44.8	14.1	....	......
1832	18 59 41.6	40.5	+ 3.80	+ 0.99	...	5	45.2	13.2	....	......
1833	31 22 57.4	60.1	+ 3.81	+ 0.74	+ 0.18	4	43.7	8.2	15 Lyncis......	7348
1834	43 59 7.1	...	+ 3.81	+ 0.63	...	4	51.9	...	....	7349
1835	32 14 54.3	54.3	+ 3.82	+ 0.73	− 0.01	6	44.0	11.5	....	......
1836	45 54 13.9	12.8	+ 3.83	+ 0.62	...	4	45.7	15.2	....	......
1837	20 9 16.2	15.1	+ 3.89	+ 0.96	...	4	44.2	13.1	....	7359
1838	31 12 10.1	...	+ 3.89	+ 0.75	...	3	49.5	...	....	7360
1839	31 4 42.1	...	+ 3.90	+ 0.75	...	2	53.7	...	....	7366
1840	51 53 42.1	43.0	+ 3.91	+ 0.59	...	3	51.1	12.1	....	......
1841	43 32 10.8	...	+ 3.92	+ 0.64	...	3	52.5	...	....	7369
1842	32 13 13.9	13.8	+ 3.95	+ 0.75	...	3	42.5	14.2	....	......
1843	43 6 0.1	...	+ 3.95	+ 0.64	...	2	52.1	...	....	7376
1844	32 10 41.6	40.8	+ 3.96	+ 0.73	...	3	44.5	11.2	....	......
1845	20 19 34.6	35.0	+ 3.96	+ 0.93	...	3	46.5	13.1	....	7378
1846	20 35 19.7	19.7	+ 3.98	+ 0.92	...	4	47.9	13.2	....	7381
1847	76 37 51.4	...	+ 3.99	+ 0.48	...	2	55.1	...	38 Geminorum	......
1848	44 42 41.4	41.4	+ 4.02	+ 0.61	+ 0.01	4	43.6	9.1	16 Lyncis......	7391
1849	48 5 46.4	45.0	+ 4.08	+ 0.61	...	4	48.1	14.1	....	......
1850	26 7 6.9	6.8	+ 4.10	+ 0.81	...	4	45.7	15.2	....	7400

Magnitude.	Estimates of Magnitude.	Mean Right Ascension 1845.0.		Precession 1845.0.	Secular Variation	Adopted Proper Motion.
R.		R.	G.			
		h. m. s.	s.	s.	s.	s.
8.9	6	6 47 37.40	...	+ 6.838	— 0.066	......
7.9	6	6 47 49.09	49.11	+ 4.099	— 0.011	......
8.2	4	6 47 52.78	52.70	+ 5.146	— 0.029	......
6.8	17	6 48 16.63	22.46	+ 6.855	— 0.066	......
7.1	4	6 48 19.97	20.04	+ 4.269	— 0.014	......
6.2	11	6 48 28.85	28.72	+ 4.101	— 0.011	......
7.2	5	6 48 30.54	30.20	+ 4.941	— 0.023	......
9.4	4	6 48 43.36	...	+ 4.251	— 0.014	......
7.8	6	6 49 0.24	...	+ 4.250	— 0.014	......
8.7	7	6 49 5.80	...	+ 4.262	— 0.015	......
9.1	6	6 49 23.58	...	+ 4.264	— 0.015	......
7.4	6	6 49 31.47	31.70	+ 4.259	— 0.011	......
7.1	7	6 49 56.15	55.73	+ 5.170	— 0.031	......
7.3	74	6 50 19.43	20.16	+81.280	—22.435	— 0.323
8.6	6	6 50 22.68	...	+ 4.485	— 0.018	......
8.7	4	6 50 29.31	28.77	+ 4.941	— 0.023	......
8.0	6	6 52 12.02	11.73	+ 4.490	— 0.017	......
6.1	9	6 52 19.03	18.74	+ 5.328	— 0.034	+ 0.008
7.1	5	6 52 27.83	27.93	+ 4.479	— 0.017	......
1.7	A	6 52 32.13	...	+ 2.355	— 0.001	......
8.7	5	6 52 34.00	...	+ 5.358	— 0.033	......
7.2	7	6 53 10.02	9.88	+ 4.193	— 0.014	......
8.0	1	6 53 19.57	...	+ 4.795	— 0.023	......
7.0	7	6 53 19.71	19.67	+ 4.795	— 0.023	......
6.7	6	6 53 31.21	...	+ 4.514	— 0.018	......
8.5	6	6 54 30.37	32.16	+ 4.478	— 0.017	......
4.3	13	6 54 54.83	...	+ 3.563	— 0.006	— 0.001
4.7	A	6 55 32.73	...	+ 2.389	— 0.001	......
6.3	4	6 55 41.96	42.33	+11.774	— 0.314	......
6.4	5	6 55 43.21	42.81	+ 5.413	— 0.040	+ 0.003
7.9	5	6 55 50.32	...	+ 5.409	— 0.035	......
6.6	7	6 55 51.28	50.55	+ 7.077	— 0.083	......
9.0	5	6 56 16.47	...	+ 5.094	— 0.030	......
6.6	9	6 56 56.41	56.07	+ 4.334	— 0.014	......
7.6	3	6 57 20.04	...	+ 5.110	— 0.031	......

Ordinal Number.	Mean North Polar Distance 1845.0.		Precession 1845.0.	Secular Variation.	Adopted Proper Motion.	Observations of N.P.D.			Names.	Oeltzen Argelander Number.
						No.	Mean year.			
R.	R.	G.				R.	R.	G.		
	° ′ ″	″	″	″	″		1800 +			
1851	19 8 42.0	...	+ 4.14	+ 0.97	...	3	48.2	...	....	7409
1852	51 48 44.2	42.3	+ 4.15	+ 0.57	...	4	48.1	10.2	....	......
1853	32 12 7.6	5.0	+ 4.16	+ 0.73	...	3	44.1	13.3	....	7415
1854	19 3 18.3	18.8	+ 4.19	+ 0.95	...	18	51.5	13.1	....	7422
1855	47 29 1.1	3.1	+ 4.20	+ 0.61	...	3	44.8	12.1	....	......
1856	51 44 28.9	28.8	+ 4.21	+ 0.58	+ 0.10	4	45.7	10.2	62 Aurigæ	......
1857	34 56 14.7	11.6	+ 4.21	+ 0.69	...	3	44.5	11.2	....	7427
1858	47 53 56.4	...	+ 4.23	+ 0.61	...	4	49.7	...	....	......
1859	47 55 34.8	...	+ 4.25	+ 0.61	...	3	51.2	...	....	......
1860	47 36 41.7	...	+ 4.26	+ 0.61	...	3	49.1	...	....	......
1861	47 33 29.6	...	+ 4.29	+ 0.61	...	3	49.8	...	....	......
1862	47 42 8.8	9.9	+ 4.30	+ 0.60	...	4	48.9	12.1	....	......
1863	31 51 33.3	31.8	+ 4.33	+ 0.72	...	5	43.6	11.1	....	7451
1864	0 57 21.2	21.0	+ 4.37	+ 11.34	...	43	45.5	7.1	*Bic. 7. 3. 20.*	......
1865	42 40 53.3	...	+ 4.37	+ 0.64	...	4	50.4	...	....	7458
1866	34 53 27.1	24.8	+ 4.38	+ 0.70	...	4	45.7	11.2	....	7461
1867	42 31 34.8	34.2	+ 4.53	+ 0.64	...	3	44.1	11.2	....	7485
1868	29 58 39.5	39.5	+ 4.54	+ 0.76	+ 0.02	6	46.5	11.1	....	7488
1869	42 44 2.3	0.9	+ 4.55	+ 0.63	...	4	45.2	11.2	....	7492
1870	118 45 53.4	...	+ 4.56	+ 0.33	+ 0.02	11	49.2	...	21 Can. Maj. ε	......
1871	29 38 58.9	...	+ 4.56	+ 0.76	...	3	45.2	...	....	7494
1872	49 12 0.2	3.8	+ 4.61	+ 0.59	...	3	44.5	11.6	....	......
1873	37 1 1.0	...	+ 4.62	+ 0.67	...	3	43.5	...	....	7501
1874	37 1 4.3	2.1	+ 4.62	+ 0.67	+ 0.02	4	45.4	11.1	....	......
1875	42 0 14.0	...	+ 4.64	+ 0.63	...	3	47.9	...	....	......
1676	42 42 5.2	2.2	+ 4.73	+ 0.64	...	4	46.9	11.2	....	7522
1877	69 12 29.1	...	+ 4.76	+ 0.50	+ 0.01	7	49.1	...	43 Geminor. ζ	......
1878	117 42 58.7	...	+ 4.81	+ 0.34	+ 0.01	4	52.1	...	22 Can. Maj. ..	......
1879	8 28 45.4	45.8	+ 4.83	+ 1.69	...	4	43.7	7.5	....	......
1880	28 58 21.3	20.5	+ 4.83	+ 0.77	...	4	44.1	9.1	17 Lyncis	......
1881	29 1 14.6	...	+ 4.84	+ 0.77	...	4	45.1	...	....	......
1882	17 56 34.6	35.7	+ 4.85	+ 1.04	...	5	47.5	10.2	....	......
1883	32 39 26.1	...	+ 4.87	+ 0.72	...	3	50.9	...	....	......
1884	45 43 37.3	36.1	+ 4.93	+ 0.64	...	4	43.7	11.2	....	......
1885	32 24 31.0	...	+ 4.96	+ 0.72	...	3	48.8	..	....	7564

Ordinal Number.		Magnitude.	Estimates of Magnitude.	Mean Right Ascension 1845.0.		Precession 1845.0.	Secular Variation	Adopted Proper Motion.	Observations of R.A.		
R.	G.	R.		R.	G.				No. R.	Mean year. R.	G.
				h. m. s.	s.	s.	s.	s.		1800 +	
1886	1267	7.6	6	6 57 54.42	54.40	+ 4.342	— 0.017	......	3	45.5	11.2
1887	1259	4.9	6	6 58 6.96	5.99	+13.163	— 0.452	+ 0.009	5	43.3	8.0
1888	1266	7.3	6	6 58 11.65	12.95	+ 5.556	— 0.043	......	4	44.6	10.2
1889	1268	7.8	5	6 58 43.32	42.86	+ 4.976	— 0.031	......	3	45.1	11.1
1890	...	8.2	4	6 59 9.69	...	+ 4.618	— 0.022	......	3	48.1	...
1891	...	6.6	5	7 0 5.04	...	+ 4.610	— 0.022	......	3	47.5	...
1892	1270	7.6	6	7 0 26.43	26.30	+ 4.164	— 0.017	......	3	44.8	12.1
1893	1269	7.2	3	7 0 33.66	33.31	+ 4.895	— 0.020	......	3	44.5	11.1
1894	...	7.4	6	7 0 41.08	...	+ 5.537	— 0.043	......	3	48.2	...
1895	1271	7.0	8	7 0 53.64	53.59	+ 4.319	— 0.020	......	7	44.1	11.2
1896	1273	4.7	7	7 0 59.15	58.92	+ 4.135	— 0.017	+ 0.005	11	50.0	8.0
1897	...	4.0	1	7 1 16.01	...	+ 3.829	— 0.010	— 0.003	2	40.1	...
1898	1272	5.5	7	7 1 17.33	17.08	+ 4.701	— 0.026	......	5	44.9	10.2
1899	1275	7.8	5	7 1 21.41	21.22	+ 4.325	— 0.020	......	3	47.2	11.2
1900	1274	7.4	5	7 1 54.86	54.46	+ 5.305	— 0.037	......	4	44.9	13.1
1901	1277	7.1	5	7 2 5.02	4.53	+ 4.477	— 0.017	......	3	47.8	11.1
1902	...	4.0	1	7 2 5.48	...	+ 2.438	— 0.001	......	2	54.2	...
1903	1276	5.1	6	7 2 21.25	21.25	+ 5.292	— 0.040	......	5	45.4	11.1
1904	1279	8.4	3	7 3 8.42	8.42	+ 4.088	— 0.017	......	2	46.2	13.2
1905	...	7.4	6	7 3 26.27	...	+ 4.699	— 0.025	......	3	45.8	...
1906	...	7.0	1	7 3 57.72	...	+ 3.447	— 0.006	......	1	52.1	...
1907	1281	6.0	8	7 4 18.85	18.57	+ 4.473	— 0.020	......	4	44.3	11.1
1908	1282	6.9	6	7 4 20.33	20.24	+ 4.385	— 0.020	......	4	46.1	13.1
1909	1280	7.6	6	7 4 24.99	24.66	+ 4.732	— 0.026	......	4	47.1	11.1
1910	...	5.3	2	7 4 28.05	...	+ 3.449	— 0.007	......	1	57.1	...
1911	...	7.7	6	7 4 58.57	...	+ 3.437	— 0.006	......	4	53.6	...
1912	1283	7.1	3	7 5 11.72	11.45	+ 5.221	— 0.040	......	5	43.5	10.2
1913	1284	5.9	9	7 5 22.72	22.51	+ 4.735	— 0.029	......	5	44.0	11.1
1914	1285	7.3	7	7 5 43.66	43.13	+ 5.238	— 0.040	+ 0.011	5	45.8	9.2
1915	1278	6.6	7	7 6 9.26	9.29	+11.341	— 0.354	......	5	46.7	7.5
1916	1286	6.4	6	7 6 24.45	23.90	+ 5.247	— 0.043	......	5	45.9	9.2
1917	...	5.4	7	7 6 44.50	...	+ 4.582	— 0.024	......	3	47.5	...
1918	1287	7.4	6	7 6 46.46	46.53	+ 4.369	— 0.020	......	3	47.1	14.1
1919	1288	7.0	7	7 7 6.95	6.83	+ 4.112	— 0.017	......	3	45.4	12.1
1920	...	8.1	3	7 7 13.69	...	+ 4.911	— 0.034	......	3	51.4	...

| Ordinal Number. | Mean North Polar Distance 1845.0. | | Precession 1845.0. | Secular Variation. | Adopted Proper Motion. | Observations of N.P.D. | | | Names. | Oeltzen-Argelander Number. |
R.	R.	G.				No. R.	Mean year. R.	G.		
	o ′ ″	″	″	″	″		1800 +			
1886	45 30 12.6	12.1	+ 5.01	+ 0.60	...	5	48.1	11.2	....	......
1887	7 18 37.7	36.8	+ 5.03	+ 1.87	+ 0.02	7	42.6	8.0	....	......
1888	27 29 36.6	32.6	+ 5.04	+ 0.79	...	4	44.6	10.2	....	......
1889	34 8 40.6	37.6	+ 5.08	+ 0.70	...	3	44.5	11.1	....	7581
1890	39 51 21.5	...	+ 5.12	+ 0.65	...	3	46.8	...	....	7593
1891	39 57 50.9	...	+ 5.20	+ 0.65	...	4	48.1	...	....	7605
1892	49 42 29.1	27.1	+ 5.23	+ 0.59	...	3	49.5	12.1	....	......
1893	35 15 29.8	29.2	+ 5.24	+ 0.70	...	4	44.6	11.1	....	......
1894	27 36 36.0	...	+ 5.25	+ 0.79	...	3	46.9	...	....	7614
1895	45 54 32.3	30.9	+ 5.27	+ 0.62	...	4	46.5	11.2	....	......
1896	50 25 59.2	61.5	+ 5.27	+ 0.58	...	6	47.5	8.0	63 Aurigæ.....	......
1897	59 30 25.1	...	+ 5.30	+ 0.54	+ 0.05	1	47.2	...	46 Geminor. τ	......
1898	38 19 19.8	17.5	+ 5.30	+ 0.66	...	5	47.0	10.2	....	7622
1899	45 45 42.6	41.1	+ 5.30	+ 0.59	...	3	43.9	11.2	....	......
1900	29 58 8.1	7.4	+ 5.35	+ 0.74	...	3	43.2	13.1	....	......
1901	42 28 55.9	57.0	+ 5.37	+ 0.64	...	4	45.7	11.1	....	......
1902	116 9 2.6	...	+ 5.36	+ 0.34	− 0.01	7	53.0	...	25 Can. Maj. δ	......
1903	30 5 41.2	41.0	+ 5.39	+ 0.75	+ 0.29	5	44.5	11.1	18 Lyncis......	......
1904	51 38 14.6	14.1	+ 5.45	+ 0.56	...	3	49.8	13.2	....	......
1905	38 17 31.5	...	+ 5.48	+ 0.67	...	5	48.3	...	....	7663
1906	74 34 2.2	...	+ 5.53	+ 0.48	...	2	55.1	...	....	......
1907	42 29 32.9	25.1	+ 5.55	+ 0.61	...	10	50.1	11.1	....	......
1908	44 19 48.2	47.8	+ 5.55	+ 0.59	...	4	46.1	13.1	....	7675
1909	37 41 59.5	56.0	+ 5.56	+ 0.65	...	4	43.7	11.1	....	7676
1910	73 35 0.6	...	+ 5.57	+ 0.48	...	2	52.1	...	51 Geminorum	......
1911	73 53 21.5	...	+ 5.61	+ 0.48	...	2	54.1	...	....	......
1912	30 48 53.4	53.4	+ 5.63	+ 0.73	+ 0.07	6	48.8	10.2	44 Camelopardi	7694
1913	37 36 11.3	7.0	+ 5.64	+ 0.65	...	7	46.7	11.1	....	7698
1914	30 36 17.5	17.0	+ 5.67	+ 0.73	...	4	44.7	9.2	45 Camelopardi	7705
1915	8 48 24.3	24.2	+ 5.71	+ 1.60	...	7	45.0	7.5	....	......
1916	30 28 30.0	29.2	+ 5.73	+ 0.73	...	3	44.1	9.2	46 Camelopardi	7714
1917	40 15 58.6	...	+ 5.76	+ 0.64	...	4	48.1	...	....	7728
1918	44 36 2.7	0.2	+ 5.76	+ 0.61	...	4	46.2	14.1	....	7729
1919	50 51 15.7	16.0	+ 5.79	+ 0.57	...	4	49.6	12.1	....	......
1920	34 48 17.9	...	+ 5.80	+ 0.70	...	2	51.1	...	....	7737

Magnitude.	Estimates of Magnitude.	Mean Right Ascension 1845.0.		Precession 1845.0.	Secular Variation	Adopted Proper Motion.
R.		R.	G.			
		h. m. s.	s.	s.	s.	s.
9.1	5	7 7 14.46	...	+ 4.912	— 0.034	......
6.1	2	7 7 14.97	15.00	+ 4.189	— 0.017	......
7.5	8	7 7 49.69	...	+ 7.351	— 0.115	— 0.015
4.5	2	7 7 56.34	...	+ 2.444	— 0.001	......
7.8	6	7 7 57.08	...	+ 7.351	— 0.115	......
7.1	5	7 8 18.28	17.88	+ 4.103	— 0.017	......
6.3	5	7 8 40.95	40.59	+ 5.298	— 0.046	......
7.4	4	7 8 45.37	...	+ 9.634	— 0.246	......
6.0	8	7 10 3.44	3.54	+ 4.368	— 0.020	......
6.7	5	7 10 5.71	5.88	+ 4.257	— 0.017	......
7.3	5	7 10 10.62	10.11	+ 4.930	— 0.031	......
6.5	5	7 10 11.94	11.71	+ 4.929	— 0.034	......
8.1	5	7 10 13.11	12.81	+ 4.933	— 0.034	......
7.8	5	7 10 22.10	22.23	+ 4.613	— 0.023	......
7.9	6	7 10 23.72	23.51	+ 4.613	— 0.023	......
3.6	14	7 10 51.71	...	+ 3.591	— 0.009	......
6.7	6	7 11 37.94	37.79	+ 4.110	— 0.020	......
5.1	4	7 11 40.73	40.80	+ 4.030	— 0.017	......
7.7	7	7 11 47.11	47.16	+ 4.254	— 0.020	......
6.5	4	7 12 2.45	2.04	+ 6.013	— 0.066	......
7.3	4	7 12 25.83	...	+ 5.016	— 0.037	......
7.4	3	7 12 33.45	...	+ 5.016	— 0.037	......
7.6	6	7 12 37.59	37.14	+ 6.032	— 0.069	......
8.6	6	7 13 22.00	21.79	+ 4.275	— 0.020	......
5.2	5	7 13 23.82	23.61	+ 4.172	— 0.020	+ 0.003
8.5	5	7 13 29.78	29.78	+ 4.937	— 0.037	......
7.3	6	7 14 36.89	36.71	+ 6.893	— 0.109	......
8.9	6	7 14 38.48	...	+ 4.269	— 0.021	......
5.6	8	7 14 41.84	40.94	+ 6.330	— 0.083	......
5.0	5	7 15 0.25	0.24	+ 4.553	— 0.026	+ 0.005
8.9	8	7 15 30.67	30.33	+ 4.492	— 0.029	......
7.9	6	7 15 38.19	38.27	+ 4.325	— 0.023	......
7.0	6	7 15 58.66	58.59	+ 4.272	— 0.023	......
4.0	1	7 16 5.57	...	+ 3.745	— 0.012	......
7.2	5	7 16 7.75	...	+ 5.969	— 0.069	......

Ordinal Number.	Mean North Polar Distance 1845.0.			Precession 1845.0.	Secular Variation.	Adopted Proper Motion.	Observations of N.P.D.			Names.	Oeltzen-Argelander Number.
							No.	Mean year.			
R.	R.		G.				R.	R.	G.		
	° ′ ″		″	″	″	″		1800 +			
1921	34 48 0.1		...	+ 5.80	+ 0.70	...	2	51.7	...	....	7737
1922	48 50 52.5		53.7	+ 5.80	+ 0.58	...	5	46.9	8.5	64 Aurigæ	......
1923	16 37 57.3		...	+ 5.85	+ 1.02	...	3	49.8	...	....	7748
1924	116 5 19.7		...	+ 5.86	+ 0.34	...	2	52.1	...	27 Can. Maj. (2)	......
1925	16 37 53.2		...	+ 5.86	+ 1.02	...	3	49.8	...	....	7749
1926	51 3 15.3		16.1	+ 5.89	+ 0.57	...	3	43.8	12.2	....	......
1927	29 49 10.5		10.3	+ 5.92	+ 0.74	+ 0.01	5	45.5	10.2	47 Camelopardi	7760
1928	11 0 37.8		...	+ 5.93	+ 1.33	...	3	52.9	...	....	7755
1929	44 29 31.7		32.6	+ 6.03	+ 0.59	...	4	46.9	14.1	....	......
1930	47 3 46.1		42.9	+ 6.04	+ 0.59	...	4	45.2	14.2	....	......
1931	34 25 53.9		52.8	+ 6.04	+ 0.67	+ 0.04	3	44.2	13.2	....	......
1932	34 26 3.0		2.6	+ 6.05	+ 0.69	...	5	46.8	13.1	19 Lyncis......	7785
1933	34 22 28.9		27.7	+ 6.05	+ 0.69	...	3	45.5	13.1	....	7786
1934	39 34 4.8		5.1	+ 6.06	+ 0.64	+ 0.05	3	44.5	13.2	20 Lyncis (1st)	......
1935	39 34 1.0		58.2	+ 6.06	+ 0.64	...	4	44.6	13.2	20 Lyncis (2d)	......
1936	67 44 15.9		...	+ 6.10	+ 0.50	+ 0.02	14	47.6	...	55 Geminor. δ	......
1937	50 43 3.5		4.8	+ 6.17	+ 0.58	...	4	48.1	12.2	....	......
1938	52 57 14.5		14.9	+ 6.17	+ 0.56	...	4	46.7	9.2	65 Aurigæ	......
1939	47 3 0.2		59.4	+ 6.18	+ 0.59	...	5	48.2	14.2	....	......
1940	23 22 22.9		20.8	+ 6.20	+ 0.83	...	3	42.8	10.6	....	7810
1941	33 8 12.9		...	+ 6.23	+ 0.70	...	2	53.2	...	....	7819
1942	33 8 ...		...	......	...	...	...	...	...	....	7821
1943	23 12 36.5		33.9	+ 6.25	+ 0.84	...	5	46.2	10.5	....	7823
1944	46 28 59.7		59.2	+ 6.31	+ 0.59	...	3	47.5	14.2	....	......
1945	49 2 8.2		8.3	+ 6.31	+ 0.57	...	5	44.9	9.2	66 Aurigæ	......
1946	34 11 17.7		16.1	+ 6.32	+ 0.68	...	4	45.7	15.1	....	......
1947	18 19 45.6		43.5	+ 6.41	+ 0.94	...	4	44.1	11.2	....	7863
1948	46 32 54.3		...	+ 6.41	+ 0.60	...	3	49.8	...	....	......
1949	21 13 40.2		41.2	+ 6.42	+ 0.88	+ 0.07	5	45.6	8.1	....	......
1950	40 29 16.8		18.2	+ 6.45	+ 0.64	+ 0.09	4	43.7	10.2	21 Lyncis......	7869
1951	41 38 39.6		39.6	+ 6.49	+ 0.63	...	4	49.2	13.2	....	7878
1952	45 13 14.2		10.2	+ 6.50	+ 0.60	...	5	48.2	13.2	....	......
1953	46 26 25.1		26.2	+ 6.53	+ 0.60	...	3	44.5	14.1	....	......
1954	61 53 58.3		...	+ 6.54	+ 0.52	...	2	56.2	...	60 Geminor. ι	......
1955	23 33 23.0		...	+ 6.54	+ 0.83	...	3	46.5	...	....	7890

| Ordinal Number. | | Magnitude. | Estimates of Magnitude. | Mean Right Ascension 1845.0. | | Precession 1845.0 | Secular Variation | Adopted Proper Motion. | Observations of R.A. | | |
R.	G.	R.		R.	G.				No.	Mean year. R.	G.
				h. m. s.	s.	s.	s.	s.		1800 +	
1956	1310	7.6	6	7 16 33.71	33.57	+ 6.936	− 0.109	......	4	45.0	11.2
1957	1315	8.3	6	7 16 48.23	48.05	+ 4.490	− 0.029	......	3	46.8	13.1
1958	1317	7.1	9	7 17 1.94	1.61	+ 4.091	− 0.020	......	6	49.5	12.2
1959	1316	7.1	5	7 17 12.19	12.31	+ 4.483	− 0.026	......	3	45.5	13.1
1960	1318	6.4	5	7 17 17.63	17.36	+ 4.496	− 0.026	......	4	46.7	13.1
1961	...	7.6	7	7 17 25.81	...	+ 4.165	− 0.019	......	4	46.6	...
1962	...	2.7	A	7 17 57.99	...	+ 2.372	− 0.001	− 0.004	3	54.2	...
1963	1319	6.5	3	7 18 4.54	4.25	+ 5.448	− 0.054	......	4	47.7	11.1
1964	1320	5.7	8	7 18 8.83	8.15	+ 4.571	− 0.029	......	7	48.6	9.1
1965	...	9.3	5	7 18 18.96	...	+ 4.544	− 0.027	......	2	46.7	...
1966	1314	7.7	7	7 18 20.92	20.86	+ 8.165	− 0.186	......	6	47.3	11.1
1967	...	8.7	7	7 18 40.96	...	+ 4.547	− 0.027	......	3	46.5	...
1968	...	7.2	6	7 18 54.89	...	+ 4.527	− 0.027	......	4	48.7	...
1969	1322	7.8	5	7 19 28.01	28.36	+ 4.079	− 0.020	......	3	46.8	13.2
1970	1325	7.2	5	7 19 41.21	41.00	+ 4.069	− 0.014	......	3	49.7	13.2
1971	1321	8.7	6	7 19 55.55	55.94	+ 5.986	− 0.074	......	2	46.6	11.1
1972	1324	7.2	12	7 20 44.37	44.17	+ 5.997	− 0.074	......	10	45.9	11.1
1973	1326	6.9	10	7 21 23.70	23.59	+ 4.093	− 0.020	......	7	50.0	12.2
1974	...	8.0	5	7 21 27.02	...	+ 6.023	− 0.078	......	2	45.2	...
1975	1323	7.3	7	7 21 50.25	50.08	+ 8.059	− 0.186	......	4	47.4	10.2
1976	1327	8.2	7	7 22 56.22	55.80	+ 6.443	− 0.094	......	5	46.7	11.2
1977	1328	6.8	9	7 23 15.19	14.79	+ 5.953	− 0.077	......	7	45.2	10.2
1978	1330	6.0	8	7 24 8.49	8.18	+ 4.927	− 0.037	......	5	46.3	13.1
1979	...	8.4	9	7 24 30.73	...	+25.329	− 2.657	......	7	54.0	...
1980	...	8.8	6	7 24 40.94	...	+ 5.952	− 0.077	......	3	45.5	...
1981	...	3.4	3	7 24 41.70	...	+ 3.856	− .0.015	− 0.013	6	49.1	...
1982	...	...	...	7 24 42.14	...	+ 3.856	− 0.015	− 0.013	63	46.3	...
1983	...	5.4	11	7 24 45.51	...	+ 3.431	− 0.008	− 0.004	15	49.3	...
1984	1331	7.2	7	7 24 56.27	56.24	+ 4.796	− 0.037	.... .	4	46.6	13.2
1985	1332	6.7	7	7 25 0.62	0.43	+ 4.247	− 0.023	......	4	47.6	12.2
1986	...	6.1	5	7 25 15.55	...	+ 4.383	− 0.026	......	3	46.5	...
1987	1333	8.1	5	7 25 47.61	47.68	+ 4.883	− 0.040	......	3	44.7	15.2
1988	...	4.6	4	7 26 21.83	...	+ 3.710	− 0.012	− 0.001	2	42.1	...
1989	1335	7.0	7	7 26 36.61	35.92	+ 5.214	− 0.051	+ 0.005	5	43.6	9.2
1990	1338	6.6	6	7 26 40.54	40.49	+ 4.125	− 0.026	......	3	46.2	12.2

Ordinal Number. R.	Mean North Polar Distance 1845.0. R. (° ′ ″)	G. (″)	Precession 1845.0. (″)	Secular Variation. (″)	Adopted Proper Motion. (″)	Observations of N.P.D. No. R.	Mean year. R. (1800+)	G.	Names.	Oeltzen-Argelander Number.
1956	18 5 36.4	33.8	+ 6.57	+ 0.94	...	4	43.7	11.2	....	7897
1957	41 38 3.7	4.7	+ 6.59	+ 0.60	...	3	51.5	13.1	....	....
1958	51 1 44.9	43.6	+ 6.61	+ 0.55	...	4	48.4	12.2	....	....
1959	41 46 12.7	11.9	+ 6.63	+ 0.62	...	4	46.2	13.1	....	......
1960	41 30 29.0	27.4	+ 6.64	+ 0.63	...	4	46.9	13.1	....	7517
1961	49 2 10.6	...	+ 6.65	+ 0.57	...	3	46.3	...	....	......
1962	119 0 14.2	...	+ 6.69	+ 0.33	...	6	53.5	...	31 Can. Maj. η	......
1963	27 55 26.6	22.3	+ 6.70	+ 0.75	...	3	43.8	11.1	....	......
1964	40 0 52.0	52.9	+ 6.71	+ 0.64	+ 0.08	4	43.7	9.1	22 Lyncis	....
1965	40 30 0.0	...	+ 6.72	+ 0.62	...	3	49.2	...	....	7936
1966	13 52 58.1	51.9	+ 6.72	+ 1.14	...	4	45.4	11.1	....	7932
1967	40 26 55.7	...	+ 6.75	+ 0.62	...	4	49.7	...	....	7937
1968	40 48 26.1	...	+ 6.77	+ 0.62	...	3	47.2	...	....	7944
1969	51 14 49.6	44.1	+ 6.82	+ 0.57	...	3	50.8	13.2	....	....
1970	51 30 55.3	50.8	+ 6.83	+ 0.55	...	3	47.5	13.2	....	....
1971	23 18 37.0	33.5	+ 6.85	+ 0.81	...	4	48.4	11.1	....	7966
1972	23 12 18.3	16.4	+ 6.92	+ 0.82	...	5	45.1	11.1	....	7983
1973	50 47 3.3	3.2	+ 6.97	+ 0.55	...	3	46.9	12.2	....	....
1974	22 59 53.0	...	+ 6.98	+ 0.83	...	4	47.4	...	....	7989
1975	14 5 42.6	36.2	+ 7.01	+ 1.11	...	4	45.4	10.2	....	7993
1976	20 20 28.4	23.8	+ 7.10	+ 0.90	...	5	47.3	11.2	....	8011
1977	23 25 49.6	46.8	+ 7.13	+ 0.83	...	6	46.8	10.2	....	....
1978	33 54 40.9	40.0	+ 7.20	+ 0.67	...	5	46.0	13.1	....	8041
1979	3 12 24.6	...	+ 7.23	+ 3.43	...	3	52.5	...	....	....
1980	23 22 58.2	...	+ 7.24	+ 0.81	...	4	46.9	...	....	....
1981	57 46 40.7	...	+ 7.24	+ 0.52	+ 0.08	4	52.2	...	66 Gem. α (1st)	......
1982	57 46 38.8	...	+ 7.24	+ 0.52	+ 0.08	31	45.9	...	66 Gem. α (2d)	......
1983	73 50 43.2	...	+ 7.25	+ 0.47	...	2	45.1	...	68 Geminorum	......
1984	35 49 25.0	20.4	+ 7.26	+ 0.64	...	4	44.2	13.2	....	....
1985	46 38 4.7	3.0	+ 7.27	+ 0.58	...	5	45.2	12.2	....	......
1986	43 29 5.4	...	+ 7.29	+ 0.59	...	4	46.7	...	....	......
1987	34 27 16.1	13.3	+ 7.33	+ 0.65	...	4	43.9	15.2	....	8063
1988	62 45 53.9	...	+ 7.38	+ 0.50	+ 0.11	1	47.2	...	69 Geminor. υ	....
1989	30 5 42.0	42.3	+ 7.40	+ 0.71	...	4	43.7	9.2	48 Camelopardi	8078
1990	49 38 6.4	6.4	+ 7.40	+ 0.54	...	3	44.5	12.2	....	......

Magnitude.	Estimates of Magnitude.	Mean Right Ascension 1845.0.		Precession 1845.0.	Secular Variation	Adopted Proper Motion.
R.		R.	G.			
		h. m. s.	s.	s.	s.	s.
6.8	6	7 26 53.00	52.76	+ 6.425	− 0.100	......
6.9	5	7 26 53.89	53.68	+ 4.795	− 0.037	......
8.4	7	7 27 3.54	4.89	+10.808	− 0.409	......
7.3	4	7 27 40.09	40.15	+ 4.060	− 0.020	......
5.9	5	7 27 58.37	58.59	+ 5.010	− 0.049	+ 0.015
7.3	5	7 28 1.47	...	+ 4.219	− 0.024	......
7.4	5	7 28 1.49	...	+ 4.219	− 0.024	......
8.2	7	7 28 5.13	4.92	+ 5.807	− 0.074	......
8.0	6	7 28 18.68	18.58	+ 4.061	− 0.023	......
8.0	6	7 28 38.85	38.14	+ 7.490	− 0.160	......
8.7	4	7 28 49.72	49.56	+ 4.844	− 0.040	......
8.0	3	7 29 12.40	12.06	+ 5.821	− 0.077	......
6.9	7	7 29 21.92	21.50	+ 4.843	− 0.040	......
7.3	6	7 29 32.94	32.54	+ 7.500	− 0.163	......
6.9	4	7 29 44.26	44.32	+ 4.466	− 0.031	......
6.2	8	7 29 47.97	48.21	+ 4.060	− 0.020	..?...
5.7	5	7 29 51.70	51.76	+ 5.131	− 0.054	......
6.8	6	7 30 22.25	21.31	+10.557	− 0.406	− 0.225
7.1	5	7 30 50.11	49.76	+ 6.372	− 0.103	......
7.7	11	7 30 50.61	...	+16.649	− 1.270	......
7.8	6	7 31 6.32	6.17	+ 5.777	− 0.077	......
7.9	6	7 31 6.63	6.29	+ 5.777	− 0.077	......
1.0	A	7 31 11.22	...	+ 3.191	− 0.006	− 0.048
7.7	5	7 31 34.51	32.69	+ 9.983	− 0.366	......
5.7	7	7 31 47.99	47.70	+ 5.812	− 0.077	+ 0.003
5.6	5	7 32 18.56	18.56	+ 4.578	− 0.034	......
6.1	4	7 32 22.98	22.38	+ 5.504	− 0.069	......
9.2	5	7 32 29.30	...	+ 4.268	− 0.026	......
7.2	6	7 32 50.56	50.80	+ 4.263	− 0.026	......
7.4	18	7 33 38.61	...	+21.171	− 2.244	......
6.6	6	7 34 5.63	4.59	+10.204	− 0.397	......
6.9	5	7 34 24.36	...	+ 4.604	− 0.035	......
7.2	6	7 34 31.11	31.25	+ 5.250	− 0.060	......
4.0	4	7 35 5.02	...	+ 3.634	− 0.012	− 0.005
7.3	7	7 35 9.67	9.20	+ 6.872	− 0.137	......

Ordinal Number. R.	Mean North Polar Distance 1845.0. R.	G.	Precession 1845.0.	Secular Variation.	Adopted Proper Motion.	Observations of N.P.D. No. R.	Mean year. R.	G.	Names.	Oeltzen-Argelander Number.
	o ' "	"	"	"	"		1800 +			
1991	20 18 48.8	44.8	+ 7.42	+ 0.87	...	15	47.5	11.1	....	8080
1992	35 45 19.1	14.6	+ 7.42	+ 0.64	...	4	44.7	13.2	....	8083
1993	9 7 1.5	2.7	+ 7.43	+ 1.45	...	4	45.2	7.1	....	......
1994	51 23 59.7	59.7	+ 7.48	+ 0.53	...	2	48.2	13.1	....	......
1995	32 34 15.6	16.2	+ 7.51	+ 0.68	...	4	46.9	9.5	23 Lyncis......	8099
1996	47 11 56.4	...	+ 7.51	+ 0.57	...	2	52.2	...	....	......
1997	47 10 51.2	...	+ 7.51	+ 0.57	...	2	52.2	...	....	......
1998	24 21 37.0	35.7	+ 7.52	+ 0.79	...	5	48.6	11.2	....	......
1999	51 19 24.8	22.0	+ 7.54	+ 0.55	...	3	48.2	13.0	....	......
2000	15 38 57.3	56.7	+ 7.56	+ 1.01	...	4	45.2	14.1	....	......
2001	34 53 45.9	42.5	+ 7.58	+ 0.66	...	3	52.5	14.2	....	8113
2002	24 12 31.8	27.4	+ 7.61	+ 0.79	...	2	45.7	11.2	....	......
2003	34 53 4.6	4.0	+ 7.62	+ 0.65	...	3	46.6	11.2	....	8122
2004	15 35 33.2	31.8	+ 7.64	+ 1.02	...	4	47.2	14.1	....	......
2005	41 30 49.2	43.1	+ 7.65	+ 0.59	...	3	46.8	14.2	....	8132
2006	51 18 25.7	25.9	+ 7.66	+ 0.55	...	4	48.4	12.8	....	......
2007	30 56 4.5	4.6	+ 7.66	+ 0.68	+ 0.08	4	46.9	10.6	24 Lyncis......	8136
2008	9 21 39.9	39.2	+ 7.70	+ 1.39	− 0.06	4	43.9	7.3	....	......
2009	20 28 53.2	48.6	+ 7.74	+ 0.85	...	4	45.2	11.1	....	8152
2010	5 11 22.1	...	+ 7.74	+ 2.18	...	4	52.7	...	....	......
2011	24 29 1.8	58.9	+ 7.76	+ 0.77	...	4	45.4	11.2	....	8161
2012	24 28 46.7	44.3	+ 7.76	+ 0.77	...	4	43.7	11.2	....	8162
2013	84 22 55.0	...	+ 7.77	+ 0.43	+ 1.08	26	45.2	...	10 Can. Min. α	......
2014	10 6 7.7	4.8	+ 7.80	+ 1.35	...	4	49.2	9.6	....	8170
2015	24 10 59.6	58.6	+ 7.82	+ 0.78	...	4	44.7	11.2	51 Camelopardi	8179
2016	39 12 22.4	21.9	+ 7.86	+ 0.61	+ 0.04	5	44.6	10.2	....	8189
2017	26 48 14.5	13.5	+ 7.87	+ 0.75	...	4	43.9	9.2	49 Camelopardi	8191
2018	45 45 14.7	...	+ 7.88	+ 0.57	...	2	52.2	...	....	......
2019	45 50 43.4	43.5	+ 7.91	+ 0.59	...	4	47.2	14.2	....	......
2020	3 52 38.8	...	+ 7.97	+ 2.83	...	6	51.4	...	....	......
2021	9 45 0.1	59.3	+ 8.00	+ 1.37	+ 0.02	4	43.9	10.0	....	8213
2022	38 36 31.1	...	+ 8.03	+ 0.62	...	4	48.4	...	....	8222
2023	29 19 53.2	51.6	+ 8.04	+ 0.71	...	4	46.7	13.1	....	8229
2024	65 14 8.8	...	+ 8.08	+ 0.48	+ 0.05	1	47.2	...	77 Geminor. κ	......
2025	17 50 9.3	5.6	+ 8.09	+ 0.92	...	5	47.0	11.1	....	8239

Mean Right Ascension 1845.0.		Precession 1845.0.	Secular Variation	Adopted Proper Motion.
R.	G.			
h. m. s.	s.	s.	s.	s.
7 35 10.63	10.14	+ 8.829	— 0.277	......
7 35 17.84	...	+ 5.142	— 0.053	......
7 35 28.78	28.86	+ 8.805	— 0.274	......
7 35 49.50	...	+ 3.731	— 0.014	— 0.049
7 36 41.93	41.83	+ 5.245	— 0.060	......
7 37 8.74	...	+ 3.487	— 0.010	— 0.008
7 37 52.91	52.46	+ 8.815	— 0.286	......
7 38 49.99	49.78	+ 5.164	— 0.051	......
7 38 51.43	51.39	+ 4.773	— 0.043	......
7 38 58.81	58.40	+ 4.812	— 0.043	......
7 39 0.03	5.02	+15.645	— 1.163	......
7 39 7.07	6.19	+ 6.858	— 0.134	......
7 39 13.24	12.17	+ 9.975	— 0.403	......
7 39 48.36	47.86	+ 6.817	— 0.131	......
7 40 8.66	8.22	+ 9.862	— 0.391	......
7 40 11.96	...	+ 4.838	— 0.047	......
7 40 41.28	...	+ 5.397	— 0.068	......
7 41 31.05	30.79	+ 7.373	— 0.180	......
7 41 44.34	...	+ 5.383	— 0.068	......
7 41 54.36	53.77	+ 4.801	— 0.043	......
7 42 12.70	12.55	+ 5.174	— 0.060	......
7 43 8.96	8.92	+ 5.161	— 0.063	......
7 43 11.77	11.31	+ 4.396	— 0.034	......
7 43 24.37	24.32	+ 4.405	— 0.031	......
7 43 51.03	50.72	+ 4.914	— 0.051	+ 0.005
7 43 53.54	53.38	+ 4.248	— 0.029	......
7 43 59.95	59.86	+ 4.247	— 0.026	......
7 44 0.25	...	+ 3.686	— 0.015	— 0.004
7 45 57.77	57.51	+ 5.654	— 0.086	......
7 47 22.34	22.00	+ 4.238	— 0.029	......
7 48 7.57	...	+15.367	— 1.310	......
7 48 18.75	18.55	+ 5.088	— 0.060	......
7 48 25.51	25.06	+ 5.194	— 0.063	......
7 48 34.40	33.92	+ 5.456	— 0.080	......
7 48 38.59	...	+ 5.686	— 0.080	....

Ordinal Number.	Mean North Polar Distance 1845.0.		Precession 1845.0.	Secular Variation.	Adopted Proper Motion	Observations of N.P.D.			Names.	Oeltzen-Argelander Number.
R.	R.	G.				No. R.	Mean year. R.	G.		
	° ′ ″	″	″	″	″		1800 +			
2026	11 59 25.2	26.9	+ 8.09	+ 1.18	...	3	44.9	14.1	...,.................	8237
2027	30 32 38.9	...	+ 8.10	+ 0.68	...	3	50.5	...	....	......
2028	12 2 . 7.6	8.6	+ 8.12	+ 1.19	...	4	45.2	14.1	....	8243
2029	61 36 16.5	...	+ 8.14	+ 0.50	+ 0.06	23	46.1	...	78 Geminor. β	......
2030	29 16 55.9	57.1	+ 8.21	+ 0.69	...	3	44.8	13.1	....	8268
2031	71 7 2.1	...	+ 8.25	+ 0.46	+ 0.05	2	45.2	...	81 Geminor. g	......
2032	11 57 24.7	23.2	+ 8.31	+ 1.19	...	4	45.9	14.1	....	......
2033	30 6 49.5	46.1	+ 8.38	+ 0.68	...	5	49.0	13.2	....	......
2034	35 29 29.6	30.3	+ 8.38	+ 0.62	...	4	45.6	14.2	....	......
2035	34 53 5.3	5.2	+ 8.39	+ 0.62	...	4	47.1	12.2	....	8307
2036	5 30 56.5	57.0	+ 8.40	+ 2.11	...	23	47.6	7.7	....	......
2037	17 45 46.5	46.8	+ 8.40	+ 0.89	...	5	48.2	10.8	....	8308
2038	9 58 8.0	1.5	+ 8.41	+ 1.32	...	5	47.6	11.2	....	......
2039	17 55 35.3	36.0	+ 8.46	+ 0.91	...	4	44.2	10.8	....	8320
2040	10 6 40.5	41.3	+ 8.49	+ 1.33	+ 0.10	5	42.2	9.7	....	......
2041	34 24 8.6	...	+ 8.49	+ 0.64	...	3	48.5	...	....	8325
2042	27 28 9.9	...	+ 8.53	+ 0.72	...	5	51.0	...	....	8329
2043	15 40 45.3	43.1	+ 8.60	+ 0.99	...	6	46.5	11.2	....	8345
2044	27 33 44.7	...	+ 8.61	+ 0.72	...	6	50.7	...	....	8353
2045	34 53 20.4	16.6	+ 8.63	+ 0.64	...	7	47.3	12.2	....	8361
2046	29 49 42.5	41.7	+ 8.65	+ 0.68	...	3	45.8	13.2	....	8364
2047	29 55 26.6	24.8	+ 8.72	+ 0.67	...	4	46.7	13.2	....	8375
2048	42 13 9.8	10.5	+ 8.73	+ 0.58	...	5	45.0	9.2	25 Lyncis......	8379
2049	42 2 24.1	24.3	+ 8.74	+ 0.56	+ 0.02	4	44.2	8.2	26 Lyncis......	8380
2050	33 5 43.7	43.0	+ 8.78	+ 0.65	+ 0.02	12	48.8	9.7	52 Camelopardi	......
2051	45 35 13.4	13.7	+ 8.78	+ 0.55	...	4	47.2	11.2	....	......
2052	45 36 37.9	38.3	+ 8.79	+ 0.55	...	4	45.7	11.2	....	......
2053	62 50 16.7	...	+ 8.79	+ 0.48	+ 0.05	2	54.2	...	83 Geminor. ϕ	......
2054	24 50 33.0	31.2	+ 8.94	+ 0.72	...	8	47.3	10.8	....	8425
2055	45 36 54.1	54.1	+ 9.05	+ 0.55	...	4	43.5	11.2	....	......
2056	5 31 52.0	...	+ 9.12	+ 1.94	...	7	49.6	...	....	......
2057	30 32 21.5	21.8	+ 9.13	+ 0.66	...	4	44.7	13.2	....	......
2058	29 15 33.9	34.0	+ 9.14	+ 0.68	+ 0.03	5	43.8	9.2	53 Camelopardi	......
2059	26 29 31.4	31.6	+ 9.15	+ 0.71	...	6	44.9	12.7	....	8460
2060	24 26 37.6	...	+ 9.15	+ 0.75	...	5	52.6	...	....	......

Magnitude.	Estimates of Magnitude.	Mean Right Ascension 1845.0.		Precession 1845.0.	Secular Variation	Adopted Proper Motion.
		R.	G.			
		h. m. s.	s.	s.	s.	s.
8.0	7	7 48 41.30	40.60	+ 5.456	− 0.080	......
7.4	6	7 48 47.38	...	+ 6.777	− 0.176	......
6.9	3	7 48 50.48	49.60	+ 5.252	− 0.066	......
7.0	5	7 49 0.68	0.62	+ 4.760	− 0.046	......
6.2	4	7 49 56.20	55.82	+ 4.946	− 0.054	......
7.6	4	7 50 38.60	38.01	+ 4.733	− 0.049	
8.4	5	7 51 24.59	24.64	+ 4.733	− 0.046	
7.9	6	7 51 26.79	...	+13.536	− 0.972	
8.7	7	7 51 57.74	...	+18.839	− 2.114	
8.1	6	7 52 5.62	...	+ 4.294	− 0.032	
7.7	6	7 52 27.82	27.94	+ 4.813	− 0.049	......
7.0	7	7 52 27.98	28.12	+ 4.972	− 0.057	......
6.9	6	7 53 2.10	1.83	+ 5.084	− 0.063	......
8.0	5	7 53 9.63	9.08	+ 6.422	− 0.134	......
8.3	7	7 53 29.61	...	+ 4.248	− 0.031	......
6.3	6	7 53 58.19	58.22	+12.496	− 0.820	......
6.4	5	7 54 10.98	9.47	+ 6.325	− 0.129	......
6.9	10	7 54 13.85	13.66	+ 4.061	− 0.029	......
8.2	7	7 54 33.43	32.71	+ 7.876	− 0.257	......
7.0	7	7 54 58.64	58.30	+ 5.715	− 0.097	+ 0.012
7.1	3	7 55 8.65	...	+ 4.790	− 0.053	......
6.5	7	7 56 24.54	24.32	+ 4.186	− 0.031	......
4.9	5	7 56 46.33	46.14	+ 4.561	− 0.043	......
7.8	9	7 57 8.20	8.23	+ 7.816	− 0.257	......
6.8	6	7 57 14.44	...	+ 4.779	− 0.054	......
5.4	8	7 57 18.32	18.17	+ 4.986	− 0.060	......
5.6	5	7 57 18.44	18.00	+ 6.094	− 0.120	+ 0.007
8.2	5	7 58 18.83	18.70	+ 4.992	− 0.066	......
6.2	4	7 58 43.43	43.17	+ 4.148	− 0.031	......
7.4	5	7 58 58.05	...	+ 4.588	− 0.046	......
7.9	6	7 59 34.23	...	+ 4.580	− 0.046	......
5.8	10	7 59 54.00	53.96	+ 7.791	− 0.257	+ 0.020
9.0	5	7 59 58.46	57.55	+ 7.850	− 0.263	......
3.0	A	8 0 56.81	...	+ 2.559	− 0.001	− 0.002
6.7	5	8 0 56.85	...	+ 4.847	− 0.058	......

Ordinal Number. R.	Mean North Polar Distance 1845.0. R.	G.	Precession 1845.0.	Secular Variation.	Adopted Proper Motion.	Observations of N.P.D. No. R.	Mean year. R. 1800 +	G.	Names.	Oeltzen-Argelander Number.
	o ′ ″	″	″	″	″					
2061	26 29 25.3	26.2	+ 9.16	+ 0.71	...	5	47.0	12.6	....	8464
2062	17 47 7.4	...	+ 9.17	+ 0.87	...	4	47.1	...	....	8466
2063	28 35 26.6	27.7	+ 9.17	+ 0.68	− 0.01	5	45.9	8.2	....	......
2064	35 7 21.4	19.6	+ 9.18	+ 0.61	...	5	43.5	11.1	....	8473
2065	32 18 16.1	13.6	+ 9.25	+ 0.62	...	5	44.4	9.7	54 Camelopardi	8490
2066	35 26 53.3	51.6	+ 9.31	+ 0.61	...	4	44.7	11.1	....	......
2067	35 24 54.0	53.2	+ 9.37	+ 0.61	...	4	45.0	11.1	....	......
2068	6 26 32.9	...	+ 9.37	+ 1.75	...	3	48.5	...	....	......
2069	4 16 54.0	...	+ 9.41	+ 2.43	...	5	51.6	...	....	......
2070	43 57 20.1	...	+ 9.42	+ 0.55	...	4	47.2	...	....	8526
2071	34 5 16.3	13.0	+ 9.45	+ 0.62	...	4	46.1	19.3	....	......
2072	31 47 42.3	38.1	+ 9.45	+ 0.63	...	6	46.9	11.2	....	8531
2073	30 19 17.5	15.4	+ 9.49	+ 0.64	...	4	46.4	12.7	....	......
2074	19 21 19.6	18.8	+ 9.50	+ 0.81	...	5	47.0	11.2	....	......
2075	44 57 58.4	...	+ 9.53	+ 0.55	...	4	52.7	...	....	......
2076	7 6 22.3	20.6	+ 9.57	+ 1.63	...	6	43.7	7.2	....	......
2077	19 50 27.1	30.9	+ 9.58	+ 0.81	...	4	44.4	11.5	....	......
2078	49 49 42.1	42.5	+ 9.59	+ 0.53	...	4	46.1	11.1	....	......
2079	13 43 5.2	0.0	+ 9.61	+ 1.01	...	5	48.0	13.2	....	8561
2080	23 53 52.1	50.9	+ 9.64	+ 0.72	...	6	44.5	9.2	....	8568
2081	34 15 45.0	...	+ 9.66	+ 0.61	...	3	51.9	...	....	8570
2082	46 18 2.0	1.6	+ 9.75	+ 0.51	...	6	46.5	10.2	28 Lyncis......	......
2083	38 3 10.0	11.3	+ 9.78	+ 0.57	...	6	45.2	9.2	27 Lyncis......	8600
2084	13 47 55.7	51.4	+ 9.81	+ 1.00	...	5	44.0	13.2	....	8602
2085	34 18 2.0	...	+ 9.81	+ 0.62	...	3	51.8	...	....	8612
2086	31 18 19.1	15.2	+ 9.82	+ 0.62	...	5	44.6	11.2	....	8615
2087	21 4 42.6	42.5	+ 9.82	+ 0.77	...	7	44.8	8.5	55 Camelopardi	8613
2088	31 10 15.4	13.9	+ 9.90	+ 0.63	...	5	45.1	11.2	....	......
2089	47 7 16.7	14.0	+ 9.93	+ 0.52	...	5	46.0	11.1	....	......
2090	37 24 28.0	...	+ 9.95	+ 0.58	...	4	47.7	...	....	8635
2091	37 31 18.5	...	+ 9.99	+ 0.58	...	5	51.0	...	....	8646
2092	13 46 52.1	51.0	+ 10.02	+ 1.00	...	6	44.7	13.1	....	8649
2093	13 36 56.6	54.3	+ 10.02	+ 0.99	...	4	46.2	13.2	....	8655
2094	113 51 40.7	...	+ 10.10	+ 0.32	− 0.08	3	47.5	...	15 Argûs.......	......
2095	33 0 53.8	...	+ 10.10	+ 0.61	...	7	45.7	...	....	8669

Ordinal Number.		Magnitude.	Estimates of Magnitude.	Mean Right Ascension 1845.0.			Precession 1845.0.	Secular Variation.	Adopted Proper Motion.	Observations of R.A.		
										No.	Mean year.	
R.	G.	R.		R.		G.				R.	R.	G.
				h. m. s.		s.	s.	s.	s.		1800 +	
2096	1416	6.5	6	8 1 4.14		4.12	+ 4.011	− 0.026	......	5	47.4	11.1
2097	1414	6.9	5	8 1 4.57		4.45	+ 5.743	− 0.109	......	3	45.5	10.9
2098	1412	8.4	10	8 1 22.00		21.56	+ 7.822	− 0.260	......	5	44.3	13.1
2099	...	8.6	13	8 1 24.54		...	+20.932	− 1.956	......	10	54.1	...
2100	1413	7.1	8	8 1 25.69		25.71	+ 6.353	− 0.149	......	3	46.5	10.9
2101	1415	5.5	4	8 1 26.99		26.42	+ 4.840	− 0.057	......	5	46.7	9.2
2102	1420	6.7	4	8 2 43.86		43.60	+ 5.131	− 0.074	......	5	48.0	10.2
2103	...	5.6	2	8 3 19.03		...	+ 3.445	− 0.012	+ 0.004	7	48.5	...
2104	...	6.9	5	8 3 19.34		...	+ 3.445	− 0.012	+ 0.004	3	54.1	...
2105	1417	6.5	7	8 3 21.92		20.54	+ 7.442	− 0.231	......	3	46.2	13.2
2106	1419	6.1	5	8 3 28.02		27.92	+ 6.796	− 0.180	......	3	44.8	9.2
2107	...	8.3	7	8 3 43.61		...	+ 5.032	− 0.066	......	3	52.5	...
2108	...	6.5	4	8 4 6.58		...	+ 5.026	− 0.066	+ 0.003	4	49.2	...
2109	1421	6.9	3	8 4 8.33		8.19	+ 4.156	− 0.034	......	3	44.8	11.1
2110	...	7.1	3	8 4 16.40		...	+ 8.211	− 0.315	......	2	51.7	...
2111	1422	5.0	4	8 4 55.27		54.81	+ 5.054	− 0.069	......	5	46.0	9.2
2112	...	7.6	6	8 5 1.49		...	+ 5.386	− 0.090	......	3	52.5	...
2113	...	7.1	7	8 5 6.61		...	+ 4.307	− 0.037	......	3	46.9	...
2114	...	8.4	3	8 5 19.00		...	+ 5.415	− 0.093	......	2	50.7	...
2115	1424	5.6	4	8 5 44.67		44.46	+ 5.307	− 0.083	+ 0.005	5	46.1	8.5
2116	1423	7.0	6	8 5 48.79		48.27	+ 5.893	− 0.123	......	3	47.2	10.2
2117	...	8.2	5	8 6 4.19		...	+ 6.120	− 0.128	......	3	49.2	...
2118	...	8.8	5	8 7 1.20		...	+ 6.094	− 0.126	......	3	51.9	...
2119	...	7.6	4	8 7 51.72		...	+ 4.870	− 0.063	......	2	51.6	...
2120	1426	5.6	5	8 7 52.70		51.74	+ 4.900	− 0.069	......	3	43.9	8.2
2121	...	3.9	4	8 8 6.27		...	+ 3.263	− 0.009	......	4	51.8	...
2122	1425	7.2	6	8 8 32.53		31.94	+ 6.083	− 0.137	......	4	46.3	10.2
2123	...	6.9	6	8 9 3.43		...	+ 8.740	− 0.358	......	2	50.6	...
2124	1427	6.1	7	8 9 39.77		39.19	+ 5.116	− 0.074	......	5	43.3	10.7
2125	1418	7.5	60	8 9 46.15		54.51	+17.675	− 2.188	......	72	48.1	7.2
2126	...	7.9	4	8 9 55.15		...	+ 4.318	− 0.039	......	4	52.4	...
2127	...	8.5	4	8 10 2.95		...	+ 4.318	− 0.039	......	3	52.8	...
2128	...	7.3	5	8 11 24.27		...	+ 4.861	− 0.063	......	2	50.7	...
2129	...	8.6	8	8 11 38.15		...	+18.081	− 2.344	......	4	50.3	...
2130	1429	5.8	5	8 12 2.32		1.82	+ 4.597	− 0.054	......	5	47.3	8.2

Ordinal Number.	Mean North Polar Distance 1845.0		Precession 1845.0.	Secular Variation.	Adopted Proper Motion.	Observations of N.P.D.				Names.	Oeltzen-Argelander Number.
						No.	Mean year.				
R.	R.	G.				R.	R.	G.			
	° ′ ″	″	″	″	″		1800 +				
2096	50 48 49.3	47.3	+ 10.11	+ 0.51	...	4	46.2	11.1	....	......
2097	23 21 43.3	40.2	+ 10.11	+ 0.73	...	4	45.4	10.9	....	8673
2098	13 38 46.4	44.1	+ 10.13	+ 0.99	...	7	48.1	13.1	....	8676
2099	3 41 45.1	...	+ 10.14	+ 2.63	...	6	53.2	...	....	......
2100	19 21 36.2	33.5	+ 10.14	+ 0.81	...	6	46.7	10.9	....	8679
2101	33 5 24.9	23.1	+ 10.14	+ 0.62	...	9	44.7	9.2	....	8682
2102	29 9 30.3	28.3	+ 10.23	+ 0.63	...	4	43.2	10.2	56 Camelopardi	......
2103	71 53 22.6	...	+ 10.28	+ 0.43	+ 0.11	4	51.9	...	16 Cancri ζ (1st)	......
2104	71 53 27.2	...	+ 10.28	+ 0.43	+ 0.11	3	54.2	...	16 Cancri ζ (2d)	......
2105	14 42 33.9	34.7	+ 10.28	+ 0.94	...	6	45.9	13.2	....	8717
2106	17 7 17.1	15.1	+ 10.29	+ 0.86	...	4	43.7	9.2	....	8724
2107	30 18 22.7	...	+ 10.31	+ 0.63	...	5	49.8	...	....	8734
2108	30 20 39.9	...	+ 10.34	+ 0.63	...	3	47.8	...	....	8737
2109	46 30 4.2	3.3	+ 10.34	+ 0.52	...	3	44.5	11.1	....	......
2110	12 33 27.6	...	+ 10.35	+ 1.01	...	4	51.7	...	....	8739
2111	29 57 39.1	39.5	+ 10.40	+ 0.63	...	5	43.4	9.2	29 Lyncis......	8754
2112	26 16 2.3	...	+ 10.40	+ 0.67	...	3	46.8	...	....	8758
2113	42 43 53.8	...	+ 10.41	+ 0.54	...	4	47.2	...	....	8759
2114	25 57 59.3	...	+ 10.42	+ 0.67	...	3	51.6	...	....	8763
2115	27 1 17.6	17.8	+ 10.46	+ 0.66	...	5	45.7	8.5	57 Camelopardi	8773
2116	21 59 53.9	51.1	+ 10.47	+ 0.75	...	5	47.4	10.2	....	8775
2117	20 29 29.2	...	+ 10.48	+ 0.76	...	3	44.9	...	....	8778
2118	20 36 11.8	...	+ 10.55	+ 0.76	...	4	45.7	...	....	8795
2119	32 13 6.4	...	+ 10.62	+ 0.60	...	4	49.7	...	....	8810
2120	31 46 49.7	49.2	+ 10.62	+ 0.61	− 0.05	4	42.9	8.2	30 Lyncis......	8812
2121	80 20 29.4	...	+ 10.64	+ 0.40	+ 0.06	2	47.7	...	17 Cancri β...	......
2122	20 35 35.8	34.5	+ 10.67	+ 0.76	...	5	45.8	10.2	....	8824
2123	11 16 31.1	...	+ 10.70	+ 1.07	...	4	50.2	...	....	8832
2124	28 53 7.3	6.5	+ 10.75	+ 0.63	...	6	46.5	10.7	....	8843
2125	4 25 3.9	58.7	+ 10.76	+ 2.23	...	18	48.6	7.2	....	......
2126	42 5 58.8	...	+ 10.77	+ 0.53	...	3	51.9	...	....	8846
2127	42 6 9.9	...	+ 10.78	+ 0.53	...	2	52.7	...	....	8849
2128	32 5 48.3	...	+ 10.87	+ 0.59	...	4	49.0	...	....	8878
2129	4 16 32.1	...	+ 10.89	+ 2.21	...	4	49.8	...	....	......
2130	36 17 14.7	11.0	+ 10.92	+ 0.55	+ 0.04	5	43.9	8.2	....	8884

Magnitude.	Estimates of Magnitude.	Mean Right Ascension 1845.0.		Precession 1845.0.	Secular Variation	Adopted Proper Motion.	Observations of R.A.		
R.	R.	R.	G.				No. R.	Mean year. R.	G.
		h. m. s.	s.	s.	s.	s.		1800 +	
4.7	12	8 12 12.33	12.06	+ 4.140	− 0.034	.....	9	49.6	9.2
7.4	6	8 12 13.62	13.43	+ 5.813	− 0.117	......	4	43.9	11.1
6.3	8	8 14 11.99	11.79	+ 4.091	− 0.034	......	5	43.4	11.2
8.8	7	8 14 13.64	13.67	+ 4.090	− 0.034	......	4	46.2	11.2
5.5	8	8 15 4.29	4.34	+ 5.794	− 0.120	......	4	43.9	10.2
8.8	4	8 15 46.40	...	+ 6.963	− 0.213	......	3	51.5	...
6.9	9	8 16 28.37	28.09	+ 4.012	− 0.031	......	6	49.0	11.2
8.5	4	8 16 35.24	...	+11.901	− 0.910	......	4	50.0	...
6.7	7	8 16 46.75	47.95	+ 4.222	− 0.040	......	4	45.9	13.2
3.8	8	8 17 20.17	19.80	+ 5.081	− 0.080	− 0.019	4	43.9	8.8
7.3	8	8 17 26.11	...	+ 6.917	− 0.212	......	5	50.3	...
6.2	8	8 17 28.04	27.73	+ 6.074	− 0.149	......	4	44.4	12.2
9.0	5	8 17 28.36	...	+ 4.008	− 0.029	......	3	49.9	...
7.0	6	8 17 45.92	47.10	+11.764	− 0.897	......	8	47.7	7.3
7.5	8	8 18 26.47	26.24	+ 5.768	− 0.120	......	4	44.2	12.2
5.9	6	8 18 35.97	...	+ 7.245	− 0.260	......	4	50.2	...
8.0	7	8 19 43.33	43.06	+ 4.558	− 0.054	......	4	45.2	11.2
...	...	8 19 58.11	...	+ 3.358	− 0.011	......	3	55.2	...
8.0	7	8 20 31.00	31.00	+ 6.091	− 0.149	......	4	44.4	11.2
4.9	6	8 20 39.47	39.01	+ 5.486	− 0.111	......	5	44.9	8.2
7.3	9	8 20 46.50	46.40	+ 4.005	− 0.031	......	5	49.4	13.1
7.3	3	8 20 52.62	52.44	+ 4.001	− 0.031	......	3	44.9	13.1
7.0	4	8 20 53.59	53.35	+ 4.554	− 0.051	......	3	45.5	11.2
8.9	4	8 21 6.50	...	+ 5.617	− 0.113	......	4	52.1	...
9.0	2	8 21 7.20	...	+ 5.616	− 0.113	......	1	52.1	...
8.7	6	8 21 12.46	...	+ 6.919	− 0.220	......	3	46.4	...
8.6	3	8 21 22.00	...	+ 5.625	− 0.114	......	2	50.2	...
6.7	6	8 21 25.00	24.78	+ 4.894	− 0.069	......	3	47.6	12.2
8.8	6	8 21 27.82	27.23	+ 6.107	− 0.151	......	3	50.1	11.1
7.1	12	8 21 42.83	42.65	+ 6.100	− 0.151	......	9	46.3	11.1
5.8	9	8 22 19.78	19.11	+ 6.902	− 0.229	......	5	45.4	10.2
7.4	6	8 22 44.61	...	+14.241	− 1.490	......	6	51.6	...
5.2	5	8 22 45.10	...	+ 3.436	− 0.013	− 0.006	10	47.2	...
6.3	5	8 22 49.50	49.72	+ 3.935	− 0.029	......	4	45.2	10.2
7.6	4	8 23 32.55	...	+ 4.181	− 0.038	......	3	51.5	...

Ordinal Number.	Mean North Polar Distance 1845.0.		Precession 1845.0.	Secular Variation.	Adopted Proper Motion.	Observations of N.P.D.			Names.	Oeltzen-Argelander Number.
R.	R.	G.				No. R.	Mean year. R.	G.		
	o ' "	"	"	"	"		1800 +			
2131	46 19 11.7	10.7	+ 10.93	+ 0.48	...	5	43.2	9.2	31 Lyncis......	......
2132	22 13 12.9	13.7	+ 10.94	+ 0.71	...	5	44.8	11.1	....	8889
2133	47 30 5.0	4.8	+ 11.09	+ 0.51	...	4	44.2	11.2	....	......
2134	47 31 18.5	17.6	+ 11.09	+ 0.51	...	4	43.7	11.2	....	......
2135	22 12 1.2	59.7	+ 11.14	+ 0.68	...	6	45.9	10.2	....	8930
2136	15 54 12.2	...	+ 11.19	+ 0.84	...	3	45.2	...	....	......
2137	49 36 25.0	23.8	+ 11.25	+ 0.49	...	4	45.0	11.2	....	......
2138	7 8 28.4	...	+ 11.26	+ 1.44	...	4	47.0	...	....	......
2139	43 49 47.9	34.7	+ 11.27	+ 0.50	...	4	44.0	13.2	....	8963
2140	28 46 13.7	12.7	+ 11.31	+ 0.61	+ 0.13	6	45.2	8.8	1 Urs. Maj. o .	8976
2141	16 0 29.3	...	+ 11.32	+ 0.81	...	4	47.2	...	....	8975
2142	20 10 5.1	3.3	+ 11.32	+ 0.73	...	5	46.0	12.2	....	8978
2143	49 39 18.6	...	+ 11.32	+ 0.48	...	2	47.7	...	....	......
2144	7 13 39.9	40.7	+ 11.34	+ 1.43	...	6	46.1	7.3	....	......
2145	22 11 31.4	28.4	+ 11.39	+ 0.69	...	5	47.2	12.2	....	9000
2146	14 45 25.9	...	+ 11.40	+ 0.89	...	3	49.8	...	....	9003
2147	36 21 53.9	51.6	+ 11.48	+ 0.53	...	5	48.2	11.2	....	9015
2148	75 16 51.9	...	+ 11.50	+ 0.40	...	1	46.1	...	29 Cancri......	......
2149	19 53 57.0	53.4	+ 11.54	+ 0.73	...	5	47.8	11.2	....	......
2150	24 20 1.9	2.0	+ 11.54	+ 0.63	+ 0.08	4	44.9	8.2	2 Urs. Maj. A.	9037
2151	49 25 49.4	48.9	+ 11.55	+ 0.45	...	4	47.0	13.1	....	......
2152	49 15 36.2	36.6	+ 11.57	+ 0.49	...	3	47.3	13.1	....	......
2153	36 21 58.3	53.5	+ 11.57	+ 0.55	...	5	49.4	11.2	....	9041
2154	23 11 57.5	...	+ 11.58	+ 0.67	...	2	49.7	...	....	9044
2155	23 12 26.8	...	+ 11.58	+ 0.67	...	2	50.2	...	....	9046
2156	15 49 29.3	...	+ 11.59	+ 0.81	...	4	47.5	...	....	9047
2157	23 5 5.3	...	+ 11.60	+ 0.67	...	3	52.5	...	....	9052
2158	30 52 22.6	21.6	+ 11.61	+ 0.60	...	3	45.6	12.2	....	9053
2159	19 44 49.7	44.4	+ 11.61	+ 0.74	...	4	47.2	11.1	....	......
2160	19 46 34.9	29.5	+ 11.62	+ 0.71	...	4	45.0	11.1	....	......
2161	15 50 16.6	11.5	+ 11.67	+ 0.83	...	5	46.4	10.2	....	9068
2162	5 33 11.1	...	+ 11.70	+ 1.69	...	6	52.9	...	....	......
2163	71 23 9.2	...	+ 11.70	+ 0.41	+ 0.06	3	48.9	...	31 Cancri θ ...	......
2164	51 27 26.6	19.2	+ 11.70	+ 0.45	...	3	46.8	10.2	....	......
2165	44 16 46.9	...	+ 11.76	+ 0.50	...	4	52.7	...	....	

Magnitude.	Estimates of Magnitude.	Mean Right Ascension 1845.0		Precession 1845.0	Secular Variation	Adopted Proper Motion.	Observations of R.A.		
R.	R.	R.	G.				No. R.	Mean year. R.	G.
		h. m. s.	s.	s.	s.	s.		1800 +	
8.7	8	8 24 54.09	...	+ 9.878	— 0.643	......	3	52.5	...
5.3	6	8 25 21.98	22.09	+ 5.439	— 0.106	— 0.004	5	44.8	8.7
8.9	6	8 25 37.98	38.08	+ 4.094	— 0.037	......	3	47.8	13.2
7.1	6	8 25 47.36	48.08	+ 4.127	— 0.109	......	3	46.4	10.2
6.9	6	8 25 50.92	...	+ 6.749	— 0.212	......	3	50.1	...
9.1	5	8 26 13.58	...	+ 9.864	— 0.639	......	2	51.7	...
6.4	8	8 26 30.26	30.09	+ 4.964	— 0.080	......	5	46.6	12.2
5.0	4	8 26 36.06	35.61	+ 5.356	— 0.103	......	5	46.5	8.7
7.3	5	8 26 37.11	...	+ 4.247	— 0.042	......	3	50.2	...
5.2	5	8 26 45.86	45.87	+ 4.542	— 0.054	......	5	44.0	11.2
6.6	7	8 27 26.91	26.92	+ 4.513	— 0.057	......	4	44.4	13.1
7.6	4	8 27 31.00	31.08	+ 6.124	— 0.166	......	3	45.5	11.1
6.3	7	8 27 46.54	46.58	+ 4.501	— 0.051	......	3	44.9	13.1
9.2	5	8 27 57.40	57.57	+ 9.496	— 0.571	......	3	44.9	7.6
7.2	4	8 28 38.01	...	+ 5.254	— 0.101	......	5	47.0	...
8.1	5	8 28 40.89	40.84	+ 4.127	— 0.040	......	4	46.9	13.3
8.4	8	8 28 54.13	54.11	+ 4.128	— 0.040	......	3	46.9	13.3
7.4	7	8 28 57.70	...	+ 6.744	— 0.218	......	3	49.8	...
9.0	4	8 29 8.10	...	+ 5.245	— 0.096	......	2	49.7	...
7.9	6	8 29 31.33	31.27	+ 4.023	— 0.034	......	5	47.0	10.2
8.7	4	8 29 55.15	...	+ 5.234	— 0.096	......	2	49.7	...
5.7	5	8 30 16.97	16.58	+ 4.182	— 0.040	......	5	46.6	9.2
8.7	7	8 30 20.45	20.31	+ 4.146	— 0.040	......	4	46.2	14.2
7.8	14	8 30 34.98	...	+18.795	— 3.052	......	14	52.5	...
7.6	6	8 30 37.70	37.46	+ 3.976	— 0.031	......	4	44.7	11.2
7.9	6	8 31 8.30	8.17	+ 4.142	— 0.040	......	6	47.5	14.2
6.3	6	8 32 11.87	...	+ 4.217	— 0.042	......	4	48.0	...
7.6	7	8 32 22.80	23.00	+ 9.423	— 0.589	......	5	45.3	7.5
8.0	5	8 32 24.96	...	+ 4.298	— 0.045	......	3	45.8	...
8.3	4	8 32 25.46	...	+ 4.297	— 0.045	......	2	50.7	...
7.6	3	8 33 26.50	...	+10.398	— 0.754	......	3	49.6	...
7.2	6	8 33 55.02	...	+ 6.797	— 0.240	......	3	48.6	...
8.3	5	8 34 20.17	...	+15.752	— 2.052	......	5	51.8	...
6.5	5	8 34 42.21	41.92	+ 5.561	— 0.129	......	4	43.2	10.7
8.1	3	8 35 4.44	...	+ 3.439	— 0.014	......	3	53.2	...

Ordinal Number.	Mean North Polar Distance 1845.0.			Precession 1845.0.	Secular Variation.	Adopted Proper Motion.	Observations of N.P.D.			Names.	Oeltzen-Argelander Number.
R.	R.		G.				No.	Mean year.			
							R.	R.	G.		
	o ′ ″		″	″	″	″		1800 +			
2166	8 57 48.6		...	+ 11.85	+ 1.14	...	5	49.0	...	....	....
2167	24 27 2.4		2.0	+ 11.88	+ 0.63	− 0.05	5	44.6	8.7	3 Ursæ Majoris	9102
2168	46 24 20.4		19.6	+ 11.90	+ 0.50	...	3	45.9	13.2	....	....
2169	46 53 28.2		27.2	+ 11.91	+ 0.46	...	5	45.0	10.2	....	....
2170	16 17 31.1		...	+ 11.92	+ 0.79	...	5	49.4	...	....	9113
2171	8 59 4.1		...	+ 11.95	+ 1.12	...	3	52.9	...	....	....
2172	29 31 30.2		28.9	+ 11.96	+ 0.57	...	5	47.4	12.2	....	....
2173	25 8 14.6		14.7	+ 11.97	+ 0.63	− 0.02	6	46.2	8.7	4 Urs. Maj. π.	9126
2174	42 20 43.1		...	+ 11.97	+ 0.50	...	4	51.5	...	....	9128
2175	36 3 53.1		51.7	+ 11.98	+ 0.52	...	4	43.7	11.2	....	9130
2176	36 32 18.4		17.8	+ 12.03	+ 0.52	...	4	45.2	13.1	....	9140
2177	19 17 34.4		31.6	+ 12.03	+ 0.70	...	5	48.0	11.1	....	9139
2178	36 45 3.9		3.5	+ 12.05	+ 0.51	...	4	44.5	13.1	....	9145
2179	9 26 13.3		13.4	+ 12.06	+ 1.10	...	3	44.9	7.6	....	....
2180	26 0 9.4		...	+ 12.12	+ 0.63	...	3	44.2	...	....	9155
2181	45 13 6.7		5.1	+ 12.13	+ 0.51	...	5	47.6	13.3	....	9157
2182	45 10 13.0		10.9	+ 12.14	+ 0.50	...	6	49.0	13.3	....	9162
2183	16 9 36.8		...	+ 12.14	+ 0.78	...	5	43.8	...	....	9161
2184	26 3 25.2		...	+ 12.15	+ 0.60	...	3	43.6	...	....	9170
2185	48 5 39.3		39.5	+ 12.17	+ 0.45	...	3	45.5	10.2	....	....
2186	26 6 50.6		...	+ 12.20	+ 0.60	...	2	43.7	...	....	9186
2187	43 37 40.0		40.7	+ 12.23	+ 0.49	− 0.06	5	46.8	9.2	34 Lyncis	9193
2188	44 33 48.3		48.1	+ 12.23	+ 0.48	...	4	43.7	14.2	....	9199
2189	3 51 4.9		...	+ 12.25	+ 2.17	...	7	52.8	...	....	....
2190	49 26 23.6		23.9	+ 12.26	+ 0.48	...	4	43.2	11.2	....	....
2191	44 35 26.6		27.4	+ 12.28	+ 0.45	...	3	44.9	14.2	....	9211
2192	42 32 56.8		...	+ 12.36	+ 0.48	...	4	43.2	...	....	....
2193	9 24 11.4		10.5	+ 12.37	+ 1.09	...	9	45.3	7.5	....	....
2194	40 35 6.0		...	+ 12.37	+ 0.49	...	2	47.2	...	....	9231
2195	40 35 13.7		...	+ 12.37	+ 0.49	...	2	47.8	...	....	....
2196	8 8 31.5		...	+ 12.45	+ 1.19	...	3	44.2	...	....	....
2197	15 41 7.3		...	+ 12.47	+ 0.78	...	4	49.0	...	....	....
2198	4 42 36.3		...	+ 12.51	+ 1.71	...	6	52.4	...	....	......
2199	42 43 49.8		47.7	+ 12.53	+ 0.63	...	6	46.2	10.7	....	....
2200	70 24 40.0		...	+ 12.55	+ 0.40	...	1	53.2	...	....	....

Magnitude.	Estimates of Magnitude.	Mean Right Ascension 1845.0.		Precession 1845.0.	Secular Variation	Adopted Proper Motion.
	R.	R.	G.			
		h. m. s.	s.	s.	s.	s.
7.6	4	8 35 46.04	...	+ 5.191	— 0.095	......
4.4	10	8 35 52.18	...	+ 3.422	— 0.014	— 0.002
7.1	7	8 36 9.11	9.00	+ 6.063	— 0.169	......
8.2	6	8 37 11.51	...	+ 5.001	— 0.089	......
3.7	11	8 38 33.95	...	+ 3.196	— 0.009	— 0.013
7.3	7	8 38 59.28	59.21	+ 3.900	— 0.031	......
7.6	9	8 39 11.80	...	+ 4.117	— 0.039	......
7.9	5	8 39 15.32	...	+ 4.112	— 0.039	......
9.0	6	8 39 31.78	...	+ 4.115	— 0.039	......
8.8	7	8 40 6.46	...	+14.974	— 1.943	......
7.9	5	8 40 19.12	19.25	+ 4.060	— 0.040	......
5.7	10	8 40 32.95	32.10	+ 5.036	— 0.097	......
7.6	6	8 41 28.71	...	+ 4.554	— 0.061	......
4.9	7	8 41 31.45	31.23	+ 4.064	— 0.040	......
6.3	5	8 41 38.03	...	+ 4.120	— 0.040	......
7.8	6	8 41 50.63	...	+ 4.104	— 0.040	......
5.8	5	8 41 53.74	53.77	+ 4.005	— 0.034	......
6.5	22	8 41 55.92	...	+14.221	— 2.013	......
8.6	4	8 42 40.24	...	+ 7.137	— 0.309	......
7.2	5	8 43 1.30	1.35	+ 6.052	— 0.177	......
8.7	4	8 43 9.23	8.92	+ 4.954	— 0.089	......
9.0	7	8 43 10.54	10.19	+ 3.999	— 0.037	......
5.7	4	8 43 15.97	15.45	+ 5.259	— 0.111	+ 0.003
7.2	4	8 43 18.24	...	+ 5.354	— 0.116	......
8.1	6	8 43 46.50	...	+ 9.943	— 0.740	......
8.0	5	8 43 52.96	...	+ 8.763	— 0.530	......
7.4	6	8 44 22.99	22.72	+ 3.937	— 0.034	......
9.1	7	8 44 27.41	...	+ 9.970	— 0.744	......
8.5	7	8 45 3.27	3.46	+ 4.934	— 0.089	......
7.2	5	8 45 6.01	5.83	+ 5.391	— 0.123	......
7.3	6	8 45 58.70	58.57	+ 5.125	+ 0.103	......
7.2	7	8 46 0.36	...	+ 4.120	— 0.042	......
7.3	4	8 46 4.97	5.10	+ 5.117	— 0.109	......
8.7	6	8 46 17.89	...	+ 7.168	— 0.314	......
5.6	9	8 46 18.91	18.83	+ 4.114	— 0.043	......

Ordinal Number. R.	Mean North Polar Distance 1845.0. R.		G.	Precession 1845.0.	Secular Variation.	Adopted Proper Motion.	Observations of N.P.D. No. R.	Mean year. R. 1800 +	G.	Names.	Oeltzen-Argelander Number.
	° ′ ″		″	″	″	″					
2201	26 6 53.9		...	+ 12.60	+ 0.59	...	4	44.5	...	....	9278
2202	71 16 48.2		...	+ 12.61	+ 0.39	+ 0.24	5	45.4	...	47 Cancri δ....	....
2203	19 8 6.1		4.1	+ 12.63	+ 0.69	...	6	46.5	11.2	....	....
2204	28 11 5.4		...	+ 12.71	+ 0.57	...	5	46.6	...	....	9296
2205	83 0 58.6		...	+ 12.79	+ 0.36	+ 0.04	11	51.4	...	11 Hydræ ε ...	....
2206	51 5 18.1		19.9	+ 12.82	+ 0.43	...	5	48.2	10.8	....	....
2207	44 27 13.0		...	+ 12.83	+ 0.46	...	5	49.0	...	....	....
2208	44 43 38.0		...	+ 12.84	+ 0.46	...	3	46.2	...	....	....
2209	44 27 31.1		...	+ 12.86	+ 0.46	...	4	49.8	...	....	9331
2210	4 54 55.2		...	+ 12.90	+ 1.69	...	3	51.6	...	....	....
2211	45 55 36.5		34.7	+ 12.91	+ 0.44	...	5	44.5	11.2	....	....
2212	27 27 50.8		51.4	+ 12.93	+ 0.57	...	6	45.2	9.2	5 Urs. Maj. b .	9341
2213	34 28 23.5		...	+ 12.99	+ 0.51	...	3	47.6	...	....	9357
2214	45 42 4.4		4.7	+ 12.99	+ 0.44	− 0.03	5	43.2	10.9	35 Lyncis......	....
2215	44 6 40.0		...	+ 13.00	+ 0.46	...	4	52.7	...	....	9361
2216	44 31 33.5		...	+ 13.01	+ 0.47	...	4	52.7	...	....	....
2217	47 25 10.0		8.1	+ 13.02	+ 0.66	...	4	44.2	13.2	....	....
2218	5 12 43.8		...	+ 13.02	+ 1.50	...	7	52.8	...	....	....
2219	13 59 0.8		...	+ 13.07	+ 0.79	...	3	44.6	...	....	....
2220	18 45 32.6		30.4	+ 13.09	+ 0.66	...	4	47.7	11.2	....	9379
2221	28 14 47.4		41.5	+ 13.10	+ 0.54	...	4	46.5	13.1	....	9383
2222	47 26 7.5		9.2	+ 13.10	+ 0.43	...	4	48.3	13.2	....	....
2223	24 48 33.9		35.2	+ 13.11	+ 0.58	+ 0.13	6	46.5	8.5	6 Ursæ Majoris	9384 .
2224	23 53 25.3		...	+ 13.11	+ 0.59	...	2	48.7	...	....	9386
2225	8 21 27.5		...	+ 13.14	+ 1.10	...	4	43.5	...	....	....
2226	10 3 24.4		...	+ 13.15	+ 0.96	...	5	50.0	...	....	9393
2227	49 16 41.2		35.0	+ 13.18	+ 0.42	...	3	44.9	10.8	....	....
2228	8 18 20.8		...	+ 13.18	+ 1.10	...	4	44.0	...	....	.....
2229	28 19 38.7		34.5	+ 13.22	+ 0.52	...	3	44.6	13.2	....	9408
2230	23 24 30.7		29.6	+ 13.23	+ 0.59	...	4	45.0	12.2	....	....
2231	25 58 48.5		47.6	+ 13.28	+ 0.54	...	4	45.2	11.2	....	9422
2232	43 38 56.7		...	+ 13.29	+ 0.45	...	4	46.2	...	....	9424
2233	26 3 17.8		15.6	+ 13.29	+ 0.55	...	3	45.9	11.2	....	9425
2234	13 43 1.5		...	+ 13.30	+ 0.77	...	3	44.9	..	....	....
2235	43 46 44.1		42.4	+ 13.30	+ 0.42	...	5	48.0	9.3	....	9430

Ordinal Number.		Magnitude.	Estimates of Magnitude.	Mean Right Ascension 1845.0.		Precession 1845.0.	Secular Variation	Adopted Proper Motion.	Observations of R.A.		
R.	G.		R.	R.	G.				No. R.	Mean year. R.	G.
				h. m. s.	s.	s.	s.	s.		1800 +	
2236	1487	5.8	6	8 46 25.92	25.84	+ 3.933	— 0.034	.....	5	46.4	10.2
2237	...	6.9	5	8 46 40.70	...	+ 4.069	— 0.040	......	4	50.2	...
2238	1488	7.4	6	8 47 1.39	1.39	+ 3.966	— 0.037	......	4	46.7	14.2
2239	1480	6.3	5	8 47 36.34	36.15	+ 9.680	— 0.720	......	4	45.2	7.9
2240	1491	8.9	5	8 47 42.02	41.79	+ 4.200	— 0.049	......	2	47.8	13.3
2241	1490	4.4	7	8 48 29.06	28.06	+ 5.552	— 0.143	+ 0.006	5	45.1	8.6
2242	1492	2.9	5	8 48 34.10	34.00	+ 4.197	— 0.046	— 0.047	31	46.3	7.3
2243	1489	7.1	6	8 48 35.31	35.32	+ 6.104	— 0.189	......	5	43.7	10.3
2244	1493	8.3	7	8 48 37.38	37.33	+ 4.204	— 0.049	......	4	49.2	13.2
2245	...	6.6	5	8 48 52.82	...	+ 4.107	— 0.042	......	4	47.2	...
2246	...	4.4	5	8 50 0.29	...	+ 3.288	— 0.012	......	12	47.3	...
2247	1495	4.5	12	8 50 33.46	33.28	+ 3.968	— 0.037	— 0.040	11	48.1	7.6
2248	1496	6.4	7	8 50 38.50	38.42	+ 3.844	— 0.031	......	6	47.6	10.2
2249	1494	7.8	4	8 50 44.56	44.61	+ 4.256	— 0.049	......	3	46.2	12.3
2250	...	8.7	7	8 50 44.87	...	+ 4.261	— 0.049	......	4	52.7	...
2251	1497	8.5	6	8 51 14.19	14.17	+ 4.027	— 0.037	......	3	48.6	13.2
2252	1498	6.7	6	8 51 40.30	40.30	+ 3.900	— 0.037	......	4	45.2	13.1
2253	1500	7.1	9	8 52 8.93	8.71	+ 4.258	— 0.051	......	4	46.7	12.2
2254	1499	7.5	7	8 52 17.36	17.19	+ 4.786	— 0.089	......	3	44.5	11.2
2255	1502	7.4	5	8 52 22.73	22.70	+ 3.868	— 0.034	......	5	47.8	13.2
2256	1501	6.0	8	8 52 36.70	36.23	+ 4.457	— 0.066	......	3	45.5	9.2
2257	1503	3.9	10	8 53 1.04	1.01	+ 4.143	— 0.046	......	12	49.7	7.3
2258	1504	7.4	4	8 53 36.18	36.20	+ 3.841	— 0.034	......	3	45.2	14.2
2259	...	9.0	8	8 53 39.12	...	+ 4.018	— 0.040	......	4	48.6	...
2260	1506	7.0	5	8 53 51.71	51.12	+ 3.838	— 0.111	......	4	48.9	13.2
2261	1507	7.0	7	8 54 10.37	10.33	+ 4.008	— 0.043	......	5	46.4	13.2
2262	...	6.8	5	8 54 22.41	...	+ 4.284	— 0.053	......	3	47.9	...
2263	1509	7.1	5	8 54 34.88	35.16	+ 4.006	— 0.046	......	5	47.1	13.2
2264	...	6.3	5	8 54 37.75	...	+ 4.742	— 0.081	......	3	47.3	...
2265	1508	5.7	5	8 54 40.53	40.48	+ 4.188	— 0.049	......	5	44.9	11.2
2266	1505	5.0	6	8 54 42.08	42.10	+ 5.403	— 0.137	......	6	42.5	10.7
2267	...	7.4	4	8 55 32.98	...	+ 4.227	— 0.050	......	3	50.2	...
2268	...	7.0	4	8 55 50.14	...	+ 6.029	— 0.210	......	4	47.8	...
2269	1512	7.9	7	8 55 59.59	59.84	+ 3.850	— 0.034	......	4	46.3	10.3
2270	1511	7.2	5	8 56 12.08	12.16	+ 4.311	— 0.057	......	4	47.4	11.2

Ordinal Number. R.	Mean North Polar Distance 1845.0. R.	G.	Precession 1845.0.	Secular Variation.	Adopted Proper Motion.	Observations of M.P.D. No. R.	Mean year. R.	G.	Names.	Oeltzen-Argelander Number.
	° ′ ″	″	″	″	″		1800 +			
2236	49 12 34.4	31.0	+ 13.31	+ 0.41	...	4	44.2	10.2	....	......
2237	45 0 9.2	...	+ 13.33	+ 0.44	...	4	49.7	...	....	9437
2238	48 4 13.9	13.0	+ 13.36	+ 0.44	...	4	45.2	14.2	....	......
2239	8 33 41.0	40.2	+ 13.40	+ 1.09	...	5	45.6	7.9	....	......
2240	41 21 29.3	27.2	+ 13.40	+ 0.45	...	3	48.9	13.3	....	9450
2241	21 46 22.2	22.9	+ 13.45	+ 0.60	...	6	45.9	8.6	8 Urs. Maj. ρ .	9457
2242	41 21 16.1	17.5	+ 13.46	+ 0.46	+ 0.28	12	43.7	7.3	9 Urs. Maj. ι .	9463
2243	18 5 34.3	33.6	+ 13.46	+ 0.77	...	5	45.0	10.3	....	9458
2244	41 8 7.3	6.4	+ 13.46	+ 0.45	...	4	47.0	13.2	....	9469
2245	43 39 56.3	...	+ 13.48	+ 0.45	...	4	44.5	...	....	9472
2246	77 32 46.3	...	+ 13.55	+ 0.35	+ 0.04	8	43.3	...	65 Cancri α ...	......
2247	47 36 27.8	27.1	+ 13.58	+ 0.40	+ 0.27	10	43.2	7.6	10 Urs. Maj...	......
2248	51 47 48.2	49.4	+ 13.59	+ 0.41	...	4	45.7	10.2	....	......
2249	39 39 27.1	24.0	+ 13.59	+ 0.43	...	5	45.6	12.3	....	9493
2250	39 36 41.7	...	+ 13.59	+ 0.43	...	5	48.0	...	....	9494
2251	45 43 2.0	0.0	+ 13.62	+ 0.40	...	3	43.9	13.2	....	......
2252	49 40 54.7	50.9	+ 13.66	+ 0.42	...	4	44.0	13.1	....	......
2253	39 26 49.3	51.0	+ 13.69	+ 0.46	...	6	47.0	12.2	....	9509
2254	28 24 7.1	5.6	+ 13.70	+ 0.53	...	4	44.7	11.2	....	......
2255	50 44 20.0	17.6	+ 13.70	+ 0.40	...	5	49.4	13.2	....	......
2256	35 6 37.0	37.4	+ 13.72	+ 0.48	...	6	46.7	9.2	....	9519
2257	42 14 6.9	7.5	+ 13.74	+ 0.43	+ 0.09	5	43.2	7.3	12 Urs. Maj. κ	9526
2258	51 32 43.8	38.4	+ 13.78	+ 0.40	...	3	46.2	14.2	....	......
2259	45 42 0.1	...	+ 13.78	+ 0.42	...	4	47.2	...	....	......
2260	50 38 58.4	57.6	+ 13.79	+ 0.39	...	5	50.2	13.2	....	......
2261	45 56 55.2	54.5	+ 13.81	+ 0.40	...	5	47.4	13.2	....	......
2262	38 33 47.3	...	+ 13.82	+ 0.45	...	5	48.4	...	....	......
2263	45 55 53.3	49.5	+ 13.85	+ 0.44	...	5	47.6	13.2	....	......
2264	30 2 33.6	...	+ 13.85	+ 0.50	...	4	47.7	..	....	9540
2265	40 51 30.4	30.0	+ 13.85	+ 0.44	...	5	46.6	11.2	....	......
2266	22 30 37.9	37.0	+ 13.85	+ 0.57	+ 0.06	5	45.6	10.7	11 Urs. Maj. σ¹	9541
2267	39 46 32.4	...	+ 13.90	+ 0.44	+ 0.05	3	48.2	...	....	9554
2268	18 1 2.2	...	+ 13.92	+ 0.63	...	3	45.5	...	....	9563
2269	50 56 47.3	45.8	+ 13.93	+ 0.39	...	5	49.4	10 3	....	......
2270	37 45 16.9	14.6	+ 13.94	+ 0.44	...	5	47.2	11 2	....	9571

Ordinal Number		Magnitude	Estimates of Magnitude	Mean Right Ascension 1845.0		Precession 1845.0	Secular Variation	Adopted Proper Motion	Observations of R.A.		
R.	G.	R.		R.	G.				No.	Mean year R.	G.
				h. m. s.	s.	s.	s.	s.		1800 +	
2271	1513	5.2	10	8 56 39.13	38.99	+ 3.848	− 0.034	......	9	48.7	9.4
2272	1510	5.1	8	8 56 40.36	39.35	+ 5.415	− 0.140	......	8	47.3	10.7
2273	...	8.3	17	8 56 40.64	...	+25.257	− 7.400	......	14	53.5	...
2274	1514	6.9	6	8 56 55.98	55.08	+ 3.843	− 0.034	......	3	45.2'	10.3
2275	1516	4.7	11	8 57 54.26	54.07	+ 4.301	− 0.057	− 0.012	5	45.6	11.2
2276	1515	4.3	8	8 58 4.58	3.56	+ 5.036	− 0.111	+ 0.012	5	45.4	8.3
2277	...	6.6	7	8 58 50.95	...	+ 6.044	− 0.220	......	4	44.9	...
2278	...	5.5	6	8 59 20.78	...	+ 3.259	− 0.011	− 0.002	3	44.6	...
2279	...	8.5	7	8 59 22.98	...	+ 4.110	− 0.046	......	4	47.7	...
2280	1517	6.0	7	9 0 9.63	9.93	+ 6.276	− 0.229	......	3	44.6	11.2
2281	...	9.1	4	9 0 15.20	...	+ 4.890	− 0.097	......	3	48.2	...
2282	1518	7.5	6	9 0 22.43	22.08	+ 4.868	− 0.094	......	4	44.0	12.2
2283	1519	8.0	6	9 0 23.90	23.94	+ 4.868	− 0.097	......	5	45.6	12.2
2284	1520	8.1	8	9 0 54.97	54.93	+ 3.872	− 0.031	......	7	47.9	13.3
2285	...	9.3	6	9 1 3.04	...	+ 4.870	− 0.095	......	3	51.5	...
2286	1521	5.4	7	9 2 1.93	1.68	+ 4.836	− 0.094	+ 0.012	7	48.5	8.2
2287	1523	7.6	7	9 3 9.34	8.94	+ 4.092	− 0.046	......	3	44.5	11.2
2288	1524	5.5	8	9 3 38.62	38.56	+ 3.964	− 0.040	......	10	48.2	10.3
2289	1522	6.8	6	9 3 46.04	45.92	+ 6.459	− 0.263	......	4	44.7	13.2
2290	...	7.3	4	9 3 46.17	...	+ 4.319	− 0.059	......	2	48.7	...
2291	...	7.9	3	9 3 47.58	...	+ 4.319	− 0.059	......	2	50.2	...
2292	1525	5.1	4	9 4 18.09	17.70	+ 4.519	− 0.074	......	4	44.5	9.5
2293	1526	5.0	6	9 4 59.85	59.11	+ 4.374	− 0.063	+ 0.004	7	47.9	8.8
2294	1527	6.8	8	9 5 10.37	10.66	+ 3.825	− 0.034	......	4	44.7	11.2
2295	...	8.1	30	9 5 19.14	...	+27.097	− 9.366	......	34	52.5	...
2296	...	7.6	7	9 5 24.81	...	+ 6.653	− 0.287	......	2	48.7	...
2297	...	4.4	5	9 6 17.81	...	+ 3.117	− 0.008	+ 0.013	9	50.3	...
2298	1528	6.1	11	9 7 5.68	7.66	+ 4.068	− 0.046	− 0.008	7	45.5	11.3
2299	...	7.8	7	9 7 15.15	...	+ 6.641	− 0.291	......	5	49.8	...
2300	...	8.7	6	9 8 5.73	...	+ 6.694	− 0.300	......	3	49.9	...
2301	1529	7.3	6	9 8 34.46	34.46	+ 4.673	− 0.086	+ 0.015	5	46.0	10.2
2302	1530	7.0	9	9 8 51.20	51.23	+ 4.064	− 0.049	......	5	44.0	11.3
2303	1531	8.2	6	9 8 59.54	59.43	+ 3.897	− 0.040	......	3	45.6	11.2
2304	1532	6.7	6	9 9 33.34	33.12	+ 4.276	− 0.060	......	4	44.8	12.2
2305	1533	6.1	10	9 9 56.31	55.98	+ 4.223	− 0.057	......	8	47.8	9.2

Ordinal Number.	Mean North Polar Distance 1845.0.			Precession 1845.0.	Secular Variation.	Adopted Proper Motion.	Observations of M.P.D.			Names.	Oeltzen-Argelander Number.
							No.	Mean year.			
R.	R.		G.				R.	R.	G.		
	° ′ ″		″	″	″	″		1800 +			
2271	50 55 57.6		56.9	+ 13.97	+ 0.39	...	4	45.0	9.4	....	......
2272	22 14 33.6		32.1	+ 13.97	+ 0.56	+ 0.11	5	44.2	10.7	13 Urs. Maj. σ^2	9578
2273	2 28 31.4		...	+ 13.97	+ 2.57	...	5	52.8	...	....	......
2274	51 6 20.8		18.5	+ 13.99	+ 0.40	...	3	46.2	10.3	....	......
2275	37 46 28.4		28.1	+ 14.05	+ 0.44	+ 0.05	8	48.4	11.2	15 Urs. Maj. f	9596
2276	25 51 41.4		42.1	+ 14.06	+ 0.53	+ 0.09	5	43.2	8.3	14 Urs. Maj. τ	9598
2277	17 42 54.4		...	+ 14.11	+ 0.63	...	5	45.1	...	....	9614
2278	78 42 41.6		...	+ 14.14	+ 0.34	...	3	44.6	...	76 Cancri κ....	......
2279	42 21 59.5		...	+ 14.15	+ 0.42	...	3	45.6	...	....	9632
2280	16 25 11.7		8.1	+ 14.19	+ 0.65	...	5	47.2	11.2	....	9640
2281	27 25 46.0		...	+ 14.20	+ 0.51	...	3	48.2	...	....	......
2282	27 41 49.6		46.4	+ 14.20	+ 0.49	...	4	44.5	12.2	....	9644
2283	27 41 27.7		20.6	+ 14.20	+ 0.48	...	4	44.5	12.2	....	9647
2284	49 35 6.6		2.9	+ 14.23	+ 0.37	...	3	43.9	13.3	....	......
2285	27 36 24.1		...	+ 14.24	+ 0.52	...	4	52.8	...	....	9657
2286	27 56 37.8		38.7	+ 14.31	+ 0.50	+ 0.06	8	47.8	8.2	16 Urs. Maj. c	9676
2287	42 22 38.1		39.3	+ 14.37	+ 0.40	...	6	46.6	11.2	....	9691
2288	46 8 51.4		50.5	+ 14.40	+ 0.41	+ 0.05	6	45.7	10.3	36 Lyncis......	......
2289	15 20 23.1		20.7	+ 14.41	+ 0.65	...	6	46.6	13.2	....	......
2290	36 39 17.4		...	+ 14.41	+ 0.45	...	4	49.0	...	....	9703
2291	36 39 5.3		...	+ 14.41	+ 0.45	...	4	50.2	...	....	9704
2292	32 37 15.3		16.3	+ 14.44	+ 0.44	+ 0.07	7	44.3	9.5	17 Urs. Maj.....	9709
2293	35 20 35.3		34.7	+ 14.49	+ 0.45	− 0.06	13	45.8	9.5	18 Urs. Maj. e	9720
2294	50 45 26.5		28.7	+ 14.50	+ 0.39	...	4	45.3	11.2	....	......
2295	2 12 1.0		...	+ 14.51	+ 2.73	...	10	52.2	...	....	......
2296	14 26 28.8		...	+ 14.51	+ 0.66	...	5	50.2	...	....	......
2297	87 2 6.9		...	+ 14.56	+ 0.31	+ 0.32	5	51.4	...	22 Hydræ θ...	......
2298	42 32 27.9		27.9	+ 14.61	+ 0.39	...	12	49.2	11.3	....	......
2299	14 22 26.1		...	+ 14.62	+ 0.66	...	4	50.7	...	....	......
2300	14 6 49.1		...	+ 14.68	+ 0.66	...	5	51.6	...	....	......
2301	29 34 14.2		12.8	+ 14.70	+ 0.46	...	6	46.9	10.2	20 Urs. Maj. ..	......
2302	42 24 33.1		31.1	+ 14.72	+ 0.40	...	7	47.2	11.3	....	9778
2303	47 39 14.6		14.5	+ 14.72	+ 0.36	...	5	47.2	11.2	....	......
2304	36 54 1.6		59.7	+ 14.76	+ 0.42	...	6	47.6	12.2	....	9784
2305	38 5 25.2		27.9	+ 14.78	+ 0.41	− 0.10	6	45.5	9.2	....	9789

Magnitude.	Estimates of Magnitudes.	Mean Right Ascension 1845.0.		Precession 1845.0.	Secular Variation	Adopted Proper Motion.
		R.	G.			
R.	R.	h. m. s.	s.	s.	s.	s.
8.1	5	9 10 15.24	15.37	+ 3.832	− 0.037	......
7.8	5	9 10 15.53	...	+ 4.216	− 0.056	......
6.0	7	9 10 17.74	17.86	+ 4.477	− 0.074	......
6.7	1	9 10 19.47	...	+ 3.369	− 0.015	− 0.012
6.6	9	9 11 8.41	8.98	+ 4.001	− 0.046	......
6.4	7	9 11 15.62	15.61	+ 3.793	− 0.034	......
6.3	5	9 11 22.84	...	+ 6.605	− 0.297	......
6.7	4	9 11 26.02	26.26	+ 3.832	− 0.034	......
9.1	6	9 11 28.99	...	+ 3.850	− 0.036	......
7.2	4	9 11 32.60	...	+ 3.848	− 0.036	......
8.5	6	9 11 43.47	...	+ 4.203	− 0.056	......
9.7	3	9 11 56.09	...	+ 4.144	− 0.054	......
6.9	5	9 11 56.21	56.33	+ 4.144	− 0.054	+ 0.009
7.6	3	9 12 38.96	...	+ 3.842	− 0.036	......
8.4	14	9 13 7.22	...	+12.343	− 1.666	......
6.2	5	9 13 11.09	11.07	+ 4.944	− 0.111	......
7.1	5	9 14 7.31	...	+ 4.161	− 0.054	......
6.1	7	9 14 8.56	8.13	+ 4.212	− 0.060	......
4.5	8	9 14 28.94	27.72	+ 9.360	− 0.846	− 0.063
9.1	10	9 14 36.24	...	+ 4.317	− 0.066	......
7.7	5	9 14 36.85	36.48	+ 4.317	− 0.066	+ 0.005
8.4	6	9 15 16.60	...	+ 5.946	− 0.225	......
9.0	5	9 16 2.24	...	+ 4.056	− 0.049	......
7.5	10	9 16 38.28	38.23	+ 4.056	− 0.054	......
7.5	6	9 17 7.50	...	+ 5.885	− 0.218	......
8.3	6	9 17 37.62	...	+ 3.984	− 0.045	......
7.6	6	9 17 53.49	...	+ 5.243	− 0.136	......
9.1	3	9 17 54.38	...	+ 5.242	− 0.136	......
8.0	5	9 17 59.38	...	+ 5.169	− 0.129	......
5.9	13	9 18 28.92	28.69	+ 3.976	− 0.046	......
8.1	7	9 18 31.55	31.19	+ 3.975	− 0.046	......
7.9	2	9 18 38.27	...	+ 5.181	......	......
6.5	5	9 18 40.24	40.76	+ 4.373	− 0.071	.....
3.6	5	9 19 14.60	14.56	+ 4.818	− 0.109	+ 0.011
2.6	3	9 19 58.26	...	+ 2.949	− 0.003	− 0.004

Ordinal Number.	Mean North Polar Distance 1845.0.		Precession 1845.0.	Secular Variation.	Adopted Proper Motion.	Observations of N.P.D.			Names.	Oeltzen-Argelander Number.
	R.	G.				No. R.	Mean year R.	Mean year G.		
	° ′ ″	″	″	″	″		1800 +			
2306	49 48 29.1	26.4	+ 14.80	+ 0.37	...	3	43.5	13.3	....	....
2307	38 2 57.9	...	+ 14.80	+ 0.42	...	4	45.2	...	....	9792
2308	32 38 55.6	55.4	+ 14.80	+ 0.43	...	6	45.9	12.2	....	....
2309	71 38 27.1	...	+ 14.80	+ 0.33	...	3	54.2	...	83 Cancri......	....
2310	43 58 38.0	34.4	+ 14.86	+ 0.40	...	4	43.5	13.2	....	9808
2311	51 9 34.7	33.2	+ 14.86	+ 0.36	...	3	46.2	11.2	....	....
2312	14 14 33.0	...	+ 14.87	+ 0.66	...	5	51.0	...	....	9810
2313	49 40 48.5	47.6	+ 14.87	+ 0.37	...	4	48.2	13.3	....	....
2314	48 57 42.7	...	+ 14.87	+ 0.38	...	4	51.2	...	....	....
2315	49 3 45.4	...	+ 14.88	+ 0.38	...	4	48.7	...	....	....
2316	38 19 51.4	...	+ 14.89	+ 0.42	...	3	44.2	...	....	9812
2317	39 47 56.2	...	+ 14.90	+ 0.40	...	3	45.9	...	....	....
2318	39 48 2.0	0.9	+ 14.90	+ 0.40	+ 0.04	5	45.5	10.2	....	9818
2319	49 7 42.6	...	+ 14.94	+ 0.38	...	5	50.4	...	....	....
2320	5 28 52.7	...	+ 14.97	+ 1.17	...	7	52.9	...	....	....
2321	25 23 50.2	48.5	+ 14.97	+ 0.47	...	4	45.2	11.2	....	9834
2322	39 3 40.1	...	+ 15.03	+ 0.40	...	3	49.2	...	....	9842
2323	37 45 55.8	54.8	+ 15.03	+ 0.41	...	5	45.6	11.3	....	....
2324	7 59 50.8	50.7	+ 15.04	+ 0.89	...	17	49.6	7.2	...ι Draconis	....
2325	35 19 14.0	...	+ 15.05	+ 0.40	...	4	48.3	...	21 Urs. Maj. (1)	....
2326	35 19 17.8	16.9	+ 15.05	+ 0.40	...	5	47.8	9.2	21 Urs. Maj. (2)	9849
2327	17 0 52.8	...	+ 15.10	+ 0.57	...	3	46.3	...	....	9862
2328	41 39 13.6	...	+ 15.14	+ 0.39	...	3	47.2	...	....	9877
2329	41 33 40.9	40.1	+ 15.17	+ 0.38	...	5	43.2	11.2	....	9887
2330	17 12 54.9	...	+ 15.20	+ 0.55	...	4	45.7	...	....	9891
2331	43 34 41.7	...	+ 15.23	+ 0.38	...	5	48.2	...	....	9896
2332	21 47 10.5	...	+ 15.24	+ 0.50	...	4	48.7	...	....	9900
2333	21 47 31.0	...	+ 15.24	+ 0.50	...	2	48.7	...	....	....
2334	22 17 35.8	...	+ 15.25	+ 0.50	...	6	53.3	...	....	9905
2335	43 43 23.4	21.5	+ 15.28	+ 0.38	+ 0.14	18	49.0	10.2	41 Lyncis......	9916
2336	43 44 44.8	40.0	+ 15.28	+ 0.37	...	6	46.6	10.3	....	9918
2337	22 27 ...	...	....	...	...	...	...	...	....	9920
2338	33 34 54.5	51.6	+ 15.29	+ 0.41	...	4	44.2	11.2	....	....
2339	26 15 55.0	54.7	+ 15.32	+ 0.45	...	6	45.9	7.7	23 Urs. Maj. h	9930
2340	97 59 24.3	...	+ 15.36	+ 0.28	− 0.03	18	46.1	...	30 Hydræ a...	....

Ordinal Number.		Magnitude.	Estimates of Magnitude.	Mean Right Ascension 1845.0.			Precession 1845.0.	Secular Variation	Adopted Proper Motion.	Observations of R.A.		
R.	G.	R.		R.		G.				No.	Mean year.	
										R.	R.	G.
				h. m. s.		s.	s.	s.	s.		1800 +	
2341	...	5.6	2	9 20 5.82		...	+ 2.989	− 0.004	......	2	58.2	...
2342	1549	5.6	6	9 20 8.26		6.69	+ 5.859	− 0.223	+ 0.012	4	46.2	9.2
2343	...	7.9	8	9 20 14.96		...	+11.950	− 1.645	......	6	51.9	...
2344	1551	8.3	4	9 20 16.62		16.53	+ 4.041	− 0.051	......	4	48.6	11.2
2345	1550	4.9	6	9 20 40.15		40.14	+ 5.489	− 0.177	......	4	43.1	10.2
2346	...	9.0	6	9 21 3.16		...	+11.846	− 1.620	......	6	51.9	...
2347	...	8.2	6	9 21 19.51		...	+ 5.125	− 0.130	......	4	52.1	...
2348	...	8.6	6	9 21 21.33		...	+ 5.125	− 0.130	......	3	53.2	...
2349	...	7.8	6	9 21 38.28		...	+ 4.779	− 0.108	......	2	48.7	...
2350	...	8.6	9	9 21 49.64		...	+11.772	− 1.611	......	6	51.9	...
2351	1552	7.7	4	9 22 12.47		12.52	+ 4.047	− 0.054	......	3	44.9	11.2
2352	1553	8.0	7	9 22 17.74		17.71	+ 4.041	− 0.051	......	5	44.2	11.2
2353	1554	3.4	4	9 22 27.17		26.79	+ 4.171	− 0.060	− 0.111	14	43.9	7.3
2354	...	7.4	6	9 22 39.31		...	+ 5.802	− 0.213	− 0.019	4	47.2	...
2355	...	8.0	11	9 22 41.25		...	+11.168	− 1.376	......	8	53.4	...
2356	...	4.5	1	9 22 52.12		...	+ 3.441	− 0.019	− 0.004	1	53.1	...
2357	...	6.6	5	9 23 3.99		...	+ 3.951	− 0.045	......	3	50.2	...
2358	...	8.2	8	9 23 18.76		...	+11.400	− 1.490	......	6	53.7	...
2359	...	7.2	6	9 23 25.85		...	+ 4.266	− 0.065	......	3	44.9	...
2360	...	5.3	9	9 23 35.21		...	+ 3.249	− 0.012	− 0.009	12	48.6	...
2361	...	7.7	4	9 23 52.66		...	+ 3.941	− 0.045	......	2	51.7	...
2362	1556	4.5	6	9 24 10.13		10.08	+ 4.175	− 0.054	......	5	43.2	9.2
2363	1555	7.4	7	9 24 16.41		16.46	+ 4.573	− 0.106	......	4	44.8	10.7
2364	1560	5.3	7	9 25 22.41		22.34	+ 3.778	− 0.037	− 0.005	4	44.8	13.2
2365	1557	7.9	6	9 25 25.20		25.15	+ 5.361	− 0.171	......	3	44.6	11.3
2366	1558	7.3	7	9 25 31.52		31.00	+ 4.388	− 0.074	......	4	46.0	12.2
2367	1559	7.5	6	9 25 31.64		31.57	+ 4.036	− 0.051	......	3	45.6	11.3
2368	...	8.1	9	9 26 30.11		...	+20.698	− 6.212	......	3	51.2	...
2369	1561	6.9	6	9 27 38.74		38.90	+ 7.248	− 0.460	+ 0.016	3	44.9	13.3
2370	1563	5.2	9	9 28 32.79		32.04	+ 5.745	− 0.226	......	5	46.4	9.2
2371	1562	6.0	9	9 28 35.05		35.37	+ 7.648	− 0.540	......	6	46.4	7.5
2372	1565	5.8	5	9 28 39.92		39.89	+ 3.781	− 0.037	+ 0.003	6	44.6	10.3
2373	1564	6.0	7	9 28 52.26		52.82	+ 5.313	− 0.169	......	4	44.7	11.3
2374	1566	7.5	4	9 29 15.03		14.77	+ 4.203	− 0.066	......	3	45.2	12.2
2375	1567	6.6	5	9 29 18.47		18.40	+ 3.855	− 0.043	......	4	46.1	13.2

Ordinal Number.	Mean North Polar Distance 1845.0.			Precession 1845.0.	Secular Variation.	Adopted Proper Motion.	Observations of N.P.D.			Names.	Oeltzen-Argelander Number.
R.	R.		G.				No.	Mean year.			
							R.	R.	G.		
	° ′ ″		″	″	″	″		1800 +			
2341	95 23 50.0		...	+ 15.43	+ 0.28	...	2	52.3	...	....	......
2342	17 6 44.4		44.8	+ 15.37	+ 0.55	+ 0.10	5	47.0	9.2	22 Urs. Maj. ...	9945
2343	5 31 11.8		...	+ 15.38	+ 1.06	...	6	51.1	...	....	......
2344	41 27 12.9		11.4	+ 15.38	+ 0.38	...	4	46.0	11.2	....	......
2345	19 29 37.3		37.9	+ 15.40	+ 0.51	− 0.04	17	50.4	10.2	24 Urs. Maj. *d*	9951
2346	5 33 44.7		...	+ 15.42	+ 1.05	...	2	49.7	...	....	......
2347	22 31 30.7		...	+ 15.44	+ 0.49	...	3	52.5	...	....	9959
2348	22 31 26.2		...	+ 15.44	+ 0.49	...	3	52.6	...	....	......
2349	26 29 29.8		...	+ 15.45	+ 0.45	...	4	47.2	...	....	......
2350	5 35 11.7		...	+ 15.46	+ 1.04	...	6	51.4	...	....	......
2351	40 59 18.6		17.3	+ 15.48	+ 0.35	...	4	45.7	11.2	....	......
2352	41 9 15.5		14.6	+ 15.49	+ 0.37	...	4	44.3	11.2	....	9972
2353	37 37 11.1		13.5	+ 15.50	+ 0.37	+ 0.57	8	44.4	7.3	25 Urs. Maj. *θ*	......
2354	17 13 52.3		...	+ 15.51	+ 0.53	+ 0.12	4	45.2	...	....	9979
2355	5 58 20.0		...	+ 15.52	+ 0.98	...	5	52.9	...	....	......
2356	66 21 8.9		...	+ 15.52	+ 0.32	...	1	56.3	...	4 Leonis λ......	......
2357	43 48 15.5		...	+ 15.53	+ 0.37	...	3	50.2	...	....	9990
2358	5 47 24.8		...	+ 15.54	+ 1.00	...	4	50.0	...	....	......
2359	35 16 14.6		...	+ 15.55	+ 0.39	...	3	45.3	...	....	......
2360	78 1 0.3		...	+ 15.56	+ 0.30	+ 0.08	10	47.9	...	5 Leonis ξ	......
2361	44 1 45.8		...	+ 15.58	+ 0.36	...	3	51.6	...	....	10002
2362	37 15 48.3		48.1	+ 15.60	+ 0.39	+ 0.04	4	43.2	9.2	26 Urs. Maj. ...	10010
2363	26 31 26.9		27.9	+ 15.60	+ 0.43	...	5	47.8	10.7	....	10014
2364	49 41 38.6		38.6	+ 15.66	+ 0.34	+ 0.05	4	45.9	13.2	....	......
2365	20 1 16.2		12.2	+ 15.66	+ 0.48	...	3	45.3	11.3	....	10027
2366	32 20 33.8		35.0	+ 15.67	+ 0.40	...	4	43.5	12.2	....	10028
2367	40 49 23.5		23.3	+ 15.67	+ 0.37	...	5	47.2	11.3	....	......
2368	2 41 44.0		...	+ 15.72	+ 1.87	...	9	52.8	...	....	......
2369	11 9 55.9		55.4	+ 15.79	+ 0.67	...	4	44.0	13.3	....	10049
2370	17 2 54.5		55.2	+ 15.83	+ 0.51	+ 0.05	8	46.4	9.2	27 Urs. Maj. ...	10077
2371	10 9 34.9		34.0	+ 15.83	+ 0.68	...	6	47.2	7 5	....	10072
2372	49 4 3.3		2.9	+ 15.84	+ 0.33	...	5	44.6	10.3	42 Lyncis......	......
2373	20 3 44.5		40.6	+ 15.85	+ 0.47	...	4	43.7	11.3	....	10084
2374	35 48 9.0		3.4	+ 15.87	+ 0.37	...	4	43.5	12.2	....	10090
2375	46 9 31.4		27.1	+ 15.87	+ 0.33	...	3	43.9	13.2	....	......

Magnitude.	Estimates of Magnitude.	Mean Right Ascension 1845.0.		Precession 1845.0.	Secular Variation.	Adopted Proper Motion.
R.		R.	G.			
		h. m. s.	s.	s.	s.	s.
7.7	4	9 29 39.96	...	+ 4.441	— 0.081	......
7.4	6	9 29 57.60	57.42	+ 4.193	— 0.066	......
8.0	6	9 31 21.83	...	+ 3.830	— 0.040	......
7.1	6	9 31 45.37	45.13	+ 3.738	— 0.034	......
7.1	7	9 31 55.62	55.16	+ 3.856	— 0.046	......
7.1	8	9 32 10.57	10.71	+ 4.011	— 0.054	......
6.6	6	9 32 20.39	...	+ 4.847	— 0.114	......
6.3	6	9 32 21.14	21.16	+ 4.219	— 0.069	......
6.0	4	9 32 22.98	22.93	+ 3.754	— 0.037	......
6.5	8	9 32 29.69	29.65	+ 3.997	— 0.051	......
7.6	4	9 32 47.41	...	+ 4.143	— 0.038	......
4.2	15	9 32 52.46	...	+ 3.220	— 0.011	— 0.013
6.9	5	9 33 39.39	39.13	+ 4.889	— 0.129	......
6.6	8	9 33 55.76	55.11	+ 4.728	— 0.111	......
5.4	5	9 35 30.19	29.66	+ 4.323	— 0.080	......
7.0	4	9 35 39.97	...	+ 4.682	— 0.107	— 0.009
9.0	7	9 36 26.58	...	+ 4.873	— 0.120	......
6.9	7	9 36 37.12	...	+ 4.796	— 0.114	......
6.7	11	9 36 45.96	45.77	+ 3.875	— 0.046	+ 0.003
2.9	11	9 37 2.62	...	+ 3.426	— 0.020	— 0.004
6.2	8	9 38 9.73	9.67	+ 4.838	— 0.126	......
5.6	13	9 38 33.92	33.76	+ 3.892	— 0.049	+ 0.027
4.0	6	9 39 55.05	55.20	+ 4.386	— 0.036	— 0.033
7.3	6	9 40 38.38	...	+ 3.855	— 0.044	......
6.6	8	9 40 41.37	41.25	+ 3.719	— 0.037	......
4.5	5	9 41 31.25	30.65	+ 4.146	— 0.069	......
7.0	6	9 41 55.05	...	+ 4.733	— 0.112	......
7.7	4	9 42 15.30	...	+ 3.712	— 0.035	......
6.5	10	9 42 49.73	...	+11.126	— 1.693	......
6.6	6	9 42 56.92	59.64	+ 3.672	— 0.034	......
7.1	5	9 43 1.86	...	+ 4.019	— 0.057	......
8.4	24	9 43 41.35	...	+24.917	—10.966	......
6.0	5	9 43 41.48	41.10	+ 4.470	— 0.094	......
3.7	5	9 43 56.25	...	+ 3.447	— 0.021	— 0.021
6.1	9	9 44 22.91	22.16	+ 5.606	— 0.231	— 0.032

Ordinal Number.	Mean North Polar Distance 1845.0.		Precession 1845.0.	Secular Variation.	Adopted Proper Motion.	Observations of N.P.D.			Names.	Oeltzen-Argelander Number.
R.	R.	G.				No.	Mean year.			
						R.	R.	G.		
	° ′ ″	″	″	″			1800 +			
2376	30 42 44.6	...	+ 15.90	+ 0.40	...	3	50.6	...	....	10097
2377	35 56 18.9	18.1	+ 15.91	+ 0.37	...	3	46.2	12.2	....	10100
2378	46 43 7.7	...	+ 15.98	+ 0.34	...	3	45.5	...	....	......
2379	50 20 40.5	34.4	+ 16.01	+ 0.34	...	4	48.0	13.2	....	......
2380	45 39 42.5	41.6	+ 16.01	+ 0.33	...	5	47.0	11.3	....	......
2381	40 30 51.9	44.6	+ 16.03	+ 0.36	...	5	47.9	11.2	....	10145
2382	24 18 47.2	...	+ 16.03	+ 0.42	...	4	48.3	...	....	10146
2383	34 55 58.7	55.9	+ 16.03	+ 0.35	...	4	46.5	11.2	....	10150
2384	49 32 21.5	21.1	+ 16.03	+ 0.30	+ 0.06	3	44.5	9.4	43 Lyncis......	......
2385	40 51 58.7	57.4	+ 16.04	+ 0.34	...	4	47.3	12.3	....	10153
2386	48 19 15.7	...	+ 16.06	+ 0.34	...	3	51.9	...	....	......
2387	79 24 20.1	...	+ 16.06	+ 0.28	+ 0.04	11	47.4	...	14 Leonis o ...	......
2388	23 39 56.1	52.8	+ 16.10	+ 0.41	...	4	46.2	11.2	....	10173
2389	25 38 17.1	14.8	+ 16.12	+ 0.41	...	6	44.9	8.6	28 Urs. Maj. ...	10178
2390	32 9 50.7	52.0	+ 16.20	+ 0.37	...	6	47.2	9.3	....	10193
2391	26 2 9.5	...	+ 16.21	+ 0.40	...	4	48.0	...	... .	10194
2392	23 28 53.8	...	+ 16.25	+ 0.43	...	4	48.5	...	....	10204
2393	24 23 39.8	...	+ 16.26	+ 0.42	...	5	47.4	...	....	10211
2394	44 10 9.3	8.0	+ 16.27	+ 0.34	+ 0.14	9	48.5	10.7	14 Leo. Min...	10212
2395	65 30 53.5	...	+ 16.28	+ 0.29	+ 0.02	16	44.4	...	17 Leonis ε ...	......
2396	23 41 22.3	20.0	+ 16.33	+ 0.40	...	5	45.4	11.2	....	10232
2397	43 15 37.3	36.3	+ 16.35	+ 0.31	+ 0.10	14	50.0	9.3	15 Leo. Min. ...	10242
2398	30 14 9.4	9.8	+ 16.43	+ 0.38	+ 0.18	7	45.2	7.4	29 Urs. Maj. υ	10256
2399	44 11 36.0	...	+ 16.46	+ 0.32	...	3	47.9	...	....	10277
2400	49 38 59.8	57.8	+ 16.46	+ 0.30	...	6	45.6	10.3	16 Leo. Min. ...	......
2401	35 12 55.2	55.4	+ 16.50	+ 0.33	+ 0.02	6	45.1	8.3	30 Urs. Maj. φ	10290
2402	24 29 11.9	...	+ 16.52	+ 0.39	...	5	47.0	...	....	10299
2403	49 39 19.8	...	+ 16.54	+ 0.31	...	4	45.7	...	....	......
2404	5 20 32.7	...	+ 16.57	+ 0.86	...	5	51.5	...	....	......
2405	51 21 41.1	38.7	+ 16.58	+ 0.31	...	4	45.5	10.3	17 Leo. Min. ...	......
2406	38 39 10.5	...	+ 16.58	+ 0.33	...	4	51.7	...	....	10312
2407	1 57 50.5	...	+ 16.61	+ 2.04	...	6	51.2	...	....	......
2408	28 9 26.0	25.9	+ 16.62	+ 0.39	...	5	44.8	11.2	....	10324
2409	63 15 56.7	...	+ 16.63	+ 0.28	+ 0.06	10	52.5	...	24 Leonis μ...	......
2410	16 23 17.0	15.2	+ 16.64	+ 0.44	+ 0.01	6	45.2	11.2	....	10332

Ordinal Number.		Magnitude.	Estimates of Magnitude.	Mean Right Ascension 1845.0.			Precession 1845.0.	Secular Variation	Adopted Proper Motion.	Observations of R.A.		
R.	G.	R.		R.		G.				No. R.	Mean year R.	G.
				h. m. s.		s.	s.	s.	s.		1800 +	
2411	1587	5.7	3	9 45	33.97	33.39	+ 3.968	− 0.057	......	4	41.7	9.3
2412	1588	6.9	7	9 45	55.31	55.29	+ 4.123	− 0.069	......	4	44.6	11.2
2413	1589	8.2	6	9 45	56.67	56.47	+ 3.832	− 0.046	......	3	44.6	11.2
2414	...	8.9	6	9 46	9.05	...	+ 5.805	− 0.261	......	3	48.6	...
2415	1590	5.9	8	9 46	22.26	22.05	+ 4.255	− 0.080	......	5	43.4	11.3
2416	...	7.1	12	9 47	19.58	...	+ 5.898	− 0.280	− 0.011	7	50.8	...
2417	1591	6.4	6	9 48	8.59	8.48	+ 3.827	− 0.049	......	6	46.5	10.3
2418	1592	5.3	11	9 48	10.14	9.92	+ 3.720	− 0.040	......	12	47.9	8.3
2419	1593	6.8	7	9 48	37.15	36.70	+ 3.961	− 0.057	......	5	43.8	11.2
2420	1594	5.7	4	9 49	8.76	8.68	+ 4.206	− 0.077	......	4	41.8	11.2
2421	1595	7.2	8	9 50	28.36	27.90	+ 3.739	− 0.043	......	5	47.2	12.3
2422	1596	7.8	7	9 51	7.81	8.38	+ 4.140	− 0.074	......	4	43.7	12.2
2423	...	8.5	6	9 52	0.96	...	+ 5.725	− 0.265	......	4	49.8	...
2424	...	5.2	6	9 52	1.17	...	+ 3.179	− 0.010	− 0.003	9	44.6	...
2425	1597	7.3	6	9 52	46.83	46.39	+ 3.928	− 0.057	......	5	43.9	10.3
2426	...	8.1	6	9 52	47.70	...	+ 3.828	− 0.047	......	4	51.7	...
2427	1598	6.5	4	9 53	10.64	10.39	+ 3.933	− 0.057	......	5	44.9	10.3
2428	...	7.5	5	9 53	18.33	...	+ 3.821	− 0.047	......	3	51.9	...
2429	1599	8.4	7	9 53	37.05	36.97	+ 3.630	− 0.034	......	3	44.9	13.3
2430	.1600	7.2	7	9 53	53.00	52.66	+ 3.716	− 0.043	......	3	44.6	13.0
2431	1601	5.9	3	9 54	15.90	15.86	+ 4.052	− 0.069	......	5	42.9	11.2
2432	1602	7.7	6	9 54	25.70	25.58	+ 4.111	− 0.074	......	5	43.8	12.2
2433	...	9.6	4	9 54	28.50	...	+ 4.111	− 0.074	......	4	47.8	...
2434	1603	7.0	7	9 54	36.00	36.33	+ 3.629	− 0.034	......	4	46.2	13.3
2435	...	6.5	6	9 54	58.25	...	+ 3.994	− 0.062	......	4	51.8	...
2436	...	7.1	4	9 55	9.96	...	+ 3.935	− 0.057	......	3	46.9	...
2437	1604	8.1	6	9 55	28.58	28.27	+ 3.959	− 0.060	......	4	47.1	11.2
2438	1605	7.7	6	9 55	43.21	42.90	+ 3.943	− 0.057	......	3	44.1	11.1
2439	1606	7.0	7	9 55	59.51	59.46	+ 4.111	− 0.071	......	3	47.5	12.3
2440	1607	8.2	5	9 56	23.01	23.26	+ 4.104	− 0.074	......	3	44.1	12.3
2441	1608	7.2	5	9 56	34.79	34.92	+ 3.652	− 0.037	......	3	44.6	13.0
2442	1610	7.6	7	9 57	11.03	10.88	+ 3.648	− 0.034	......	3	47.6	11.2
2443	...	7.4	4	9 57	28.63	...	+ 3.771	− 0.045	......	4	51.7	...
2444	1609	6.3	8	9 57	41.38	41.08	+ 4.509	− 0.114	......	7	45.8	11.2
2445	1611	8.2	6	9 57	43.68	43.62	+ 3.616	− 0.037	......	2	50.2	13.2

Ordinal Number.	Mean North Polar Distance 1845.0.		Precession 1845.0.	Secular Variation.	Adopted Proper Motion.	Observations of N.P.D.			Names.	Oeltzen-Argelander Number.
						No.	Mean year.			
R.	R.	G.				R.	R.	G.		
	° ′ ″	″	″	″	″		1800 +			
2411	39 27 4.8	6.7	+ 16.70	+ 0.31	...	7	45.4	9.3	31 Urs. Maj. ...	10351
2412	35 1 31.7	30.2	+ 16.72	+ 0.33	...	5	45.2	11.2	....	10356
2413	44 5 19.5	17.7	+ 16.72	+ 0.30	...	4	42.8	11.2	....	10357
2414	15 5 43.1	...	+ 16.73	+ 0.47	...	4	50.0	...	....	10359
2415	31 50 51.5	50.9	+ 16.74	+ 0.33	+ 0.04	6	46.9	11.3	....	10366
2416	14 30 8.4	...	+ 16.78	+ 0.47	+ 0.04	6	50.6	...	....	10373
2417	43 51 0.7	57.8	+ 16.83	+ 0.31	...	4	44.0	10.3	....	10385
2418	48 12 33.9	31.3	+ 16.83	+ 0.30	...	6	44.6	8.3	19 Leo. Min. ...	....
2419	39 8 18.9	19.8	+ 16.85	+ 0.31	...	4	44.7	11.2	....	10391
2420	32 26 59.5	59.1	+ 16.88	+ 0.34	...	5	44.7	11.2	....	....
2421	46 56 35.1	31.4	+ 16.93	+ 0.27	...	5	45.4	12.3	....	....
2422	33 39 18.1	3.1	+ 16.96	+ 0.30	...	5	47.5	12.2	....	....
2423	14 56 37.7	...	+ 17.00	+ 0.47	...	3	47.9	...	....	10439
2424	81 12 52.3	...	+ 17.00	+ 0.24	+ 0.03	5	44.5	...	29 Leonis π ...	....
2425	39 22 36.0	34.9	+ 17.04	+ 0.29	...	6	45.0	10.3	....	10451
2426	42 53 41.0	...	+ 17.04	+ 0.29	...	4	51.8	...	....	10453
2427	39 8 46.3	44.5	+ 17.06	+ 0.29	...	6	45.0	10.3	....	10458
2428	43 3 29.7	...	+ 17.06	+ 0.29	...	3	51.9	...	....	10460
2429	51 21 46.7	48.2	+ 17.08	+ 0.27	...	4	48.8	13.3	....	....
2430	47 14 48.0	46.5	+ 17.09	+ 0.27	...	5	46.7	13.0	....	....
2431	35 21 43.4	42.0	+ 17.11	+ 0.30	+ 0.04	7	45.7	11.2	....	10469
2432	33 45 54.4	54.7	+ 17.12	+ 0.31	...	3	43.3	12.2	....	....
2433	33 45 55.8	...	+ 17.12	+ 0.31	...	2	42.8	...	....	....
2434	51 13 41.3	36.9	+ 17.13	+ 0.28	...	3	46.6	13.3	....	....
2435	36 52 50.5	...	+ 17.14	+ 0.30	...	4	52.7	...	....	....
2436	38 42 0.0	...	+ 17.15	+ 0.29	...	3	43.6	...	....	10492
2437	37 51 36.4	35.1	+ 17.17	+ 0.30	...	4	45.2	11.2	....	10498
2438	38 19 55.1	53.8	+ 17.18	+ 0.30	...	4	46.0	11.1	....	10499
2439	33 28 52.2	52.6	+ 17.19	+ 0.30	...	5	46.3	12.3	....	10504
2440	33 35 25.8	26.8	+ 17.21	+ 0.31	...	4	44.0	12.3	....	10509
2441	49 40 1.3	0.3	+ 17.22	+ 0.27	...	3	43.9	13.0	....	....
2442	49 44 38.8	38.3	+ 17.24	+ 0.25	...	4	44.5	11.2	....	....
2443	44 11 16.5	...	+ 17.26	+ 0.28	...	4	51.8	...	....	10532
2444	25 17 37.1	37.4	+ 17.27	+ 0.34	...	4	44.5	11.2	....	10541
2445	51 13 25.0	25.8	+ 17.27	+ 0.27	...	4	48.8	13.2	....	....

Magnitude.	Estimates of Magnitude.	Mean Right Ascension 1845.0.		Precession 1845.0.	Secular Variation	Adopted Proper Motion.
R.		R.	G.			
		h. m. s.	s.	s.	s.	s.
8.2	7	9 58 6.42	6.56	+ 3.620	— 0.037	......
7.3	7	9 58 33.58	33.44	+ 4.488	— 0.109	......
3.8	4	9 58 52.64	...	+ 3.283	— 0.015	— 0.004
7.4	7	9 59 7.21	7.10	+ 3.918	— 0.060	......
8.4	7	9 59 25.86	...	+ 4.077	— 0.071	......
7.8	8	10 0 2.85	2.59	+ 3.615	— 0.037	......
1.3	A	10 0 6.81	...	+ 3.221	— 0.012	— 0.019
7.2	8	10 0 24.24	24.19	+ 3.872	— 0.054	......
6.4	6	10 1 37.09	37.07	+ 3.652	— 0.040	......
6.5	8	10 1 50.84	55.64	+ 3.862	— 0.054	......
6.1	8	10 2 0.54	0.82	+ 3.587	— 0.037	......
7.4	6	10 2 7.34	7.16	+ 3.673	— 0.040	......
6.8	5 .	10 3 48.67	48.33	+ 3.879	— 0.057	......
6.8	2	10 3 53.04	...	+ 8.831	— 0.944	......
5.9	7	10 4 22.55	22.60	+ 4.224	— 0.089	......
6.7	4	10 5 19.14	19.18	+ 4.224	— 0.086	......
5.8	73	10 6 7.72	8.66	+10.401	— 1.834	— 0.079
8.2	17	10 6 7.86	...	+14.626	— 4.044	......
5.6	5	10 6 42.41	42.37	+ 4.487	— 0.120	......
8.1	7	10 6 49.53	49.62	+ 3.673	— 0.043	......
7.4	7	10 7 17.88	17.57	+ 3.639	— 0.040	......
8.8	6	10 7 18.92	18.61	+ 3.640	— 0.040	......
3.6	6	10 7 43.68	43.49	+ 3.671	— 0.043	— 0.015
6.6	8	10 7 58.83	59.02	+ 3.640	— 0.040	......
5.6	2	10 8 21.43	...	+ 3.232	— 0.013	+ 0.003
7.3	6	10 8 40.18	40.06	+ 4.766	— 0.160	......
7.1	7	10 9 5.76	5.55	+ 3.871	— 0.060	......
5.9	5	10 9 8.40	8.22	+ 4.735	— 0.154	— 0.015
6.6	6	10 9 10.81	10.83	+ 3.666	— 0.043	......
6.7	9	10 9 24.40	24.16	+ 3.687	— 0.046	+ 0.009
8.8	6	10 9 32.01	...	+11.972	— 2.589	......
7.2	7	10 10 12.71	12.47	+ 4.735	— 0.160	......
6.1	6	10 10 27.13	27.19	+ 3.948	— 0.066	......
8.3	6	10 10 50.77	...	+ 8.409	— 0.902	......
2.7	1	10 11 25.23	...	+ 3.300	— 0.017	+ 0.019

Ordinal Number. R.	Mean North Polar Distance 1845.0 R.	G.	Precession 1845.0	Secular Variation	Adopted Proper Motion	Observations of N.P.D. No. R.	Mean year R. 1800+	G.	Names.	Oeltzen-Argelander Number.
2446	50 57 4.7	0.1	+ 17.28	+ 0.25	...	3	47.6	13.3	....	......
2447	25 29 28.0	28.9	+ 17.30	+ 0.31	...	4	43.8	13.2	....	......
2448	72 29 2.6	...	+ 17.32	+ 0.24	...	1	47.3	...	30 Leonis η ...	......
2449	38 25 24.6	24.4	+ 17.33	+ 0.28	...	5	47.1	11.1	....	10559
2450	33 41 46.3	...	+ 17.34	+ 0.30	...	3	46.6	...	....	......
2451	50 48 43.5	39.4	+ 17.37	+ 0.26	...	3	47.9	13.3	....	......
2452	77 16 38.8	...	+ 17.37	+ 0.23	− 0.01	47	46.9	...	32 Leonis α ...	......
2453	39 44 1.2	59.9	+ 17.39	+ 0.29	...	5	47.4	11.3	....	10587
2454	48 34 44.6	42.8	+ 17.44	+ 0.26	...	4	46.5	13.2	....	......
2455	39 45 49.9	33.4	+ 17.45	+ 0.27	...	5	43.4	11.3	....	10603
2456	51 50 13.0	12.0	+ 17.46	+ 0.27	...	3	45.9	14.3	....	......
2457	47 30 22.5	21.0	+ 17.46	+ 0.26	...	5	43.7	12.3	....	......
2458	38 44 23.8	21.0	+ 17.53	+ 0.26	...	4	44.2	10.5	....	10637
2459	6 25 29.8	...	+ 17.54	+ 0.60	...	3	48.8	...	....	......
2460	29 14 58.4	58.0	+ 17.56	+ 0.30	...	6	46.9	11.2	....	10651
2461	29 4 52.5	50.3	+ 17.60	+ 0.30	...	5	44.8	11.2	....	10665
2462	4 58 1.0	59.0	+ 17.63	+ 0.75	+ 0.05	56	51.2	7.3	....	......
2463	3 9 24.1	...	+ 17.63	+ 0.92	...	7	52.0	...	....	......
2464	24 7 18.4	17.9	+ 17.65	+ 0.29	+ 0.04	6	45.9	8.3	32 Urs. Maj. ...	10686
2465	46 25 56.4	52.9	+ 17.66	+ 0.25	...	3	45.0	13.3	....	......
2466	47 57 15.3	14.0	+ 17.68	+ 0.25	...	4	43.3	11.3	....	......
2467	47 55 28.0	26.6	+ 17.68	+ 0.25	...	5	47.5	11.3	....	......
2468	46 18 51.1	50.2	+ 17.70	+ 0.26	+ 0.06	5	42.7	7.1	33 Urs. Maj. λ	......
2469	47 45 40.9	39.4	+ 17.70	+ 0.22	...	5	45.2	10.3	....	......
2470	75 30 2.1	...	+ 17.72	+ 0.22	+ 0.04	1	52.2	...	37 Leonis	......
2471	20 12 21.8	21.3	+ 17.73	+ 0.31	...	4	45.8	11.2	....	10707
2472	37 49 18.9	18.2	+ 17.75	+ 0.25	...	4	44.0	11.3	....	10711
2473	20 28 36.8	34.8	+ 17.75	+ 0.31	+ 0.06	3	43.2	11.2	....	10713
2474	46 10 33.0	29.4	+ 17.75	+ 0.23	...	3	44.9	12.9	....	......
2475	45 9 57.0	62.6	+ 17.76	+ 0.23	+ 0.42	5	47.3	12.3	....	10717
2476	3 58 55.2	...	+ 17.77	+ 0.81	...	4	50.4	...	....	......
2477	20 17 52.8	46.9	+ 17.79	+ 0.29	...	6	46.6	11.2	....	10728
2478	35 0 29.7	27.1	+ 17.80	+ 0.24	...	6	46.9	10.3	....	10734
2479	6 32 49.4	...	+ 17.82	+ 0.54	...	4	44.3	...	....	......
2480	69 22 35.8	...	+ 17.84	+ 0.22	+ 0.15	4	53.2	...	41 Leonis γ (1st)	......

Magnitude.	Estimates of Magnitude.	Mean Right Ascension 1845.0.		Precession 1845.0.	Secular Variation	Adopted Proper Motion.
R.		R.	G.			
		h. m. s.	s.	s.	s.	s.
4·9	4	10 11 25.66	...	+ 3.300	— 0.017	+ 0.023
5.2	9	10 11 36.49	34.55	+ 8.287	— 1.049	— 0.106
7.5	15	10 11 43.92	...	+10.293	— 1.824	......
6.6	5	10 11 45.49	45.05	+ 3.630	— 0.040	+ 0.004
4.8	6	10 12 52.94	52.84	+ 4.445	— 0.123	+ 0.005
5.9	6	10 12 56.50	56.58	+ 3.612	— 0.040	......
3.4	11	10 13 4.52	4.36	+ 3.617	— 0.040	— 0.008
6.4	3	10 13 29.88	...	+ 3.239	— 0.014	— 0.002
7.1	8	10 14 0.34	...	+ 4.346	— 0.090	......
8.7	7	10 16 9.68	...	+ 3.858	— 0.061	......
7.9	6	10 16 34.55	...	+ 7.591	— 0.853	......
6.2	12	10 18 15.88	15.72	+ 3.594	— 0.040	......
6.5	6	10 18 28.18	25.49	+ 3.744	— 0.051	......
6.7	6	10 18 28.49	28.21	+ 3.747	— 0.054	......
5.9	6	10 18 49.44	48.30	+ 4.378	— 0.123	......
6.4	8	10 19 14.54	...	+ 3.659	— 0.043	......
6.0	1	10 19 27.68	...	+ 3.176	— 0.010	— 0.002
6.3	10	10 19 35.53	...	+ 4.289	— 0.110	......
6.1	7	10 19 41.21	42.18	+ 6.768	— 0.626	— 0.004
7.6	8	10 20 31.93	32.02	+ 3.784	— 0.057	......
4.9	3	10 20 40.05	40.13	+ 3.927	— 0.071	......
6.9	8	10 20 56.22	55.86	+ 3.561	— 0.040	......
5.7	7	10 21 2.48	2.35	+ 3.535	— 0.037	+ 0.003
4.8	6	10 21 45.10	43.51	+ 5.386	— 0.300	+ 0.004
7.4	7	10 21 59.02	58.79	+ 3.532	— 0.037	......
7.1	7	10 22 7.20	6.95	+ 3.677	— 0.051	......
7.9	11	10 22 15.77	...	+10.169	— 1.970	......
7.8	7	10 22 20.80	20.89	+ 3.605	— 0.043	......
7.4	4	10 23 13.61	13.79	+ 3.617	— 0.046	......
4.7	6	10 24 10.19	10.21	+ 3.545	— 0.040	......
7.3	9	10 24 16.17	14.96	+ 3.716	— 0.051	......
4.4	10	10 24 38.79	...	+ 3.166	— 0.010	......
7.1	8	10 24 51.89	51.58	+ 3.710	— 0.054	......
5.6	8	10 25 8.14	7.80	+ 3.927	— 0.074	+ 0.012
8.9	7	10 25 56.07	...	+ 3.562	— 0.038	......

Ordinal Number. R.	Mean North Polar Distance 1845.0.		Precession 1845.0.	Secular Variation.	Adopted Proper Motion.	Observations of N.P.D.			Names.	Oeltzen-Argelander Number.
	R.	G.				No. R.	Mean year. R.	Mean year. G.		
	° ′ ″	″	″	″	″		1800 +			
2481	69 22 37.2	...	+ 17.84	+ 0.22	+ 0.15	2	54.3	...	41 Leonis γ (2d)	......
2482	6 39 29.2	31.5	+ 17.85	+ 0.55	+ 0.07	6	44.8	7.5	.3.d.Carmd	......
2483	4 48 53.3	...	+ 17.85	+ 0.64	...	9	49.5	...	....	......
2484	47 22 26.7	27.2	+ 17.85	+ 0.21	...	4	45.5	9.3	....	......
2485	23 39 10.2	11.2	+ 17.90	+ 0.28	+ 0.06	6	45.9	8.3	..3.d.H.kmey	10772
2486	47 59 9.5	4.4	+ 17.91	+ 0.24	+ 0.01	5	45.7	11.2	....	......
2487	47 43 23.0	22.4	+ 17.91	+ 0.23	− 0.03	7	45.1	7.0	34 Urs. Maj. μ	......
2488	74 14 43.1	...	+ 17.93	+ 0.21	+ 0.01	1	52.2	...	42 Leonis......	......
2489	25 3 35.3	...	+ 17.96	+ 0.28	...	7	48.1	...	....	10788
2490	36 35 33.2	...	+ 18.03	+ 0.25	...	4	47.8	...	....	10812
2491	7 11 4.4	...	+ 18.05	+ 0.48	...	3	49.9	...	....	......
2492	47 36 32.4	28.6	+ 18.11	+ 0.21	...	7	46.4	10.6	....	......
2493	40 23 23.7	53.2	+ 18.11	+ 0.20	...	6	46.3	11.2	....	......
2494	40 14 55.5	53.5	+ 18.11	+ 0.20	...	5	45.4	11.2	....	10845
2495	23 35 0.7	59.2	+ 18.13	+ 0.26	+ 0.02	6	46.3	9.3	35 Ursæ Majoris	10849
2496	43 59 54.7	...	+ 18.14	+ 0.23	...	4	49.8	...	....	10857
2497	79 26 59.3	...	+ 18.16	+ 0.20	+ 0.01	1	49.3	...	45 Leonis......	......
2498	24 57 0.0	...	+ 18.16	+ 0.27	...	8	48.5	...	....	10861
2499	8 42 40.6	38.7	+ 18.17	+ 0.44	...	5	45.4	7.2	....	......
2500	38 12 54.7	52.0	+ 18.20	+ 0.24	...	5	47.1	12.3	....	......
2501	33 13 37.4	36.0	+ 18.20	+ 0.23	...	6	42.3	8.3	36 Ursæ Majoris	10885
2502	48 44 17.3	17.1	+ 18.21	+ 0.21	...	4	45.0	11.3	....	......
2503	50 17 0.9	1.1	+ 18.22	+ 0.23	+ 0.02	4	44.2	10.3	32 Leo. Min...	......
2504	13 29 30.9	28.3	+ 18.24	+ 0.33	...	5	49.9	9.3	.g.Drac..	10892
2505	50 11 7.5	3.2	+ 18.25	+ 0.21	...	5	47.7	10.3	./.................	......
2506	42 19 56.1	56.1	+ 18.25	+ 0.21	...	5	47.2	11.2	....	10895
2507	4 27 12.8	...	+ 18.26	+ 0.61	...	3	49.5	...	....	......
2508	45 56 34.3	35.5	+ 18.26	+ 0.20	...	5	47.5	11.3	....	......
2509	45 1 23.8	22.6	+ 18.29	+ 0.20	...	3	45.6	11.2	....	10911
2510	48 46 43.5	43.5	+ 18.33	+ 0.20	...	6	46.3	9.3	....	......
2511	40 1 24.2	28.7	+ 18.33	+ 0.21	...	5	48.3	12.3	....	10928
2512	79 53 51.2	...	+ 18.34	+ 0.19	+ 0.03	13	44.9	...	47 Leonis ρ....	......
2513	40 5 41.5	41.4	+ 18.35	+ 0.21	...	3	45.2	12.3	....	10939
2514	32 7 16.7	17.0	+ 18.36	+ 0.22	...	8	48.4	8.7	37 Ursæ Majoris	10942
2515	47 19 51.8	...	+ 18.39	+ 0.21	...	4	48.3	...	....	......

Ordinal Number.		Magnitude.	Estimates of Magnitude.	Mean Right Ascension 1845.0.			Precession 1845.0.	Secular Variation	Adopted Proper Motion.	Observations of R.A.		
R.	G.	R.		R.		G.				No. R.	Mean year. R.	G.
				h. m. s.		s.	s.	s.	s.		1800 +	
2516	1661	6.8	9	10 26	0.35	0.16	+ 3.562	− 0.040	......	4	44.5	11.3
2517	1663	8.0	6	10 26	7.31	7.05	+ 3.544	− 0.040	......	3	43.9	10.9
2518	...	7.1	3	10 26	13.22	...	+ 3.630	− 0.043	......	3	51.5	...
2519	...	9.5	7	10 26	23.11	...	+ 3.562	− 0.038	......	3	52.6	...
2520	...	5.6	7	10 26	42.70	...	+ 3.142	− 0.009	......	3	56.2	...
2521	1664	8.4	5	10 26	54.06	54.34	+ 3.919	− 0.077	......	3	46.9	13.0
2522	1665	6.5	5	10 27	27.06	27.10	+ 3.886	− 0.071	......	4	44.1	12.0
2523	...	6.8	3	10 27	35.64	...	+ 2.855	+ 0.005	− 0.027	2	54.3	...
2524	1662	7.0	4	10 27	50.62	52.01	+ 6.461	− 0.600	+ 0.042	4	43.3	7.4
2525	...	7.1	4	10 27	51.44	...	+ 3.638	− 0.044	......	5	45.7	...
2526	1666	6.6	5	10 28	8.72	8.60	+ 4.008	− 0.089	......	3	47.3	11.3
2527	1667	7.7	6	10 28	30.93	31.03	+ 3.898	− 0.074	. ....	4	47.8	13.3
2528	...	7.8	6	10 29	6.90	...	+ 3.523	− 0.036	......	4	52.7	...
2529	1668	5.6	7	10 29	26.77	56.62	+ 3.791	− 0.051	......	5	46.2	11.2
2530	...	7.9	7	10 29	36.60	...	+ 3.518	− 0.036	......	4	52.5	...
2531	1670	6.3	12	10 30	14.82	14.67	+ 3.479	− 0.034	− 0.021	8	49.3	10.3
2532	1669	5.4	5	10 30	41.73	41.82	+ 4.411	− 0.143	......	3	44.6	12.3
2533	1672	5.0	3	10 31	18.17	18.16	+ 4.231	− 0.120	......	4	43.2	9.0
2534	1671	8.3	6	10 31	21.26	20.82	+ 4.413	− 0.146	......	3	44.6	12.3
2535	1674	8.0	9	10 31	28.94	28.19	+ 3.774	− 0.066	......	5	46.0	11.8
2536	1675	8.5	5	10 31	30.79	30.83	+ 3.539	− 0.040	......	4	45.5	11.3
2537	...	9.6	6	10 31	35.40	...	+ 4.405	− 0.140	......	5	54.0	...
2538	...	7.6	6	10 31	43.33	...	+ 3.528	− 0.037	......	3	52.2	...
2539	1673	4.7	6	10 31	52.98	51.95	+ 4.439	− 0.151	+ 0.003	5	46.2	8.3
2540	1676	7.5	5	10 33	3.94	3.58	+ 4.042	− 0.097	......	3	46.6	11.2
2541	...	Var.	17	10 33	35.28	...	+ 4.392	− 0.142	......	8	51.1	...
2542	1677	5.5	6	10 33	53.54	53.48	+ 3.855	− 0.074	+ 0.006	4	43.3	10.3
2543	...	6.0	5	10 34	13.29	...	+ 4.293	− 0.128	......	3	51.6	...
2544	1678	5.7	9	10 34	24.88	24.88	+ 3.593	− 0.049	− 0.025	9	49.9	13.3
2545	...	7.0	1	10 34	37.56	...	+ 3.107	− 0.006	− 0.008	2	42.3	...
2546	...	9.7	3	10 34	46.88	...	+ 3.593	− 0.045	......	3	48.3	...
2547	1679	7.4	10	10 34	53.06	52.92	+ 3.591	− 0.046	− 0.025	8	49.6	13.3
2548	1680	8.1	7	10 35	37.33	37.20	+ 3.631	− 0.049	......	5	48.0	14.3
2549	1682	8.4	5	10 36	8.55	8.37	+ 3.561	− 0.046	......	5	46.3	12.0
2550	1683	7.2	8	10 36	11.51	11.36	+ 3.572	− 0.046	......	5	46.4	12.3

Ordinal Number.	Mean North Polar Distance 1845.0. R.	G.	Precession 1845.0.	Secular Variation.	Adopted Proper Motion.	Obs. of N.P.D. No.	Mean year. R.	G.	Names.	Oeltzen-Argelander Number.
	o ′ ″	″	″	″	″		1800 +			
2516	47 17 30.6	31.6	+ 18.39	+ 0.19	...	5	47.5	11.3	....	......
2517	48 19 23.3	20.3	+ 18.40	+ 0.21	...	4	44.7	10.9	....	......
2518	43 32 48.4	...	+ 18.40	+ 0.22	...	2	51.8	...	....	10955
2519	47 17 29.1	...	+ 18.40	+ 0.21	...	4	43.3	...	....	......
2520	82 15 3.1	...	+ 18.40	+ 0.18	— 0.06	1	41.3	...	48 Leonis......	......
2521	31 53 29.5	24.6	+ 18.42	+ 0.21	...	5	47.1	13.0	....	10964
2522	32 46 2.7	2.6	+ 18.44	+ 0.21	...	4	43.3	12.0	....	......
2523	112 22 43.9	...	+ 18.44	+ 0.16	— 0.35	5	53.5	...	....	......
2524	8 46 5.4	5.4	+ 18.45	+ 0.36	+ 0.02	5	45.0	7.4	....	......
2525	42 38 58.8	...	+ 18.45	+ 0.22	...	5	47.0	...	....	10981
2526	29 3 53.0	44.9	+ 18.46	+ 0.21	...	3	42.9	11.3	....	10985
2527	32 5 38.0	34.3	+ 18.48	+ 0.22	...	3	43.9	13.3	....	......
2528	48 45 33.6	...	+ 18.49	+ 0.20	...	4	51.5	...	....	......
2529	35 31 29.9	25.9	+ 18.51	+ 0.16	...	4	43.0	11.2	....	......
2530	48 52 27.4	...	+ 18.51	+ 0.20	...	4	52.8	...	....	......
2531	51 17 2.7	1.8	+ 18.54	+ 0.19	+ 0.03	7	49.7	10.3	38 Leo. Min...	......
2532	20 44 58.1	56.4	+ 18.55	+ 0.23	...	5	45.2	12.3	....	11015
2533	23 28 26.3	26.9	+ 18.57	+ 0.22	+ 0.10	7	43.7	9.0	38 Ursæ Majoris	11022
2534	20 35 22.7	22.8	+ 18.58	+ 0.25	...	4	45.3	12.3	....	11025
2535	35 33 57.7	55.2	+ 18.58	+ 0.21	...	5	45.5	11.8	....	......
2536	47 2 32.0	31.3	+ 18.58	+ 0.19	...	3	44.6	11.3	....	......
2537	20 39 35.2	...	+ 18.58	+ 0.24	...	1	53.7	...	....	11029?
2538	47 39 58.9	...	+ 18.58	+ 0.20	...	3	51.9	...	....	......
2539	20 6 56.5	56.6	+ 18.59	+ 0.23	+ 0.05	7	45.3	8.3	*[handwritten note]*	11038
2540	26 58 45.8	45.2	+ 18.63	+ 0.21	...	4	45.5	11.2	....	11048
2541	20 24 49.4	...	+ 18.65	+ 0.24	...	9	51.6	...	R Ursæ Majoris	......
2542	31 59 20.2	19.5	+ 18.65	+ 0.18	+ 0.07	6	45.0	10.3	39 Ursæ Majoris	11064
2543	21 46 41.2	...	+ 18.66	+ 0.23	...	3	51.0	...	....	11067
2544	42 59 0.9	56.4	+ 18.67	+ 0.17	...	5	43.1	13.3	....	11071
2545	85 36 30.0	...	+ 18.67	+ 0.16	— 0.01	4	43.8	...	34 Sextantis...	......
2546	42 54 14.7	...	+ 18.68	+ 0.19	...	2	49.8	...	....	11075
2547	42 58 49.3	45.6	+ 18.68	+ 0.16	...	3	43.9	13.3	....	11077
2548	40 38 34.1	32.8	+ 18.71	+ 0.18	...	5	46.7	14.3	....	11083
2549	44 13 6.9	6.4	+ 18.73	+ 0.19	...	3	44.9	12.0	....	11092
2550	43 37 18.6	18.0	+ 18.73	+ 0.18	...	4	44.8	12.3	....	11093

Magnitude.	Estimates of Magnitude.	Mean Right Ascension 1845.0.		Precession 1845.0.	Secular Variation	Adopted Proper Motion.
R.	R.	R.	G.			
		h. m. s.	s.	s.	s.	s.
7.2	6	10 36 14.50	13.83	+ 3.827	− 0.071	+ 0.005
7.2	9	10 36 25.12	25.13	+ 3.501	− 0.040	......
6.1	6	10 36 37.00	36.95	+ 3.837	− 0.074	......
8.0	6	10 37 28.02	...	+ 3.545	− 0.041	......
7.2	7	10 37 53.15	53.00	+ 3.520	− 0.043	......
7.2	8	10 38 55.30	55.07	+ 5.046	− 0.289	......
7.3	6	10 39 3.63	3.28	+ 3.542	− 0.046	......
6.9	6	10 39 6.57	...	+ 3.485	− 0.036	......
6.9	8	10 39 7.30	6.98	+ 3.465	− 0.037	......
8.6	11	10 39 15.88	...	+ 8.540	− 1.505	......
7.5	5	10 39 56.14	55.94	+ 3.524	− 0.040	......
7.9	8	10 40 30.88	31.02	+ 3.482	− 0.040	......
7.8	15	10 40 31.45	31.42	+ 3.507	− 0.040	......
8.9	7	10 41 8.80	8.50	+ 4.349	− 0.154	......
5.8	6	10 41 35.38	34.95	+ 3.771	− 0.071	......
5.6	6	10 41 36.32	35.72	+ 3.851	− 0.089	......
4.0	6	10 41 58.77	...	+ 2.947	+ 0.003	+ 0.006
8.4	5	10 42 9.43	9.45	+ 3.558	− 0.049	......
6.3	8	10 42 48.44	50.97	+ 4.330	− 0.151	......
6.5	7	10 42 55.24	54.99	+ 3.617	− 0.054	......
6.7	7	10 43 10.01	9.72	+ 3.662	− 0.060	......
6.4	7	10 43 12.06	11.73	+ 3.660	− 0.060	......
5.0	3	10 44 9.12	8.79	+ 3.700	− 0.063	......
8.5	5	10 44 37.75	...	+ 3.993	− 0.102	......
7.8	6	10 44 41.80	...	+ 3.701	− 0.065	......
7.9	6	10 44 49.77	...	+ 3.557	− 0.045	......
8.3	5	10 45 1.96	1.86	+ 3.942	− 0.097	......
4.7	5	10 45 2.17	1.93	+ 3.485	− 0.040	......
7.5	7	10 45 43.43	43.61	+ 3.455	− 0.040	......
9.0	7	10 46 3.11	3.60	+ 4.290	− 0.151	......
9.0	5	10 46 32.21	32.14	+ 3.453	− 0.040	......
7.0	6	10 46 54.39	54.16	+ 3.749	− 0.074	......
7.4	6	10 47 10.21	...	+ 4.817	− 0.257	......
8.0	5	10 47 16.14	...	+ 3.511	− 0.042	− 0.005
5.8	6	10 47 21.71	21.55	+ 5.135	− 0.349	− 0.019

Ordinal Number.	Mean North Polar Distance 1845.0.		Precession 1845.0.	Secular Variation.	Adopted Proper Motion.	Observations of N.P.D.	Mean year.		Names.	Oeltzen-Argelander Number.
R.	R.	G.				No. R.	R.	G.		
	° ′ ″	″	″	″	″		1800 +			
2551	32 16 1.9	2.4	+ 18.73	+ 0.20	...	6	45.6	9.3	40 Ursæ Majoris	11094
2552	47 52 41.1	39.7	+ 18.74	+ 0.19	...	4	45.3	14.3	....	....
2553	31 49 6.7	6.9	+ 18.74	+ 0.19	+ 0.09	5	44.5	10.3	41 Ursæ Majoris	11097
2554	45 4 55.7	...	+ 18.77	+ 0.18	...	3	44.3	...	....	....
2555	46 9 34.6	34.1	+ 18.78	+ 0.17	...	5	45.9	11.3	....	....
2556	13 11 11.2	8.7	+ 18.81	+ 0.24	...	6	45.2	13.3	....	11127
2557	44 22 55.7	55.1	+ 18.81	+ 0.15	...	3	44.3	11.2	....	11130
2558	48 4 25.9	...	+ 18.82	+ 0.17	...	5	51.6	...	....	....
2559	49 26 27.1	24.4	+ 18.82	+ 0.17	...	5	45.5	10.3	....	....
2560	4 49 11.8	...	+ 18.82	+ 0.40	...	6	52.4	...	....	....
2561	45 15 13.3	12.6	+ 18.84	+ 0.16	...	4	45.2	12.3	....	11138
2562	47 47 31.2	32.0	+ 18.86	+ 0.16	...	5	46.7	12.3	....	....
2563	46 6 53.8	53.2	+ 18.86	+ 0.16	...	5	47.2	11.3	....	....
2564	19 24 57.0	50.5	+ 18.88	+ 0.21	...	4	48.0	13.3	....	11151
2565	32 35 56.3	56.5	+ 18.89	+ 0.17	...	4	44.7	9.3	43 Ursæ Majoris	11155
2566	29 51 30.6	31.8	+ 18.89	+ 0.17	+ 0.07	4	43.0	8.3	42 Ursæ Majoris	11157
2567	105 23 2.4	...	+ 18.90	+ 0.14	− 0.07	3	54.2	...	Hydræ ν	....
2568	42 22 59.2	58.0	+ 18.91	+ 0.17	...	4	46.3	11.2	....	11166
2569	19 19 20.8	15.9	+ 18.92	+ 0.18	...	7	46.2	13.3	....	11178
2570	38 54 39.9	37.8	+ 18.93	+ 0.17	...	4	45.3	10.3	....	11181
2571	36 36 47.0	44.9	+ 18.94	+ 0.17	...	5	45.9	11.3	....	11185
2572	36 40 24.9	20.4	+ 18.94	+ 0.17	...	4	42.7	11.3	....	11186
2573	34 35 33.1	32.3	+ 18.97	+ 0.17	+ 0.02	5	42.3	9.3	44 Ursæ Majoris	11198
2574	25 3 31.4	...	+ 18.98	+ 0.18	...	3	50.0	...	....	11205
2575	34 22 29.3	...	+ 18.98	+ 0.17	...	3	46.6	...	....	11208
2576	41 30 23.8	...	+ 18.99	+ 0.17	...	3	49.6	...	....	11213
2577	26 13 35.5	36.5	+ 18.99	+ 0.17	...	3	44.9	12.3	....	....
2578	45 59 10.7	11.1	+ 18.99	+ 0.15	+ 0.06	8	44.8	7.3	45 Urs. Maj. ω	....
2579	47 50 22.6	24.5	+ 19.01	+ 0.15	...	4	46.3	12.3	....	....
2580	19 9 49.4	45.2	+ 19.02	+ 0.19	...	4	46.3	13.3	....	11229
2581	47 42 59.3	62.5	+ 19.03	+ 0.14	...	4	47.0	12.3	....	....
2582	31 40 14.5	13.3	+ 19.04	+ 0.15	...	4	46.8	11.2	....	11233
2583	13 27 3.8	...	+ 19.05	+ 0.22	...	3	46.7	...	....	....
2584	43 24 17.6	...	+ 19.05	+ 0.16	− 0.01	4	49.2	...	....	11244
2585	11 24 7.4	5.9	+ 19.05	+ 0.21	+ 0.04	4	44.8	13.3	....	11245

Ordinal Number.		Magnitude.	Estimates of Magnitude.	Mean Right Ascension 1845.0		Precession 1845.0	Secular Variation	Adopted Proper Motion.	Observations of R.A.		
									No.	Mean year.	
R.	G.	R.		R.	G.				R.	R.	G.
				h. m. s.	s.	s.	s.	s.		1800 +	
2586	1711	6.1	5	10 47 22.68	22.62	+ 3.456	− 0.040	+ 0.005	5	48.6	10.3
2587	1708	7.9	8	10 47 40.06	40.92	+ 5.113	− 0.340	......	5	47.7	14.3
2588	1710	8.8	9	10 47 43.74	43.30	+ 4.771	− 0.254	......	5	48.9	14.3
2589	1713	8.4	9	10 48 3.26	2.62	+ 4.244	− 0.154	......	4	48.3	13.3
2590	1715	7.1	6	10 48 18.28	18.39	+ 3.443	− 0.037	......	4	46.0	12.3
2591	1714	7.1	7	10 48 19.19	18.14	+ 4.252	− 0.154	......	5	53.0	13.3
2592	1712	9.1	6	10 48 20.07	19.71	+ 4.765	− 0.214	......	3	52.6	14.3
2593	1716	8.0	5	10 48 47.20	47.11	+ 3.598	− 0.054	......	3	47.2	16.3
2594	...	7.7	31	10 50 0.41	...	+18.199	−11.697	......	32	52.1	...
2595	1717	7.0	6	10 50 5.43	5.73	+ 3.486	− 0.049	......	3	45.9	11.3
2596	1718	5.5	10	10 50 46.14	45.65	+ 3.419	− 0.037	− 0.028	7	49.5	9.3
2597	1719	6.3	6	10 51 14.62	14.85	+ 3.889	− 0.097	......	3	45.9	11.9
2598	1721	6.3	7	10 51 16.84	16.74	+ 3.582	− 0.051	......	3	44.6	16.3
2599	1722	6.1	7	10 51 19.04	18.94	+ 3.484	− 0.043	......	3	46.3	11.3
2600	1723	5.9	5	10 51 32.10	32.25	+ 3.447	− 0.040	......	3	46.0	11.2
2601	1720	7.3	7	10 51 52.16	52.37	+ 4.673	− 0.249	......	4	46.2	14.3
2602	1724	6.8	6	10 51 52.77	52.65	+ 3.442	− 0.040	......	3	45.6	11.2
2603	...	7.8	9	10 51 57.01	...	+ 3.458	− 0.039	......	5	53.0	...
2604	1725	5.5	6	10 52 8.16	8.32	+ 3.398	− 0.034	......	3	45.3	10.3
2605	...	4.0	A	10 52 14.00	...	+ 2.947	+ 0.005	......	1	42.4	...
2606	1726	1.7	1	10 52 26.99	26.61	+ 3.673	− 0.069	+ 0.010	5	45.6	7.0
2607	...	5.4	9	10 52 33.33	...	+ 3.100	− 0.006	− 0.002	8	47.6	...
2608	1727	6.5	7	10 52 55.83	54.47	+ 4.182	− 0.140	......	5	46.7	13.3
2609	1728	7.8	9	10 53 24.91	25.35	+ 4.767	− 0.277	......	4	50.3	13.6
2610	...	7.2	8	10 53 44.67	...	+ 3.802	− 0.088	......	4	45.8	...
2611	1729	2.0	A	10 54 6.79	6.62	+ 3.801	− 0.086	− 0.017	23	42.6	7.3
2612	...	7.3	10	10 54 39.83	...	+ 9.183	− 2.322	......	5	53.8	...
2613	1730	7.3	9	10 54 51.64	51.89	+ 3.447	− 0.040	......	5	45.8	11.2
2614	1731	7.9	8	10 55 12.46	13.08	+ 3.381	− 0.034	......	4	44.5	12.3
2615	1732	7.2	6	10 55 38.49	38.78	+ 3.378	− 0.034	......	3	44.6	12.3
2616	1733	6.1	6	10 55 53.18	52.90	+ 3.370	− 0.031	......	5	46.2	9.3
2617	...	7.6	8	10 56 5.99	...	+ 3.369	− 0.031	......	4	48.8	...
2618	1734	7.4	10	10 56 57.80	57.30	+ 3.435	− 0.037	......	8	47.5	11.3
2619	...	4.8	12	10 57 1.26	...	+ 3.122	− 0.007	− 0.024	12	51.6	...
2620	1736	7.5	7	10 57 59.07	58.84	+ 3.427	− 0.037	......	5	46.3	11.3

Ordinal Number.	Mean North Polar Distance 1845.0.		Precession 1845.0.	Secular Variation.	Adopted Proper Motion	Observations of N.P.D.			Names.	Oeltzen Argelander Number.
R.	R.	G.				No. R.	Mean year. R.	G.		
	° ′ ″	″	″	″	″		1800 +			
2586	47 9 44.3	41.7	+ 19.05	+ 0.13	+ 0.02	4	43.7	10.3	....	....
2587	11 28 47.2	44.7	+ 19.06	+ 0.21	...	6	48.2	14.3	....	11251
2588	13 41 55.8	53.8	+ 19.06	+ 0.19	...	4	48.5	14.3	....	....
2589	19 21 37.3	34.7	+ 19.07	+ 0.17	...	5	48.3	13.3	....	11260
2590	47 49 10.9	8.4	+ 19.08	+ 0.14	...	3	44.9	12.3	....	....
2591	19 11 0.6	51.2	+ 19.08	+ 0.18	...	4	42.3	13.3	....	11266
2592	13 44 35.9	34.5	+ 19.08	+ 0.20	...	4	50.1	14.3	....	....
2593	37 42 53.2	17.2	+ 19.09	+ 0.14	...	3	44.2	16.3	....	....
2594	1 31 17.7	...	+ 19.13	+ 0.80	...	8	50.3	...	....	....
2595	43 58 21.7	18.4	+ 19.13	+ 0.15	...	4	45.3	11.3	....	....
2596	48 44 35.6	36.8	+ 19.14	+ 0.12	...	6	47.8	9.3	47 Urs. Maj. ..	....
2597	25 44 49.1	46.6	+ 19.16	+ 0.16	...	3	45.3	11.9	....	11305
2598	37 40 3.3	27.9	+ 19.16	+ 0.15	...	5	46.3	16.3	....	11306
2599	43 38 39.4	39.5	+ 19.16	+ 0.14	...	4	47.3	11.3	....	....
2600	46 15 11.5	5.7	+ 19.17	+ 0.14	...	4	47.3	11.2	....	....
2601	13 43 35.3	33.3	+ 19.18	+ 0.21	...	3	45.3	14.3	....	11319
2602	46 26 15.9	17.1	+ 19.18	+ 0.15	...	3	44.6	11.2	....	....
2603	45 15 29.9	...	+ 19.18	+ 0.14	...	4	52.8	...	....	11322
2604	49 57 23.1	22.6	+ 19.18	+ 0.13	...	5	47.9	10.3	49 Urs. Maj. ..	....
2605	107 28 27.4	...	+ 19.18	+ 0.12	...	1	55.3	...	7 Crateris α....	....
2606	32 47 17.7	17.3	+ 19.19	+ 0.15	...	16	50.8	7.0	48 Urs. Maj. β	11332
2607	85 33 4.9	...	+ 19.19	+ 0.13	+ 0.03	8	45.6	...	58 Leonis d....	....
2608	19 8 9.9	9.2	+ 19.20	+ 0.17	...	4	48.3	13.3	....	11343
2609	12 42 51.1	49.7	+ 19.22	+ 0.21	...	5	48.3	13.6	....	11350
2610	27 30 38.9	...	+ 19.23	+ 0.17	...	7	46.0	...	....	....
2611	27 24 49.0	48.9	+ 19.23	+ 0.15	+ 0.09	38	46.5	7.3	50 Urs. Maj. α	11365
2612	3 31 19.8	...	+ 19.24	+ 0.38	...	6	51.8	...	....	....
2613	44 50 1.7	59.0	+ 19.25	+ 0.13	...	5	47.7	11.2	....	....
2614	50 12 19.0	17.9	+ 19.26	+ 0.13	...	4	50.1	12.3	....	....
2615	50 17 51.6	53.5	+ 19.27	+ 0.13	...	4	47.3	12.3	....	....
2616	50 55 30.1	29.8	+ 19.28	+ 0.14	...	4	45.1	9.3	51 Urs. Maj. ..	....
2617	50 55 10.2	...	+ 19.28	+ 0.13	...	4	49.1	...	....	....
2618	44 51 47.5	48.4	+ 19.31	+ 0.15	...	3	44.6	11.3	....	11412
2619	81 49 38.4	...	+ 19.31	+ 0.12	+ 0.08	10	50.1	...	63 Leonis χ....	....
2620	45 2 54.8	54.5	+ 19.32	+ 0.13	...	4	45.8	11.3	....	11434

Ordinal Number.		Magnitude.	Estimates of Magnitude.	Mean Right Ascension 1845.0.		Precession 1845.0.	Secular Variation	Adopted Proper Motion.	Observations of R.A.		
									No.	Mean year.	
R.	G.	R.	R.	R.	G.				R.	R.	G.
				h. m. s.	s.	s.	s.	s.		1800 +	
2621	1735	7.1	10	10 58 3.71	2.96	+ 4.844	− 0.323	......	6	46.6	13.3
2622	1737	7.5	7	10 58 57.30	57.53	+ 3.548	− 0.056	......	3	45.7	11.8
2623	1738	8.3	6	10 59 54.49	54.27	+ 3.565	− 0.059	......	4	46.1	12.3
2624	1739	7.0	9	11 0 17.79	17.73	+ 3.514	− 0.054	......	4	44.7	11.3
2625	1740	7.1	8	11 0 42.51	42.23	+ 3.556	− 0.063	......	5	45.3	12.3
2626	1741	3.3	12	11 0 55.64	55.41	+ 3.415	− 0.037	− 0.007	12	48.7	7.4
2627	1742	6.0	8	11 0 56.52	56.54	+ 3.399	− 0.037	......	5	46.1	10.3
2628	...	8.0	4	11 1 41.76	...	+ 3.857	− 0.104	......	3	51.9	...
2629	...	8.1	3	11 1 46.02	...	+ 3.854	− 0.104	......	3	52.8	...
2630	...	6.3	8	11 2 12.76	...	+ 3.944	− 0.122	......	3	49.2	...
2631	1743	6.7	7	11 2 29.40	29.25	+ 3.544	− 0.060	......	5	45.4	12.3
2632	1744	8.3	10	11 2 58.81	59.04	+ 3.384	− 0.037	......	6	46.9	11.3
2633	1745	6.9	8	11 3 10.37	10.47	+ 3.384	− 0.037	......	4	47.5	11.8
2634	1746	6.7	7	11 3 41.20	41.03	+ 3.547	− 0.063	......	4	44.8	10.6
2635	...	7.9	6	11 4 20.80	...	+ 3.415	− 0.042	......	3	51.6	...
2636	1747	6.8	7	11 4 32.62	33.04	+ 4.742	− 0.329	......	4	45.5	13.3
2637	1748	7.8	7	11 4 38.51	38.40	+ 3.505	− 0.057	......	3	44.0	11.0
2638	1749	6.7	7	11 5 3.93	3.74	+ 3.355	− 0.034	......	3	46.0	11.3
2639	1750	7.6	5	11 5 36.31	36.19	+ 3.449	− 0.057	......	4	46.3	11.0
2640	...	2.7	2	11 5 51.44	...	+ 3.192	− 0.015	+ 0.011	42	44.6	...
2641	...	7.8	6	11 6 6.02	...	+ 3.373	− 0.037	......	4	47.2	...
2642	1751	7.7	7	11 6 26.81	26.70	+ 3.389	− 0.040	......	3	47.3	14.3
2643	...	7.7	5	11 6 32.41	...	+ 3.315	− 0.029	......	4	51.7	...
2644	1752	8.5	7	11 6 54.30	54.41	+ 3.396	− 0.040	......	3	48.3	14.3
2645	1753	8.1	5	11 6 59.91	59.94	+ 3.357	− 0.037	......	3	44.1	13.3
2646	1754	7.9	7	11 7 1.78	1.60	+ 3.395	− 0.040	......	3	49.6	14.3
2647	...	8.2	4	11 7 6.97	...	+ 3.485	− 0.051	......	3	50.9	...
2648	1755	6.9	5	11 7 7.20	6.21	+ 3.485	− 0.051	......	3	50.6	10.6
2649	1756	8.0	5	11 7 14.67	14.75	+ 3.357	− 0.037	......	3	48.1	13.3
2650	...	5.6	2	11 7 45.24	...	+ 3.146	− 0.010	......	2	53.3	...
2651	1757	6.0	5	11 7 56.17	56.47	+ 3.433	− 0.046	......	2	48.8	13.1
2652	1758	8.1	5	11 7 56.18	56.07	+ 3.353	− 0.034	......	3	51.6	13.3
2653	1759	7.5	9	11 8 18.68	18.45	+ 3.345	− 0.031	......	4	48.2	11.3
2654	1760	8.0	5	11 8 35.63	35.33	+ 3.409	− 0.046	......	3	47.0	11.3
2655	...	5.1	6	11 8 47.15	...	+ 3.055	− 0.001	− 0.009	6	48.6	...

Ordinal Number. R.	Mean North Polar Distance 1845.0. R.	G.	Precession 1845.0.	Secular Variation.	Adopted Proper Motion.	Observations of N.P.D. No. R.	Mean year. B. (1800 +)	G.	Names.	Oeltzen-Argelander Number.
	° ′ ″	″	″	″	″					
2621	11 22 30.1	29.2	+ 19.32	+ 0.17	...	5	45.5	13.3	....	....
2622	36 20 28.9	27.8	+ 19.35	+ 0.14	...	5	46.1	11.8	....	....
2623	35 0 36.8	34.5	+ 19.36	+ 0.13	...	4	45.8	12.3	....	11459
2624	37 46 57.7	55.7	+ 19.38	+ 0.13	...	5	47.2	11.3	....	11473
2625	35 3 17.3	16.8	+ 19.38	+ 0.13	...	6	47.0	12.3	....	11483
2626	44 39 41.9	42.7	+ 19.39	+ 0.12	+ 0.08	9	46.6	7.4	52 Urs. Maj. ψ	11489
2627	45 57 11.7	9.6	+ 19.39	+ 0.12	...	6	46.6	10.3	....	....
2628	23 8 31.1	...	+ 19.41	+ 0.15	...	2	52.3	...	....	11505
2629	23 7 48.2	...	+ 19.41	+ 0.15	...	2	51.3	...	....	11507
2630	20 53 16.8	...	+ 19.42	+ 0.14	...	5	47.5	...	....	11509
2631	35 0 44.0	43.5	+ 19.43	+ 0.13	...	4	44.7	12.3	....	11520
2632	46 19 53.0	45.1	+ 19.44	+ 0.12	...	6	46.3	11.3	....	....
2633	46 19 0.6	51.5	+ 19.44	+ 0.11	...	5	46.1	11.8	....	....
2634	34 15 52.3	51.0	+ 19.45	+ 0.11	...	5	45.1	10.6	....	....
2635	42 56 6.0	...	+ 19.46	+ 0.13	...	4	51.8	...	....	11560
2636	10 50 51.6	50.4	+ 19.47	+ 0.16	...	4	45.3	13.3	....	11561
2637	36 18 22.6	20.3	+ 19.47	+ 0.11	...	5	47.3	11.0	....	11563
2638	48 4 10.4	10.7	+ 19.48	+ 0.11	...	4	46.0	11.3	....	....
2639	36 12 32.8	27.0	+ 19.49	+ 0.11	...	5	44.7	11.0	....	11573
2640	68 37 38.7	...	+ 19.50	+ 0.11	+ 0.14	4	47.2	...	68 Leonis δ....	....
2641	45 49 21.5	...	+ 19.50	+ 0.11	...	5	44.9	...	....	....
2642	44 5 34.7	30.9	+ 19.51	+ 0.11	...	4	47.0	14.3	....	11583
2643	51 34 39.4	...	+ 19.51	+ 0.09	...	4	51.8	...	....	....
2644	43 18 22.4	21.8	+ 19.52	+ 0.11	...	5	47.1	14.3	....	11598
2645	46 48 57.2	57.0	+ 19.52	+ 0.10	...	4	46.8	13.3	....	....
2646	43 18 5.5	3.6	+ 19.52	+ 0.10	...	5	47.1	14.3	....	11601
2647	36 22 55.3	...	+ 19.52	+ 0.10	...	1	49.4	...	....	....
2648	36 23 7.3	7.7	+ 19.52	+ 0.10	...	4	44.3	10.5	....	11604
2649	46 42 25.0	21.6	+ 19.53	+ 0.12	...	3	45.3	13.3	....	....
2650	73 50 51.2	...	+ 19.54	+ 0.10	...	1	53.2	...	73 Leonis n....	....
2651	39 40 44.4	41.5	+ 19.54	+ 0.12	...	3	45.3	13.1	....	11621
2652	46 48 4.5	3.0	+ 19.54	+ 0.10	...	3	50.3	13.3	....	....
2653	47 25 44.3	44.3	+ 19.54	+ 0.08	...	5	48.1	11.3	....	....
2654	41 13 3.3	1.4	+ 19.55	+ 0.10	...	3	48.3	11.3	....	11625
2655	92 48 18.4	...	+ 19.55	+ 0.10	+ 0.04	3	54.3	...	74 Leonis φ...	....

Ordinal Number.		Magnitude.	Estimates of Magnitude.	Mean Right Ascension 1845.0		Precession 1845.0.	Secular Variation	Adopted Proper Motion.	Observations of R.A.		
R.	G.	R.		R.	G.				No. R	Mean year R.	G.
				h. m. s.	s.	s.	s.	s.		1800 +	
2656	...	8.3	3	11 8 52.25	...	+ 3.342	− 0.035	......	2	50.8	...
2657	...	7.3	6	11 9 14.03	...	+ 3.780	− 0.105	......	2	51.8	...
2658	1761	7.2	7	11 9 33.53	33.34	+ 3.520	− 0.063	......	4	45.8	11.8
2659	1762	7.1	6	11 9 49.62	49.32	+ 3.640	− 0.086	......	3	45.7	10.7
2660	1763	6.6	6	11 9 53.48	53.09	+ 3.342	− 0.034	......	4	46.5	12.3
2661	1764	5.1	7	11 10 40.08	39.88	+ 3.301	− 0.031	......	8	47.8	8.3
2662	1765	6.4	6	11 11 20.55	20.56	+ 3.766	− 0.109	......	3	45.3	13.3
2663	...	3.4	5	11 11 35.84	...	+ 3.000	− 0.004	− 0.009	4	52.2	...
2664	...	7.0	7	11 11 56.89	...	+ 3.356	− 0.039	......	4	51.8	...
2665	1766	7.1	8	11 12 13.31	13.51	+ 3.432	− 0.049	......	5	44.9	11.3
2666	1767	7.6	6	11 12 27.92	27.68	+ 3.534	− 0.071	......	3	46.0	11.2
2667	...	7.4	2	11 12 59.73	...	+ 3.097	− 0.005	......	3	55.3	...
2668	1768	7.2	8	11 13 5.98	5.57	+ 3.308	− 0.034	......	9	48.2	12.3
2669	...	4.5	6	11 13 8.64	...	+ 3.103	− 0.006	− 0.009	13	46.8	...
2670	1769	8.0	8	11 13 9.01	8.91	+ 3.307	− 0.031	......	4	47.7	12.3
2671	1770	7.9	8	11 13 16.20	16.27	+ 3.352	− 0.040	......	2	44.3	12.3
2672	1771	6.0	7	11 13 35.54	35.08	+ 3.651	− 0.094	......	3	44.6	10.3
2673	1772	6.5	9	11 14 14.49	14.56	+ 3.302	− 0.029	......	5	45.9	11.3
2674	1773	5.5	7	11 14 18.05	17.71	+ 3.329	− 0.037	+ 0.003	4	43.3	9.3
2675	1774	6.9	9	11 15 29.88	30.52	+ 3.272	− 0.029	......	7	49.3	11.3
2676	...	4.3	11	11 15 50.60	...	+ 3.122	− 0.008	+ 0.007	9	53.5	...
2677	...	5.7	1	11 16 47.43	...	+ 3.026	− 0.003	......	4	42.4	...
2678	1775	7.7	8	11 17 3.89	4.14	+ 3.306	− 0.034	......	4	47.7	12.3
2679	1776	5.7	6	11 17 10.40	9.79	+ 3.448	− 0.057	......	7	45.7	8.3
2680	1777	7.8	4	11 17 40.81	40.73	+ 3.304	− 0.034	......	3	45.3	12.3
2681	1779	9.1	7	11 18 34.29	34.44	+ 3.754	− 0.126	......	4	47.8	13.3
2682	1778	8.4	4	11 18 46.71	45.24	+ 4.748	− 0.451	......	4	46.9	7.8
2683	1780	7.8	6	11 18 48.17	48.53	+ 3.444	− 0.060	......	3	44.1	14.3
2684	...	7.3	8	11 19 1.30	...	+ 6.131	− 1.060	......	4	52.1	...
2685	1781	7.3	5	11 19 23.78	23.71	+ 3.259	− 0.029	......	3	46.6	10.3
2686	...	5.5	7	11 19 58.02	...	+ 3.085	− 0.004	......	14	48.1	...
2687	1783	5.6	4	11 20 10.67	10.29	+ 3.516	− 0.077	− 0.017	5	45.4	11.3
2688	...	7.5	6	11 20 13.35	...	+ 3.265	− 0.030	......	3	50.3	...
2689	1784	7.1	6	11 20 25.33	25.45	+ 3.289	− 0.034	......	4	47.6	12.3
2690	1785	7.4	6	11 20 34.12	33.81	+ 3.276	− 0.031	......	3	45.0	11.3

Ordinal Number.	Mean North Polar Distance 1845.0.			Precession 1845.0.	Secular Variation.	Adopted Proper Motion.	Observations of N.P.D.				Names.	Oeltzen-Argelander Number.
R.	R.		G.				No.	Mean year.				
							R.	R.	G.			
	° ′ ″		″	″	″	″		1800 +				
2656	47 22 53.3		...	+ 19.55	+ 0.10	...	3	49.0	...		....	....
2657	22 28 9.9		...	+ 19.56	+ 0.12	...	5	51.7	...		....	11632
2658	32 57 32.1		32.6	+ 19.57	+ 0.10	...	4	45.5	11.8		....	11637
2659	26 58 21.5		20.6	+ 19.58	+ 0.12	...	4	44.5	10.7		....	11640
2660	46 50 11.3		10.1	+ 19.58	+ 0.11	...	4	43.7	12.3		....	....
2661	50 57 54.4		54.5	+ 19.59	+ 0.09	+ 0.09	6	45.3	8.3		55 Urs. Maj. ..	....
2662	22 2 59.5		57.3	+ 19.60	+ 0.10	...	5	45.9	13.3		....	11668
2663	103 56 27.7		...	+ 19.61	+ 0.09	− 0.18	3	54.3	...		12 Crateris δ .	....
2664	44 9 11.4		...	+ 19.62	+ 0.10	...	6	52.1	...		....	11678
2665	37 23 11.4		6.9	+ 19.62	+ 0.10	...	4	43.5	11.3		....	11680
2666	30 40 8.0		7.5	+ 19.62	+ 0.09	...	4	45.8	11.2		....	11682
2667	84 16 13.4		...	+ 19.63	+ 0.09	...	1	51.3	...		....	....
2668	48 43 5.5		3.7	+ 19.63	+ 0.07	...	4	45.3	12.3		....	....
2669	83 7 19.2		...	+ 19.63	+ 0.09	+ 0.03	7	45.1	...		77 Leonis σ ...	....
2670	48 52 12.9		13.4	+ 19.63	+ 0.07	...	5	48.3	12.3		....	....
2671	43 49 9.5		8.3	+ 19.63	+ 0.07	...	4	46.8	12.3		....	11700
2672	24 49 20.3		21.2	+ 19.64	+ 0.09	...	5	46.7	10.3		....	11702
2673	48 58 30.7		31.8	+ 19.65	+ 0.07	...	5	47.1	11.3		....	....
2674	45 40 3.0		3.9	+ 19.66	+ 0.09	...	7	45.1	9.3		56 Urs. Maj. ..	....
2675	51 54 52.3		54.3	+ 19.68	+ 0.09	...	5	48.1	11.3		....	....
2676	78 37 4.0		...	+ 19.69	+ 0.09	+ 0.07	5	53.5	...		78 Leonis ι ...	....
2677	100 0 36.6		...	+ 19.70	+ 0.08	...	1	58.3	...		14 Crateris ε ..	....
2678	46 31 17.6		21.5	+ 19.70	+ 0.08	...	6	46.1	12.3		....	....
2679	33 18 2.1		1.8	+ 19.71	+ 0.10	− 0.04	7	45.7	8.3		....	11747
2680	46 24 58.6		56.9	+ 19.71	+ 0.07	...	4	44.8	12.3		....	....
2681	19 21 27.7		27.4	+ 19.72	+ 0.07	...	5	47.5	13.3		....	11765
2682	8 6 39.1		41.2	+ 19.72	+ 0.09	...	4	43.8	7.8		....	....
2683	32 34 20.5		18.9	+ 19.72	+ 0.05	...	5	45.5	14.3		....	11768
2684	4 26 27.2		...	+ 19.73	+ 0.15	...	6	52.1	...		....	....
2685	51 12 20.5		16.8	+ 19.73	+ 0.05	...	3	49.0	10.3		....	....
2686	86 17 26.7		...	+ 19.74	+ 0.08	+ 0.02	3	48.6	...		84 Leonis τ ...	....
2687	27 22 45.4		48.4	+ 19.75	+ 0.07	− 0.13	4	43.8	11.3		....	11785
2688	49 50 22.9		...	+ 19.75	+ 0.08	...	3	46.3	...		....	....
2689	46 21 5.2		2.5	+ 19.76	+ 0.07	...	5	47.7	12.3		....	....
2690	47 58 11.4		14.9	+ 19.76	+ 0.07	...	4	47.5	11.3		....	....

Ordinal Number.		Magnitude.	Estimates of Magnitude.	Mean Right Ascension 1845.0.		Precession 1845.0.	Secular Variation	Adopted Proper Motion.	Observations of R.A.		
R.	G.	R.		R.	G.				No. R.	Mean year. R.	G.
				h. m. s.	s.	s.	s.	s.		1800 +	
2691	1782	6.0	6	11 20 39.95	41.99	+ 4.690	− 0.043	......	5	43.8	7.3
2692	1786	5.5	5	11 20 42.31	41.92	+ 3.263	− 0.029	......	4	47.0	9.3
2693	1787	6.0	7	11 21 0.83	0.99	+ 3.427	− 0.057	......	4	45.3	14.3
2694	1788	7.1	6	11 21 33.05	32.76	+ 3.391	− 0.054	......	2	46.8	13.3
2695	1789	8.3	5	11 21 37.03	37.13	+ 3.282	− 0.031	......	2	48.3	12.3
2696	...	7.1	5	11 21 55.25	...	+ 3.248	− 0.028	......	4	50.3	...
2697	1792	6.6	6	11 21 55.91	55.82	+ 3.311	− 0.040	......	3	46.9	14.3
2698	1791	7.3	5	11 21 59.58	59.29	+ 3.418	− 0.057	......	2	49.8	14.3
2699	1794	6.9	4	11 22 6.74	7.53	+ 3.286	− 0.034	......	2	47.9	10.3
2700	1793	6.0	11	11 22 6.74	6.65	+ 3.282	− 0.037	+ 0.011	7	50.9	9.3
2701	1790	3.7	5	11 22 8.02	8.08	+ 3.680	− 0.120	......	6	44.7	7.6
2702	...	5.6	2	11 22 24.02	...	+ 3.062	− 0.001	......	6	42.2	...
2703	1795	7.1	5	11 22 25.64	25.11	+ 3.267	− 0.034	......	2	48.3	11.3
2704	1796	6.9	5	11 22 26.30	27.10	+ 3.319	− 0.040	......	3	47.0	13.3
2705	...	7.4	9	11 22 39.35	...	+ 6.587	− 1.573	......	7	52.6	...
2706	...	6.6	5	11 22 39.98	...	+ 3.325	− 0.042	......	3	47.0	...
2707	1797	5.3	5	11 23 31.53	31.14	+ 3.467	− 0.074	......	5	44.5	11.3
2708	1798	7.2	8	11 23 32.11	32.19	+ 3.263	− 0.031	......	3	45.9	11.3
2709	1799	7.8	6	11 26 13.26	12.64	+ 3.329	− 0.049	......	3	44.0	12.4
2710	1800	5.9	4	11 26 30.64	30.33	+ 3.355	− 0.051	......	5	43.0	11.3
2711	1801	9.1	6	11 26 40.15	39.89	+ 3.489	− 0.083	......	3	46.0	14.3
2712	1802	5.2	4	11 26 53.65	53.23	+ 3.604	− 0.117	+ 0.023	7	43.9	10.3
2713	...	7.6	5	11 27 18.89	...	+ 3.522	− 0.095	......	3	52.0	...
2714	1803	6.7	6	11 27 50.11	49.64	+ 3.986	− 0.237	......	4	44.8	13.3
2715	1805	9.1	5	11 28 40.15	39.91	+ 3.239	− 0.034	......	3	46.0	15.2
2716	1804	7.1	7	11 28 41.42	40.55	+ 3.428	− 0.077	......	5	45.4	11.9
2717	1806	7.4	5	11 28 55.54	55.84	+ 3.433	− 0.080	......	4	44.7	13.6
2718	...	4.7	6	11 29 0.93	...	+ 3.070	− 0.002	− 0.003	12	46.7	...
2719	1807	6.0	5	11 29 28.29	28.19	+ 3.293	− 0.046	......	3	44.3	12.3
2720	1808	8.0	9	11 29 36.77	36.23	+ 3.450	− 0.083	......	4	48.3	14.3
2721	1809	6.7	8	11 30 3.57	3.42	+ 3.447	− 0.086	......	3	45.3	14.3
2722	1810	5.9	9	11 30 3.84	3.88	+ 3.241	− 0.034	......	9	49.3	9.3
2723	1811	6.4	3	11 30 13.01	12.82	+ 3.260	− 0.040	......	5	46.0	10.3
2724	...	8.6	7	11 30 33.18	...	+ 3.247	− 0.034	......	2	44.2	...
2725	1812	7.0	6	11 30 34.12	35.75	+ 3.247	− 0.034	......	3	46.5	13.1

Ordinal Number.	Mean North Polar Distance 1845.0.		Precession 1845.0.	Secular Variation.	Adopted Proper Motion.	Observations of N.P.D.			Names.	Oeltzen-Argelander Number.
R.	R.	G.				No. R.	Mean year. R.	G.		
	o ′ ″	″	″	″	″		1800 +			
2691	8 1 14.0	14.1	+ 19.76	+ 0.11	...	5	46.3	7.3	[illegible]	......
2692	49 48 38.0	37.8	+ 19.76	+ 0.07	...	3	44.9	9.3	57 Urs. Maj. ...	......
2693	32 24 27.5	27.7	+ 19.77	+ 0.09	...	3	46.3	14.3	....	11798
2694	34 46 57.1	52.6	+ 19.77	+ 0.07	...	5	48.3	13.3	....	11804
2695	46 29 4.8	4.8	+ 19.77	+ 0.06	...	3	46.0	12.3	....	......
2696	51 11 30.0	...	+ 19.78	+ 0.08	...	3	48.0	...	....	......
2697	42 29 24.5	23.8	+ 19.78	+ 0.07	...	3	46.6	14.3	....	......
2698	32 24 1.1	3.0	+ 19.78	+ 0.07	...	3	45.9	14.3	....	11811
2699	45 34 13.9	15.9	+ 19.78	+ 0.07	...	4	50.0	10.3	....	......
2700	45 58 34.9	36.5	+ 19.78	+ 0.07	− 0.04	8	50.5	9.3	58 Urs. Maj. ...	......
2701	19 48 51.3	50.9	+ 19.78	+ 0.08	+ 0.06	6	47.6	7.6	1 Draconis λ ..	11815
2702	92 8 55.9	...	+ 19.78	+ 0.07	...	3	56.3	...	87 Leonis e ...	......
2703	47 51 17.1	16.4	+ 19.78	+ 0.05	...	4	51.3	11.3	....	......
2704	41 12 50.0	46.4	+ 19.78	+ 0.05	...	4	49.8	13.3	....	11818
2705	3 31 45.2	...	+ 19.79	+ 0.16	...	4	52.3	...	....	......
2706	40 21 17.0	...	+ 19.79	+ 0.08	...	3	46.0	...	....	11821
2707	28 3 35.4	32.2	+ 19.80	+ 0.07	...	6	44.4	11.3	....	11840
2708	47 42 34.4	36.4	+ 19.80	+ 0.06	...	7	46.7	11.3	....	......
2709	37 10 33.7	38.0	+ 19.84	+ 0.07	...	4	48.5	12.4	....	11879
2710	34 21 31.7	30.9	+ 19.84	+ 0.06	...	4	43.3	11.3	....	11883
2711	24 49 33.8	32.7	+ 19.85	+ 0.08	...	4	45.3	14.3	....	11885
2712	19 48 55.4	54.8	+ 19.85	+ 0.08	+ 0.12	7	45.6	10.3	2 Draconis	11887
2713	22 48 0.1	...	+ 19.86	+ 0.07	...	4	51.5	...	....	11896
2714	11 32 51.2	51.4	+ 19.86	+ 0.08	...	4	44.3	13.3	....	11899
2715	47 6 12.7	10.3	+ 19.87	+ 0.05	...	3	44.9	15.2	....	......
2716	26 56 49.8	49.6	+ 19.87	+ 0.06	...	6	47.3	11.9	....	11909
2717	26 25 51.4	51.1	+ 19.87	+ 0.06	...	3	44.7	13.6	....	......
2718	89 58 6.2	...	+ 19.87	+ 0.06	− 0.03	3	51.3	...	91 Leonis υ ...	......
2719	38 31 24.0	21.4	+ 19.88	+ 0.05	...	4	45.8	12.3	....	11920
2720	24 57 56.7	57.6	+ 19.88	+ 0.06	...	5	47.7	14.3	....	11924
2721	24 47 43.2	43.8	+ 19.88	+ 0.05	...	5	48.5	14.3	....	11932
2722	45 30 55.6	54.6	+ 19.88	+ 0.05	...	5	45.9	9.3	59 Urs. Maj. ...	......
2723	42 18 24.0	24.0	+ 19.88	+ 0.05	+ 0.05	4	45.8	10.3	60 Urs. Maj. ...	11935
2724	44 2 4.2	...	+ 19.89	+ 0.05	...	5	46.5	...	....	......
2725	44 2 3.4	4.1	+ 19.89	+ 0.05	...	4	47.8	13.1	....	11940

Ordinal Number.		Magnitude.	Estimates of Magnitude.	Mean Right Ascension 1845.0.		Precession 1845.0.	Secular Variation	Adopted Proper Motion.	Observations of R.A.		
R.	G.	R.	R.	R.	G.				No.	Mean year.	
									R.	R.	G.
				h. m. s.	s.	s.	s.	s.		1800 +	
2726	...	7.8	5	11 30 42.03	...	+ 3.223	− 0.031	......	3	52.0	...
2727	1813	7.5	6	11 31 31.00	30.84	+ 3.242	− 0.034	......	2	46.8	13.1
2728	1814	7.1	8	11 31 42.85	43.14	+ 3.397	− 0.071	......	4	47.1	14.4
2729	1815	7.8	5	11 31 49.00	48.61	+ 3.222	− 0.031	......	2	46.8	15.3
2730	1816	6.5	3	11 31 56.55	56.32	+ 3.340	− 0.060	......	4	47.5	11.3
2731	1817	7.4	5	11 32 32.48	32.83	+ 3.367	− 0.066	......	3	49.3	14.3
2732	...	6.9	5	11 33 31.60	...	+ 3.209	− 0.031	......	3	52.6	...
2733	1819	5.4	4	11 33 46.41	45.80	+ 3.441	− 0.091	......	4	43.3	9.3
2734	...	9.3	7	11 33 46.25	...	+ 5.376	− 1.124	......	6	53.9	...
2735	1818	9.5	7	11 33 56.92	53.84	+ 4.587	− 0.646	......	4	48.7	8.4
2736	1820	8.0	6	11 34 20.09	20.20	+ 3.218	− 0.031	......	5	46.3	13.3
2737	1821	6.7	5	11 35 23.90	23.68	+ 3.202	− 0.031	......	4	44.8	10.3
2738	...	8.1	11	11 35 32.31	...	+ 5.329	− 1.165	......	10	52.5	...
2739	...	7.4	5	11 36 22.05	...	+ 3.406	− 0.090	......	3	50.6	...
2740	1822	8.1	5	11 37 24.81	26.34	+ 3.219	− 0.037	......	4	45.8	14.4
2741	1823	3.9	7	11 37 50.71	50.54	+ 3.217	− 0.037	− 0.013	7	47.1	7.2
2742	...	4.5	6	11 37 53.57	...	+ 3.087	− 0.005	......	10	51.2	...
2743	1824	7.2	5	11 38 35.10	34.48	+ 3.341	− 0.077	......	3	47.9	11.3
2744	1825	5.2	3	11 38 35.95	35.76	+ 3.258	− 0.051	......	5	45.2	11.3
2745	1826	6.8	4	11 38 43.71	43.51	+ 3.306	− 0.066	......	4	43.7	12.3
2746	...	7.5	4	11 40 40.82	...	+ 3.347	− 0.091	......	3	51.6	...
2747	...	9.0	2	11 40 ...	...	+ 3.347	− 0.091	......	...	...	...
2748	...	2.0	A	11 41 9.03	...	+ 3.100	− 0.009	− 0.036	45	45.1	...
2749	...	10.1	25	11 41 46.75	...	+ 3.154	− 0.026	......	10	53.2	...
2750	1827	6.8	4	11 41 59.54	59.11	+ 3.220	− 0.049	......	2	45.8	11.3
2751	...	3.6	11	11 42 37.38	...	+ 3.075	− 0.002	+ 0.048	17	48.2	...
2752	1828	7.1	6	11 42 54.37	53.50	+ 3.399	− 0.097	......	4	50.1	13.3
2753	1829	9.6	5	11 43 4.56	4.13	+ 3.179	− 0.029	......	3	49.7	12.3
2754	1830	6.5	44	11 44 1.67	1.46	+ 3.145	− 0.029	+ 0.344	31	51.1	11.3
2755	...	7.8	5	11 44 52.38	...	+ 3.166	− 0.036	......	3	47.3	...
2756	...	7.9	2	11 45 32.86	...	+ 3.151	− 0.031	......	3	51.6	...
2757	1831	2.3	A	11 45 39.04	38.67	+ 3.188	− 0.046	+ 0.011	26	41.9	7.1
2758	1832	6.8	4	11 45 46.81	46.26	+ 3.144	− 0.029	......	4	45.4	9.3
2759	...	9.2	28	11 46 2.63	...	+ 3.135	− 0.025	......	16	52.8	...
2760	...	9.6	15	11 46 21.64	...	+ 3.136	− 0.025	......	10	53.2	...

Ordinal Number.	Mean North Polar Distance 1845.0.			Precession 1845.0.	Secular Variation.	Adopted Proper Motion.	Observations of N.P.D.			Names.	Oeltzen-Argelander Number.
	R.						No.	Mean year.			
R.	R.		G.				R.	R.	G.		
	° ′ ″		″	″	″	″		1800 +			
2726	47 59 53.0		...	+ 19.89	+ 0.06	...	3	52.0	...	....	....
2727	43 59 6.3		4.7	+ 19.90	+ 0.05	...	4	46.6	13.1	....	11958
2728	26 44 36.8		37.1	+ 19.91	+ 0.07	...	4	46.3	14.4	....	11962
2729	47 6 54.6		55.5	+ 19.91	+ 0.07	...	3	45.0	15.3	....	......
2730	31 10 18.8		19.1	+ 19.91	+ 0.07	...	7	45.7	11.3	....	11966
2731	28 17 51.7		52.2	+ 19.91	+ 0.06	...	3	45.0	14.3	....	......
2732	47 54 5.0		...	+ 19.92	+ 0.06	...	3	52.6	...	....	......
2733	22 23 51.8		51.1	+ 19.92	+ 0.04	− 0.05	6	44.1	9.3	3 Draconis.....	11992
2734	3 47 18.0		...	+ 19.92	+ 0.09	...	3	52.0	...	....	......
2735	5 42 34.4		28.6	+ 19.93	+ 0.09	...	4	45.3	8.4	....	......
2736	45 21 0.7		58.6	+ 19.93	+ 0.05	...	3	43.6	13.3	....	11998
2737	47 25 2.0		1.8	+ 19.94	+ 0.04	...	5	45.9	10.3	....	......
2738	3 36 27.7		...	+ 19.94	+ 0.08	...	9	51.7	...	....	......
2739	22 16 34.0		...	+ 19.95	+ 0.05	...	3	49.0	...	....	12032
2740	41 27 37.1		29.3	+ 19.95	+ 0.04	...	4	43.3	14.4	....	12045
2741	41 21 41.1		40.4	+ 19.96	+ 0.04	...	6	42.5	7.2	63 Urs. Maj. χ	12051
2742	82 36 8.6		...	+ 19.96	+ 0.04	+ 0.21	5	51.7	...	3 Virginis ν....	....
2743	24 44 45.8		46.8	+ 19.97	+ 0.04	...	5	45.1	11.3	....	12063
2744	33 30 34.4		34.4	+ 19.97	+ 0.04	...	4	42.6	11.3	....	....
2745	27 44 9.4		8.6	+ 19.97	+ 0.04	...	6	46.0	12.3	....	12066
2746	21 48 37.5		...	+ 19.98	+ 0.04	...	1	49.3	...	....	12087
2747	21 48 46.9		...	+ 19.98	+ 0.04	...	2	50.8	...	....	....
2748	74 33 42.6		...	+ 19.98	+ 0.04	+ 0.10	2	40.3	...	94 Leonis β...	....
2749	51 13 50.6		...	+ 19.99	+ 0.04	...	17	52.3	...	....	....
2750	34 53 11.5		11.0	+ 19.99	+ 0.02	...	3	43.6	11.3	....	....
2751	87 21 42.9		...	+ 19.99	+ 0.03	+ 0.28	10	49.0	...	5 Virginis β...	....
2752	20 18 11.1		7.2	+ 20.00	+ 0.03	...	4	43.3	13.3	....	12106
2753	42 4 52.2		52.0	+ 20.00	+ 0.02	...	3	45.6	12.3	....	......
2754	51 10 11.2		9.0	+ 20.00	+ 0.01	+ 5.70	32	51.0	11.3	....	......
2755	42 34 46.0		...	+ 20.01	+ 0.03	...	4	46.8	...	....	......
2756	46 13 15.5		...	+ 20.01	+ 0.03	...	3	51.4	...	....	......
2757	35 26 37.0		35.7	+ 20.01	+ 0.02	...	6	43.9	7 1	64 Urs. Maj. γ	12152
2758	48 13 20.5		17.5	+ 20.02	+ 0.03	...	3	42.3	9 3	....	......
2759	51 11 1.6		...	+ 20.02	+ 0.03	...	14	52.3	...	....	......
2760	51 5 57.6		...	+ 20.02	+ 0.03	...	6	51.6	...	....	......

Ordinal Number.		Magnitude.	Estimates of Magnitude.	Mean Right Ascension 1845.0.		Precession 1845.0	Secular Variation	Adopted Proper Motion.	Observations of R.A.		
R.	G.	R.	R.	R.	G.				No. R.	Mean year. R.	G.
				h. m. s.	s.	s.	s.	s.		1800 +	
2761	1833	6.7	8	11 47 0.96	0.33	+ 3.152	− 0.034	+ 0.006	5	48.4	9.3
2762	1834	7.2	8	11 47 6.63	5.80	+ 3.151	− 0.037	……	4	48.3	9.3
2763	1835	5.6	3	11 47 50.71	50.54	+ 3.181	− 0.051	+ 0.003	4	43.7	10.3
2764	1836	7.1	4	11 48 1.16	0.95	+ 3.132	− 0.029	……	3	43.9	12.4
2765	1837	7.3	6	11 48 21.08	20.82	+ 3.133	− 0.029	……	4	45.8	13.3
2766	…	7.8	3	11 48 27.00	…	+ 3.144	− 0.035	……	2	51.8	…
2767	1838	6.1	2	11 48 45.59	45.45	+ 3.195	− 0.063	……	3	42.3	12.3
2768	1839	8.3	6	11 48 52.63	52.52	+ 3.127	− 0.026	……	4	44.8	11.3
2769	1840	7.1	5	11 49 5.57	5.57	+ 3.126	− 0.031	……	3	47.0	11.3
2770	…	8.6	3	11 49 11.69	…	+ 3.139	− 0.035	……	3	52.0	…
2771	1841	6.7	7	11 49 15.27	15.65	+ 3.125	− 0.026	……	5	46.0	11.3
2772	1842	8.1	4	11 49 39.07	40.53	+ 3.474	− 0.260	……	3	47.7	7.3
2773	1843	6.5	4	11 50 13.87	13.49	+ 3.179	− 0.057	……	4	43.3	12.3
2774	…	9.9	4	11 50 31.64	…	+ 4.546	− 1.546	……	4	53.7	…
2775	…	8.0	9	11 50 52.63	…	+ 4.494	− 1.540	……	6	53.0	…
2776	1844	7.7	5	11 51 12.17	12.21	+ 3.167	− 0.063	……	4	44.3	12.3
2777	…	8.6	4	11 51 48.23	…	+ 3.136	− 0.046	……	2	51.8	…
2778	…	8.3	4	11 51 59.10	…	+ 3.209	− 0.103	……	3	52.7	…
2779	…	6.0	1	11 52 0.83	…	+ 3.074	− 0.003	− 0.002	1	41.2	…
2780	…	8.3	5	11 52 1.66	…	+ 3.522	− 0.031	……	2	46.8	…
2781	…	8.6	5	11 52 2.66	…	+ 3.209	− 0.103	……	3	52.3	…
2782	1845	6.2	4	11 52 4.59	4.04	+ 3.387	− 0.257	……	5	44.4	7.9
2783	…	7.5	5	11 52 24.87	…	+ 3.115	− 0.031	……	3	52.6	…
2784	1846	6.8	6	11 52 48.52	48.29	+ 3.193	− 0.094	……	3	47.0	10.4
2785	…	4.7	6	11 52 55.93	…	+ 3.075	− 0.004	……	10	49.2	…
2786	1847	5.7	3	11 54 13.53	13.15	+ 3.102	− 0.029	− 0.032	4	43.7	9.3
2787	…	8.7	7	11 54 23.40	…	+ 3.102	− 0.030	……	3	44.2	…
2788	…	6.8	4	11 54 36.48	…	+ 3.100	− 0.030	− 0.017	3	46.1	…
2789	1848	9.2	5	11 55 17.02	12.49	+ 3.343	− 0.380	……	3	43.9	7.6
2790	…	7.4	5	11 55 19.81	…	+ 3.277	− 0.259	……	2	51.9	…
2791	1849	7.7	4	11 56 2.18	2.01	+ 3.114	− 0.060	……	3	45.3	8.4
2792	1850	6.3	36	11 56 48.75	50.07	+ 3.369	− 0.614	……	41	50.2	7.6
2793	1851	7.4	8	11 57 12.04	12.48	+ 3.144	− 0.143	……	4	47.8	13.3
2794	1852	6.1	5	11 57 17.14	14.92	+ 3.143	− 0.149	……	4	45.3	13.3
2795	…	4.4	4	11 57 18.86	…	+ 3.073	− 0.005	− 0.013	4	47.8	…

Ordinal Number. R.	Mean North Polar Distance 1845.0.		Precession 1845.0.	Secular Variation.	Adopted Proper Motion.	Observations of N.P.D.			Names.	Oeltzen-Argelander Number.
	R.	G.				No. R.	Mean year R.	G.		
	° ′ ″	″	″	″	″		1800 +			
2761	42 39 40.1	38.9	+ 20.02	+ 0.03	+ 0.02	5	44.3	9.3	65 Urs. Maj...	....
2762	42 40 5.2	3.4	+ 20.02	+ 0.03	...	6	44.0	9.3	....	....
2763	32 32 19.9	19.7	+ 20.03	+ 0.03	...	6	42.8	10.3	66 Urs. Maj. ...	12176
2764	48 29 18.0	18.7	+ 20.03	+ 0.02	...	3	43.6	12.4	....	....
2765	47 7 24.8	23.5	+ 20.03	+ 0.02	...	3	43.0	13.3	....	....
2766	42 26 23.4	...	+ 20.03	+ 0.03	...	2	52.8	...	....	....
2767	27 35 11.7	10.0	+ 20.03	+ 0.01	...	4	43.1	12.3	....	12190
2768	48 46 52.7	51.4	+ 20.03	+ 0.01	...	4	45.3	11.3	....	....
2769	48 50 53.0	53.6	+ 20.03	+ 0.01	...	3	43.0	11.3	....	....
2770	42 34 5.4	...	+ 20.03	+ 0.02	...	2	52.4	...	....	....
2771	48 47 26.1	24.0	+ 20.03	+ 0.01	...	4	43.3	11.3	....	....
2772	8 30 12.4	12.9	+ 20.04	+ 0.03	...	4	44.3	7.3	....	....
2773	27 40 21.1	21.3	+ 20.04	+ 0.02	...	5	45.3	12.3	....	12212
2774	2 8 30.4	...	+ 20.04	+ 0.03	...	2	54.9	...	....	....
2775	2 8 33.0	...	+ 20.04	+ 0.03	...	4	52.3	...	....	....
2776	27 48 7.8	6.5	+ 20.04	+ 0.01	...	4	44.3	12.3	....	12220
2777	35 44 19.3	...	+ 20.04	+ 0.02	...	4	51.8	...	....	....
2778	18 28 38.0	...	+ 20.04	+ 0.02	...	2	51.8	...	....	12234
2779	85 28 51.7	...	+ 20.04	+ 0.01	+ 0.02	1	54.3	...	7 Virginis b ...	....
2780	45 47 33.2	...	+ 20.04	+ 0.02	...	4	47.3	...	....	....
2781	18 29 7.3	...	+ 20.04	+ 0.02	...	2	52.3	...	....	12236
2782	8 16 57.0	55.1	+ 20.04	+ 0.01	...	4	43.8	7.9	....	....
2783	44 30 24.6	...	+ 20.04	+ 0.01	...	4	52.8	...	....	12243
2784	18 54 0.4	59.8	+ 20.04	0.00	...	3	44.0	10.4	....	12250
2785	82 31 16.0	...	+ 20.04	+ 0.01	+ 0.04	2	52.3	...	8 Virginis π...	....
2786	46 5 39.4	40.9	+ 20.05	0.00	− 0.05	5	42.9	9.3	67 Urs. Maj....	....
2787	45 59 46.8	...	+ 20.05	+ 0.01	...	4	47.3	...	....	....
2788	46 1 50.2	...	+ 20.05	0.00	+ 0.58	3	42.9	...	....	....
2789	5 45 18.9	17.6	+ 20.05	+ 0.01	...	3	44.3	7.6	....	....
2790	7 26 55.6	...	+ 20.05	+ 0.01	...	3	48.0	...	....	....
2791	27 44 1.7	1.8	+ 20.05	0.00	...	4	45.8	8.4	....	....
2792	3 33 13.6	17.0	+ 20.05	0.00	...	16	47.9	7.6	....	....
2793	12 22 17.4	13.8	+ 20.05	0.00	...	5	44.9	13.3	....	12304
2794	12 13 39.5	35.1	+ 20.05	0.00	...	4	43.8	13.3	....	12309
2795	80 24 21.1	...	+ 20.05	0.00	+ 0.02	2	50.3	...	9 Virginis o ...	....

Ordinal Number.		Magnitude.	Estimates of Magnitude.	Mean Right Ascension 1845.0.			Precession 1845.0.	Secular Variation	Adopted Proper Motion.	Observations of R.A.		
R.	G.	R.	R.	R.		G.				No.	Mean year.	
										R.	R.	G.
				h. m. s.		s.	s.	s.	s.		1800 +	
2796	...	7.7	6	11 57 39.78		...	+ 3.088	— 0.040	......	4	48.8	...
2797	...	8.5	5	11 57 40.68		...	+ 3.088	— 0.040	......	3	52.7	...
2798	...	7.9	3	11 57 41.45		...	+ 3.088	— 0.044	......	2	51.8	...
2799	1853	6.1	3	11 57 47.85		47.75	+ 3.096	— 0.060	......	4	43.7	10.3
2800	...	7.5	4	12 1 29.93		...	+ 3.058	— 0.043	......	4	51.7	...
2801	1854	7.4	5	12 1 36.14		35.88	+ 3.062	— 0.026	......	4	45.8	10.9
2802	1855	7.4	4	12 1 49.88		50.48	+ 3.061	— 0.026	......	3	44.1	11.3
2803	...	6.8	7	12 2 23.83		...	+ 3.003	— 0.132	......	3	48.0	...
2804	...	9.1	6	12 2 42.03		...	+ 2.995	— 0.134	......	3	52.3	...
2805	...	9.6	6	12 2 55.47		...	+ 2.998	— 0.136	......	4	53.6	...
2806	1856	7.6	6	12 3 18.94		18.76	+ 3.054	— 0.023	......	3	45.9	11.3
2807	...	9.0	10	12 3 35.51		...	+ 2.969	— 0.133	......	6	50.6	...
2808	1858	5.9	8	12 3 54.63		55.22	+ 2.895	— 0.209	......	4	46.2	7.3
2809	1857	6.2	2	12 3 59.63		58.91	+ 3.033	— 0.046	......	5	45.8	9.3
2810	...	9.0	8	12 4 15.03		...	+ 2.949	— 0.135	......	4	51.5	...
2811	...	6.7	8	12 4 26.01		...	+ 2.945	— 0.131	+ 0.025	4	48.3	...
2812	...	8.7	6	12 4 26.69		...	+ 2.895	— 0.209	......	4	46.0	...
2813	1859	5.4	6	12 4 51.95		50.55	+ 2.931	— 0.137	+ 0.007	5	46.3	8.3
2814	...	9.0	5	12 5 8.11		...	+ 3.044	— 0.025	......	3	50.9	...
2815	...	7.8	6	12 6 18.80		...	+ 2.113	— 0.290	......	4	52.9	...
2816	1860	8.0	11	12 6 22.41		18.95	+ 2.694	— 0.246	......	12	50.8	8.4
2817	1861	6.4	3	12 7 1.01		0.40	+ 3.014	— 0.037	......	5	45.2	9.3
2818	1863	5.7	5	12 7 42.48		42.18	+ 2.939	— 0.080	......	4	47.4	10.3
2819	1862	3.5	2	12 7 43.73		43.28	+ 2.998	— 0.043	+ 0.015	5	45.6	7.1
2820	...	2.0	A	12 7 50.68		...	+ 3.084	+ 0.009	— 0.008	3	42.4	...
2821	...	9.2	5	12 8 19.71		...	+ 3.027	— 0.026	......	3	53.4	...
2822	1864	5.0	4	12 8 20.57		20.32	+ 3.027	— 0.026	+ 0.003	4	43.3	8.3
2823	1865	6.3	5	12 8 21.36		20.74	+ 2.907	— 0.089	......	4	47.1	13.3
2824	1866	8.5	7	12 9 12.77		14.11	+ 2.957	— 0.060	......	4	46.3	14.3
2825	...	7.8	6	12 9 20.15		...	+ 2.727	— 0.144	......	3	49.6	...
2826	...	8.8	6	12 9 23.25		...	+ 2.911	— 0.077	......	3	52.7	...
2827	...	7.5	5	12 9 23.72		...	+ 2.725	— 0.144	+ 0.016	4	49.1	...
2828	...	7.5	7	12 10 41.74		...	+ 2.913	— 0.076	......	3	52.6	...
2829	...	6.1	3	12 10 43.84		...	+ 3.070	+ 0.001	......	1	47.3	...
2830	...	8.6	6	12 10 51.60		...	+ 3.013	— 0.025	......	4	50.5	...

Ordinal Number.	Mean North Polar Distance 1845.0.			Precession 1845.0.	Secular Variation.	Adopted Proper Motion.	Observations of N.P.D.				Names.	Oeltzen-Argelander Number.
							No.	Mean year.				
R.	R.		G.				R.	R.		G.		
	° ′ ″		″	″	″	″		1800 +				
2796	37 12 21.2		...	+ 20.05	0.00	...	4	48.3		...	....	....
2797	37 12 21.1		...	+ 20.05	0.00	...	3	48.7		...	....	....
2798	36 15 44.4		...	+ 20.05	0.00	...	3	52.0		...	....	....
2799	26 12 2.5		59.2	+ 20.05	0.00	...	5	43.5		10.3	....	12318
2800	35 44 16.9		...	+ 20.05	0.00	...	3	50.0		...	....	12387
2801	50 30 8.8		7.8	+ 20.05	0.00	...	5	46.7		10.9	....	....
2802	48 52 57.7		55.8	+ 20.05	0.00	...	5	45.9		11.3	....	....
2803	11 44 58.2		...	+ 20.05	0.00	...	4	46.3		...	....	12404
2804	11 47 7.9		...	+ 20.05	0.00	...	3	52.3		...	....	12411
2805	11 40 0.5		...	+ 20.05	0.00	...	2	53.4		...	....	12418
2806	50 0 29.1		30.8	+ 20.05	0.00	...	4	45.3		11.3	....	....
2807	11 42 40.7		...	+ 20.05	0.00	...	4	48.1		...	....	12428
2808	7 25 39.8		39.2	+ 20.05	0.00	...	6	45.7		7.3	*264 Cam.*	....
2809	32 4 56.9		57.5	+ 20.05	0.00	...	5	43.1		9.3	68 Urs. Maj. ...	12435
2810	11 36 39.7		...	+ 20.05	− 0.01	...	4	46.4		...	....	12442
2811	11 41 50.3		...	+ 20.05	− 0.01	...	4	46.8		...	....	12452
2812	7 25 24.8		...	+ 20.05	− 0.01	...	4	43.8		...	....	....
2813	11 31 21.0		20.6	+ 20.05	− 0.01	...	10	49.7		8.3	*4 Dec.*	12459
2814	48 53 15.4		...	+ 20.05	− 0.01	...	2	48.3		...	....	....
2815	2 12 20.3		...	+ 20.04	− 0.01	...	5	52.2		...	....	....
2816	5 38 7.1		4.8	+ 20.04	− 0.02	...	5	47.3		8.4	....	....
2817	35 42 8.6		8.2	+ 20.04	− 0.02	...	6	44.8		9.3	1 Can. Ven. ...	12487
2818	18 56 13.8		13.0	+ 20.04	− 0.03	...	4	44.8		10.3	....	12499
2819	32 6 20.5		20.3	+ 20.04	− 0.02	...	6	42.0		7.1	69 Urs. Maj. δ	12500
2820	106 40 52.5		...	+ 20.04	− 0.02	− 0.02	2	54.3		...	4 Corvi γ	....
2821	48 28 38.4		...	+ 20.04	− 0.02	...	2	52.3		...	2 Can. Ven. (1)	....
2822	48 28 34.8		34.2	+ 20.04	− 0.02	...	5	43.7		8.3	2 Can. Ven. (2)	....
2823	16 35 10.3		6.9	+ 20.04	− 0.03	...	3	43.6		13.3	....	....
2824	25 30 39.9		42.3	+ 20.04	− 0.02	...	4	45.3		14.3	....	12517
2825	9 0 58.6		...	+ 20.04	− 0.02	...	3	47.7		...	....	....
2826	18 59 30.7		...	+ 20.04	− 0.02	...	4	53.6		...	....	12522
2827	9 0 48.3		...	+ 20.04	− 0.02	− 0.03	3	47.7		...	....	....
2828	20 20 35.5		...	+ 20.04	− 0.02	...	4	52.3		...	....	12534
2829	89 55 31.6		...	+ 20.03	− 0.02	...	2	56.3		...	13 Virginis	....
2830	48 13 20.4		...	+ 20.03	− 0.02	...	3	50.3		...	....	....

Ordinal Number.		Magnitude.	Estimates of Magnitude.	Mean Right Ascension 1845.0.		Precession 1845.0.	Secular Variation	Adopted Proper Motion.	Observations of R.A.		
R.	G.		R.	R.	G.				No. R.	Mean year R.	G.
				h. m. s.	s.	s.	s.	s.		1800 +	
2831	...	9.3	3	12 10 54.42	...	+ 2.885	— 0.076	....	3	50.9	...
2832	...	7.5	5	12 11 48.30	...	+ 3.008	— 0.026	....	3	51.0	...
2833	1868	5.8	7	12 11 49.49	49.40	+ 2.793	— 0.100	+ 0.022	4	48.4	10.8
2834	...	4.2	11	12 11 58.75	...	+ 3.070	— 0.001	— 0.007	25	48.1	...
2835	1869	5.2	3	12 12 9.48	9.41	+ 2.987	— 0.031	+ 0.006	6	42.7	9.3
2836	1871	6.6	28	12 12 15.90	17.67	+ 1.553	— 0.080	+ 0.325	39	49.7	7.3
2837	1870	7.8	5	12 12 16.76	16.61	+ 3.000	— 0.029	....	4	47.3	11.3
2838	...	5.4	6	12 12 28.70	...	+ 3.065	+ 0.001	— 0.016	4	53.8	...
2839	1867	7.0	6	12 12 29.75	29.82	+ 3.011	— 0.031	....	3	44.9	12.3
2840	1872	7.6	7	12 12 59.70	59.79	+ 2.927	— 0.049	....	3	47.7	12.7
2841	1873	7.2	4	12 13 11.40	11.17	+ 2.909	— 0.054	....	3	47.0	14.3
2842	1875	6.4	2	12 13 18.57	18.49	+ 2.944	— 0.040	+ 0.004	4	47.7	10.3
2843	1874	7.8	6	12 13 20.52	20.28	+ 3.007	— 0.023	....	3	48.0	12.3
2844	...	7.6	4	12 14 8.10	...	+ 2.997	— 0.025	....	2	51.8	...
2845	1876	8.5	6	12 14 8.62	9.61	+ 2.911	— 0.051	....	2	49.8	13.3
2846	1884	6.5	47	12 14 25.47	22.80	— 0.271	+ 1.809	— 0.152	63	48.3	7.3
2847	1879	7.6	9	12 14 30.98	26.99	+ 2.232	— 0.154	....	8	50.8	8.1
2848	1877	6.8	5	12 14 38.42	37.95	+ 2.906	— 0.051	....	3	43.9	13.0
2849	1878	9.6	6	12 14 44.64	44.13	+ 2.927	— 0.046	....	3	52.0	14.4
2850	1880	8.5	4	12 14 56.11	56.19	+ 2.904	— 0.051	....	2	48.4	12.8
2851	1881	6.2	3	12 16 8.77	8.57	+ 2.981	— 0.026	....	4	43.3	9.3
2852	1882	7.9	5	12 16 13.89	13.41	+ 2.986	— 0.026	....	3	44.1	13.4
2853	...	7.8	4	12 16 20.15	...	+ 2.934	— 0.039	....	3	51.7	...
2854	1883	5.0	5	12 16 28.44	28.42	+ 2.945	— 0.037	....	5	46.2	11.8
2855	...	7.5	5	12 16 45.86	...	+ 2.971	— 0.027	....	3	53.0	...
2856	1885	7.4	5	12 16 58.80	58.71	+ 2.981	— 0.023	....	3	45.7	12.3
2857	1886	8.5	4	12 17 2.96	2.49	+ 2.860	— 0.054	....	2	45.8	11.3
2858	1887	5.5	7	12 17 37.22	37.00	+ 2.908	— 0.043	....	5	46.3	9.6
2859	1889	8.5	7	12 17 40.59	37.43	+ 1.997	— 0.109	....	5	47.6	8.3
2860	1888	6.3	5	12 17 50.71	50.48	+ 2.850	— 0.054	....	3	44.3	11.3
2861	1890	5.3	8	12 18 12.09	12.00	+ 2.981	— 0.023	....	11	48.5	8.4
2862	1892	8.2	7	12 18 57.42	55.78	+ 1.966	— 0.080	....	5	46.2	7.9
2863	1891	7.1	5	12 19 6.29	5.92	+ 2.905	— 0.040	....	4	45.9	10.4
2864	1893	6.6	7	12 19 38.29	39.28	+ 2.701	— 0.074	....	3	45.7	13.3
2865	...	7.0	2	12 19 52.85	...	+ 3.012	— 0.013	....	2	57.3	...

Ordinal Number.	Mean North Polar Distance 1845.0.		Precession 1845.0.	Secular Variation.	Adopted Proper Motion.	Observations of N.P.D.			Names.	Oeltzen Argelander Number.
	R.	G.				No. R.	Mean year. R. (1800 +)	G.		
2831	19 2 22.4	...	+ 20.03	— 0.02	...	2	47.3	...	....	12539
2832	48 11 49.8	...	+ 20.03	— 0.02	...	4	48.3	...	....	......
2833	13 58 44.1	42.4	+ 20.03	— 0.03	...	9	51.0	10.8	....	12557
2834	89 48 17.7	...	+ 20.03	— 0.02	+ 0.03	5	51.1	...	15 Virginis η .	......
2835	40 9 16.3	20.0	+ 20.03	— 0.03	...	4	42.8	9.3	3 Can. Ven. ...	12555
2836	2 42 8.2	7.1	+ 20.03	— 0.01	...	8	48.7	7.3	....	......
2837	45 31 48.1	49.8	+ 20.03	— 0.03	...	3	46.3	11.3	....	......
2838	85 49 26.3	...	+ 20.02	— 0.02	+ 0.07	3	54.4	...	16 Virginis c ..	......
2839	51 14 10.9	13.1	+ 20.02	— 0.06	...	4	44.8	12.3	....	......
2840	27 49 45.2	44.0	+ 20.02	— 0.04	...	4	48.3	12.7	....	12564
2841	25 28 7.4	7.6	+ 20.02	— 0.04	...	3	45.0	14.3	....	12567
2842	31 16 20.9	19.5	+ 20.02	— 0.04	+ 0.06	4	42.3	10.3	70 Urs. Maj. ..	......
2843	51 6 55.2	56.4	+ 20.02	— 0.04	...	3	51.4	12.3	....	......
2844	48 25 47.5	...	+ 20.02	— 0.03	...	3	51.7	...	....	......
2845	27 22 52.7	43.5	+ 20.02	— 0.03	...	4	46.3	13.3	....	12580
2846	1 26 27.4	26.5	+ 20.01	— 0.01	— 0.07	67	44.3	7.3	....	......
2847	5 45 57.8	55.0	+ 20.01	— 0.04	...	3	44.0	8.1	....	......
2848	27 32 54.6	52.4	+ 20.01	— 0.05	...	5	46.1	13.0	....	12587
2849	31 3 23.5	20.7	+ 20.01	— 0.05	...	3	52.0	14.4	....	......
2850	27 40 6.0	2.5	+ 20.01	— 0.04	...	2	44.8	12.8	....	12590
2851	46 35 52.1	54.0	+ 20.00	— 0.05	...	3	45.7	9.3	4 Can. Ven. ...	......
2852	48 25 15.4	16.6	+ 20.00	— 0.05	...	3	46.0	13.4	....	......
2853	34 58 56.0	...	+ 20.00	— 0.03	...	4	52.6	...	....	12611
2854	37 34 42.6	43.3	+ 20.00	— 0.04	...	5	44.7	11.3	5 Can. Ven. ...	12615
2855	46 3 8.4	...	+ 20.00	— 0.03	...	3	52.0	...	....	......
2856	47 48 25.3	26.6	+ 20.00	— 0.04	...	3	45.0	12.3	....	......
2857	25 20 52.0	51.9	+ 20.00	— 0.03	...	3	43.3	11.3	....	12623
2858	32 21 43.4	43.1	+ 19.99	— 0.05	...	5	43.6	7.6	71 Urs. Maj. ...	......
2859	5 29 13.9	12.6	+ 19.99	— 0.05	...	4	50.3	8.3	....	......
2860	25 20 16.9	16.8	+ 19.99	— 0.05	...	4	43.6	11.3	....	12635
2861	50 7 14.9	14.9	+ 19.99	— 0.05	+ 0.04	6	45.6	8.4	6 Can. Ven. ...	......
2862	5 42 45.2	42.7	+ 19.99	— 0.03	...	5	44.7	7.9	....	......
2863	33 58 55.5	56.2	+ 19.98	— 0.05	...	4	45.8	10.4	72 Urs. Maj. ..	......
2864	17 12 38.6	38.1	+ 19.98	— 0.05	...	4	45.8	13.3	....	12654
2865	63 13 42.9	...	+ 19.98	— 0.04	...	2	53.4	...	....	......

Magnitude.	Estimates of Magnitude.	Mean Right Ascension 1845.0.		Precession 1845.0.	Secular Variation	Adopted Proper Motion.
R.	R.	R.	G.			
		h. m. s.	s.	s.	s.	s.
6.6	7	12 19 56.29	56.15	+ 2.965	— 0.023	......
5.6	3	12 20 11.49	11.10	+ 2.892	— 0.040	......
7.0	5	12 21 10.83	...	+ 2.920	— 0.033	......
3.0	1	12 21 51.20	...	+ 3.106	+ 0.010	......
7.1	8	12 22 22.17	22.00	+ 2.752	— 0.057	......
9.0	8	12 22 25.96	25.70	+ 2.900	— 0.034	......
5.8	8	12 22 41.67	41.79	+ 2.848	— 0.043	......
6.3	8	12 22 41.94	42.19	+ 2.898	— 0.037	— 0.013
6.0	4	12 22 47.49	46.86	+ 2.844	— 0.043	......
5.2	7	12 23 17.07	16.67	+ 2.696	— 0.063	......
6.2	6	12 23 26.69	26.40	+ 2.883	— 0.034	......
6.9	11	12 23 28.64	28.43	+ 2.954	— 0.020	......
5.0	A	12 24 5.66	...	+ 3.108	+ 0.010	— 0.027
6.0	2	12 25 47.16	...	+ 3.093	+ 0.006	— 0.009
6.4	7	12 25 55.94	55.91	+ 2.948	— 0.020	......
7.5	3	12 26 11.35	...	+ 2.918	— 0.026	......
2.3	A	12 26 15.42	...	+ 3.133	+ 0.014	— 0.008
4.4	10	12 26 22.33	21.54	+ 2.931	— 0.023	— 0.069
4.1	5	12 26 50.05	50.12	+ 2.626	— 0.060	......
5.2	5	12 28 8.44	8.41	+ 2.598	— 0.060	+ 0.019
7.2	8	12 28 15.66	15.45	+ 2.929	— 0.023	......
7.2	6	12 28 27.29	...	+ 2.895	— 0.026	......
7.5	8	12 29 21.12	20.73	+ 1.979	— 0.054	......
7.0	8	12 30 45.39	45.23	+ 2.808	— 0.034	......
9.0	9	12 31 0.22	0.14	+ 2.890	— 0.029	......
7.3	5	12 31 10.74	...	+ 2.882	— 0.026	......
5.5	3	12 31 15.32	...	+ 3.092	+ 0.005	......
6.1	4	12 31 18.12	18.03	+ 2.907	— 0.026	......
8.2	7	12 32 15.82	15.34	+ 2.737	— 0.043	......
9.3	7	12 33 22.00	22.17	+ 2.727	— 0.040	......
8.0	7	12 33 25.15	24.46	+ 2.728	— 0.040	......
7.6	7	12 33 47.04	...	+ 2.540	— 0.051	......
4.5	1	12 33 48.31	...	+ 3.072	+ 0.002	......
4.4	2	12 33 48.67	...	+ 3.072	+ 0.002	— 0.037
7.5	5	12 34 4.50	5.29	+ 2.653	— 0.043	......

Ordinal Number.	Mean North Polar Distance 1845.0.		Precession 1845.0.	Secular Variation.	Adopted Proper Motion.	Observations of N.P.D.			Names.	Oeltzen-Argelander Number.
						No.	Mean year.			
R.	R.	G.				R.	R.	G.		
	° ′ ″	″	″	″	″		1800 +			
2866	47 47 9.2	9.9	+ 19.98	− 0.05	...	5	47.3	12.3	....	......
2867	33 25 43.0	43.1	+ 19.98	− 0.04	+ 0.04	4	43.3	9.4	73 Urs. Maj. ...	12663
2868	39 30 24.5	...	+ 19.96	− 0.04	...	4	49.9	...	....	12674
2869	105 39 8.4	...	+ 19.96	− 0.04	+ 0.16	5	51.9	...	7 Corvi δ	......
2870	22 14 54.6	54.1	+ 19.96	− 0.04	...	4	46.3	13.3	....	12688
2871	37 33 13.7	13.7	+ 19.96	− 0.04	...	5	48.6	12.0	....	12689
2872	30 44 27.3	27.2	+ 19.96	− 0.04	− 0.06	7	45.8	9.6	74 Urs. Maj. ...	12691
2873	37 36 29.7	29.2	+ 19.96	− 0.04	...	4	45.1	11.8	7 Can. Ven. ...	12692
2874	30 22 27.1	25.6	+ 19.95	− 0.05	...	4	43.1	10.4	75 Urs. Maj. ..	12695
2875	19 56 22.4	23.4	+ 19.95	− 0.05	+ 0.12	10	49.8	9.4	4 Draconis.....	12700
2876	36 4 25.1	33.0	+ 19.95	− 0.05	...	4	47.6	11.3	....	12703
2877	49 33 39.5	38.0	+ 19.95	− 0.05	...	5	47.9	12.3	....	......
2878	105 20 13.6	...	+ 19.95	− 0.05	+ 0.07	1	48.4	...	8 Corvi η	......
2879	98 35 47.0	...	+ 19.93	− 0.05	...	2	55.9	...	21 Virginis q .	......
2880	51 4 28.1	28.2	+ 19.93	− 0.05	...	4	45.9	12.4	....	......
2881	45 2 41.8	...	+ 19.93	− 0.05	...	4	51.8	...	....	12749
2882	112 32 19.8	...	+ 19.92	− 0.05	+ 0.07	3	48.3	...	9 Corvi β	......
2883	47 47 56.6	57.5	+ 19.92	− 0.05	− 0.30	9	47.5	8.3	8 Can. Ven. β	......
2884	19 21 25.0	25.3	+ 19.92	− 0.05	+ 0.03	7	44.6	7.2	5 Draconis κ..	12755
2885	19 7 23.6	23.4	+ 19.90	− 0.05	+ 0.01	4	43.3	9.3	6 Draconis	12772
2886	49 27 39.2	36.2	+ 19.90	− 0.05	...	3	43.6	10.4	....	......
2887	43 21 55.4	...	+ 19.90	− 0.05	...	4	49.9	...	....	12776
2888	8 53 40.5	39.6	+ 19.89	− 0.05	...	7	45.5	7.5	....	......
2889	34 17 37.1	35.8	+ 19.87	− 0.08	...	6	46.4	11.3	....	12823
2890	45 2 33.9	35.6	+ 19.87	− 0.07	...	5	47.5	12.4	....	......
2891	43 55 42.4	...	+ 19.87	− 0.06	...	5	51.7	...	....	12830
2892	97 8 29.5	...	+ 19.86	− 0.06	+ 0.04	4	52.9	...	26 Virginis χ .	......
2893	48 16 19.2	19.0	+ 19.87	− 0.06	+ 0.06	5	44.4	9.6	9 Can. Ven. ...	......
2894	29 23 57.4	59.3	+ 19.86	− 0.06	...	5	46.5	13.4	....	12847
2895	29 28 45.2	46.9	+ 19.85	− 0.05	...	4	47.9	13.4	....	12875
2896	29 37 20.7	18.3	+ 19.85	− 0.05	...	5	48.3	13.4	....	12878
2897	20 20 50.2	...	+ 19.84	− 0.05	...	5	54.0	...	....	......
2898	90 35 53.1	...	+ 19.84	− 0.07	...	4	52.4	...	29 Virginis γ (n.)	......
2899	90 35 56.5	...	+ 19.84	− 0.07	+ 0.05	4	51.1	...	29 Virginis γ (s.)	......
2900	25 22 41.2	40.3	+ 19.84	− 0.05	...	3	44.3	13.3	....	12893

| Ordinal Number | | Magnitude. | Estimates of Magnitude. | Mean Right Ascension 1845.0 | | Precession 1845.0 | Secular Variation | Adopted Proper Motion | Observations of R.A. | | |
| | | | | | | | | | No. | Mean year | |
R.	G.	R.		R.	G.				R.	R.	G.
				h. m. s.	s.	s.	s.	s.		1800 +	
2901	...	7.0	6	12 34 13.71	...	+ 2.832	— 0.028	......	3	51.0	...
2902	1917	6.0	6	12 34 46.24	45.88	+ 2.664	— 0.043	......	6	46.3	10.6
2903	1918	6.2	6	12 36 14.88	14.83	+ 2.674	— 0.040	......	5	47.3	10.4
2904	...	7.5	7	12 36 43.22	...	+ 2.706	— 0.036	......	3	51.6	...
2905	1923	7.4	8	12 37 5.69	8.80	+ 0.834	+ 0.154	......	6	47.9	8.2
2906	1919	6.4	8	12 37 7.40	7.24	+ 2.855	— 0.023	......	6	47.2	11.3
2907	...	Var.	13	12 37 8.16	...	+ 2.665	— 0.039	......	8	51.3	...
2908	1920	6.9	6	12 37 12.59	12.43	+ 2.862	— 0.023	......	3	45.0	12.7
2909	1921	6.0	10	12 37 38.88	38.58	+ 2.886	— 0.020	— 0.033	7	48.3	9.3
2910	1922	5.3	7	12 37 50.04	49.79	+ 2.840	— 0.026	......	5	47.6	11.4
2911	1924	7.6	7	12 39 29.00	28.85	+ 2.849	— 0.023	......	4	45.3	13.0
2912	1927	6.3	5	12 40 30.00	28.39	+ 1.503	+ 0.006	......	5	46.3	6.7
2913	1926	6.1	6	12 40 40.71	40.19	+ 2.594	— 0.040	......	4	45.6	11.0
2914	1925	6.8	6	12 40 42.08	42.29	+ 2.778	— 0.029	......	5	46.2	12.9
2915	1928	5.4	7	12 41 13.04	12.77	+ 2.489	— 0.043	......	4	43.3	9.7
2916	1929	6.5	11	12 41 33.03	32.88	+ 2.790	— 0.026	......	6	49.5	9.3
2917	1930	6.1	7	12 41 53.40	52.89	+ 2.629	— 0.034	......	4	44.8	11.0
2918	...	6.8	7	12 42 29.92	...	+ 2.781	— 0.025	......	3	45.3	...
2919	1931	6.1	9	12 42 48.28	48.34	+ 2.874	— 0.017	......	5	46.5	11.4
2920	...	6.8	7	12 43 4.53	...	+ 2.705	— 0.030	......	3	45.3	...
2921	...	7.8	9	12 44 9.86	...	+ 2.829	— 0.021	......	4	48.8	...
2922	...	7.0	5	12 44 18.33	...	+ 2.547	— 0.036	......	2	49.9	...
2923	...	7.3	6	12 46 11.79	...	+ 2.778	— 0.024	......	3	44.9	...
2924	...	5.4	3	12 46 18.15	...	+ 3.112	+ 0.007	— 0.002	8	42.0	...
2925	1932	2.8	5	12 47 11.60	11.25	+ 2.652	— 0.031	+ 0.013	6	43.4	6.9
2926	...	7.5	6	12 47 21.50	...	+ 2.769	— 0.024	......	3	44.2	...
2927	...	3.4	4	12 47 47.91	...	+ 3.049	0.000	— 0.030	7	51.5	...
2928	1933	6.2	6	12 47 51.05	50.87	+ 2.762	— 0.023	......	4	46.8	11.3
2929	1937	6.2	22	12 47 56.17	54.88	+ 0.308	+ 0.246	......	19	50.9	6.6
2930	1940	5.5	15	12 48 3.96	2.85	+ 0.303	+ 0.243	......	14	50.1	6.6
2931	1934	8.3	6	12 48 4.56	3.62	+ 2.642	— 0.031	......	2	48.8	13.4
2932	...	6.7	3	12 48 44.99	...	+ 2.840	— 0.017	......	3	54.4	...
2933	1935	3.0	7	12 48 46.26	45.84	+ 2.840	— 0.017	— 0.023	32	46.9	7.3
2934	...	6.2	4	12 48 50.97	...	+ 2.654	— 0.029	......	3	48.9	...
2935	1936	7.6	5	12 48 52.16	52.27	+ 2.634	— 0.029	......	3	46.9	13.4

Ordinal Number.	Mean North Polar Distance 1845.0.			Precession 1845.0.	Secular Variation.	Adopted Proper Motion.	Observations of N.P.D.				Names.	Oeltzen-Argelander Number.
R.	R.		G.				No. R.	Mean year.				
								R.	G.			
	° ′ ″		″	″	″	″		1800 +				
2901	39 51 35.5		...	+ 19.83	− 0.06	...	4	49.4	...		....	12899
2902	26 26 6.6		6.8	+ 19.83	− 0.05	+ 0.05	5	42.3	10.6		76 Urs. Maj. ..	12911
2903	27 59 44.8		42.7	+ 19.80	− 0.06	...	5	44.5	10.4		....	12931
2904	30 16 46.1		...	+ 19.80	− 0.06	...	5	51.3	...		....	......
2905	5 30 19.1		18.8	+ 19.79	− 0.04	...	6	44.3	8.2		....	......
2906	45 2 50.8		51.7	+ 19.79	− 0.08	...	6	46.7	11.3		....	12948
2907	28 3 25.7		...	+ 19.79	− 0.06	...	8	49.0	...		S Urs. Maj. ...	......
2908	46 1 25.8		25.1	+ 19.79	− 0.08	...	5	46.8	12.7		....	......
2909	49 52 40.7		40.8	+ 19.78	− 0.09	− 0.16	5	46.5	9.3		10 Can. Ven...	......
2910	43 42 40.9		41.8	+ 19.78	− 0.09	...	5	46.8	11.4		....	12961
2911	45 59 55.3		50.7	+ 19.75	− 0.09	...	4	45.3	13.0		....	......
2912	8 31 45.2		42.0	+ 19.74	− 0.05	...	4	42.8	6.7		....	......
2913	26 22 19.2		17.4	+ 19.74	− 0.08	...	7	45.2	11.0		....	12998
2914	38 59 43.8		43.1	+ 19.74	− 0.08	...	4	45.3	12.9		....	12999
2915	22 21 45.7		43.4	+ 19.73	− 0.08	...	5	45.2	9.7		7 Draconis	13005
2916	40 41 13.3		15.2	+ 19.72	− 0.09	...	6	47.3	9.3		11 Can. Ven...	13008
2917	28 50 1.4		1.8	+ 19.72	− 0.08	...	6	46.3	11.0		....	13015
2918	40 24 49.7		...	+ 19.71	− 0.07	...	5	45.7	...		....	13028
2919	51 38 18.1		20.9	+ 19.71	− 0.07	...	5	47.2	11.4		....	......
2920	34 23 51.3		...	+ 19.70	− 0.07	...	5	47.7	...		....	13040
2921	46 40 56.0		...	+ 19.68	− 0.08	...	5	49.9	...		....	......
2922	26 10 12.5		...	+ 19.68	− 0.07	...	5	43.8	...		....	13058
2923	42 30 3.2		...	+ 19.64	− 0.08	...	4	43.9	...		....	13086
2924	98 41 46.8		...	+ 19.64	− 0.09	+ 0.04	2	48.4	...		40 Virginis ψ.	......
2925	33 11 52.0		52.8	+ 19.63	− 0.09	+ 0.05	11	50.1	6.9		77 Urs. Maj. ε	13103
2926	42 22 48.1		...	+ 19.63	− 0.08	...	5	47.2	...		....	13105
2927	85 45 30.5		...	+ 19.62	− 0.09	+ 0.09	3	52.0	...		43 Virginis δ..	......
2928	41 57 41.4		41.6	+ 19.62	− 0.09	...	4	45.3	11.3		....	13110
2929	5 44 22.0		21.7	+ 19.62	− 0.01	...	10	50.8	6.6		32 Caml	......
2930	5 44 40.1		40.1	+ 19.62	− 0.01	...	5	45.7	6.6		....	......
2931	33 3 19.9		21.1	+ 19.62	− 0.08	...	5	45.5	13.4		....	13117
2932	50 50 50.5		...	+ 19.60	− 0.10	...	1	58.3	...		12Can.Ven.α(1)	......
2933	50 50 36.2		35.6	+ 19.60	− 0.10	− 0.06	4	46.1	7.3		12Can.Ven.α(2)	......
2934	34 11 54.7		...	+ 19.60	− 0.08	...	5	47.7	...		....	13126
2935	32 57 52.2		51.6	+ 19.60	− 0.09	...	3	45.0	13.4		....	13127

Magnitude.	Estimates of Magnitude.	Mean Right Ascension 1845.0.		Precession 1845.0	Secular Variation	Adopted Proper Motion.
R.		R.	G.			
		h. m. s.	s.	s.	s.	s.
5.5	6	12 49 17.22	17.13	+ 2.421	− 0.037	+ 0.014
7.2	7	12 49 28.31	28.24	+ 2.790	− 0.020	......
8.6	5	12 49 28.92	...:	+ 2.662	− 0.029	......
6.5	7	12 49 29.17	29.25	+ 2.662	− 0.029	......
8.5	4	12 49 38.57	...	+ 2.768	− 0.022	......
6.2	6	12 50 2.33	2.35	+ 2.759	− 0.023	......
7.5	7	12 50 49.95	49.74	+ 2.285	− 0.037	......
6.8	5	12 50 59.93	59.83	+ 2.337	− 0.037	......
6.9	6	12 51 42.98	42.66	+ 2.813	− 0.017	......
7.4	7	12 52 24.46	24.05	+ 2.258	− 0.034	......
7.2	6	12 52 40.98	...	+ 0.455	+ 0.170	......
8.3	6	12 53 13.86	15.27	+ 2.242	− 0.034	......
5.6	12	12 54 2.76	2.83	+ 2.318	− 0.034	......
5.1	6	12 54 3.74	3.38	+ 2.585	− 0.029	+ 0.011
6.2	6	12 54 12.24	...	+ 1.784	− 0.016	......
6.5	7	12 55 42.53	42.86	+ 2.397	− 0.031	− 0.011
7.4	7	12 55 42.64	...	+ 2.734	− 0.021	......
7.0	7	12 56 17.34	17.26	+ 2.495	− 0.029	......
8.2	7	12 56 19.63	19.59	+ 2.698	− 0.026	......
7.1	8	12 56 48.42	48.15	+ 2.755	− 0.020	......
7.6	5	12 57 29.16	...	+ 2.790	− 0.017	......
7.2	10	12 58 37.81	37.75	+ 2.782	− 0.014	......
7.3	4	12 58 51.32	51.04	+ 2.685	− 0.020	......
8.4	8	12 58 51.85	...	− 0.040	+ 0.298	......
5.7	5	12 58 53.31	53.01	+ 2.717	− 0.020	......
8.5	8	12 59 7.87	7.23	+ 2.680	− 0.020	......
5.5	2	12 59 47.06	...	+ 3.130	+ 0.009	......
6.6	9	13 0 1.50	1.54	+ 1.874	− 0.017	......
8.1	8	13 0 3.61	3.67	+ 2.799	− 0.014	......
6.1	6	13 0 14.75	14.35	+ 2.392	− 0.029	......
4.9	9	13 1 55.92	...	+ 3.099	+ 0.006	− 0.004
7.9	23	13 2 17.21	...	− 3.187	+ 1.545	......
6.1	5	13 2 29.52	29.56	+ 2.786	− 0.017	......
5.9	3	13 2 33.67	33.34	+ 2.774	− 0.017	......
7.1	2	13 2 53.74	53.52	+ 2.771	− 0.017	......

Ordinal Number.	Mean North Polar Distance 1845.0.			Precession 1845.0.	Secular Variation.	Adopted Proper Motion.	Observations of N.P.D.				Names.	Oeltzen-Argelander Number.
R.	R.		G.				No. R.	Mean year. R.		G.		
	° ′ ″		″	″	″	″		1800 +				
2936	23 43 10.8		11.0	+ 19.59	− 0.09	+ 0.06	5	43.4	9.3		8 Draconis.....	13137
2937	45 36 29.4		28.4	+ 19.59	− 0.10	...	4	45.4	12.4		....	......
2938	35 3 37.8		...	+ 19.59	− 0.09	...	3	51.7	...		....	......
2939	35 3 37.9		37.6	+ 19.59	− 0.09	+ 0.02	5	47.6	10.4		....	13145
2940	43 32 48.1		...	+ 19.58	− 0.08	...	3	52.0	...		....	13148
2941	42 58 52.6		51.6	+ 19.58	− 0.09	...	5	48.4	11.3		....	13153
2942	20 32 36.8		34.6	+ 19.56	− 0.09	...	5	48.7	14.0		....	......
2943	21 55 7.3		5.6	+ 19.56	− 0.08	...	3	47.7	13.3		....	13168
2944	49 19 4.0		5.3	+ 19.54	− 0.12	...	3	47.0	15.3		....	......
2945	20 27 21.9		22.8	+ 19.53	− 0.09	...	4	46.3	14.0		....	13191
2946	6 38 34.0		...	+ 19.53	− 0.02	...	3	52.0	...		....	......
2947	20 23 17.5		26.1	+ 19.52	− 0.07	...	3	45.1	14.0		....	13207
2948	22 33 56.4		56.3	+ 19.50	− 0.09	+ 0.02	9	48.7	9.3		9 Draconis.....	13221
2949	32 47 49.6		47.4	+ 19.50	− 0.10	...	9	47.0	10.4		78 Urs. Maj. ...	13222
2950	13 41 28.7		...	+ 19.49	− 0.06	...	5	49.2	...		....	......
2951	25 33 21.3		21.3	+ 19.46	− 0.11	− 0.02	4	44.6	13.3		....	13238
2952	43 46 50.9		...	+ 19.46	− 0.09	...	6	51.7	...		....	13237
2953	29 26 55.9		56.2	+ 19.45	− 0.11	...	4	44.3	10.3		....	13255
2954	41 11 52.9		52.9	+ 19.45	− 0.11	...	4	45.9	12.3		....	......
2955	46 9 31.7		31.6	+ 19.44	− 0.11	...	5	47.8	11.3		....	......
2956	49 50 37.4		...	+ 19.43	− 0.10	...	4	46.4	...		....	......
2957	49 33 56.2		57.8	+ 19.40	− 0.12	...	5	47.8	15.0		....	......
2958	41 23 16.4		12.4	+ 19.40	− 0.10	...	4	45.3	12.4		....	13292
2959	6 13 52.1		...	+ 19.40	0.00	...	5	51.8	...		....	......
2960	43 54 5.4		5.9	+ 19.40	− 0.10	...	4	44.3	11.3		....	13293
2961	41 8 26.5		24.1	+ 19.39	− 0.11	...	5	48.8	12.4		....	13301
2962	99 54 34.9		...	+ 19.37	− 0.12	+ 0.02	1	55.3	...		49 Virginis g ..	......
2963	16 8 40.3		40.6	+ 19.36	− 0.11	...	5	47.7	13.4		....	13324
2964	51 54 9.8		10.6	+ 19.36	− 0.14	...	4	46.9	12.3		....	......
2965	27 7 33.6		33.0	+ 19.36	− 0.12	+ 0.03	5	47.1	10.4		....	13328
2966	94 42 36.6		...	+ 19.32	− 0.12	+ 0.04	4	52.1	...		51 Virginis θ .	......
2967	3 16 53.3		...	+ 19.32	+ 0.13	...	9	50.2	...		....	......
2968	51 44 57.3		59.6	+ 19.31	− 0.13	...	3	46.0	11.3		....	......
2969	50 38 19.1		19.1	+ 19.31	− 0.12	...	3	46.4	3.4		15 Can. Ven...	......
2970	50 26 56.4		56.0	+ 19.30	− 0.13	...	3	46.7	9.3		16 Can. Ven...	......

Magnitude.	Estimates of Magnitude.	Mean Right Ascension 1845.0.		Precession 1845.0.	Secular Variation	Adopted Proper Motion.
R.		R.	G.			
		h. m. s.	s.	s.	s.	s.
5.9	4	13 2 55.66	55.74	+ 2.773	− 0.017	......
6.9	4	13 3 10.59	...	+ 2.495	− 0.024	......
6.8	6	13 3 49.78	49.53	+ 2.347	− 0.029	......
7.1	7	13 4 25.97	25.74	+ 2.741	− 0.017	......
6.9	8	13 5 51.06	50.83	+ 2.711	− 0.020	......
9.4	5	13 5 51.63	...	+ 1.673	− 0.006	....
8.7	5	13 5 52.03	...	+ 1.673	− 0.006	......
8.0	7	13 6 26.81	...	+ 2.659	− 0.019	......
5.0	5	13 6 40.85	40.71	+ 2.737	− 0.017	......
8.2	4	13 6 52.68	...	+ 2.653	− 0.019	......
7.9	7	13 7 8.72	8.23	+ 2.464	− 0.026	......
7.0	8	13 7 15.54	14.68	+ 2.462	− 0.026	......
7.1	10	13 7 40.93	41.42	+ 2.101	− 0.020	......
8.9	5	13 7 51.90	...	+ 2.100	− 0.022	......
6.8	9	13 8 9.50	10.12	+ 2.095	− 0.020	......
6.4	11	13 8 33.39	33.65	+ 2.719	− 0.017	......
6.9	7	13 9 5.14	4.59	+ 1.719	− 0.009	......
8.9	8	13 10 2.36	...	+ 2.567	− 0.020	......
5.4	3	13 10 18.49	...	+ 3.197	+ 0.013	− 0.075
5.3	9	13 10 35.12	35.25	+ 2.713	− 0.016	......
8.1	5	13 10 58.50	...	+ 2.574	− 0.020	......
8.2	5	13 11 5.69	...	+ 2.711	− 0.016	......
6.3	4	13 11 7.35	6.38	+ 0.405	+ 0.146	......
5.2	5	13 11 38.51	38.22	+ 2.571	− 0.023	......
7.4	7	13 12 41.90	...	+ 2.633	− 0.018	......
5.7	5	13 13 21.88	21.72	+ 2.705	− 0.014	......
7.9	4	13 13 44.18	43.90	+ 2.023	− 0.017	......
6.8	7	13 14 4.22	...	+ 2.648	− 0.016	......
7.2	5	13 14 8.74	8.52	+ 2.730	− 0.014	......
7.6	33	13 14 15.90	11.40	− 12.962	+ 12.106	.....
9.0	5	13 14 51.88	51.68	+ 2.708	− 0.014	......
6.6	5	13 15 16.60	...	+ 2.643	− 0.016	......
7.0	6	13 15 54.94	54.62	+ 1.880	− 0.014	......
7.7	3	13 16 28.35	28.45	+ 2.700	− 0.014	......
7.6	7	13 16 31.73	31.44	+ 2.500	− 0.020	....

Ordinal Number.	Mean North Polar Distance 1845.0.		Precession 1845.0.	Secular Variation.	Adopted Proper Motion.	Observations of N.P.D.			Names.	Oeltzen-Argelander Number.
	R.	G.				No. R.	Mean year. 1800 +			
R.	R.	G.				R.	R.	G.		
	° ′ ″	″	″	″	″					
2971	50 40 32.3	32.2	+ 19.30	− 0.13	− 0.04	5	43.2	8.4	17 Can. Ven...	......
2972	32 20 30.4	...	+ 19.30	− 0.10	...	4	49.1	...	....	......
2973	26 56 39.7	36.3	+ 19.28	− 0.11	...	4	45.3	10.4	....	13387
2974	48 22 54.0	54.1	+ 19.27	− 0.11	...	3	43.7	12.4	18 Can. Ven...	......
2975	46 33 0.9	2.1	+ 19.23	+ 0.13	...	5	47.8	11.3	....	......
2976	15 12 49.8	...	+ 19.23	− 0.07	...	1	52.4	...	....	13417
2977	15 12 23.3	...	+ 19.23	− 0.07	...	3	52.0	...	....	13418
2978	42 40 55.2	...	+ 19.23	− 0.11	...	3	52.0	...	....	13425
2979	49 1 28.5	29.3	+ 19.21	− 0.13	...	5	46.0	8.4	....	......
2980	42 41 58.0	...	+ 19.21	− 0.11	...	3	52.4	...	....	13428
2981	32 29 44.9	44.3	+ 19.20	− 0.11	...	5	45.3	10.3	....	13433
2982	32 28 5.7	3.8	+ 19.20	− 0.11	...	4	46.1	10.4	....	13436
2983	21 52 5.9	5.1	+ 19.19	− 0.08	...	4	46.4	10.4	....	13444
2984	21 54 40.2	...	+ 19.18	− 0.09	...	3	46.4	...	....	13448
2985	21 53 24.9	23.4	+ 19.17	− 0.11	...	4	46.4	10.4	....	13455
2986	48 19 28.1	28.2	+ 19.16	− 0.14	− 0.02	4	45.3	9.4	19 Can. Ven...	......
2987	16 22 43.0	40.1	+ 19.15	− 0.08	...	4	46.6	13.4	....	......
2988	38 36 38.2	...	+ 19.13	− 0.11	...	5	52.4	...	....	13483
2989	107 26 50.0	...	+ 19.12	− 0.14	+ 1.04	3	54.4	...	61 Virginis	......
2990	48 36 34.2	54.8	+ 19.11	− 0.13	...	7	47.2	9.3	20 Can. Ven...	......
2991	39 25 18.4	...	+ 19.10	− 0.11	...	3	46.4	...	....	13502
2992	48 39 4.4	...	+ 19.10	− 0.12	...	4	45.9	...	....	......
2993	8 42 29.0	28.5	+ 19.10	− 0.02	...	4	44.3	7.7	....	......
2994	39 30 3.4	25.1	+ 19.08	− 0.13	...	5	45.6	9.4	21 Can. Ven...	13514
2995	43 39 22.2	...	+ 19.05	− 0.12	...	4	51.8	...	....	13528
2996	49 2 2.7	2.6	+ 19.03	− 0.15	...	4	46.3	9.4	23 Can. Ven...	......
2997	21 59 25.1	23.6	+ 19.02	− 0.12	...	3	44.0	10.4	....	13542
2998	45 11 47.5	...	+ 19.01	− 0.12	...	4	51.9	...	....	13552
2999	51 19 44.0	45.6	+ 19.01	− 0.15	...	4	47.9	11.4	....	......
3000	1 31 17.1	15.8	+ 19.01	+ 0.71	...	20	49.1	6.7	....	......
3001	49 48 20.9	23.0	+ 19.00	− 0.12	...	3	47.4	12.4	....	......
3002	45 17 3.8	...	+ 18.98	− 0.12	...	5	52.2	...	....	13570
3003	20 5 0.2	58.9	+ 18.96	− 0.11	...	5	47.1	14.3	....	13573
3004	49 45 36.3	37.4	+ 18.95	− 0.13	...	3	45.0	12.4	....	......
3005	37 32 7.9	6.9	+ 18.94	− 0.15	...	4	43.6	15.2	....	13585

Magnitude.	Estimates of Magnitude.	Mean Right Ascension 1845.0.		Precession 1845.0.	Secular Variation	Adopted Proper Motion.
R.	R.	R.	G.			
		h. m. s.	s.	s.	s.	s.
7.8	6	13 16 39.02	38.78	+ 2.601	− 0.017	......
6.4	6	13 16 52.08	51.73	+ 2.728	− 0.014	......
1.0	A	13 17 2.12	...	+ 3.151	+ 0.009	− 0.005
3.5	4	13 17 40.48	40.20	+ 2.418	− 0.020	+ 0.017
5.3	9	13 17 41.38	41.50	+ 2.418	− 0.020	+ 0.014
7.9	6	13 18 40.57	40.45	+ 2.410	− 0.020	......
5.0	4	13 19 0.43	59.98	+ 2.405	− 0.023	+ 0.016
6.2	7	13 19 37.06	36.73	+ 2.585	− 0.017	......
7.9	6	13 20 1.02	0.68	+ 2.060	− 0.014	......
6.6	6	13 20 41.47	42.77	+ 2.122	− 0.017	− 0.015
7.3	31	13 21 9.31	11.45	− 2.905	+ 1.131	......
6.8	5	13 21 35.48	35.17	+ 2.657	− 0.014	......
7.4	5	13 21 43.57	42.84	+ 1.535	0.000	......
7.0	5	13 21 50.00	50.15	+ 2.485	− 0.017	......
6.8	6	13 21 51.35	51.05	+ 2.042	− 0.017	......
7.0	4	13 21 57.31	56.99	+ 2.042	− 0.014	......
5.8	4	13 22 11.04	10.73	+ 1.516	+ 0.006	+ 0.004
7.6	11	13 22 12.77	...	− 1.998	+ 0.723	......
6.5	3	13 22 21.19	...	+ 3.117	+ 0.007	......
6.7	4	13 22 22.82	22.37	+ 2.478	− 0.020	......
8.4	4	13 22 24.55	24.43	+ 1.527	+ 0.006	......
7.5	7	13 22 31.00	30.88	+ 2.535	− 0.017	......
8.4	6	13 22 31.40	...	+ 1.063	+ 0.048	......
5.9	3	13 22 45.22	45.15	+ 2.227	− 0.020	......
8.2	2	13 22 48.02	...	+ 3.128	+ 0.008	......
7.4	4	13 22 50.55	50.00	+ 1.688	− 0.003	......
8.1	4	13 23 8.47	...	+ 2.224	− 0.017	......
7.1	4	13 23 42.83	42.45	+ 1.689	− 0.003	......
8.2	6	13 23 53.46	...	+ 2.585	− 0.015	......
6.5	1	13 23 54.97	...	+ 3.116	+ 0.007	......
6.5	7	13 24 31.94	32.20	+ 2.622	− 0.014	......
6.3	1	13 24 48.62	...	+ 3.150	+ 0.009	− 0.004
7.3	7	13 25 25.26	24.73	+ 2.529	− 0.014	......
6.3	5	13 25 41.73	41.30	+ 0.450	+ 0.017	− 0.029
7.8	7	13 25 51.71	51.57	+ 2.605	− 0.017	......

Ordinal Number.	Mean North Polar Distance 1845.0.		Precession 1845.0.	Secular Variation.	Adopted Proper Motion.	Observations of N.P.D.			Names.	Oeltzen-Argelander Number.
R.	R.	G.				No. R.	Mean year R.	G.		
	° ′ ″	″	″	″	″		1800 +			
3006	43 3 56.0	55.8	+ 18.94	− 0.14	...	3	46.1	12.4	....	13537
3007	52 9 16.7	18.9	+ 18.93	− 0.14	...	4	45.9	11.4	....	....
3008	100 21 1.4	...	+ 18.93	− 0.15	+ 0.04	27	47.7	...	67 Virginis α..	....
3009	34 15 50.3	49.2	+ 18.91	− 0.14	+ 0.04	12	47.4	6.8	79 Urs.Maj.ζ(1)	13602
3010	34 16 1.9	1.8	+ 18.91	− 0.14	+ 0.05	8	46.3	13.5	79 Urs.Maj.ζ(2)	....
3011	34 17 36.4	36.6	+ 18.88	− 0.14	...	4	44.4	13.4	....	13619
3012	34 12 11.2	10.6	+ 18.87	− 0.14	+ 0.03	6	46.0	8.3	80 Urs. Maj. g.	13624
3013	43 9 49.1	49.2	+ 18.86	− 0.13	...	3	44.0	12.4	....	13630
3014	24 20 46.5	47.8	+ 18.85	− 0.10	...	4	48.1	14.3	....	....
3015	25 56 28.9	38.0	+ 18.82	− 0.12	...	4	48.4	10.4	....	13639?
3016	4 26 8.2	7.6	+ 18.81	+ 0.15	...	22	49.0	7.9	....	....
3017	48 27 48.0	46.4	+ 18.79	− 0.16	...	3	43.7	15.0	....	....
3018	16 55 14.4	12.8	+ 18.79	− 0.10	...	2	49.4	13.4	....	13655
3019	38 36 36.0	38.2	+ 18.79	− 0.14	...	3	45.7	11.4	....	13658
3020	24 27 39.8	40.8	+ 18.79	− 0.11	...	4	46.4	14.4	....	13560
3021	24 28 37.6	39.0	+ 18.78	− 0.13	...	3	45.4	14.4	....	13662
3022	16 48 8.9	8.9	+ 18.78	− 0.09	...	3	45.8	13.4	....	13670
3023	5 17 24.2	...	+ 18.78	+ 0.10	...	3	52.2	...	....	. . ....
3024	95 40 4.5	...	+ 18.77	− 0.16	...	1	56.4	...	72 Virginis l¹.	....
3025	38 28 28.4	26.1	+ 18.77	− 0.15	...	3	42.7	11.4	....	13672
3026	16 56 58.7	53.2	+ 18.77	− 0.09	...	2	44.9	13.4	....	13674
3027	41 21 0.1	58.8	+ 18.77	− 0.13	...	4	48.9	12.3	....	13675
3028	13 12 39.5	...	+ 18.77	− 0.06	...	3	52.0	...	....	....
3029	29 15 9.2	8.8	+ 18.76	− 0.13	+ 0.02	4	41.8	9.4	....	13681
3030	97 3 40.6	...	+ 18.78	− 0.16	...	1	41.4	...	....	....
3031	18 52 39.9	39.2	+ 18.76	− 0.09	...	3	43.0	10.4	....	13684
3032	29 16 13.0	...	+ 18.75	− 0.11	...	2	52.4	...	....	13690
3033	19 4 12.1	11.1	+ 18.73	− 0.11	...	2	47.4	10.4	....	13696
3034	44 36 51.8	...	+ 18.73	− 0.11	...	2	51.9	...	....	13697
3035	95 27 13.7	...	+ 18.72	− 0.16	...	2	56.4	...	74 Virginis l².	....
3036	47 5 39.2	1.2	+ 18.71	− 0.14	...	3	45.0	9.4	....	....
3037	99 21 53.4	...	+ 18.69	− 0.17	+ 0.03	1	49.4	...	76 Virginis h..	....
3038	41 57 57.3	56.8	+ 18.67	− 0.17	...	3	45.7	12.3	....	13720
3039	10 33 17.7	17.6	+ 18.67	− 0.03	− 0.02	3	44.3	8.1	....	....
3040	46 28 11.1	11.3	+ 18.66	− 0.16	...	3	45.7	15.2	....	....

Magnitude.	Estimates of Magnitude.	Mean Right Ascension 1845.0.		Precession 1845.0.	Secular Variation	Adopted Proper Motion.
	R.	R.	G.			
		h. m. s.	s.	s.	s.	s.
7.5	1	13 26 10.87	...	+ 3.137	+ 0.009	......
8.9	3	13 26 28.34	...	+ 2.484	− 0.016	......
8.2	4	13 26 28.65	...	+ 2.484	− 0.016	......
8.1	7	13 26 42.07	...	+ 2.579	− 0.015	......
7.8	5	13 26 45.16	44.86	+ 2.510	− 0.017	......
4.1	5	13 26 48.00	...	+ 3.068	+ 0.004	− 0.019
7.3	7	13 27 17.09	...	+ 2.550	− 0.015	......
6.9	5	13 27 30.59	30.43	+ 2.658	− 0.014	......
5.6	8	13 27 52.30	52.27	+ 2.680	− 0.011	+ 0.011
4.9	6	13 28 6.84	6.86	+ 2.476	− 0.017	......
5.8	5	13 28 9.39	9.05	+ 2.322	− 0.020	+ 0.004
6.8	4	13 28 37.92	37.73	+ 2.566	− 0.014	......
6.7	5	13 30 21.29	21.03	+ 2.452	− 0.017	......
6.9	6	13 30 26.69	...	+ 2.376	− 0.016	......
8.2	2	13 30 48.06	...	+ 2.362	− 0.016	......
8.3	6	13 30 53.69	53.92	+ 2.601	− 0.014	......
7.7	7	13 30 58.68	58.34	+ 2.588	− 0.014	......
6.9	7	13 31 7.05	...	+ 2.373	− 0.016	......
9.2	5	13 31 12.78	13.03	+ 2.636	− 0.011	......
7.8	8	13 31 17.35	17.84	+ 2.635	− 0.014	......
8.7	5	13 31 25.80	25.45	+ 2.476	− 0.017	......
6.6	5	13 31 29.94	29.82	+ 2.417	− 0.014	......
7.8	6	13 31 52.09	...	+ 2.409	− 0.015	......
7.3	4	13 32 25.19	24.72	+ 1.783	− 0.006	......
8.2	6	13 32 50.78	...	+ 2.523	− 0.013	......
7.9	5	13 32 51.33	51.08	+ 2.470	− 0.017	......
6.6	5	13 33 7.82	7.85	+ 2.379	− 0.017	......
6.0	7	13 33 28.03	27.82	+ 1.435	+ 0.011	......
5.9	2	13 33 29.13	...	+ 3.144	+ 0.009	− 0.004
5.7	3	13 33 30.23	30.00	+ 2.348	− 0.017	− 0.011
7.8	2	13 33 50.49	...	+ 2.523	− 0.013	......
6.5	6	13 34 40.98	40.78	+ 2.211	− 0.017	......
5.2	4	13 34 51.10	51.23	+ 2.289	− 0.014	......
6.2	4	13 35 52.24	52.06	+ 2.573	− 0.014	......
8.2	6	13 36 32.24	...	− 4.904	+ 1.663	......

Ordinal Number.	Mean North Polar Distance 1845.0.		Precession 1845.0.	Secular Variation.	Adopted Proper Motion.	Observations of N.P.D.			Names.	Oeltzen-Argelander Number.
R.	R.	G.				No. R.	Mean year. R.	G.		
	° ′ ″	″	″	″	″		1800 +			
3041	97 49 17.0	...	+ 18.66	− 0.16	...	1	41.3	...	....	......
3042	40 3 36.6	...	+ 18.64	− 0.13	...	1	52.4	...	....	13740
3043	40 3 40.5	...	+ 18.64	− 0.13	...	4	49.2	...	....	13741
3044	44 54 34.4	...	+ 18.63	− 0.14	...	4	47.9	...	....	......
3045	41 26 31.6	31.7	+ 18.63	− 0.16	...	3	47.7	13.9	....	......
3046	89 48 6.1	...	+ 18.63	− 0.17	− 0.06	4	53.9	...	79 Virginis ζ..	......
3047	43 36 17.6	...	+ 18.62	− 0.14	...	4	51.8	...	....	13756
3048	50 24 55.9	56.9	+ 18.61	− 0.16	...	3	46.4	12.4	....	......
3049	52 1 16.8	18.6	+ 18.60	− 0.15	...	4	46.9	13.4	....	......
3050	40 11 22.8	23.5	+ 18.59	− 0.14	...	6	45.0	8.2	24 Can. Ven...	13774
3051	33 51 20.4	38.3	+ 18.59	− 0.13	...	5	42.8	9.4	81 Urs. Maj....	......
3052	45 0 32.2	34.7	+ 18.58	− 0.13	...	5	41.6	11.4	....	13788
3053	39 43 14.9	13.3	+ 18.51	− 0.16	...	3	43.7	10.4	....	13809
3054	36 31 8.6	...	+ 18.51	− 0.13	...	4	49.1	...	....	13812
3055	36 33 ...	...	....	...	...	...	...	...	....	13817
3056	47 46 7.7	7.1	+ 18.49	− 0.18	...	3	43.7	11.4	....	......
3057	47 0 26.3	22.7	+ 18.49	− 0.17	...	4	44.1	12.3	....	......
3058	36 36 55.5	...	+ 18.49	− 0.13	− 0.13	5	51.6	...	....	13820
3059	50 1 40.5	35.6	+ 18.48	− 0.18	...	3	45.0	15.0	....	......
3060	50 1 30.1	25.7	+ 18.48	− 0.17	...	3	45.4	15.0	....	......
3061	41 9 39.5	35.2	+ 18.48	− 0.15	...	2	48.4	15.4	....	13822
3062	38 29 41.2	39.4	+ 18.47	− 0.17	− 0.07	5	47.4	10.4	....	......
3063	38 15 0.5	...	+ 18.46	− 0.14	...	4	48.4	...	....	13833
3064	22 10 17.1	15.4	+ 18.45	− 0.11	...	3	47.4	14.4	....	13842
3065	44 13 49.6	...	+ 18.43	− 0.14	...	3	52.7	...	....	13848
3066	41 18 54.7	53.6	+ 18.43	− 0.16	...	3	47.7	15.4	....	13850
3067	37 24 27.5	28.7	+ 18.42	− 0.15	...	3	46.4	14.4	....	......
3068	17 58 5.9	5.1	+ 18.41	− 0.09	...	4	45.9	13.4	....	......
3069	97 55 9.1	...	+ 18.41	− 0.18	...	7	43.1	...	82 Virginis m .	......
3070	36 17 37.3	57.0	+ 18.41	− 0.14	...	5	42.8	9.1	82 Urs. Maj....	13862
3071	44 13 31.2	...	+ 18.40	− 0.14	...	3	52.0	...	....	13863
3072	32 0 27.1	27.1	+ 18.37	− 0.13	...	4	44.1	10.4	....	13881
3073	34 31 56.5	14.7	+ 18.37	− 0.12	...	6	44.5	9.4	83 Urs. Maj....	......
3074	47 32 34.2	33.1	+ 18.32	− 0.18	...	5	42.8	12.4	....	......
3075	3 56 2.6	...	+ 18.30	+ 0.29	...	4	54.2	...	....	......

Magnitude.	Estimates of Magnitude.	Mean Right Ascension 1845.0.		Precession 1845.0.	Secular Variation	Adopted Proper Motion.
R.	R.	R.	G.			
		h. m. s.	s.	s.	s.	s.
6.1	8	13 36 40.23	39.68	+ 1.863	− 0.009	......
7.2	7	13 36 41.69	42.19	− 0.081	+ 0.171	......
6.9	6	13 36 45.14	44.62	+ 2.242	− 0.017	......
6.5	8	13 37 0.39	...	+ 2.496	− 0.013	......
6.7	6	13 37 21.05	20.43	+ 1.829	− 0.009	......
6.3	6	13 37 53.83	53.60	+ 2.339	− 0.017	......
8.3	6	13 38 20.76	20.72	+ 2.083	− 0.009	......
7.4	7	13 38 21.24	20.94	+ 2.232	− 0.017	......
7.5	7	13 38 33.67	33.75	+ 2.068	− 0.009	......
9.0	6	13 38 36.33	36.20	+ 2.582	− 0.011	......
9.2	4	13 39 19.69	19.80	+ 1.419	+ 0.014	......
8.7	8	13 39 24.73	10.09	− 16.366	+ 12.671	......
7.7	6	13 39 25.82	25.47	+ 2.567	− 0.014	......
6.6	5	13 39 29.15	28.37	+ 2.215	− 0.011	......
6.3	4	13 39 36.06	36.00	+ 2.610	− 0.011	......
6.0	5	13 39 38.41	38.86	+ 2.565	− 0.014	......
6.0	6	13 40 18.42	18.55	+ 2.606	− 0.011	......
8.7	5	13 40 22.51	22.17	+ 2.564	− 0.014	......
6.0	3	13 40 48.15	47.97	+ 2.251	− 0.014	......
2.3	3	13 41 25.53	25.38	+ 2.386	− 0.011	− 0.012
6.0	1	13 41 27.60	...	+ 3.249	+ 0.014	− 0.009
6.6	5	13 41 32.24	31.91	+ 2.539	− 0.011	..... .
7.7	8	13 41 51.23	50.84	+ 2.360	− 0.014	......
6.2	6	13 42 3.68	4.34	+ 0.151	+ 0.134	− 0.013
7.1	6	13 42 12.32	...	+ 2.530	− 0.013	......
6.8	7	13 43 38.55	...	+ 2.519	− 0.012	......
7.9	7	13 44 21.52	21.28	+ 2.523	− 0.011	......
6.1	5	13 44 42.70	42.01	+ 1.948	− 0.009	......
6.6	6	13 45 7.76	7.50	+ 2.073	− 0.009	......
6.6	7	13 46 34.54	34.42	+ 2.547	− 0.011	......
7.0	7	13 46 52.98	52.93	+ 2.510	− 0.011	......
4.8	2	13 46 54.28	53.44	+ 1.752	0.000	+ 0.002
5.9	9	13 47 3.91	1.10	− 2.239	+ 0.603	......
6.6	8	13 47 11.42	12.05	+ 1.493	+ 0.009	......
3.0	A	13 47 18.30	...	+ 2.860	− 0.003	− 0.004

| Ordinal Number. | Mean North Polar Distance 1845.0. | | Precession 1845.0. | Secular Variation. | Adopted Proper Motion. | Observations of N.P.D. | | | Names. | Oeltzen-Argelander Number. |
R.	R.	G.				No. R.	Mean year. R.	G.		
	° ′ ″	″	″	″	″		1800 +			
3076	24 23 36.1	36.8	+ 18.30	− 0.11	...	5	47.2	14.4	....	13907
3077	9 51 35.5	35.1	+ 18.29	− 0.02	...	6	45.7	7.7	....	13913
3078	33 29 23.0	23.9	+ 18.29	− 0.16	...	3	44.0	11.4	....	13908 ?
3079	43 41 53.5	...	+ 18.28	− 0.15	...	3	51.7	...	....	13917
3080	23 56 40.4	41.1	+ 18.27	− 0.13	...	4	44.9	14.4	....	13923
3081	37 9 16.2	15.5	+ 18.25	− 0.16	...	5	47.8	13.9	....	13929
3082	29 23 40.3	41.6	+ 18.24	− 0.12	...	3	46.7	13.4	....	13938
3083	33 35 4.5	5.8	+ 18.24	− 0.13	...	4	47.1	10.4	....	13939
3084	29 4 26.9	26.5	+ 18.23	− 0.13	...	5	48.4	12.4	....	13946
3085	48 47 54.0	53.0	+ 18.23	− 0.16	...	3	48.0	15.3	....	....
3086	18 47 9.5	8.7	+ 18.20	− 0.10	...	2	51.4	14.9	....	13957
3087	1 39 20.9	20.7	+ 18.20	+ 1.15	...	4	45.9	8.4	....	....
3088	48 10 56.0	55.2	+ 18.20	− 0.16	...	3	48.1	12.3	....	....
3089	33 19 37.0	22.9	+ 18.20	− 0.13	...	5	48.6	10.4	....	13963
3090	50 43 4.1	6.7	+ 18.19	− 0.17	...	5	49.0	15.4	....	....
3091	48 7 54.9	53.1	+ 18.19	− 0.17	...	4	43.7	12.4	....	....
3092	50 40 47.7	47.5	+ 18.17	− 0.16	...	4	48.1	15.4	....	....
3093	48 16 14.6	12.9	+ 18.16	− 0.17	...	2	51.9	12.4	....	....
3094	34 47 28.9	45.3	+ 18.15	− 0.15	...	5	43.2	9.4	84 Urs. Maj....	13980
3095	39 54 41.3	41.4	+ 18.12	− 0.17	+ 0.03	34	43.4	6.9	85 Urs. Maj. η	13988
3096	107 21 35.7	...	+ 18.12	− 0.20	+ 0.03	1	54.3	...	89 Virginis	....
3097	47 10 32.0	32.1	+ 18.12	− 0.16	...	5	42.8	11.4	....	....
3098	38 59 13.2	15.5	+ 18.10	− 0.18	...	4	46.9	11.4	....	13997
3099	11 9 33.8	33.2	+ 18.10	− 0.01	− 0.07	5	46.4	13.4	....	14003
3100	46 53 13.1	...	+ 18.09	− 0.14	...	3	47.7	...	....	....
3101	46 40 17.8	...	+ 18.04	− 0.16	...	4	48.9	...	....	....
3102	47 4 31.7	33.4	+ 18.01	− 0.18	...	5	47.6	12.3	....	....
3103	27 44 10.9	8.0	+ 18.00	− 0.13	...	4	44.1	13.8	....	14032
3104	30 41 29.1	30.7	+ 17.98	− 0.15	...	6	45.4	10.4	....	14038
3105	48 53 44.2	45.3	+ 17.93	− 0.16	...	4	44.9	11.4	....	....
3106	47 3 0.4	59.1	+ 17.91	− 0.18	...	4	44.2	12.4	....	....
3107	24 30 35.8	36.0	+ 17.91	− 0.13	+ 0.04	5	42.8	8.4	10 Draconis i .	14062
3108	6 28 16.0	17.7	+ 17.91	+ 0.15	+ 0.09	9	46.6	7.8	....	....
3109	20 54 54.9	53.0	+ 17.91	− 0.08	...	6	46.0	10.4	....	14068
3110	70 49 23.3	...	+ 17.89	− 0.19	+ 0.36	2	46.9	...	8 Boötis η.....	....

Ordinal Number		Magnitude.	Estimates of Magnitude.	Mean Right Ascension 1845.0			Precession 1845.0.	Secular Variation	Adopted Proper Motion.	Observations of R.A.		
R.	G.	R.		R.		G.				No.	Mean year.	
										R.	R.	G.
				h. m. s.		s.	s.	s.	s.		1800 +	
3111	2061	8.5	9	13 47	23.75	23.61	+ 1.490	+ 0.009	......	5	46.5	10.4
3112	2062	5.8	3	13 48	8.57	8.72	+ 2.218	− 0.014	+ 0.012	5	44.3	9.4
3113	...	6.3	2	13 49	17.76	...	+ 2.678	− 0.008	......	2	57.3	...
3114	...	7.1	7	13 49	18.05	...	+ 2.551	− 0.010	......	3	51.7	...
3115	...	7.3	6	13 50	24.89	...	+ 2.339	− 0.012	......	3	46.7	...
3116	2064	7.8	6	13 50	36.69	36.52	+ 2.449	− 0.011	......	4	47.9	15.4
3117	2066	6.8	6	13 50	39.75	39.07	− 0.367	+ 0.189	......	6	46.4	7.9
3118	2067	7.3	5	13 52	25.78	26.10	+ 1.804	− 0.003	......	3	46.4	12.3
3119	2068	6.7	6	13 52	42.96	42.63	+ 1.871	− 0.003	......	4	45.8	10.4
3120	2069	7.8	6	13 53	17.35	17.16	+ 2.483	− 0.009	......	5	48.0	11.4
3121	2071	7.0	8	13 53	27.14	24.89	− 1.195	+ 0.329	......	4	47.4	7.7
3122	...	4.3	1	13 53	45.90	...	+ 3.044	+ 0.004	+ 0.005	5	45.2	...
3123	...	7.8	4	13 53	57.51	...	+ 2.227	− 0.008	......	4	48.9	...
3124	2070	6.6	6	13 54	10.89	10.78	+ 1.658	0.000	......	3	45.4	13.4
3125	...	8.4	6	13 54	11.06	...	+ 0.839	+ 0.045	......	4	51.6	...
3126	...	7.9	7	13 55	33.43	...	− 0.496	+ 0.198	......	4	45.1	...
3127	2072	7.6	9	13 55	50.44	50.40	+ 2.438	− 0.011	......	5	47.0	11.4
3128	...	7.4	3	13 56	47.84	...	+ 3.253	+ 0.014	......	3	56.4	...
3129	...	7.0	1	13 56	48.92	...	+ 3.165	+ 0.010	......	1	57.4	...
3130	2073	6.3	8	13 57	13.46	13.24	+ 2.241	− 0.011	......	4	44.9	10.4
3131	2074	9.3	7	13 57	16.26	15.34	+ 1.324	+ 0.014	......	3	45.4	12.4
3132	...	4.5	1	13 57	33.66	...	+ 3.389	+ 0.021	+ 0.007	5	42.4	...
3133	...	7.5	7	13 57	47.45	...	+ 0.755	+ 0.052	......	3	45.7	...
3134	2075	6.3	4	13 58	26.23	26.22	+ 1.311	+ 0.020	......	5	43.0	12.4
3135	2079	9.9	9	13 58	51.89	50.19	− 2.936	+ 0.654	......	6	53.9	8.4
3136	...	9.3	1	13 59	36.62	...	+ 3.193	+ 0.011	......	1	58.3	...
3137	...	8.5	4	13 59	39.86	...	+ 0.762	+ 0.048	......	4	48.0	...
3138	2076	4.0	4	14 0	11.80	11.77	+ 1.627	+ 0.006	......	10	48.1	6.9
3139	2077	7.2	7	14 1	2.54	2.18	+ 2.445	− 0.011	......	5	45.1	10.4
3140	2078	5.0	6	14 1	43.81	43.75	+ 2.403	− 0.011	......	5	45.6	9.4
3141	...	8.5	13	14 1	53.07	...	− 6.520	+ 1.867	......	8	54.1	...
3142	2080	5.9	3	14 2	29.67	29.58	+ 2.253	− 0.011	......	4	43.3	9.3
3143	...	9.2	5	14 2	31.89	...	+ 2.493	− 0.008	......	2	49.9	...
3144	...	7.9	6	14 2	51.56	...	+ 2.400	− 0.008	......	5	46.1	...
3145	...	9.1	4	14 3	2.15	...	+ 2.397	− 0.008	......	2	50.9	...

| Ordinal Number. | Mean North Polar Distance 1845.0. | | Precession 1845.0. | Secular Variation. | Adopted Proper Motion. | Observations of N.P.D. | | | Names. | Oelzen-Argelander Number. |
	R.	G.				No. R.	Mean year R.	Mean year G.		
	° ′ ″	″	″	″	″		1300 +			
3111	20 54 28.0	28.1	+ 17.89	− 0.12	...	5	46.6	10.4	....	14070
3112	35 30 27.0	42.9	+ 17.86	− 0.17	...	5	42.7	9.4	86 Urs. Maj. ...	14085
3113	57 12 30.5	...	+ 17.84	− 0.18	...	2	53.4	...	....	......
3114	49 46 29.2	...	+ 17.81	− 0.17	...	4	49.9	...	....	......
3115	40 13 38.6	...	+ 17.77	− 0.16	...	4	46.4	...	....	14106
3116	44 57 31.2	31.3	+ 17.76	− 0.19	...	4	44.9	15.4	....	...−..
3117	10 14 22.8	21.5	+ 17.76	+ 0.01	...	7	45.8	7.9	..................؛	14111
3118	26 27 7.0	7.7	+ 17.69	− 0.13	...	4	43.5	12.3	....	14137
3119	27 45 37.2	43.0	+ 17.68	− 0.13	...	4	43.9	10.4	....	14142
3120	47 11 49.8	51.9	+ 17.65	− 0.19	...	4	44.7	11.4	....	......
3121	8 28 11.7	11.7	+ 17.64	+ 0.05	...	6	46.4	10.4	....	......
3122	87 42 9.9	...	+ 17.63	− 0.21	+ 0.07	2	48.9	...	93 Virginis τ .	......
3123	37 5 20.6	...	+ 17.62	− 0.15	...	3	49.1	...	....	14162
3124	24 21 7.8	7.8	+ 17.62	− 0.11	...	5	47.4	13.4	....	14166
3125	15 58 41.5	...	+ 17.62	− 0.06	...	3	50.1	...	....	14167
3126	10 16 2.3	...	+ 17.56	+ 0.04	...	5	48.0	...	....	14197
3127	45 41 29.1	33.2	+ 17.55	− 0.17	...	5	47.6	11.4	....	......
3128	105 35 26.5	...	+ 17.51	− 0.23	...	3	53.1	...	....	......
3129	98 18 11.8	...	+ 17.50	− 0.22	...	1	41.3	...	....	......
3130	38 16 51.4	51.8	+ 17.49	− 0.16	...	5	48.4	10.4	....	14213
3131	20 33 3.1	2.4	+ 17.49	− 0.09	...	4	50.7	12.4	....	14214
3132	115 55 57.9	...	+ 17.47	− 0.24	+ 0.14	5	52.4	...	49 Hydræ π...	......
3133	15 51 6.8	...	+ 17.46	− 0.05	...	5	46.2	...	....	14217
3134	20 34 26.9	26.8	+ 17.44	− 0.09	...	5	43.2	12.4	....	14229
3135	6 17 45.3	46.3	+ 17.42	+ 0.22	...	4	49.4	8.4	....	......
3136	100 24 47.8	...	+ 17.38	− 0.24	...	1	43.3	...	....	......
3137	16 6 53.8	...	+ 17.38	− 0.06	...	4	46.9	...	....	14262
3138	24 52 55.1	53.5	+ 17.36	− 0.12	...	6	43.2	6.9	11 Draconis α	14272
3139	47 9 39.9	40.0	+ 17.32	− 0.20	...	4	44.4	10.4	....	......
3140	45 24 22.4	21.7	+ 17.29	− 0.19	...	6	44.0	9.4	....	......
3141	4 2 38.9	...	+ 17.28	+ 0.47	...	5	52.8	...	....	......
3142	39 48 27.8	46.9	+ 17.26	− 0.17	...	5	43.0	9.3	13 Boötis	......
3143	49 44 11.2	...	+ 17.26	− 0.18	...	3	51.1	...	....	......
3144	45 31 11.1	...	+ 17.24	− 0.18	...	3	48.1	...	....	......
3145	45 27 47.4	...	+ 17.23	− 0.18	...	2	48.9	...	....	......

Magnitude.	Estimates of Magnitude.	Mean Right Ascension 1845.0.		Precession 1845.0.	Secular Variation	Adopted Proper Motion.
R.	R.	R.	G.			
		h. m. s.	s.	s.	s.	s.
8.3	5	14 3 44.01	...	+ 0.449	+ 0.075	......
6.7	4	14 3 57.83	58.27	+ 1.874	− 0.003	......
7.9	10	14 4 0.88	0.51	+ 2.487	− 0.009	......
7.1	6	14 4 15.30	...	+ 0.411	+ 0.075	......
4.4	4	14 4 38.22	...	+ 3.186	+ 0.010	......
6.6	7	14 5 23.07	22.94	+ 2.420	− 0.009	......
6.2	3	14 5 46.24	45.47	+ 0.407	+ 0.086	......
8.1	6	14 5 56.34	...	+ 2.416	− 0.008	......
6.8	5	14 6 7.46	7.07	+ 1.893	− 0.003	......
7.6	4	14 6 7.99	...	+ 2.373	− 0.008	......
7.8	5	14 6 22.18	...	+ 1.803	− 0.001	......
7.3	21	14 6 30.71	27.80	− 8.390	+ 2.863	......
7.0	1	14 7 ...	...	......	......	......
6.6	5	14 7 3.35	2.99	+ 1.179	+ 0.026	......
8.9	5	14 7 27.66	...	+ 2.487	− 0.007	......
8.6	6	14 7 40.56	40.40	+ 2.480	− 0.009	......
7.3	4	14 7 48.85	...	+ 2.804	− 0.002	......
4.0	A	14 7 53.66	...	+ 3.135	+ 0.008	......
7.3	5	14 7 54.61	...	+ 2.147	− 0.006	......
5.6	1	14 7 55.63	55.26	+ 2.147	− 0.006	+ 0.009
6.1	4	14 8 8.39	8.19	+ 2.426	− 0.009	......
7.2	5	14 8 10.24	10.29	+ 2.475	− 0.009	......
1.0	A	14 8 35.63	...	+ 2.811	− 0.002	− 0.079
6.3	7	14 8 46.98	...	+ 2.816	− 0.002	+ 0.004
5.2	3	14 9 12.36	12.60	+ 1.090	+ 0.026	+ 0.019
7.1	7	14 9 14.18	...	+ 2.463	− 0.007	......
5.1	3	14 9 33.12	32.83	− 0.380	+ 0.160	......
6.8	3	14 9 50.95	...	+ 2.109	− 0.007	......
6.8	4	14 10 3.81	...	+ 2.319	− 0.007	......
6.2	6	14 10 5.68	...	+ 2.457	− 0.007	......
4.0	A	14 10 29.39	29.15	+ 2.303	− 0.009	− 0.018
5.3	2	14 10 40.58	40.55	+ 2.144	− 0.003	......
5.3	6	14 10 43.94	...	+ 3.232	+ 0.012	− 0.002
8.1	4	14 11 47.59	47.04	+ 2.467	− 0.006	......
6.3	4	14 11 50.22	50.40	+ 2.138	− 0.006	......

Ordinal Number.	Mean North Polar Distance 1845.0.		Precession 1845.0.	Secular Variation.	Adopted Proper Motion.	Observations of N.P.D.			Names.	Oeltzen-Argelander Number.
R.	R.	G.				No. R.	Mean year. R.	G.		
	° ′ ″	″	″	″	″		1800 +			
3146	14 41 29.8	...	+ 17.20	− 0.03	...	4	46.4	...	....	14328
3147	29 55 35.8	33.7	+ 17.19	− 0.15	...	4	45.9	10.4	....	14332
3148	49 44 16.8	16.7	+ 17.19	− 0.20	...	4	46.9	13.4	....	......
3149	14 32 28.4	...	+ 17.18	− 0.03	...	3	45.4	...	....	14342
3150	99 32 58.2	...	+ 17.16	− 0.24	...	6	46.3	...	98 Virginis κ..	......
3151	46 55 43.7	43.9	+ 17.13	− 0.19	...	4	46.4	12.4	....	......
3152	14 40 18.7	18.2	+ 17.11	− 0.04	...	6	41.7	9.4	3 Ursæ Minoris	14371
3153	46 51 27.5	...	+ 17.10	− 0.18	...	3	47.4	...	....	......
3154	30 43 4.9	2.5	+ 17.09	− 0.17	...	4	46.4	11.4	....	......
3155	45 4 54.0	...	+ 17.09	− 0.18	...	2	51.4	...	....	......
3156	28 51 44.4	...	+ 17.09	− 0.13	...	2	52.4	...	....	14377
3157	3 30 3.7	4.6	+ 17.08	+ 0.69	...	7	50.5	7.7	....	......
3158	60 9 44.4	...	+ 17.05	− 0.21	...	1	52.4	...	....	......
3159	20 24 21.7	19.0	+ 17.05	− 0.10	...	3	44.7	12.4	....	14386
3160	50 27 12.5	...	+ 17.03	− 0.19	...	2	51.3	...	....	......
3161	50 9 40.4	40.1	+ 17.02	− 0.21	...	3	52.8	13.4	....	......
3162	69 22 23.8	...	+ 17.01	− 0.22	...	2	53.4	...	....	......
3163	95 15 29.1	...	+ 17.01	− 0.24	+ 0.41	1	57.4	...	99 Virginis ι...	......
3164	37 29 5.2	...	+ 17.01	− 0.18	...	4	43.4	...	17 Boötis κ (1st)	......
3165	37 29 0.2	59.4	+ 17.01	− 0.18	+ 0.02	4	45.2	7.8	17 Boötis κ (2d)	14397
3166	47 45 3.7	0.4	+ 17.00	− 0.20	...	3	44.4	12.4	....	......
3167	49 59 54.8	55.1	+ 17.00	− 0.20	...	3	47.1	13.4	....	......
3168	70 0 28.1	...	+ 16.97	− 0.22	+ 1.93	12	43.7	...	16 Boötis α ...	......
3169	70 21 48.5	...	+ 16.97	− 0.22	+ 0.06	5	53.4	...	....	......
3170	19 50 20.5	19.6	+ 16.95	− 0.10	+ 0.06	4	43.1	8.4	....	14415
3171	49 36 3.0	...	+ 16.95	− 0.19	...	3	49.1	...	....	......
3172	11 43 29.1	28.9	+ 16.93	+ 0.01	...	3	41.0	8.4	4 Ursæ Minoris	14421
3173	36 44 29.2	...	+ 16.92	− 0.16	...	3	47.8	...	....	......
3174	43 42 53.8	...	+ 16.91	− 0.18	...	2	51.9	...	....	14427
3175	49 32 3.9	...	+ 16.91	− 0.19	...	4	48.9	...	....	......
3176	43 11 52.2	52.6	+ 16.89	− 0.19	− 0.15	4	43.2	8.0	19 Boötis λ....	......
3177	37 54 57.6	56.4	+ 16.89	− 0.16	− 0.08	3	41.4	8.5	21 Boötis ι....	14431
3178	102 39 18.3	...	+ 16.88	− 0.25	− 0.02	5	42.9	...	100 Virginis λ	......
3179	50 18 51.1	52.4	+ 16.83	− 0.20	...	2	50.9	11.4	....	......
3180	37 58 26.3	24.8	+ 16.83	− 0.17	...	4	44.9	9.4	....	14445

Magnitude.	Estimates of Magnitude.	Mean Right Ascension 1845.0.		Precession 1845.0.	Secular Variation	Adopted Proper Motion.
R.	R.	R.	G.			
		h. m. s.	s.	s.	s.	s.
7.0	5	14 11 53.82	...	+ 2.021	— 0.004	......
7.0	4	14 12 19.02	...	+ 2.117	— 0.006	......
7.1	7	14 12 33.55	33.40	+ 2.468	— 0.009	......
7.1	5	14 12 45.95	45.52	+ 2.394	— 0.009	......
8.1	5	14 12 55.93	55.47	+ 1.219	+ 0.020	......
6.8	7	14 13 5.40	...	+ 2.106	— 0.006	......
6.8	5	14 13 25.87	25.72	+ 2.464	— 0.009	......
7.0	5	14 13 47.21	46.98	+ 1.995	— 0.003	......
8.0	6	14 15 0.49	...	+ 2.088	— 0.005	......
6.7	1	14 15 5.75	...	+ 3.214	+ 0.011	— 0.004
8.2	6	14 15 56.30	...	+ 1.488	+ 0.013	......
7.7	8	14 16 26.90	...	+ 2.348	— 0.006	......
7.7	6	14 16 45.97	45.99	+ 2.028	— 0.003	......
7.3	1	14 16 51.43	...	+ 3.441	+ 0.021	......
6.8	6	14 16 52.76	52.76	+ 1.162	+ 0.020	......
7.4	10	14 17 3.83	3.86	+ 2.484	— 0.006	
7.4	7	14 17 32.14	31.89	+ 2.337	— 0.006	
7.2	6	14 18 8.20	8.14	+ 1.145	+ 0.023	
7.3	5	14 18 10.60	10.13	+ 1.664	+ 0.006	
7.8	8	14 18 22.73	...	+ 2.242	— 0.006	
6.2	6	14 19 9.65	9.56	+ 2.451	— 0.006	......
4.5	5	14 19 55.19	54.76	+ 2.069	— 0.003	— 0.029
7.1	6	14 20 4.11	3.48	+ 2.003	— 0.003	......
8.5	5	14 20 29.25	...	+ 1.998	— 0.002	......
9.2	6	14 20 31.87	31.70	— 0.374	+ 0.146	......
8.1	7	14 21 9.07	...	+ 2.233	— 0.005	......
7.2	7	14 22 12.35	...	+ 2.141	— 0.005	......
7.2	6	14 22 42.45	42.41	+ 2.409	— 0.006	......
6.2	3	14 23 14.27	14.15	+ 2.120	— 0.003	— 0.030
6.4	7	14 23 21.06	21.03	+ 2.289	— 0.006	......
6.5	5	14 23 30.21	29.69	+ 2.353	— 0.003	......
8.8	6	14 23 47.45	47.44	— 0.430	+ 0.146	......
7.5	5	14 24 43.03	42.70	+ 1.641	+ 0.003	......
9.0	5	14 25 1.12	0.84	+ 2.398	— 0.006	......
8.5	5	14 25 5.19	...	+ 2.392	— 0.005	......

Ordinal Number.	Mean North Polar Distance 1845.0			Precession 1845.0	Secular Variation.	Adopted Proper Motion.	Observations of N.P.D.			Names.	Oeltzen-Argelander Number.
							No.	Mean year			
R.	R.		G.				R.	R.	G.		
	° ′ ″		″	″	″			1800 +			
3181	34 44	11.1	...	+ 16.82	— 0.16	...	3	45.7	...	....	14447
3182	37 25	42.7	...	+ 16.81	— 0.17	...	3	42.0	...	....	......
3183	50 31	1.9	6.2	+ 16.79	— 0.21	...	4	47.9	11.4	....	......
3184	47 16	33.9	31.6	+ 16.78	— 0.21	...	4	45.2	12.4	....	......
3185	21 35	30.7	30.9	+ 16.77	— 0.12	...	3	46.1	12.4	....	14458
3186	37 15	2.5	...	+ 16.77	— 0.17	...	5	47.2	...	....	......
3187	50 29	27.8	29.5	+ 16.75	— 0.21	...	5	49.0	11.4	....	......
3188	34 25	16.5	17.8	+ 16.73	— 0.18	...	3	45.1	10.4	....	14464
3189	37 6	54.8	...	+ 16.67	— 0.17	...	4	45.2	...	....	......
3190	101 0	11.9	...	+ 16.66	— 0.26	+ 0.09	1	41.2	...	2 Libræ	......
3191	25 17	18.1	...	+ 16.63	— 0.12	...	5	51.0	...	....	14498
3192	46 4	54.5	...	+ 16.61	— 0.19	...	4	49.4	...	....	......
3193	35 46	15.4	17.9	+ 16.59	— 0.17	...	4	45.9	11.4	....	14511
3194	116 8	43.7	...	+ 16.58	— 0.28	...	2	53.4	...	....	......
3195	21 30	27.9	27.7	+ 16.58	— 0.11	...	4	45.1	12.4	....	14515
3196	52 5	19.3	22.8	+ 16.58	— 0.20	...	4	47.4	13.4	... .	......
3197	45 50	6.8	5.6	+ 16.55	— 0.21	...	3	44.4	12.4	....	......
3198	21 29	24.7	23.9	+ 16.52	— 0.11	...	7	44.5	12.4	....	14536
3199	28 19	30.2	24.9	+ 16.52	— 0.15	...	4	43.4	10.4	....	......
3200	42 31	34.8	...	+ 16.51	— 0.18	...	5	51.8	...	....	14538 ?
3201	50 54	16.1	14.7	+ 16.47	— 0.21	...	4	44.4	10.4	....	......
3202	37 25	50.2	51.2	+ 16.43	— 0.19	+ 0.41	7	44.6	7.0	23 Boötis θ ...	14563
3203	35 42	38.9	37.0	+ 16.43	— 0.16	...	4	44.7	11.4	....	14565
3204	35 34	59.9	...	+ 16.43	— 0.16	...	2	51.9	...	....	14572
3205	12 35	34.5	34.4	+ 16.40	+ 0.02	...	3	48.4	14.4	....	14573
3206	42 41	23.0	...	+ 16.37	— 0.18	...	4	52.4	...	....	14578 ?
3207	39 54	29.6	...	+ 16.31	— 0.18	...	5	49.2	...	....	14588
3208	49 41	16.7	16.3	+ 16.29	— 0.22	...	4	44.4	10.4	....	......
3209	39 27	32.3	32.6	+ 16.27	— 0.17	...	7	45.0	9.4	24 Boötis g ...	......
3210	45 2	42.0	41.8	+ 16.26	— 0.20	...	5	46.0	10.4	....	14605
3211	47 30	6.5	1.2	+ 16.25	— 0.21	...	5	44.0	11.4	....	......
3212	12 38	12.4	12.9	+ 16.24	+ 0.04	...	3	45.8	14.4	....	14611
3213	28 55	18.6	19.1	+ 16.19	— 0.15	...	3	45.1	13.4	....	14623 ?
3214	49 36	57.8	57.5	+ 16.17	— 0.22	...	3	44.0	12.4	....	......
3215	49 23	55.9	...	+ 16.16	— 0.21	...	3	51.7	...	....	......

Ordinal Number		Magnitude	Estimates of Magnitude	Mean Right Ascension 1845.0		Precession 1845.0	Secular Variation	Adopted Proper Motion	Observations of R.A.		
R.	G.	R.		R.	G.				No.	R.	G.
				h. m. s.	s.	s.	s.	s.		1800 +	
3216	2120	3.5	7	14 25 50.12	50.11	+ 2.427	− 0.006	− 0.004	15	50.7	7.5
3217	2126	9.0	7	14 26 18.08	17.63	− 0.523	+ 0.157	......	3	50.4	14.4
3218	2122	8.3	5	14 26 55.05	54.91	+ 1.623	+ 0.006	......	3	50.1	13.4
3219	2121	6.3	6	14 27 0.33	0.12	+ 2.453	− 0.006	......	5	48.8	11.4
3220	...	8.0	5	14 27 2.61	...	+ 2.121	− 0.005	......	3	51.7	...
3221	2123	5.9	5	14 27 5.76	6.14	+ 1.438	+ 0.009	......	4	45.9	10.4
3222	2128	9.6	7	14 27 19.02	18.89	− 0.497	+ 0.117	......	4	53.7	14.4
3223	2125	6.4	6	14 27 30.67	30.49	+ 1.628	+ 0.003	......	4	47.6	13.4
3224	2124	6.8	7	14 27 48.62	48.58	+ 2.302	− 0.006	......	4	47.1	10.4
3225	2130	4.4	5	14 27 55.71	55.26	− 0.251	+ 0.123	+ 0.009	6	46.0	7.0
3226	2129	7.4	6	14 28 16.68	16.34	+ 0.995	+ 0.026	......	3	45.7	15.1
3227	...	6.8	4	14 28 25.64	...	+ 1.977	− 0.003	......	3	49.7	...
3228	2127	6.7	5	14 28 26.23	26.16	+ 2.191	− 0.003	......	3	48.7	12.4
3229	...	5.9	4	14 29 14.54	...	+ 2.103	− 0.004	......	2	48.9	...
3230	...	7.3	5	14 29 19.73	...	− 1.172	+ 0.235	......	3	52.1	...
3231	2131	6.5	5	14 29 34.94	34.04	+ 1.783	+ 0.003	......	4	44.1	13.4
3232	2132	6.5	4	14 30 20.90	20.05	+ 1.232	+ 0.017	......	2	46.9	12.5
3233	2134	7.2	5	14 30 53.17	52.90	+ 1.401	+ 0.011	......	4	47.4	10.4
3234	2133	6.7	7	14 31 1.96	2.03	+ 2.293	− 0.006	......	4	43.9	10.4
3235	...	8.2	6	14 31 24.64	...	+ 2.241	− 0.004	......	4	52.1	...
3236	...	7.7	6	14 31 33.14	...	+ 2.237	− 0.004	......	4	52.9	...
3237	2140	8.4	5	14 32 21.20	21.08	− 0.573	+ 0.151	......	3	48.4	14.4
3238	2135	5.5	4	14 32 23.19	23.30	+ 2.265	− 0.006	......	5	44.1	9.4
3239	2136	6.9	5	14 32 51.36	51.30	+ 2.002	0.000	......	5	45.5	11.4
3240	2137	5.8	10	14 33 4.21	4.05	+ 2.240	− 0.006	− 0.009	11	50.4	9.4
3241	2138	6.6	3	14 33 20.35	20.56	+ 1.899	0.000	+ 0.017	6	44.6	10.5
3242	2139	7.6	5	14 33 47.67	47.48	+ 2.402	− 0.003	......	4	44.9	10.4
3243	...	8.9	5	14 34 34.22	...	+ 2.356	− 0.004	......	3	47.7	...
3244	2141	7.4	5	14 34 47.87	47.75	+ 2.398	− 0.006	......	3	48.1	10.4
3245	...	7.7	4	14 34 52.91	...	+ 2.095	− 0.004	......	3	51.7	...
3246	2142	8.1	7	14 35 10.90	10.69	+ 2.336	− 0.006	......	4	48.0	11.4
3247	...	7.4	4	14 35 26.94	...	+ 2.199	− 0.003	......	3	51.8	...
3248	2143	9.0	7	14 36 4.53	4.23	+ 2.315	− 0.006	......	4	49.6	12.4
3249	...	9.4	4	14 36 11.16	...	+ 2.346	− 0.004	......	4	52.2	...
3250	...	9.1	8	14 36 14.43	...	− 22.528	+ 11.071	......	5	51.9	...

Ordinal Number.	Mean North Polar Distance 1845.0.		Precession 1845.0.	Secular Variation.	Adopted Proper Motion.	Observations of N.P.D.				Names.	Oeltzen-Argelander Number.
	R.	G.				No. R.	Mean year. R.	G.			
	° ′ ″	″	″	″	″		1800 +				
3216	51 0 40.2	40.5	+ 16.13	− 0.22	− 0.14	6	42.4	7.5	27 Boötis γ ...	......
3217	12 29 49.8	48.5	+ 16.11	+ 0.05	...	4	49.9	14.4	....	14643
3218	28 54 55.1	55.9	+ 16.07	− 0.16	...	2	44.9	13.4	....	14654 ?
3219	52 21 13.6	12.6	+ 16.07	− 0.22	...	4	45.4	11.4	....	......
3220	40 7 50.7	...	+ 16.06	− 0.18	...	4	51.9	...	....	14656
3221	26 7 39.4	39.1	+ 16.06	− 0.14	...	4	44.4	10.4	....	......
3222	12 39 37.8	37.3	+ 16.05	+ 0.03	...	3	50.3	14.4	....	......
3223	29 5 22.6	22.4	+ 16.04	− 0.16	...	5	47.6	13.4	....	14660
3224	46 18 39.7	41.2	+ 16.02	− 0.23	...	4	45.4	10.4	....	......
3225	13 36 54.3	53.9	+ 16.02	+ 0.01	...	6	44.9	7.0	5 Urs. Min. ...	14666
3226	21 13 59.1	57.6	+ 16.00	− 0.10	...	4	46.9	15.1	....	14669
3227	36 25 10.2	...	+ 15.99	− 0.17	− 0.30	3	47.7	...	....	......
3228	42 31 57.3	55.4	+ 15.99	− 0.21	+ 0.04	4	43.6	12.4	....	14673
3229	39 57 13.5	...	+ 15.95	− 0.19	...	3	48.1	...	....	14685
3230	10 48 55.6	...	+ 15.94	+ 0.11	...	4	46.2	...	....	14693
3231	32 14 39.2	32.5	+ 15.93	− 0.18	...	3	44.4	13.4	....	......
3232	23 55 35.9	36.7	+ 15.90	− 0.10	...	4	42.9	12.5	....	14710
3233	26 6 14.6	13.3	+ 15.86	− 0.15	...	4	45.2	10.4	....	14719
3234	46 29 26.7	25.5	+ 15.86	− 0.20	...	5	45.0	10.4	....	......
3235	44 42 15.0	...	+ 15.83	− 0.20	...	4	50.9	...	....	......
3236	44 30 44.3	...	+ 15.83	− 0.20	...	4	50.4	...	....	14729 ?
3237	12 45 14.4	16.6	+ 15.79	+ 0.06	...	3	46.4	14.4	....	......
3238	45 41 12.2	14.1	+ 15.79	− 0.19	...	5	43.8	9.4	....	......
3239	37 45 0.0	0.7	+ 15.76	− 0.18	...	3	44.7	11.4	....	14745
3240	44 55 25.9	25.7	+ 15.74	− 0.23	...	9	50.0	9.4	33 Boötis	......
3241	35 18 17.4	18.6	+ 15.73	− 0.18	...	4	43.4	10.5	....	14752
3242	51 13 16.0	18.1	+ 15.70	− 0.24	...	3	46.1	10.4	....	......
3243	49 26 31.1	...	+ 15.66	− 0.21	...	2	47.4	...	....	......
3244	51 11 25.3	33.0	+ 15.65	− 0.23	...	4	46.4	10.4	....	......
3245	40 37 33.3	...	+ 15.64	− 0.19	...	2	51.9	...	....	14763
3246	48 46 8.7	10.3	+ 15.63	− 0.22	...	4	45.4	11.4	....	......
3247	43 54 49.1	...	+ 15.62	− 0.20	...	2	52.0	...	....	14777 ?
3248	48 5 57.2	55.4	+ 15.58	− 0.23	...	3	48.7	12.4	....	......
3249	49 16 43.4	...	+ 15.59	− 0.22	...	4	49.9	...	....	......
3250	1 53 2.5	...	+ 15.59	+ 2.07	...	4	51.7	...	....	......

Ordinal Number.		Magnitude.	Estimates of Magnitude.	Mean Right Ascension 1845.0.		Precession 1845.0.	Secular Variation	Adopted Proper Motion.	Observations of R.A.		
									No.	Mean year.	
R.	G.	R.		R.	G.				R.	R.	G.
				h. m. s.	s.	s.	s.	s.		1800 +	
3251	2144	9.3	7	14 36 29.92	32.05	+ 2.311	− 0.006	......	4	54.1	12.4
3252	...	8.9	4	14 36 57.80	...	+ 2.341	− 0.004	......	3	52.7	...
3253	...	9.7	4	14 37 13.79	...	− 2.289	+ 0.397	......	3	54.4	...
3254	...	8.9	5	14 37 31.24	...	− 2.280	+ 0.399	......	4	54.2	...
3255	2145	6.0	5	14 37 43.76	43.63	+ 2.329	− 0.006	......	4	46.4	11.4
3256	2147	7.7	5	14 38 3.71	3.17	+ 0.295	+ 0.069	......	3	50.7	13.4
3257	2146	6.1	4	14 38 11.89	10.91	+ 1.474	+ 0.009	......	4	47.2	10.4
3258	...	2.3	1	14 38 13.12	...	+ 2.623	− 0.002	− 0.005	54	47.7	...
3259	...	6.5	4	14 38 47.68	...	+ 2.191	− 0.004	+ 0.046	3	49.7	...
3260	2148	8.7	4	14 39 35.03	35.28	+ 2.391	− 0.006	......	2	48.9	12.4
3261	2149	7.4	7	14 39 39.05	39.25	+ 2.269	− 0.006	......	6	45.3	10.4
3262	2150	7.0	5	14 40 13.79	13.34	+ 1.468	+ 0.009	......	4	48.2	10.4
3263	2151	8.1	8	14 41 55.56	55.39	+ 2.384	− 0.006	......	5	49.0	12.2
3264	...	3.7	2	14 42 18.88	...	+ 3.309	+ 0.014	− 0.007	20	46.3	...
3265	2152	6.2	6	14 43 1.65	2.15	+ 2.377	− 0.003	......	4	47.4	11.4
3266	...	9.1	5	14 43 26.40	...	+ 1.947	0.000	......	2	51.9	...
3267	2153	6.0	4	14 43 47.33	47.16	+ 2.138	− 0.003	......	5	47.3	9.4
3268	...	7.2	6	14 44 4.89	...	+ 2.122	− 0.003	......	3	46.4	...
3269	2154	6.0	7	14 44 22.57	23.07	+ 2.386	− 0.003	......	6	48.4	10.4
3270	2156	7.3	5	14 44 24.82	24.61	+ 1.821	+ 0.003	......	4	48.1	13.4
3271	2155	6.9	7	14 44 25.23	25.28	+ 2.046	0.000	......	5	45.6	9.4
3272	...	7.4	8	14 44 25.47	...	+ 2.046	0.000	......	4	46.6	...
3273	2157	6.6	5	14 44 30.57	30.24	+ 1.943	− 0.003	......	5	48.7	12.4
3274	2161	7.4	5	14 45 4.52	4.15	+ 0.254	+ 0.069	......	2	46.9	9.4
3275	...	6.9	4	14 45 19.93	...	+ 1.896	0.000	......	3	50.8	...
3276	2158	7.5	5	14 45 36.17	35.96	+ 2.335	− 0.006	......	2	47.9	11.4
3277	2159	9.3	4	14 45 36.43	36.39	+ 1.941	+ 0.003	......	2	50.4	12.4
3278	2160	7.8	5	14 45 47.22	46.72	+ 1.930	0.000	......	3	49.4	12.4
3279	...	7.4	8	14 45 51.75	...	+ 2.167	− 0.002	......	4	52.6	...
3280	2162	6.7	5	14 46 35.45	35.08	+ 2.113	− 0.003	......	5	46.3	10.4
3281	2170	8.0	4	14 46 42.89	40.23	− 4.302	+ 0.726	......	3	50.7	7.9
3282	2163	8.2	4	14 47 8.82	8.88	+ 1.052	+ 0.023	......	3	50.1	14.5
3283	2164	5.5	7	14 47 30.76	30.34	+ 1.529	+ 0.009	− 0.002	8	49.6	10.5
3284	2165	7.3	4	14 47 38.61	38.59	+ 1.038	+ 0.026	......	2	48.4	14.5
3285	...	7.0	1	14 47 52.51	...	+ 3.501	+ 0.020	......	1	57.3	...

Ordinal Number. R.	Mean North Polar Distance 1845.0.		Precession 1845.0.	Secular Variation.	Adopted Proper Motion.	Observations of N.P.D.			Names.	Oeltzen-Argelander Number.
	R.	G.				No. R.	Mean year. R.	Mean year. G.		
	° ′ ″	″	″	″	″		1800 +			
3251	48 11 10.4	27.0	+ 15.56	− 0.23	...	4	49.1	12.4	....	......
3252	49 13 31.7	...	+ 15.53	− 0.22	...	3	48.1	...	....	......
3253	8 58 45.2	...	+ 15.52	+ 0.21	...	1	53.4	...	....	......
3254	8 59 8.0	...	+ 15.50	+ 0.21	...	2	51.4	...	....	......
3255	48 52 56.0	58.3	+ 15.49	− 0.23	...	5	43.8	11.4	....	......
3256	17 2 39.1	35.9	+ 15.47	− 0.04	...	3	44.8	13.4	....	14809
3257	28 4 33.9	31.3	+ 15.46	− 0.16	...	5	44.5	10.4	....	14810?
3258	62 16 9.2	...	+ 15.46	− 0.24	− 0.01	3	47.1	...	36 Boötis ε....	......
3259	44 9 22.9	...	+ 15.43	− 0.20	+ 0.05	4	47.7	...	....	14821
3260	51 36 36.1	37.3	+ 15.38	− 0.25	...	3	50.4	12.4	....	......
3261	46 57 53.4	56.7	+ 15.38	− 0.23	...	4	44.4	10.4	....	......
3262	28 14 40.8	37.2	+ 15.35	− 0.15	...	4	43.9	10.4	....	14844
3263	51 40 50.1	51.4	+ 15.25	− 0.24	...	3	45.8	12.2	....	......
3264	105 23 38.6	...	+ 15.23	− 0.31	+ 0.06	9	45.5	...	9 Libræ α²	......
3265	51 32 50.2	55.4	+ 15.19	− 0.24	...	4	45.5	11.4	....	......
3266	37 54 27.3	...	+ 15.17	− 0.18	...	3	48.4	...	....	......
3267	43 14 7.8	7.4	+ 15.15	− 0.21	+ 0.09	6	45.9	9.4	38 Boötis h ...	14875
3268	42 46 28.4	...	+ 15.13	− 0.20	...	5	46.8	...	....	14883
3269	52 5 19.7	25.0	+ 15.11	− 0.25	...	3	45.1	10.4	....	......
3270	35 7 25.8	24.6	+ 15.11	− 0.19	...	4	46.2	13.4	....	......
3271	40 38 23.4	24.3	+ 15.11	− 0.21	− 0.05	5	45.4	9.4	39 Boötis (1st)	14889
3272	40 38 20.2	...	+ 15.11	− 0.21	...	5	46.6	...	39 Boötis (2d)	14890
3273	37 58 53.6	53.6	+ 15.10	− 0.21	...	3	44.7	12.4	....	......
3274	17 23 15.1	15.5	+ 15.08	− 0.02	+ 0.03	4	46.7	9.4	6 Urs. Min. ...	......
3275	36 56 50.9	...	+ 15.06	− 0.18	...	4	50.2	...	....	14900
3276	50 15 21.3	21.0	+ 15.04	− 0.24	...	4	45.9	11.4	....	......
3277	38 2 56.8	55.1	+ 15.04	− 0.20	...	3	44.3	12.4	....	......
3278	37 49 45.5	42.5	+ 15.03	− 0.20	...	3	47.1	12.4	....	......
3279	44 25 47.5	...	+ 15.03	− 0.21	...	4	51.9	...	....	14906
3280	42 52 59.4	58.3	+ 14.99	− 0.20	...	3	46.4	10.4	....	......
3281	6 52 38.6	36.9	+ 14.97	+ 0.39	...	3	46.1	7.9	....	......
3282	23 49 12.4	18.2	+ 14.95	− 0.12	...	2	50.0	14.5	....	......
3283	30 4 27.7	30.4	+ 14.93	− 0.16	− 0.07	4	48.2	10.5	....	......
3284	23 42 56.7	55.1	+ 14.03	− 0.10	...	2	47.9	14.5	....	......
3285	115 39 12.7	...	+ 14.90	− 0.34	...	2	53.4	...	....	......

Ordinal Number.		Magnitude.	Estimates of Magnitude.	Mean Right Ascension 1845.0.		Precession 1845.0.	Secular Variation	Adopted Proper Motion.	Observations of R.A.		
R.	G.	R.	R.	R.	G.				No. R.	Mean year. R.	G.
				h. m. s.	s.	s.	s.	s.		1800 +	
3286	2166	7.3	5	14 48 3.37	3.12	+ 1.725	+ 0.006	......	3	46.7	13.4
3287	...	5.3	3	14 48 22.04	...	+ 3.241	+ 0.011	− 0.001	6	51.4	...
3288	2167	7.3	7	14 49 7.62	6.91	+ 2.098	0.000	......	6	46.5	10.4
3289	...	6.9	5	14 50 9.19	...	+ 2.263	− 0.003	......	3	47.8	...
3290	2168	8.6	4	14 50 16.43	16.17	+ 2.212	− 0.003	......	4	48.9	11.4
3291	2169	8.4	7	14 50 18.44	18.46	+ 2.214	− 0.006	......	4	48.9	11.4
3292	2172	2.8	6	14 51 13.33	12.69	− 0.271	+ 0.103	......	17	41.9	7.0
3293	2171	5.8	5	14 51 14.53	15.30	+ 1.978	+ 0.003	......	5	44.7	10.5
3294	...	7.3	6	14 52 8.53	...	+ 2.155	− 0.002	......	3	51.7	...
3295	...	8.1	7	14 52 29.42	...	+ 2.256	− 0.003	......	6	51.9	...
3296	...	5.0	A	14 52 41.96	...	+ 3.197	+ 0.010	− 0.006	2	51.9	...
3297	...	6.3	4	14 53 29.66	...	+ 2.292	− 0.003	......	3	47.8	...
3298	2173	6.1	8	14 53 40.42	40.33	+ 2.302	− 0.003	......	6	48.4	9.4
3299	...	7.0	1	14 54 29.06	...	+ 3.229	+ 0.011	......	2	56.4	...
3300	2174	6.8	8	14 54 32.56	32.43	+ 2.141	0.000	......	4	47.0	10.4
3301	...	7.6	7	14 54 57.01	...	+ 1.775	+ 0.004	......	4	53.4	...
3302	...	7.2	6	14 54 58.45	...	+ 1.775	+ 0.004	......	5	52.5	...
3303	...	3.3	A	14 55 0.57	...	+ 3.494	+ 0.019	......	1	40.1	...
3304	2175	9.4	7	14 55 1.17	1.18	+ 1.688	+ 0.006	......	4	46.9	13.4
3305	2177	5.0	4	14 55 8.30	7.79	+ 0.938	+ 0.029	......	4	46.1	8.4
3306	2176	6.4	6	14 55 21.54	21.44	+ 2.046	+ 0.003	......	5	45.8	10.4
3307	2179	7.2	7	14 56 1.74	1.19	+ 1.681	+ 0.006	......	3	45.4	13.4
3308	2178	3.5	1	14 56 6.48	6.49	+ 2.262	− 0.006	......	6	48.9	8.8
3309	2180	7.0	4	14 56 7.70	7.60	− 0.523	+ 0.123	......	2	44.9	13.9
3310	2184	6.9	4	14 56 51.42	51.56	− 1.638	+ 0.237	......	3	52.1	14.4
3311	...	8.6	4	14 56 52.84	...	+ 2.134	− 0.002	......	3	50.1	...
3312	2181	7.0	6	14 57 30.56	30.17	+ 0.961	+ 0.026	......	4	47.1	14.5
3313	...	6.6	5	14 57 38.07	...	+ 2.126	− 0.002	......	3	50.4	...
3314	2182	5.8	5	14 57 49.83	50.63	+ 1.393	+ 0.009	......	3	49.4	10.5
3315	2185	6.9	6	14 57 59.91	59.56	− 0.558	+ 0.123	......	3	45.8	13.9
3316	2186	9.5	4	14 58 28.34	27.87	− 0.576	+ 0.120	......	2	47.9	13.5
3317	...	7.0	4	14 58 40.41	...	+ 2.017	0.000	......	3	48.0	...
3318	2183	5.4	5	14 58 40.91	40.42	+ 2.017	0.000	− 0.045	4	46.5	9.4
3319	2187	6.5	6	14 59 49.81	49.57	+ 1.391	+ 0.011	......	4	48.9	10.5
3320	2189	8.0	4	14 59 58.91	58.35	+ 0.888	+ 0.031	....	4	47.0	12.5

Ordinal Number. R.	Mean North Polar Distance 1845.0.		Precession 1845.0.	Secular Variation.	Adopted Proper Motion.	Observations of M.P.D.			Names.	Oeltzen-Argelander Number.
	R.	G.				No. R.	Mean year. R.	G.		
	o ′ ″	″	″	″	″		1800 +			
3286	33 37 9.5	9.7	+ 14.90	− 0.18	...	3	46.8	13.4	....	......
3287	100 46 47.5	...	+ 14.88	− 0.32	+ 0.03	2	53.9	...	15 Libræ ξ^2...	......
3288	42 46 24.3	23.2	+ 14.84	− 0.21	...	3	46.1	10.4	....	$\overline{14953}$
3289	48 14 10.9	...	+ 14.78	− 0.22	...	3	47.4	...	....	......
3290	46 30 47.2	46.5	+ 14.77	− 0.22	...	4	44.7	11.4	....	......
3291	46 34 46.0	46.9	+ 14.77	− 0.22	...	4	44.4	11.4	....	......
3292	15 12 40.7	40.3	+ 14.71	+ 0.01	...	24	45.9	7.0	7 Urs. Min. β	14985
3293	39 44 8.0	8.7	+ 14.71	− 0.21	+ 0.27	5	44.5	10.5	....	14984
3294	44 54 33.9	...	+ 14.66	− 0.21	...	4	51.9	...	....	14991
3295	48 17 6.2	...	+ 14.64	− 0.22	...	3	49.1	...	....	......
3296	97 53 59.7	...	+ 14.62	− 0.32	+ 0.02	2	52.9	...	19 Libræ δ	......
3297	49 44 12.4	...	+ 14.57	− 0.23	...	4	47.7	...	....	......
3298	50 7 1.8	2.5	+ 14.57	− 0.23	− 0.03	4	44.1	9.4	40 Boötis	......
3299	99 46 39.2	...	+ 14.52	− 0.32	...	1	50.4	...	....	......
3300	44 47 45.6	45.4	+ 14.52	− 0.21	...	6	46.7	10.4	....	15014
3301	35 30 41.7	...	+ 14.49	− 0.18	...	3	51.8	...	....	15018
3302	35 31 20.7	...	+ 14.49	− 0.18	...	3	51.8	...	....	15019
3303	114 40 6.8	...	+ 14.48	− 0.35	...	2	55.5	...	20 Libræ	......
3304	33 46 50.6	51.7	+ 14.48	− 0.19	...	3	45.1	13.4	....	......
3305	23 26 57.4	57.8	+ 14.47	− 0.13	...	4	43.4	8.4	[handwritten]	......
3306	42 6 28.7	28.7	+ 14.46	− 0.23	...	4	44.9	10.4	....	15025
3307	33 46 3.1	3.9	+ 14.42	− 0.19	...	5	47.0	13.4	....	......
3308	48 59 41.6	40.9	+ 14.42	− 0.24	...	5	44.1	8.8	42 Boötis β...	......
3309	14 29 49.0	49.1	+ 14.42	+ 0.05	...	4	43.9	13.9	....	15037
3310	11 11 59.3	59.6	+ 14.37	+ 0.15	...	3	44.8	14.4	....	15047 ?
3311	44 52 52.2	...	+ 14.37	− 0.22	...	3	49.1	...	....	......
3312	23 54 34.7	33.8	+ 14.33	− 0.12	...	4	46.7	14.5	....	15052
3313	44 44 48.0	...	+ 14.32	− 0.22	...	3	48.8	...	....	15053
3314	29 11 5.6	7.2	+ 14.31	− 0.16	...	3	44.1	10.5	....	15056
3315	14 28 56.7	55.9	+ 14.30	+ 0.04	+ 0.02	4	46.2	13.9	8 Urs. Min. ...	15065
3316	14 26 40.3	38.8	+ 14.28	+ 0.07	...	2	44.4	13.5	....	15070
3317	41 44 25.7	...	+ 14.26	− 0.22	...	4	50.9	...	44 Boötis i (1)	15073
3318	41 44 23.7	24.9	+ 14.26	− 0.22	− 0.02	3	43.1	9.4	44 Boötis i (2)	15074
3319	29 22 7.1	7.0	+ 14.19	− 0.15	...	3	47.4	10.5	....	15087
3320	23 25 40.4	41.5	+ 14.18	− 0.11	...	2	45.9	12.5	....	......

Ordinal Number.		Magnitude.	Estimates of Magnitude.	Mean Right Ascension 1845.0.			Precession 1845.0.	Secular Variation.	Adopted Proper Motion.	Observations of R.A.		
R.	G.	R.	R.	R.		G.				No. R.	Mean year R.	G.
				h. m. s.		s.	s.	s.	s.		1800 +	
3321	2191	7.0	3	15 0 17.39		18.24	+ 0.092	+ 0.074	− 0.063	3	47.4	9.4
3322	2188	5.5	5	15 0 17.88		17.91	+ 1.991	+ 0.003	......	6	49.6	10.4
3323	2190	7.2	6	15 0 33.92		33.29	+ 0.902	+ 0.029	......	4	47.8	12.5
3324	2210	7.1	21	15 0 36.76		33.42	−12.812	+ 3.451	......	22	51.6	7.6
3325	2196	5.4	5	15 1 13.63		8.05	− 4.833	+ 0.760	......	5	47.0	7.6
3326	2193	9.7	3	15 1 33.11		31.97	− 0.632	+ 0.126	......	2	47.9	13.5
3327	2192	6.0	4	15 1 37.46		36.92	+ 0.878	+ 0.031	......	5	45.5	12.5
3328	...	5.8	5	15 1 51.36		...	+ 1.701	+ 0.003	......	3	48.4	...
3329	...	5.3	4	15 3 23.88		...	+ 3.404	+ 0.015	− 0.002	2	41.4	...
3330	2194	6.4	8	15 3 24.61		24.44	+ 1.900	+ 0.003	......	6	46.1	10.4
3331	2195	8.2	5	15 4 12.36		11.62	+ 0.873	+ 0.029	......	5	44.4	12.5
3332	2197	6.7	8	15 4 54.74		54.22	+ 1.116	+ 0.017	......	4	45.9	10.4
3333	2200	7.2	5	15 6 1.12		1.01	− 0.423	+ 0.106	+ 0.014	4	47.2	9.5
3334	2199	6.8	6	15 6 4.08		4.29	+ 0.852	+ 0.031	......	6	44.7	12.5
3335	2198	8.2	6	15 6 25.20		25.09	+ 1.942	+ 0.006	......	3	46.4	12.4
3336	2201	6.2	12	15 7 41.56		41.40	+ 2.283	− 0.003	......	12	50.6	11.4
3337	2202	7.2	7	15 7 42.81		42.66	+ 1.940	+ 0.003	......	4	48.2	12.4
3338	2207	8.0	6	15 7 46.10		45.21	+ 0.275	+ 0.057	......	3	48.4	15.4
3339	2203	7.9	6	15 7 49.55		50.07	+ 1.587	+ 0.006	......	4	49.4	10.5
3340	2213	6.8	9	15 7 58.29		55.71	− 7.175	+ 1.249	......	12	51.6	7.6
3341	2204	7.1	6	15 8 7.18		7.16	+ 1.890	+ 0.003	......	7	45.9	9.4
3342	2205	6.7	5	15 8 28.82		28.92	+ 2.136	0.000	......	3	48.4	10.5
3343	2206	5.9	3	15 8 34.35		33.97	+ 2.164	− 0.003	......	3	47.5	10.4
3344	...	2.0	Λ	15 8 40.42		...	+ 3.222	+ 0.010	− 0.009	25	44.8	...
3345	2209	7.5	6	15 8 52.15		52.57	+ 1.581	+ 0.009	......	4	50.3	10.5
3346	2208	6.9	3	15 9 3.78		3.55	+ 2.278	− 0.003	......	2	48.9	11.4
3347	2212	8.0	6	15 9 12.60		12.19	+ 0.841	+ 0.031	......	4	48.3	12.5
3348	2211	8.2	6	15 9 35.84		35.88	+ 1.572	+ 0.006	......	3	49.5	10.5
3349	...	6.6	6	15 11 7.01		...	+ 1.824	+ 0.003	......	2	52.0	...
3350	...	7.9	5	15 11 58.70		...	+ 0.679	+ 0.035	......	3	49.7	...
3351	...	8.2	5	15 12 34.98		...	− 0.281	+ 0.080	......	3	51.7	...
3352	2214	5.4	7	15 12 53.11		51.19	+ 0.610	+ 0.040	......	5	46.4	10.4
3353	2215	8.4	6	15 13 29.01		29.17	+ 1.100	+ 0.017	......	3	45.1	13.4
3354	...	8.2	10	15 13 50.00		...	− 7.562	+ 1.310	......	6	51.2	...
3355	2216	6.9	7	15 14 24.35		24.17	+ 2.182	+ 0.003	......	4	46.9	10.4

Ordinal Number.	Mean North Polar Distance 1845.0.		Precession 1845.0.	Secular Variation.	Adopted Proper Motion.	Observations of N.P.D.			Names.	Oeltzen-Argelander Number.
R.	R.	G.				No.	Mean year.			
						R.	R.	G.		
	° ′ ″	″	″	″	″		1800 +			
3321	17 37 44.6	42.9	+ 14.16	− 0.02	− 0.13	4	49.2	9.4	9 Ursæ Minoris	......
3322	41 14 51.3	52.6	+ 14.16	− 0.22	...	3	43.4	10.4	47 Boötis *k* ...	15091
3323	23 36 38.1	35.2	+ 14.15	− 0.09	...	6	43.8	12.5	....	......
3324	3 24 56.2	55.8	+ 14.15	+ 1.41	...	12	51.1	7.6	....	......
3325	6 51 23.8	13.7	+ 14.10	+ 0.48	...	7	46.4	7.6	....	......
3326	14 24 56.9	54.6	+ 14.08	+ 0.04	...	3	48.8	13.5	....	15114
3327	23 28 38.8	37.8	+ 14.08	− 0.10	...	8	42.2	12.5	....	15113
3328	34 50 41.4	...	+ 14.06	− 0.18	...	3	46.1	...	....	15117
3329	109 12 5.4	...	+ 13.96	− 0.36	+ 0.04	1	48.4	...	24 Libræ ι¹....	......
3330	39 20 58.1	58.2	+ 13.96	− 0.23	...	4	45.7	10.4	....	15137
3331	23 39 58.1	53.1	+ 13.92	− 0.10	...	4	46.5	12.5	....	15149
3332	26 17 24.2	23.6	+ 13.88	− 0.11	...	5	45.8	10.4	....	15161
3333	15 30 53.2	53.2	+ 13.80	+ 0.03	...	5	43.4	9.5	10 Urs. Min. ...	15180
3334	23 37 17.1	15.9	+ 13.80	− 0.10	...	4	43.9	12.5	....	15179
3335	40 43 15.0	14.8	+ 13.78	− 0.20	...	4	47.7	12.4	....	15184
3336	51 9 6.7	7.5	+ 13.70	− 0.24	...	5	46.0	11.4	....	......
3337	40 50 19.0	21.3	+ 13.70	− 0.19	...	5	46.4	12.4	....	15195
3338	19 15 56.2	56.8	+ 13.69	− 0.05	...	5	49.4	15.4	....	15203
3339	33 23 30.2	29.7	+ 13.69	− 0.17	...	4	46.7	10.5	....	15201
3340	5 27 5.0	4.8	+ 13.68	+ 0.78	...	4	46.9	7.6	....	......
3341	39 38 37.5	37.6	+ 13.67	− 0.21	...	4	46.2	9.4	....	......
3342	46 22 26.7	29.7	+ 13.65	− 0.22	...	3	45.4	10.5	....	......
3343	47 14 54.4	54.2	+ 13.64	− 0.24	...	6	45.1	10.4	....	......
3344	98 48 26.2	...	+ 13.63	− 0.34	+ 0.01	6	52.8	...	27 Libræ β....	......
3345	33 22 23.5	23.5	+ 13.62	− 0.18	...	4	47.7	10.5	....	15216
3346	51 7 24.5	26.6	+ 13.61	− 0.25	...	3	46.8	11.4	....	......
3347	23 46 48.3	48.6	+ 13.60	− 0.10	...	3	47.8	12.5	....	15223
3348	33 18 6.7	4.7	+ 13.57	− 0.19	...	4	48.5	10.5	....	15226
3349	38 29 10.0	...	+ 13.48	− 0.19	...	4	52.0	...	....	......
3350	22 33 54.1	...	+ 13.42	− 0.07	...	3	47.4	...	....	15259
3351	16 33 6.7	...	+ 13.38	+ 0.03	...	2	47.4	...	....	......
3352	22 3 49.2	36.1	+ 13.36	− 0.09	...	6	45.1	10.4	....	15264
3353	26 54 5.0	5.5	+ 13.32	− 0.13	...	4	46.9	13.4	....	15276
3354	5 22 34.0	...	+ 13.29	+ 0.81	...	4	46.4	...	....	......
3355	48 27 38.5	45.5	+ 13.26	− 0.25	...	5	47.2	10.4	....	......

Ordinal Number		Magnitude.	Estimates of Magnitude.	Mean Right Ascension 1845.0		Precession 1845.0	Secular Variation	Adopted Proper Motion.	Observations of R.A.		
R.	G.	R.		R.	G.				No. R.	Mean year R.	Mean year G.
				h. m. s.	s.	s.	s.	s.		1800 +	
3356	...	7.2	4	15 14 29.03	...	+ 1.073	+ 0.020	......	3	46.5	...
3357	2217	7.7	7	15 14 38.47	38.61	+ 1.841	+ 0.006	......	6	50.3	11.4
3358	2218	8.8	5	15 15 17.31	16.83	+ 1.742	+ 0.003	......	3	49.1	12.4
3359	2219	8.5	6	15 15 27.25	26.69	+ 1.118	+ 0.020	......	3	48.8	13.5
3360	...	6.2	5	15 15 31.92	...	+ 1.757	+ 0.003	......	3	46.1	...
3361	2220	7.5	6	15 16 15.20	15.01	+ 1.176	+ 0.017	......	3	52.1	14.5
3362	...	7.8	7	15 16 31.71	...	− 11.751	+ 2.486	......	4	54.2	...
3363	2222	8.1	5	15 16 34.86	34.86	+ 1.112	+ 0.017	......	3	49.8	14.0
3364	...	7.2	4	15 16 43.14	...	+ 1.252	+ 0.013	......	3	53.5	...
3365	...	7.3	6	15 16 44.22	...	− 5.686	+ 0.778	......	4	53.0	...
3366	...	8.0	4	15 16 45.20	...	+ 2.219	− 0.001	......	3	51.8	...
3367	...	7.2	2	15 16 50.13	...	+ 1.249	+ 0.013	......	1	51.5	...
3368	...	9.2	3	15 16 53.00	...	+ 1.256	+ 0.013	......	2	54.4	...
3369	2221	5.5	5	15 16 53.49	53.38	+ 2.217	0.000	......	4	48.0	10.5
3370	2223	7.5	6	15 16 58.35	58.23	+ 1.731	+ 0.006	......	4	47.0	12.4
3371	2224	6.6	5	15 17 3.92	3.68	+ 1.079	+ 0.017	......	3	48.8	13.0
3372	2225	7.4	6	15 17 9.65	9.09	− 0.007	+ 0.069	......	2	49.0	10.4
3373	2228	5.4	2	15 17 15.77	15.38	− 0.124	+ 0.074	......	3	44.8	8.0
3374	...	9.0	1	15 17 39.67	...	+ 1.178	+ 0.009	......	1	51.4	...
3375	...	8.2	4	15 18 6.17	...	+ 1.961	+ 0.002	......	2	52.4	...
3376	2229	8.5	4	15 18 20.83	21.04	+ 1.734	+ 0.009	......	2	52.4	12.4
3377	2226	4.6	2	15 18 38.13	38.23	+ 2.276	− 0.003	− 0.010	3	42.0	10.4
3378	2227	7.0	3	15 18 39.56	39.83	+ 2.277	− 0.003	......	2	45.4	10.4
3379	...	5.7	1	15 19 31.56	...	+ 3.368	+ 0.013	......	1	53.3	...
3380	2231	6.3	7	15 19 44.63	44.50	+ 1.096	+ 0.017	......	4	47.7	14.3
3381	...	5.8	5	15 20 4.04	...	+ 0.980	+ 0.020	......	3	46.1	...
3382	2230	7.0	5	15 20 6.54	6.47	+ 1.948	+ 0.003	......	4	47.1	11.4
3383	...	7.1	5	15 20 24.54	...	+ 1.000	+ 0.021	......	2	54.2	...
3384	2233	7.9	4	15 20 31.74	31.99	+ 1.129	+ 0.014	......	2	45.4	14.4
3385	2232	7.4	4	15 20 40.86	40.63	+ 2.049	+ 0.003	......	3	45.8	10.5
3386	2236	3.1	3	15 21 1.31	1.14	− 0.168	+ 0.074	+ 0.018	7	44.0	6.9*
3387	...	7.6	5	15 21 5.58	...	+ 2.057	+ 0.001	......	3	48.7	...
3388	2234	7.2	6	15 21 16.20	17.73	+ 1.207	+ 0.014	......	4	47.7	13.1
3389	2235	3.1	4	15 21 29.39	29.18	+ 1.321	+ 0.011	......	4	45.9	7.3
3390	...	7.0	6	15 21 33.85	...	+ 1.998	+ 0.001	......	4	47.2	...

Ordinal Number. R.	Mean North Polar Distance 1845.0.		Precession 1845.0.	Secular Variation.	Adopted Proper Motion.	Observations of M.P.D.			Names.	Oeltzen-Argelander Number.
	R. (° ′ ″)	G. (″)	(″)	(″)	(″)	No. R.	Mean year R. (1800 +)	G.		
3356	26 39 45.8	...	+ 13.25	− 0.11	...	3	44.4	...	....	15291
3357	39 13 21.0	22.6	+ 13.24	− 0.23	...	5	46.4	11.4	....	15293
3358	37 9 14.5	16.6	+ 13.20	− 0.21	...	3	48.8	12.4	....	......
3359	27 16 40.8	41.3	+ 13.19	− 0.14	...	3	48.5	13.5	....	......
3360	37 28 51.1	...	+ 13.19	− 0.19	...	5	46.4	...	....	......
3361	28 3 47.8	47.9	+ 13.14	− 0.14	...	3	47.5	14.5	....	......
3362	3 54 8.9	...	+ 13.12	+ 1.30	...	4	52.9	...	....	......
3363	27 18 44.3	45.3	+ 13.12	− 0.13	...	3	46.4	14.0	....	......
3364	29 6 5.7	...	+ 13.11	− 0.13	...	2	52.9	...	....	15316
3365	6 35 31.3	...	+ 13.11	+ 0.60	...	3	52.1	...	....	......
3366	49 55 48.0	...	+ 13.11	− 0.24	...	4	43.7	...	....	......
3367	29 3 43.8	...	+ 13.10	− 0.13	...	2	52.0	...	....	15318
3368	29 4 58.4	...	+ 13.10	− 0.13	...	2	52.0	...	....	15321
3369	49 51 45.1	43.8	+ 13.10	− 0.24	...	5	43.4	10.5	....	......
3370	37 5 56.4	54.6	+ 13.09	− 0.21	...	3	44.5	12.4	....	......
3371	26 58 7.4	7.6	+ 13.08	− 0.14	...	3	45.1	13.0	....	......
3372	18 13 32.4	33.2	+ 13.08	0.00	...	4	48.7	10.4	12 Urs. Min...	......
3373	17 36 49.1	50.0	+ 13.07	0.00	− 0.03	5	44.9	12.5	11 Urs. Min.}	15328
3374	28 9 22.3	...	+ 13.05	− 0.12	...	2	54.2	...	....	......
3375	42 32 24.0	...	+ 13.02	− 0.22	...	2	52.0	...	....	......
3376	37 17 41.3	40.8	+ 13.00	− 0.20	...	2	50.4	12.4	....	......
3377	52 4 33.4	35.3	+ 12.98	− 0.26	− 0.08	5	44.8	10.4	51 Boötis μ ...	......
3378	52 6 20.1	25.5	+ 12.98	− 0.26	...	3	47.2	10.4	....	......
3379	106 10 17.0	...	+ 12.91	− 0.38	...	1	55.4	...	32 Libræ ζ¹ ...	......
3380	27 24 0.6	59.2	+ 12.90	− 0.15	...	4	47.0	14.3	....	15357
3381	26 6 13.7	...	+ 12.88	− 0.11	...	3	48.8	...	....	15361
3382	42 23 27.3	26.9	+ 12.88	− 0.24	+ 0.03	3	46.8	11.4	....	15360
3383	26 19 15.3	...	+ 12.86	− 0.11	...	3	50.8	...	....	......
3384	27 52 7.3	10.6	+ 12.85	− 0.15	...	3	49.1	14.4	....	......
3385	45 9 10.3	9.7	+ 12.84	− 0.25	...	4	49.7	10.5	....	15369
3386	17 36 52.6	51.4	+ 12.82	0.00	− 0.06	5	45.9	6.9	13 Urs. Min. γ	15373
3387	45 26 58.7	...	+ 12.81	− 0.23	...	3	48.8	...	....	......
3388	28 54 42.7	48.2	+ 12.80	− 0.16	...	3	43.7	13.1	....	......
3389	30 29 20.9	21.4	+ 12.79	− 0.15	...	4	43.4	7.3	12 Draconis ι .	15380
3390	43 51 21.1	...	+ 12.78	− 0.22	...	3	45.5	...	....	15383

Ordinal Number.		Magnitude.	Estimates of Magnitudes.	Mean Right Ascension 1845.0.		Precession 1845.0.	Secular Variation	Adopted Proper Motion.	Observations of R.A.		
R.	G.	R.	R.	R.	G.				No. R.	Mean year. R.	G.
				h. m. s.	s.	s.	s.	s.		1800 +	
3391	2237	6.8	8	15 22 45.69	45.53	+ 2.225	0.000	……	4	48.4	10.5
3392	2238	7.5	7	15 22 46.89	47.16	− 0.542	+ 0.100	……	4	48.9	10.4
3393	…	7.3	6	15 24 26.46	…	+ 2.183	0.000	……	3	51.8	…
3394	2239	6.7	5	15 24 27.50	27.16	+ 1.904	+ 0.003	……	4	46.4	11.4
3395	…	8.4	6	15 24 38.48	…	+ 2.189	0.000	……	3	53.1	…
3396	2241	6.0	5	15 24 47.47	47.31	+ 1.175	+ 0.017	……	2	45.0	13.1
3397	2243	6.7	6	15 24 56.09	55.85	+ 1.041	+ 0.020	……	3	47.2	14.4
3398	2240	6.7	6	15 24 57.23	57.05	+ 1.540	+ 0.006	……	3	44.7	12.0
3399	…	8.8	8	15 25 5.63	…	− 0.557	+ 0.094	……	4	52.0	…
3400	2242	5.0	7	15 25 21.81	21.86	+ 2.151	0.000	……	5	47.1	9.4
3401	…	5.0	A	15 25 42.74	…	+ 3.246	+ 0.010	+ 0.019	1	49.3	…
3402	2245	6.8	5	15 25 49.25	49.05	+ 1.082	+ 0.017	……	3	47.1	13.1
3403	2244	4.9	7	15 26 14.20	14.12	+ 2.146	0.000	……	3	46.8	9.4
3404	2246	6.3	6	15 26 37.35	37.37	+ 1.044	+ 0.017	……	3	50.8	13.1
3405	…	4.3	A	15 26 51.84	…	+ 3.337	+ 0.012	+ 0.002	4	52.2	…
3406	2247	9.0	6	15 26 56.60	56.25	+ 1.565	+ 0.006	……	3	52.1	12.5
3407	2248	8.8	7	15 27 44.95	44.86	+ 1.567	+ 0.006	……	3	48.4	12.4
3408	…	2.0	A	15 28 7.57	…	+ 2.528	0.000	+ 0.009	42	42.6	…
3409	2250	5.8	5	15 28 46.15	46.35	+ 0.832	+ 0.026	……	3	48.1	13.4
3410	2252	9.3	7	15 29 1.83	1.85	+ 0.836	+ 0.023	……	3	52.1	13.4
3411	2251	7.0	6	15 29 32.92	32.76	+ 2.027	+ 0.003	……	4	50.0	14.5
3412	2249	5.5	4	15 29 33.79	33.51	+ 2.196	− 0.003	……	3	46.8	8.4
3413	2253	6.8	3	15 29 51.26	51.19	+ 2.057	0.000	……	4	47.6	10.5
3414	2283	6.9	40	15 30 4.57	1.10	−24.740	+ 8.423	……	47	50.5	8.1
3415	…	7.3	6	15 30 25.95	…	+ 2.168	0.000	……	3	51.8	…
3416	…	6.9	5	15 30 31.59	…	+ 2.168	0.000	……	2	52.0	…
3417	2254	7.4	3	15 30 36.00	35.83	+ 1.794	+ 0.006	……	2	45.9	10.4
3418	2255	6.4	8	15 31 10.36	10.31	+ 1.581	+ 0.009	……	4	47.0	11.4
3419	…	7.4	5	15 31 37.15	…	+ 0.844	+ 0.028	……	3	51.4	…
3420	2257	5.7	7	15 31 58.39	58.28	+ 1.537	+ 0.006	……	5	45.0	12.4
3421	2256	5.1	8	15 32 15.75	15.75	+ 2.145	0.000	+ 0.005	8	47.0	9.4
3422	…	5.3	2	15 33 1.71	…	+ 3.442	+ 0.014	− 0.003	3	41.7	…
3423	2258	6.7	7	15 33 7.69	7.44	+ 2.031	+ 0.003	……	6	47.9	10.5
3424	2259	6.2	5	15 33 18.54	18.35	+ 1.908	+ 0.003	+ 0.011	3	48.8	10.0
3425	2263	7.0	6	15 33 33.00	31.78	+ 0.370	+ 0.043	……	3	48.8	14.5

Ordinal Number.	Mean North Polar Distance 1845.0.		Precession 1845.0.	Secular Variation.	Adopted Proper Motion.	Observations of N.P.D.			Names.	Oeltzen-Argelander Number.
R.	R.	G.				No. R.	Mean year. R.	G.		
	o ′ ″	″	″	″	″		1800 +			
3391	50 44 16.4	16.4	+ 12.71	− 0.25	...	5	48.1	10.5	....	......
3392	15 58 43.7	47.3	+ 12.71	+ 0.08	...	4	46.4	10.4	14 Urs. Min. ...	......
3393	49 33 28.9	...	+ 12.59	− 0.25	...	3	52.1	...	....	......
3394	41 45 7.3	6.9	+ 12.59	− 0.22	...	5	46.0	11.4	....	15412
3395	49 46 18.8	...	+ 12.58	− 0.25	...	4	53.0	...	....	......
3396	28 47 35.7	36.2	+ 12.57	− 0.13	...	4	47.0	13.1	....	15419
3397	27 11 13.3	13.0	+ 12.56	− 0.12	...	4	46.0	14.4	....	15424
3398	34 16 20.1	20.3	+ 12.56	− 0.17	...	4	47.0	12.0	....	15423
3399	16 2 32.6	...	+ 12.54	+ 0.06	...	5	47.6	...	....	......
3400	48 38 7.3	8.0	+ 12.52	− 0.27	− 0.01	6	46.2	9.4	52 Boötis ν¹...	......
3401	99 31 42.4	...	+ 12.50	− 0.37	+ 0.23	1	54.4	...	37 Libræ	......
3402	27 44 25.8	26.2	+ 12.49	− 0.15	...	3	44.1	13.1	....	15434
3403	48 34 17.3	18.1	+ 12.46	− 0.27	− 0.01	5	46.9	9.4	53 Boötis ν²...	......
3404	27 22 7.4	8.2	+ 12.45	− 0.10	...	5	43.0	13.1	....	15444
3405	104 16 5.4	...	+ 12.43	− 0.38	− 0.02	2	49.5	...	38 Libræ γ ...	......
3406	34 53 50.7	50.4	+ 12.42	− 0.19	...	3	43.5	12.5	....	......
3407	35 0 9.1	7.0	+ 12.36	− 0.20	...	5	43.2	12.4	....	......
3408	62 45 36.0	...	+ 12.34	− 0.29	+ 0.07	1	41.1	...	5 Cor. Bor. α.	......
3409	25 16 7.7	10.2	+ 12.29	− 0.11	− 0.01	3	44.1	13.4	....	15473
3410	25 19 43.4	47.4	+ 12.17	− 0.12	...	4	48.0	13.4	....	15479
3411	45 24 58.6	59.2	+ 12.24	− 0.24	...	4	47.0	14.5	....	......
3412	50 28 18.4	19.5	+ 12.24	− 0.26	− 0.01	5	44.2	8.4	6 Cor. Bor. μ.	......
3413	46 18 58.7	61.1	+ 12.22	− 0.24	...	5	43.8	10.5	....	......
3414	2 11 6.0	7.5	+ 12.20	+ 3.08	...	11	48.9	8.1	[handwritten note]	......
3415	49 39 17.8	...	+ 12.17	− 0.25	...	3	51.8	...	....	......
3416	49 41 1.5	...	+ 12.17	− 0.25	...	3	51.8	...	....	......
3417	39 47 5.0	5.6	+ 12.17	− 0.21	...	3	45.4	10.4	....	15499
3418	35 33 45.3	43.9	+ 12.12	− 0.21	...	4	47.7	11.4	....	......
3419	25 34 35.5	...	+ 12.10	− 0.09	...	4	52.0	...	....	......
3420	34 51 19.8	19.5	+ 12.07	− 0.19	...	4	45.2	12.4	....	......
3421	49 8 19.7	19.8	+ 12.05	− 0.26	− 0.08	5	44.8	9.4	54 Boötis φ...	......
3422	109 10 18.8	...	+ 11.99	− 0.40	+ 0.12	1	46.5	...	43 Libræ κ	......
3423	45 53 16.5	16.2	+ 11.99	− 0.24	...	3	46.8	10.5	....	......
3424	42 41 20.6	20.9	+ 11.98	− 0.22	+ 0.13	4	48.0	10.0	....	......
3425	21 40 31.6	24.3	+ 11.96	− 0.05	...	3	47.1	14.5	....	15529

Ordinal Number.		Magnitude.	Estimates of Magnitude.	Mean Right Ascension 1845.0.			Precession 1845.0.	Secular Variation	Adopted Proper Motion.	Observations of R.A.		
R.	G.	R.	R.	R.		G.				No.	Mean year.	
										R.	R.	G.
				h. m. s.		s.	s.	s.	s.		1800 +	
3426	2260	5.9	8	15 33 33.50		33.39	+ 1.536	+ 0.006	......	5	45.8	12.4
3427	...	8.3	4	15 33 51.17		...	+ 2.019	+ 0.001	......	3	51.8	...
3428	2262	6.2	3	15 34 2.72		2.73	+ 1.746	+ 0.006	......	7	47.0	11.4
3429	2261	7.0	4	15 34 4.06		3.72	+ 1.900	+ 0.003	......	3	48.2	10.4
3430	...	8.4	6	15 34 4.71		...	+ 2.063	+ 0.001	......	3	52.8	...
3431	...	7.8	3	15 34 12.34		...	+ 2.060	+ 0.001	......	2	52.5	...
3432	2264	7.2	4	15 35 8.79		8.38	+ 2.016	+ 0.003	......	4	48.2	10.5
3433	2265	7.8	6	15 35 12.51		12.31	+ 1.342	+ 0.011	......	4	52.9	14.4
3434	...	6.0	A	15 35 21.73		...	+ 3.362	+ 0.012	+ 0.001	3	53.4	...
3435	2266	7.4	7	15 35 24.87		24.78	+ 1.345	+ 0.011	......	4	51.0	14.4
3436	2267	6.8	6	15 35 44.66		44.40	+ 1.311	+ 0.009	......	2	45.4	13.5
3437	2268	5.1	4	15 36 8.10		6.98	− 1.961	+ 0.197	......	5	45.3	7.5
3438	...	2.3	A	15 36 38.23		...	+ 2.939	+ 0.004	+ 0.009	41	45.7	...
3439	...	7.4	7	15 38 8.49		...	+ 0.185	+ 0.047	......	3	51.7	...
3440	2271	6.8	6	15 38 11.27		11.07	− 0.214	+ 0.069	......	3	51.1	10.4
3441	2275	7.0	7	15 38 25.28		27.15	− 3.777	+ 0.394	......	4	50.2	7.9
3442	2276	7.5	7	15 38 38.08		39.61	− 3.782	+ 0.397	......	4	50.2	8.4
3443	2270	5.9	7	15 38 38.14		38.11	+ 1.630	+ 0.006	− 0.004	5	48.6	9.4
3444	2269	8.4	6	15 38 38.28		38.35	+ 1.885	+ 0.006	......	5	51.2	12.4
3445	...	7.1	7	15 39 33.93		...	− 4.062	+ 0.414	......	4	50.1	...
3446	2272	7.7	7	15 39 58.30		58.25	+ 1.596	+ 0.006	......	4	47.1	11.4
3447	2273	7.4	5	15 40 18.23		19.16	+ 1.590	+ 0.006	......	3	46.5	11.4
3448	...	7.2	8	15 40 56.18		...	+ 2.048	+ 0.001	......	4	51.9	...
3449	2274	8.1	6	15 41 8.91		8.86	+ 1.603	+ 0.006	......	3	46.2	11.4
3450	...	5.0	A	15 41 40.01		...	+ 3.590	+ 0.017	− 0.005	2	40.8	...
3451	2277	7.2	8	15 42 5.09		5.43	+ 1.869	+ 0.006	......	6	49.4	10.4
3452	2278	7.9	5	15 42 44.04		43.75	+ 1.173	+ 0.014	......	2	46.9	12.9
3453	...	6.4	5	15 42 53.04		...	+ 1.435	+ 0.008	......	4	46.7	...
3454	2286	6.9	6	15 43 7.85		4.63	− 5.646	+ 0.634	......	4	49.9	8.1
3455	...	8.1	6	15 43 49.90		...	+ 0.123	+ 0.048	......	3	51.8	...
3456	...	6.0	1	15 43 53.70		...	+ 1.437	+ 0.008	......	3	49.7	...
3457	2282	7.2	7	15 44 16.81		16.42	+ 0.156	+ 0.046	......	3	50.7	10.4
3458	2280	5.1	2	15 44 18.98		18.71	+ 0.885	+ 0.020	......	6	43.9	9.9
3459	2279	7.6	7	15 44 26.63		26.30	+ 1.151	+ 0.014	......	4	47.3	13.0
3460	2281	6.4	8	15 44 33.34		32.97	+ 1.143	+ 0.011	....	4	47.3	12.8

Ordinal Number. R.	Mean North Polar Distance 1845.0.			Precession 1845.0.	Secular Variation.	Adopted Proper Motion.	Observations of N.P.D.			Names.	Oeltzen-Argelander Number.
	R.		G.				No. R.	Mean year. 1800 + R.	G.		
	° ′ ″		″	″	″	″					
3426	34 58 54.2		52.6	+ 11.96	− 0.19	...	4	48.7	12.4	....	15528
3427	45 37 43.0		...	+ 11.94	− 0.24	...	2	51.9	...	....	....
3428	39 4 6.9		7.1	+ 11.92	− 0.23	...	2	45.5	11.4	....	15536
3429	42 33 59.8		59.2	+ 11.92	− 0.24	...	3	49.8	10.4	....	....
3430	46 52 9.8		...	+ 11.92	− 0.24	...	3	53.1	...	....	....
3431	46 47 55.4		...	+ 11.91	− 0.24	...	2	52.5	...	....	....
3432	45 39 15.2		17.8	+ 11.85	− 0.24	...	3	50.1	10.5	....	....
3433	31 58 28.9		29.5	+ 11.84	− 0.17	...	3	49.1	14.4	....	15549
3434	105 10 27.8		...	+ 11.86	− 0.40	+ 0.06	3	50.8	...	44 Libræ η ...	....
3435	32 2 1.5		1.0	+ 11.83	− 0.16	...	4	46.7	14.4	....	15553
3436	31 34 22.7		23.1	+ 11.80	− 0.18	...	5	47.3	13.5	....	....
3437	12 8 13.6		12.2	+ 11.78	+ 0.23	...	5	45.1	7.5	15 Urs. Min. θ	15565
3438	83 4 56.1		...	+ 11.74	− 0.35	− 0.05	11	41.1	...	24 Serpentis a	....
3439	20 40 54.5		...	+ 11.63	− 0.02	...	6	47.8	...	....	15594
3440	18 20 44.3		46.6	+ 11.63	+ 0.01	...	5	46.6	10.4	....	....
3441	9 2 32.5		36.4	+ 11.61	+ 0.44	...	4	45.5	7.9	....	....
3442	9 2 29.6		30.9	+ 11.60	+ 0.46	...	4	46.0	8.4	....	....
3443	37 8 52.2		53.7	+ 11.60	− 0.20	...	5	45.7	9.4	....	15601
3444	42 36 25.9		26.5	+ 11.60	− 0.23	...	3	45.2	12.4	....	....
3445	8 43 5.9		...	+ 11.53	+ 0.48	...	5	50.7	...	....	....
3446	36 36 29.4		31.1	+ 11.50	− 0.21	...	5	47.3	11.4	....	....
3447	36 31 53.7		54.2	+ 11.48	− 0.20	...	4	43.7	11.4	....	....
3448	47 2 53.3		...	+ 11.44	− 0.25	...	5	51.9	...	....	....
3449	36 50 18.4		17.2	+ 11.42	− 0.20	...	5	47.1	11.4	....	....
3450	115 16 29.5		...	+ 11.39	− 0.43	+ 0.02	3	56.5	...	1 Scorpii b.....	....
3451	42 31 59.5		59.9	+ 11.35	− 0.24	...	3	46.1	10.4	....	....
3452	30 12 14.6		14.1	+ 11.31	− 0.14	...	4	47.5	12.9	....	15649
3453	34 2 54.7		...	+ 11.29	− 0.17	...	3	46.3	...	....	15653
3454	7 13 45.7		44.8	+ 11.28	+ 0.69	...	7	49.3	8.1	....	....
3455	20 35 37.9		...	+ 11.23	− 0.01	...	3	47.2	...	....	....
3456	34 8 48.6		...	+ 11.22	− 0.17	...	3	46.8	...	....	15666
3457	20 50 31.2		32.8	+ 11.19	− 0.04	...	5	48.1	10.4	....	....
3458	26 55 12.2		12.8	+ 11.19	− 0.12	+ 0.05	5	42.9	9.9	....	15672
3459	30 2 19.0		20.0	+ 11.18	− 0.15	...	5	50.1	13.0	....	15673
3460	29 57 15.7		15.4	+ 11.18	− 0.13	...	6	47.0	12.8	....	15676

Magnitude.	Estimates of Magnitude.	Mean Right Ascension 1845.0.		Precession 1845.0.	Secular Variation	Adopted Proper Motion.
R.		R.	G.			
		h. m. s.	s.	s.	s.	s.
5.0	1	15 45 0.57	...	+ 3.396	+ 0.012	+ 0.009
7.2	6	15 45 42.00	...	+ 2.030	+ 0.001	......
7.2	6	15 47 6.56	6.51	+ 1.566	+ 0.009	......
5.0	6	15 47 19.04	19.09	+ 2.030	0.000	+ 0.040
8.9	7	15 47 47.42	...	+ 1.889	+ 0.002	......
7.5	8	15 48 15.21	15.11	+ 1.888	+ 0.006	......
6.9	6	15 48 21.14	20.07	− 3.611	+ 0.337	......
5.2	4	15 48 40.63	40.46	+ 1.386	+ 0.009	......
5.3	7	15 49 27.98	28.07	+ 1.998	+ 0.003	.....
3.0	A	15 49 29.28	...	+ 3.612	+ 0.016	− 0.003
4.0	4	15 49 43.54	42.37	− 2.355	+ 0.209	+ 0.029
5.1	5	15 50 9.41	9.34	+ 2.176	0.000	+ 0.004
6.0	5	15 50 17.66	17.68	+ 2.017	+ 0.003	+ 0.007
4.0	2	15 51 10.70	...	+ 3.531	+ 0.014	......
7.0	11	15 52 2.21	...	−10.794	+ 1.487	......
6.3	7	15 52 2.52	2.54	+ 2.114	+ 0.003	......
8.0	8	15 52 7.26	5.87	− 3.774	+ 0.349	......
6.3	7	15 52 49.76	49.75	+ 1.152	+ 0.014	......
7.3	2	15 53 50.83	...	+ 3.634	+ 0.016	......
5.4	6	15 54 7.16	7.77	+ 1.430	+ 0.009	......
6.0	6	15 54 40.71	40.60	+ 1.693	+ 0.003	......
6.7	8	15 55 25.06	...	+ 2.123	0.000	......
9.0	6	15 55 37.75	...	+ 1.693	+ 0.004	......
7.9	6	15 55 39.78	...	+ 1.689	+ 0.004	......
8.3	7	15 55 43.02	42.34	− 0.617	+ 0.080	......
3.0	1	15 56 25.99	...	+ 3.473	+ 0.012	......
7.0	5	15 56 38.18	38.26	+ 2.091	+ 0.003	......
7.1	7	15 57 13.73	13.82	− 0.652	+ 0.077	......
4.8	4	15 57 58.43	58.10	+ 1.857	+ 0.003	......
5.5	7	15 58 8.52	8.42	+ 1.521	+ 0.006	......
8.0	6	15 58 14.80	...	− 1.579	+ 0.161	......
6.9	9	15 58 47.14	47.11	− 1.565	+ 0.131	+ 0.019
3.9	2	15 58 59.51	59.63	+ 1.149	+ 0.011	− 0.027
7.8	6	15 59 7.12	7.40	+ 1.065	+ 0.020	......
7.0	5	15 59 36.02	37.71	+ 2.114	+ 0.003	......

Ordinal Number.	Mean North Polar Distance 1845.0.			Precession 1845.0.	Secular Variation.	Adopted Proper Motion.	Observations of N.P.D.				Names.	Oeltzen-Argelander Number.
	R.	R.	G.				No. R.	Mean year. R.	G.			
	o ′ ″		″	″	″	″		1800 +				
3461	106 16 10.8		...	+ 11.14	− 0.41	− 0.12	2	49.4	...		46 Libræ θ	......
3462	46 58 0.3		...	+ 11.09	− 0.24	...	4	46.4	...		....	......
3463	36 37 36.7		34.0	+ 10.99	− 0.19	...	4	44.2	10.5		....	......
3464	47 6 41.8		42.7	+ 10.97	− 0.27	− 0.58	6	46.4	9.5		1 Herculis χ...	......
3465	43 29 6.5		...	+ 10.93	− 0.23	...	4	48.0	...		....	15712
3466	43 29 58.3		58.5	+ 10.90	− 0.25	...	6	47.6	10.5		....	15718
3467	9 32 8.4		9.9	+ 10.90	+ 0.45	...	5	46.9	8.0		18 Urs. Min...	......
3468	33 42 48.3		51.7	+ 10.87	− 0.19	...	6	44.1	8.5		....	15726
3469	46 24 24.9		25.9	+ 10.81	− 0.26	− 0.06	6	45.5	10.4		2 Herculis	......
3470	115 39 46.5		...	+ 10.81	− 0.44	+ 0.04	1	58.4	...		6 Scorpii π ...	......
3471	11 43 54.5		54.0	+ 10.79	+ 0.26	...	22	43.7	6.9		16 Urs. Min. ζ	15743
3472	51 36 7.4		8.3	+ 10.76	− 0.29	− 0.09	5	46.7	9.4		12 Cor. Bor. λ	......
3473	46 58 48.0		48.3	+ 10.75	− 0.27	...	6	45.5	9.5		4 Herculis	......
3474	112 10 31.4		...	+ 10.69	− 0.44	...	2	48.0	...		7 Scorpii δ	......
3475	4 40 30.8		...	+ 10.63	+ 1.30	...	6	51.7	...		....	......
3476	49 51 31.4		33.2	+ 10.62	− 0.28	...	4	45.0	10.4		....	......
3477	9 24 25.3		26.9	+ 10.62	+ 0.33	...	5	47.7	8.4		....	......
3478	30 38 22.0		22.7	+ 10.57	− 0.13	...	5	44.9	8.5		....	......
3479	116 16 22.4		...	+ 10.49	− 0.45	...	2	53.5	...		....	......
3480	34 48 37.3		41.5	+ 10.47	− 0.18	...	4	45.5	9.4		....	15799
3481	39 40 30.0		28.7	+ 10.43	− 0.21	...	5	46.1	10.5		....	......
3482	50 23 6.7		...	+ 10.37	− 0.26	...	5	51.9	...		....	......
3483	39 43 25.5		...	+ 10.35	− 0.21	...	4	46.5	...		....	......
3484	39 39 47.0		...	+ 10.35	− 0.21	...	5	46.3	...		....	......
3485	17 15 4.8		1.1	+ 10.35	+ 0.07	...	5	48.1	10.5		....	15817
3486	109 22 33.0		...	+ 10.29	− 0.43	+ 0.02	5	49.7	...		8 Scorpii β (1st)	......
3487	49 32 41.2		42.1	+ 10.28	− 0.27	...	4	44.9	10.4		....	......
3488	17 9 57.5		57.7	+ 10.23	+ 0.06	...	5	45.7	10.5		....	15837
3489	43 31 48.8		48.0	+ 10.18	− 0.24	...	6	45.5	8.5		6 Herculis υ...	......
3490	36 39 5.4		4.1	+ 10.17	− 0.19	...	8	46.1	9.4		....	......
3491	13 55 32.2		...	+ 10.16	+ 0.20	...	5	46.7	...		....	15854
3492	13 59 2.3		1.4	+ 10.12	+ 0.19	+ 0.02	6	47.5	9.5		17 Urs. Min...	15865
3493	31 1 8.8		8.4	+ 10.10	− 0.16	− 0.33	6	44.3	6.9		13 Draconis θ	......
3494	29 56 30.4		32.1	+ 10.09	− 0.15	...	5	47.7	12.5		....	......
3495	50 25 18.4		20.3	+ 10.06	− 0.26	...	3	47.2	10.4		....	......

Ordinal Number.		Magnitude.	Estimates of Magnitude.	Mean Right Ascension 1845.0.			Precession 1845.0.	Secular Variation	Adopted Proper Motion.	Observations of R.A.		
R.	G.	R.	R.	R.		G.				No. R.	Mean year. R.	G.
				h. m. s.		s.	s.	s.	s.		1800 +	
3496	2307	7.1	7	15 59 45.22		45.07	+ 0.198	+ 0.040	......	3	50.4	10.5
3497	2315	7.4	9	15 59 57.30		55.83	− 6.946	+ 0.714	......	4	51.0	7.5
3498	...	6.0	7	16 0 21.01		...	+ 1.076	+ 0.014	......	4	47.2	...
3499	2309	7.2	6	16 2 9.60		49.25	+ 1.015	+ 0.009	......	3	48.8	12.5
3500	2310	7.3	4	16 2 23.05		22.78	+ 1.780	+ 0.003	......	3	46.8	10.5
3501	...	7.7	4	16 2 43.21		...	+ 1.705	+ 0.004	......	3	51.7	...
3502	...	4.2	2	16 2 59.62		...	+ 3.473	+ 0.012	− 0.002	3	49.8	...
3503	2312	8.7	4	16 3 29.98		29.86	− 0.235	+ 0.051	......	2	52.4	12.0
3504	2311	4.7	6	16 3 53.39		53.38	+ 1.887	+ 0.003	......	10	49.2	8.5
3505	...	8.7	6	16 3 54.54		...	− 0.746	+ 0.091	......	2	52.0	...
3506	2314	6.7	5	16 4 53.85		53.72	+ 1.644	+ 0.006	......	3	46.8	10.5
3507	2313	7.7	4	16 4 58.17		58.16	+ 2.053	+ 0.003	......	3	47.0	10.4
3508	2316	6.7	6	16 5 23.01		22.70	+ 1.928	+ 0.006	+ 0.014	3	48.3	9.5
3509	2319	6.9	8	16 5 24.63		24.17	− 0.276	+ 0.054	......	4	50.0	12.2
3510	...	8.8	6	16 5 34.09		...	− 0.276	+ 0.054	......	2	51.5	...
3511	2320	5.6	1	16 5 55.48		55.51	+ 0.130	+ 0.040	......	4	45.6	8.5
3512	...	7.3	6	16 5 58.92		...	+ 1.756	+ 0.004	......	4	53.7	...
3513	...	6.7	4	16 6 1.04		...	+ 1.165	+ 0.012	......	2	46.0	...
3514	...	7.8	6	16 6 1.30		...	− 6.849	+ 0.663	......	3	49.9	...
3515	...	3.0	A	16 6 13.71		...	+ 3.138	+ 0.006	− 0.006	24	43.8	...
3516	2317	6.4	3	16 6 40.03		40.28	+ 2.102	+ 0.003	......	3	47.9	11.5
3517	2318	5.6	6	16 6 39.98		39.82	+ 1.981	+ 0.003	......	4	48.0	10.4
3518	2322	6.7	6	16 7 18.05		17.59	+ 1.006	+ 0.014	......	3	45.8	12.5
3519	2323	7.0	5	16 7 36.33		36.16	+ 0.673	+ 0.026	......	2	49.0	10.5
3520	2321	7.0	4	16 7 42.00		41.94	+ 2.133	+ 0.003	......	3	51.1	10.5
3521	2324	7.9	5	16 8 8.08		8.32	+ 1.018	+ 0.014	......	3	52.5	12.5
3522	...	7.2	8	16 8 23.36		...	− 8.277	+ 0.850	......	6	50.5	...
3523	...	6.9	27	16 8 42.70		...	−12.793	+ 1.748	......	34	51.6	...
3524	...	6.2	7	16 8 44.44		...	− 2.136	+ 0.170	......	4	50.5	...
3525	...	6.6	4	16 11 27.29		...	+ 2.056	+ 0.002	......	3	48.5	...
3526	...	3.3	A	16 11 46.80		...	+ 3.631	+ 0.014	− 0.003	2	40.9	...
3527	2326	6.5	5	16 11 51.82		51.57	+ 0.190	+ 0.040	......	4	44.6	10.5
3528	2325	7.2	5	16 12 0.76		0.31	+ 1.453	+ 0.009	......	4	45.5	10.4
3529	...	7.7	7	16 12 29.41		...	− 0.779	+ 0.089	......	3	51.8	...
3530	2327	8.2	6	16 12 34.10		33.54	+ 0.26c	+ 0.037	......	4	48.1	12.5

Ordinal Number.	Mean North Polar Distance 1845.0.		Precession 1845.0.	Secular Variation.	Adopted Proper Motion.	Observations of N.P.D.			Names.	Oeltzen-Argelander Number.
R.	R.	G.				No. R.	Mean year. R.	G.		
	o ′ ″	″	″	″	″		1800 +			
3496	21 56 32.2	31.2	+ 10.05	− 0.02	...	5	47.3	10.5	....	15877
3497	6 35 37.9	38.0	+ 10.03	+ 0.88	...	6	49.6	7.5	....	....
3498	30 9 44.7	...	+ 10.00	− 0.13	...	4	44.8	...	....	....
3499	29 32 6.1	6.8	+ 9.86	− 0.22	...	4	46.0	12.5	....	....
3500	42 4 45.2	45.6	+ 9.84	− 0.25	...	5	46.3	10.5	....	15917
3501	40 30 5.1	...	+ 9.82	− 0.22	...	4	46.0	...	....	15922
3502	109 3 10.2	...	+ 9.80	− 0.44	+ 0.03	2	49.5	...	14 Scorpii ν ...	......
3503	19 27 54.4	55.3	+ 9.76	+ 0.02	...	4	44.5	12.0	....	15934
3504	44 39 21.2	22.6	+ 9.73	− 0.25	− 0.02	7	46.7	8.5	11 Herculis φ	15935
3505	17 1 46.9	...	+ 9.73	+ 0.09	...	5	52.9	...	....	15941
3506	39 24 40.1	43.3	+ 9.65	− 0.23	...	5	46.9	10.5	....	15956
3507	49 2 29.1	32.1	+ 9.65	− 0.26	...	3	44.5	10.4	....	......
3508	45 45 49.0	52.3	+ 9.62	− 0.25	+ 0.34	4	46.0	9.5	14 Herculis ...	......
3509	19 19 29.5	29.9	+ 9.61	+ 0.01	...	5	46.9	12.2	....	15968
3510	19 19 25.3	...	+ 9.61	+ 0.01	...	4	50.7	...	....	15970
3511	21 46 52.4	52.9	+ 9.57	− 0.04	− 0.07	5	45.3	8.5	....	15978
3512	41 47 20.1	...	+ 9.57	− 0.22	...	5	51.9	...	....	15977
3513	31 39 24.0	...	+ 9.57	− 0.14	...	4	47.0	...	....	......
3514	6 45 19.2	...	+ 9.57	+ 0.88	...	4	49.0	...	....	......
3515	93 17 25.7	...	+ 9.55	− 0.40	+ 0.13	4	40.4	...	1 Ophiuchi δ .	......
3516	50 32 34.1	34.5	+ 9.52	− 0.27	...	3	47.1	11.5	....	......
3517	47 13 31.1	33.5	+ 9.52	− 0.25	...	5	44.9	10.4	....	......
3518	29 43 30.3	28.7	+ 9.47	− 0.14	...	5	47.7	12.5	....	......
3519	26 11 17.9	17.7	+ 9.44	− 0.11	...	3	43.9	10.5	....	16006
3520	51 31 53.7	54.4	+ 9.44	− 0.28	...	4	47.8	10.5	....	......
3521	29 55 9.1	5.2	+ 9.40	− 0.15	...	3	44.8	12.5	....	......
3522	5 56 38.3	...	+ 9.38	+ 1.06	...	3	48.9	...	....	......
3523	4 15 46.3	...	+ 9.36	+ 1.65	...	9	50.3	...	....	......
3524	12 47 45.2	...	+ 9.36	+ 0.27	...	6	48.1	...	....	......
3525	49 34 41.4	...	+ 9.14	− 0.26	...	4	47.4	...	....	......
3526	115 12 53.5	...	+ 9.12	− 0.47	− 0.01	3	48.2	...	20 Scorpii σ ...	......
3527	22 27 45.7	45.1	+ 9.11	− 0.04	...	4	44.4	10.5	....	16056
3528	36 22 31.7	28.0	+ 9.10	− 0.21	...	4	44.5	10.4	....	16057
3529	17 12 50.2	...	+ 9.07	+ 0.10	...	4	50.0	...	....	......
3530	22 59 34.5	30.9	+ 9.06	− 0.04	...	5	46.7	12.5	....	......

Ordinal Number.		Magnitude.	Estimates of Magnitude.	Mean Right Ascension 1845.0.		Precession 1845.0.	Secular Variation	Adopted Proper Motion.	Observations of R.A.		
R.	G.	R.		R.	G.				No. R.	Mean year R.	G.
				h. m. s.	s.	s.	s.	. s.		1800 +	
3531	2329	7.7	4	16 13 43.21	43.85	+ 0.286	+ 0.034	+ 0.041	4	46.9	11.2
3532	...	7.6	6	16 14 5.46	...	+ 1.991	+ 0.002	......	3	51.8	...
3533	2328	5.6	10	16 14 36.62	37.03	+ 2.062	+ 0.003	......	8	48.5	11.4
3534	2332	5.3	5	16 14 40.72	40.37	+ 0.984	+ 0.023	......	5	44.4	8.5
3535	2330	6.1	6	16 14 51.69	51.58	+ 1.670	+ 0.003	......	4	47.0	9.5
3536	...	5.5	3	16 15 2.46	...	+ 3.499	+ 0.011	− 0.004	3	48.5	...
3537	...	4.8	4	16 15 5.07	...	+ 2.645	+ 0.002	......	14	50.4	...
3538	2331	4.7	4	16 15 5.15	4.97	+ 1.798	+ 0.003	......	5	44.5	7.0
3539	2334	5.9	6	16 15 19.40	18.67	− 1.839	+ 0.126	......	6	45.9	7.9
3540	2335	8.2	5	16 16 14.87	14.02	− 1.034	+ 0.086	......	2	50.5	12.5
3541	2333	7.0	4	16 16 29.63	29.32	+ 1.507	+ 0.006	......	5	46.7	10.4
3542	2336	6.2	7	16 16 30.26	30.61	− 1.611	+ 0.117	− 0.013	5	45.6	11.5
3543	2337	6.4	8	16 17 9.19	9.24	− 1.068	+ 0.086	. ....	7	46.1	12.5
3544	2338	6.2	6	16 18 14.91	14.97	− 0.062	+ 0.043	......	2	49.0	10.5
3545	...	1.3	A	16 19 54.79	...	+ 3.663	+ 0.014	− 0.001	17	47.5	...
3546	...	7.7	5	16 19 57.32	...	+ 2.114	+ 0.002	......	3	51.8	...
3547	2339	7.2	8	16 19 59.65	59.54	+ 1.857	+ 0.003	......	5	47.5	11.4
3548	2340	6.8	6	16 20 35.92	35.56	+ 1.480	+ 0.003	......	5	45.6	10.4
3549	...	8.8	7	16 20 37.93	...	+ 1.306	+ 0.009	......	3	52.8	...
3550	...	7.8	5	16 20 43.29	...	+ 0.808	+ 0.019	......	3	52.2	...
3551	...	8.6	3	16 20 48.78	...	+ 0.782	+ 0.019	......	2	52.0	...
3552	...	7.0	7	16 20 56.10	...	+ 1.291	+ 0.009	......	4	48.0	...
3553	2343	5.9	4	16 21 2.44	2.00	+ 1.300	+ 0.009	......	4	46.8	8.5
3554	2342	7.4	6	16 21 4.92	4.79	+ 1.512	+ 0.006	......	5	47.2	11.0
3555	2341	6.8	6	16 21 9.37	9.02	+ 2.008	+ 0.003	......	4	47.0	10.5
3556	2345	6.1	5	16 21 44.68	44.47	+ 0.778	+ 0.017	......	5	45.8	10.4
3557	2346	2.8	4	16 21 54.19	53.92	+ 0.795	+ 0.017	......	18	41.9	6.8
3558	2349	4.9	7	16 22 6.00	5.98	− 1.850	+ 0.117	......	3	47.8	7.8
3559	2344	6.8	5	16 22 8.15	8.34	+ 1.704	+ 0.003	......	2	47.5	11.5
3560	2347	5.7	4	16 22 11.58	11.70	− 0.179	+ 0.046	......	5	47.6	10.5
3561	...	4.5	1	16 22 16.40	...	+ 3.425	+ 0.009	− 0.001	2	51.0	...
3562	2348	4.9	9	16 23 33.26	33.15	+ 1.962	+ 0.003	+ 0.005	12	50.8	8.5
3563	...	6.3	1	16 23 49.77	...	+ 2.606	+ 0.002	......	1	56.5	...
3564	2350	7.3	6	16 24 6.51	6.39	+ 1.510	+ 0.006	......	4	45.0	10.5
3565	...	8.6	5	16 24 39.30	...	+ 1.648	+ 0.004	......	3	48.6	...

Ordinal Number. R.	Mean North Polar Distance 1845.0. R.	G.	Precession 1845.0.	Secular Variation.	Adopted Proper Motion	No. R.	Mean year. R.	G.	Names.	Oeltzen Argelander Number.
	° ′ ″	″	″	″	″		1800 +			
3531	23 14 18.7	17.6	+ 8.97	− 0.05	...	5	45.9	11.2	....	16081
3532	47 57 53.3	....	+ 8.94	− 0.26	...	5	51.9	...	....	....
3533	49 55 1.9	3.7	+ 8.90	− 0.27	...	6	44.5	11.4	....	....
3534	29 52 3.3	4.8	+ 8.89	− 0.15	...	7	45.1	8.5	....	16098
3535	40 35 18.0	19.7	+ 8.88	− 0.23	...	5	46.5	9.5	....	16100
3536	109 40 8.8	...	+ 8.87	− 0.46	+ 0.06	1	48.5	...	4 Ophiuchi ψ.	....
3537	70 28 42.8	...	+ 8.86	− 0.35	...	1	56.5	...	20 Herculis γ.	....
3538	43 18 53.2	53.9	+ 8.86	− 0.25	...	8	48.6	7.0	22 Herculis τ.	....
3539	13 44 5.4	5.3	+ 8.85	+ 0.25	...	7	47.1	7.9	19 Urs. Min...	16111
3540	16 19 34.0	30.0	+ 8.77	+ 0.13	...	5	47.7	12.5	....	16126
3541	37 35 27.1	25.7	+ 8.75	− 0.21	...	4	46.5	10.4	....	16128
3542	14 24 28.7	27.7	+ 8.75	+ 0.21	...	6	46.5	11.5	20 Urs. Min...	16131
3543	16 13 40.6	41.1	+ 8.70	+ 0.14	...	5	46.6	12.5	....	16138
3544	21 4 36.4	37.9	+ 8.61	− 0.01	...	5	46.3	10.5	....	....
3545	116 4 56.1	...	+ 8.48	− 0.48	+ 0.03	19	48.3	...	21 Scorpii a...	....
3546	51 43 58.6	...	+ 8.48	− 0.26	...	5	51.9	...	....	....
3547	44 57 12.2	13.4	+ 8.47	− 0.27	− 0.05	5	46.3	11.4	....	16178
3548	37 21 18.8	18.4	+ 8.43	− 0.19	...	5	47.1	10.4	....	16183
3549	34 29 2.5	...	+ 8.43	− 0.17	...	4	48.5	...	....	16185
3550	28 12 21.4	...	+ 8.42	− 0.11	...	5	48.3	...	....	16188
3551	27 56 56.9	...	+ 8.41	− 0.10	...	2	52.5	...	....	16190
3552	34 17 54.0	...	+ 8.40	− 0.17	...	3	45.9	...	....	16194
3553	34 26 25.5	26.6	+ 8.39	− 0.19	...	3	45.2	8.5	....	16198
3554	37 55 47.8	47.8	+ 8.39	− 0.20	...	4	45.5	11.0	....	16200
3555	48 50 9.6	8.1	+ 8.38	− 0.28	...	4	45.3	10.5	....	....
3556	27 57 0.2	0.0	+ 8.34	− 0.10	...	4	43.2	10.4	....	16210
3557	28 8 1.6	1.0	+ 8.32	− 0.12	− 0.08	6	47.5	6.8	14 Draconis η.	16212
3558	13 53 25.7	24.9	+ 8.31	+ 0.25	− 0.26	5	47.1	7.8	21 Urs. Min. η	16216
3559	41 41 52.2	56.8	+ 8.31	− 0.22	...	3	45.9	11.5	....	....
3560	20 31 57.6	56.5	+ 8.30	+ 0.02	...	5	47.9	10.5	....	....
3561	106 16 12.0	...	+ 8.29	− 0.45	+ 0.03	1	48.5	...	8 Ophiuchi ϕ.	....
3562	47 46 26.5	25.3	+ 8.19	− 0.27	− 0.07	5	46.9	8.5	30 Herculis y..	....
3563	69 10 36.3	...	+ 8.18	− 0.34	...	1	52.5	...	....	....
3564	38 3 51.6	53.4	+ 8.13	− 0.26	...	4	46.0	10.5	....	16240
3565	40 40 55.8	...	+ 8.10	− 0.21	...	3	51.8	...	....	....

Magnitude.	Estimates of Magnitude.	Mean Right Ascension 1845.0.		Precession 1845.0.	Secular Variation	Adopted Proper Motion.
R.	R.	R.	G.			
		h. m. s.	s.	s.	s.	s.
6.4	7	16 24 46.50	46.38	+ 1.519	+ 0.009	......
7.8	7	16 24 49.73	49.69	+ 1.500	+ 0.009	......
6.3	6	16 25 51.00	50.72	+ 1.645	+ 0.006	......
7.1	3	16 25 52.99	53.33	+ 1.694	+ 0.003	......
3.3	A	16 26 14.56	...	+ 3.719	+ 0.014	......
7.9	6	16 26 53.30	...	+ 0.857	+ 0.014	......
7.2	4	16 27 2.08	1.87	− 0.650	+ 0.057	......
7.0	7	16 27 19.21	...	+ 2.023	+ 0.002	......
6.8	5	16 28 17.17	16.95	+ 2.093	0.000	......
4.9	7	16 28 18.72	18.47	− 0.155	+ 0.040	+ 0.005
8.3	7	16 28 49.85	49.67	− 3.413	+ 0.206	......
6.7	5	16 28 51.92	51.41	+ 1.576	+ 0.003	......
4.3	7	16 29 6.55	6.24	+ 1.930	+ 0.003	......
6.7	6	16 30 12.36	12.02	+ 1.456	+ 0.006	......
5.6	4	16 30 14.91	14.61	+ 0.827	+ 0.017	......
5.9	8	16 31 40.16	40.08	+ 1.745	+ 0.006	......
6.0	5	16 32 31.77	31.75	+ 1.410	+ 0.006	......
5.8	6	16 32 34.27	34.15	+ 1.409	+ 0.006	......
7.8	7	16 32 34.82	...	+ 1.409	+ 0.006	......
6.9	7	16 32 48.80	48.61	+ 2.032	+ 0.003	......
7.1	5	16 33 7.33	...	+ 0.571	+ 0.020	......
7.6	5	16 33 21.95	21.31	+ 0.494	+ 0.023	......
6.9	5	16 34 19.04	...	+ 1.629	+ 0.004	......
5.7	10	16 34 29.41	29.54	− 3.512	+ 0.194	− 0.019
4.9	4	16 34 32.56	32.65	+ 1.626	+ 0.006	......
5.1	9	16 34 52.94	52.88	+ 1.201	+ 0.009	......
5.8	7	16 35 22.20	21.87	+ 0.582	+ 0.020	......
5.9	7	16 37 23.89	24.20	− 2.692	+ 0.140	......
7.4	8	16 37 32.70	...	+ 1.182	+ 0.008	......
3.5	11	16 37 35.10	34.69	+ 2.049	+ 0.003	......
6.8	6	16 38 22.23	...	+ 1.565	+ 0.004	......
6.0	6	16 39 48.61	48.23	+ 1.209	+ 0.006	......
5.4	4	16 39 51.53	51.22	+ 0.391	+ 0.023	......
7.5	10	16 40 23.99	23.82	− 2.842	+ 0.140	......
7.2	6	16 40 31.15	...	+ 1.046	+ 0.004	......

Ordinal Number. R.	Mean North Polar Distance 1845.0. R.	G.	Precession 1845.0.	Secular Variation.	Adopted Proper Motion.	Observations of N.P.D. No. R.	Mean year. R.	G.	Names.	Oeltzen-Argelander Number.
	° ′ ″	″	″	″	″		1800 +			
3566	38 15 4.4	3.7	+ 8.09	− 0.22	...	4	46.5	10.5	....	16251
3567	37 54 27.7	26.2	+ 8.09	− 0.21	...	4	47.5	10.5	....	16252
3568	40 41 57.6	56.1	+ 8.01	− 0.22	...	5	45.9	9.5	34 Herculis ...	......
3569	41 41 56.8	45.9	+ 8.00	− 0.25	...	4	46.5	11.5	....	16272
3570	117 53 17.2	...	+ 7.98	− 0.50	+ 0.02	1	48.5	...	23 Scorpii τ...	......
3571	29 1 29.8	...	+ 7.92	− 0.12	...	4	49.0	...	....	......
3572	18 16 15.5	15.5	+ 7.91	+ 0.07	...	3	44.8	12.5	....	16290
3573	49 33 23.6	...	+ 7.89	− 0.27	...	5	51.9	...	....	......
3574	51 35 7.8	11.6	+ 7.81	− 0.30	...	4	46.8	10.5	....	......
3575	20 53 48.3	47.9	+ 7.81	+ 0.01	− 0.04	5	45.7	7.5	15 Draconis A	16306
3576	10 45 53.3	52.3	+ 7.77	+ 0.46	...	4	47.0	12.5	....	......
3577	39 31 45.7	46.0	+ 7.77	− 0.21	...	4	45.3	9.9	....	16315
3578	47 14 24.5	24.4	+ 7.74	− 0.28	− 0.05	5	43.0	7.5	35 Herculis σ.	......
3579	37 26 20.9	21.0	+ 7.66	− 0.20	...	5	46.9	10.4	....	16340
3580	28 51 3.0	1.4	+ 7.65	− 0.13	...	5	44.9	10.5	....	16341
3581	43 4 13.2	13.8	+ 7.54	− 0.24	...	6	47.8	10.5	....	16359
3582	36 47 11.6	11.4	+ 7.47	− 0.19	− 0.02	6	45.7	8.5	16 Draconis...	16375
3583	36 45 44.5	43.5	+ 7.47	− 0.18	...	5	47.1	8.5	17 Draconis (1)	16377
3584	36 45 45.3	...	+ 7.47	− 0.18	...	4	47.0	...	17 Draconis (2)	......
3585	50 6 31.9	30.4	+ 7.45	− 0.27	...	5	48.1	11.5	....	......
3586	26 25 39.4	...	+ 7.42	− 0.10	...	4	47.0	...	....	16387
3587	25 44 56.4	54.9	+ 7.40	− 0.08	...	4	46.5	10.4	....	16400
3588	40 49 43.5	...	+ 7.32	− 0.22	...	5	47.1	...	....	......
3589	10 42 39.2	44.0	+ 7.31	+ 0.48	...	6	46.8	12.5	....	16420
3590	40 45 57.0	59.5	+ 7.30	− 0.24	...	6	47.5	8.5	42 Herculis ...	......
3591	33 40 46.2	50.1	+ 7.28	− 0.16	...	5	46.1	10.5	....	......
3592	26 36 53.1	50.2	+ 7.24	− 0.08	...	6	45.5	10.4	....	......
3593	12 14 58.1	66.8	+ 7.07	+ 0.36	...	5	45.9	10.5	....	16451
3594	33 32 0.4	...	+ 7.06	− 0.16	...	6	48.9	...	....	......
3595	50 46 47.5	47.1	+ 7.06	− 0.28	+ 0.07	5	44.7	6.3	44 Herculis η.	......
3596	39 45 55.5	...	+ 6.99	− 0.21	...	5	49.3	...	....	16461
3597	34 1 23.4	26.7	+ 6.87	− 0.19	...	6	46.2	8.5	....	......
3598	25 6 58.4	59.7	+ 6.87	− 0.06	...	7	45.1	8.5	18 Draconis y.	16485
3599	12 0 25.6	25.8	+ 6.83	+ 0.40	...	7	47.1	10.5	....	16491
3600	39 50 54.9	...	+ 6.82	− 0.21	...	4	47.5	...	....	......

Ordinal Number.		Magnitude.	Estimates of Magnitude.	Mean Right Ascension 1845.0.		Precession 1845.0.	Secular Variation	Adopted Proper Motion.	Observations of R.A.		
R.	G.	R.		R.	G.				No. R.	Mean year. R.	G.
				h. m. s.	s.	s.	s.	s.		1800 +	
3601	2379	8.0	9	16 41 32.81	32.25	− 2.832	+ 0.143	......	3	46.2	10.5
3602	2377	5.0	3	16 42 21.81	21.32	+ 1.124	+ 0.009	......	5	44.6	8.5
3603	2376	6.1	5	16 42 22.41	22.30	+ 1.914	+ 0.002	......	6	47.0	10.5
3604	...	7.1	6	16 42 26.59	...	+ 1.229	+ 0.007	......	3	47.2	...
3605	2382	6.9	10	16 42 31.20	30.31	− 2.891	+ 0.143	......	6	46.9	10.5
3606	...	7.0	8	16 43 17.53	...	− 1.049	+ 0.065	......	4	51.7	...
3607	...	7.9	7	16 43 25.36	...	+ 1.912	+ 0.002	......	4	50.7	...
3608	...	7.1	6	16 43 40.92	...	+ 1.219	+ 0.007	+ 0.035	4	46.6	...
3609	2380	5.1	4	16 44 42.11	42.02	+ 1.748	+ 0.006	......	4	45.0	8.6
3610	...	7.4	2	16 44 50.29	...	+ 3.676	+ 0.010	......	1	54.6	...
3611	2381	6.2	8	16 44 51.59	51.72	+ 1.860	+ 0.003	......	5	45.6	10.6
3612	2384	6.9	4	16 45 14.60	14.25	+ 1.062	+ 0.009	......	4	46.4	12.5
3613	2388	6.7	7	16 45 25.45	26.16	− 1.397	+ 0.071	......	4	47.1	11.4
3614	2386	7.3	5	16 45 32.95	32.61	+ 0.510	+ 0.017	......	4	47.6	13.5
3615	...	7.3	7	16 45 34.70	...	+ 1.036	+ 0.009	......	4	46.1	...
3616	2383	6.3	5	16 45 38.40	38.61	+ 1.922	0.000	......	6	47.7	10.5
3617	2387	6.3	6	16 45 58.53	58.51	+ 0.494	+ 0.020	......	4	45.3	13.5
3618	2385	7.7	7	16 46 11.32	11.17	+ 1.914	+ 0.003	......	4	48.8	10.5
3619	...	9.0	6	16 46 31.48	...	+ 0.893	+ 0.011	......	4	53.8	...
3620	...	7.6	2	16 46 32.50	...	+ 0.893	+ 0.011	......	2	52.0	...
3621	...	8.2	8	16 46 36.47	...	− 2.977	+ 0.148	......	4	52.1	...
3622	...	8.0	5	16 47 50.85	...	+ 1.143	+ 0.007	......	4	47.3	...
3623	...	7.6	6	16 48 15.43	...	+ 1.813	+ 0.003	......	3	51.8	...
3624	2389	7.0	6	16 48 38.71	38.16	+ 1.880	+ 0.006	......	4	46.0	10.5
3625	...	7.1	7	16 49 52.34	...	+ 1.713	+ 0.003	+ 0.016	3	47.2	...
3626	2391	6.0	10	16 50 4.99	3.40	− 2.817	+ 0.120	......	5	45.6	12.5
3627	...	8.0	5	16 50 32.32	...	+ 1.724	+ 0.003	......	2	48.5	...
3628	...	10.0	1	16 50 34.20	...	+ 3.364	+ 0.008	......	1	56.4	...
3629	...	Var.	7	16 50 49.00	...	+ 3.356	+ 0.008	......	4	48.5	...
3630	...	7.0	8	16 51 45.36	...	+ 1.669	+ 0.003	......	4	50.5	...
3631	2390	6.7	5	16 51 55.63	55.24	+ 0.800	+ 0.014	......	5	44.5	8.5
3632	2392	6.3	8	16 52 57.25	57.18	+ 1.887	+ 0.006	......	5	46.4	10.5
3633	2393	7.1	5	16 53 14.14	15.70	+ 0.626	+ 0.017	......	5	45.1	10.6
3634	...	3.7	9	16 54 21.69	...	+ 2.294	+ 0.001	− 0.005	31	48.8	...
3635	2398	7.7	7	16 54 23.44	22.81	− 1.935	+ 0.083	......	5	46.3	10.5

Ordinal Number.	Mean North Polar Distance 1845.0.			Precession 1845.0.	Secular Variation.	Adopted Proper Motion.	Observations of N.P.D.				Names.	Oeltzen-Argelander Number.
R.	R.		G.				No. R.	Mean year.				
								R.	R.	G.		
	° ′ ″		″	″	″	″		1800 +				
3601	12 2 36.7		35.3	+ 6.73	+ 0.38	...	7	47.9	10.5		....	16503
3602	32 56 21.8		24.0	+ 6.66	− 0.17	...	5	45.5	8.5		....	16514
3603	47 28 54.4		54.5	+ 6.66	− 0.28	...	4	45.5	10.5		....	......
3604	34 24 12.7		...	+ 6.66	− 0.17	...	3	46.9	...		....	16517
3605	11 56 46.0		42.4	+ 6.65	+ 0.39	...	6	46.5	10.5		....	16526
3606	17 2 26.0		...	+ 6.59	+ 0.15	...	5	51.9	...		....	16536
3607	47 29 31.1		...	+ 6.58	− 0.26	...	4	49.0	...		....	......
3608	34 18 48.8		...	+ 6.55	− 0.17	+ 0.03	5	50.3	...		....	16538
3609	43 44 38.3		37.0	+ 6.47	− 0.25	...	6	45.3	8.6		52 Herculis ...	16549
3610	115 33 59.9		...	+ 6.46	− 0.51	...	3	52.5	...		....	......
3611	46 17 59.5		60.5	+ 6.46	− 0.26	...	5	46.5	10.6		....	......
3612	32 14 19.2		16.6	+ 6.43	− 0.14	...	4	45.0	12.5		....	......
3613	15 49 58.0		56.8	+ 6.41	+ 0.19	...	4	45.8	11.4		....	16565
3614	26 20 30.6		31.8	+ 6.40	− 0.08	...	5	47.5	13.5		....	16567
3615	31 54 57.2		...	+ 6.40	− 0.14	...	4	43.0	...		....	......
3616	47 50 23.4		27.2	+ 6.39	− 0.28	...	4	44.4	10.5		....	......
3617	26 11 59.1		61.7	+ 6.36	− 0.09	...	4	45.3	13.5		....	16570
3618	47 39 27.4		29.3	+ 6.35	− 0.26	...	4	45.5	10.5		....	......
3619	30 12 59.1		...	+ 6.32	− 0.12	...	2	52.0	...		....	......
3620	30 13 46.6		...	+ 6.32	− 0.12	...	2	52.1	...		....	......
3621	11 50 59.2		...	+ 6.31	+ 0.42	...	4	47.0	...		....	......
3622	33 24 29.4		...	+ 6.21	− 0.16	...	3	48.5	...		....	......
3623	45 20 35.3		...	+ 6.17	− 0.25	...	4	52.0	...		....	......
3624	46 54 19.8		9.0	+ 6.14	− 0.27	...	5	45.1	10.5		....	......
3625	43 12 27.4		...	+ 6.04	− 0.24	+ 0.03	5	49.1	...		....	16627
3626	12 13 23.8		30.3	+ 6.02	+ 0.38	...	6	46.5	12.5		....	......
3627	43 28 30.9		...	+ 5.98	− 0.24	...	4	49.8	...		....	......
3628	102 57 20.7		...	+ 5.97	− 0.48	...	1	51.5	...		....	......
3629	102 38 59.9		...	+ 5.96	− 0.48	...	5	48.9	...		....	......
3630	42 23 8.5		...	+ 5.88	− 0.24	...	5	50.1	...		....	16649
3631	29 23 18.4		18.1	+ 5.87	− 0.11	...	5	45.9	8.5		....	16656
3632	47 14 43.1		40.6	+ 5.78	− 0.27	...	5	45.1	10.5		....	......
3633	27 39 10.9		9.6	+ 5.76	− 0.09	...	6	46.5	10.5		....	......
3634	58 50 28.7		...	+ 5.66	− 0.32	− 0.04	3	53.5	..		58 Herculis ε .	......
3635	14 22 14.2		13.6	+ 5.66	− 0.26	...	5	46.9	10.5		....	16697

Mean Right Ascension 1845.0.		Precession 1845.0.	Secular Variation	Adopted Proper Motion.	Observations of R.A.		
					No.	Mean year.	
R.	G.				R.	R.	G.
h. m. s.	s.	s.	s.	s.		1800 +	
16 54 48.33	48.52	+ 0.593	+ 0.014	......	5	46.5	10.6
16 54 52.67	52.54	+ 2.018	0.000	......	4	47.0	10.5
16 55 8.81	8.67	− 1.280	+ 0.057	......	2	46.0	11.6
16 55 11.39	11.08	+ 0.270	+ 0.020	+ 0.033	5	45.1	8.5
16 55 40.10	39.48	+ 0.280	+ 0.020	......	5	45.1	9.5
16 55 53.46	53.11	− 0.065	+ 0.029	......	3	44.8	13.5
16 55 56.89	57.10	− 0.600	+ 0.040	......	3	45.6	10.6
16 56 31.31	31.41	+ 1.097	+ 0.011	......	3	44.2	8.5
16 56 43.19	43.39	− 1.179	+ 0.049	......	4	46.5	11.4
16 56 56.43	56.39	− 0.060	+ 0.026	......	2	48.5	13.5
16 57 34.82	34.13	− 1.583	+ 0.063	......	3	44.3	12.4
16 57 47.68	46.92	− 1.958	+ 0.077	......	5	46.1	10.5
16 58 56.39	55.09	− 1.682	+ 0.066	......	2	50.6	12.5
16 59 1.90	1.25	− 0.327	+ 0.031	......	4	49.5	13.5
16 59 5.26	4.15	− 1.650	+ 0.063	......	6	47.0	12.5
16 59 23.64	23.79	− 1.247	+ 0.057	......	5	46.6	11.5
16 59 55.52	55.26	− 0.368	+ 0.029	......	4	47.1	13.5
17 0 15.49	14.48	− 1.594	+ 0.060	......	5	48.2	12.5
17 0 21.88	21.76	+ 1.822	+ 0.006	......	4	47.5	10.5
17 0 28.98	...	+ 1.327	+ 0.005	......	3	51.8	...
17 0 43.23	...	+ 1.582	+ 0.003	......	3	47.5	...
17 0 45.23	...	+ 1.675	+ 0.003	......	4	53.0	...
17 1 14.01	...	+ 3.305	+ 0.005	......	5	50.1	...
17 1 29.64	...	+ 3.429	+ 0.006	......	8	48.9	...
17 2 3.53	2.95	− 6.482	+ 0.294	+ 0.009	19	42.1	7.0
17 2 7.60	7.41	+ 1.243	+ 0.006	− 0.011	5	45.6	8.1
17 2 7.68	...	+ 1.243	+ 0.006	......	3	46.9	...
17 2 19.60	19.33	+ 0.696	+ 0.017	......	3	44.3	13.5
17 2 43.56	43.59	+ 1.955	0.000	......	5	44.0	8.5
17 3 37.18	36.27	− 2.966	+ 0.103	......	4	48.0	12.5
17 3 40.44	40.33	− 1.282	+ 0.051	......	5	47.9	10.8
17 4 29.18	...	+ 1.465	+ 0.003	+ 0.007	3	48.9	...
17 4 35.55	35.33	+ 0.679	+ 0.014	......	4	45.0	13.5
17 4 36.29	36.07	− 1.319	+ 0.051	......	5	46.4	10.8
17 4 40.33	...	+ 0.955	+ 0.007	+ 0.019	2	47.0	...

Ordinal Number. R.	Mean North Polar Distance 1845.0.		Precession 1845.0.	Secular Variation.	Adopted Proper Motion.	Observations of N.P.D.			Names.	Oeltzen Argelander Number.
	R.	G.				No. R.	Mean year. R.	G.		
	° ′ ″	″	″	″	″		1800 +			
3636	27 23 29.4	29.2	+ 5.63	− 0.08	...	5	45.3	10.6	....	......
3637	50 40 19.2	23.1	+ 5.62	− 0.29	...	3	44.8	10.5	....	......
3638	16 26 42.1	39.1	+ 5.60	+ 0.18	...	5	49.9	11.6	....	......
3639	24 37 41.0	41.9	+ 5.60	− 0.03	− 0.03	9	42.7	8.5	19 Draconis h^1	......
3640	24 43 28.7	28.8	+ 5.55	− 0.06	...	4	43.0	9.5	20 Draconis h^2	......
3641	22 17 0.8	59.6	+ 5.54	+ 0.01	...	4	46.0	13.5	....	......
3642	19 17 38.3	34.0	+ 5.53	+ 0.08	...	5	48.1	10.6	....	16720
3643	33 4 55.4	56.8	+ 5.48	− 0.17	...	5	45.9	8.5	....	16723
3644	16 50 27.2	27.4	+ 5.47	+ 0.17	...	5	47.5	11.4	....	......
3645	22 20 32.5	36.0	+ 5.45	+ 0.01	...	3	46.2	13.5	....	......
3646	15 28 9.9	9.4	+ 5.39	+ 0.21	...	4	45.8	12.4	....	......
3647	14 22 1.7	58.7 ·	+ 5.36	+ 0.22	...	4	45.5	10.5	....	......
3648	15 10 59.7	60.7	+ 5.28	+ 0.23	...	4	49.8	12.5	....	......
3649	20 47 28.2	26.1	+ 5.27	+ 0.03	...	3	48.2	13.5	....	16766
3650	15 17 21.5	19.6	+ 5.27	+ 0.23	...	6	46.9	12.5	....	......
3651	16 38 24.0	23.5	+ 5.24	+ 0.17	...	4	47.0	11.5	....	16775
3652	20 35 13.6	10.2	+ 5.20	+ 0.06	...	5	45.5	13.5	....	16782
3653	15 29 3.1	0.0	+ 5.17	+ 0.22	...	4	44.6	12.5	....	......
3654	45 58 26.5	27.9	+ 5.16	− 0.26	...	4	45.0	10.5	....	......
3655	36 33 17.6	·...	+ 5.15	− 0.18	...	3	52.2	...	....	16790
3656	40 58 47.9	...	+ 5.13	− 0.22	+ 0.19	4	48.0	...	....	16794
3657	42 49 10.6	...	+ 5.11	− 0.23	...	4	52.0	...	....	16796
3658	100 18 56.1	...	+ 5.09	− 0.46	...	2	48.5	...	....	......
3659	105 31 38.1	...	+ 5.06	− 0.48	− 0.12	4	50.5	...	35 Ophiuchi η	......
3660	7 43 2.7	3.2	+ 5.02	+ 0.93	...	24	43.2	7.0	22 Urs. Min. ϵ	......
3661	35 19 26.8	28.0	+ 5.01	− 0.18	...	4	48.6	8.1	21 Drac. μ (1)	......
3662	35 19 23.8	...	+ 5.01	− 0.18	...	6	45.9	...	21 Drac. μ (2)	......
3663	28 36 20.0	21.0	+ 4.99	− 0.11	...	5	46.7	13.5	....	16821
3664	49 16 40.7	41.7	+ 4.96	− 0.28	...	7	46.9	8.5	....	......
3665	12 7 26.9	28.3	+ 4.88	+ 0.41	...	5	46.3	12.5	....	16849
3666	16 35 24.6	24.5	+ 4.88	+ 0.18	...	4	42.3	10.5	....	16848
3667	38 57 30.4	...	+ 4.81	− 0.21	− 0.04	4	48.0	...	....	16862
3668	28 29 30.8	33.2	+ 4.80	− 0.10	...	3	46.2	13.5	....	16867
3669	16 28 32.8	31.7	+ 4.80	+ 0.19	...	4	44.5	10.3	....	16869
3670	31 31 37.8	...	+ 4.79	− 0.13	+ 0.10	3	47.2	...	....	......

Magnitude.	Estimates of Magnitude.	Mean Right Ascension 1845.0.		Precession 1845.0	Secular Variation	Adopted Proper Motion.
R.	R.	R.	G.			
		h. m. s.	s.	s.	s.	s.
6.6	6	17 4 49.36	...	+ 1.147	+ 0.006	− 0.003
7.1	5	17 5 16.76	16.00	− 1.931	+ 0.066	......
...	...	17 5 49.65	...	+ 3.716	+ 0.008	− 0.037
6.8	7	17 6 19.53	19.24	+ 0.690	+ 0.014	......
6.2	7	17 6 35.34	35.17	− 1.963	+ 0.066	......
7.0	2	17 6 42.09	...	+ 3.713	+ 0.008	− 0.036
6.7	6	17 6 54.78	54.72	+ 1.902	+ 0.003	......
6.4	6	17 7 8.64	...	+ 1.745	+ 0.002	......
3.0	1	17 7 34.93	...	+ 2.732	+ 0.001	− 0.003
7.2	5	17 7 40.29	40.12	+ 1.816	+ 0.003	......
8.1	7	17 7 59.87	60.40	− 2.965	+ 0.100	......
6.9	6	17 8 15.18	15.14	+ 2.008	0.000	......
3.0	6	17 8 21.04	20.58	+ 0.156	+ 0.017	......
7.4	5	17 8 57.23	...	+ 1.741	+ 0.002	......
8.0	21	17 9 15.03	...	−11.560	+ 0.635	......
7.6	4	17 9 58.05	...	+ 1.748	+ 0.002	......
7.7	6	17 11 12.16	...	+ 0.447	+ 0.013	......
5.7	9	17 11 12.95	12.43	+ 0.500	+ 0.014	+ 0.007
7.7	5	17 11 13.91	...	+ 1.110	+ 0.006	......
5.0	2	17 11 43.23	...	+ 3.570	+ 0.006	+ 0.017
5.6	2	17 12 29.75	...	+ 3.675	+ 0.007	− 0.003
7.3	5	17 12 52.07	...	+ 1.518	+ 0.003	+ 0.026
6.0	9	17 13 11.17	11.08	+ 2.011	+ 0.003	......
7.0	6	17 13 23.82	...	+ 0.441	+ 0.013	......
6.8	7	17 14 12.04	11.86	+ 0.717	+ 0.009	......
6.3	8	17 14 37.09	37.17	+ 0.721	+ 0.011	......
7.0	3	17 14 56.65	...	+ 2.152	0.000	......
6.8	6	17 15 21.41	...	+ 1.738	+ 0.002	......
5.5	3	17 15 58.54	58.64	+ 1.692	+ 0.003	......
5.5	7	17 16 38.72	38.36	+ 1.963	+ 0.003	......
5.5	1	17 16 54.64	...	+ 3.656	+ 0.006	......
7.2	6	17 17 52.39	...	+ 0.390	+ 0.013	......
9.0	6	17 18 15.27	...	+ 0.364	+ 0.013	......
6.7	4	17 18 38.88	38.35	− 0.966	+ 0.034	......
6.8	6	17 18 49.43	49.36	+ 2.016	+ 0.006	......

Ordinal Number. R.	Mean North Polar Distance 1845.0.			Precession 1845.0.	Secular Variation.	Adopted Proper Motion.	Observations of N.P.D.			Names.	Oeltzen-Argelander Number.
	R.		G.				No. R.	Mean year. R.	G.		
	o ′ ″		″	″	″	″		1800 +			
3671	34 2 0.2		...	+ 4.78	— 0.16	+ 0.03	3	47.6	...	....	16873
3672	14 33 37.1		34.4	+ 4.74	+ 0.26	...	3	44.9	10.6	....	16885
3673	116 22 2.8		...	+ 4.66	— 0.53	+ 1.12	2	53.5	...	36 Ophiuc. A (2)	......
3674	28 38 46.1		47.6	+ 4.65	— 0.11	...	3	45.9	13.5	....	16896
3675	14 29 29.7		25.9	+ 4.63	+ 0.27	...	5	46.1	10.6	....	16900
3676	116 18 57.6		...	+ 4.62	— 0.53	+ 1.15	1	58.5	...	30 Scorpii	......
3677	48 4 51.0		50.0	+ 4.60	— 0.28	...	3	44.2	10.5	....	......
3678	44 29 9.4		...	+ 4.58	— 0.25	...	4	52.0	...	....	......
3679	75 25 43.7		...	+ 4.55	— 0.39	— 0.04	1	47.6	...	64 Herculis a.	......
3680	46 5 0.8		8.8	+ 4.54	— 0.26	...	5	47.9	10.5	....	......
3681	12 10 41.7		41.3	+ 4.51	+ 0.42	...	5	47.5	12.5	....	16918
3682	50 49 50.3		50.0	+ 4.49	— 0.29	...	4	46.5	11.5	....	......
3683	24 5 39.4		40.7	+ 4.48	— 0.03	...	4	43.3	6.8	22 Draconis ζ.	16923
3684	44 26 42.1		...	+ 4.43	— 0.25	...	4	50.5	...	....	......
3685	5 5 37.6		...	+ 4.40	+ 1.65	...	7	52.3	...	....	......
3686	44 38 2.8		...	+ 4.34	— 0.25	...	3	49.9	...	....	......
3687	26 28 27.8		...	+ 4.24	— 0.06	...	4	46.8	...	....	16974
3688	26 56 53.5		55.0	+ 4.24	— 0.07	...	14	46.9	9.6	....	16975
3689	33 41 23.3		...	+ 4.23	— 0.15	...	4	52.0	...	....	......
3690	110 56 25.8		...	+ 4.19	— 0.51	+ 0.21	4	51.5	...	40 Ophiuchi ξ	......
3691	114 50 18.5		...	+ 4.13	— 0.52	— 0.02	3	50.8	...	42 Ophiuchi θ	......
3692	40 8 24.6		...	+ 4.10	— 0.22	+ 0.21	3	46.5	...	....	16995
3693	51 1 35.4		37.6	+ 4.07	— 0.29	...	4	47.8	10.5	....	......
3694	26 28 26.6		...	+ 4.05	— 0.06	...	4	49.6	...	....	17002
3695	29 7 11.5		13.4	+ 3.98	— 0.11	...	5	46.3	10.5	....	17011
3696	29 9 49.6		49.4	+ 3.95	— 0.09	...	6	46.5	10.5	....	17020
3697	54 28 13.3		...	+ 3.91	— 0.31	...	1	53.6	...	....	......
3698	44 32 10.5		...	+ 3.88	— 0.25	...	4	51.6	...	....	......
3699	43 36 15.8		17.9	+ 3.83	— 0.24	...	4	42.6	8.5	74 Herculis ...	17041
3700	49 52 11.6		8.2	+ 3.77	— 0.29	...	4	43.5	10.5	....	......
3701	114 1 30.1		...	+ 3.75	— 0.52	+ 0.12	1	55.5	...	44 Ophiuchi b	......
3702	26 7 17.8		...	+ 3.67	— 0.06	...	3	47.5	...	....	......
3703	25 54 47.6		...	+ 3.63	— 0.06	...	4	51.0	...	....	......
3704	18 2 53.4		54.1	+ 3.60	+ 0.14	...	4	44.0	10.0	....	......
3705	51 16 28.0		29.0	+ 3.58	— 0.31	...	3	44.2	10.5	....	......

Magnitude.	Estimates of Magnitude.	Mean Right Ascension 1845.0.		Precession 1845.0.	Secular Variation	Adopted Proper Motion.
R.		R.	G.			
		h. m. s.	s.	s.	s.	s.
8.1	5	17 19 27.38	...	+ 1.992	+ 0.001	......
7.1	6	17 19 29.84	...	+ 1.991	+ 0.001	......
7.6	4	17 19 51.18	...	− 0.365	+ 0.020	......
6.4	8	17 20 41.92	...	+ 1.030	+ 0.005	+ 0.003
7.4	7	17 20 49.44	49.26	− 0.743	+ 0.023	......
7.1	9	17 21 22.02	22.24	− 0.531	+ 0.023	......
7.1	7	17 22 32.17	31.67	− 0.543	+ 0.020	......
6.1	5	17 22 37.90	37.63	+ 1.584	0.000	......
6.2	8	17 23 41.46	...	+ 0.767	+ 0.006	......
6.5	5	17 23 45.70	...	+ 0.892	+ 0.005	......
9.1	5	17 24 52.55	...	− 0.542	+ 0.019	......
6.6	10	17 25 29.69	29.66	+ 2.000	+ 0.003	......
2.6	2	17 26 56.00	55.78	+ 1.351	+ 0.003	......
7.4	6	17 27 14.43	...	− 1.797	+ 0.047	......
2.0	A	17 27 44.46	...	+ 2.772	+ 0.001	+ 0.004
7.6	7	17 27 56.69	...	+ 0.795	+ 0.005	......
6.1	8	17 28 12.35	12.50	+ 1.905	+ 0.003	......
4.8	8	17 29 7.58	7.82	+ 1.157	+ 0.003	+ 0.030
4.5	6	17 29 12.96	12.77	+ 1.158	+ 0.003	+ 0.017
6.5	7	17 30 59.37	...	+ 0.975	+ 0.004	......
7.9	6	17 31 24.86	...	− 0.360	+ 0.014	......
6.3	6	17 31 25.84	25.18	− 4.662	+ 0.091	......
8.2	7	17 32 24.48	...	− 0.324	+ 0.014	......
8.0	8	17 32 29.09	28.75	+ 1.567	+ 0.003	......
5.7	8	17 32 34.61	34.60	+ 1.560	+ 0.003	......
5.4	6	17 32 35.45	35.45	− 0.254	+ 0.014	− 0.007
7.9	6	17 32 56.10	56.19	+ 1.835	+ 0.003	......
7.1	8	17 33 23.67	23.43	+ 1.801	0.000	......
5.4	9	17 33 23.77	23.10	+ 0.573	+ 0.009	+ 0.037
7.0	7	17 33 50.57	50.25	+ 0.512	+ 0.009	......
5.0	A	17 34 8.65	...	+ 3.596	+ 0.003	− 0.010
7.0	7	17 34 54.02	54.06	+ 1.783	+ 0.003	......
8.0	5	17 35 4.97	...	+ 1.567	+ 0.002	......
4.2	5	17 35 5.44	5.32	+ 1.690	+ 0.003	......
2.5	1	17 35 49.09	...	+ 2.962	+ 0.001	− 0.005

Ordinal Number.	Mean North Polar Distance 1845.0. R.	G.	Precession 1845.0.	Secular Variation.	Adopted Proper Motion.	No. R.	Mean year. R.	Mean year. G.	Names.	Oeltzen-Argelander Number.
	° ′ ″	″	″	″	″		1800 +			
3706	50 40 21.1	...	+ 3.53	− 0.28	...	3	51.9	...	....	....
3707	50 38 54.9	...	+ 3.52	− 0.28	...	3	51.9	...	....	....
3708	20 58 14.6	...	+ 3.49	+ 0.06	...	3	48.2	...	....	17093
3709	32 50 47.1	...	+ 3.42	− 0.15	− 0.06	4	47.0	...	....	17110
3710	19 3 47.3	47.0	+ 3.41	+ 0.10	...	5	45.5	10.5	....	....
3711	20 5 55.9	55.1	+ 3.36	+ 0.06	...	6	45.9	10.5	....	17123
3712	20 3 28.6	28.7	+ 3.26	+ 0.07	...	6	46.6	10.5	....	17147
3713	41 36 26.5	27.0	+ 3.25	− 0.25	...	5	44.0	8.6	77 Herculis x.	17146
3714	29 49 14.4	...	+ 3.16	− 0.11	...	4	47.0	...	....	....
3715	31 13 2.2	...	+ 3.16	− 0.14	...	3	45.9	...	....	17161
3716	20 5 36.3	...	+ 3.06	+ 0.08	...	4	45.5	...	....	17178
3717	50 59 55.2	54.4	+ 3.01	− 0.29	...	5	47.2	11.5	....	....
3718	37 34 53.8	53.6	+ 2.88	− 0.21	...	7	43.7	6.8	23 Draconis β	....
3719	15 12 28.8	...	+ 2.86	+ 0.26	...	5	51.9	...	....	....
3720	77 19 20.5	...	+ 2.81	− 0.40	+ 0.20	17	52.4	...	55 Ophiuchi a	....
3721	30 11 34.2	...	+ 2.80	− 0.11	...	3	47.6	...	....	17236
3722	48 38 37.1	34.7	+ 2.77	− 0.29	...	6	46.3	12.5	....	....
3723	34 42 29.4	29.9	+ 2.69	− 0.18	...	6	44.9	7.5	24 Draconis ν^1	17258
3724	34 43 11.3	11.6	+ 2.69	− 0.16	...	4	43.9	7.5	25 Draconis ν^2	17260
3725	32 20 14.5	...	+ 2.53	− 0.14	...	4	43.5	...	....	17297
3726	21 8 31.8	...	+ 2.49	+ 0.05	...	3	48.9	...	....	17303
3727	9 44 4.2	3.3	+ 2.49	+ 0.66	...	3	45.5	7.6	....	17306
3728	21 21 17.2	...	+ 2.41	+ 0.05	...	4	46.1	...	....	17321
3729	41 26 24.8	21.5	+ 2.40	− 0.24	...	5	45.4	10.5	....	17320
3730	41 19 18.6	20.0	+ 2.39	− 0.24	− 0.03	12	49.4	10.5	82 Herculis y.	17323
3731	21 46 0.4	0.9	+ 2.39	+ 0.03	− 0.11	7	47.1	9.6	27 Draconis f.	17329
3732	47 4 25.4	25.7	+ 2.36	− 0.28	...	5	46.7	11.5	....	....
3733	46 18 33.9	32.2	+ 2.32	− 0.27	...	4	43.0	10.6	....	....
3734	28 0 23.8	16.4	+ 2.32	− 0.10	+ 0.36	6	47.5	9.6	26 Draconis ...	....
3735	27 26 33.3	33.1	+ 2.28	− 0.09	...	4	45.8	10.0	....	....
3736	111 36 6.5	...	+ 2.26	− 0.52	− 0.04	3	52.2	...	58 Ophiuchi ...	....
3737	45 54 51.6	54.5	+ 2.19	− 0.27	...	3	44.9	10.6	....	....
3738	41 28 16.2	...	+ 2.18	− 0.23	...	4	47.1	...	....	17369
3739	43 54 31.0	30.3	+ 2.18	− 0.23	...	5	45.2	7.6	85 Herculis ι..	17370
3740	85 21 46.1	...	+ 2.11	− 0.43	− 0.17	8	53.3	...	69 Ophiuchi β	....

Ordinal Number.		Magnitude.	Estimates of Magnitude.	Mean Right Ascension 1845.0.			Precession 1845.0.	Secular Variation	Adopted Proper Motion.	Observations of R.A.		
R.	G.	R.	R.	R.	G.					No. R.	Mean year. R.	G.
				h. m. s.	s.		s.	s.	s.		1800 +	
3741	2457	6.2	7	17 35 56.29	55.82		+ 1.806	+ 0.003	......	5	43.6	10.5
3742	2458	6.9	9	17 36 21.37	21.25		+ 1.883	0.000	......	6	47.5	11.5
3743	2460	7.4	6	17 36 58.77	58.14		− 1.667	+ 0.031	......	5	46.6	9.6
3744	...	7.3	8	17 37 18.11	...		− 0.320	+ 0.010	......	4	47.9	...
3745	...	8.0	8	17 37 26.75	...		− 0.301	+ 0.010	......	5	48.7	...
3746	...	5.7	2	17 37 48.34	...		+ 3.771	+ 0.003	− 0.010	1	42.5	...
3747	2461	4.9	10	17 37 51.87	51.37		− 0.366	+ 0.009	+ 0.003	5	45.4	6.7
3748	2459	6.2	7	17 38 30.00	29.99		+ 1.778	+ 0.003	......	5	45.5	10.5
3749	...	7.3	22	17 38 56.08	...		−11.368	+ 0.258	......	18	53.2	...
3750	...	8.6	17	17 39 27.86	...		−108.029	+15.871	......	10	53.3	...
3751	...	7.5	5	17 39 30.69	...		− 1.060	+ 0.018	......	3	51.9	...
3752	...	8.5	7	17 39 31.40	...		+ 1.778	+ 0.001	......	4	49.1	...
3753	2462	8.2	4	17 39 42.13	42.03		+ 1.947	0.000	......	3	44.2	11.6
3754	2463	8.1	7	17 40 0.41	0.55		+ 1.989	0.000	......	4	48.0	10.6
3755	...	8.2	7	17 40 6.12	...		− 9.227	+ 0.169	......	5	51.7	...
3756	...	8.1	6	17 40 19.13	...		+ 1.975	0.000	......	3	44.9	...
3757	2476	7.6	6	17 40 23.70	21.15		− 8.526	+ 0.126	......	5	48.4	7.6
3758	2464	6.5	5	17 40 44.14	44.15		+ 1.994	+ 0.003	......	4	45.8	10.6
3759	2465	6.7	9	17 40 51.49	51.32		+ 1.976	0.000	......	5	47.4	10.5
3760	2466	7.7	7	17 42 55.89	55.96		+ 1.950	0.000	......	5	44.7	11.5
3761	2467	7.0	10	17 42 58.65	58.51		+ 1.607	+ 0.003	......	6	46.6	12.5
3762	2468	8.5	5	17 43 21.30	20.92		+ 1.955	+ 0.003	......	3	46.2	11.5
3763	2469	7.8	5	17 43 26.18	26.06		+ 1.775	+ 0.003	......	4	47.0	10.6
3764	2470	7.0	7	17 43 49.57	49.42		+ 1.608	+ 0.003	......	5	46.5	12.5
3765	...	7.2	3	17 44 7.17	...		− 1.154	+ 0.018	......	3	48.6	...
3766	...	6.6	3	17 44 26.96	...		+ 3.327	+ 0.001	− 0.003	3	52.9	...
3767	...	8.2	3	17 44 37.78	...		+ 3.327	+ 0.001	......	3	52.9	...
3768	2475	4.9	6	17 44 42.35	42.07		− 1.090	+ 0.017	......	5	45.5	7.6
3769	2477	6.4	10	17 44 44.08	43.70		− 1.092	+ 0.020	......	8	49.7	7.6
3770	2471	7.8	5	17 45 8.45	8.52		+ 1.869	+ 0.003	......	4	48.1	12.6
3771	2472	5.3	4	17 45 22.30	22.04		+ 1.433	+ 0.003	......	5	45.0	9.6
3772	2474	6.9	6	17 46 0.05	0.08		+ 1.565	+ 0.003	......	4	43.2	10.8
3773	2473	6.2	5	17 46 12.24	12.15		+ 1.945	0.000	......	5	45.4	10.5
3774	...	7.6	2	17 46 43.95	...		+ 3.743	+ 0.002	......	2	55.5	...
3775	2478	8.3	7	17 46 44.17	44.21		+ 1.565	+ 0.003	......	4	47.4	11.5

Ordinal Number. R.	Mean North Polar Distance 1845.0.		Preces- sion 1845.0.	Secular Variation.	Adopted Proper Motion.	Observations of N.P.D.			Names.	Oeltzen- Argelander Number.
	R.	G.				No. R.	Mean year. R.	G.		
	o ′ ″	″	″	″	″		1800 +			
3741	46 26 59.5	63.2	+ 2.10	− 0.27	...	6	46.3	10.5	....	....
3742	48 15 55.9	57.8	+ 2.07	− 0.26	...	5	47.3	11.5	....	....
3743	15 40 49.1	49.0	+ 2.01	+ 0.24	...	4	44.0	9.6	29 Draconis ...	....
3744	21 25 26.0	...	+ 1.98	+ 0.05	...	4	46.6	...	....	17413
3745	21 32 4.4	...	+ 1.97	+ 0.05	...	3	45.9	...	....	17419
3746	117 45 55.4	...	+ 1.94	− 0.55	+ 0.02	1	53.5	...	3 Sagittarii	....
3747	21 10 17.4	16.6	+ 1.93	+ 0.04	− 0.31	19	46.9	6.7	28 Draconis ω	17426
3748	45 50 41.5	43.8	+ 1.88	− 0.25	...	5	46.7	10.5	....	....
3749	5 16 2.8	...	+ 1.84	+ 1.65	...	6	51.2	...	....	....
3750	0 41 12.2	...	+ 1.79	+15.70	...	8	52.6	...	....	....
3751	17 51 49.2	...	+ 1.79	+ 0.16	...	4	52.1	...	....	....
3752	45 51 3.4	...	+ 1.79	− 0.26	...	3	47.9	...	....	....
3753	49 52 25.1	23.7	+ 1.77	− 0.29	...	3	45.6	11.6	....	....
3754	50 56 30.2	30.9	+ 1.75	− 0.28	...	4	49.6	10.6	....	....
3755	6 10 55.6	...	+ 1.74	+ 1.34	...	5	51.4	...	....	....
3756	50 34 24.8	...	+ 1.72	− 0.29	...	3	48.2	...	....	....
3757	6 33 11.5	16.5	+ 1.71	+ 1.22	...	5	47.0	7.6	....	....
3758	51 3 15.9	15.7	+ 1.68	− 0.30	...	3	45.3	10.6	....	....
3759	50 36 55.2	57.5	+ 1.67	− 0.30	...	4	49.3	10.5	....	....
3760	49 58 11.8	16.2	+ 1.49	− 0.29	...	5	47.1	11.5	....	....
3761	42 19 54.7	54.8	+ 1.49	− 0.23	...	5	45.5	12.5	....	17509
3762	50 5 34.4	33.5	+ 1.45	− 0.30	...	3	43.3	11.5	....	....
3763	45 50 25.5	27.8	+ 1.45	− 0.25	...	5	48.5	10.6	....	....
3764	42 21 42.8	42.8	+ 1.41	− 0.25	...	4	46.0	12.5	....	17522
3765	17 31 39.1	...	+ 1.39	+ 0.16	...	3	45.3	...	....	17531?
3766	100 51 20.5	...	+ 1.36	− 0.48	+ 0.18	1	52.6	...	....	....
3767	100 19 40.6	...	+ 1.34	− 0.48	...	1	52.6	...	....	....
3768	17 46 37.8	38.1	+ 1.34	+ 0.16	+ 0.28	11	48.2	7.6	31 Drac. ψ¹ (1)	17540
3769	17 46 8.2	7.1	+ 1.33	+ 0.14	+ 0.26	4	47.6	7.6	31 Drac. ψ¹ (2)	17543
3770	47 59 46.4	46.6	+ 1.30	− 0.26	...	6	44.8	12.6	....	....
3771	39 10 46.3	49.4	+ 1.28	− 0.21	− 0.19	6	46.6	9.6	30 Draconis ...	....
3772	41 33 41.2	41.5	+ 1.22	− 0.24	...	8	48.4	10.8	88 Herculis z .	....
3773	49 53 8.1	8.2	+ 1.21	− 0.27	...	4	42.8	10.5	....	....
3774	116 44 18.9	...	+ 1.16	− 0.54	...	2	52.5	...	....	....
3775	41 33 38.4	40.1	+ 1.16	− 0.23	...	3	45.6	11.5	....	....

Ordinal Number.		Magnitude.	Estimates of Magnitude.	Mean Right Ascension 1845.0.		Precession 1845.0.	Secular Variation	Adopted Proper Motion.	Observations of R.A.		
R.	G.	R.	R.	R.	G.				No. R.	Mean year R.	G.
				h. m. s.	s.	s.	s.	s.		1800 +	
3776	...	7.5	6	17 46 54.52	...	+ 1.025	+ 0.002	......	4	48.4	...
3777	2479	5.7	6	17 47 2.30	2.32	+ 1.950	+ 0.003	......	5	43.8	10.5
3778	2480	7.5	7	17 47 25.01	24.88	+ 1.830	+ 0.003	......	5	47.5	12.5
3779	2481	6.8	6	17 47 43.56	43.29	+ 1.654	+ 0.003	......	5	46.4	11.6
3780	2482	8.0	6	17 47 54.74	54.65	+ 1.662	0.000	......	3	45.6	11.6
3781	2483	7.5	7	17 48 8.56	8.45	+ 1.857	0.000	......	4	45.1	12.6
3782	...	8.8	6	17 48 10.34	...	+ 1.654	0.000	......	3	48.5	...
3783	...	9.2	4	17 48 14.39	...	+ 1.858	0.000	......	3	52.9	...
3784	2484	4.9	6	17 48 15.39	15.37	+ 1.949	+ 0.003	......	6	47.3	10.5
3785	...	8.5	3	17 48 18.47	...	+ 1.552	+ 0.001	......	3	49.9	...
3786	...	8.4	3	17 49 0.51	...	+ 1.042	+ 0.001	......	3	51.9	...
3787	2485	7.2	6	17 49 15.83	15.81	+ 1.839	+ 0.003	......	4	47.1	12.5
3788	...	8.4	7	17 49 52.59	...	+ 1.558	0.000	......	3	48.3	...
3789	2486	7.6	8	17 50 14.30	13.95	+ 1.707	+ 0.003	......	4	46.6	10.6
3790	2487	7.9	6	17 50 16.75	16.76	+ 1.723	+ 0.003	......	4	48.5	10.6
3791	...	5.3	1	17 50 19.87	...	+ 3.658	+ 0.001	− 0.005	4	47.7	...
3792	...	4.2	3	17 50 29.71	...	+ 3.300	+ 0.001	......	8	53.6	...
3793	2488	3.4	6	17 50 51.07	50.96	+ 1.021	+ 0.001	+ 0.014	5	44.8	6.9
3794	2489	8.2	3	17 51 35.63	35.51	+ 1.389	0.000	......	3	43.9	11.6
3795	2490	7.0	8	17 52 13.87	13.55	+ 1.733	0.000	......	5	47.1	10.0
3796	...	9.4	7	17 52 16.71	...	−22.165	+ 0.293	......	5	52.4	...
3797	2491	6.1	5	17 52 21.75	21.68	+ 1.716	0.000	......	4	43.6	10.6
3798	...	8.2	8	17 52 50.42	...	−22.217	+ 0.283	......	6	52.2	...
3799	2492	2.3	1	17 53 0.55	0.44	+ 1.390	+ 0.003	......	50	44.4	6.9
3800	2493	6.7	4	17 53 16.58	16.34	+ 1.805	+ 0.003	......	5	44.8	10.5
3801	...	7.6	8	17 53 26.55	...	+ 1.569	0.000	......	4	48.1	...
3802	...	7.8	6	17 54 8.45	...	+ 1.735	0.000	......	3	46.9	...
3803	2494	6.8	7	17 54 26.71	26.55	+ 1.711	+ 0.003	......	5	46.9	11.5
3804	...	7.2	5	17 54 27.49	...	+ 1.183	+ 0.001	......	3	48.9	...
3805	...	7.8	6	17 54 28.04	...	+ 1.813	0.000	......	3	48.6	...
3806	...	6.9	6	17 54 55.43	...	+ 1.813	0.000	......	4	47.0	...
3807	2495	8.0	6	17 55 4.72	4.10	+ 1.518	+ 0.003	......	5	45.7	11.6
3808	...	7.5	6	17 55 4.72	...	+ 0.489	+ 0.002	......	3	51.9	...
3809	...	7.6	5	17 55 9.85	...	+ 0.487	+ 0.002	......	3	51.9	...
3810	...	7.4	4	17 55 12.94	...	+ 3.712	+ 0.001	......	3	55.6	...

Ordinal Number.	Mean North Polar Distance 1845.0.			Precession 1845.0.	Secular Variation.	Adopted Proper Motion.	Observations of N.P.D.				Names.	Oeltzen-Argelander Number.
	R.	R.	G.				No. R.	Mean year R.	G.			
	° ′ ″		″	″	″	″		1800 +				
3776	33 7 42.7		...	+ 1.15	− 0.15	...	2	45.6	...		....	17580
3777	49 58 51.0	51.5		+ 1.13	− 0.30	...	3	44.9	10.5		....	....
3778	47 6 14.4	13.5		+ 1.10	− 0.27	...	3	45.6	12.5		....	....
3779	43 18 49.0	43.3		+ 1.07	− 0.25	...	3	46.9	11.6		....	17589
3780	43 29 6.1	4.3		+ 1.06	− 0.23	...	4	46.8	11.6		....	17592
3781	47 45 5.8	7.5		+ 1.04	− 0.26	...	3	47.3	12.6		....	....
3782	43 19 10.6	...		+ 1.04	− 0.24	...	3	43.6	...		....	17608
3783	47 45 36.9	...		+ 1.03	− 0.27	...	2	51.1	...		....	....
3784	49 57 35.0	34.6		+ 1.03	− 0.28	...	5	45.4	10.5		90 Herculis *f*.	....
3785	41 20 20.5	...		+ 1.02	− 0.23	...	3	52.9	...		....	17611
3786	33 21 33.9	...		+ 0.96	− 0.15	...	2	44.6	...		....	17621
3787	47 19 16.8	17.9		+ 0.94	− 0.27	...	3	44.6	12.5		....	....
3788	41 27 7.2	...		+ 0.88	− 0.23	...	4	49.8	...		....	....
3789	44 25 6.5	6.6		+ 0.85	− 0.26	...	4	47.6	10.6		....	17639
3790	44 45 17.1	18.8		+ 0.85	− 0.25	...	4	48.3	10.6		....	17640
3791	113 47 43.8	...		+ 0.85	− 0.53	+ 0.04	2	56.6	...		4 Sagittarii	....
3792	99 44 56.4	...		+ 0.83	− 0.48	...	2	52.6	...		64 Ophiuchi *ν*	....
3793	33 6 3.6	4.5		+ 0.80	− 0.15	− 0.07	7	45.4	6.9		32 Draconis *ξ*	17650
3794	38 28 42.6	42.8		+ 0.73	− 0.22	...	4	42.8	11.6		....	17663
3795	44 59 29.6	30.8		+ 0.68	− 0.25	...	4	44.5	10.0		....	....
3796	3 1 48.1	...		+ 0.68	+ 3.23	...	3	52.6	...		....	....
3797	44 37 38.9	37.5		+ 0.67	− 0.25	...	4	45.6	10.5		....	17673
3798	3 1 31.3	...		+ 0.63	+ 3.24	...	3	51.9	...		....	....
3799	38 29 26.6	27.1		+ 0.61	− 0.21	+ 0.04	34	46.7	6.9		33 Draconis *γ*	17685
3800	46 33 59.2	61.0		+ 0.59	− 0.26	...	4	42.8	10.5		....	....
3801	41 41 15.0	...		+ 0.57	− 0.23	...	4	48.8	...		....	17690
3802	45 2 56.7	...		+ 0.51	− 0.25	...	3	45.6	...		....	....
3803	44 30 44.2	46.8		+ 0.49	− 0.24	...	4	43.1	11.5		....	17703
3804	35 19 7.6	...		+ 0.49	− 0.17	...	4	49.6	...		....	....
3805	46 51 23.2	...		+ 0.48	− 0.26	...	3	53.2	...		....	....
3806	46 45 27.7	...		+ 0.44	− 0.26	...	4	47.0	...		....	... ..
3807	40 43 40.6	41.2		+ 0.43	− 0.23	...	4	45.8	11.6		....	....
3808	27 22 41.7	...		+ 0.43	− 0.06	...	3	52.3	...		....	17718
3809	27 21 50.6	...		+ 0.42	− 0.06	...	2	52.6	...		....	17719
3810	115 36 18.8	...		+ 0.41	− 0.54	...	2	52.5	...		....	....

Ordinal Number.		Magnitude.	Estimates of Magnitude.	Mean Right Ascension 1845.0.			Precession 1845.0.	Secular Variation	Adopted Proper Motion.	Observations of R.A.		
R.	G.	R.		R.		G.				No.	Mean year.	
										R.	R.	G.
				h. m. s.		s.	s.	s.	s.		1800 +	
3811	...	8.1	5	17 55 24.17		...	+ 3.286	0.000	......	4	53.0	...
3812	...	9.0	6	17 55 25.53		...	+ 1.569	0.000	......	4	47.1	...
3813	...	7.5	7	17 55 30.00		...	− 2.746	+ 0.020	......	4	46.3	...
3814	2496	5.8	7	17 55 30.68		30.80	+ 1.709	0.000	......	6	47.9	11.5
3815	...	3.3	A	17 55 51.23		...	+ 3.855	+ 0.001	− 0.004	4	51.3	...
3816	2501	5.1	7	17 56 23.42		23.29	− 2.710	+ 0.006	......	5	45.0	8.6
3817	...	8.6	6	17 56 32.64		...	+ 1.564	0.000	......	4	46.6	...
3818	...	8.5	6	17 56 32.67		...	+ 0.512	+ 0.002	......	3	51.9	...
3819	2497	7.5	6	17 56 40.69		40.62	+ 1.717	+ 0.003	......	3	45.9	11.5
3820	...	7.2	4	17 57 1.29		...	+ 1.561	0.000	......	3	43.6	...
3821	...	8.3	5	17 57 14.33		...	+ 3.286	0.000	......	4	53.0	...
3822	2498	8.6	7	17 57 39.22		39.11	+ 1.780	+ 0.003	......	4	46.6	13.6
3823	2499	7.4	7	17 57 49.09		48.65	+ 1.812	+ 0.003	......	6	45.8	10.5
3824	2504	6.1	6	17 57 52.48		52.35	− 1.049	+ 0.003	......	4	45.9	7.7
3825	2500	7.2	8	17 57 56.85		56.76	+ 1.768	0.000	......	6	46.6	13.6
3826	...	7.9	4	17 58 33.29		...	+ 1.570	0.000	......	2	48.2	...
3827	...	8.2	4	17 59 3.88		...	+ 3.284	0.000	......	5	52.9	...
3828	2502	6.4	5	17 59 6.08		5.74	+ 1.561	0.000	......	8	47.4	8.6
3829	...	8.9	4	17 59 8.57		...	+ 1.561	0.000	......	3	51.8	...
3830	...	7.3	7	17 59 19.09		...	+ 3.708	0.000	......	2	56.6	...
3831	2503	7.6	3	17 59 27.79		27.63	+ 1.862	0.000	......	4	46.1	10.6
3832	2505	6.6	7	17 59 40.87		40.66	+ 1.945	0.000	......	6	47.0	10.5
3833	2506	7.2	6	17 59 45.87		45.15	+ 1.830	0.000	......	3	45.0	9.6
3834	2507	7.2	6	18 0 5.41		4.89	+ 1.825	0.000	......	4	44.7	9.6
3835	...	7.7	4	18 0 8.86		...	+ 1.056	0.000	......	3	51.9	...
3836	...	8.5	4	18 0 10.72		...	+ 1.056	0.000	......	4	51.9	...
3837	...	8.8	6	18 0 11.16		...	+ 1.056	0.000	......	4	53.8	...
3838	2508	6.4	8	18 0 10.89		10.91	+ 1.870	0.000	......	6	47.2	10.6
3839	2509	7.9	6	18 0 41.40		41.06	+ 1.988	0.000	......	4	47.2	11.7
3840	...	8.9	4	18 0 41.78		...	+ 1.573	0.000	......	4	52.6	...
3841	2510	7.7	11	18 0 51.64		51.71	+ 1.579	0.000	......	6	48.2	12.6
3842	2511	8.7	5	18 1 4.74		4.65	+ 1.576	0.000	......	4	50.6	12.6
3843	2512	7.8	7	18 1 30.20		30.17	+ 1.934	0.000	......	4	46.6	10.5
3844	2513	7.2	5	18 1 32.20		32.03	+ 1.514	0.000	......	5	46.6	12.0
3845	2514	7.7	7	18 2 7.75		7.60	+ 1.804	0.000	......	4	45.5	12.6

Ordinal Number.	Mean North Polar Distance 1845.0		Precession 1845.0.	Secular Variation.	Adopted Proper Motion.	Observations of N.P.D.			Names.	Oeltzen-Argelander Number.
R.	R.	G.				No. R.	Mean year R.	Mean year G.		
	° ′ ″	″	″	″	″		1800 +			
3811	99 14 57.3	...	+ 0.40	− 0.48	...	2	52.6	...	....	......
3812	41 41 36.4	...	+ 0.40	− 0.23	...	3	47.6	...	....	17721
3813	12 56 39.7	...	+ 0.39	+ 0.40	...	5	43.1	...	....	17734
3814	44 29 18.2	18.5	+ 0.39	− 0.25	...	4	43.1	11.5	....	17726
3815	120 25 10.6	...	+ 0.36	− 0.56	+ 0.23	2	46.7	...	10 Sagittarii γ^2	......
3816	13 1 17.7	15.5	+ 0.32	+ 0.41	− 0.24	9	43.0	8.6	35 Draconis...	17752
3817	41 35 8.0	...	+ 0.30	− 0.23	...	4	45.1	...	....	17748
3818	27 35 38.0	...	+ 0.30	− 0.06	...	4	52.1	...	....	17753
3819	44 38 44.7	44.1	+ 0.29	− 0.25	...	4	43.8	11.5	....	......
3820	41 31 52.5	...	+ 0.26	− 0.23	...	5	45.2	...	....	17761
3821	99 16 3.9	...	+ 0.24	− 0.48	...	2	52.6	...	....	......
3822	46 1 1.1	0.9	+ 0.21	− 0.25	...	3	44.3	13.6	....	......
3823	46 43 57.7	58.5	+ 0.19	− 0.27	...	3	44.2	10.5	....	......
3824	17 58 55.1	55.9	+ 0.19	+ 0.17	...	4	44.8	7.7	34 Draconis ψ^2	17777
3825	45 45 50.8	50.7	+ 0.18	− 0.25	...	4	46.5	13.6	....	......
3826	41 42 7.1	...	+ 0.13	− 0.23	...	4	49.1	...	....	17789
3827	99 11 25.4	...	+ 0.08	− 0.48	...	1	52.5	...	....	......
3828	41 32 25.4	25.5	+ 0.08	− 0.23	...	5	43.4	8.6	....	17800
3829	41 32 38.6	...	+ 0.08	− 0.23	...	4	50.1	...	....	......
3830	115 29 15.4	...	+ 0.05	− 0.54	...	2	52.5	...	....	......
3831	47 54 42.0	46.1	+ 0.05	− 0.26	...	3	45.6	10.6	....	......
3832	49 55 30.0	31.3	+ 0.03	− 0.28	...	4	44.6	10.5	....	......
3833	47 8 50.2	50.6	+ 0.02	− 0.27	...	4	46.5	9.6	....	......
3834	47 3 8.3	7.4	− 0.01	− 0.27	...	3	46.2	9.6	....	......
3835	33 34 46.8	...	− 0.01	− 0.15	...	2	51.1	...	....	17819
3836	33 34 10.0	...	− 0.02	− 0.15	...	2	51.6	...	....	17821
3837	33 34 14.6	...	− 0.02	− 0.15	...	2	50.6	...	....	......
3838	48 4 2.8	7.6	− 0.02	− 0.28	...	3	44.8	10.6	....	......
3839	51 0 48.9	48.4	− 0.06	− 0.29	...	3	47.3	11.7	....	......
3840	41 47 4.5	...	− 0.06	− 0.23	...	3	52.9	...	....	......
3841	41 52 31.0	29.5	− 0.08	− 0.24	...	5	48.4	12.6	....	17838
3842	41 50 11.8	11.1	− 0.09	− 0.22	...	3	50.9	12.6	....	17841
3843	49 39 14.0	14.5	− 0.13	− 0.28	...	5	50.4	10.5	....	......
3844	40 40 9.0	9.8	− 0.13	− 0.21	...	5	47.8	12.0	....	17849
3845	46 33 49.2	49.6	− 0.19	− 0.27	...	3	45.6	12.6	....	......

Ordinal Number.		Magnitude.	Estimates of Magnitude.	Mean Right Ascension 1845.0.			Precession 1845.0.	Secular Variation	Adopted Proper Motion.	Observations of R.A.		
R.	G.	R.	R.	R.		G.				No. R.	Mean year. R.	G.
				h. m.　s.		s.	s.	s.	s.		1800 +	
3846	2515	7.6	6	18	2 13.08	12.83	+ 1.507	0.000	......	4	44.1	12.1
3847	2516	7.9	7	18	2 15.45	15.15	+ 1.504	0.000	......	4	44.1	12.0
3848	2517	4.9	.3	18	2 48.77	48.55	+ 1.804	0.000	......	5	44.4	12.6
3849	2518	6.4	6	18	3 14.32	14.12	+ 1.494	0.000	......	4	44.1	11.5
3850	2519	8.1	7	18	3 34.73	34.36	+ 1.986	0.000	......	5	47.9	11.7
3851	2520	7.0	7	18	3 45.95	45.70	+ 1.775	0.000	......	5	47.2	10.5
3852	2521	7.3	8	18	4 14.29	14.02	+ 1.799	− 0.003	......	4	44.1	12.6
3853	...	4.7	9	18	4 29.72	...	+ 3.586	− 0.001	− 0.004	40	49.9	...
3854	2523	7.9	7	18	4 49.21	48.28	+ 1.029	0.000	......	4	44.4	9.7
3855	2522	8.0	9	18	5 9.17	8.99	+ 1.986	0.000	......	5	46.6	11.7
3856	2524	7.6	7	18	5 45.49	45.56	+ 1.990	0.000	......	4	46.1	11.7
3857	...	7.9	5	18	5 50.90	...	+ 1.566	0.000	......	4	49.6	...
3858	...	6.7	6	18	5 53.56	...	+ 0.305	− 0.002	......	4	47.6	...
3859	2525	7.1	8	18	6 4.89	4.45	+ 1.985	0.000	......	5	46.6	11.7
3860	2526	7.1	6	18	6 14.29	14.29	+ 0.936	0.000	......	4	46.6	10.6
3861	...	8.8	7	18	6 36.47	...	+ 0.374	− 0.002	......	4	50.6	...
3862	...	7.9	6	18	6 41.53	...	+ 0.345	− 0.002	......	3	48.9	...
3863	2528	7.0	5	18	7 16.46	15.96	+ 1.072	0.000	......	5	44.5	9.7
3864	2527	6.3	2	18	7 21.07	20.35	+ 1.214	0.000	......	5	44.5	8.6
3865	...	8.4	6	18	7 44.67	...	+ 1.894	0.000	......	4	47.1	...
3866	2529	6.5	7	18	7 47.26	47.16	+ 1.904	0.000	......	6	48.5	11.5
3867	2530	6.3	5	18	7 54.70	54.67	+ 1.998	0.000	......	5	44.6	11.7
3868	...	7.1	6	18	8 12.99	...	+ 1.890	0.000	......	3	45.9	...
3869	...	8.7	5	18	8 20.02	...	+ 1.816	0.000	......	3	48.2	...
3870	2534	7.3	9	18	8 32.07	32.53	− 2.197	− 0.011	......	5	47.5	10.6
3871	2531	8.0	7	18	8 33.91	33.63	+ 1.530	0.000	......	3	44.9	12.5
3872	2532	7.2	8	18	8 48.17	47.88	+ 1.811	0.000	......	5	45.2	10.5
3873	...	6.9	3	18	9 6.40	...	+ 3.712	− 0.001	......	3	54.6	...
3874	...	7.6	7	18	9 23.12	...	+ 1.814	0.000	......	3	47.0	...
3875	2548	8.5	6	18	9 53.75	53.73	− 8.528	− 0.080	......	4	49.2	7.9
3876	...	8.3	5	18	10 48.53	...	− 4.343	− 0.032	......	4	50.9	...
3877	2533	6.0	6	18	10 49.55	49.67	+ 1.863	0.000	......	6	47.0	11.5
3878	2536	6.9	11	18	10 59.28	58.76	+ 1.528	0.000	......	5	45.9	12.6
3879	2535	6.5	10	18	11 5.39	5.65	+ 1.727	0.000	......	11	49.8	10.5
3880	2546	6.0	9	18	11 37.37	41.11	− 4.481	− 0.037	......	9	48.8	7.6

Ordinal Number.	Mean North Polar Distance 1845.0.			Precession 1845.0.	Secular Variation.	Adopted Proper Motion.	Observations of N.P.D.			Names.	Oeltzen-Argelander Number.
	R.	R.	G.				No.	Mean year.			
							R.	R.	G.		
	° ′ ″		″	″	″	″		1800 +			
3846	40 33 1.2		2.2	− 0.19	− 0.21	...	4	43.3	12.1	....	17869
3847	40 29 41.4		40.1	− 0.20	− 0.23	...	4	45 1	12.0	....	17872
3848	46 33 17.4		17.1	− 0.25	− 0.27	...	4	43.3	12.6	....	......
3849	40 18 36.5		37.2	− 0.28	− 0.21	...	4	43.0	11.5	....	17898
3850	50 57 32.1		33.9	− 0.31	− 0.28	...	3	44.9	11.7	....	......
3851	45 54 40.4		42.7	− 0.33	− 0.26	...	6	46.2	10.5	....	......
3852	46 27 46.5		48.9	− 0.37	− 0.26	...	5	46.6	12.6	....	......
3853	111 5 35.0		...	− 0.39	− 0.52	...	5	51.6	...	13 Sagittarii μ	......
3854	33 13 26.8		30.5	− 0.42	− 0.15	...	4	46.1	9.7	....	17926
3855	50 57 11.6		10.9	− 0.45	− 0.29	...	4	46.3	11.7	....	......
3856	51 4 12.8		14.7	− 0.50	− 0.28	...	6	48.8	11.7	....	......
3857	41 37 50.2		...	− 0.51	− 0.23	...	5	48.8	...	....	......
3858	25 48 8.8		...	− 0.52	− 0.04	...	3	47.0	...	....	......
3859	50 55 56.0		56.5	− 0.53	− 0.28	...	5	47.6	11.7	....	......
3860	32 2 52.8		53.5	− 0.54	− 0.12	...	5	45.4	10.6	....	17947
3861	26 22 15.5		...	− 0.58	− 0.05	...	3	47.0	...	....	......
3862	26 7 27.0		...	− 0.59	− 0.05	...	3	49.2	...	....	......
3863	33 46 0.6		0.9	− 0.64	− 0.17	...	5	46.5	9.7	....	17967
3864	35 45 29.5		37.0	− 0.64	− 0.17	...	5	44.3	8.6	....	17969
3865	48 39 14.4		...	− 0.68	− 0.27	...	3	45.9	...	....	......
3866	48 53 21.7		22.0	− 0.68	− 0.27	...	4	43.3	11.5	....	......
3867	51 15 59.0		60.3	− 0.69	− 0.29	...	4	45.0	11.7	....	......
3868	48 33 33.5		...	− 0.72	− 0.27	...	5	49.0	...	....	......
3869	46 48 24.9		...	− 0.73	− 0.27	...	2	46.1	...	....	......
3870	14 14 0.3		0.5	− 0.75	+ 0.26	...	5	47.8	10.6	....	18000
3871	40 56 23.5		21.4	− 0.75	− 0.23	...	5	48.0	12.5	....	17999
3872	46 42 31.9		30.7	− 0.77	− 0.27	...	4	46.1	10.5	....	......
3873	115 39 20.9		...	− 0.80	− 0.54	...	2	52.5	...	....	......
3874	46 45 23.4		...	− 0.82	− 0.27	...	4	45.6	...	....	......
3875	6 34 8.1		8.4	− 0.87	+ 1.23	...	4	48.1	7.9	....	......
3876	10 12 42.9		...	− 0.95	+ 0.63	...	3	47.7	...	....	......
3877	47 53 24.9		26.0	− 0.95	− 0.28	...	5	46.4	11.5	....	......
3878	40 53 38.4		40.8	− 0.96	− 0.22	...	4	46.1	12.6	....	18045
3879	44 50 8.8		5.3	− 0.97	− 0.25	...	4	46.6	10.5	....	18047
3880	10 1 37.3		38.3	− 1.02	+ 0.66	− 0.05	7	43.5	7.6	40 Draconis ...	......

Magnitude.	Estimates of Magnitude. R.	Mean Right Ascension 1845.0. R. h. m. s.	G. s.	Precession 1845.0. s.	Secular Variation s.	Adopted Proper Motion. s.
6.2	5	18 11 39.99	...	+ 2.902	0.000	......
6.0	12	18 11 43.76	47.49	− 4.483	− 0.037	......
6.8	5	18 11 58.25	57.60	+ 1.051	0.000	......
8.3	8	18 12 5.55	5.77	+ 1.942	0.000	......
5.8	9	18 12 11.94	12.35	+ 1.915	0.000	......
7.4	8	18 12 42.32	42.20	+ 1.284	0.000	......
7.3	12	18 12 47.30	47.27	+ 1.940	0.000	......
8.3	8	18 12 48.90	...	− 4.453	− 0.036	......
7.1	7	18 12 56.45	56.19	+ 1.533	0.000	......
5.7	7	18 13 0.28	59.33	+ 0.291	0.000	+ 0.052
7.0	6	18 13 57.91	57.53	+ 1.672	0.000	......
8.1	7	18 14 6.65	...	+ 1.916	0.000	......
8.0	7	18 14 56.83	56.45	+ 1.562	0.000	......
7.3	6	18 14 58.69	...	+ 1.871	0.000	......
7.9	5	18 15 17.94	...	+ 1.871	0.000	......
6.2	4	18 15 58.32	...	+ 2.644	0.000	......
6.1	6	18 16 11.05	10.99	− 0.350	− 0.006	......
5.9	7	18 16 18.35	17.85	+ 1.407	0.000	......
7.4	6	18 16 56.56	56.36	+ 1.905	0.000	......
8.3	12	18 16 58.18	...	−10.498	− 0.185	......
7.9	7	18 17 10.64	10.55	+ 1.860	0.000	......
6.3	7	18 17 14.14	14.06	+ 1.501	− 0.002	......
7.3	6	18 17 21.00	...	− 9.375	− 0.153	......
7.9	7	18 17 22.18	21.78	+ 1.939	0.000	......
4.9	8	18 17 34.91	34.66	+ 1.534	0.000	......
6.6	8	18 17 50.73	49.84	+ 1.410	− 0.003	......
6.8	5	18 17 53.09	52.51	− 0.345	− 0.006	......
7.5	6	18 18 14.48	14.41	+ 1.790	0.000	......
4.1	3	18 18 24.31	...	+ 3.706	− 0.003	− 0.005
6.7	5	18 18 34.63	34.55	+ 1.397	0.000	......
7.2	5	18 18 39.14	38.96	+ 1.677	0.000	......
7.5	5	18 18 48.11	47.98	+ 1.164	0.000	......
5.1	4	18 19 7.51	7.52	+ 1.975	0.000	− 0.003
6.7	8	18 19 21.61	21.42	+ 1.792	0.000	......
6.6	5	18 19 23.10	22.89	+ 1.855	0.000	......

Ordinal Number. R.	Mean North Polar Distance 1845.0. R.	Mean North Polar Distance 1845.0. G.	Precession 1845.0.	Secular Variation.	Adopted Proper Motion.	Observations of N.P.D. No. R.	Observations of N.P.D. Mean year. R. 1800 +	Observations of N.P.D. Mean year. G. 1800 +	Names.	Oeltzen-Argelander Number.
3881	82 47 53.9	...	— 1.02	— 0.42	...	2	52.6	...	....	......
3882	10 1 25.5	26.2	— 1.03	+ 0.66	— 0.06	10	49.8	7.6	41 Draconis...	......
3883	33 27 47.2	49.4	— 1.05	— 0.16	...	5	47.6	9.7	....	18061
3884	49 47 59.6	60.2	— 1.06	— 0.29	...	3	45.7	11.6	....	......
3885	49 7 15.9	20.6	— 1.07	— 0.28	...	4	45.6	8.6	....	......
3886	36 45 32.8	34.4	— 1.11	— 0.18	...	4	47.2	10.5	....	......
3887	49 45 15.4	17.7	— 1.12	— 0.29	...	4	47.7	11.5	....	......
3888	10 3 42.0	...	— 1.12	+ 0.64	...	4	48.1	...	....	......
3889	40 57 45.1	45.3	— 1.13	— 0.22	...	3	45.6	12.6	....	18084
3890	25 39 17.2	17.6	— 1.14	— 0.06	— 0.01	5	47.8	9.6	36 Draconis...	18087
3891	43 39 9.5	8.5	— 1.22	— 0.24	...	4	45.6	11.6	....	18104
3892	49 8 10.1	...	— 1.23	— 0.28	...	4	48.6	...	....	......
3893	41 29 55.8	61.9	— 1.31	— 0.24	...	4	46.1	12.6	....	18116
3894	48 3 54.2	...	— 1.31	— 0.27	...	3	48.3	...	....	......
3895	48 3 46.2	...	— 1.34	— 0.27	...	3	48.9	...	....	......
3896	72 14 50.6	...	— 1.39	— 0.38	...	2	52.7	...	....	......
3897	21 18 4.4	3.8	— 1.41	+ 0.07	+ 0.06	4	47.1	8.6	37 Draconis...	18143
3898	38 43 5.0	5.8	— 1.43	— 0.22	...	4	43.8	9.7	....	18147
3899	48 51 30.0	27.9	— 1.48	— 0.27	...	4	46.5	12.7	....	......
3900	5 36 41.0	...	— 1.48	+ 1.60	...	4	48.1	...	....	......
3901	47 47 6.0	7.3	— 1.50	— 0.27	...	3	47.0	11.6	....	......
3902	40 20 51.6	53.7	— 1.51	— 0.23	...	4	46.6	10.6	....	18161
3903	6 6 44.0	...	— 1.52	+ 1.36	...	4	51.4	...	....	......
3904	49 41 57.6	65.2	— 1.52	— 0.29	...	4	46.1	12.7	....	......
3905	40 57 15.2	18.7	— 1.54	— 0.23	...	4	47.6	8.6	....	18168
3906	38 46 18.1	19.1	— 1.56	— 0.21	...	5	46.2	9.7	....	18171
3907	21 19 13.7	10.0	— 1.56	+ 0.06	+ 0.08	5	47.6	9.6	38 Draconis...	18175
3908	46 8 44.4	43.7	— 1.59	— 0.25	...	3	45.9	11.6	....	......
3909	115 30 1.4	...	— 1.61	— 0.54	+ 0.24	5	50.8	...	22 Sagittarii λ	......
3910	38 32 3.7	3.7	— 1.62	— 0.19	...	3	45.6	10.2	....	18193
3911	43 43 9.5	11.5	— 1.63	— 0.25	...	3	45.3	11.5	....	......
3912	34 56 48.5	47.1	— 1.64	— 0.16	...	3	46.3	12.6	....	......
3913	50 34 25.8	26.8	— 1.67	— 0.28	...	3	46.9	10.5	2 Lyræ μ	......
3914	46 10 24.9	24.6	— 1.69	— 0.26	...	4	47.1	11.5	....	......
3915	47 36 49.8	50.4	— 1.69	— 0.26	...	4	48.1	11.7	....	......

Magnitude.	Estimates of Magnitude.	Mean Right Ascension 1845.0.		Precession 1845.0.	Secular Variation	Adopted Proper Motion.
R.	R.	R.	G.			
		h. m. s.	s.	s.	s.	s.
6.8	6	18 19 59.86	...	− 0.123	− 0.006	......
6.1	2	18 20 ...	...	......	... ..	......
8.0	5	18 20 1.16	1.15	+ 1.213	− 0.003	......
8.0	6	18 20 20.58	...	− 5.773	− 0.102	......
8.1	6	18 20 30.03	30.66	+ 1.990	0.000	......
7.7	12	18 20 31.70	...	−14.493	− 0.368	......
8.5	5	18 20 39.08	39.06	+ 1.682	0.000	......
7.2	6	18 21 16.37	...	+ 1.556	− 0.001	......
7.0	6	18 21 19.78	19.79	+ 1.496	0.000	......
6.9	6	18 21 28.84	...	− 0.895	− 0.014	− 0.013
8.4	5	18 21 33.86	34.48	+ 1.990	0.000	......
5.4	4	18 21 38.77	38.60	+ 0.880	− 0.003	− 0.009
8.0	5	18 21 43.01	...	+ 0.880	− 0.003	......
7.4	4	18 22 7.56	...	+ 1.657	− 0.001	......
4.5	90	18 22 20.01	20.04	−19.286	− 0.616	+ 0.048
8.1	6	18 22 20.07	20.87	+ 1.693	0.000	......
8.9	5	18 22 41.04	41.20	+ 1.372	0.000	......
4.4	5	18 22 58.38	58.30	− 0.849	− 0.012	......
8.3	5	18 23 0.32	0.34	+ 1.374	0.000	......
8.2	5	18 23 22.15	...	+ 1.737	− 0.001	......
7.7	7	18 23 27.50	27.26	+ 1.694	0.000	......
7.8	7	18 23 32.28	32.19	+ 1.794	0.000	......
7.5	5	18 23 34.40	33.85	+ 1.500	− 0.003	......
8.4.	6	18 23 38.11	38.19	+ 1.785	0.000	......
7.3	5	18 23 42.56	42.43	+ 1.779	0.000	......
3.7	5	18 23 50.60	50.41	− 1.189	− 0.019	+ 0.117
7.7	5	18 23 54.88	54.61	+ 1.186	− 0.003	......
7.6	3	18 23 56.01	...	+ 1.397	− 0.002	......
7.1	3	18 24 15.11	...	+ 1.677	− 0.001	......
8.8	6	18 24 23.30	...	− 5.728	− 0.118	......
7.7	5	18 24 24.54	24.32	+ 1.794	0.000	......
7.3	5	18 24 25.84	25.84	+ 1.250	− 0.003	......
7.0	4	18 24 33.98	33.89	+ 0.803	− 0.006	......
7.4	5	18 24 59.67	59.70	+ 1.700	0.000	......
7.6	6	18 25 8.66	8.49	+ 1.379	0.000	......

Ordinal Number.	Mean North Polar Distance 1845.0.		Precession 1845.0.	Secular Variation.	Adopted Proper Motion	Observations of N.P.D.				Names.	Oeltzen-Argelander Number.
	R.	G.				No. R.	Mean year. R.	G.			
R.	R.	G.	"	"	"	R.	R.	G.			
	° ′ ″	″	″	″	″		1800 +				
3916	22 38 26.0	...	− 1.75	+ 0.02	...	4	49.1	...	....	18218
3917	83 53 46.9	...	− 1.75	− 0.42	...	2	52.7	...	....	....
3918	35 39 31.7	33.0	− 1.75	− 0.18	...	3	46.0	10.6	....	18216
3919	8 33 50.8	...	− 1.78	+ 0.84	...	2	48.2	...	....	....
3920	50 57 52.7	53.1	− 1.79	− 0.28	...	3	47.3	13.6	....	....
3921	4 20 9.4	...	− 1.79	+ 2.11	...	6	49.9	...	....	....
3922	43 49 5.2	4.9	− 1.80	− 0.23	...	3	45.6	11.6	....	....
3923	41 19 33.5	...	− 1.86	− 0.22	...	4	52.1	...	....	18235
3924	40 13 14.2	11.9	− 1.86	− 0.26	...	3	45.6	12.6	....	18238
3925	18 33 38.0	...	− 1.88	+ 0.13	− 0.08	3	48.0	...	....	18244
3926	50 56 4.1	6.5	− 1.88	− 0.27	...	3	50.6	13.6	....	....
3927	31 17 15.4	16.8	− 1.89	− 0.12	− 0.05	3	44.2	7.7	39 Draconis b	18246
3928	31 15 53.8	...	− 1.89	− 0.12	...	2	44.5	...	....	18248
3929	43 16 58.4	...	− 1.93	− 0.23	...	3	52.0	...	....	18257
3930	3 24 20.5	21.2	− 1.95	+ 2.77	− 0.03	167	44.3	6.9	23 Urs. Min. δ	....
3931	44 1 2.2	9.1	− 1.95	− 0.24	...	4	46.1	13.6	....	18260
3932	38 4 21.3	25.1	− 1.98	− 0.19	...	4	47.6	10.7	....	18270
3933	18 44 48.4	47.2	− 2.01	+ 0.11	...	3	43.7	6.9	43 Draconis φ	18275
3934	38 5 40.4	41.4	− 2.01	− 0.20	...	3	47.0	10 7	....	18274
3935	44 55 41.3	...	− 2.04	− 0.25	...	3	48.6	...	....	....
3936	44 1 48.8	50.1	− 2.05	− 0.25	...	3	46.6	13.6	....	18276
3937	46 10 15.2	16.0	− 2.06	− 0.27	...	4	46.3	11.5	....	....
3938	40 16 47.2	51.8	− 2.06	− 0.23	...	3	47.2	10.6	....	18277
3939	45 58 0.1	59.6	− 2.06	− 0.25	...	3	50.7	13.5	....	....
3940	45 50 28.9	28.7	− 2.07	− 0.26	...	3	48.3	13.5	....	....
3941	17 20 11.2	9.7	− 2.08	+ 0.16	+ 0.35	4	47.3	6.8	44 Draconis χ	....
3942	35 12 44.9	45.4	− 2.09	− 0.18	...	3	46.6	12.6	....	18282
3943	38 28 6.9	...	− 2.09	− 0.20	...	3	51.6	...	....	18283
3944	43 40 34.8	...	− 2.12	− 0.24	...	3	49.7	...	....	18286
3945	8 35 30.0	...	− 2.13	+ 0.84	...	3	47.7	...	....	....
3946	46 10 3.9	8.2	− 2.13	− 0.26	...	3	46.2	11.5	....	....
3947	36 8 47.9	46.7	− 2.13	− 0.17	...	3	45.7	10.5	....	18291
3948	30 23 24.4	29.8	− 2.15	− 0.13	...	3	44.0	12.6	....	18293
3949	44 7 14.1	14.5	− 2.18	− 0.24	...	3	47.6	13.5	....	18301
3950	38 9 17.1	16.1	− 2.20	− 0.21	...	4	47.4	13.7	....	18306

Magnitude.	Estimates of Magnitude.	Mean Right Ascension 1845.0.		Precession 1845.0.	Secular Variation	Adopted Proper Motion.
R.	R.	R.	G.			
		h. m. s.	s.	s.	s.	s.
5.4	6	18 25 32.20	32.29	+ 0.159	— 0.006	+ 0.014
6.2	5	18 25 34.11	33.90	+ 0.819	— 0.006	......
7.1	5	18 25 34.78	34.95	+ 1.920	0.000	......
7.7	5	18 25 47.17	46.97	+ 1.940	0.000	......
7.3	4	18 26 0.97	0.94	+ 1.916	0.000	......
8.0	5	18 26 32.40	32.51	+ 1.945	0.000	......
8.1	4	18 26 58.06	57.85	+ 1.792	0.000	......
6.9	6	18 27 21.05	20.63	+ 1.701	0.000	......
7.7	5	18 27 32.07	31.60	+ 2.005	0.000	......
7.3	7	18 27 40.28	39.93	+ 2.006	0.000	......
7.3	7	18 27 41.12	...	— 5.704	— 0.116	......
6.9	5	18 27 55.22	55.19	+ 1.712	0.000	..... .
6.0	29	18 28 5.57	4.93	—21.997	— 1.177	+ 0.085
7.0	8	18 28 6.90	6.69	+ 1.940	0.000	......
7.9	6	18 28 10.40	10.19	+ 1.790	0.000	......
7.1	6	18 28 11.68	...	+ 1.955	— 0.001	......
7.0	5	18 28 14.32	14.23	+ 1.697	0.000	......
7.4	4	18 28 19.20	...	— 0.925	— 0.023	......
8.3	10	18 28 32.21	...	—26.104	— 1.472	......
6.6	4	18 28 38.67	38.49	+ 1.373	— 0.002	......
8.5	2	18 28 41.28	...	+ 3.705	— 0.004	......
8.1	5	18 29 8.31	7.80	+ 0.227	— 0.009	......
8.4	4	18 29 16.21	15.90	+ 0.824	— 0.003	......
8.5	6	18 29 18.83	...	+ 1.356	— 0.003	......
6.9	4	18 29 24.94	24.74	+ 1.692	0.000	......
9.0	7	18 29 27.03	26.71	+ 1.770	0.000	......
7.8	6	18 29 44.59	44.53	+ 0.837	— 0.006	......
5.0	5	18 29 54.15	54.06	+ 1.034	— 0.006	......
8.7	4	18 29 54.58	54.74	+ 1.775	0.000	......
7.5	6	18 29 56.67	56.34	+ 0.532	— 0.006	......
7.2	11	18 30 10.38	10.38	+ 2.006	0.000	......
9.2	7	18 30 22.77	...	+ 1.360	0.000	......
5.0	5	18 30 25.75	25.25	+ 1.360	0.000	......
7.5	6	18 30 34.22	34.42	+ 1.950	0.000	......
8.0	6	18 30 37.15	36.94	+ 1.933	0.000	......

Ordinal Number.	Mean North Polar Distance 1845.0.			Precession 1845.0.	Secular Variation.	Adopted Proper Motion.	Observations of N.P.D.				Names.	Oeltzen-Argelander Number.
							No.	Mean year.				
R.	R.		G.				R.	R.	G.			
	° ′ ″		″	″	″	″		1800 +				
3951	24 31 57.0		57.6	— 2.23	— 0.02	+ 0.06	3	46.0	8.7		42 Draconis...	18312
3952	30 33 10.7		11.2	— 2.23	— 0.11	...	4	49.9	12.6		....	18314
3953	49 7 43.4		44.2	— 2.23	— 0.27	...	3	47.0	11.6		....	....
3954	49 36 54.1		52.6	— 2.25	— 0.27	...	3	45.3	12.7		....	....
3955	49 0 5.1		6.0	— 2.27	— 0.27	...	3	47.0	11.6		....	....
3956	49 44 25.9		27.1	— 2.32	— 0.29	...	3	47.3	12.7		....	....
3957	46 5 26.0		26.6	— 2.35	— 0.25	...	3	47.0	13.5		....	....
3958	44 7 22.6		23.0	— 2.39	— 0.25	...	3	45.6	12.8		....	18345
3959	51 14 54.9		56.4	— 2.40	— 0.28	...	2	48.2	11.6		....	....
3960	51 16 37.2		33.7	— 2.41	— 0.27	...	4	51.1	11.6		....	....
3961	8 36 4.3		...	— 2.42	+ 0.83	...	3	47.7	...		....	....
3962	44 20 20.5		22.1	— 2.44	— 0.25	...	3	47.2	12.8		....	18356
3963	3 1 48.3		47.9	— 2.45	+ 3.13	...	18	47.8	7.0		24 Ursæ Minoris	....
3964	49 34 59.4		58.8	— 2.45	— 0.27	...	4	46.6	12.7		....	....
3965	46 1 43.8		43.9	— 2.46	— 0.26	...	3	45.2	13.5		....	....
3966	49 57 27.4		...	— 2.46	— 0.28	...	4	52.1	...		....	....
3967	44 1 20.4		20.1	— 2.46	— 0.23	...	3	45.6	12.8		....	18364
3968	18 22 19.8		...	— 2.47	+ 0.14	...	3	48.3	...		....	....
3969	2 36 13.1		...	— 2.49	+ 3.77	...	2	50.2	...		....	....
3970	37 59 55.3		56.9	— 2.50	— 0.20	...	3	43.3	10.6		....	....
3971	115 32 48.5		...	— 2.50	— 0.54	...	2	52.7	...		....	....
3972	25 0 43.5		46.9	— 2.54	— 0.02	...	4	43.6	10.2		....	18384
3973	30 32 47.5		44.7	— 2.55	— 0.11	...	2	50.2	12.6		....	....
3974	37 43 22.2		...	— 2.56	— 0.19	...	2	45.1	...		....	18386
3975	43 54 0.5		0.5	— 2.57	— 0.25	...	3	45.0	12.8		....	18387
3976	45 33 12.5		10.2	— 2.57	— 0.25	...	2	49.1	13.7		....	....
3977	30 41 41.5		40.2	— 2.60	— 0.13	...	3	45.3	12.6		....	....
3978	33 4 16.2		17.9	— 2.61	— 0.15	...	3	44.6	7.7		45 Draconis d	18397
3979	45 40 8.1		5.2	— 2.61	— 0.25	...	2	50.2	13.7		....	....
3980	27 34 45.8		46.2	— 2.61	— 0.07	...	4	50.9	14.5		....	18399
3981	51 13 41.8		41.5	— 2.63	— 0.28	...	6	51.2	11.6		....	....
3982	37 46 2.2		...	— 2.66	— 0.21	...	3	53.0	...		....	18408
3983	37 46 2.7		4.2	— 2.66	— 0.21	...	4	43.4	9.6		....	18409
3984	49 47 32.4		33.9	— 2.67	— 0.29	...	3	47.0	12.7		....	....
3985	49 21 14.7		18.2	— 2.67	— 0.27	...	3	47.3	12.7		....	....

Ordinal Number		Magnitude.	Estimates of Magnitude.	Mean Right Ascension 1845.0.		Precession 1845.0.	Secular Variation	Adopted Proper Motion.	Observations of R.A.		
R.	G.	R.	R.	R.	G.				No. R.	Mean year R.	G.
				h. m. s.	s.	s.	s.	s.		1800 +	
3986	2614	7.8	5	18 30 41.30	40.96	+ 1.434	− 0.003	......	3	48.3	12.7
3987	2617	6.9	7	18 30 46.77	46.74	+ 0.188	− 0.006	......	6	46.3	14.2
3988	...	9.5	5	18 30 56.52	...	+ 0.093	− 0.011	......	3	51.3	...
3989	...	8.1	11	18 30 57.68	...	−39.894	− 3.520	......	5	51.2	...
3990	2615	7.3	6	18 31 9.77	9.83	+ 1.838	0.000	......	4	47.9	13.5
3991	2622	8.6	5	18 31 26.70	26.90	+ 0.197	− 0.009	......	3	49.3	14.6
3992	...	8.8	5	18 31 27.98	...	+ 1.776	− 0.002	......	3	49.0	...
3993	2616	1.0	A	18 31 41.40	41.17	+ 2.011	0.000	+ 0.017	22	45.4	6.7
3994	...	7.2	3	18 31 46.20	...	+ 1.806	− 0.002	......	2	47.2	...
3995	2618	6.4	5	18 32 0.97	0.74	+ 1.831	0.000	......	3	46.6	13.5
3996	2619	8.5	5	18 32 3.43	3.42	+ 1.782	0.000	......	3	49.0	13.7
3997	2621	8.5	3	18 32 9.20	9.27	+ 1.779	0.000	......	2	46.6	13.7
3998	2620	8.6	5	18 32 9.79	9.67	+ 1.853	0.000	......	3	45.0	13.6
3999	2623	6.2	3	18 32 59.44	59.37	+ 1.979	0.000	......	3	45.3	12.6
4000	2624	8.3	9	18 33 9.87	8.89	+ 1.857	0.000	......	4	46.9	13.6
4001	2625	8.1	7	18 33 46.18	45.80	+ 1.204	− 0.003	......	4	48.1	10.0
4002	2630	8.0	7	18 34 6.94	7.49	+ 0.409	− 0.006	......	3	46.1	10.7
4003	2626	9.5	6	18 34 22.94	22.78	+ 1.763	0.000	......	3	46.2	13.7
4004	2627	6.2	8	18 34 33.38	33.12	+ 1.929	0.000	......	5	46.4	11.6
4005	...	8.5	8	18 34 56.75	...	+ 1.851	− 0.001	......	4	51.8	...
4006	2629	6.6	8	18 34 57.02	57.13	+ 2.029	0.000	+ 0.015	4	46.1	13.6
4007	...	8.3	7	18 35 5.93	...	− 7.353	− 0.204	......	4	51.2	...
4008	...	7.5	3	18 35 18.96	...	+ 1.367	0.000	......	3	54.6	...
4009	2632	7.6	8	18 35 18.98	18.74	+ 1.367	0.000	......	7	48.6	12.6
4010	2631	8.2	9	18 35 20.39	20.41	+ 1.841	0.000	......	6	48.5	13.6
4011	...	8.0	6	18 35 22.05	...	+ 0.452	− 0.010	......	3	48.9	...
4012	...	7.5	6	18 35 22.06	...	− 2.269	− 0.061	......	3	48.3	...
4013	...	8.2	4	18 35 24.60	...	+ 2.162	− 0.004	......	2	47.2	...
4014	2634	7.9	5	18 35 29.67	28.91	+ 1.177	0.000	......	4	47.0	9.6
4015	2633	8.5	8	18 35 35.30	35.36	+ 1.839	0.000	......	4	47.9	13.6
4016	2640	5.8	5	18 35 43.90	43.64	+ 0.192	− 0.009	......	5	46.2	14.1
4017	...	9.0	5	18 35 45.09	...	+ 1.848	− 0.002	......	2	52.1	...
4018	2635	8.7	8	18 35 57.43	57.27	+ 1.846	0.000	......	7	49.0	13.6
4019	...	4.0	2	18 35 58.21	...	+ 3.747	− 0.006	+ 0.004	2	41.5	...
4020	2641	5.9	7	18 36 9.44	9.26	+ 0.546	− 0.006	......	4	46.7	14.5

Ordinal Number.	Mean North Polar Distance 1845.0.		Preces-sion 1845.0.	Secular Variation.	Adopted Proper Motion.	Observations of N.P.D.			Names.	Oeltzen-Argelander Number.
R.	R.	G.				No. R.	Mean year. R.	Mean year. G.		
	° ′ ″	″	″	″	″		1800 +			
3986	39 0 33.4	36.9	− 2.68	− 0.22	...	2	50.2	12.7	....	18412
3987	24 41 1.4	2.9	− 2.69	− 0.04	...	2	45.1	14.2	....	....
3988	23 59 26.1	...	− 2.70	− 0.01	...	2	48.6	...	....	....
3989	1 45 58.1	...	− 2.70	+ 5.76	...	7	51.6	...	....	....
3990	47 4 11.7	11.8	− 2.72	− 0.27	...	3	45.6	13.5	....	....
3991	24 44 55.7	60.1	− 2.74	− 0.02	...	3	48.6	14.6	....	....
3992	45 39 35.2	...	− 2.74	− 0.25	...	2	48.1	...	....	....
3993	51 21 26.5	27.1	− 2.76	− 0.28	− 0.28	7	47.9	6.7	3 Lyræ α	....
3994	46 19 51.1	...	− 2.77	− 0.25	...	3	47.3	...	....	....
3995	46 54 24.7	23.8	− 2.79	− 0.26	...	3	47.0	13.5	....	....
3996	45 46 24.9	28.3	− 2.80	− 0.27	...	3	50.6	13.7	....	....
3997	45 42 58.5	52.6	− 2.80	− 0.24	...	3	50.0	13.7	....	....
3998	47 23 21.6	22.7	− 2.80	− 0.25	...	2	49.7	13.6	....	....
3999	50 27 55.2	57.2	− 2.88	− 0.29	...	3	45.3	12.6	....	....
4000	47 28 14.4	18.4	− 2.89	− 0.26	...	5	47.6	13.6	....	....
4001	35 19 7.1	8.4	− 2.94	− 0.16	...	3	45.6	10.0	....	18462
4002	26 25 22.8	13.5	− 2.97	− 0.04	...	4	47.2	10.7	....	18474
4003	45 19 33.4	35.9	− 3.00	− 0.26	...	3	47.0	13.7	....	....
4004	49 12 13.5	14.5	− 3.01	− 0.27	...	4	45.1	11.6	....	....
4005	47 18 0.4	...	− 3.05	− 0.26	...	4	52.1	...	....	....
4006	51 46 24.5	27.0	− 3.05	− 0.30	...	4	48.1	13.6	....	....
4007	7 13 38.0	...	− 3.06	+ 1.07	...	3	47.0	...	....	....
4008	37 47 ...	...	......	...	...	...	...	...	....	18493
4009	37 47 40.8	41.4	− 3.08	− 0.20	...	4	46.4	12.6	....	....
4010	47 3 26.1	29.5	− 3.08	− 0.26	...	4	48.7	13.6	....	....
4011	26 46 45.5	...	− 3.08	− 0.07	...	5	48.2	...	....	18496
4012	13 53 44.2	...	− 3.08	+ 0.33	...	3	48.0	...	....	18500
4013	34 41 35.6	...	− 3.09	− 0.16	...	3	45.4	...	....	....
4014	34 53 46.4	49.6	− 3.09	− 0.16	...	3	45.6	9.6	....	18499
4015	47 0 58.4	61.5	− 3.10	− 0.26	...	5	48.8	13.6	....	....
4016	24 39 0.2	3.8	− 3.11	− 0.02	...	4	45.8	14.1	....	18510
4017	47 14 8.8	...	− 3.12	− 0.27	...	3	50.0	...	....	....
4018	47 10 53.9	54.5	− 3.13	− 0.26	...	3	48.3	13.6	....	....
4019	117 8 38.3	...	− 3.13	− 0.54	− 0.01	4	53.1	...	27 Sagittarii φ	....
4020	27 36 49.9	51.0	− 3.15	− 0.07	...	3	46.2	14.5	....	18517

Ordinal Number		Magnitude	Estimates of Magnitude	Mean Right Ascension 1845.0		Precession 1845.0	Secular Variation	Adopted Proper Motion	Observations of R.A.		
R.	G.		R.	R.	G.				No. R.	Mean year R.	G.
				h. m. s.	s.	s.	s.	s.		1800 +	
4021	2638	6.1	6	18 36 19.14	19.25	+ 1.378	0.000	+ 0.015	4	45.4	12.6
4022	...	7.1	5	18 36 20.85	...	+ 3.762	− 0.006	......	1	55.5	...
4023	2636	8.1	8	18 36 25.03	24.99	+ 1.950	0.000	......	4	46.6	11.7
4024	2637	7.1	5	18 36 25.78	25.67	+ 1.790	0.000	......	6	46.2	12.7
4025	2642	6.7	4	18 36 31.42	31.05	+ 0.730	− 0.006	......	4	44.8	12.7
4026	2639	6.6	5	18 36 39.62	39.34	+ 1.940	0.000	......	5	46.2	11.6
4027	2655	5.3	7	18 37 12.02	10.84	− 2.843	− 0.060	......	4	46.7	9.7
4028	2645	6.7	5	18 37 17.51	17.59	+ 0.437	+ 0.437	......	4	46.7	10.6
4029	...	8.5	7	18 37 25.10	...	− 7.341	− 0.224	......	4	51.2	...
4030	2643	8.3	7	18 37 57.69	57.63	+ 2.031	− 0.003	......	5	46.1	13.6
4031	2644	6.5	5	18 38 6.66	6.57	+ 1.966	− 0.003	......	5	47.2	11.7
4032	2649	8.3	6	18 38 15.98	15.96	+ 0.409	− 0.006	......	3	47.0	10.7
4033	2646	7.2	8	18 38 22.17	22.10	+ 1.762	0.000	......	4	46.9	12.7
4034	...	9.1	6	18 38 22.43	...	+ 1.762	0.000	......	3	54.6	...
4035	2647	7.1	7	18 38 36.26	36.04	+ 1.636	0.000	......	4	47.4	12.6
4036	2648	6.4	7	18 38 50.77	50.61	+ 2.027	0.000	......	4	46.1	13.6
4037	...	9.2	4	18 39 1.09	...	+ 2.024	− 0.001	......	2	51.1	...
4038	...	8.1	3	18 39 9.17	...	+ 1.812	− 0.002	......	3	49.4	...
4039	2650	6.7	4	18 39 12.31	12.03	+ 1.984	0.000	......	4	45.8	8.6
4040	2651	6.5	3	18 39 14.52	14.33	+ 1.986	0.000	......	4	45.5	8.6
4041	...	8.1	7	18 39 25.29	...	+ 1.155	− 0.004	......	4	53.4	...
4042	2658	5.8	5	18 39 34.70	34.55	+ 0.530	− 0.006	......	5	47.5	10.6
4043	2657	5.0	6	18 39 37.83	37.84	+ 1.162	− 0.003	......	4	47.9	7.7
4044	2652	7.0	6	18 39 40.55	40.39	+ 1.635	0.000	......	3	49.3	12.6
4045	...	8.6	4	18 39 44.83	...	+ 1.800	− 0.002	......	3	50.8	...
4046	2654	8.1	5	18 39 49.26	49.03	+ 1.766	0.000	......	3	45.0	12.7
4047	2653	7.5	4	18 39 55.09	55.23	+ 2.035	0.000	......	2	48.0	13.6
4048	...	7.9	5	18 39 55.27	...	+ 1.169	− 0.004	......	3	49.3	...
4049	2656	7.3	6	18 39 55.31	55.52	+ 1.813	0.000	......	3	50.0	13.5
4050	...	7.3	1	18 39 56.00	...	+ 3.751	− 0.006	......	1	56.5	...
4051	2659	7.0	3	18 40 10.85	10.78	+ 1.277	− 0.003	......	3	44.4	14.5
4052	...	7.9	5	18 40 38.56	...	+ 1.709	− 0.002	......	3	48.0	...
4053	2660	7.9	6	18 40 44.06	44.06	+ 1.917	0.000	......	3	47.0	11.6
4054	2661	9.4	8	18 40 48.39	38.08	+ 1.697	0.000	......	5	46.2	13.7
4055	...	7.1	5	18 40 49.79	...	+ 3.631	− 0.005	......	3	56.6	...

| Ordinal Number. | Mean North Polar Distance 1845.0. | | Precession 1845.0. | Secular Variation. | Adopted Proper Motion. | Observations of N.P.D. | | | Names. | Oeltzen-Argelander Number. |
	R.	G.				No. R.	Mean year R.	G.		
	° ′ ″	″	″	″	″		1800 +			
4021	37 56 51.5	52.8	− 3.16	− 0.19	− 0.03	4	44.4	12.6	....	18523
4022	117 39 16.3	...	− 3.15	− 0.54	...	2	52.7	...	....	......
4023	49 40 19.2	23.2	− 3.17	− 0.27	...	4	46.6	11.7	....	......
4024	45 52 26.5	28.9	− 3.17	− 0.25	...	3	43.6	12.7	....	......
4025	29 25 55.0	57.1	− 3.18	− 0.10	...	3	43.9	12.7	....	......
4026	49 25 38.1	37.5	− 3.19	− 0.27	...	3	44.4	11.6	....	......
4027	12 34 43.9	44.3	− 3.24	+ 0.39	...	3	50.3	9.7	....	18543
4028	26 36 36.5	36.8	− 3.25	− 0.07	...	3	44.9	10.6	.................7..	18539
4029	7 13 17.8	...	− 3.26	+ 1.06	...	3	47.7	...	....	......
4030	51 46 55.9	57.7	− 3.31	− 0.30	...	4	49.1	13.6	....	......
4031	50 51 8.4	7.9	− 3.32	− 0.29	...	3	47.0	11.7	....	......
4032	26 21 9.4	9.5	− 3.33	− 0.05	...	3	49.0	10.7	....	......
4033	45 13 33.6	34.3	− 3.34	− 0.25	...	4	46.4	12.7	....	18564
4034	45 13 8.8	...	− 3.34	− 0.25	...	3	48.0	...	....	18565
4035	42 34 44.7	46.3	− 3.36	− 0.23	...	3	45.9	12.3	....	......
4036	51 37 21.4	23.2	− 3.38	− 0.28	...	3	47.6	13.5	....	......
4037	51 33 41.3	...	− 3.40	− 0.29	...	2	51.1	...	....	......
4038	46 18 36.2	...	− 3.41	− 0.26	...	2	45.6	...	....	......
4039	50 29 20.0	20.0	− 3.41	− 0.27	− 0.04	3	45.3	8.6	4 Lyræ ε¹......	......
4040	50 32 44.9	46.2	− 3.42	− 0.29	− 0.09	3	49.7	8.6	5 Lyræ ε²......	......
4041	34 31 40.6	...	− 3.43	− 0.16	...	3	51.0	...	....	......
4042	27 24 14.0	16.2	− 3.44	− 0.06	...	3	45.9	10.6	....	......
4043	34 36 57.0	57.3	− 3.45	− 0.16	...	5	44.8	7.7	46 Draconis c.	......
4044	42 32 20.9	19.9	− 3.45	− 0.22	...	4	47.4	12.6	....	18586
4045	46 2 32.1	...	− 3.46	− 0.26	...	2	48.1	...	....	......
4046	45 16 7.7	9.4	− 3.47	− 0.26	...	2	46.6	12.7	....	18593
4047	51 50 30.4	30.4	− 3.47	− 0.27	...	2	48.6	13.6	....	......
4048	34 42 19.9	...	− 3.47	− 0.16	...	3	48.4	...	....	......
4049	46 19 28.9	29.3	− 3.47	− 0.24	...	3	47.7	13.5	....	......
4050	117 17 35.9	...	− 3.49	− 0.54	...	2	52.7	...	....	......
4051	36 17 5.1	2.2	− 3.50	− 0.19	...	4	45.4	14.5	....	18598
4052	44 1 31.4	...	− 3.54	− 0.25	...	2	44.6	...	....	18604
4053	48 45 23.2	24.4	− 3.55	− 0.29	...	3	47.3	11.6	....	......
4054	43 46 49.7	32.1	− 3.55	− 0.28	...	3	46.3	13.7	....	......
4055	113 1 8.0	...	− 3.55	− 0.52	...	1	52.7	...	....	......

Ordinal Number.		Magnitude.	Estimates of Magnitude.	Mean Right Ascension 1845.0.		Precession 1845.0.	Secular Variation.	Adopted Proper Motion.	Observations of R.A.		
R.	G.	R.	R.	R.	G.				No. R.	Mean year. R.	G.
				h. m. s.	s.	s.	s.	s.		1800 +	
4056	...	8.4	5	18 41 27.71	...	+ 1.806	− 0.002	......	3	53.6	...
4057	2662	8.7	7	18 41 8.15	8.36	+ 2.036	0.000	......	4	49.0	13.7
4058	2664	6.5	5	18 41 15.81	15.55	+ 1.916	0.000	......	3	45.3	11.6
4059	2663	8.1	5	18 41 18.60	18.45	+ 2.035	0.000	......	3	50.9	13.7
4060	...	7.9	6	18 41 32.76	...	+ 1.801	− 0.002	......	3	51.6	...
4061	2665	8.4	5	18 41 35.51	35.12	+ 1.816	0.000	......	3	44.4	13.6
4062	...	8.2	6	18 41 36.80	...	− 7.032	− 0.234	......	3	53.0	...
4063	2666	6.9	4	18 41 44.61	44.60	+ 1.826	− 0.003	......	3	47.6	13.5
4064	...	7.3	1	18 41 45.57	...	+ 3.751	− 0.006	......	2	55.6	...
4065	2668	8.4	5	18 42 0.10	0.47	+ 2.036	0.000	......	2	48.2	13.7
4066	...	7.3	5	18 42 10.72	...	− 1.178	− 0.043	......	2	52.6	...
4067	2670	5.9	6	18 42 28.60	28.24	+ 0.711	0.000	......	4	46.2	12.6
4068	2669	6.7	6	18 42 34.93	34.74	+ 1.702	− 0.003	......	3	44.6	11.7
4069	...	7.8	14	18 43 14.31	...	−18.319	− 1.182	......	7	51.3	...
4070	2671	6.2	5	18 43 15.28	14.87	+ 1.339	− 0.003	. ....	5	44.8	8.6
4071	2672	7.0	4	18 43 29.63	29.39	+ 1.546	0.000	......	4	46.9	10.2
4072	...	7.0	6	18 43 37.12	...	+ 1.565	− 0.003	......	4	45.8	...
4073	...	8.4	11	18 43 40.75	...	−55.301	− 8.725	......	8	52.8	...
4074	2673	8.7	5	18 43 47.51	47.70	+ 1.973	0.000	......	2	47.2	13.6
4075	2708	7.1	6	18 43 50.85	50.81	− 8.006	− 0.309	......	5	49.0	7.6
4076	...	6.5	2	18 43 59.83	...	+ 2.230	− 0.001	......	1	53.6	...
4077	2675	7.0	6	18 44 3.73	3.40	+ 1.754	0.000	......	5	46.2	12.7
4078	...	6.5	1	18 44 5.74	...	+ 2.239	− 0.001	......	3	56.6	...
4079	2674	8.7	6	18 44 7.98	7.93	+ 1.954	0.000	......	3	45.9	13.6
4080	2677	5.6	4	18 44 11.03	10.47	+ 1.582	− 0.003	......	4	46.6	9.7
4081	2681	8.4	8	18 44 13.91	13.59	+ 0.737	− 0.006	......	4	48.7	13.7
4082	...	3.9	11	18 44 21.46	...	+ 2.212	− 0.001	− 0.002	61	46.1	...
4083	2676	7.6	6	18 44 22.02	21.81	+ 2.036	0.000	......	4	47.1	12.7
4084	...	7.7	3	18 44 23.00	...	− 0.615	− 0.027	......	2	48.7	...
4085	2712	6.4	8	18 44 28.09	27.61	− 7.690	− 0.270	......	6	49.5	7.6
4086	2679	8.4	9	18 44 35.28	35.31	+ 1.752	0.000	......	5	49.6	12.7
4087	2678	7.2	5	18 44 37.80	37.68	+ 1.823	0.000	......	3	44.3	13.5
4088	2680	7.6	5	18 44 47.85	47.68	+ 1.948	0.000	......	3	44.6	13.6
4089	...	5.2	3	18 44 48.68	...	+ 3.625	− 0.006	− 0.004	1	49.6	...
4090	...	6.5	7	18 44 54.90	...	− 0.660	− 0.026	......	4	48.2	...

Ordinal Number.	Mean North Polar Distance 1845.0.		Precession 1845.0.	Secular Variation.	Adopted Proper Motion.	Observations of N.P.D.			Names.	Oeltzen-Argelander Number.
R.	R.	G.				No. R.	Mean year. R.	G.		
	° ′ ″	″	″	″	″		1800 +			
4056	46 9 10.8	...	− 3.57	− 0.25	...	2	45.1	...	....	....
4057	51 50 30.9	33.7	− 3.58	− 0.29	...	3	49.3	13.7	....	....
4058	48 43 18.2	19.5	− 3.59	− 0.27	...	4	44.9	11.6	....	....
4059	51 48 35.7	34.4	− 3.59	− 0.28	...	2	48.6	13.7	....	....
4060	46 1 44.4	...	− 3.61	− 0.25	...	3	46.7	...	....	....
4061	46 20 52.0	52.3	− 3.62	− 0.26	...	3	44.3	13.6	....	....
4062	7 24 57.6	...	− 3.62	+ 1.01	...	3	47.7	...	....	....
4063	46 36 15.6	15.1	− 3.63	− 0.25	...	4	46.7	13.5	....	....
4064	117 20 14.3	...	− 3.64	− 0.54	...	2	52.7	...	....	....
4065	51 48 22.3	23.6	− 3.65	− 0.28	...	3	50.0	13.7	....	....
4066	17 11 38.3	...	− 3.67	+ 0.16	...	3	48.0	...	....	18623
4067	29 6 54.8	56.0	− 3.70	− 0.11	...	4	44.6	12.6	....	18628
4068	43 51 8.2	6.7	− 3.70	− 0.23	...	4	45.6	11.7	....	18629
4069	3 30 48.4	...	− 3.76	+ 2.62	...	10	50.8	...	....	....
4070	37 10 49.1	48.7	− 3.76	− 0.18	...	6	45.6	8.6	....	18640
4071	40 44 15.4	17.1	− 3.78	− 0.21	...	5	46.2	10.2	....	18646
4072	41 5 47.8	...	− 3.79	− 0.22	...	4	45.1	...	....	....
4073	1 17 20.7	...	− 3.80	+ 8.12	...	5	52.6	...	....	....
4074	50 6 42.0	39.9	− 3.81	− 0.28	...	3	49.0	13.6	....	....
4075	6 45 28.5	30.4	− 3.81	+ 1.15	...	4	45.4	7.6	....	....
4076	57 21 43.7	...	− 3.82	− 0.32	...	1	53.6	...	8 Lyræ ν¹......	....
4077	44 54 54.7	57.4	− 3.83	− 0.24	...	4	46.1	12.7	....	18653?
4078	57 37 29.3	...	− 3.83	− 0.32	...	1	53.7	...	9 Lyræ ν²......	....
4079	49 35 57.9	60.3	− 3.84	− 0.28	...	3	47.3	13.6	....	....
4080	41 24 26.7	30.2	− 3.84	− 0.22	...	3	44.3	9.7	....	18656
4081	29 21 14.5	16.2	− 3.85	− 0.11	...	4	50.9	13.7	....	18657
4082	56 48 48.8	...	− 3.86	− 0.32	+ 0.03	4	48.9	...	10 Lyræ β.....	....
4083	51 44 55.3	57.0	− 3.86	− 0.29	...	3	46.9	12.7	....	....
4084	19 35 42.1	...	− 3.86	+ 0.07	...	2	48.7	...	....	18663
4085	6 57 9.1	8.7	− 3.87	+ 1.08	...	5	42.6	7.6	....	....
4086	44 51 10.8	10.5	− 3.88	− 0.25	...	4	43.6	12.7	....	18665
4087	46 26 34.3	35.5	− 3.88	− 0.25	...	3	44.4	13.5	....	....
4088	49 26 25.7	25.4	− 3.89	− 0.26	...	3	44.4	13.6	....	....
4089	112 55 47.6	...	− 3.90	− 0.52	+ 0.01	4	53.4	...	32 Sagittarii ν¹	....
4090	19 22 18.4	...	− 3.90	+ 0.09	+ 0.09	4	49.2	...	....	18675

Magnitude.	Estimates of Magnitude.	Mean Right Ascension 1845.0.		Precession 1845.0.	Secular Variation	Adopted Proper Motion.
	R.	R.	G.			
		h. m. s.	s.	s.	s.	s.
7.0	6	18 44 54·97	...	− 2.859	− 0.083	......
8.5	5	18 44 57.81	57.67	+ 0.746	− 0.009	......
7.2	4	18 45 29.18	28.86	+ 2.002	0.000	......
8.6	6	18 45 37.89	37.94	+ 1.917	− 0.003	......
4.0	1	18 45 39.08	...	+ 3.723	− 0.007	......
7.2	6	18 45 42.53	42.31	+ 1.859	0.000	......
7.2	4	18 46 1.83	1.75	+ 1.815	0.000	......
7.1	4	18 46 5.90	4.76	+ 2.030	0.000	......
7.3	6	18 46 15.78	15.55	+ 2.004	0.000	......
9.1	5	18 46 23.29	23.06	+ 1.962	0.000	......
6.0	1	18 46 35.31	...	+ 3.462	− 0.005	......
8.3	7	18 46 36.60	36.54	+ 1.455	− 0.003	......
7.3	8	18 46 50.72	50.69	+ 1.921	0.000	......
7.4	7	18 46 55.99	55.91	+ 1.763	0.000	......
7.5	7	18 47 6.19	6.16	+ 1.261	− 0.003	......
6.6	6	18 47 8.73	8.77	+ 1.924	0.000	......
7.3	6	18 47 33.25	33.42	+ 1.827	− 0.003	......
7.8	6	18 47 40.21	40.29	+ 1.462	0.000	......
5.4	5	18 48 6.56	6.25	+ 1.348	− 0.006	......
7.3	6	18 48 16.46	16.30	+ 1.828	0.000	......
6.6	7	18 48 17.56	17.49	+ 1.941	0.000	......
6.9	5	18 48 23.45	23.48	+ 0.745	− 0.006	......
7.8	5	18 48 25.26	24.52	+ 1.343	− 0.003	......
8.6	7	18 48 34.78	34.79	+ 1.862	0.000	......
6.4	7	18 48 38.98	38.85	+ 1.864	0.000	......
8.0	6	18 48 47.49	47.31	+ 1.811	0.000	......
7.7	5	18 48 48.72	48.55	+ 1.968	0.000	......
8.2	7	18 48 53.55	...	+ 0.878	− 0.006	......
4.5	3	18 48 54.63	54.15	+ 0.878	− 0.006	+ 0.005
7.3	7	18 49 13.76	13.60	+ 1.933	0.000	......
5.3	5	18 49 23.12	22.98	+ 1.485	0.000	......
7.5	7	18 49 25.56	25.26	+ 1.488	0.000	......
9.2	6	18 49 30.95	30.94	+ 0.743	− 0.009	......
5.0	5	18 49 36.66	37.06	− 1.455	− 0.046	......
5.9	6	18 49 54.47	54.14	+ 1.919	0.000	......

Ordinal Number.	Mean North Polar Distance 1845.0.			Precession 1845.0.	Secular Variation.	Adopted Proper Motion.	Observations of N.P.D.			Names.	Oeltzen-Argelander Number.
							No.	Mean year.			
R.	R.		G.				R.	R.	G.		
	° ′ ″		″	″	″	″		1800 +			
4091	12 28 7.1		...	− 3.90	+ 0.40	...	4	52.1	...	....	18678
4092	29 26 30.3		32.8	− 3.91	− 0.11	...	2	49.7	13.7	....	18673
4093	50 50 22.1		23.5	− 3.95	− 0.27	...	3	47.4	12.7	....	....
4094	48 40 21.5		20.7	− 3.97	− 0.28	...	3	46.0	12.7	....	....
4095	116 28 58.4		...	− 3.97	− 0.53	+ 0.08	2	46.6	...	34 Sagittarii σ	....
4096	47 16 7.6		6.8	− 3.97	− 0.25	...	4	45.1	11.6	....	....
4097	46 13 27.6		27.7	− 4.00	− 0.25	...	3	44.4	13.5	....	....
4098	51 33 27.0		28.4	− 4.01	− 0.27	...	3	47.7	12.6	....	....
4099	50 51 45.1		46.6	− 4.02	− 0.28	...	3	47.3	11.7	....	....
4100	49 46 48.8		50.4	− 4.03	− 0.27	...	3	46.3	13.6	....	....
4101	106 33 36.5		...	− 4.08	− 0.49	...	2	52.7	...	....	....
4102	39 2 10.7		12.5	− 4.05	− 0.20	...	3	46.3	12.6	....	18694
4103	48 43 8.9		9.6	− 4.07	− 0.27	...	5	48.1	12.7	....	....
4104	45 2 59.4		61.2	− 4.08	− 0.25	...	4	47.6	12.7	....	18701
4105	35 52 50.7		51.0	− 4.09	− 0.17	...	4	47.1	10.6	....	18703
4106	48 48 7.8		7.7	− 4.10	− 0.28	...	4	44.9	12.7	....	....
4107	46 28 34.3		34.5	− 4.13	− 0.25	...	3	45.7	13.5	....	....
4108	39 7 12.7		12.4	− 4.14	− 0.20	...	3	47.0	12.6	....	18714
4109	37 13 23.9		32.0	− 4.18	− 0.19	...	4	44.1	9.7	....	18720
4110	46 28 26.6		24.9	− 4.19	− 0.25	...	3	47.0	13.5	....	....
4111	49 11 42.2		44.8	− 4.19	− 0.26	...	4	47.1	13.6	....	....
4112	29 20 51.9		53.3	− 4.20	− 0.09	...	3	43.9	13.7	....	18725
4113	37 7 14.9		41.7	− 4.20	− 0.17	...	3	46.3	9.7	....	18726
4114	47 15 22.4		19.6	− 4.22	− 0.27	...	4	48.7	11.6	....	....
4115	47 17 16.1		15.7	− 4.22	− 0.25	...	4	44.6	11.6	....	....
4116	46 3 51.8		52.9	− 4.24	− 0.26	...	3	45.3	13.5	....	....
4117	49 52 7.6		9.2	− 4.24	− 0.28	...	3	47.3	13.6	....	....
4118	30 47 30.3		...	− 4.25	− 0.13	...	4	51.6	...	47 Draconis o(1)	....
4119	30 47 59.6		60.2	− 4.25	− 0.13	− 0.01	5	47.2	6.3	47 Draconis o(2)	....
4120	48 58 5.8		6.8	− 4.28	− 0.29	...	3	46.6	13.1	....	....
4121	39 28 56.0		56.7	− 4.29	− 0.21	...	5	45.1	12.5	....	18740
4122	39 31 59.8		60.3	− 4.29	− 0.21	...	5	46.5	12.5	....	18742
4123	29 18 21.3		22.2	− 4.30	− 0.11	...	3	46.4	13.7	....	18743
4124	16 5 46.9		47.1	− 4.31	+ 0.20	− 0.13	4	43.7	8.5	....	....
4125	48 35 33.4		34.9	− 4.33	− 0.26	...	4	47.6	11.7	....	....

Magnitude.	Estimates of Magnitude. R.	Mean Right Ascension 1845.0. R.	G.	Precession 1845.0.	Secular Variation	Adopted Proper Motion.
		h. m. s.	s.	s.	s.	s.
9.0	6	18 50 8.69	...	+ 1.978	— 0.001	......
8.2	7	18 50 13.14	13.14	+ 1.978	— 0.001	......
7.0	8	18 50 18.94	18.88	+ 1.976	— 0.001	......
4.4	8	18 50 37.14	36.91	+ 1.822	— 0.001	......
8.4	7	18 50 40.24	40.08	+ 1.975	— 0.001	......
5.7	6	18 50 41.88	41.97	+ 1.586	— 0.003	......
8.5	5	18 50 49.76	...	+ 1.812	— 0.002	......
6.2	5	18 51 4.95	4.25	+ 1.040	— 0.006	......
7.5	7	18 51 16.05	...	+ 1.810	— 0.002	......
5.3	7	18 51 20.51	20.21	— 1.880	— 0.057	......
7.5	4	18 52 31.53	31.76	+ 1.901	— 0.002	......
7.4	6	18 52 33.40	33.09	+ 1.738	— 0.002	......
8.0	6	18 52 53.74	53.37	+ 1.740	— 0.002	......
8.4	7	18 53 8.52	...	+ 2.013	— 0.001	......
7.4	7	18 53 9.60	9.43	+ 2.000	— 0.001	......
7.3	5	18 53 17.68	17.40	+ 1.995	— 0.001	......
7.3	7	18 53 32.09	31.94	+ 0.749	— 0.006	......
6.5	7	18 53 42.37	42.10	+ 1.961	— 0.001	......
8.5	5	18 53 54.82	...	— 4.412	— 0.163	......
6.4	6	18 53 59.35	59.18	+ 2.017	— 0.001	......
5.6	6	18 54 7.67	7.63	+ 1.021	— 0.006	......
8.5	4	18 54 14.09	...	— 4.391	— 0.162	......
8.0	6	18 54 20.52	19.64	+ 0.608	— 0.009	......
7.9	7	18 54 23.08	22.92	+ 1.923	— 0.001	......
6.4	4	18 54 55.02	54.59	+ 0.991	— 0.006	+ 0.003
7.6	8	18 54 57.32	57.09	+ 1.570	— 0.003	......
7.6	4	18 55 12.80	12.72	+ 2.015	— 0.001	......
6.7	7	18 55 12.86	...	— 0.829	— 0.045	......
6.7	5	18 55 14.49	14.11	+ 1.962	— 0.001	......
7.5	4	18 55 14.79	...	+ 3.690	— 0.008	......
4.7	8	18 55 23.60	...	+ 3.593	— 0.007	+ 0.001
7.7	5	18 55 24.60	24.46	+ 1.995	— 0.001	......
7.4	4	18 55 26.23	26.21	+ 1.994	— 0.001	......
8.0	5	18 55 33.35	33.29	+ 1.923	— 0.001	......
6.0	4	18 55 43.55	42.67	+ 0.610	— 0.009	......

| Ordinal Number. | Mean North Polar Distance 1845.0. | | Precession 1845.0. | Secular Variation. | Adopted Proper Motion. | Observations of N.P.D. | | | Names. | Oeltzen-Argelander Number. |
R.	R.	G.				No. R.	Mean year R.	G.		
	° ′ ″	″	″	″	″		1800 +			
4126	50 4 10.2	...	− 4.35	− 0.28	...	4	50.2	...	....	......
4127	50 3 29.5	32.1	− 4.36	− 0.28	...	4	47.9	13.6	....	......
4128	50 1 13.0	13.6	− 4.37	− 0.29	...	3	45.7	13.6	....	......
4129	46 15 18.7	23.7	− 4.39	− 0.25	...	4	42.6	8.7	13 Lyræ	......
4130	49 59 44.7	46.0	− 4.40	− 0.29	...	3	46.0	13.6	....	......
4131	41 19 55.2	56.5	− 4.40	− 0.22	+ 0.12	3	43.6	10.7	....	18761
4132	46 1 21.4	...	− 4.41	− 0.25	...	3	46.4	...	....	......
4133	32 42 32.2	31.9	− 4.43	− 0.14	...	4	44.4	9.7	....	18766
4134	45 58 22.7	...	− 4.45	− 0.25	...	4	46.7	...	....	......
4135	14 45 7.8	9.9	− 4.46	+ 0.25	− 0.02	13	50.6	7.7	50 Draconis...·	18779
4136	48 5 43.4	41.9	− 4.56	− 0.28	...	3	44.3	12.7	....	......
4137	44 20 58.4	58.4	− 4.56	− 0.25	...	4	45.1	12.7	....	18792
4138	44 22 25.7	25.3	− 4.59	− 0.25	...	4	44.4	12.7	....	18794
4139	50 54 42.7	...	− 4.61	− 0.28	...	4	43.7	...	....	......
4140	50 33 54.5	54.3	− 4.61	− 0.28	...	3	47.3	13.6	....	......
4141	50 25 47.6	49.3	− 4.62	− 0.28	...	3	45.0	13.6	....	......
4142	29 15 26.5	28.1	− 4.64	− 0.10	...	5	47.3	13.7	....	......
4143	49 31 50.5	50.8	− 4.66	− 0.29	...	4	44.1	11.6	....	......
4144	9 51 35.0	...	− 4.67	+ 0.63	...	3	47.7	...	....	18809
4145	50 59 37.9	38.6	− 4.68	− 0.28	...	4	46.6	11.7	....	......
4146	32 23 20.9	19.6	− 4.69	− 0.14	...	6	46.2	8.7	48 Draconis...	......
4147	9 52 42.3	...	− 4.70	+ 0.63	...	3	47.7	...	....	18814
4148	27 49 21.8	25.3	− 4.71	− 0.09	...	5	46.4	9.7	....	18811
4149	48 34 27.8	28.0	− 4.71	− 0.26	...	4	44.1	13.5	....	......
4150	31 59 11.1	12.2	− 4.76	− 0.14	...	4	46.6	12.6	....	......
4151	40 53 34.3	35.6	− 4.76	− 0.21	...	5	48.1	11.4	....	18820
4152	50 52 48.5	50.6	− 4.78	− 0.27	...	3	46.9	11.7	....	......
4153	18 24 56.3	...	− 4.78	+ 0.13	...	5	47.0	...	....	18829?
4154	49 31 50.2	51.3	− 4.79	− 0.29	...	3	45.0	11.6	....	......
4155	115 27 14.5	...	− 4.80	− 0.52	...	1	53.7	...	....	......
4156	111 57 44.7	...	− 4.80	− 0.51	+ 0.05	7	50.3	...	39 Sagittarii o	......
4157	50 22 16.1	16.8	− 4.80	− 0.28	...	3	47.0	13.6	....	......
4158	50 20 59.5	60.7	− 4.80	− 0.27	...	3	47.1	13.6	....	......
4159	48 31 56.0	54.9	− 4.81	− 0.26	...	4	47.5	13.6	....	......
4160	27 48 44.4	43.6	− 4.83	− 0.09	...	4	41.3	9.7	....	18835

Magnitude.	Estimates of Magnitude.	Mean Right Ascension 1845.0.		Precession 1845.0.	Secular Variation	Adopted Proper Motion.
R.		R.	G.			
		h. m. s.	s.	s.	s.	s.
8.1	6	18 55 50.03	...	− 1.535	− 0.060	......
6.8	6	18 55 55.50	55.37	+ 1.900	− 0.001	......
8.0	6	18 56 9.57	9.46	+ 1.935	− 0.001	......
5.0	10	18 56 16.59	16.12	− 0.715	− 0.031	+ 0.007
6.5	4	18 56 28.70	....	− 4.099	− 0.152	......
7.7	5	18 56 40.74	40.91	+ 1.811	− 0.001	......
7.1	5	18 56 41.02	41.03	+ 1.932	− 0.001	......
8.5	5	18 56 49.33	49.47	+ 1.258	− 0.004	......
7.4	14	18 56 49.90	49.48	− 1.414	− 0.034	......
7.1	2	18 56 52.08	52.11	+ 1.640	− 0.002	......
5.7	3	18 57 3.22	3.47	+ 1.694	− 0.003	+ 0.017
6.1	4	18 57 39.29	39.30	+ 1.191	− 0.005	− 0.002
7.9	8	18 57 56.36	56.22	+ 1.994	− 0.001	......
3.5	2	18 58 17.19	...	+ 2.756	− 0.002	− 0.006
6.4	6	18 58 28.15	28.47	+ 1.412	− 0.004	......
8.0	6	18 58 29.23	29.22	+ 1.996	− 0.001	......
8.2	7	18 58 42.66	...	− 1.958	− 0.046	......
7.5	6	18 58 43.70	43.53	− 1.958	− 0.046	......
8.5	5	18 58 45.59	...	− 4.232	− 0.163	......
7.7	5	18 58 53.18	53.44	+ 1.989	− 0.001	......
8.5	5	18 59 9.57	9.57	+ 1.930	− 0.002	......
7.6	7	18 59 44.27	44.03	+ 1.562	− 0.003	......
7.8	6	18 59 50.86	50.29	+ 1.939	− 0.001	......
6.7	5	18 59 54.94	54.28	+ 0.842	− 0.006	......
8.4	5	18 59 56.94	56.56	+ 1.990	− 0.001	......
7.3	5	19 0 1.69	1.44	+ 1.747	− 0.003	......
8.5	5	19 0 15.29	...	− 7.616	− 0.387	......
8.9	7	19 0 16.33	16.33	+ 1.940	− 0.001	......
4.4	9	19 0 32.59	...	+ 3.572	− 0.007	− 0.004
7.6	6	19 0 36.14	36.04	+ 1.284	− 0.003	......
8.5	6	19 0 56.77	...	+ 1.943	− 0.002	......
8.1	4	19 1 7.95	7.66	+ 2.058	− 0.002	......
6.8	7	19 1 9.56	9.47	+ 1.550	− 0.003	......
6.7	7	19 1 15.64	15.42	+ 1.942	− 0.002	......
5.3	3	19 1 26.14	25.99	+ 1.349	− 0.006	......

| Ordinal Number. | Mean North Polar Distance 1845.0. | | Precession 1845.0. | Secular Variation. | Adopted Proper Motion. | Observations of N.P.D. | | | Names. | Oeltzen-Argelander Number. |
| | R. | G. | | | | No. R. | Mean year R. | Mean year G. | | |
	° ′ ″	″	″	″	″		1800 +			
4161	15 44 19.7	...	— 4.84	+ 0.22	...	4	48.7	...	....	....
4162	47 57 31.0	29.6	— 4.85	— 0.27	...	3	45.7	12.7	....	....
4163	48 48 13.3	14.7	— 4.86	— 0.26	...	4	47.7	13.5	....	....
4164	18 54 41.3	42.2	— 4.87	+ 0.11	...	12	46.0	6.9	52 Draconis υ.	18839
4165	10 15 4.4	...	— 4.89	+ 0.58	...	8	51.4	...	....	18845
4166	45 50 0.2	2.8	— 4.91	— 0.26	...	3	47.0	12.7	....	....
4167	48 43 53.5	53.6	— 4.91	— 0.27	...	4	44.1	13.5	....	....
4168	35 33 45.7	42.8	— 4.92	— 0.17	...	3	49.0	14.5	....	18846
4169	16 7 10.8	14.2	— 4.92	+ 0.18	...	9	49.3	12.6	....	18847
4170	42 10 59.4	58.9	— 4.92	— 0.21	...	3	46.0	8.6	....	....
4171	43 16 56.8	55.8	— 4.94	— 0.24	+ 0.06	6	46.0	10.7	16 Lyræ........	18849
4172	34 33 44.0	45.0	— 4.99	— 0.16	+ 0.06	3	43.2	8.7	49 Draconis...	18858
4173	50 16 17.7	19.7	— 5.02	— 0.29	...	4	46.9	13.6	....	....
4174	76 21 44.1	...	— 5.05	— 0.39	+ 0.07	2	48.2	...	17 Aquilæ ζ...	....
4175	37 57 42.5	43.1	— 5.06	— 0.19	...	3	45.0	10.7	....	....
4176	50 18 57.7	59.9	— 5.06	— 0.27	...	3	47.0	13.6	....	....
4177	14 25 28.0	...	— 5.08	+ 0.29	...	3	45.7	...	....	....
4178	14 25 23.6	25.2	— 5.08	+ 0.29	...	4	47.2	12.8	....	....
4179	10 2 29.4	...	— 5.09	+ 0.59	...	3	47.7	...	....	18886
4180	50 6 40.7	42.5	— 5.09	— 0.29	...	3	47.0	13.7	....	....
4181	48 36 31.2	33.6	— 5.12	— 0.27	...	3	45.3	13.6	....	....
4182	40 35 48.7	49.0	— 5.17	— 0.22	...	4	46.4	12.6	....	18900
4183	48 48 6.6	7.0	— 5.18	— 0.28	...	5	45.9	13.6	....	....
4184	30 5 59.2	60.2	— 5.18	— 0.11	...	6	46.9	9.7	....	....
4185	50 6 22.5	24.9	— 5.19	— 0.29	...	3	47.4	13.7	....	....
4186	44 18 39.2	38.8	— 5.19	— 0.24	...	4	44.7	11.6	....	18906
4187	6 52 34.0	...	— 5.21	+ 1.07	...	4	52.2	...	....	....
4188	48 48 41.9	47.2	— 5.21	— 0.26	...	5	48.3	13.6	....	....
4189	111 15 51.6	...	— 5.24	— 0.50	+ 0.03	9	49.5	...	41 Sagittarii π	....
4190	35 50 30.5	30.6	— 5.24	— 0.17	...	4	44.9	10.6	....	....
4191	48 52 34.7	...	— 5.27	— 0.27	...	4	52.1	...	....	....
4192	51 52 56.3	56.1	— 5.28	— 0.27	...	3	48.0	12.4	....	....
4193	40 18 43.7	45.1	— 5.29	— 0.22	...	4	44.8	12.7	....	....
4194	48 49 22.2	23.2	— 5.30	— 0.28	...	5	46.9	13.6	....	....
4195	36 50 23.1	22.9	— 5.31	— 0.18	...	5	45.6	7.1	51 Draconis...	18930

Ordinal Number.		Magnitude.	Estimates of Magnitude.	Mean Right Ascension 1845.0.			Precession 1845.0.	Secular Variation	Adopted Proper Motion.	Observations of R.A.		
										No.	Mean year.	
R.	G.	R.		R.		G.				R.	R.	G.
				h. m. s.		s.	s.	s.	s.		1800 +	
4196	2767	8.6	6	19 1 36.12		36.22	+ 1.938	— 0.002	.....	3	47.3	13.6
4197	2771	6.7	5	19 1 47.00		46.36	+ 0.661	— 0.012	......	5	46.2	9.8
4198	2769	7.3	7	19 2 15.52		15.01	+ 1.957	— 0.002	......	4	44.7	11.7
4199	2775	7.2	7	19 2 19.65		18.63	— 1.394	— 0.051	......	4	44.2	12.6
4200	2773	8.3	5	19 2 30.00		29.84	+ 1.817	— 0.003	......	3	45.6	12.7
4201	2772	7.3	6	19 2 30.40		30.13	+ 1.867	— 0.003	......	5	44.1	11.6
4202	2770	7.3	6	19 2 31.11		30.93	+ 2.040	— 0.001	......	5	46.2	10.7
4203	2774	7.0	8	19 2 58.01		57.74	+ 2.031	— 0.001	......	7	47.4	10.7
4204	...	...	...	19 4 ...		...	......	......	......	...	...	...
4205	2784	6.7	6	19 4 24.11		24.17	— 2.417	— 0.094	— 0.017	5	45.1	9.6
4206	2776	8.3	7	19 4 32.66		32.82	+ 1.539	— 0.003	......	3	45.9	12.7
4207	2777	7.0	6	19 4 35.66		35.55	+ 1.533	— 0.003	......	5	46.0	12.7
4208	...	6.6	88	19 4 36.34		...	—17.953	— 1.730	......	86	50.8	...
4209	2778	6.3	7	19 4 48.06		48.00	+ 1.416	— 0.004	......	3	45.0	11.6
4210	2779	7.9	8	19 4 55.65		55.19	+ 1.226	— 0.007	......	4	46.1	12.6
4211	2781	7.3	7	19 5 9.48		9.24	+ 1.231	— 0.007	......	3	47.4	12.6
4212	...	8.1	5	19 5 29.56		...	+ 2.044	— 0.002	......	3	47.0	...
4213	2780	7.9	5	19 5 34.66		34.43	+ 2.035	— 0.002	......	4	46.6	10.7
4214	...	7.0	5	19 5 35.30		...	+ 1.924	— 0.002	......	3	49.9	...
4215	...	8.1	4	19 5 52.99		...	+ 2.049	— 0.002	......	3	46.7	...
4216	...	8.2	5	19 5 53.18		...	+ 2.049	— 0.002	......	4	53.6	...
4217	...	7.6	8	19 5 57.48		...	+ 1.935	— 0.002	......	4	50.6	...
4218	2783	7.0	5	19 6 13.45		12.95	+ 1.637	— 0.003	......	4	46.9	11.8
4219	2782	6.2	6	19 6 14.55		14.37	+ 1.989	— 0.002	......	4	44.7	11.7
4220	...	...	...	19 6 ...		...	......	......	......	...	...	...
4221	2785	7.1	6	19 7 13.60		13.25	+ 1.958	— 0.002	......	5	46.4	11.7
4222	2786	8.2	7	19 7 29.76		29.29	+ 1.234	— 0.006	......	4	44.6	12.7
4223	...	7.9	5	19 7 35.81		...	+ 1.983	— 0.002	......	2	48.1	...
4224	2787	6.8	7	19 7 53.06		52.88	+ 1.693	— 0.003	.....;	4	45.6	11.6
4225	2789	6.6	6	19 8 4.22		4.44	+ 1.570	— 0.003	......	5	44.8	9.8
4226	...	6.9	8	19 8 5.13		...	+ 1.570	— 0.003	......	3	41.1	...
4227	2788	9.0	6	19 8 17.29		18.53	+ 1.998	— 0.002	......	4	45.6	10.7
4228	...	8.1	8	19 8 27.23		...	— 4.742	— 0.241	......	4	49.7	...
4229	2790	5.0	3	19 8 28.95		28.91	+ 2.040	— 0.002	......	5	44.8	9.7
4230	...	5.3	2	19 8 33.88		...	+ 3.515	— 0.008	— 0.004	3	48.5	...

Ordinal Number. R.	Mean North Polar Distance 1845.0. R.	G.	Precession 1845.0.	Secular Variation.	Adopted Proper Motion.	Observations of N.P.D. No. R.	Mean year. R. (1800+)	G.	Names.	Oeltzen-Argelander Number.
4196	48 43 21.5	22.8	− 5.33	− 0.28	...	4	47.2	13.6	....	......
4197	28 8 16.2	18.4	− 5.34	− 0.09	...	4	43.6	9.8	....	18943
4198	49 11 11.5	12.6	− 5.38	− 0.27	...	4	46.6	11.7	....	......
4199	16 5 25.9	24.7	− 5.39	+ 0.19	...	5	44.5	12.6	....	......
4200	45 46 11.5	12.7	− 5.40	− 0.25	...	4	47.2	12.7	....	......
4201	46 55 40.2	41.7	− 5.40	− 0.25	...	4	43.1	11.6	....	......
4202	51 18 50.8	51.7	− 5.40	− 0.27	...	3	44.4	10.7	....	......
4203	51 5 19.9	21.7	− 5.44	− 0.28	...	3	45.6	10.7	....	......
4204	117 7 45.1	...	− 5.56	− 0.52	...	3	53.7	...	....	......
4205	13 10 28.8	26.0	− 5.56	+ 0.34	...	9	47.3	9.6	....	18992
4206	39 59 26.9	28.5	− 5.57	− 0.20	...	4	45.2	12.7	....	18990
4207	39 53 2.4	3.6	− 5.58	− 0.22	...	4	43.9	12.7	....	18991
4208	3 29 41.9	...	− 5.58	+ 2.52	...	29	49.8	...	....	......
4209	37 49 10.2	7.8	− 5.59	− 0.18	...	6	47.6	11.6	....	......
4210	34 50 57.4	58.4	− 5.61	− 0.18	...	5	46.6	12.6	....	18998
4211	34 55 5.2	6.1	− 5.63	− 0.19	...	6	45.1	12.6	....	19002
4212	51 20 49.0	...	− 5.65	− 0.29	...	3	45.4	...	....	......
4213	51 4 57.6	58.5	− 5.66	− 0.29	...	3	45.3	10.7	....	......
4214	48 13 50.8	...	− 5.66	− 0.27	...	3	49.4	...	....	......
4215	51 28 10.7	...	− 5.68	− 0.29	...	2	43.7	...	....	......
4216	51 28 9.2	...	− 5.68	− 0.29	...	1	47.7	...	....	......
4217	48 28 40.5	...	− 5.69	− 0.27	...	5	49.7	...	....	......
4218	41 48 34.6	33.5	− 5.71	− 0.22	...	3	43.6	11.8	....	......
4219	49 49 30.7	31.1	− 5.72	− 0.29	...	5	44.5	11.7	....	......
4220	115 55 49.7	...	− 5.75	− 0.52	...	3	53.7	...	....	......
4221	49 1 12.0	12.6	− 5.80	− 0.27	...	4	43.6	11.7	....	......
4222	34 52 40.7	41.4	− 5.82	− 0.17	...	4	45.7	12.7	....	19042
4223	49 37 41.6	...	− 5.83	− 0.28	...	3	48.3	...	....	......
4224	42 53 6.1	5.7	− 5.85	− 0.22	...	5	47.0	11.6	....	......
4225	40 25 57.2	22.6	− 5.87	− 0.22	...	4	43.1	9.3	....	19051
4226	40 25 49.4	...	− 5.87	− 0.22	...	6	48.7	...	....	19052
4227	50 1 13.2	15.1	− 5.89	− 0.28	...	3	46.4	10.7	....	......
4228	9 17 10.2	...	− 5.90	+ 0.66	...	4	48.2	...	....	......
4229	51 7 3.3	2.8	− 5.90	− 0.27	− 0.05	3	45.7	9.7	20 Lyræ η.....	......
4230	109 13 22.3	...	− 5.91	− 0.49	− 0.01	1	46.7	...	43 Sagittarii d	......

Magnitude.	Estimates of Magnitude.	Mean Right Ascension 1845.0.		Precession 1845.0.	Secular Variation	Adopted Proper Motion.
R.	R.	R.	G.			
		h. m. s.	s.	s.	s.	s.
5.0	2	19 8 44.48	44.25	+ 1.134	— 0.006	......
7.6	5	19 8 56.34	...	+ 1.988	— 0.002	......
6.4	3	19 9 10.35	10.50	+ 0.240	— 0.020	......
8.6	6	19 9 11.12	10.75	+ 1.244	— 0.006	......
7.1	6	19 9 17.32	...	— 0.816	— 0.079	......
8.7	5	19 9 18.08	...	+ 1.959	— 0.002	......
7.2	5	19 9 21.05	...	+ 1.075	— 0.010	......
9.3	5	19 9 21.24	5.24	+ 1.993	— 0.002	......
8.6	5	19 9 23.24	22.83	+ 1.961	— 0.002	......
7.2	6	19 9 37.81	37.60	+ 1.649	— 0.003	......
8.0	5	19 10 5.94	...	+ 2.006	— 0.002	......
8.2	6	19 10 6.95	6.75	+ 1.381	— 0.006	......
7.1	5	19 10 13.25	13.19	+ 1.631	— 0.003	......
7.6	5	19 10 13.64	...	— 0.855	— 0.051	......
7.7	4	19 10 18.77	18.68	+ 1.799	— 0.003	......
6.7	9	19 10 34.73	34.62	+ 1.997	— 0.002	......
7.6	5	19 10 47.78	47.74	+ 1.794	— 0.003	......
5.0	4	19 11 9.01	8.68	+ 1.076	— 0.009	......
6.5	5	19 11 16.77	16.46	+ 1.564	— 0.003	......
8.5	6	19 11 28.40	27.83	+ 1.716	— 0.003	......
9.2	4	19 11 35.16	...	+ 1.718	— 0.003	......
7.9	4	19 11 38.96	...	+ 1.610	— 0.003	......
6.7	6	19 11 51.49	...	— 8.414	— 0.543	......
8.4	6	19 11 56.61	56.37	+ 1.261	— 0.006	......
6.8	7	19 12 4.09	3.76	+ 1.965	— 0.002	......
7.4	6	19 12 4.48	...	— 0.839	— 0.051	......
...	...	19 12 ...	...	......	......	......
7.4	4	19 12 14.00	13.97	+ 1.600	— 0.003	......
7.4	5	19 12 14.49	14.17	+ 1.654	— 0.003	......
6.4	7	19 12 24.54	24.40	+ 1.721	— 0.003	......
8.2	4	19 12 26.91	26.75	+ 1.712	— 0.003	......
3.6	5	19 12 30.21	30.11	+ 0.019	— 0.026	+ 0.022
9.0	6	19 12 31.77	...	+ 1.925	— 0.002	......
7.9	3	19 12 34.21	...	+ 1.276	— 0.007	......
8.9	3	19 12 37.78	...	+ 1.617	— 0.004	......

Ordinal Number.	Mean North Polar Distance 1845.0.		Precession 1845.0.	Secular Variation.	Adopted Proper Motion.	Observations of N.P.D.			Names.	Oeltzen-Argelander Number.
R.	R.	G.				No. R.	Mean year. R.	G.		
	° ′ ″	″	″	″	″		1800 +			
4231	33 24 11.2	11.4	− 5.92	− 0.14	− 0.05	5	46.3	7.7	53 Draconis...	19061
4232	49 41 52.1	...	− 5.94	− 0.28	...	3	46.3	...	....	....
4233	24 16 50.8	52.0	− 5.96	− 0.03	...	5	45.6	8.6	55 Draconis...	19072
4234	34 57 9.2	7.9	− 5.96	− 0.17	...	4	46.2	12.7	....	19071
4235	18 10 51.3	...	− 5.97	+ 0.11	...	4	52.1	...	....	19073
4236	48 57 37.0	...	− 5.97	− 0.27	...	3	44.3	...	....	....
4237	32 36 27.9	...	− 5.97	− 0.15	...	3	47.0	...	....	....
4238	49 48 42.9	21.2	− 5.98	− 0.28	...	3	44.6	10.7	....	....
4239	49 0 21.4	22.1	− 5.98	− 0.27	...	3	43.9	11.7	....	....
4240	41 54 58.8	58.3	− 6.00	− 0.23	...	3	45.6	11.8	....	19078
4241	50 9 19.9	...	− 6.04	− 0.28	...	2	45.6	...	....	....
4242	37 3 13.3	13.8	− 6.04	− 0.19	...	3	48.3	12.6	....	....
4243	41 32 51.2	52.0	− 6.05	− 0.23	...	3	45.9	10.7	....	19088
4244	17 59 21.3	...	− 6.05	+ 0.12	...	3	52.0	...	....	19090
4245	45 5 37.5	40.2	− 6.06	− 0.26	...	3	46.7	11.7	....	....
4246	49 54 30.9	31.1	− 6.08	− 0.28	...	4	42.6	10.2	....	....
4247	44 56 4.4	5.9	− 6.10	− 0.25	...	3	45.3	11.7	....	....
4248	32 33 40.0	39.7	− 6.13	− 0.16	+ 0.09	11	44.9	7.6	54 Draconis...	19097
4249	40 12 1.6	2.5	− 6.14	− 0.22	...	3	45.0	9.8	....	....
4250	43 12 37.9	35.1	− 6.15	− 0.23	...	3	45.7	12.6	....	19100
4251	43 16 13.0	...	− 6.16	− 0.24	...	3	49.3	...	....	19101
4252	41 5 33.9	...	− 6.16	− 0.22	...	2	48.6	...	....	19102
4253	6 19 11.2	...	− 6.18	+ 1.17	...	3	48.3	...	....	....
4254	35 6 8.4	7.5	− 6.19	− 0.17	...	3	47.3	12.7	....	19107
4255	49 0 38.5	39.0	− 6.20	− 0.26	...	3	46.3	11.7	....	....
4256	18 1 11.4	...	− 6.20	+ 0.12	...	3	52.0	...	....	19112
4257	119 48 30.4	...	− 6.21	− 0.53	...	2	53.7	...	....	....
4258	40 51 4.2	3.3	− 6.22	− 0.23	...	3	45.0	10.8	....	19113
4259	41 55 4.0	3.6	− 6.22	− 0.24	...	3	46.7	11.8	....	....
4260	43 17 21.9	32.6	− 6.23	− 0.23	...	4	48.2	12.6	....	19116
4261	43 5 39.2	40.1	− 6.23	− 0.22	...	2	49.2	12.6	....	19117
4262	22 36 39.9	41.0	− 6.24	− 0.01	− 0.07	13	51.6	6.7	57 Draconis δ.	19121
4263	48 0 34.4	...	− 6.24	− 0.26	...	4	51.9	...	....	....
4264	35 18 45.2	...	− 6.24	− 0.19	...	2	51.2	...	....	19123
4265	41 9 55.2	...	− 6.25	− 0.22	...	2	49.2	...	....	19125

Ordinal Number.		Magnitude.	Estimates of Magnitude.	Mean Right Ascension 1845.0.		Precession 1845.0.	Secular Variation	Adopted Proper Motion.	Observations of R.A.		
R.	G.	R.		R.	G.				No.	Mean year.	
									R.	R.	G.
				h. m. s.	s.	s.	s.	s.		1800 +	
4266	...	4.4	4	19 12 40.86	...	+ 3.486	− 0.008	− 0.003	5	45.9	...
4267	...	8.3	6	19 12 41.88	...	+ 1.937	− 0.002	....	3	51.0	...
4268	...	8.5	4	19 13 0.25	...	+ 1.654	− 0.004	....	2	51.7	...
4269	...	9.3	6	19 13 4.25	...	+ 1.937	− 0.002	....	4	53.9	...
4270	...	7.8	3	19 13 10.05	...	+ 1.938	− 0.002	....	2	52.1	...
4271	2813	3.8	3	19 13 31.04	30.82	+ 1.381	− 0.006	+ 0.004	5	45.5	6.8
4272	2812	6.6	6	19 13 47.36	47.14	+ 2.003	− 0.002	....	5	46.8	10.7
4273	...	8.0	6	19 13 47.38	...	+ 1.942	− 0.002	....	3	53.0	...
4274	...	8.2	5	19 14 21.33	...	+ 1.971	− 0.002	....	2	48.7	...
4275	2814	7.1	7	19 14 26.38	26.42	+ 2.007	− 0.002	....	5	48.8	10.6
4276	...	7.7	6	19 14 27.88	...	+ 1.563	− 0.004	....	4	48.7	...
4277	...	7.7	5	19 14 28.72	...	+ 1.969	− 0.002	....	3	50.7	...
4278	2815	6.3	6	19 14 29.75	29.68	+ 1.598	− 0.003	....	5	44.9	10.7
4279	2819	8.2	7	19 14 37.27	37.00	+ 0.571	− 0.017	....	4	47.2	12.7
4280	2816	8.6	8	19 14 42.74	42.66	+ 1.379	− 0.006	....	4	44.1	12.6
4281	2825	5.0	6	19 14 47.66	48.22	− 2.124	− 0.094	....	4	48.2	8.7
4282	2817	8.4	7	19 14 48.93	48.47	+ 1.383	− 0.006	....	3	44.3	11.8
4283	...	9.2	7	19 14 50.10	...	+ 2.022	− 0.002	....	4	52.7	...
4284	2818	6.7	6	19 15 13.24	13.09	+ 2.022	− 0.002	....	4	45.6	11.6
4285	2821	6.8	6	19 15 21.74	21.02	+ 0.594	− 0.014	....	5	46.9	10.9
4286	...	8.9	6	19 15 37.95	...	+ 1.921	− 0.002	....	3	46.6	...
4287	...	...	...	19 15 50.27	...	+ 3.654	− 0.010	....	1	40.5	...
4288	2820	6.7	4	19 16 5.74	5.95	+ 1.916	− 0.002	....	4	46.7	11.7
4289	2822	6.3	4	19 16 11.12	10.61	+ 1.325	− 0.006	....	4	44.8	8.6
4290	2823	8.1	4	19 16 20.20	19.79	+ 1.389	− 0.006	....	3	47.0	11.8
4291	2824	7.2	5	19 16 28.92	28.82	+ 1.562	− 0.004	....	4	44.4	10.6
4292	2826	8.9	5	19 16 42.45	42.44	+ 1.110	− 0.006	....	2	48.2	12.8
4293	2827	5.5	9	19 17 25.48	25.22	+ 1.101	− 0.009	....	5	45.7	12.8
4294	...	7.9	8	19 17 38.18	...	− 6.399	− 0.360	....	4	49.1	...
4295	...	3.6	2	19 17 40.93	...	+ 3.008	− 0.004	+ 0.014	43	46.0	...
4296	...	9.1	6	19 17 43.38	...	+ 0.473	− 0.021	....	4	51.2	...
4297	...	9.0	3	19 17 48.56	...	+ 0.489	− 0.020	....	2	52.1	...
4298	2829	6.8	7	19 17 50.82	50.74	+ 1.452	− 0.005	....	3	45.6	10.7
4299	2828	6.9	5	19 18 4.27	3.97	+ 1.908	− 0.002	....	3	45.3	11.7
4300	...	7.4	7	19 18 28.42	...	− 4.424	− 0.229	....	3	50.0	...

Ordinal Number.	Mean North Polar Distance 1845.0.			Precession 1845.0.	Secular Variation.	Adopted Proper Motion.	Observations of N.P.D.			Names.	Oeltzen-Argelander Number.
							No.	Mean year.			
R.	R.		G.				R.	R.	G.		
	° ′ ″		″	″	″	″		1800 +			
4266	108	7	59.1	...	— 6.25	— 0.48	— 0.03	3	46.3	...	44 Sagittarii ρ¹	......
4267	48	15	11.4	...	— 6.25	— 0.27	...	3	51.3	...	....	......
4268	41	52	19.2	...	— 6.28	— 0.23	...	4	54.2	...	....	......
4269	48	15	9.2	...	— 6.28	— 0.27	...	3	51.4	...	....	......
4270	48	16	24.9	...	— 6.29	— 0.27	...	3	51.0	...	....	......
4271	36	54	55.7	56.0	— 6.32	— 0.18	+ 0.09	4	44.6	6.8	1 Cygni κ......	19136
4272	49	55	20.6	21.4	— 6.34	— 0.26	...	3	42.3	10.7	....	......
4273	48	21	24.8	...	— 6.35	— 0.27	...	3	51.0	...	....	......
4274	49	3	37.7	...	— 6.39	— 0.27	...	3	47.3	...	....	......
4275	50	1	2.7	3.7	— 6.40	— 0.28	...	3	46.0	10.6	....	......
4276	40	3	18.4	...	— 6.40	— 0.22	...	4	45.7	...	....	......
4277	49	0	44.8	...	— 6.40	— 0.27	...	3	45.7	...	....	......
4278	40	42	54.9	58.1	— 6.40	— 0.21	...	5	46.4	10.7	....	19145
4279	26	53	10.2	11.5	— 6.41	— 0.07	...	4	47.7	12.7	....	19147
4280	36	49	35.9	30.4	— 6.42	— 0.19	...	4	46.6	12.6	....	19148
4281	13	42	6.0	5.1	— 6.43	+ 0.30	+ 0.14	3	44.3	8.7	59 Draconis...	......
4282	36	53	26.3	24.5	— 6.43	— 0.19	...	5	45.7	11.8	....	19149
4283	50	22	8.8	...	— 6.43	— 0.28	...	3	47.6	...	....	......
4284	50	21	40.2	40.1	— 6.46	— 0.27	...	3	45.0	11.6	....	......
4285	27	4	25.2	25.5	— 6.48	— 0.11	...	5	45.8	10.9	....	19159
4286	47	44	6.6	...	— 6.50	— 0.26	...	3	49.4	...	....	......
4287	114	48	12.9	...	— 6.51	— 0.50	+ 0.03	3	56.6	...	47 Sagittarii χ¹	......
4288	47	36	5.3	6.3	— 6.53	— 0.10	...	4	45.7	11.7	....	......
4289	35	54	38.6	37.5	— 6.54	— 0.17	...	6	45.3	8.6	....	......
4290	36	55	33.9	33.7	— 6.56	— 0.20	...	4	45.6	11.8	....	19176
4291	39	57	4.5	5.5	— 6.57	— 0.22	...	3	43.3	10.6	....	......
4292	32	47	17.5	19.4	— 6.59	— 0.15	...	4	46.6	12.8	....	19183
4293	32	38	48.1	49.1	— 6.64	— 0.13	...	12	45.3	12.8	....	19192
4294	7	35	6.3	...	— 6.66	+ 0.88	...	4	48.2	...	....	......
4295	87	11	22.4	...	— 6.67	— 0.41	— 0.10	12	52.4	...	30 Aquilæ δ...	......
4296	25	53	18.3	...	— 6.67	— 0.06	...	4	48.1	...	....	19196
4297	26	1	22.6	...	— 6.68	— 0.06	...	2	51.2	...	....	......
4298	37	55	8.6	8.9	— 6.68	— 0.19	...	5	45.2	10.7	....	......
4299	47	19	21.5	22.1	— 6.70	— 0.26	...	3	44.3	11.7	....	......
4300	9	32	23.0	...	— 6.73	+ 0.60	...	4	48.2	...	....	......

Ordinal Number.		Magnitude.	Estimates of Magnitudes.	Mean Right Ascension 1845.0.		Precession 1845.0.	Secular Variation	Adopted Proper Motion.	Observations of R.A.		
R.	G.	R.		R.	G.				No. R.	Mean year. R.	G.
				h. m. s.	s.	s.	s.	s.		1800 +	
4301	2830	8.0	7	19 18 29.23	29.21	+ 1.766	− 0.003	......	4	48.6	12.6
4302	2840	4.4	9	19 18 29.84	29.55	− 1.066	− 0.057	− 0.028	5	45.4	7.7
4303	2835	6.9	6	19 18 33.80	33.14	+ 0.447	− 0.017	......	3	48.7	9.7
4304	2833	6.4	7	19 18 35.80	35.13	+ 1.097	− 0.006	......	5	46.2	11.1
4305	...	7.6	7	19 18 47.23	...	+ 1.725	− 0.003	......	3	52.0	...
4306	2831	7.1	5	19 18 51.79	52.00	+ 2.054	− 0.002	......	4	47.9	11.6
4307	2832	6.0	5	19 19 2.62	2.32	+ 1.893	− 0.003	......	5	45.3	11.7
4308	...	8.1	5	19 19 17.75	...	+ 2.014	− 0.002	......	2	47.7	...
4309	2834	7.0	6	19 19 18.48	17.93	+ 1.828	− 0.003	......	3	47.7	10.8
4310	2836	6.6	6	19 19 19.86	19.90	+ 1.573	− 0.003	......	5	44.7	10.3
4311	...	8.2	8	19 19 27.57	...	+ 1.830	− 0.003	......	4	50.7	...
4312	2837	7.4	7	19 19 32.18	31.96	+ 1.762	− 0.003	......	4	46.6	12.6
4313	...	7.6	8	19 19 37.76	...	− 4.426	− 0.232	......	5	50.1	...
4314	2839	7.2	6	19 19 37.97	37.88	+ 1.291	− 0.005	......	3	45.6	12.6
4315	2842	4.8	5	19 19 51.56	51.45	+ 0.323	− 0.020	+ 0.009	5	45.1	6.9
4316	2838	8.2	7	19 19 55.78	55.41	+ 1.890	− 0.002	......	4	47.1	11.7
4317	2841	7.0	6	19 20 28.60	28.55	+ 1.577	− 0.003	......	5	44.9	10.3
4318	...	7.6	4	19 20 31.47	...	+ 1.920	− 0.003	......	5	51.4	...
4319	2843	7.9	8	19 21 4.26	4.23	+ 1.940	− 0.002	......	4	48.6	12.8
4320	2844	6.4	7	19 21 12.97	12.89	+ 1.833	− 0.003	......	4	45.9	10.8
4321	2845	7.0	6	19 21 17.47	17.31	+ 1.829	− 0.003	......	4	44.7	10.8
4322	2846	7.4	5	19 21 29.16	28.87	+ 2.031	− 0.002	......	4	45.6	11.6
4323	2847	7.9	8	19 21 36.12	35.81	+ 1.277	− 0.006	......	5	46.3	12.7
4324	...	7.2	8	19 21 51.82	...	− 1.092	− 0.079	......	5	47.6	...
4325	2848	7.6	7	19 22 22.34	22.32	+ 1.946	− 0.002	......	4	45.6	12.8
4326	...	9.1	5	19 22 35.16	...	+ 1.587	− 0.004	......	3	45.3	...
4327	2850	7.5	5	19 22 40.67	40.43	+ 1.312	− 0.006	......	3	45.0	11.7
4328	2849	7.4	4	19 22 40.91	41.23	+ 1.588	− 0.004	......	3	45.7	10.6
4329	2852	6.4	5	19 22 58.32	57.81	+ 1.091	− 0.009	+ 0.003	5	45.3	9.7
4330	...	7.6	5	19 23 18.17	...	− 2.066	− 0.106	......	2	51.2	...
4331	2851	6.9	8	19 23 22.71	22.50	+ 2.035	− 0.002	......	6	46.3	11.6
4332	2854	5.5	4	19 23 38.18	38.11	+ 1.471	− 0.005	......	5	44.4	8.6
4333	2853	8.0	6	19 23 44.77	45.06	+ 2.036	− 0.002	......	4	46.2	11.6
4334	...	7.2	8	19 24 33.95	...	− 2.119	− 0.110	......	5	50.7	...
4335	...	8.0	8	19 24 35.97	...	− 1.996	− 0.105	......	4	49.9	...

Ordinal Number.	Mean North Polar Distance 1845.0.		Precession 1845.0.	Secular Variation.	Adopted Proper Motion.	Observations of N.P.D.			Names.	Oeltzen-Argelander Number.
						No.	Mean year.			
R.	R.	G.				R.	R.	G.		
	° ′ ″	″	″	″	″		1800 +			
4301	44 0 31.1	28.6	− 6.73	− 0.22	...	3	45.7	12.6	....	19207
4302	16 56 2.7	5.4	− 6.74	+ 0.14	− 0.08	12	51.2	7.7	60 Draconis τ	19213
4303	25 54 7.8	7.7	− 6.74	− 0.06	...	5	45.6	9.7	....	19210
4304	32 31 48.3	51.5	− 6.74	− 0.14	...	3	45.6	11.1	....	19209
4305	43 6 7.8	...	− 6.76	− 0.24	...	4	52.2	...	....	19216?
4306	51 5 14.2	12.4	− 6.77	− 0.29	...	3	45.4	11.6	....	....
4307	46 54 40.1	40.0	− 6.78	− 0.25	...	4	44.2	11.7	....	....
4308	49 58 37.0	...	− 6.80	− 0.28	...	4	47.4	...	....	....
4309	45 22 10.0	10.4	− 6.80	− 0.24	...	4	46.2	10.8	....	....
4310	40 1 45.7	47.9	− 6.80	− 0.20	...	4	46.9	10.3	....	19222
4311	45 23 55.0	...	− 6.82	− 0.25	...	4	50.2	...	....	....
4312	43 51 48.6	48.5	− 6.82	− 0.23	...	5	47.4	12.6	....	19228
4313	9 31 11.6	...	− 6.83	+ 0.60	...	3	47.7	...	....	....
4314	35 13 53.0	51.6	− 6.84	− 0.21	...	4	46.7	12.6	....	19229
4315	24 35 0.9	1.6	− 6.85	− 0.05	− 0.02	5	45.3	6.9	58 Draconis π	19232
4316	46 46 52.1	49.4	− 6.85	− 0.25	...	3	46.4	11.7	....	....
4317	40 3 43.1	43.9	− 6.90	− 0.22	...	5	47.1	10.3	....	19238
4318	47 30 47.8	...	− 6.90	− 0.26	...	4	50.2	...	....	....
4319	47 58 59.8	64.2	− 6.95	− 0.27	...	4	47.4	12.8	....	....
4320	45 22 25.5	22.9	− 6.96	− 0.25	...	5	45.2	10.8	....	....
4321	45 17 44.0	42.4	− 6.96	− 0.25	...	4	44.9	10.8	....	....
4322	50 20 52.2	54.0	− 6.98	− 0.27	...	3	45.7	11.6	....	....
4323	34 57 6.2	4.8	− 6.99	− 0.17	...	3	45.3	12.7	....	19252
4324	16 44 54.5	...	− 7.01	+ 0.15	...	5	46.7	...	....	19261
4325	48 4 55.5	55.8	− 7.04	− 0.26	...	3	46.0	12.8	....	....
4326	40 9 24.7	...	− 7.07	− 0.22	...	3	43.7	...	....	....
4327	35 25 30.0	27.4	− 7.08	− 0.18	...	4	43.6	11.7	....	19270
4328	40 10 10.7	11.4	− 7.08	− 0.22	...	4	44.2	10.6	....	....
4329	32 17 0.2	3.2	− 7.10	− 0.14	...	6	47.0	9.7	....	19274
4330	13 40 44.4	...	− 7.13	+ 0.28	...	4	50.2	...	....	19283
4331	50 22 31.2	31.6	− 7.14	− 0.29	...	4	46.7	11.6	....	....
4332	37 59 35.9	35.3	− 7.16	− 0.20	...	5	44.9	8.6	7 Cygni ι¹	....
4333	50 22 52.0	51.1	− 7.17	− 0.28	...	3	46.7	11.6	....	....
4334	13 30 34.3	...	− 7.23	+ 0.29	...	4	50.2	...	....	19297
4335	13 49 30.1	...	− 7.24	+ 0.27	...	4	49.2	...	....	19300

Ordinal Number.		Magnitude.	Estimates of Magnitude.	Mean Right Ascension 1845.0.		Precession 1845.0.	Secular Variation.	Adopted Proper Motion.	Observations of R.A.		
R.	G.	R.		R.	G.				No. R.	Mean year R.	G.
				h. m. s.	s.	s.	s.	s.		1800 +	
4336	2855	7.4	8	19 24 44.83	44.89	+ 1.325	— 0.006	......	4	46.9	11.7
4337	...	8.0	3	19 25 32.59	...	+ 2.143	— 0.003	......	2	46.2	...
4338	2856	6.9	9	19 25 34.68	34.55	+ 1.789	— 0.003	......	5	46.9	10.8
4339	2858	7.8	6	19 25 42.60	42.47	+ 1.629	— 0.004	......	4	46.1	10.7
4340	2857	7.4	5	19 25 43.33	43.15	+ 1.921	— 0.002	......	3	45.3	11.7
4341	2859	4.0	8	19 25 47.77	47.52	+ 1.511	— 0.006	......	11	49.7	6.8
4342	2860	7.1	7	19 26 19.74	19.63	+ 1.924	— 0.003	......	4	46.6	11.7
4343	2861	7.0	5	19 26 24.58	24.46	+ 1.783	— 0.003	......	4	47.1	10.8
4344	...	6.0	1	19 26 36.70	...	+ 3.651	— 0.012	— 0.002	2	52.1	...
4345	2862	7.0	8	19 26 45.33	44.99	+ 1.678	— 0.004	......	4	47.1	10.1
4346	2864	6.5	4	19 26 52.32	51.95	+ 1.291	— 0.006	......	5	44.7	12.6
4347	2863	7.4	9	19 26 54.79	54.63	+ 1.597	— 0.004	......	5	47.6	11.8
4348	...	6.0	8	19 26 58.71	...	— 2.004	— 0.109	......	5	48.7	...
4349	...	7.8	7	19 27 5.95	...	— 3.212	— 0.178	......	4	49.7	...
4350	2865	5.6	7	19 27 13.03	12.89	+ 1.592	— 0.004	......	4	44.7	11.8
4351	...	5.3	1	19 27 16.17	...	+ 3.654	— 0.012	+ 0.002	5	48.3	...
4352	2866	9.2	7	19 27 16.35	16.47	+ 1.686	— 0.003	......	3	46.7	12.6
4353	2868	8.4	7	19 27 32.04	31.34	+ 1.282	— 0.006	......	4	48.2	12.7
4354	2867	8.7	6	19 27 34.41	33.97	+ 1.680	— 0.003	......	3	46.7	12.6
4355	...	7.6	9	19 27 54.95	...	— 2.687	— 0.149	......	5	51.2	...
4356	2871	7.7	7	19 27 55.73	55.91	+ 1.601	— 0.004	......	4	46.7	11.8
4357	...	6.0	7	19 27 56.69	...	+ 1.273	— 0.008	......	5	46.7	...
4358	2869	9.0	6	19 27 57.09	57.05	+ 1.798	— 0.003	......	3	49.4	12.7
4359	2872	6.6	6	19 28 5.34	4.96	+ 1.305	— 0.005	......	3	47.6	12.6
4360	...	8.9	5	19 28 7.04	...	+ 1.788	— 0.003	......	4	48.1	...
4361	2870	6.6	7	19 28 12.53	12.21	+ 2.087	— 0.002	......	5	46.6	9.7
4362	2873	7.7	8	19 28 29.22	28.84	+ 1.800	— 0.003	......	4	47.2	12.7
4363	2875	5.9	4	19 28 33.44	35.01	+ 1.067	— 0.009	......	5	46.2	9.7
4364	2874	8.1	6	19 28 42.86	42.33	+ 1.954	— 0.002	......	3	46.3	12.8
4365	2876	6.3	5	19 29 25.53	25.44	+ 1.652	— 0.004	......	4	44.9	9.8
4366	...	7.9	5	19 29 25.85	...	+ 0.646	— 0.018	......	4	52.2	...
4367	...	9.6	5	19 29 29.73	...	+ 0.646	— 0.018	......	3	53.0	...
4368	...	8.4	5	19 29 32.86	...	+ 0.646	— 0.018	......	4	53.4	...
4369	2877	5.7	6	19 29 38.01	38.05	+ 1.954	— 0.002	......	4	43.5	12.8
4370	2878	6.5	6	19 29 49.96	49.82	+ 1.893	— 0.002	......	5	45.4	10.7

Ordinal Number.	Mean North Polar Distance 1845.0. R.		Precession 1845.0.	Secular Variation.	Adopted Proper Motion.	Observations of N.P.D. No. R.	Mean year. 1800 +		Names.	Oeltzen-Argelander Number.
	R. (o ' ")	G. (")	(")	(")	(")	R.	R.	G.		
4336	35 32 19.1	18.0	— 7.25	— 0.18	...	5	47.0	11.7		19298
4337	47 9 24.0	...	— 7.31	— 0.25	...	4	50.1	...		......
4338	44 10 30.4	32.3	— 7.32	— 0.25	...	5	45.4	10.8		19308
4339	40 48 51.2	55.1	— 7.33	— 0.23	...	6	47.5	10.7		19311
4340	47 17 8.2	9.6	— 7.33	— 0.27	...	5	46.4	11.7		......
4341	38 35 54.6	53.9	— 7.33	— 0.19	— 0.13	11	45.5	6.8	10 Cygni ι^2 ...	......
4342	47 20 22.6	24.1	— 7.38	— 0.27	...	5	46.7	11.7		......
4343	43 59 40.7	40.5	— 7.38	— 0.23	...	4	45.1	10.8		19321
4344	115 3 11.3	...	— 7.40	— 0.49	...	3	54.6	...	51 Sagittarii h^1	......
4345	41 44 41.1	41.3	— 7.41	— 0.22	...	6	46.7	10.1		......
4346	34 54 30.4	36.6	— 7.42	— 0.17	....	4	46.6	12.6		......
4347	40 7 47.3	49.4	— 7.42	— 0.20	...	6	45.5	11.8		19333
4348	13 45 3.9	...	— 7.43	+ 0.27	...	4	48.6	...		19336
4349	11 10 39.1	...	— 7.44	+ 0.44	....	4	48.2	...		......
4350	40 1 23.3	26.0	— 7.45	— 0.22	...	5	47.7	11.3		19337
4351	115 13 10.8	...	— 7.45	— 0.49	— 0.02	6	51.3	...	52 Sagittarii h^2	......
4352	41 53 10.0	11.3	— 7.45	— 0.21	...	4	47.9	12.5		19338
4353	34 44 20.7	19.6	— 7.47	— 0.16	...	3	45.7	12.7		......
4354	41 45 2.8	14.9	— 7.48	— 0.23	...	5	48.4	12.6		19342
4355	12 9 2.8	...	— 7.51	+ 0.38	...	3	50.4	...		19362
4356	40 9 41.1	52.5	— 7.51	— 0.22	...	3	45.6	11.8		19349
4357	34 35 47.2	...	— 7.51	— 0.17	...	5	47.4	...		19353
4358	44 16 42.0	38.1	— 7.51	— 0.24	...	3	47.7	12.7		19351
4359	35 4 14.7	19.5	— 7.52	— 0.18	...	4	43.7	12.6		19359
4360	44 1 16.4	...	— 7.52	— 0.24	...	3	46.3	...		19360
4361	51 34 20.8	23.0	— 7.53	— 0.28	...	3	47.7	9.7		......
4362	44 17 38.7	39.6	— 7.55	— 0.23	...	4	46.7	12.7		19368
4363	31 43 38.3	24.7	— 7.56	— 0.14	...	5	46.5	9.7		19370
4364	47 58 31.6	34.7	— 7.57	— 0.26	...	4	48.4	12.8		......
4365	41 4 22.7	24.2	— 7.63	— 0.23	...	3	44.0	9.8		19378
4366	27 0 59.5	...	— 7.63	— 0.08	...	2	52.2	...		19380
4367	27 0 57.9	...	— 7.64	— 0.08	...	2	52.2	...		19383
4368	27 1 6.4	...	— 7.64	— 0.08	...	2	52.2	...		19386
4369	47 55 26.2	28.6	— 7.64	— 0.25	...	4	46.2	12.8		......
4370	46 23 32.2	34.2	— 7.66	— 0.25	...	4	44.9	10.7		......

Magnitude.	Estimates of Magnitude.	Mean Right Ascension 1845.0		Precession 1845.0	Secular Variation	Adopted Proper Motion.
R.		R.	G.			
		h. m. s.	s.	s.	s.	s.
6.5	5	19 30 15.35	15.41	+ 1.707	− 0.003	......
7.9	6	19 30 16.51	...	+ 2.022	− 0.002	.....
5.8	4	19 30 18.92	18.82	+ 1.551	− 0.004	......
8.6	4	19 30 20.40	19.69	+ 1.892	− 0.003	......
7.8	6	19 30 33.11	32.42	+ 1.012	− 0.009	......
8.1	5	19 30 34.25	...	+ 0.947	− 0.012	......
8.7	4	19 30 40.11	...	+ 1.789	− 0.003	......
8.5	6	19 30 40.31	40.27	+ 1.962	− 0.002	......
6.6	5	19 30 43.94	...	+ 0.947	− 0.012	......
8.0	6	19 30 46.02	46.15	+ 1.959	− 0.002	......
9.1	5	19 30 46.43	...	+ 1.790	− 0.003	......
7.8	6	19 30 52.29	...	+ 1.790	− 0.003	......
8.8	6	19 30 52.81	52.59	+ 2.012	− 0.002	......
6.0	6	19 30 57.12	55.39	− 3.448	− 0.200	......
7.9	4	19 31 9.17	8.79	+ 1.548	− 0.005	......
7.2	5	19 31 19.84	...	+ 1.979	− 0.002	......
7.4	6	19 31 20.18	19.89	+ 2.011	− 0.002	......
7.6	7	19 31 24.88	24.78	+ 2.013	− 0.002	......
8.1	5	19 31 27.37	27.38	+ 2.015	− 0.002	......
6.6	6	19 31 29.76	29.74	+ 2.106	− 0.002	......
6.3	3	19 31 36.54	36.37	+ 1.907	− 0.002	......
6.8	7	19 31 46.68	46.41	+ 1.608	− 0.004	......
5.6	5	19 31 49.82	50.16	+ 1.867	− 0.002	......
6.7	5	19 31 51.71	51.71	+ 2.100	− 0.002	......
8.5	5	19 32 8.92	...	+ 2.018	− 0.002	......
4.8	3	19 32 17.01	16.90	+ 1.611	− 0.004	......
4.4	7	19 32 38.87	38.39	− 0.200	− 0.040	+ 0.096
Var.	7	19 32 39.33	39.14	+ 1.613	− 0.004	......
8.0	6	19 32 41.18	...	− 0.572	− 0.057	......
9.8	6	19 32 41.27	...	+ 1.612	− 0.004	......
6.0	4	19 33 6.96	6.17	+ 0.651	− 0.018	......
5.8	5	19 33 38.53	38.24	+ 1.662	− 0.004	......
5.3	9	19 33 39.01	...	+ 3.433	− 0.009	......
7.9	5	19 33 43.43	...	− 3.521	− 0.215	......
9.2	6	19 33 57.14	...	+ 1.905	− 0.003	......

Ordinal Number. R.	Mean North Polar Distance 1845.0.		Precession 1845.0.	Secular Variation.	Adopted Proper Motion.	Observations of N.P.D.			Names.	Oeltzen-Argelander Number.
	R.	G.				No. R.	Mean year. R.	G.		
	° ′ ″	″	″	″	″		1800 +			
4371	42 10 15.9	14.5	− 7.69	− 0.21	...	5	47.5	10.6	....	19395
4372	49 39 17.7	...	− 7.70	− 0.27	...	3	50.0	...	....	....
4373	39 5 36.0	34.2	− 7.70	− 0.21	+ 0.10	4	42.2	12.6	....	19398
4374	46 20 43.6	45.7	− 7.70	− 0.25	...	3	45.7	10.7	....	....
4375	30 56 28.9	31.0	− 7.72	− 0.14	...	4	46.7	9.8	....	19403
4376	30 10 21.0	...	− 7.72	− 0.12	...	1	52.7	...	....	19404
4377	43 55 17.9	...	− 7.73	− 0.23	...	1	52.7	...	....	19405
4378	48 5 1.6	4.1	− 7.73	− 0.26	...	2	45.1	12.8	....	....
4379	30 10 42.2	...	− 7.73	− 0.12	...	2	51.6	...	....	19410
4380	47 58 30.4	33.2	− 7.73	− 0.24	...	3	47.3	12.8	....	....
4381	43 54 28.6	...	− 7.74	− 0.23	...	2	51.7	...	....	19411
4382	43 54 47.7	...	− 7.74	− 0.23	...	2	51.6	...	....	19412
4383	49 22 33.1	35.5	− 7.74	− 0.25	...	3	48.4	12.7	....	....
4384	10 42 49.6	48.5	− 7.75	+ 0.46	...	4	49.4	9.8	....	....
4385	39 0 5.1	8.4	− 7.77	− 0.21	...	2	44.1	12.6	....	19425
4386	48 27 6.0	...	− 7.78	− 0.26	...	4	45.6	...	....	....
4387	49 20 0.9	0.6	− 7.78	− 0.26	...	3	45.0	12.7	....	....
4388	49 22 39.0	38.4	− 7.79	− 0.27	...	5	45.8	12.7	....	....
4389	49 25 13.3	14.8	− 7.79	− 0.26	...	4	50.7	12.7	....	....
4390	51 57 38.6	40.6	− 7.79	− 0.26	...	5	47.8	13.6	....	....
4391	46 38 17.3	18.8	− 7.80	− 0.24	...	3	44.6	8.6	....	....
4392	40 6 24.3	25.1	− 7.82	− 0.22	− 0.02	4	43.2	11.6	....	19441
4393	45 38 43.6	41.1	− 7.82	− 0.24	...	3	45.0	10.7	....	....
4394	51 45 6.8	7.9	− 7.82	− 0.26	...	3	50.0	13.6	....	....
4395	49 28 9.9	...	− 7.85	− 0.27	...	3	49.0	...	....	....
4396	40 8 7.8	11.0	− 7.86	− 0.22	− 0.15	4	45.1	6.9	13 Cygni θ	19452
4397	20 36 9.0	10.7	− 7.89	+ 0.03	+ 1.79	12	50.8	7.5	61 Draconis σ	19457
4398	40 8 48.6	47.8	− 7.89	− 0.22	...	5	53.1	11.6	R Cygni	....
4399	18 39 20.4	...	− 7.89	+ 0.09	...	3	54.0	...	....	19458
4400	40 7 21.2	...	− 7.89	− 0.22	...	3	54.0	...	....	....
4401	26 54 35.4	37.0	− 7.92	− 0.07	...	3	43.7	9.7	....	....
4402	41 4 20.0	26.1	− 7.97	− 0.22	...	8	48.5	8.7	....	19472
4403	106 28 54.3	...	− 7.97	− 0.46	− 0.02	6	48.0	...	55 Sagittarii e^2	....
4404	10 32 41.5	...	− 7.97	+ 0.47	...	3	47.7	...	....	19473
4405	46 27 54.4	...	− 7.99	− 0.25	...	4	48.7	...	....	....

Magnitude.	Estimates of Magnitude.	Mean Right Ascension 1845.0.		Precession 1845.0.	Secular Variation	Adopted Proper Motion.
R.		R.	G.			
		h. m. s.	s.	s.	s.	s.
7.2	4	19 34 4.22	...	+ 1.344	— 0.007	......
7.2	5	19 34 9.17	8.78	+ 1.562	— 0.006	......
8.3	8	19 34 14.21	14.19	+ 2.103	— 0.002	......
7.8	7	19 34 14.21	14.27	+ 1.908	— 0.002	......
9.1	5	19 34 23.30	23.27	+ 2.094	— 0.002	......
5.7	6	19 34 23.85	23.89	+ 1.949	— 0.002	+ 0.005
7.9	7	19 34 59.55	59.32	+ 1.572	— 0.006	......
5.8	6	19 35 11.91	11.40	+ 1.348	— 0.007	......
7.4	7	19 35 55.50	55.18	+ 2.112	— 0.002	......
6.3	6	19 35 56.61	56.41	— 0.529	— 0.053	......
5.3	5	19 36 3.28	2.79	+ 1.842	— 0.003	......
9.4	8	19 36 3.44	...	+ 2.044	— 0.002	......
6.8	8	19 36 20.19	20.13	+ 2.058	— 0.002	......
8.7	5	19 36 23.71	23.64	+ 2.036	— 0.002	......
6.4	7	19 36 39.60	39.70	+ 2.050	— 0.002	......
9.0	5	19 36 54.64	54.89	+ 2.049	— 0.002	......
7.8	6	19 37 3.46	3.60	+ 1.617	— 0.004	......
8.0	8	19 37 14.55	14.53	+ 2.060	— 0.002	......
8.3	5	19 37 16.84	16.87	+ 2.061	— 0.002	......
7.6	6	19 37 21.48	21.08	+ 1.005	— 0.012	......
9.8	4	19 37 26.92	27.31	+ 2.056	— 0.002	......
6.9	8	19 37 40.40	40.17	+ 2.035	— 0.002	......
5.9	3	19 37 41.70	41.33	+ 1.610	— 0.004	— 0.022
6.5	2	19 37 43.57	43.24	+ 2.108	— 0.002	......
5.9	5	19 37 44.42	44.38	+ 1.611	— 0.004	— 0.016
7.0	9	19 37 44.58	44.47	+ 2.062	— 0.002	......
7.3	7	19 38 12.56	...	+ 1.773	— 0.003	.....
6.9	6	19 38 21.07	20.45	— 1.176	— 0.077	......
7.1	7	19 38 22.61	...	+ 2.073	— 0.002	......
6.1	5	19 38 34.74	34.54	+ 1.998	— 0.002	......
8.7	6	19 38 40.36	40.78	+ 2.065	— 0.002	......
7.7	6	19 38 47.53	...	+ 1.774	— 0.003	......
3.0	1	19 38 53.41	...	+ 2.851	— 0.003	......
7.8	5	19 39 23.73	23.26	+ 1.507	— 0.005	......
8.8	7	19 39 30.11	30.32	+ 2.063	— 0.002	....

Ordinal Number.	Mean North Polar Distance 1845.0.			Precession 1845.0.	Secular Variation.	Adopted Proper Motion.	Observations of N.P.D.				Names.	Oeltzen-Argelander Number.
	R.	R.	G.				No. R.	Mean year. R.	G.			
	° ′ ″		″	″	″	″		1800 +				
4406	35 23 33.1		...	— 8.00	— 0.18	...	3	45.7	...	....	19475
4407	39 6 59.8		62.1	— 8.01	— 0.21	...	4	46.7	11.8	....	19476
4408	51 42 39.0		39.0	— 8.01	— 0.26	...	4	48.7	13.6	....	....
4409	46 30 49.2		52.9	— 8.01	— 0.23	...	4	45.9	10.7	....	....
4410	51 27 29.5		32.5	— 8.03	— 0.28	...	2	47.2	13.6	....	....
4411	47 32 13.1		13.0	— 8.03	— 0.26	— 0.07	5	45.5	10.6	14 Cygni.......	....
4412	39 15 0.1		2.0	— 8.08	— 0.21	...	3	45.3	11.8	....	19492
4413	35 23 16.5		15.0	— 8.09	— 0.17	...	5	44.7	8.6	....	19497
4414	51 54 7.0		8.3	— 8.15	— 0.28	...	5	45.8	12.2	....	....
4415	18 44 25.1		22.1	— 8.15	+ 0.08	...	5	47.9	9.7	....	19512
4416	44 50 22.7		25.9	— 8.16	— 0.24	...	4	44.4	12.6	....	....
4417	49 58 5.9		...	— 8.16	— 0.27	...	4	52.2	...	....	....
4418	50 20 22.5		23.7	— 8.18	— 0.26	...	3	45.6	13.6	....	....
4419	49 43 7.8		5.9	— 8.19	— 0.26	...	3	44.3	12.7	....	....
4420	50 6 34.1		36.1	— 8.21	— 0.27	...	3	45.7	13.7	....	....
4421	50 4 0.4		4.7	— 8.23	— 0.27	...	3	50.0	13.7	....	....
4422	39 58 59.8		60.1	— 8.24	— 0.21	...	4	46.4	10.7	....	....
4423	50 20 17.8		20.2	— 8.25	— 0.25	...	3	46.4	13.7	....	....
4424	50 21 53.2		55.6	— 8.26	— 0.27	...	4	46.7	13.7	....	....
4425	30 31 12.3		40.2	— 8.27	— 0.14	...	4	47.7	12.7	....	....
4426	50 13 21.2		20.3	— 8.27	— 0.26	...	2	50.2	13.7	....	....
4427	49 38 38.2		37.5	— 8.29	— 0.27	...	5	46.5	12.7	....	....
4428	39 49 56.8		57.8	— 8.29	— 0.20	+ 0.16	4	42.6	9.5	16 Cygni c.....	....
4429	51 41 39.5		41.9	— 8.29	— 0.26	...	3	44.7	10.3	....	....
4430	39 50 23.4		25.3	— 8.30	— 0.22	+ 0.21	4	43.9	9.5	....	....
4431	50 22 10.6		12.3	— 8.30	— 0.28	...	4	48.7	13.6	....	....
4432	43 9 27.6		...	— 8.33	— 0.23	...	4	52.2	...	....	19561
4433	15 58 37.9		39.6	— 8.34	+ 0.17	...	5	48.6	9.7	....	....
4434	50 37 38.1		...	— 8.35	— 0.27	...	3	46.3	...	....	....
4435	48 35 45.4		47.2	— 8.36	— 0.25	...	3	46.3	11.7	....	....
4436	50 24 56.5		56.7	— 8.37	— 0.27	...	3	45.0	13.8	....	....
4437	43 7 24.6		...	— 8.38	— 0.23	...	4	52.2	...	....	19570
4438	79 45 37.2		...	— 8.39	— 0.38	...	5	49.5	...	50 Aquilæ γ...	....
4439	37 48 27.2		28.7	— 8.43	— 0.21	...	4	46.7	11.8	....	....
4440	50 17 6.4		9.6	— 8.43	— 0.25	...	3	48.0	13.8	....	....

Ordinal Number.		Magnitude.	Estimates of Magnitude.	Mean Right Ascension 1845.0.		Precession 1845.0.	Secular Variation	Adopted Proper Motion.	Observations of R.A.		
R.	G.	R.	R.	R.	G.				No. R.	Mean year. R.	G.
				h. m. s.	s.	s.	s.	s.		1800 +	
4441	2928	6.3	7	19 39 33.51	33.59	+ 2.040	— 0.002	.....	5	46.2	12.6
4442	...	9.0	6	19 39 47.94	...	+ 2.069	— 0.002	......	2	47.1	...
4443	2931	7.4	7	19 39 55.39	54.78	+ 1.506	— 0.005	......	5	46.4	11.8
4444	...	9.5	4	19 40 0.29	...	+ 2.056	— 0.002	......	2	45.2	...
4445	2932	3.5	4	19 40 7.74	7.76	+ 1.869	— 0.002	+ 0.006	5	45.0	7.0
4446	2935	5.9	3	19 40 13.15	12.17	+ 1.158	— 0.010	......	4	45.5	8.6
4447	...	8.6	10	19 40 21.97	...	—25.473	— 5.258		8	51.5	...
4448	2936	6.0	8	19 40 29.47	29.30	+ 1.229	— 0.009	......	6	47.0	11.7
4449	2933	7.2	5	19 40 31.25	30.94	+ 2.048	— 0.002	......	4	47.2	12.6
4450	2934	7.2	6	19 40 33.85	33.62	+ 2.072	— 0.002	......	3	46.0	11.9
4451	2937	7.5	5	19 41 24.75	24.48	+ 1.896	— 0.002	......	2	46.7	12.7
4452	2938	8.9	6	19 41 35.75	35.94	+ 2.074	— 0.002	......	4	48.1	10.7
4453	2939	6.8	5	19 41 43.60	43.25	+ 1.905	— 0.002	......	3	45.4	12.7
4454	2941	5.9	8	19 42 55.12	55.01	+ 1.754	— 0.003	......	4	43.8	10.8
4455	...	6.0	4	19 43 11.25	...	+ 3.495	— 0.011	— 0.003	6	47.3	...
4456	...	1.3	A	19 43 13.17	...	+ 2.891	— 0.003	+ 0.036	92	46.1	...
4457	2942	7.0	8	19 43 20.93	20.70	+ 2.077	— 0.002	......	4	45.2	10.7
4458	...	10.0	5	19 43 22.95	...	+ 1.760	— 0.003	......	3	49.1	...
4459	...	9.8	6	19 43 30.85	...	+ 1.759	— 0.003	......	3	46.8	...
4460	2948	8.5	6	19 43 31.65	41.53	— 0.059	— 0.043	......	3	49.0	12.8
4461	2947	8.6	5	19 43 36.88	35.76	— 0.081	— 0.043	......	3	48.4	12.8
4462	2943	6.3	8	19 43 58.42	58.23	+ 2.120	— 0.002	+ 0.003	8	46.8	9.7
4463	2944	7.9	7	19 44 4.47	4.12	+ 1.910	— 0.002	......	4	47.2	12.7
4464	...	8.2	4	19 44 4.85	...	+ 1.910	— 0.002	......	2	50.7	...
4465	2945	7.9	7	19 44 16.00	15.75	+ 1.241	— 0.009	.....	5	45.3	11.8
4466	2946	6.9	6	19 44 16.68	16.46	+ 1.253	— 0.009	......	3	46.6	11.7
4467	2952	6.1	7	19 44 30.15	30.15	— 0.050	— 0.037	......	5	47.3	12.8
4468	2949	5.2	7	19 45 4.48	4.31	+ 2.122	— 0.002	......	4	47.7	9.8
4469	2950	5.5	6	19 45 18.12	17.92	+ 2.057	— 0.002	......	4	46.7	8.6
4470	2953	6.3	4	19 45 29.46	29.30	+ 1.075	— 0.009	......	2	46.7	12.7
4471	2951	8.1	7	19 45 40.59	40.48	+ 2.096	— 0.002	......	4	50.1	13.6
4472	...	7.2	6	19 45 49.54	...	+ 0.908	— 0.016	......	2	50.1	...
4473	2954	7.7	5	19 46 0.60	0.56	+ 1.918	— 0.002	......	3	47.7	12.7
4474	...	7.8	5	19 46 5.39	...	+ 2.054	— 0.002	......	3	52.0	...
4475	2955	7.8	3	19 46 10.53	10.30	+ 2.097	— 0.002	......	2	47.7	13.6

Ordinal Number.	Mean North Polar Distance 1845.0.		Precession 1845.0.	Secular Variation.	Adopted Proper Motion.	Observations of N.P.D.			Names.	Oeltzen-Argelander Number.
						No.	Mean year.			
R.	R.	G.				R.	R.	G.		
	° ′ ″	″	″	″	″		1800 +			
4441	49 39 16.1	15.9	− 8.44	− 0.26	...	5	44.7	12.6	....	......
4442	50 26 15.1	...	− 8.46	− 0.27	...	4	48.2	...	....	......
4443	37 45 41.1	41.8	− 8.47	− 0.20	...	4	45.0	11.8	....	......
4444	50 4 53.9	...	− 8.47	− 0.27	...	2	46.1	...	....	......
4445	45 14 40.7	42.8	− 8.49	− 0.25	...	5	43.0	7.0	18 Cygni δ....	......
4446	32 21 5.0	4.7	− 8.49	− 0.14	...	5	45.3	8.6	....	19593
4447	2 25 42.2	...	− 8.50	+ 3.36	...	6	51.7	...	....	......
4448	33 19 48.7	50.6	− 8.51	− 0.15	...	5	45.5	11.7	....	19600
4449	49 49 12.6	13.0	− 8.51	− 0.25	...	5	45.0	12.6	....	......
4450	50 29 12.2	14.9	− 8.52	− 0.27	...	5	45.4	11.9	....	......
4451	45 48 46.1	47.8	− 8.59	− 0.25	...	3	46.7	12.7	....	......
4452	50 28 44.8	49.6	− 8.60	− 0.26	...	4	49.9	10.7	....	......
4453	46 1 49.3	51.2	− 8.61	− 0.24	...	4	44.0	12.7	....	......
4454	42 28 24.8	24.5	− 8.71	− 0.24	...	8	47.6	10.8	....	19635
4455	109 26 0.5	...	− 8.73	− 0.46	+ 0.06	2	48.2	...	57 Sagittarii...	......
4456	81 32 12.1	...	− 8.73	− 0.38	− 0.38	28	48.4	...	53 Aquilæ α...	......
4457	50 28 9.9	12.5	− 8.74	− 0.27	...	4	46.2	10.7	....	......
4458	42 33 19.5	...	− 8.74	− 0.23	...	2	48.2	...	....	19644
4459	42 32 16.2	...	− 8.75	− 0.23	...	4	44.9	...	....	19651
4460	21 1 39.9	38.5	− 8.75	+ 0.06	...	4	49.1	12.8	....	19653
4461	20 53 20.0	30.3	− 8.76	+ 0.06	...	3	48.3	12.3	....	19657
4462	51 40 36.7	37.6	− 8.79	− 0.28	...	4	47.2	9.7	....	......
4463	46 0 27.6	27.1	− 8.80	− 0.25	...	3	44.7	12.7	....	......
4464	46 0 36.8	...	− 8.80	− 0.25	...	3	43.7	...	....	......
4465	33 17 1.6	1.5	− 8.81	− 0.15	...	4	45.4	11.8	....	......
4466	33 28 14.7	12.5	− 8.81	− 0.15	...	5	45.5	11.7	....	......
4467	21 2 31.3	31.0	− 8.83	+ 0.01	...	5	47.7	12.8	....	19676
4468	51 40 23.3	24.7	− 8.88	− 0.29	− 0.12	3	45.7	9.8	19 Cygni.......	......
4469	49 47 30.3	29.8	− 8.89	− 0.25	...	5	43.0	8.6	....	......
4470	30 58 12.4	19.0	− 8.91	− 0.14	...	5	46.2	12.7	....	19695
4471	50 51 51.1	50.5	− 8.92	− 0.26	...	3	48.4	13.6	....	......
4472	28 58 37.0	...	− 8.93	− 0.12	...	4	46.7	...	....	19704
4473	46 4 2.6	2.9	− 8.95	− 0.25	...	4	46.7	12.7	....	......
4474	49 39 35.8	...	− 8.95	− 0.27	...	5	52.1	...	....	......
4475	50 51 32.7	35.4	− 8.96	− 0.26	...	3	49.7	13.6	....	......

Ordinal Number.		Magnitude.	Estimates of Magnitude.	Mean Right Ascension 1845.0.		Precession 1845.0.	Secular Variation	Adopted Proper Motion.	Observations of R.A.		
R.	G.	R.		R.	G.				No. R.	Mean year. R.	G.
				h. m. s.	s.	s.	s.	s.		1800 +	
4476	...	7.8	23	19 46 13.86	...	−13.036	− 1.734	......	23	52.0	...
4477	...	9.0	5	19 46 25.85	...	+ 2.093	− 0.002	......	2	48.2	...
4478	2956	7.6	4	19 46 35.61	35.29	+ 2.033	− 0.002	......	3	48.7	11.7
4479	...	8.2	4	19 46 39.13	...	+ 1.927	− 0.003	......	3	51.4	...
4480	2957	6.5	7	19 46 41.64	41.15	+ 1.790	− 0.003	......	3	44.9	11.8
4481	2958	5.1	3	19 46 44.30	43.87	+ 1.508	− 0.005	......	4	46.2	7.7
4482	2959	8.3	3	19 47 12.13	11.84	+ 2.124	− 0.002	......	3	47.0	12.6
4483	2960	8.1	5	19 47 22.79	22.83	+ 2.129	− 0.002	......	3	47.0	12.6
4484	...	5.0	2	19 47 25.84	...	+ 3.694	− 0.015	......	2	53.5	...
4485	2961	7.7	9	19 47 32.13	32.04	+ 2.126	− 0.002	......	7	45.4	12.6
4486	2962	5.7	5	19 47 33.24	33.23	+ 1.767	− 0.003	......	5	46.7	10.7
4487	2965	8.0	6	19 47 41.40	41.65	+ 0.813	− 0.017	......	3	48.0	12.8
4488	...	4.2	6	19 47 41.95	...	+ 2.944	− 0.004	+ 0.002	65	47.5	...
4489	...	8.5	21	19 47 58.31	...	−12.955	− 1.715	......	19	51.7	...
4490	2968	6.8	6	19 47 58.35	58.23	+ 0.937	− 0.015	......	5	45.3	10.8
4491	2980	8.4	6	19 48 1.71	2.11	− 3.783	− 0.269	......	3	52.0	13.6
4492	2963	8.6	6	19 48 3.72	3.51	+ 1.761	− 0.003	......	4	47.7	10.7
4493	2964	7.2	6	19 48 22.51	22.20	+ 2.037	− 0.002	......	3	47.0	11.7
4494	2967	6.3	7	19 48 26.02	26.07	+ 1.776	− 0.003	......	5	47.1	10.7
4495	2969	8.4	5	19 48 35.20	34.86	+ 1.931	− 0.003	......	4	43.2	12.7
4496	2966	7.6	5	19 48 35.38	35.12	+ 2.042	− 0.002	......	3	48.3	11.7
4497	2970	8.4	8	19 48 36.29	35.98	+ 1.928	− 0.003	......	5	47.1	12.7
4498	2974	4.0	8	19 48 40.07	39.92	− 0.175	− 0.047	+ 0.015	5	46.2	6.8
4499	2971	7.4	6	19 48 54.73	54.81	+ 1.879	− 0.003	......	3	48.4	14.6
4500	...	5.5	4	19 49 9.36	...	+ 3.408	− 0.010	− 0.001	2	49.7	...
4501	2972	7.5	4	19 49 19.75	19.69	+ 2.035	− 0.002	......	3	44.7	11.7
4502	...	8.8	5	19 49 28.12	...	+ 0.936	− 0.015	......	3	47.7	...
4503	2973	8.2	7	19 49 29.98	29.75	+ 2.109	− 0.002	......	4	47.1	13.6
4504	2975	7.8	5	19 49 54.10	54.12	+ 1.775	− 0.003	......	4	48.1	10.7
4505	2976	5.1	5	19 50 6.20	5.98	+ 1.236	− 0.009	......	4	44.1	9.7
4506	2978	7.1	4	19 50 8.14	7.89	+ 1.191	− 0.009	......	3	47.0	10.8
4507	...	6.4	5	19 50 17.10	...	+ 2.084	− 0.002	......	3	51.4	...
4508	...	5.1	5	19 50 19.26	...	+ 2.142	− 0.001	+ 0.002	3	50.0	...
4509	2977	6.6	5	19 50 26.74	26.65	+ 1.794	− 0.003	......	3	47.7	10.7
4510	2979	7.8	5	19 50 42.12	41.78	+ 1.638	− 0.004	......	3	48.8	11.4

Ordinal Number.	Mean North Polar Distance 1845.0.		Precession 1845.0.	Secular Variation.	Adopted Proper Motion.	Observations of N.P.D.			Names.	Oeltzen-Argelander Number.
						No.	Mean year.			
R.	R.	G.				R.	R.	G.		
	° ′ ″	″	″	″	″		1800 +			
4476	4 14 46.7	...	− 8.97	+ 1.70	...	5	51.5	...	....	......
4477	50 44 42.8	...	− 8.98	− 0.27	...	3	48.7	...	....	......
4478	49 2 48.8	48.6	− 8.99	− 0.25	...	3	44.5	11.7	....	......
4479	46 16 14.1	...	− 9.00	− 0.25	...	2	49.2	...	....	......
4480	43 1 7.6	8.6	− 9.00	− 0.22	...	5	47.0	11.8	....	19712
4481	37 24 11.7	11.5	− 9.00	− 0.18	+ 0.07	5	43.1	7.7	20 Cygni d	19714
4482	51 34 34.3	34.0	− 9.04	− 0.27	...	2	46.2	12.6	....	......
4483	51 43 36.2	38.8	− 9.05	− 0.25	...	3	48.5	12.6	....	......
4484	117 34 30.7	...	− 9.06	− 0.48	...	4	56.7	...	59 Sagittarii b	......
4485	51 38 26.2	37.2	− 9.07	− 0.28	...	2	47.2	12.6	....	......
4486	42 27 58.2	58.7	− 9.07	− 0.23	...	3	42.3	10.7	....	19729
4487	27 50 11.4	11.9	− 9.08	− 0.09	...	3	50.0	12.8	....	......
4488	83 58 34.9	...	− 9.08	− 0.38	+ 0.47	7	51.7	...	60 Aquilæ β...	......
4489	4 15 4.7	...	− 9.10	+ 1.69	...	5	51.5	...	....	......
4490	29 11 19.1	22.4	− 9.10	− 0.11	...	2	42.7	10.8	....	19737
4491	9 51 33.9	37.2	− 9.11	+ 0.48	...	4	47.6	13.6	....	......
4492	42 17 37.8	33.7	− 9.11	− 0.23	...	3	45.0	10.7	....	19740
4493	49 2 43.2	44.6	− 9.13	− 0.25	...	3	46.7	11.7	....	......
4494	42 35 36.0	33.8	− 9.14	− 0.23	...	5	45.7	10.7	....	19746
4495	46 15 58.0	56.8	− 9.15	− 0.25	...	2	47.7	12.7	....	......
4496	49 10 25.6	27.3	− 9.15	− 0.26	...	3	46.3	11.7	....	......
4497	46 9 34.3	34.7	− 9.15	− 0.24	...	3	47.7	12.7	....	......
4498	20 7 38.3	38.7	− 9.16	+ 0.02	...	14	50.5	6.8	63 Draconis ε.	19751
4499	44 55 56.7	58.6	− 9.17	− 0.22	...	3	47.3	14.6	....	19754
4500	105 53 53.0	...	− 9.19	− 0.44	+ 0.09	5	52.7	...	61 Sagittarii g	......
4501	48 56 22.3	22.9	− 9.21	− 0.27	...	3	45.4	11.7	....	......
4502	29 5 23.1	...	− 9.22	− 0.12	...	4	47.9	...	....	19764
4503	51 0 9.0	11.0	− 9.22	− 0.27	...	3	50.0	13.6	....	......
4504	42 29 30.4	27.7	− 9.25	− 0.22	...	3	44.0	10.7	....	19775
4505	32 52 52.4	53.2	− 9.27	− 0.16	...	4	43.4	9.7	23 Cygni.......	19779
4506	32 14 17.4	18.1	− 9.27	− 0.15	...	3	44.0	10.8	....	......
4507	50 14 8.4	...	− 9.28	− 0.27	...	3	49.3	...	....	......
4508	51 55 19.3	...	− 9.28	− 0.28	...	3	47.0	...	22 Cygni.......	......
4509	42 52 2.9	0.1	− 9.29	− 0.21	...	5	47.5	10.7	....	......
4510	39 35 18.1	20.2	− 9.31	− 0.19	...	3	45.3	11.4	....	......

Ordinal Number.		Magnitude.	Estimates of Magnitude.	Mean Right Ascension 1845.0.		Precession 1845.0.	Secular Variation	Adopted Proper Motion.	Observations of R.A.		
R.	G.	R.		R.	G.				No. R.	Mean year. R.	G.
				h. m. s.	s.	s.	s.	s.		1800 +	
4511	...	6.1	5	19 50 48.66	...	+ 1.076	— 0.012	......	3	48.3	...
4512	2983	8.4	6	19 51 2.64	2.44	+ 0.832	— 0.017	......	2	48.7	12.8
4513	2987	5.3	4	19 51 37.30	37.49	+ 1.556	— 0.006	......	4	46.3	8.8
4514	2981	8.3	5	19 51 38.87	38.77	+ 2.096	— 0.001	......	3	47.6	13.6
4515	2982	8.3	7	19 51 39.77	39.50	+ 2.020	— 0.002	......	4	50.7	11.8
4516	2986	7.7	4	19 51 49.84	49.72	+ 1.935	— 0.002	......	3	48.0	12.6
4517	2984	4.7	4	19 51 50.80	50.78	+ 2.081	— 0.001	......	4	46.7	8.6
4518	2985	8.8	6	19 51 53.01	52.99	+ 2.105	— 0.001	......	3	48.3	13.6
4519	...	6.9	10	19 51 55.85	...	+ 2.146	— 0.001	+ 0.010	5	48.6	...
4520	...	8.2	6	19 51 59.25	...	+ 1.215	— 0.012	......	3	52.4	...
4521	...	7.0	4	19 52 3.38	...	+ 1.091	— 0.013	......	2	47.2	...
4522	...	7.4	6	19 52 5.99	...	+ 2.149	— 0.001	......	3	51.3	...
4523	2992	7.0	5	19 52 11.40	10.67	+ 0.992	— 0.017	......	3	45.7	9.8
4524	2988	8.0	3	19 52 11.99	12.04	+ 1.937	— 0.002	......	3	48.0	12.6
4525	2993	6.4	8	19 52 14.83	14.10	+ 1.009	— 0.014	......	4	47.1	9.8
4526	2991	6.2	9	19 52 17.34	17.15	+ 1.194	— 0.009	......	4	46.7	10.8
4527	...	7.9	3	19 52 17.96	...	+ 1.104	— 0.013	......	2	52.2	...
4528	2990	6.5	5	19 52 30.75	30.53	+ 1.640	— 0.004	......	4	45.0	10.1
4529	3007	8.6	6	19 52 31.38	31.12	— 3.681	— 0.271	......	4	51.7	13.6
4530	2994	7.9	3	19 52 32.96	32.83	+ 1.410	— 0.009	......	2	48.2	13.7
4531	2989	6.3	4	19 52 43.51	43.11	+ 2.015	— 0.002	......	5	46.4	11.8
4532	...	7.8	5	19 52 45.38	...	+ 1.212	— 0.012	......	3	50.0	...
4533	...	9.4	6	19 52 51.17	...	+ 1.934	— 0.002	......	3	54.3	...
4534	2995	8.2	6	19 52 52.79	52.57	+ 1.934	— 0.002	......	6	48.1	12.6
4535	2996	5.0	4	19 52 57.61	57.31	+ 1.153	— 0.011	......	6	46.8	10.2
4536	2999	8.2	5	19 53 2.82	2.69	+ 0.838	— 0.017	......	2	47.7	12.8
4537	...	4.8	1	19 53 7.29	...	+ 3.700	— 0.016	......	6	52.1	...
4538	...	7.1	6	19 53 15.17	...	+ 0.624	— 0.023	......	3	50.7	...
4539	2997	8.5	5	19 53 16.84	16.60	+ 1.414	— 0.006	......	2	45.7	13.7
4540	2998	8.6	6	19 53 33.73	33.65	+ 1.894	— 0.002	......	3	49.3	14.6
4541	3002	8.8	5	19 54 13.21	12.93	+ 1.406	— 0.006	......	3	45.1	13.7
4542	...	8.4	4	19 54 15.77	...	+ 1.942	— 0.002	......	3	44.2	...
4543	3000	8.0	6	19 54 26.54	26.44	+ 2.116	— 0.001	......	3	48.4	13.6
4544	3001	6.0	5	19 54 28.42	28.00	+ 1.882	— 0.002	......	3	45.0	11.7
4545	...	9.4	6	19 54 56.26	...	+ 1.576	— 0.006	......	3	51.3	...

Ordinal Number.	Mean North Polar Distance 1845.0.			Precession 1845.0.	Secular Variation.	Adopted Proper Motion.	Observations of N.P.D.				Names.	Oeltzen-Argelander Number.
R.	R.		G.				No R.	Mean year.				
								R.	G.			
	° ′ ″		″	″	″	″		1800 +				
4511	30 41 59.1		...	− 9.32	− 0.14	...	3	46.7	...		....	....
4512	27 51 45.6		47.5	− 9.34	− 0.09	...	4	50.5	12.8		....	....
4513	37 58 13.2		13.5	− 9.38	− 0.18	− 0.02	4	43.7	8.8		24 Cygni ψ ...	....
4514	50 29 25.7		29.1	− 9.39	− 0.27	...	3	48.0	13.6		....	....
4515	48. 22 15.5		17.4	− 9.39	− 0.26	...	3	45.1	11.8		....	....
4516	46 8 30.6		31.1	− 9.40	− 0.24	...	3	44.7	12.6		....	....
4517	50 2 44.7		45.4	− 9.40	− 0.25	...	3	46.0	8.6		....	....
4518	50 45 19.1		19.1	− 9.41	− 0.28	...	3	47.0	13.6		....	....
4519	51 57 20.0		...	− 9.41	− 0.28	+ 0.05	5	49.7	...		....	....
4520	32 28 25.4		...	− 9.42	− 0.15	...	3	52.0	...		....	19817?
4521	30 48 32.2		...	− 9.42	− 0.14	...	3	47.4	...		....	....
4522	52 0 46.0		...	− 9.42	− 0.28	...	3	43.4	...		....	....
4523	29 35 10.2		12.3	− 9.43	− 0.13	...	3	44.1	9.8		....	19820
4524	46 9 10.1		9.2	− 9.43	− 0.24	...	2	45.7	12.6		....	....
4525	29 47 43.5		43.8	− 9.43	− 0.12	...	4	43.1	9.8		....	19822
4526	32 9 28.0		26.1	− 9.44	− 0.16	...	5	49.1	10.8		....	19823
4527	30 57 30.1		...	− 9.44	− 0.14	...	3	51.0	...		....	....
4528	39 30 43.0		44.6	− 9.45	− 0.19	...	6	45.3	10.1		....	19825
4529	9 54 19.2		21.2	− 9.46	+ 0.46	...	4	47.6	13.6		....	....
4530	35 23 19.7		18.0	− 9.46	− 0.19	...	3	48.7	13.7		....	....
4531	48 9 17.7		18.8	− 9.47	− 0.25	...	3	43.6	11.8		....	....
4532	32 22 54.5		...	− 9.47	− 0.15	...	5	48.3	...		....	19832
4533	46 2 5.8		...	− 9.48	− 0.20	...	3	47.0	...		....	....
4534	46 1 50.8		49.1	− 9.48	− 0.20	...	3	45.7	12.6		....	....
4535	31 33 59.9		60.3	− 9.49	− 0.15	...	4	43.4	10.2		....	....
4536	27 48 52.8		53.0	− 9.49	− 0.07	...	3	50.4	12.8		....	19840
4537	118 8 5.9		...	− 9.50	− 0.47	− 0.02	3	54.6	...		62 Sagittarii c.	....
4538	25 41 26.2		...	− 9.51	− 0.08	+ 0.02	3	50.4	...		....	19843
4539	35 24 19.1		18.5	− 9.51	− 0.17	...	3	49.0	13.7		....	....
4540	45 0 45.9		47.5	− 9.54	− 0.25	...	3	47.3	14.6		....	....
4541	35 15 39.3		42.2	− 9.58	− 0.18	...	3	50.0	13.7		....	19861
4542	46 9 8.4		...	− 9.59	− 0.25	...	3	47.7	...		....	....
4543	50 53 34.1		34.4	− 9.60	− 0.25	...	4	51.4	13.6		....	....
4544	44 38 53.6		53.8	− 9.60	− 0.24	...	4	43.1	11.7		....	....
4545	38 7 16.8		...	− 9.64	− 0.20	...	3	52.4	...		....	....

Ordinal Number.		Magnitude.	Estimates of Magnitude.	Mean Right Ascension 1845.0.			Precession 1845.0.	Secular Variation	Adopted Proper Motion.	Observations of R.A.		
R.	G.	R.		R.		G.				No. R.	Mean year. R.	Mean year. G.
				h. m. s.		s.	s.	s.	s.		1800 +	
4546	...	9.1	6	19 55	0.16	...	+ 1.592	− 0.006	......	3	48.6	...
4547	3003	8.9	6	19 55	1.52	1.34	+ 1.412	− 0.006	......	3	46.7	13.8
4548	3004	6.2	4	19 55	8.78	8.70	+ 1.590	− 0.005	+ 0.006	4	45.7	8.6
4549	3008	8.0	5	19 55	9.58	9.59	+ 0.823	− 0.017	......	2	46.8	12.8
4550	...	7.3	6	19 55	21.96	...	+ 1.005	− 0.016	......	2	47.2	...
4551	3005	8.7	6	19 55	38.64	38.40	+ 2.118	− 0.001	......	3	47.0	13.6
4552	...	8.4	5	19 55	43.33	...	+ 1.581	− 0.006	......	4	51.2	...
4553	3012	8.1	5	19 55	45.86	44.81	+ 0.819	− 0.020	......	2	48.2	12.8
4554	...	7.0	6	19 55	47.74	...	+ 1.587	− 0.006	......	3	47.0	...
4555	3006	8.6	6	19 55	49.68	48.99	+ 2.065	− 0.001	......	4	47.1	10.6
4556	3011	7.2	3	19 55	49.83	49.60	+ 1.242	− 0.009	......	3	46.4	10.8
4557	...	9.0	5	19 55	57.38	...	+ 2.091	− 0.001	......	4	47.4	...
4558	3009	7.9	6	19 56	3.41	3.21	+ 2.093	− 0.001	......	5	49.1	12.7
4559	3010	7.3	5	19 56	12.41	11.91	+ 1.948	− 0.002	......	3	44.2	11.8
4560	3013	7.4	5	19 56	29.21	28.83	+ 2.075	− 0.001	......	5	48.5	10.6
4561	...	9.9	5	19 56	30.31	...	+ 2.076	− 0.001	......	3	48.0	...
4562	3019	6.2	7	19 56	31.67	31.57	+ 0.766	− 0.020	......	4	45.7	12.6
4563	3016	9.2	6	19 56	40.45	40.39	+ 1.417	− 0.007	......	4	48.5	13.8
4564	3014	6.7	5	19 56	42.03	41.89	+ 1.995	− 0.002	......	3	45.9	11.8
4565	...	9.1	6	19 56	47.16	...	+ 1.425	− 0.007	......	4	51.2	...
4566	3015	7.6	6	19 56	51.29	51.04	+ 1.901	− 0.003	......	3	45.4	14.6
4567	3021	7.8	5	19 56	51.51	51.18	+ 0.818	− 0.026	......	3	49.0	12.8
4568	3017	5.5	5	19 56	58.35	58.39	+ 1.696	− 0.003	......	6	45.4	8.7
4569	3020	8.1	5	19 57	7.58	7.52	+ 1.519	− 0.005	......	4	47.2	11.7
4570	3018	9.1	7	19 57	13.09	13.58	+ 2.124	− 0.001	......	4	48.2	13.6
4571	3022	7.7	5	19 57	36.12	36.10	+ 2.102	− 0.001	......	4	46.2	12.7
4572	3025	7.8	7	19 57	56.15	55.75	+ 0.752	− 0.017	......	4	48.7	12.6
4573	3023	8.1	5	19 57	58.75	58.60	+ 2.099	− 0.001	......	4	47.9	12.7
4574	3026	7.5	5	19 58	29.94	30.07	+ 1.265	− 0.009	......	3	46.6	10.8
4575	3024	7.5	6	19 58	35.49	35.25	+ 2.087	− 0.001	......	5	49.5	10.6
4576	3027	6.9	6	19 58	50.18	49.82	+ 1.693	− 0.003	......	3	47.6	11.7
4577	...	7.4	6	19 58	52.19	...	+ 1.684	− 0.004	......	4	49.7	...
4578	3028	8.4	7	19 59	10.17	9.88	+ 2.034	− 0.001	......	5	48.0	12.2
4579	...	7.9	5	19 59	13.79	...	+ 1.622	− 0.005	......	2	49.7	...
4580	3029	8.5	8	19 59	17.24	17.28	+ 2.134	− 0.001	......	5	45.6	13.6

Ordinal Number.	Mean North Polar Distance 1845.0.			Precession 1845.0.	Secular Variation.	Adopted Proper Motion	Observations of N.P.D.			Names.	Oeltzen Argelander Number.
R.	R.		G.				No. R.	Mean year. R.	G.		
	° ′ ″		″	″	″	″		1800 +			
4546	38 25 17.6		...	— 96.4	— 0.20	...	4	46.2	...	....	......
4547	35 15 29.1		30.6	— 9.65	— 0.18	...	4	45.7	13.8	....	19876
4548	38 22 1.3		2.0	— 9.66	— 0.21	...	4	43.4	8.6	....	....
4549	27 32 36.1		35.8	— 9.66	— 0.09	...	3	47.1	12.8	....	19379
4550	29 34 4.8		...	— 9.67	— 0.12	...	4	49.2	...	....	....
4551	50 53 12.5		13.0	— 9.70	— 0.28	...	3	48.0	13.6	....	......
4552	38 8 41.2		...	— 9.70	— 0.20	...	3	44.6	...	....	......
4553	27 27 47.2		52.2	— 9.70	— 0.09	...	3	50.7	12.8	....	19888
4554	38 16 30.4		...	— 9.71	— 0.20	...	5	44.7	...	....	......
4555	49 20 2.9		1.4	— 9.71	— 0.26	...	5	47.4	10.6	....	......
4556	32 36 49.5		49.7	— 9.71	— 0.15	...	4	45.2	10.8	....	15890
4557	50 4 20.2		...	— 9.72	— 0.27	...	2	46.2	...	....	......
4558	50 7 43.2		43.1	— 9.72	— 0.26	...	2	46.2	12.7	....	......
4559	46 9 44.6		44.5	— 9.74	— 0.25	...	3	47.3	11.8	....	......
4560	49 34 11.3		12.6	— 9.76	— 0.26	...	3	43.3	10.6	....	......
4561	49 35 7.6		...	— 9.76	— 0.26	...	2	47.2	...	....	......
4562	26 53 17.5		17.6	— 9.76	— 0.08	...	5	48.2	12.6	....	19904
4563	35 14 4.8		4.7	— 9.77	— 0.16	...	3	52.4	13.8	....	19905
4564	46 18 33.4		34.1	— 9.77	— 0.23	...	3	45.6	11.8	....	......
4565	35 21 7.2		...	— 9.78	— 0.18	...	2	51.7	...	....	......
4566	44 57 11.2		14.3	— 9.78	— 0.21	...	3	45.7	14.6	....	19907
4567	27 23 35.9		36.9	— 9.79	— 0.12	...	2	49.2	12.8	....	19911
4568	40 19 27.7		28.6	— 9.79	— 0.19	— 0.02	4	46.7	8.7	26 Cygni e	......
4569	36 55 15.9		14.5	— 9.81	— 0.19	...	3	45.7	11.7	....	......
4570	50 57 11.0		9.5	— 9.81	— 0.25	...	3	52.7	13.6	....	......
4571	50 15 32.8		32.7	— 9.84	— 0.25	...	3	47.3	12.7	....	......
4572	26 39 15.2		13.8	— 9.87	— 0.09	...	4	46.7	12.6	....	19924
4573	50 9 14.1		14.7	— 9.87	— 0.25	...	3	48.7	12.7	....	......
4574	32 46 49.4		51.2	— 9.91	— 0.15	...	5	45.7	10.3	....	19944
4575	49 46 44.8		44.9	— 9.92	— 0.26	...	3	45.1	10.5	....	......
4576	40 7 38.0		39.1	— 9.94	— 0.21	...	3	45.6	11.7	....	19957
4577	39 58 10.0		...	— 9.94	— 0.21	...	4	46.7	...	....	19960
4578	48 14 20.9		20.8	— 9.96	— 0.24	...	4	47.2	12.2	....	......
4579	38 41 51.0		...	— 9.97	— 0.20	...	4	48.2	...	....	......
4580	51 5 33.0		31.9	— 9.97	— 0.26	...	3	47.7	13.6	....	......

Magnitude.	Estimates of Magnitude.	Mean Right Ascension 1845.0.		Precession 1845.0.	Secular Variation	Adopted Proper Motion.
R.		R.	G.			
		h. m. s.	s.	s.	s.	s.
7.2	8	19 59 46.81	46.57	+ 2.085	− 0.001	......
5.1	4	19 59 49.18	48.97	+ 0.654	− 0.020	......
8.3	5	19 59 56.94	55.87	+ 2.135	− 0.001	......
7.4	6	19 59 59.34	...	+ 1.648	− 0.005	......
8.4	3	20 0 2.82	...	+ 1.624	− 0.005	......
7.9	4	20 0 31.09	...	+ 0.676	− 0.028	......
8.1	5	20 0 32.93	32.78	+ 2.113	− 0.001	......
7.4	6	20 0 34.61	...	+ 1.636	− 0.005	......
6.1	5	20 0 36.15	36.09	+ 0.679	− 0.020	......
7.1	7	20 0 51.64	51.30	+ 2.146	− 0.001	......
5.9	8	20 0 54.69	54.01	+ 1.623	− 0.004	......
8.1	7	20 0 56.54	56.37	+ 1.693	− 0.004	......
7.8	6	20 1 4.31	4.11	+ 1.391	− 0.008	......
8.2	6	20 1 9.77	7.36	+ 1.366	− 0.008	......
8.1	9	20 1 21.12	20.73	+ 0.766	− 0.017	......
6.1	5	20 1 49.82	49.82	+ 1.368	− 0.008	......
4.7	5	20 2 5.93	5.74	+ 0.299	− 0.034	+ 0.003
5.8	4	20 2 8.86	7.81	+ 1.558	− 0.006	......
8.3	5	20 2 37.50	37.26	+ 2.129	− 0.001	......
6.9	5	20 2 45.00	44.96	+ 2.037	− 0.001	......
6.4	3	20 2 46.02	45.86	+ 1.711	− 0.004	......
5.8	6	20 2 47.10	46.74	+ 0.770	− 0.020	......
8.5	5	20 2 47.99	47.53	+ 2.108	− 0.001	......
7.6	7	20 2 52.31	51.77	+ 2.030	+ 0.001	......
5.5	9	20 3 4.34	4.34	+ 0.950	− 0.017	+ 0.013
7.9	7	20 3 10.93	10.92	+ 1.918	− 0.002	......
7.3	6	20 3 18.06	17.66	+ 2.129	− 0.001	. ....
8.5	6	20 3 29.49	28.32	+ 0.793	− 0.020	......
8.1	6	20 3 32.86	...	+ 1.978	− 0.002	......
8.8	6	20 3 48.45	48.32	+ 1.440	− 0.006	......
5.9	6	20 3 51.99	51.75	− 1.543	− 0.123	......
6.5	7	20 4 12.15	11.88	+ 0.294	− 0.036	......
8.7	6	20 4 12.28	...	+ 1.986	− 0.002	......
8.5	6	20 4 12.91	12.76	+ 2.110	− 0.001	......
7.4	6	20 4 18.52	17.96	+ 1.699	− 0.004	......

Ordinal Number. R.	Mean North Polar Distance 1845.0 R.	G.	Precession 1845.0	Secular Variation.	Adopted Proper Motion.	Observations of N.P.D. No. R.	Mean year R. (1800+)	Mean year G.	Names.	Oeltzen-Argelander Number.
	o ′ ″	″	″	″	″					
4581	49 37 27.5	26.5	− 10.01	− 0.26	...	5	46.9	10.7	....	....
4582	25 36 45.2	44.9	− 10.01	− 0.07	+ 0.02	5	41.2	7.7	64 Draconis e.	....
4583	51 5 14.9	16.2	− 10.02	− 0.26	...	3	50.0	13.6	....	....
4584	39 8 57.2	...	− 10.02	− 0.21	...	5	52.1	...	....	....
4585	38 40 23.1	...	− 10.03	− 0.20	...	3	48.7	...	....	....
4586	25 46 38.7	...	− 10.07	− 0.08	...	3	44.0	...	....	....
4587	50 22 35.9	39.8	− 10.07	− 0.27	...	3	47.7	12.7	....	....
4588	38 51 43.4	...	− 10.07	− 0.20	...	4	51.1	...	....	....
4589	25 48 8.7	11.9	− 10.07	− 0.07	...	6	47.0	8.7	65 Draconis...	....
4590	51 20 45.5	47.4	− 10.09	− 0.26	...	3	45.3	13.6	....	....
4591	38 36 11.0	14.6	− 10.09	− 0.18	...	5	47.8	9.7	....	....
4592	39 59 35.9	36.2	− 10.10	− 0.21	...	3	45.6	11.7	....	20005
4593	34 31 11.8	14.1	− 10.11	− 0.18	...	4	45.9	13.7	....	....
4594	34 7 8.1	4.0	− 10.12	− 0.19	...	3	45.7	9.8	....	20012
4595	26 36 1.4	3.8	− 10.13	− 0.09	...	6	50.2	13.6	....	20017
4596	34 6 19.8	21.9	− 10.16	− 0.15	...	4	43.2	11.5	....	20027
4597	22 34 6.3	6.2	− 10.19	− 0.04	− 0.04	7	43.2	7.1	67 Draconis ρ	20041
4598	37 17 26.3	35.1	− 10.19	− 0.19	...	4	43.4	8.6	....	20038
4599	50 41 53.4	54.2	− 10.22	− 0.25	...	2	47.8	11.8	....	....
4600	48 3 51.6	53.0	− 10.23	− 0.23	...	3	45.0	10.7	....	....
4601	40 13 3.8	3.8	− 10.23	− 0.19	...	3	45.7	11.7	....	20059
4602	26 33 19.0	21.7	− 10.23	− 0.07	...	5	44.7	13.6	....	20062
4603	50 4 49.6	49.8	− 10.23	− 0.23	...	3	48.0	12.7	....	....
4604	47 50 35.2	36.8	− 10.24	− 0.24	...	4	47.4	10.7	....	....
4605	28 27 12.6	12.7	− 10.26	− 0.12	− 0.05	6	44.3	8.8	66 Draconis...	....
4606	44 54 19.1	19.5	− 10.27	− 0.24	...	4	46.5	14.6	....	....
4607	50 39 10.3	11.5	− 10.28	− 0.27	...	5	45.1	11.8	....	....
4608	26 44 51.3	58.4	− 10.29	− 0.09	...	4	50.2	13.6	....	20085
4609	46 23 25.4	...	− 10.29	− 0.25	...	5	52.1	...	....	....
4610	35 7 26.7	25.2	− 10.31	− 0.16	...	3	49.4	13.7	....	20091
4611	13 57 14.8	15.0	− 10.31	+ 0.22	+ 0.08	5	45.0	9.3	69 Draconis...	20095
4612	22 25 7.6	7.6	− 10.35	− 0.05	...	3	44.0	9.7	....	20103
4613	46 34 25.4	...	− 10.35	− 0.25	...	4	52.2	...	....	....
4614	50 1 33.6	32.2	− 10.35	− 0.27	...	3	47.4	12.7	....	....
4615	39 52 10.7	13.2	− 10.35	− 0.20	...	3	45.6	11.7	....	20107

Ordinal Number.		Magnitude.	Estimates of Magnitude.	Mean Right Ascension 1845.0.			Precession 1845.0.	Secular Variation	Adopted Proper Motion.	Observations of R.A.		
R.	G.	R.		R.		G.				No. R.	Mean year. R.	G.
				h. m. s.		s.	s.	s.	s.		1800 +	
4616	3057	7.1	7	20 4 27.14		27.08	+ 1.284	— 0.009	......	4	45.7	10.8
4617	3060	7.7	6	20 4 44.26		44.08	+ 0.800	— 0.020	......	2	47.7	13.7
4618	3058	8.2	6	20 5 0.68		0.38	+ 2.110	— 0.001	......	4	48.1	12.7
4619	...	7.0	7	20 5 4.99		...	+ 1.986	— 0.002	......	6	52.3	...
4620	...	8.7	6	20 5 7.79		...	+ 0.822	— 0.020	......	3	51.0	...
4621	3065	7.9	4	20 5 7.82		8.17	+ 0.826	— 0.020	......	2	49.2	13.7
4622	3063	8.5	5	20 5 21.42		21.38	+ 1.467	— 0.006	......	3	45.4	13.8
4623	...	8.7	4	20 5 25.74		...	+ 2.118	— 0.001	......	3	52.0	...
4624	3061	8.0	5	20 5 28.08		27.89	+ 1.928	— 0.002	......	3	44.6	14.6
4625	3062	7.7	7	20 5 40.10		39.70	+ 2.019	— 0.001	......	4	45.6	13.6
4626	3071	6.7	5	20 5 45.13		45.08	+ 1.406	— 0.006	......	3	47.0	13.7
4627	...	9.5	8	20 5 45.62		...	+ 2.123	— 0.001	......	5	53.1	...
4628	3064	7.7	7	20 5 49.24		49.11	+ 2.167	— 0.001	......	5	49.0	12.8
4629	...	10.1	9	20 5 51.85		...	+ 2.125	— 0.001	......	4	53.9	...
4630	3068	8.6	5	20 5 57.70		57.37	+ 2.016	— 0.001	......	4	50.0	13.6
4631	3070	8.4	4	20 6 0.51		0.87	+ 1.924	— 0.002	......	3	49.9	14.6
4632	3067	7.6	6	20 6 1.59		1.48	+ 2.166	— 0.001	......	3	50.7	12.7
4633	3073	8.5	6	20 6 5.52		5.37	+ 1.833	— 0.002	......	4	47.2	11.8
4634	3069	8.1	5	20 6 9.29		9.13	+ 2.173	— 0.001	......	2	48.1	12.8
4635	3075	7.5	4	20 6 14.57		14.41	+ 1.474	— 0.006	......	2	47.7	13.8
4636	3072	8.3	4	20 6 15.37		15.60	+ 2.172	0.000	......	3	50.3	12.8
4637	3074	7.0	5	20 6 18.54		17.87	+ 2.119	0.000	......	3	48.0	12.6
4638	3082	7.5	6	20 6 18.95		18.92	— 0.505	— 0.069	......	3	50.4	12.1
4639	...	6.9	8	20 6 29.08		...	+ 0.963	— 0.018	......	5	46.1	...
4640	3076	8.4	6	20 6 29.12		30.29	+ 1.922	— 0.002	......	3	53.1	14.6
4641	3085	7.1	3	20 6 34.03		33.84	— 0.762	— 0.080	......	2	47.2	10.8
4642	...	8.3	5	20 6 37.86		...	+ 1.922	— 0.002	......	3	50.0	...
4643	...	9.2	3	20 6 45.97		...	+ 2.022	— 0.002	......	2	50.7	...
4644	...	9.3	4	20 6 52.60		...	+ 2.140	0.000	......	2	49.2	...
4645	3077	7.3	3	20 7 3.80		2.94	+ 2.123	0.000	......	2	48.6	12.6
4646	3078	8.5	5	20 7 8.67		8.60	+ 2.023	— 0.001	......	3	51.1	13.6
4647	3083	8.4	6	20 7 10.48		10.20	+ 0.781	— 0.023	......	3	49.7	13.6
4648	3079	7.0	5	20 7 18.32		17.88	+ 1.841	— 0.003	......	5	46.2	11.8
4649	...	8.1	4	20 7 26.11		...	+ 2.182	0.000	......	3	49.0	...
4650	3080	7.1	3	20 7 45.12		45.25	+ 2.174	0.000	......	3	46.0	12.8

Ordinal Number.	Mean North Polar Distance 1845.0.			Precession 1845.0.	Secular Variation.	Adopted Proper Motion.	Observations of N.P.D.				Names.	Oeltzen Argelander Number.
	R.		G.				No. R.	Mean year.				
	R.							R.	G.			
	° ′ ″		″	″	″	″		1800 +				
4616	32 39	4.0	2.4	− 10.36	− 0.15	...	4	47.7	10.8	....	20110
4617	26 44	34.7	35.9	− 10.39	− 0.11	...	4	46.7	13.7	....	20118
4618	49 58	40.2	39.6	− 10.40	− 0.25	...	4	47.7	12.7	....	....
4619	46 30	49.9	...	− 10.41	− 0.25	...	3	52.0	...	....	....
4620	26 56	44.3	...	− 10.41	− 0.09	...	3	51.3	...	....	20129
4621	26 59	32.8	29.9	− 10.41	− 0.09	...	3	50.0	13.7	....	20130
4622	35 27	47.8	47.9	− 10.43	− 0.18	...	2	49.2	13.8	....	....
4623	50 10	31.7	...	− 10.43	− 0.26	...	2	52.2	...	....	....
4624	44 58	58.9	62.6	− 10.43	− 0.21	...	2	45.2	14.6	....	20139
4625	47 21	39.7	41.4	− 10.45	− 0.24	...	3	45.7	13.6	....	....
4626	34 25	42.2	43.1	− 10.46	− 0.17	...	3	44.4	13.7	....	....
4627	50 17	29.8	...	− 10.46	− 0.27	...	5	53.3	...	....	....
4628	51 38	28.6	29.6	− 10.47	− 0.28	...	3	48.7	12.8	....	....
4629	50 20	23.4	...	− 10.47	− 0.27	...	5	55.9	...	....	....
4630	47 13	34.2	35.6	− 10.47	− 0.25	...	2	50.1	13.6	....	....
4631	44 51	27.7	31.1	− 10.48	− 0.23	...	3	43.7	14.6	....	20162
4632	51 34	48.4	49.7	− 10.48	− 0.26	...	3	48.8	12.7	....	....
4633	42 38	45.5	46.5	− 10.48	− 0.21	...	4	47.7	11.8	....	....
4634	51 46	38.2	40.4	− 10.49	− 0.27	...	3	52.0	12.8	....	....
4635	35 31	4.4	5.2	− 10.50	− 0.19	...	2	50.2	13.8	....	....
4636	51 45	35.2	39.0	− 10.50	− 0.27	...	2	51.7	12.8	....	....
4637	50 7	50.4	50.1	− 10.51	− 0.29	...	3	45.4	12.6	....	....
4638	17 40	7.0	8.0	− 10.51	+ 0.05	...	3	46.0	12.1	....	20169
4639	28 22	46.6	...	− 10.52	− 0.12	...	3	46.2	...	....	20175
4640	44 44	39.7	35.3	− 10.52	− 0.24	...	3	50.1	14.5	....	20173
4641	16 32	29.7	30.2	− 10.52	+ 0.10	...	3	44.4	10.3	....	20184
4642	45 0	53.1	...	− 10.52	− 0.24	...	2	54.3	...	....	20180
4643	47 20	8.3	...	− 10.53	− 0.25	...	2	52.3	...	....	....
4644	50 43	51.1	...	− 10.54	− 0.27	...	2	50.2	...	....	....
4645	50 11	40.9	42.8	− 10.55	− 0.24	...	3	46.4	12.5	....	....
4646	47 20	49.3	52.2	− 10.56	− 0.23	...	2	48.7	13.6	....	....
4647	26 24	18.7	20.0	− 10.56	− 0.08	...	4	47.7	13.6	....	20195
4648	42 43	34.6	34.2	− 10.57	− 0.21	...	5	43.9	11.8	....	....
4649	51 58	59.3	...	− 10.58	− 0.27	...	2	47.7	...	....	....
4650	51 41	58.3	60.5	− 10.61	− 0.27	...	2	46.2	12.8	....	....

Magnitude.	Estimates of Magnitude.	Mean Right Ascension 1845.0.		Precession 1845.0.	Secular Variation	Adopted Proper Motion.
R.		R.	G.			
		h. m. s.	s.	s.	s.	s.
7.6	6	20 7 46.01	46.12	+ 2.175	0.000	......
8.0	6	20 7 50.16	...	+ 2.183	0.000	......
8.1	6	20 7 57.42	57.45	+ 1.728	— 0.003	......
5.5	4	20 8 13.00	12.82	+ 1.670	— 0.004	......
7.9	6	20 8 13.32	13.18	+ 2.000	— 0.001	......
5.2	5	20 8 25.68	25.51	+ 1.883	— 0.002	+ 0.006
6.2	5	20 8 29.81	29.71	+ 2.018	— 0.001	......
8.1	5	20 8 30.72	30.65	+ 1.734	— 0.003	......
4.2	6 ·	20 8 45.10	44.77	+ 1.887	— 0.002	......
9.0	6	20 8 45.96	45.84	+ 1.473	— 0.009	......
7.3	5	20 8 46.20	...	+ 1.889	— 0.002	......
7.8	3	20 8 56.26	55.99	+ 2.126	0.000	......
6.8	5	20 9 1.07	...	+ 2.065	— 0.001	......
5.6	6	20 9 1.90	1.91	+ 0.979	— 0.017	+ 0.015
7.7	5	20 9 6.09	...	+ 1.673	— 0.005	......
9.0	4	20 9 8.50	8.50	+ 2.023	0.000	......
8.1	6	20 9 20.12	19.88	+ 1.474	— 0.006	......
5.0	1	20 9 27.05	...	+ 3.331	— 0.010	......
8.3	7	20 9 28.47	28.50	+ 1.935	— 0.002	......
7.7	5	20 9 29.81	29.37	+ 0.848	— 0.020	......
7.4	6	20 9 32.04	31.84	+ 0.299	— 0.034	......
7.1	6	20 9 33.44	33.26	+ 1.591	— 0.004	......
8.1	6	20 9 33.52	33.58	+ 2.184	0.000	......
7.0	5	20 9 38.59	38.53	+ 1.478	— 0.006	......
7.7	5	20 9 43.01	42.76	+ 2.095	0.000	......
4.8	4	20 9 47.44	47.26	+ 1.391	— 0.009	+ 0.007
7.6	6	20 9 55.50	...	+ 1.851	— 0.003	......
7.3	4	20 9 56.56	...	+ 1.862	— 0.002	......
6.7	4	20 10 13.38	13.73	+ 0.307	— 0.037	......
7.0	5	20 10 13.39	...	+ 2.000	— 0.002	......
8.3	5	20 10 15.83	15.58	+ 1.938	— 0.003	......
6.8	5	20 10 17.30	17.36	+ 1.932	— 0.003	......
7.0	6	20 10 17.37	...	+ 1.995	— 0.002	......
6.8	6	20 10 25.67	25.63	+ 2.177	0.000	......
6.0	5	20 10 36.28	35.84	+ 1.107	— 0.014	......

Ordinal Number.	Mean North Polar Distance 1845.0.			Precession 1845.0.	Secular Variation.	Adopted Proper Motion.	Observations of N.P.D.			Names.	Oeltzen-Argelander Number.
	R.		G.				No. R.	Mean year. R.	G.		
	° ′ ″		″	″	″	″		1800 +			
4651	51 44 11.0		12.6	— 10.61	— 0.26	...	3	45.4	12.8	....	....
4652	51 59 8.8		...	— 10.61	— 0.27	...	3	48.4	...	....	....
4653	40 12 30.0		30.9	— 10.63	— 0.23	...	3	47.0	10.7	....	....
4654	39 0 2.5		3.3	— 10.64	— 0.19	...	4	43.7	8.7	....	20214
4655	46 39 18.9		17.5	— 10.64	— 0.23	...	3	48.3	13.6	....	....
4656	43 39 3.6		3.9	— 10.66	— 0.23	— 0.01	3	44.3	9.4	30 Cygni o¹...	20220
4657	47 5 18.4		18.1	— 10.67	— 0.26	...	3	45.7	13.6	....	....
4658	40 16 45.6		46.2	— 10.67	— 0.22	...	3	47.3	10.7	....	20222
4659	43 43 34.9		35.3	— 10.69	— 0.23	...	11	50.2	7.7	31 Cygni o² ...	20229
4660	35 19 25.3		24.7	— 10.69	— 0.19	...	4	50.7	13.8	....	....
4661	43 45 21.6		...	— 10.69	— 0.23	...	4	46.7	...	....	20231
4662	50 8 22.6		22.8	— 10.69	— 0.24	...	4	51.0	12.6	....	....
4663	48 21 50.7		...	— 10.70	— 0.25	...	3	52.4	...	....	....
4664	28 23 23.9		23.9	— 10.70	— 0.11	— 0.05	6	46.1	8.3	68 Draconis ...	....
4665	38 58 22.8		...	— 10.71	— 0.20	...	2	47.8	...	....	20245
4666	47 11 6.2		7.7	— 10.72	— 0.27	...	2	50.2	13.5	....	....
4667	35 17 43.3		45.5	— 10.73	— 0.19	...	4	46.7	13.3	....	....
4668	103 1 15.6		...	— 10.74	— 0.41	...	12	52.3	...	6 Capricorni α²	....
4669	44 50 58.5		60.3	— 10.74	— 0.24	...	4	51.7	14.6	....	....
4670	26 56 17.6		17.2	— 10.74	— 0.11	...	3	47.7	13.7	....	20255
4671	22 10 0.0		1.9	— 10.74	— 0.03	...	3	50.7	14.8	....	20257
4672	37 21 3.9		9.4	— 10.74	— 0.19	...	3	45.7	11.7	....	....
4673	51 51 43.8		45.9	— 10.74	— 0.26	...	3	51.7	12.8	....	....
4674	35 20 12.3		12.8	— 10.75	— 0.18	...	2	46.2	13.8	....	....
4675	49 10 20.4		21.9	— 10.75	— 0.24	...	2	49.2	11.7	....	....
4676	33 54 18.6		19.0	— 10.76	— 0.17	— 0.04	3	46.0	7.8	33 Cygni.......	20263
4677	42 45 44.8		...	— 10.76	— 0.23	...	3	44.7	...	....	20264
4678	43 1 51.4		...	— 10.76	— 0.23	...	2	47.7	...	....	....
4679	22 11 35.6		38.2	— 10.79	— 0.03	...	2	48.2	14.8	....	20272
4680	46 28 18.8		...	— 10.79	— 0.25	...	2	49.2	...	....	....
4681	44 52 41.8		44.5	— 10.79	— 0.24	...	2	52.2	14.6	....	20269
4682	44 43 54.2		54.2	— 10.79	— 0.24	...	2	44.1	14.6	....	20271
4683	46 19 59.6		...	— 10.79	— 0.25	...	3	51.4	...	....	....
4684	51 34 28.5		28.8	— 10.81	— 0.27	...	3	48.8	12.8	....	....
4685	29 49 56.6		58.2	— 10.82	— 0.13	— 0.01	3	43.6	9.1	....	....

Ordinal Number.		Magnitude.	Estimates of Magnitude.	Mean Right Ascension 1845.0.		Precession 1845.0.	Secular Variation	Adopted Proper Motion.	Observations of R.A.		
R.	G.	R.		R.	G.				No. R.	Mean year. R.	G.
				h. m. s.	s.	s.	s.	s.		1800 +	
4686	3108	4.2	3	20 10 40.75	40.56	+ 1.853	− 0.002	......	4	46.7	8.3
4687	...	8.4	7	20 10 42.58	...	+ 1.856	− 0.003	......	3	50.3	...
4688	...	8.2	6	20 10 56.40	...	+ 1.858	− 0.003	......	4	46.7	...
4689	3110	6.3	5	20 10 59.28	59.22	+ 1.941	− 0.002	......	3	49.0	14.6
4690	3109	8.3	4	20 11 2.47	2.41	+ 2.178	0.000	......	2	51.2	12.8
4691	3114	6.5	5	20 11 12.86	12.58	+ 1.743	− 0.003	......	2	49.2	10.4
4692	...	8.9	4	20 11 14.08	...	+ 2.153	0.000	......	2	49.2	...
4693	...	8.2	3	20 11 14.41	...	+ 2.153	0.000	......	3	47.7	...
4694	3113	5.3	3	20 11 24.44	24.09	+ 2.131	0.000	......	2	50.7	10.4
4695	...	7.7	3	20 11 25.32	...	− 1.826	− 0.160	......	3	52.4	...
4696	3116	7.1	4	20 11 33.07	33.20	+ 1.953	− 0.001	......	3	49.4	14.6
4697	3115	8.6	5	20 11 34.96	34.69	+ 2.029	− 0.001	......	3	50.0	13.6
4698	3123	8.7	5	20 11 35.13	34.95	+ 0.895	− 0.020	......	3	52.3	13.7
4699	...	8.7	4	20 11 35.15	...	+ 2.046	− 0.001	......	2	52.2	...
4700	3119	7.2	5	20 11 36.30	36.27	+ 1.632	− 0.003	......	3	51.0	10.8
4701	3117	7.1	4	20 11 42.80	42.37	+ 2.125	0.000	......	4	47.2	12.7
4702	3118	6.6	4	20 11 50.18	49.97	+ 2.158	0.000	......	3	47.8	12.7
4703	3120	8.1	5	20 12 1.41	1.29	+ 2.180	0.000	......	2	50.7	10.8
4704	3121	6.2	4	20 12 10.50	10.31	+ 2.052	0.000	......	3	49.0	10.8
4705	3122	8.2	5	20 12 13.89	13.58	+ 2.129	0.000	......	3	48.7	12.7
4706	3124	8.4	5	20 12 17.58	17.53	+ 2.036	0.000	......	3	51.0	13.6
4707	...	4.2	2	20 12 17.87	...	+ 3.376	− 0.011	......	6	49.3	...
4708	3129	7.1	5	20 12 18.46	18.57	+ 0.743	− 0.023	......	3	52.4	8.8
4709	...	8.5	3	20 12 19.74	...	+ 1.740	− 0.004	......	2	51.2	...
4710	3126	7.8	3	20 12 20.80	20.64	+ 1.640	− 0.004	......	2	47.7	10.8
4711	3127	8.1	5	20 12 27.47	28.32	+ 1.745	− 0.003	......	3	50.6	10.4
4712	3125	6.1	6	20 12 37.60	37.48	+ 2.123	0.000	......	3	45.4	9.8
4713	...	8.1	9	20 12 40.59	...	+ 2.138	0.000	......	5	53.9	...
4714	3128	8.3	10	20 12 51.72	51.46	+ 2.135	0.000	......	3	49.0	12.6
4715	3130	8.3	4	20 13 1.71	1.55	+ 1.967	− 0.001	......	2	51.2	11.7
4716	3131	8.3	5	20 13 3.38	3.16	+ 1.956	− 0.001	......	4	48.2	14.1
4717	...	7.7	5	20 13 7.68	...	+ 2.138	0.000	......	3	53.7	...
4718	...	7.2	5	20 13 13.27	...	− 1.912	− 0.170	+ 0.109	2	50.7	...
4719	3132	6.0	4	20 13 19.12	19.09	+ 2.181	0.000	......	3	45.3	12.8
4720	3134	8.6	5	20 13 23.52	23.53	+ 1.901	− 0.002	......	2	47.7	14.8

Ordinal Number.	Mean North Polar Distance 1845.0			Precession 1845.0.	Secular Variation.	Adopted Proper Motion.	Observations of N.P.D.			Names.	Oeltzen-Argelander Number.
	R.	R.	G.				No.	Mean year.			
							R.	R. 1800 +	G.		
	° ′ ″		″	″	″	″					
4686	42 45 35.6		34.5	− 10.82	− 0.23	...	7	47.7	8.3	32 Cygni	20286
4687	42 49 2.4		...	− 10.82	− 0.23	...	4	48.2	...	....	20287
4688	42 51 35.5		...	− 10.84	− 0.23	...	3	47.0	...	....	20292
4689	44 53 34.1		33.7	− 10.85	− 0.24	...	3	47.4	14.6	....	20293
4690	51 34 35.3		36.3	− 10.85	− 0.26	...	3	49.4	12.8	....	....
4691	40 14 33.2		33.8	− 10.86	− 0.19	...	3	46.7	10.4	....	20298
4692	50 46 40.4		...	− 10.86	− 0.26	...	2	46.7	...	....	....
4693	50 46 45.9		...	− 10.86	− 0.26	...	1	45.8	...	....	....
4694	50 6 41.5		43.1	− 10.88	− 0.26	...	2	52.2	10.4	....	....
4695	12 55 23.9		...	− 10.88	+ 0.23	...	2	51.2	...	....	....
4696	45 8 16.0		17.1	− 10.89	− 0.23	...	3	46.1	14.6	....	20314
4697	47 9 0.3		0.2	− 10.89	− 0.24	...	3	51.7	13.6	....	....
4698	27 18 0.4		0.5	− 10.89	− 0.10	...	3	51.7	13.7	....	20315
4699	47 36 21.8		...	− 10.89	− 0.25	...	2	50.7	...	....	....
4700	37 58 23.9		23.4	− 10.89	− 0.18	...	2	45.2	10.8	....	....
4701	49 53 11.2		9.2	− 10.90	− 0.25	...	3	46.7	12.7	....	....
4702	50 53 6.3		7.6	− 10.91	− 0.26	...	2	49.7	12.7	....	....
4703	51 32 40.1		39.9	− 10.92	− 0.25	...	3	52.0	10.8	....	....
4704	47 45 24.4		26.4	− 10.93	− 0.23	...	3	47.1	10.8	....	....
4705	49 58 21.9		22.7	− 10.94	− 0.25	...	2	45.2	12.7	....	....
4706	47 17 43.6		42.8	− 10.94	− 0.23	...	2	50.2	13.6	....	....
4707	105 15 59.3		...	− 10.94	− 0.41	− 0.03	3	49.0	...	9 Capricorni β	....
4708	25 42 39.0		41.0	− 10.95	− 0.10	...	4	46.2	8.8	....	20328
4709	40 5 38.8		...	− 10.95	− 0.21	...	2	51.1	...	....	20326
4710	38 4 50.1		49.0	− 10.95	− 0.20	...	2	45.2	10.8	....	....
4711	40 11 26.9		20.0	− 10.95	− 0.19	...	4	46.9	10.4	....	20333
4712	49 44 54.5		54.6	− 10.97	− 0.25	...	4	46.6	9.8	....	....
4713	50 21 32.1		...	− 10.97	− 0.26	...	5	53.1	...	....	....
4714	50 5 34.8		33.5	− 10.98	− 0.26	...	7	52.3	12.6	....	....
4715	45 24 44.1		45.0	− 11.00	− 0.24	...	3	46.0	11.7	....	....
4716	45 5 4.4		5.1	− 11.00	− 0.23	...	3	45.7	14.1	....	20346
4717	50 15 18.6		...	− 11.00	− 0.26	...	2	53.8	...	....	....
4718	12 38 25.0		...	− 11.01	+ 0.23	+ 0.02	4	45.5	...	....	....
4719	51 28 42.8		43.2	− 11.02	− 0.26	...	3	47.7	12.8	....	....
4720	43 41 25.3		27.8	− 11.03	− 0.24	...	3	51.0	14.8	....	20356

Ordinal Number		Magnitude	Estimates of Magnitude	Mean Right Ascension 1845.0		Precession 1845.0	Secular Variation	Adopted Proper Motion	Observations of R.A.		
R.	G.	R.	R.	R.	G.				No. R.	Mean year R.	G.
				h. m. s.	s.	s.	s.	s.		1800 +	
4721	...	8.9	7	20 13 29.10	...	− 10.926	− 1.565	......	7	54.2	...
4722	3133	7.4	5	20 13 31.29	31.13	+ 2.173	0.000	......	3	47.9	11.8
4723	...	8.5	5	20 13 37.53	...	+ 0.742	− 0.028	......	3	52.7	...
4724	3136	7.6	6	20 13 48.17	48.14	+ 1.912	− 0.002	......	3	48.6	14.9
4725	...	6.9	4	20 13 51.55	...	+ 1.922	− 0.002	......	2	48.7	...
4726	3135	7.7	6	20 13 52.41	52.38	+ 2.191	0.000	......	3	46.1	12.7
4727	...	7.5	5	20 13 54.90	...	+ 1.979	− 0.002	......	3	47.7	...
4728	3148	4.8	5	20 13 59.83	59.25	− 1.852	− 0.167	+ 0.003	5	46.2	7.7
4729	...	8.0	3	20 14 3.31	...	+ 1.787	− 0.003	+ 0.006	2	49.2	...
4730	3137	7.9	7	20 14 6.75	6.37	+ 2.048	0.000	......	4	51.8	11.8
4731	...	7.3	7	20 14 16.76	...	+ 2.113	0.000	......	3	52.0	...
4732	3138	7.6	6	20 14 21.60	21.25	+ 1.996	− 0.001	......	3	47.7	12.5
4733	3139	8.1	5	20 14 30.40	30.30	+ 2.189	0.000	......	3	48.7	12.7
4734	3142	6.8	5	20 14 34.88	34.94	+ 1.486	− 0.006	......	3	48.7	13.8
4735	3140	6.4	4	20 14 38.27	37.98	+ 2.172	0.000	......	5	47.3	11.8
4736	3147	7.2	5	20 14 38.25	38.63	− 0.443	− 0.074	......	3	48.1	14.7
4737	3141*	7.0	8	20 14 45.01	44.71	+ 1.962	− 0.001	......	5	43.6	13.0
4738	3143	7.1	6	20 15 0.50	0.46	+ 1.905	− 0.002	......	4	46.7	14.8
4739	3145	8.0	6	20 15 5.82	5.67	+ 1.479	− 0.009	......	3	45.0	13.8
4740	3146	8.1	6	20 15 23.42	23.34	+ 1.956	− 0.002	......	2	47.2	13.6
4741	3144	7.9	6	20 15 28.34	28.25	+ 2.186	0.000	......	3	46.8	12.8
4742	3150	5.8	7	20 15 59.06	55.02	+ 0.539	− 0.030	......	5	46.5	9.7
4743	3156	7.0	5	20 16 0.25	0.92	− 0.367	− 0.071	......	2	48.2	14.7
4744	...	6.1	6	20 16 33.96	...	+ 2.121	0.000	......	4	46.4	...
4745	3149	2.7	11	20 16 39.98	39.79	+ 2.150	0.000	......	9	48.9	6.9
4746	3153	7.4	6	20 16 56.93	56.88	+ 1.660	− 0.003	......	3	46.7	10.4
4747	3159	5.8	7	20 17 1.00	0.68	+ 1.012	− 0.017	......	6	46.6	8.8
4748	3151	5.6	9	20 17 1.88	1.66	+ 1.954	− 0.002	......	8	49.6	13.6
4749	3152	9.0	4	20 17 2.75	2.98	+ 1.944	− 0.002	......	2	46.2	13.7
4750	...	8.1	5	20 17 14.95	...	+ 2.185	0.000	......	3	51.2	...
4751	3154	5.9	4	20 17 15.31	15.13	+ 2.126	0.000	......	3	47.3	8.7
4752	3155	6.9	5	20 17 18.43	18.27	+ 2.185	0.000	......	3	48.7	11.9
4753	3158	8.2	5	20 17 22.16	22.25	+ 1.670	− 0.003	......	4	48.6	10.7
4754	3308	6.3	68	20 17 22.53	23.17	− 51.682	− 29.320	......	111	46.9	7.1
4755	...	7.2	4	20 17 34.98	...	+ 2.134	0.000	......	3	48.4	...

Ordinal Number. R.	Mean North Polar Distance 1845.0.			Precession 1845.0.	Secular Variation.	Adopted Proper Motion.	Observations of M.P.D.			Names.	Oeltzen-Argelander Number.
	R.		G.				No. R.	Mean year. R.	G.		
	° ′ ″		″	″	″	″		1800 +			
4721	4 33 41.4		...	— 11.03	+ 1.36	...	2	52.7	...	....	......
4722	51 12 37.6		38.0	— 11.04	— 0.28	...	2	50.7	11.8	....	......
4723	25 40 3.3		...	— 11.04	— 0.08	...	2	53.2	...	....	20357
4724	43 56 21.4		22.5	— 11.05	— 0.21	...	3	45.4	14.9	....	20362
4725	44 9 41.5		...	— 11.06	— 0.23	...	3	49.1	...	....	20366
4726	51 45 10.4		12.1	— 11.06	— 0.26	...	3	48.7	12.7	....	......
4727	45 36 21.1		...	— 11.06	— 0.24	...	3	48.6	...	....	......
4728	12 45 30.0		31.3	— 11.07	+ 0.23	...	5	45.3	7.7	1 Cephei κ.....	......
4729	40 59 9.0		...	— 11.07	— 0.22	...	3	50.0	...	....	......
4730	47 29 9.6		11.2	— 11.08	— 0.25	...	3	47.3	11.8	....	......
4731	49 20 48.3		...	— 11.09	— 0.26	...	4	52.2	...	....	......
4732	45 16 15.2		15.8	— 11.09	— 0.22	...	3	45.7	12.5	....	20375
4733	51 39 11.7		15.0	— 11.10	— 0.24	...	3	48.4	12.7	....	......
4734	35 5 10.0		8.9	— 11.11	— 0.17	...	4	47.2	13.8	....	......
4735	51 4 59.2		58.8	— 11.12	— 0.27	...	4	50.5	11.8	....	......
4736	17 34 47.4		48.6	— 11.12	+ 0.05	...	3	45.0	14.7	....	......
4737	45 7 17.4		17.8	— 11.13	— 0.25	...	3	47.7	13.0	....	20382
4738	43 39 1.0		2.2	— 11.14	— 0.22	...	3	45.4	14.8	....	......
4739	34 56 32.1		33.8	— 11.15	— 0.18	...	4	47.2	13.8	....	20394
4740	44 54 53.0		54.2	— 11.17	— 0.23	...	4	49.4	13.6	....	20399
4741	51 27 28.2		29.3	— 11.18	— 0.27	...	3	49.1	12.8	....	......
4742	23 38 38.4		49.6	— 11.21	— 0.06	...	6	45.4	9.7	....	20411
4743	17 52 34.3		35.1	— 11.21	+ 0.07	...	2	46.3	14.7	....	......
4744	49 21 36.0		...	— 11.26	— 0.26	...	4	46.6	...	....	......
4745	50 14 12.3		12.3	— 11.27	— 0.27	...	4	43.7	6.9	37 Cygni γ....	......
4746	38 4 53.0		53.4	— 11.28	— 0.18	...	3	46.4	10.4	....	20426
4747	28 14 2.5		2.3	— 11.29	— 0.12	...	6	45.5	8.8	71 Draconis ...	20436
4748	44 42 0.9		3.2	— 11.29	— 0.23	...	4	46.2	13.6	....	20430
4749	44 28 7.3		7.1	— 11.29	— 0.23	...	3	49.4	13.7	....	20433
4750	51 17 13.9		...	— 11.31	— 0.26	...	3	50.3	...	....	......
4751	49 28 0.8		1.1	— 11.31	— 0.26	...	4	44.7	8.7	....	......
4752	51 17 3.6		4.8	— 11.31	— 0.26	...	3	47.4	11.9	....	......
4753	38 15 11.2		10.4	— 11.32	— 0.21	...	3	46.3	10.7	....	20438
4754	1 9 18.2		20.2	— 11.32	+ 6.48	— 0.01	158	43.0	7.1	Urs. Min. λ ...	......
4755	49 41 46.2		...	— 11.33	— 0.26	...	2	48.8	...	....	......

| Magnitude. | Estimates of Magnitude. | Mean Right Ascension 1845.0. | | Precession 1845.0. | Secular Variation | Adopted Proper Motion. |
		R.	G.			
		h. m. s.	s.	s.	s.	s.
6.5	4	20 17 35.09	34.71	+ 2.060	— 0.001	......
7.0	6	20 17 40.51	40.37	+ 1.754	— 0.003	......
8.0	7	20 17 43.06	42.84	+ 2.060	— 0.001	......
9.0	.5	20 17 44.55	...	+ 1.514	— 0.006	......
8.6	6	20 17 44.57	44.52	+ 1.502	— 0.006	......
7.1	3	20 17 46.64	...	+ 2.136	0.000	......
7.5	4	20 17 58.89	...	+ 1.684	— 0.005	......
8.7	5	20 18 4.48	4.19	+ 1.962	— 0.003	......
8.9	6	20 18 14.33	...	— 0.399	— 0.088	......
7.5	5	20 18 17.66	17.16	— 0.004	— 0.051	......
8.6	10	20 18 19.66	...	+ 1.679	— 0.005	......
5.3	2	20 18 26.60	...	+ 3.443	— 0.013	— 0.002
7.4	5	20 18 33.64	33.62	+ 1.532	— 0.006	......
8.8	6	20 18 56.62	...	+ 2.175	0.000	......
6.6	5	20 19 0.98	0.47	+ 1.548	— 0.006	......
7.0	11	20 19 13.40	13.23	+ 2.160	0.000	......
8.5	7	20 19 21.87	...	+ 2.171	0.000	......
6.1	4	20 19 23.28	22.16	+ 0.301	— 0.037	......
10.0	4	20 19 27.26	27.05	+ 1.967	— 0.002	......
8.1	7	20 19 33.62	...	+ 1.614	— 0.006	......
8.0	5	20 19 39.00	...	+ 2.166	0.000	......
7.5	5	20 19 51.05	...	+ 2.173	0.000	......
7.8	5	20 19 54.09	53.96	+ 2.164	0.000	......
5.0	1	20 20 0.89	...	+ 3.432	— 0.013	— 0.006
6.9	3	20 20 2.20	1.79	+ 2.081	— 0.001	......
6.9	5	20 20 29.20	28.87	+ 2.156	0.000	......
8.1	6	20 20 44.58	44.48	+ 1.513	— 0.006	......
7.3	6	20 20 46.30	...	+ 1.538	— 0.006	......
9.2	6	20 20 52.08	52.08	+ 1.982	— 0.001	......
8.2	5	20 20 52.24	...	+ 1.037	— 0.017	— 0.002
8.0	5	20 21 2.65	2.91	+ 1.982	— 0.001	......
7.7	5	20 21 8.41	8.28	+ 2.159	0.000	......
8.5	5	20 21 17.24	17.56	+ 1.667	— 0.005	......
7.1	12	20 21 17.85	17.47	— 7.677	— 1.031	......
8.5	5	20 21 21.87	21.72	+ 1.518	— 0.006	......

Ordinal Number.	Mean North Polar Distance 1845.0.		Precession 1845.0.	Secular Variation.	Adopted Proper Motion.	Observations of N.P.D.	Mean year.		Names.	Oeltzen-Argelander Number.
	R.	G.				No. R.	R.	G.		
	° ′ ″	″	″	″	″		1800 +			
4756	47 30 49.7	53.0	− 11.33	− 0.25	...	3	45.7	11.9	....	......
4757	39 57 15.6	15.3	− 11.33	− 0.19	...	3	45.6	11.7	....	20444
4758	47 30 5.0	5.9	− 11.33	− 0.25	...	3	45.7	11.8	....	......
4759	35 16 2.1	...	− 11.34	− 0.18	...	2	51.2	...	....	......
4760	35 7 19.3	20.6	− 11.34	− 0.17	...	3	51.3	13.8	....	......
4761	49 44 15.0	...	− 11.34	− 0.25	...	3	48.0	...	....	......
4762	38 29 29.6	...	− 11.36	− 0.20	...	3	51.4	...	....	20450
4763	44 51 26.9	29.2	− 11.36	− 0.22	...	2	50.7	13.6	....	20453
4764	17 36 21.1	...	− 11.37	− 0.10	...	4	49.2	...	....	20460
4765	19 42 3.6	2.6	− 11.38	0.00	...	3	45.4	12.6	....	20462
4766	38 21 53.2	...	− 11.39	− 0.20	...	4	51.2	...	....	20458
4767	108 42 56.5	...	− 11.40	− 0.41	− 0.02	4	54.4	...	10 Capricorni π	......
4768	35 33 53.1	52.2	− 11.40	− 0.18	...	3	47.0	12.7	....	......
4769	50 49 48.5	...	− 11.42	− 0.26	...	3	52.4	...	....	......
4770	35 49 30.4	30.7	− 11.43	− 0.17	...	5	48.7	9.8	....	......
4771	50 20 52.4	52.2	− 11.45	− 0.26	...	3	46.4	10.7	....	......
4772	50 39 44.1	...	− 11.46	− 0.26	...	3	50.7	...	....	......
4773	21 36 55.8	57.7	− 11.46	− 0.04	...	5	44.5	9.7	....	20490
4774	44 52 1.8	4.4	− 11.47	− 0.25	...	3	47.0	13.6	....	20487
4775	37 58 7.8	...	− 11.48	− 0.19	...	3	45.1	...	....	......
4776	50 28 58.5	...	− 11.48	− 0.26	...	4	50.7	...	....	......
4777	50 42 35.7	...	− 11.49	− 0.26	...	4	50.0	...	....	......
4778	50 24 20.4	18.7	− 11.49	− 0.26	...	3	49.3	10.7	....	......
4779	108 19 17.2	...	− 11.50	− 0.41	+ 0.01	2	47.7	...	11 Capricorni ρ	......
4780	47 53 57.7	61.0	− 11.50	− 0.25	...	5	48.1	10.3	....	......
4781	50 6 12.2	13.9	− 11.53	− 0.25	...	3	45.7	10.4	....	......
4782	35 3 34.9	35.7	− 11.55	− 0.16	...	3	47.4	13.3	....	20516
4783	35 29 41.5	...	− 11.55	− 0.18	...	3	48.4	...	....	......
4784	45 6 28.1	31.3	− 11.56	− 0.22	...	3	47.7	14.3	....	......
4785	28 14 8.0	...	− 11.56	− 0.12	− 0.45	3	48.3	...	72 Draconis ...	20519
4786	45 5 30.1	34.2	− 11.58	− 0.24	...	3	47.4	14.8	....	......
4787	50 9 35.7	36.3	− 11.58	− 0.24	...	3	48.0	10.2	....	......
4788	37 51 52.8	48.6	− 11.60	− 0.21	...	3	45.7	10.7	....	......
4789	5 47 44.4	41.9	− 11.60	+ 0.92	...	6	49.9	7.7	....	......
4790	35 4 43.1	42.1	− 11.60	− 0.17	...	2	46.2	13.8	....	20534

Ordinal Number.		Magnitude.	Estimates of Magnitude.	Mean Right Ascension 1845.0.			Precession 1845.0.	Secular Variation	Adopted Proper Motion.	Observations of R.A.		
R.	G.	R.	R.	R.		G.				No. R.	Mean year. R.	G.
				h. m. s.		s.	s.	s.	s.		1800 +	
4791	3182	9.1	6	20 21 27.26		26.88	+ 1.193	− 0.009	......	4	47.4	13.6
4792	3181	7.0	5	20 21 31.36		31.03	+ 1.560	− 0.006	......	4	45.0	9.8
4793	...	7.4	5	20 21 45.01		...	+ 2.181	0.000	......	3	49.3	...
4794	3183	8.5	5	20 21 47.18		46.74	+ 1.195	− 0.011	....	3	48.4	13.6
4795	3184	6.5	6	20 21 52.03		51.75	+ 1.250	− 0.012	......	3	45.0	12.6
4796	...	6.5	1	20 22 ...		...	......	......	......	...	...	...
4797	3189	8.6	5	20 22 6.69		6.41	+ 1.191	− 0.012	......	3	49.0	13.6
4798	3185	9.1	5	20 22 8.12		7.90	+ 1.599	− 0.006	......	3	48.0	12.7
4799	...	7.1	4	20 22 8.12		...	+ 1.222	− 0.012	......	3	52.1	...
4800	...	7.8	5	20 22 8.45		...	+ 1.125	− 0.015	......	2	47.3	...
4801	...	8.1	5	20 22 10.61		...	+ 1.612	− 0.006	......	2	49.7	...
4802	3190	8.4	3	20 22 11.50		11.14	+ 1.189	− 0.012	......	2	50.2	13.7
4803	3188	8.2	7	22 22 13.73		13.67	+ 1.599	− 0.006	......	3	45.4	12.7
4804	3186	5.6	5	20 22 18.08		17.84	+ 1.824	− 0.003	+ 0.005	9	51.1	7.1
4805	...	8.0	4	20 22 28.03		...	+ 1.664	− 0.006	......	2	45.2	...
4806	3187	7.9	5	20 22 31.12		31.05	+ 2.155	.0.000	......	4	48.1	11.7
4807	3192	7.4	7	20 22 35.18		34.88	+ 1.213	− 0.011	......	5	49.5	13.7
4808	3191	6.7	5	20 22 38.57		38.46	+ 1.452	− 0.006	......	3	47.1	8.7
4809	...	8.8	4	20 22 41.45		...	+ 1.452	− 0.006	......	2	51.2	...
4810	...	7.3	8	20 23 19.03		...	− 10.110	− 1.547	......	5	53.5	...
4811	...	7.3	3	20 23 41.37		...	+ 1.980	− 0.002	......	2	48.2	...
4812	...	6.8	4	20 23 43.60		...	+ 1.851	− 0.002	+ 0.001	4	49.2	...
4813	3193	8.4	6	20 23 45.90		45.56	+ 2.175	0.000	......	4	48.3	10.8
4814	...	8.3	10	20 23 48.32		...	− 39.003	− 17.993	......	6	49.7	...
4815	...	8.5	5	20 23 48.99		...	+ 2.104	0.000	......	2	49.7	...
4816	...	7.8	8	20 24 1.15		...	+ 1.980	− 0.001	......	5	47.9	...
4817	...	7.7	5	20 24 2.03		...	+ 2.103	0.000	......	4	49.4	...
4818	...	7.4	6	20 24 2.55		...	+ 1.854	− 0.002	......	3	52.0	...
4819	...	7.2	4	20 24 7.33		...	+ 1.837	− 0.002	......	4	46.9	...
4820	3194	8.6	4	20 24 18.98		18.48	+ 1.584	− 0.005	......	2	50.1	12.6
4821	...	7.7	8	20 24 43.51		...	+ 1.787	− 0.003	......	4	51.2	...
4822	3199	8.2	7	20 24 45.98		45.25	+ 1.259	− 0.009	......	3	49.7	12.7
4823	...	7.8	5	20 24 47.89		...	+ 2.160	0.000	......	2	47.7	...
4824	3196	6.5	6	20 24 52.13		51.40	+ 1.976	− 0.001	......	4	46.7	9.7
4825	3195	7.6	4	20 24 54.98		54.52	+ 2.166	0.000	Adopted...	2	46.6	10.8

Ordinal Number. R.	Mean North Polar Distance 1845.0 R. (° ′ ″)	G.	Precession 1845.0	Secular Variation.	Adopted Proper Motion.	Observations of N.P.D. No. R.	Mean year. R. (1800 +)	G.	Names.	Oeltzen-Argelander Number.
4791	30 13 1.8	3.7	− 11.61	− 0.15	...	2	47.3	13.6	....	20539
4792	35 49 18.0	17.7	− 11.61	− 0.17	...	3	46.0	9.8	....	......
4793	50 46 34.8	...	− 11.62	− 0.26	...	3	51.0	...	....	......
4794	30 9 5.3	2.6	− 11.63	− 0.15	...	2	48.2	13.6	....	20544
4795	30 54 18.7	20.1	− 11.63	− 0.15	...	4	47.0	12.6	....	......
4796	105 34 11.8	...	− 11.68	− 0.40	...	1	53.3	...	....	......
4797	30 4 18.3	19.3	− 11.65	− 0.15	...	2	50.7	13.6	....	20552
4798	36 29 25.7	29.7	− 11.65	− 0.17	...	2	48.7	12.7	....	20551
4799	30 29 37.9	...	− 11.65	− 0.14	...	3	52.1	...	....	20553
4800	29 12 29.8	...	− 11.65	− 0.13	...	3	48.7	...	....	......
4801	36 43 4.5	...	− 11.66	− 0.18	...	3	48.7	...	....	20554
4802	30 2 19.7	19.8	− 11.66	− 0.14	...	2	50.7	13.7	....	20558
4803	36 28 54.6	54.0	− 11.67	− 0.21	...	5	47.5	12.7	....	20559
4804	41 7 43.1	44.2	− 11.67	− 0.22	− 0.04	9	49.4	7.1	43 Cygni ω¹...	20561
4805	37 42 41.4	...	− 11.68	− 0.19	...	2	46.3	...	....	20563
4806	49 54 4.5	4.9	− 11.68	− 0.24	...	3	48.1	11.7	....	......
4807	30 19 50.9	51.6	− 11.69	− 0.15	...	3	49.7	13.7	....	20566
4808	33 52 14.3	15.6	− 11.69	− 0.16	...	4	45.6	8.7	....	......
4809	33 52 27.4	...	− 11.69	− 0.16	...	2	47.2	...	....	......
4810	4 42 7.2	...	− 11.74	+ 1.22	...	4	53.2	...	....	......
4811	44 47 41.6	...	− 11.77	− 0.23	...	3	46.1	...	....	......
4812	41 35 38.9	...	− 11.77	− 0.22	+ 0.07	3	47.0	...	....	......
4813	50 24 58.0	60.9	− 11.77	− 0.25	...	3	46.7	10.8	....	......
4814	1 28 24.3	...	− 11.77	+ 4.61	...	5	50.3	...	....	......
4815	48 14 7.7	...	− 11.77	− 0.25	...	3	52.0	...	....	......
4816	44 46 48.3	...	− 11.79	− 0.23	...	3	47.3	...	....	......
4817	48 11 46.8	...	− 11.79	− 0.25	...	3	49.3	...	....	......
4818	41 38 51.2	...	− 11.79	− 0.22	...	4	52.2	...	....	......
4819	41 14 58.5	...	− 11.80	− 0.22	...	3	45.7	...	....	......
4820	36 0 47.6	47.0	− 11.81	− 0.18	...	3	45.4	12.6	....	20612
4821	40 3 23.9	...	− 11.84	− 0.21	...	4	45.7	...	....	20621
4822	30 46 50.3	50.5	− 11.84	− 0.14	...	3	46.6	12.7	....	20624
4823	49 51 13.2	...	− 11.84	− 0.25	...	3	47.4	...	....	......
4824	44 35 43.2	51.6	− 11.85	− 0.23	...	4	48.0	9.7	....	20625
4825	50 0 41.5	41.8	− 11.85	− 0.24	...	5	46.3	10.8	....	......

Magnitude.	Estimates of Magnitude.	Mean Right Ascension 1845.0.		Precession 1845.0.	Secular Variation	Adopted Proper Motion.
R.	R.	R.	G.			
		h. m. s.	s.	s.	s.	s.
7.8	4	20 24 56.36	56.06	+ 1.994	— 0.001	......
7.3	6	20 25 10.50	10.21	+ 2.067	0.000	......
8.8	6	20 25 14.33	13.87	+ 1.224	— 0.009	......
5.2	4	20 25 15.48	15.22	+ 1.856	— 0.002	+ 0.002
7.0	3	20 25 18.86	...	+ 2.037	— 0.001	......
7.4	9	20 25 25.94	25.75	+ 2.170	0.000	......
7.3	4	20 25 27.42	26.61	+ 0.293	— 0.040	......
8.7	5	20 25 28.48	28.16	+ 1.609	— 0.006	......
6.0	2	20 25 34.63	...	+ 1.501	— 0.007	......
6.8	5	20 25 37.06	...	+ 1.821	— 0.002	......
7.4	5	20 25 46.76	...	+ 2.186	0.000	......
7.6	5	20 25 52.22	...	— 1.098	— 0.125	......
7.4	5	20 26 2.31	1.88	+ 1.706	— 0.003	......
6.6	6	20 26 6.18	5.85	+ 1.847	— 0.002	......
7.9	6	20 26 11.12	10.79	+ 1.216	— 0.011	......
7.3	5	20 26 11.90	11.18	+ 1.583	— 0.006	......
7.0	3	20 26 25.00	...	+ 0.380	— 0.040	+ 0.022
7.8	5	20 26 27.42	27.47	+ 2.010	— 0.001	......
9.4	5	20 26 29.20	...	+ 1.589	— 0.006	......
5.2	5	20 26 31.75	31.60	+ 1.849	— 0.002	......
6.3	4	20 26 55.45	55.18	+ 1.709	— 0.003	......
7.8	5	20 26 57.24	56.79	+ 1.592	— 0.004	......
4.7	5	20 26 58.24	57.99	+ 1.014	— 0.017	+ 0.004
7.2	7	20 27 23.36	23.79	+ 2.128	0.000	......
7.1	7	20 27 28.71	28.61	+ 2.142	0.000	......
6.9	6	20 27 28.75	28.58	+ 2.084	0.000	......
9.1	8	20 27 32.57	...	+ 1.619	— 0.006	......
7.8	4	20 27 33.23	33.46	+ 2.020	— 0.001	......
6.1	5	20 27 59.03	58.99	+ 1.471	— 0.007	......
8.2	5	20 28 5.89	5.63	+ 1.620	— 0.006	......
6.4	4	20 28 15.24	...	+ 1.829	— 0.002	......
6.4	3	20 28 17.23	17.25	+ 2.135	0.000	......
7.9	5	20 28 23.34	23.08	+ 1.680	— 0.004	......
6.9	6	20 28 26.20	26.36	+ 2.017	— 0.001	......
7.9	3	20 28 38.14	37.64	+ 1.259	— 0.011	......

| Ordinal Number. | Mean North Polar Distance 1845.0. | | Precession 1845.0. | Secular Variation. | Adopted Proper Motion. | Observations of N.P.D. | | | | Names. | Oeltzen-Argelander Number. |
R.	R.	G.				No. R.	Mean year. R.	G.			
	° ′ ″	″	″	″	″		1800 +				
4826	45 4 15.9	21.3	— 11.85	— 0.22	...	3	47.4	14.8	....	......
4827	47 3 16.5	16.0	— 11.87	— 0.24	...	3	45.4	11.8	....	......
4828	30 15 31.7	32.2	— 11.88	— 0.15	...	3	46.8	13.6	....	20644
4829	41 34 1.3	2.3	— 11.88	— 0.22	— 0.02	3	43.4	6.6	45 Cygni ω²...	20643
4830	46 12 14.7	...	— 11.88	— 0.24	...	3	47.4	...	....	......
4831	50 5 37.3	37.8	— 11.89	— 0.25	...	2	45.2	10.8	....	......
4832	21 11 10.5	11.7	— 11.90	— 0.06	...	3	50.3	9.7	....	......
4833	36 23 34.4	31.7	— 11.90	— 0.21	...	2	47.8	12.7	....	20648
4834	34 27 0.9	...	— 11.90	— 0.18	...	3	46.4	...	....	......
4835	40 44 10.2	...	— 11.91	— 0.21	...	3	52.0	...	....	20653
4836	50 34 59.4	...	— 11.91	— 0.26	...	3	47.1	...	....	......
4837	14 27 55.4	...	— 11.92	+ 0.13	...	3	52.0	...	....	......
4838	38 13 34.9	34.9	— 11.93	— 0.19	...	4	49.4	11.7	....	......
4839	41 18 25.6	26.9	— 11.93	— 0.19	...	3	43.8	10.7	....	20663
4840	30 5 46.9	45.7	— 11.94	— 0.13	...	3	43.0	13.6	....	20670
4841	35 50 37.1	41.5	— 11.94	— 0.17	...	3	45.7	11.2	....	20668
4842	21 44 57.6	...	— 11.96	— 0.04	— 0.07	2	43.2	...	....	20677
4843	45 21 4.8	6.8	— 11.96	— 0.23	...	3	49.4	14.7	....	......
4844	35 55 44.7	...	— 11.96	— 0.18	...	3	51.4	...	....	20678
4845	41 18 1.8	1.2	— 11.97	— 0.22	...	4	44.7	7.7	46 Cygni ω³...	20681
4846	38 12 58.4	60.8	— 11.99	— 0.18	...	3	45.7	11.7	....	......
4847	35 55 55.4	54.0	— 11.99	— 0.17	...	4	47.9	11.2	....	20690
4848	27 31 32.7	35.0	— 11.99	— 0.12	...	4	48.7	7.2	2 Cephei θ.....	......
4849	48 38 48.1	4.6	— 12.02	— 0.22	...	3	45.4	10.8	....	......
4850	49 3 12.9	16.1	— 12.03	— 0.24	...	3	46.1	11.8	....	......
4851	47 20 2.7	5.0	— 12.03	— 0.23	...	4	49.0	11.8	....	......
4852	36 23 58.0	...	— 12.03	— 0.18	...	3	51.7	...	....	20708
4853	45 32 49.2	51.2	— 12.03	— 0.21	...	2	47.2	14.7	....	......
4854	33 44 42.1	42.3	— 12.07	— 0.17	. ....	5	44.8	8.7	....	......
4855	36 22 12.2	11.9	— 12.08	— 0.20	...	4	47.8	12.7	....	20715
4856	40 41 8.9	...	— 12.09	— 0.21	...	3	44.4	...	....	20719
4857	48 45 9.8	7.2	— 12.09	— 0.25	...	3	48.4	10.8	....	......
4858	37 30 8.5	7.2	— 12.10	— 0.20	...	3	45.6	10.7	....	20725
4859	45 21 12.5	13.2	— 12.10	— 0.23	...	7	49.1	14.7	....	......
4860	30 27 51.5	53.0	— 12.12	— 0.16	...	3	48.0	13.6	....	20732

Magnitude.	Estimates of Magnitude.	Mean Right Ascension 1845.0.		Precession 1845.0.	Secular Variation	Adopted Proper Motion.
R.		R.	G.			
		h. m. s.	s.	s.	s.	s.
5.8	4	20 28 50.27	50.02	+ 1.961	— 0.001	......
7.8	5	20 28 52.39	51.79	+ 1.972	— 0.001	......
7.2	4	20 28 52.53	52.38	+ 2.083	0.000	......
7.3	5	20 28 54.00	53.83	+ 1.233	— 0.014	......
7.5	5	20 28 56.16	56.64	+ 2.021	— 0.001	......
6.7	7	20 28 57.03	56.84	+ 1.609	— 0.004	......
6.4	3	20 29 0.86	0.61	+ 2.159	0.000	......
7.6	5	20 29 3.65	3.70	+ 1.695	— 0.004	......
7.3	5	20 29 16.25	15.77	+ 1.592	— 0.004	......
7.3	4	20 29 23.26	22.64	+ 1.695	— 0.004	......
7.8	4	20 29 24.29	...	+ 2.140	0.000	......
7.4	5	20 29 34.93	...	+ 1.708	— 0.004	......
8.7	5	20 29 39.88	...	+ 1.959	— 0.001	......
7.8	6	20 29 46.10	45.74	+ 1.959	— 0.001	......
6.5	4	20 29 46.47	46.01	+ 2.136	0.000	......
7.5	4	20 29 51.70	...	+ 1.864	— 0.002	......
8.1	6	20 30 10.68	10.77	+ 2.019	— 0.001	......
9.4	7	20 30 13.97	...	—34.993	—15.543	......
3.7	3	20 30 16.78	...	+ 2.805	— 0.002	+ 0.005
6.1	4	20 30 19.53	19.67	+ 1.747	— 0.003	+ 0.011
7.4	11	20 30 33.99	...	— 8.122	— 1.168	......
5.8	2	20 30 37.64	38.11	— 0.188	— 0.069	......
7.4	5	20 30 51.69	...	+ 2.167	0.000	......
...	...	20 31 ...	...	......	......	......
7.3	11	20 31 9.39	8.43	— 7.055	— 0.960	......
5.7	A	20 31 13.30	...	+ 3.427	— 0.014	......
8.1	9	20 31 21.53	...	+ 2.117	0.000	......
8.4	4	20 31 29.82	29.70	+ 0.610	— 0.029	......
8.1	5	20 21 32.58	...	+ 2.112	0.000	......
8.2	6	20 31 44.14	...	+ 0.183	— 0.051	......
7.1	6	20 31 56.01	55.80	+ 2.106	0.000	......
8.9	6	20 32 2.06	...	+ 2.121	0.000	......
6.6	6	20 32 3.68	4.31	+ 0.176	— 0.051	......
6.7	11	20 32 18.87	...	— 8.119	— 1.186	......
7.0	1	20 32 26.10	...	+ 2.872	— 0.003	......

| Ordinal Number. | Mean North Polar Distance 1845.0. | | Precession 1845.0. | Secular Variation. | Adopted Proper Motion. | Observations of N.P.D. | | | Names. | Oeltzen-Argelander Number. |
	R.	G.				No. R.	Mean year R.	G.		
	° ′ ″	″	″	″	″		1800 +			
4861	43 50 8.9	9.6	− 12.13	− 0.22	...	4	44.7	11.7	....	20738
4862	44 6 47.2	47.3	− 12.13	− 0.20	...	3	49.0	11.8	....	....
4863	47 9 56.7	55.1	− 12.13	− 0.24	...	3	47.7	11.8	....	....
4864	30 6 4.5	2.9	− 12.13	− 0.13	...	3	46.4	13.6	....	......
4865	45 24 29.4	27.8	− 12.13	− 0.21	...	2	45.1	14.7	....	20740
4866	36 4 18.5	19.0	− 12.13	− 0.15	...	6	49.1	12.7	....	20742
4867	49 26 0.0	1.3	− 12.14	− 0.25	...	3	47.1	11.8	....	......
4868	37 43 30.7	29.7	− 12.14	− 0.18	...	3	51.0	10.7	....	20745
4869	35 43 40.1	41.6	− 12.15	− 0.16	...	4	50.7	12.7	....	20751
4870	37 42 12.6	11.7	− 12.16	− 0.18	...	2	45.7	10.7	....	20757
4871	48 48 50.3	...	− 12.17	− 0.25	...	3	46.4	...	....	....
4872	37 55 53.6	...	− 12.18	− 0.19	...	4	50.2	...	....	20764
4873	43 41 47.0	...	− 12.18	− 0.22	...	3	47.0	...	....	20768
4874	43 41 11.2	10.4	− 12.19	− 0.22	...	3	45.7	11.7	....	20770
4875	48 38 36.2	38.4	− 12.19	− 0.24	...	4	47.7	9.7	....	....
4876	41 21 15.0	...	− 12.20	− 0.21	...	2	43.3	...	....	....
4877	45 15 31.4	32.4	− 12.22	− 0.23	...	3	51.4	14.8	....	20778
4878	1 35 44.6	...	− 12.22	+ 4.05	...	3	49.4	...	....	....
4879	75 56 24.7	...	− 12.23	− 0.32	+ 0.04	7	54.7	...	6 Delphini β .	....
4880	38 40 42.2	43.5	− 12.23	− 0.19	− 0.03	4	46.5	9.8	....	20780
4881	5 24 9.7	...	− 12.25	+ 0.93	...	5	54.1	...	....	....
4882	17 59 38.0	38.8	− 12.26	+ 0.01	...	4	43.7	8.7	....	20787
4883	49 29 28.7	...	− 12.27	− 0.25	...	3	49.3	...	....	....
4884	114 38 57.1	...	− 12.28	− 0.41	...	1	53.8	...	....	....
4885	5 57 24.7	20.5	− 12.28	+ 0.82	...	4	49.7	7.3	....	....
4886	108 40 51.5	...	− 12.29	− 0.39	− 0.02	1	49.7	...	15 Capricorni υ	....
4887	47 55 44.7	...	− 12.30	− 0.24	...	3	45.8	...	....	....
4888	23 13 20.0	21.0	− 12.31	− 0.06	...	3	45.3	12.7	....	....
4889	47 46 2.6	...	− 12.31	− 0.24	...	3	49.1	...	....	....
4890	20 3 32.4	...	− 12.33	− 0.02	...	4	48.1	...	....	20817
4891	47 32 51.3	54.5	− 12.34	− 0.23	...	4	48.3	11.9	....	....
4892	47 58 44.3	...	− 12.35	− 0.24	...	3	50.0	...	....	....
4893	19 59 58.9	58.0	− 12.35	− 0.01	...	3	46.3	8.8	....	20830
4894	5 22 23.4	...	− 12.37	+ 0.92	...	6	54.0	...	....	....
4895	79 17 51.2	...	− 12.39	− 0.33	...	1	53.7	...	....	....

Magnitude.	Estimates of Magnitude.	Mean Right Ascension 1845.0.		Precession 1845.0.	Secular Variation	Adopted Proper Motion.
R.		R.	G.			
		h. m. s.	s.	s.	s.	s.
7.2	6	20 32 29.63	29.16	+ 2.113	0.000	......
8.3	7	20 32 39.33	...	+ 2.136	0.000	......
9.2	6	20 32 41.94	...	+ 2.135	0.000	......
7.7	6	20 32 41.53	41.47	+ 0.313	− 0.040	......
7.4	6	20 32 45.18	...	+ 2.139	0.000	......
7.1	6	20 32 45.82	45.24	− 4.270	− 0.480	......
6.8	5	20 32 48.52	48.62	+ 1.704	− 0.003	......
6.8	5	20 32 55.37	54.96	+ 2.063	0.000	......
4.9	7	20 33 29.01	28.50	− 0.689	− 0.103	......
7.7	6	20 33 51.11	...	+ 1.739	− 0.003	......
5.7	8	20 33 53.14	52.90	+ 2.191	0.000	......
9.0	7	20 33 58.74	...	+ 2.191	0.000	......
6.6	5	20 34 2.08	1.70	+ 2.137	0.000	......
.6.8	7	20 34 9.52	...	+ 2.020	0.000	......
7.0	8	20 34 35.55	35.17	+ 1.246	− 0.011	......
8.2	5	20 34 40.90	...	+ 1.221	− 0.013	......
6.8	6	20 34 41.35	40.88	+ 0.331	− 0.040	......
6.5	·7	20 34 59.59	59.14	+ 1.555	− 0.006	......
6.5	6	20 35 12.41	12.24	+ 2.240	0.000	......
8.3	4	20 35 17.62	17.27	+ 1.239	− 0.011	......
7.9	5	20 35 30.66	30.51	+ 0.624	− 0.026	......
8.2	4	20 35 46.94	46.93	+ 2.073	0.000	......
1.7	A	20 36 8.98	8.69	+ 2.041	0.000	......
5.5	6	20 36 20.55	20.44	+ 2.163	0.000	......
6.7	7	20 36 21.11	21.01	− 3.410	− 0.387	+ 0.020
7.2	4	20 36 23.10	23.18	+ 1.613	− 0.003	......
5.0	1	20 36 54.47	...	+ 3.571	− 0.018	− 0.007
5.8	7	20 37 0.03	59.94	+ 1.281	− 0.011	......
7.5	6	20 37 6.84	...	+ 2.025	0.000	......
5.5	6	20 37 25.93	25.79	+ 1.847	− 0.002	......
8.6	10	20 37 41.51	...	−10.878	− 1.802	......
5.5	8	20 37 41.59	41.07	− 3.369	− 0.386	+ 0.009
8.1	5	20 38 4.18	4.51	+ 0.664	− 0.029	......
8.6	6	20 38 5.85	...	+ 2.049	0.000	......
6.1	9	20 38 10.00	8.92	− 3.120	− 0.353	+ 0.021

Ordinal Number.	Mean North Polar Distance 1845.0.		Precession 1845.0.	Secular Variation.	Adopted Proper Motion.	Observations of N.P.D.			Names.	Oeltzen-Argelander Number.
R.	R.	G.				No.	Mean year.			
						R.	R.	G.		
	° ′ ″	″	″	″	″		1800 +			
4896	47 42 9.3	15.4	− 12.38	− 0.23	...	3	45.3	11.9	....	....
4897	48 22 3.7	...	− 12.39	− 0.24	...	3	47.4	...	....	....
4898	48 20 27.7	...	− 12.40	− 0.24	...	3	47.4	...	....	....
4899	20 51 46.4	46.7	− 12.40	− 0.05	...	4	48.2	13.6	....	20837
4900	48 28 4.7	...	− 12.40	− 0.24	...	4	48.7	...	....	....
4901	8 8 47.3	45.7	− 12.40	+ 0.48	...	3	46.4	7.8	....	....
4902	37 33 59.8	59.0	− 12.40	− 0.18	...	5	49.9	10.7	....	20838
4903	46 12 33.4	34.6	− 12.41	− 0.23	...	4	48.0	10.8	....	....
4904	15 34 41.3	41.5	− 12.45	+ 0.08	+ 0.03	6	45.2	7.7	73 Draconis ...	20864
4905	38 9 57.8	...	− 12.47	− 0.19	...	3	50.4	...	....	20869
4906	49 57 57.0	57.1	− 12.48	− 0.25	...	5	46.5	11.7	....	....
4907	49 57 32.7	...	− 12.48	− 0.25	...	4	46.2	...	....	....
4908	48 17 14.4	8.5	− 12.48	− 0.22	...	5	47.5	9.7	....	....
4909	44 52 42.7	...	− 12.49	− 0.23	...	4	47.2	...	....	20879
4910	29 47 19.4	19.7	− 12.52	− 0.12	...	5	48.3	13.6	....	20892
4911	29 26 27.7	...	− 12.53	− 0.14	...	3	46.4	...	....	20900
4912	20 51 27.0	26.1	− 12.53	− 0.03	...	5	47.9	13.6	....	20904
4913	34 32 23.5	21.5	− 12.55	− 0.17	...	5	47.9	9.1	....	20913
4914	51 28 0.9	2.1	− 12.57	− 0.26	...	3	45.1	9.8	....	....
4915	29 37 40.3	41.7	− 12.57	− 0.13	...	3	46.4	13.6	....	20918
4916	23 2 27.4	28.1	− 12.59	− 0.08	...	4	48.5	12.7	....	20927
4917	46 11 31.6	33.5	− 12.61	− 0.24	...	4	46.3	10.7	....	....
4918	45 16 16.5	16.7	− 12.63	− 0.22	...	54	48.2	6.7	50 Cygni α....	20940
4919	48 50 7.4	9.0	− 12.65	− 0.26	...	5	46.3	11.9	....	....
4920	9 5 50.6	50.1	− 12.65	+ 0.39	...	4	43.7	7.8	....	....
4921	35 26 36.3	36.4	− 12.65	− 0.19	...	5	45.1	12.8	....	20944
4922	115 49 24.9	...	− 12.69	− 0.40	+ 0.17	4	53.9	....	16 Capricorni ψ	......
4923	30 3 13.5	19.7	− 12.69	− 0.14	...	5	45.3	13.6	....	20956
4924	44 43 20.6	...	− 12.70	− 0.23	...	3	45.8	...	....	....
4925	40 12 52.2	53.2	− 12.72	− 0.21	...	4	43.6	8.8	51 Cygni.......	20966
4926	4 14 3.9	...	− 12.74	+ 1.22	...	5	51.5	...	....	....
4927	9 6 47.0	47.1	− 12.74	+ 0.37	...	4	43.7	7.8	75 Draconis ...	20982
4928	23 12 2.9	2.5	− 12.76	− 0.07	...	4	45.2	12.7	....	20993
4929	45 16 19.9	...	− 12.76	− 0.20	...	3	46.8	...	....	20988
4930	9 27 19.5	19.5	− 12.76	+ 0.37	− 0.20	7	45.6	7.8	74 Draconis...	......

Magnitude.	Estimates of Magnitude.	Mean Right Ascension 1845.0.		Precession 1845.0.	Secular Variation	Adopted Proper Motion.
R.		R.	G.			
		h. m. s.	s.	s.	s.	s.
6.6	7	20 38 19.17	18.57	+ 2.153	0.000	......
6.7	6	20 38 25.64	...	+ 1.494	— 0.007	+ 0.007
6.7	4	20 38 31.76	31.71	+ 2.013	0.000	......
8.7	5	20 39 6.59	...	— 3.128	— 0.386	......
4.5	4	20 39 16.88	...	+ 3.252	— 0.010	......
7.0	5	20 39 18.57	18.37	+ 1.618	— 0.005	......
6.7	5	20 39 19.10	18.90	+ 1.516	— 0.006	......
7.5	6	20 39 20.58	...	— 0.768	— 0.120	......
6.2	6	20 39 20.95	20.61	+ 1.289	— 0.011	......
6.2	4	20 39 29.15	29.01	+ 1.980	— 0.001	......
8.5	6	20 39 34.94	34.78	+ 1.985	0.000	......
7.9	6	20 39 45.16	44.68	+ 2.150	0.000	......
6.3	7	20 40 7.73	7.49	+ 2.018	0.000	......
8.9	4	20 40 22.86	36.15	+ 0.357	— 0.043	......
8.4	7	20 40 43.71	...	+ 2.160	0.000	......
7.0	6	20 40 56.12	...	+ 1.849	— 0.002	......
5.8	6	20 41 13.79	13.94	+ 0.770	— 0.029	......
5.8	5	20 41 25.86	25.66	+ 2.016	0.000	......
Var.	30	20 41 27.89	11.25	—40.082	—22.692	......
4.9	4	20 41 30.16	30.11	+ 1.500	— 0.006	......
8.3	5	20 41 30.28	30.35	+ 1.757	— 0.003	......
7.1	6	20 41 34.69	34.50	+ 2.159	0.000	......
7.8	4	20 41 42.97	...	+ 1.996	— 0.001	......
8.2	5	20 41 44.55	44.82	+ 1.679	— 0.003	......
6.0	5	20 41 51.63	51.69	+ 1.748	— 0.003	......
7.0	7	20 41 55.88	...	— 2.102	— 0.241	— 0.010
6.2	6	20 42 1.92	1.47	+ 2.053	0.000	......
7.2	6	20 42 3.70	...	+ 1.921	0.000	......
3.5	5	20 42 7.55	7.34	+ 1.219	— 0.014	+ 0.014
8.1	7	20 42 18.46	17.92	+ 0.411	— 0.043	......
7.9	4	20 42 23.35	23.09	+ 1.549	— 0.006	......
9.0	6	20 42 31.10	...	+ 1.852	— 0.002	......
9.7	4	20 42 34.97	...	+ 1.854	— 0.002	......
7.5	6	20 42 36.13	35.49	+ 1.770	— 0.003	......
8.7	5	20 42 42.38	42.15	+ 1.424	— 0.008	......

Ordinal Number. R.	Mean North Polar Distance 1845.0. R.	Mean North Polar Distance 1845.0. G.	Precession 1845.0.	Secular Variation.	Adopted Proper Motion.	Observations of N.P.D. No. R.	Observations of N.P.D. Mean year R. (1800 +)	Observations of N.P.D. Mean year G.	Names.	Oeltzen-Argelander Number.
4931	48 20 13.8	15.6	− 12.77	− 0.21	...	4	43.7	9.7	....	......
4932	33 10 14.8	...	− 12.78	− 0.17	+ 0.02	3	47.0	...	....	20994
4933	44 14 21.9	21.4	− 12.79	− 0.22	...	3	43.4	9.9	....	20996
4934	9 24 35.7	...	− 12.83	+ 0.34	...	3	49.8	...	....	......
4935	100 3 33.1	...	− 12.84	− 0.36	...	4	46.7	...	2 Aquarii ε	......
4936	35 16 1.1	0.2	− 12.84	− 0.16	...	4	47.0	12.8	....	21008
4937	33 26 39.7	41.0	− 12.84	− 0.15	...	3	46.7	13.6	....	......
4938	14 58 22.9	...	− 12.84	+ 0.08	...	4	48.7	...	....	21012
4939	29 57 21.7	19.8	− 12.84	− 0.12	...	7	46.7	13.6	....	21009
4940	43 15 49.2	49.0	− 12.85	− 0.20	...	4	44.5	10.7	....	21010
4941	43 24 2.6	1.8	− 12.86	− 0.21	...	4	47.0	10.7	....	21016
4942	48 5 33.6	34.6	− 12.87	− 0.22	...	4	46.5	10.8	....	......
4943	44 12 25.0	25.3	− 12.90	− 0.22	...	4	46.2	9.9	....	21032
4944	20 39 5.7	24.6	− 12.91	− 0.04	...	3	52.4	12.7	....	......
4945	48 17 35.2	...	− 12.94	− 0.24	...	3	47.1	...	....	......
4946	39 53 26.6	...	− 12.95	− 0.20	...	4	52.2	...	....	21058
4947	23 54 19.4	21.9	− 12.97	− 0.09	...	5	46.2	8.7	4 Cephei.......	21067
4948	44 2 3.3	2.5	− 12.99	− 0.23	...	3	43.4	9.9	....	21073
4949	1 21 8.3	12.1	− 12.99	+ 4.64	...	14	50.2	7.8	24 Cephei (Hev.)	......
4950	32 58 29.4	28.2	− 12.99	− 0.15	+ 0.19	4	44.0	7.6	....	21078
4951	37 47 11.2	11.9	− 12.99	− 0.18	...	3	47.1	11.7	....	......
4952	48 9 27.0	28.5	− 12.99	− 0.24	...	4	47.2	10.8	....	......
4953	43 27 22.9	...	− 13.00	− 0.22	...	·3	43.4	...	....	......
4954	36 10 33.9	33.6	− 13.01	− 0.19	...	3	50.0	14.8	....	21090
4955	37 34 1.1	55.4	− 13.01	− 0.19	...	4	47.7	11.7	....	21095
4956	11 7 19.0	...	− 13.02	+ 0.23	...	4	49.7	...	....	......
4957	44 59 14.1	15.2	− 13.03	− 0.22	...	4	45.7	9.7	....	21099
4958	48 30 1.1	...	− 13.03	− 0.24	...	4	47.2	...	....	......
4959	28 45 43.2	39.4	− 13.03	− 0.13	− 0.87	4	43.7	6.7	3 Cephei η	21102
4960	20 54 26.6	27.9	− 13.04	− 0.03	...	4	50.0	12.7	....	......
4961	33 44 4.3	7.0	− 13.05	− 0.16	...	2	46.2	13.8	....	21111
4962	39 47 19.8	...	− 13.06	− 0.20	...	2	51.2	...	....	21115
4963	39 50 16.3	...	− 13.06	− 0.20	...	2	51.2	...	....	......
4964	37 57 35.3	36.6	− 13.06	− 0.18	...	4	48.2	11.8	....	21123
4965	31 37 18.8	18.2	− 13.07	− 0.15	...	2	51.7	13.6	....	......

Ordinal Number.		Magnitude.	Estimates of Magnitude.	Mean Right Ascension 1845.0.		Precession 1845.0.	Secular Variation	Adopted Proper Motion.	Observations of R.A.		
R.	G.	R.	R.	R.	G.				No. R.	Mean year. R.	G.
				h. m. s.	s.	s.	s.	s.		1800 +	
4966	3287	7.9	6	20 42 45.50	45.16	+ 2.184	0.000	......	4	49.2	12.6
4967	3290	8.2	5	20 42 52.14	52.07	+ 1.854	− 0.001	......	3	48.0	10.8
4968	...	8.0	3	20 42 54.65	...	+ 2.168	0.000	......	3	48.4	...
4969	3291	7.8	4	20 43 3.80	3.44	+ 2.184	0.000	......	2	50.1	12.6
4970	3292	7.5	6	20 43 7.85	7.82	+ 2.271	0.000	......	3	49.7	10.7
4971	3298	7.0	6	20 43 15.16	15.16	+ 1.460	− 0.008	......	3	45.4	13.6
4972	3295	6.0	5	20 43 15.16	14.81	+ 1.782	− 0.003	......	3	45.0	11.7
4973	3296	8.1	4	20 43 20.48	20.42	+ 1.626	− 0.005	......	3	49.4	12.8
4974	3301	6.5	8	20 43 34.93	34.75	+ 0.411	− 0.043	......	4	47.2	12.7
4975	3299	4.6	5	20 43 39.53	39.48	+ 2.040	0.000	......	4	46.8	8.8
4976	...	6.3	6	20 44 3.51	...	− 5.242	− 0.722	......	3	51.4	...
4977	...	5.3	2	20 44 17.45	...	+ 3.240	− 0.010	.....	3	47.4	...
4978	3304	8.8	5	20 44 31.91	31.51	+ 1.478	− 0.008	......	3	48.1	13.6
4979	3300	5.3	6	20 44 34.73	34.62	+ 2.115	0.000	+ 0.015	5	45.2	10.1
4980	...	8.0	10	20 44 35.50	...	−19.488	− 6.034	......	9	53.1	...
4981	3302	6.2	5	20 44 40.17	39.87	+ 2.024	0.000	......	3	45.3	9.9
4982	3305	7.3	5	20 44 44.28	44.40	+ 1.702	− 0.003	......	3	45.4	14.8
4983	3303	6.8	4	20 44 44.31	44.02	+ 1.862	− 0.001	......	3	44.7	10.8
4984	3306	7.6	4	20 45 2.37	1.98	+ 2.171	0.000	......	3	45.4	11.8
4985	3307	7.6	7	20 45 19.13	18.45	+ 1.453	− 0.006	......	4	46.7	13.6
4986	...	8.1	6	20 45 28.69	...	+ 1.786	− 0.004	......	3	48.6	...
4987	3309	6.5	7	20 45 34.19	33.87	+ 1.455	− 0.006	......	4	47.7	13.6
4988	...	9.1	4	20 45 43.82	...	+ 2.166	0.000	......	2	48.2	...
4989	3310	7.1	5	20 46 14.40	14.16	+ 1.576	− 0.004	......	3	44.5	13.7
4990	3312	7.7	7	20 46 24.28	23.98	+ 1.671	− 0.003	......	3	46.8	12.8
4991	3311	7.0	6	20 46 25.79	25.65	+ 1.799	− 0.002	......	4	44.6	10.7
4992	...	8.5	4	20 46 27.41	...	+ 2.132	0.000	......	3	52.0	...
4993	...	9.0	5	20 46 27.80	...	+ 2.132	0.000	......	3	54.7	...
4994	3313	6.9	7	20 46 36.70	36.45	+ 1.918	− 0.001	......	4	48.2	10.9
4995	...	7.3	4	20 46 42.14	...	+ 2.030	− 0.001	......	3	45.1	...
4996	...	8.4	4	20 46 45.90	...	+ 2.174	0.000	......	3	48.0	...
4997	...	7.9	4	20 46 47.13	...	+ 1.917	− 0.002	......	2	50.2	...
4998	3314	7.9	6	20 46 53.96	53.79	+ 2.191	0.000	......	3	47.7	12.6
4999	...	8.1	5	20 46 59.00	...	+ 1.918	− 0.001	......	3	51.1	...
5000	3315	8.1	5	20 47 21.27	20.92	+ 1.605	− 0.004	......	3	49.9	13.7

Ordinal Number.	Mean North Polar Distance 1845.0.		Precession 1845.0.	Secular Variation.	Adopted Proper Motion.	Observations of N.P.D.			Names.	Oeltzen-Argelander Number.
R.	R.	G.				No. R.	Mean year R.	Mean year G.		
	° ′ ″	″	″	″	″		1800 +			
4966	48 51 12.5	11.0	— 13.07	— 0.24	...	3	48.1	12.6	....	....
4967	39 48 14.0	15.5	— 13.08	— 0.19	...	3	46.8	10.8	....	21128
4968	48 18 49.0	...	— 13.08	— 0.23	...	2	46.8	...	....	....
4969	48 48 30.3	30.1	— 13.09	— 0.24	...	3	45.4	12.6	....	....
4970	51 42 23.4	26.0	— 13.10	— 0.25	...	4	49.7	10.7	....	....
4971	32 9 9.6	10.7	— 13.11	— 0.16	...	3	47.4	13.6	....	21142
4972	38 9 23.7	19.0	— 13.11	— 0.20	...	4	48.2	11.7	....	21140
4973	35 0 3.7	3.6	— 13.11	— 0.16	...	4	49.8	12.8	....	21147
4974	20 48 48.7	49.4	— 13.13	— 0.04	...	5	45.7	12.7	....	....
4975	44 27 30.8	31.4	— 13.13	— 0.22	...	6	48.3	8.8	55 Cygni	....
4976	6 55 10.3	...	— 13.16	+ 0.58	...	3	48.0	...	....	....
4977	99 33 39.5	...	— 13.17	— 0.36	+ 0.04	2	48.2	...	6 Aquarii μ ...	....
4978	32 18 58.6	61.4	— 13.19	— 0.15	...	2	45.2	13.6	....	21170
4979	46 31 19.5	20.1	— 13.19	— 0.23	— 0.13	10	49.9	10.1	56 Cygni	....
4980	2 33 19.4	...	— 13.19	+ 2.14	...	4	49.0	...	....	....
4981	43 54 52.4	51.3	— 13.20	— 0.21	...	4	45.7	9.9	....	....
4982	36 20 41.2	45.1	— 13.20	— 0.17	...	3	45.4	14.8	....	21177
4983	39 47 28.9	29.7	— 13.20	— 0.20	...	3	44.7	10.8	....	21175
4984	48 11 40.5	41.9	— 13.22	— 0.22	...	3	45.8	11.8	....	....
4985	31 49 57.6	60.7	— 13.24	— 0.15	...	5	44.5	13.6	....	21185
4986	37 59 23.5	...	— 13.25	— 0.19	...	3	50.1	...	....	21188
4987	31 49 38.0	38.7	— 13.26	— 0.15	...	4	45.7	13.6	....	21189
4988	47 56 50.5	...	— 13.27	— 0.23	...	3	48.1	...	....	....
4989	33 46 46.9	50.6	— 13.30	— 0.15	...	3	47.4	13.7	....	....
4990	35 33 22.3	22.3	— 13.31	— 0.16	...	4	49.7	12.8	....	21223
4991	38 11 3.5	5.2	— 13.31	— 0.17	...	3	47.0	10.7	....	21225
4992	46 49 23.0	...	— 13.31	— 0.23	...	2	51.7	...	....	....
4993	46 49 28.7	...	— 13.31	— 0.23	...	2	52.2	...	....	....
4994	40 55 28.1	26.7	— 13.33	— 0.21	...	3	45.6	10.9	....	21231
4995	43 50 48.3	...	— 13.34	— 0.22	...	3	44.7	...	....	21232
4996	48 6 3.1	...	— 13.34	— 0.23	...	2	48.3	...	....	....
4997	40 52 58.5	...	— 13.34	— 0.21	...	3	51.4	...	....	21234
4998	48 36 9.3	8.8	— 13.35	— 0.24	...	3	48.4	12.6	....	....
4999	40 53 34.8	...	— 13.36	— 0.21	...	3	51.7	...	....	21243
5000	34 12 55.7	53.8	— 13.38	— 0.18	...	3	47.7	13.7	....	21261

Ordinal Number.		Magnitude.	Estimates of Magnitude.	Mean Right Ascension 1845.0.			Precession 1845.0.	Secular Variation	Adopted Proper Motion.	Observations of R.A.		
R.	G.	R.	R.	R.		G.				No.	Mean year.	
							s.	s.	s.	R.	R.	G.
				h. m. s.		s.	s.				1800 +	
5001	3322	7.4	7	20 47 21.67		21.68	+ 0.465	− 0.037	......	4	48.2	13.7
5002	...	8.1	5	20 47 45.09		...	+ 1.917	− 0.001	......	2	52.2	...
5003	3317	5.0	4	20 47 45.89		45.43	+ 2.116	+ 0.001	......	8	47.6	9.3
5004	3320	8.6	6	20 47 46.01		45.91	+ 1.582	− 0.004	......	4	47.7	13.8
5005	3316	6.7	6	20 47 47.69		47.40	+ 2.180	+ 0.001	......	4	48.2	10.5
5006	3319	5.2	4	20 47 53.90		53.23	+ 2.090	0.000	......	5	45.6	9.7
5007	3318	7.5	5	20 47 54.67		54.63	+ 2.222	+ 0.001	......	3	47.1	11.6
5008	3321	7.2	5	20 48 0.16		0.00	+ 1.679	− 0.003	......	2	45.7	12.8
5009	...	7.9	6	20 48 6.81		...	+ 2.092	0.000	......	4	44.7	...
5010	3325	8.9	5	20 48 22.51		22.55	+ 1.585	− 0.004	......	2	48.1	13.7
5011	3323	7.4	6	20 48 24.33		23.83	+ 2.119	+ 0.001	+ 0.006	3	47.1	9.6
5012	3324	6.4	4	20 48 35.10		35.00	+ 2.235	+ 0.001	......	4	46.7	10.7
5013	3326	7.3	3	20 48 35.16		35.07	+ 1.600	− 0.004	......	3	47.3	13.7
5014	...	6.9	5	20 48 40.45		...	+ 2.096	0.000	......	2	49.2	...
5015	3328	7.3	6	20 48 40.51		40.37	+ 1.480	− 0.006	......	3	50.0	13.6
5016	3327	6.9	6	20 48 52.31		52.09	+ 1.933	0.000	......	4	48.3	10.8
5017	3329	7.5	6	20 48 52.68		52.63	+ 1.711	− 0.003	......	3	48.1	14.8
5018	3330	7.6	5	20 49 10.61		10.34	+ 2.211	+ 0.001	......	3	50.4	12.6
5019	...	8.9	5	20 49 18.79		...	+ 1.589	− 0.004	......	4	50.2	...
5020	...	7.4	5	20 49 19.66		...	+ 2.097	0.000	......	4	47.9	...
5021	3331	7.0	8	20 49 19.87		19.65	+ 2.060	+ 0.001	......	4	48.2	12.7
5022	3332	6.8	4	20 49 38.74		38.58	+ 2.184	+ 0.001	......	3	50.0	11.8
5023	...	8.8	5	20 49 41.28		...	+ 2.177	0.000	......	2	51.2	...
5024	3335	7.7	5	20 49 41.29		41.17	+ 1.619	− 0.004	......	3	51.3	13.7
5025	...	7.7	2	20 49 46.10		...	+ 2.270	+ 0.001	......	2	48.6	...
5026	3334	7.0	5	20 49 49.98		49.68	+ 2.057	+ 0.001	......	3	50.7	12.7
5027	3333	6.7	5	20 49 51.70		51.36	+ 2.157	+ 0.001	......	3	47.7	11.7
5028	...	5.9	11	20 50 35.88		...	+ 2.022	0.000	......	5	50.5	...
5029	3336	6.9	5	20 50 36.20		35.80	+ 2.158	+ 0.001	......	3	47.3	11.7
5030	...	7.1	4	20 50 40.66		...	+ 2.200	0.000	......	2	51.2	...
5031	3339	8.9	4	20 51 5.72		5.87	+ 1.598	− 0.004	......	3	47.8	13.8
5032	3337	5.6	4	20 51 6.90		6.83	+ 2.111	+ 0.001	......	6	44.7	10.7
5033	...	6.7	5	20 51 20.57		...	+ 1.882	− 0.002	......	3	47.4	...
5034	...	6.4	6	20 51 21.75		...	+ 1.958	0.000	......	3	48.3	...
5035	3338	4.4	4	20 51 23.76		23.46	+ 2.231	+ 0.001	......	5	46.4	6.6

Ordinal Number.	Mean North Polar Distance 1845.0.		Precession 1845.0.	Secular Variation.	Adopted Proper Motion.	Observations of N.P.D.				Names.	Oelzen-Argelander Number.
	R.	G.				No. R.	Mean year R.	G.			
	° ′ ″	″	″	″	″		1800 +				
5001	20 55 11.8	14.2	− 13.38	− 0.05	...	3	45.8	13.7	....	21262
5002	40 47 35.6	...	− 13.41	− 0.21	...	4	53.2	...	....	21268
5003	46 11 49.8	51.7	− 13.41	− 0.24	...	8	48.3	9.3	57 Cygni.......	....
5004	33 44 51.7	54.4	− 13.41	− 0.18	...	3	47.7	13.8	....	....
5005	48 10 27.4	29.1	− 13.41	− 0.24	...	3	43.7	10.5	....	....
5006	45 24 10.8	12.1	− 13.42	− 0.24	...	5	41.5	9.7	....	21270
5007	49 32 8.7	10.3	− 13.42	− 0.25	...	4	48.0	11.6	....	....
5008	35 31 59.0	59.8	− 13.42	− 0.18	...	4	46.0	12.8	....	21272
5009	45 25 45.9	...	− 13.43	− 0.23	...	3	44.6	...	....	....
5010	33 45 11.5	16.4	− 13.45	− 0.18	...	3	48.7	13.7	....	....
5011	46 12 0.4	2.0	− 13.45	− 0.24	...	5	46.5	9.6	....	....
5012	49 53 2.7	3.8	− 13.46	− 0.24	...	5	45.9	10.7	....	....
5013	34 0 0.8	2.5	− 13.46	− 0.17	...	3	46.4	13.7	....	21294
5014	45 28 37.4	...	− 13.46	− 0.23	...	4	46.4	...	....	....
5015	31 55 44.9	46.1	− 13.46	− 0.15	...	4	48.2	13.6	....	21295
5016	41 3 12.1	13.5	− 13.48	− 0.21	...	4	43.7	10.8	....	21298
5017	36 4 32.6	39.8	− 13.48	− 0.19	...	5	49.4	14.8	....	21299
5018	49 0 42.6	45.1	− 13.50	− 0.25	...	3	49.4	12.6	....	....
5019	33 42 24.9	...	− 13.51	− 0.17	...	3	48.1	...	....	21311 ?
5020	45 27 10.6	...	− 13.51	− 0.23	...	3	43.7	...	....	....
5021	44 21 26.1	27.1	− 13.51	− 0.23	...	5	48.9	12.7	....	21308
5022	48 4 34.2	35.1	− 13.53	− 0.24	...	4	46.9	11.8	....	....
5023	47 51 51.7	...	− 13.53	− 0.23	...	3	52.0	...	....	....
5024	34 13 29.3	30.4	− 13.53	− 0.17	...	3	45.8	13.7	....	21320
5025	50 58 2.9	...	− 13.53	− 0.24	...	3	50.0	...	....	....
5026	44 14 17.3	14.8	− 13.54	− 0.22	...	4	49.0	12.7	....	21322
5027	47 13 20.6	20.6	− 13.54	− 0.23	...	4	47.7	11.7	....	....
5028	43 10 26.8	...	− 13.58	− 0.22	...	6	51.3	...	....	21354
5029	47 10 6.5	5.9	− 13.58	− 0.20	...	3	45.0	11.7	....	....
5030	47 49 22.7	...	− 13.59	− 0.23	...	4	50.0	...	....	....
5031	33 40 41.4	42.4	− 13.61	− 0.14	...	2	47.2	13.8	....	21366
5032	45 40 9.1	9.0	− 13.62	− 0.22	...	6	42.5	10.7	....	....
5033	39 31 6.7	...	− 13.63	− 0.20	...	3	44.0	...	....	21375
5034	41 23 55.0	...	− 13.64	− 0.21	...	3	48.4	...	....	....
5035	49 25 37.7	37.7	− 13.64	− 0.24	...	4	45.0	6.6	58 Cygni ν......	....

Ordinal Number		Magnitude	Estimates of Magnitude	Mean Right Ascension 1845.0		Precession 1845.0	Secular Variation	Adopted Proper Motion	Observations of R.A.		
R.	G.	R.	R.	R.	G.				No. R.	Mean year R.	Mean year G.
				h. m. s.	s.	s.	s.	s.		1800 +	
5036	3341	5.8	8	20 51 30.48	29.79	+ 1.897	0.000	......	4	44.8	9.7
5037	3340	7.2	6	20 51 42.09	42.24	+ 2.276	+ 0.002	......	5	45.7	9.8
5038	3343	7.1	6	20 51 47.67	47.18	+ 2.194	+ 0.001	......	4	47.2	11.8
5039	3342	8.0	5	20 51 49.11	49.44	+ 2.274	+ 0.002	......	3	46.7	9.8
5040	...	8.0	5	20 51 52.60	...	+ 2.263	+ 0.002	......	4	51.2	...
5041	3344	7.6	4	20 52 5.00	4.77	+ 2.259	+ 0.002	......	3	46.3	10.9
5042	3346	6.2	5	20 52 8.35	8.05	+ 1.605	− 0.006	......	5	44.6	11.0
5043	...	8.8	4	20 52 14.39	...	+ 2.140	+ 0.001	......	3	50.3	...
5044	3345	7.3	5	20 52 23.98	23.97	+ 2.121	+ 0.001	......	4	45.5	10.7
5045	3347	8.4	6	20 52 32.18	31.93	+ 1.606	− 0.006	......	4	46.3	13.8
5046	...	7.6	5	20 52 38.89	...	+ 2.065	0.000	......	3	47.1	...
5047	...	5.8	4	20 52 46.59	...	+ 2.133	+ 0.001	+ 0.016	3	48.0	...
5048	3354	7.4	4	20 53 0.67	0.77	+ 0.973	− 0.023	......	3	48.1	12.9
5049	3348	7.3	7	20 53 4.16	3.73	+ 2.062	0.000	......	4	48.0	12.7
5050	...	7.2	6	20 53 11.68	...	+ 2.137	+ 0.001	......	3	49.3	...
5051	3359	7.8	6	20 53 11.51	11.91	+ 0.488	− 0.040	......	3	49.7	14.8
5052	...	6.9	6	20 53 21.56	...	+ 2.149	+ 0.001	......	3	50.3	...
5053	3355	7.2	6	20 53 26.50	26.31	+ 1.688	− 0.003	......	3	47.7	12.8
5054	3370	5.7	8	20 53 26.64	24.99	− 3.804	− 0.497	......	4	47.1	7.8
5055	3349	7.2	4	20 53 32.05	31.91	+ 2.076	+ 0.001	......	2	48.7	12.6
5056	3352	5.9	5	20 53 32.21	32.05	+ 1.917	0.000	......	4	47.6	8.8
5057	3353	6.9	5	20 53 40.87	40.60	+ 2.126	+ 0.001	......	3	48.7	10.7
5058	3351	6.8	7	20 53 42.04	41.76	+ 2.204	+ 0.001	......	4	46.9	11.8
5059	3358	7.8	5	20 53 43.67	43.22	+ 1.656	− 0.003	......	3	47.7	13.7
5060	3356	7.7	5	20 53 43.41	43.36	+ 2.070	+ 0.001	......	3	46.8	12.6
5061	3350	6.8	4	20 53 44.71	44.42	+ 2.306	+ 0.002	......	3	48.4	11.7
5062	3363	7.3	6	20 53 57.34	57.00	+ 0.967	− 0.026	......	2	46.3	12.9
5063	3357	6.5	3	20 54 0.11	59.22	+ 2.266	+ 0.002	......	4	46.7	10.8
5064	3361	8.4	6	20 54 6.10	6.29	+ 1.683	− 0.003	......	3	50.7	12.8
5065	3360	6.7	4	20 54 21.80	21.53	+ 2.122	+ 0.001	......	3	46.3	10.7
5066	3373*	5.1	7	20 54 25.35	26.24	− 2.401	− 0.306	− 0.008	4	47.9	8.7
5067	3362	5.2	4	20 54 33.32	33.16	+ 2.035	0.000	......	4	45.7	8.1
5068	...	7.4	5	20 54 56.74	...	+ 1.995	− 0.001	......	2	52.2	...
5069	...	8.5	5	20 55 2.93	...	+ 2.133	+ 0.001	......	3	48.0	...
5070	3364	6.4	4	20 55 9.71	9.64	+ 1.674	− 0.004	......	3	48.4	12.7

Ordinal Number.	Mean North Polar Distance 1845.0.			Precession 1845.0.	Secular Variation.	Adopted Proper Motion.	Observations of N.P.D.				Names.	Oeltzen-Argelander Number.
	R.		G.				No.	Mean year.				
R.	R.		G.				R.	R.		G.		
	° ′ ″		″	″	″	″		1800 +				
5036	39 51 53.1		54.4	− 13.65	− 0.21	...	5	47.5		9.7	....	21377
5037	50 56 0.1		1.0	− 13.66	− 0.24	...	2	45.2		9.8	....	....
5038	48 9 8.2		10.6	− 13.67	− 0.25	...	3	48.0		11.8	....	....
5039	50 53 1.1		21.9	− 13.67	− 0.24	...	2	49.7		9.8	....	....
5040	50 28 45.8		...	− 13.67	− 0.24	...	2	50.3		...	....	....
5041	50 19 26.8		26.9	− 13.69	− 0.24	...	3	48.8		10.9	....	....
5042	33 42 26.0		28.0	− 13.69	− 0.17	...	4	47.2		11.0	....	21395
5043	46 25 8.6		...	− 13.69	− 0.23	...	2	50.2		...	....	....
5044	45 48 31.9		31.0	− 13.71	− 0.24	...	3	49.1		10.7	....	....
5045	33 40 7.9		9.8	− 13.71	− 0.16	...	4	45.3		13.8	....	21405
5046	44 7 51.1		...	− 13.72	− 0.22	...	2	48.2		...	....	21408
5047	46 7 46.1		...	− 13.73	− 0.23	...	5	50.8		...	....	....
5048	24 54 26.6		26.8	− 13.74	− 0.09	...	3	46.4		12.9	....	21417
5049	43 59 48.9		50.2	− 13.74	− 0.19	...	4	46.0		12.7	....	21418
5050	46 11 3.5		...	− 13.75	− 0.23	...	3	50.0		...	....	....
5051	20 38 48.3		50.0	− 13.75	− 0.03	...	3	49.4		14.8	....	....
5052	46 32 24.0		...	− 13.76	− 0.23	...	3	50.4		...	....	....
5053	35 6 40.1		44.0	− 13.77	− 0.17	...	3	47.1		12.8	....	21431
5054	8 2 52.4		52.2	− 13.77	+ 0.39	− 0.03	9	50.0		7.8	76 Draconis...	....
5055	44 20 45.8		45.9	− 13.77	− 0.20	...	3	47.5		12.6	....	21435
5056	40 8 17.0		17.8	− 13.77	− 0.20	...	3	43.0		8.8	....	21436
5057	45 48 40.4		44.0	− 13.78	− 0.21	...	3	44.4		10.7	....	....
5058	48 16 36.6		37.5	− 13.78	− 0.21	...	3	46.4		11.8	....	....
5059	34 28 45.7		44.5	− 13.79	− 0.18	...	3	49.1		13.7	....	21443
5060	44 9 39.9		39.2	− 13.79	− 0.21	...	3	46.8		12.6	....	21439
5061	51 46 42.7		43.2	− 13.79	− 0.24	...	4	50.7		11.7	....	....
5062	24 46 12.4		11.4	− 13.80	− 0.09	...	4	51.5		12.9	....	21449
5063	50 21 6.8		16.3	− 13.80	− 0.24	...	3	48.8		10.8	....	....
5064	34 57 1.8		3.0	− 13.81	− 0.17	...	3	51.8		12.8	....	21454
5065	45 36 23.3		20.6	− 13.83	− 0.22	...	3	44.8		10.7	....	....
5066	10 1 57.5		56.5	− 13.83	+ 0.26	...	3	46.7		8.7	....	21476
5067	43 4 55.6		55.4	− 13.84	− 0.21	+ 0.01	5	43.5		8.1	59 Cygni *f¹*....	21470
5068	41 55 28.3		...	− 13.86	− 0.21	...	3	52.4		...	....	....
5069	45 50 44.3		...	− 13.87	− 0.23	...	2	45.3		...	....	....
5070	34 39 44.9		45.7	− 13.88	− 0.17	...	3	44.0		12.7	....	21479

Ordinal Number.		Magnitude.	Estimates of Magnitude.	Mean Right Ascension 1845.0.			Precession 1845.0.	Secular Variation.	Adopted Proper Motion.	Observations of R.A.		
										No.	Mean year.	
R.	G.	R.		R.		G.				R.	R.	G.
				h. m. s.		s.	s.	s.	s.		1800 +	
5071	...	8.6	5	20 55 13.18		...	+ 2.132	+ 0.001	......	3	48.7	...
5072	3365	6.9	5	20 55 24.39		23.85	+ 1.713	− 0.004	......	3	44.5	13.6
5073	...	5.2	5	20 55 34.60		...	+ 3.429	− 0.016	− 0.006	4	49.8	...
5074	...	5.5	5	20 55 35.87		...	+ 1.477	− 0.009	......	2	50.2	...
5075	3366	5.8	5	20 55 46.27		46.08	+ 2.089	+ 0.001	......	3	46.0	10.1
5076	...	7.4	8	20 55 52.85		...	+ 2.300	+ 0.002	......	4	45.7	...
5077	3368	8.2	6	20 56 3.57		3.28	+ 1.689	− 0.004	......	3	47.8	12.7
5078	...	6.7	3	20 56 12.30		...	+ 2.158	+ 0.001	......	3	47.7	...
5079	...	7.8	5	20 56 19.76		...	+ 2.044	0.000	......	3	46.7	...
5080	...	8.4	4	20 56 23.28		...	+ 1.483	− 0.009	......	2	50.3	...
5081	3367	6.5	5	20 56 24.40		23.95	+ 2.295	+ 0.002	......	3	46.4	9.7
5082	3369	8.3	5	20 56 26.59		26.27	+ 2.077	+ 0.001	......	4	48.7	12.7
5083	3377	6.5	4	20 56 28.88		28.73	− 0.594	− 0.111	......	2	50.2	12.9
5084	3371	5.9	5	20 56 52.04		51.82	+ 2.139	+ 0.001	......	3	44.7	9.9
5085	3372	6.4	34	20 57 4.18		3.87	+ 2.321	+ 0.002	......	17	52.2	11.8
5086	3374	7.2	5	20 57 4.79		4.73	+ 2.146	+ 0.001	......	3	47.3	9.9
5087	...	5.3	2	20 57 13.76		...	+ 3.378	− 0.015	+ 0.004	3	52.3	...
5088	3375	6.5	7	20 57 42.36		42.18	+ 1.629	− 0.005	......	5	44.7	13.7
5089	3384	6.9	5	20 57 42.64		42.35	− 0.522	− 0.109	......	2	46.3	12.9
5090	...	7.8	20	20 57 48.73		...	− 8.019	− 1.504	. ....	15	52.4	...
5091	3378	5.4	4	20 57 52.73		52.34	+ 1.652	− 0.005	......	5	46.7	11.8
5092	...	7.0	1	20 58 ...		...	......	......	......	...	...	...
5093	...	9.7	5	20 58 3.61		...	+ 2.241	+ 0.002	......	2	51.3	...
5094	3376	6.3	4	20 58 4.00		3.93	+ 2.241	+ 0.002	......	3	44.5	10.8
5095	3379	6.1	4	20 58 22.87		22.55	+ 1.946	0.000	......	3	45.0	10.7
5096	3380	8.0	8	20 58 28.40		28.06	+ 2.094	+ 0.001	......	4	46.7	12.7
5097	3382	8.5	6	20 58 57.27		56.86	+ 1.645	− 0.004	......	3	47.4	13.6
5098	3381	7.8	4	20 59 0.93		0.76	+ 2.106	+ 0.001	......	3	47.1	12.7
5099	3383	6.0	5	20 59 3.58		3.15	+ 1.825	− 0.001	......	3	45.1	11.7
5100	3389	8.2	6	20 59 10.63		9.85	+ 0.930	− 0.023	......	3	47.4	9.7
5101	3386	7.8	7	20 59 10.86		10.71	+ 1.777	− 0.002	......	4	47.2	12.7
5102	3385	4.0	6	20 59 17.65		17.45	+ 2.176	+ 0.002	......	9	46.6	6.7
5103	3387	7.1	5	20 59 23.79		23.20	+ 1.735	− 0.003	......	3	44.7	9.8
5104	3388	8.7	4	20 59 32.95		32.48	+ 1.947	0.000	......	3	45.4	10.7
5105	3390	8.3	6	20 59 54.74		24.61	+ 1.957	0.000	......	3	45.7	10.7

Ordinal Number.	Mean North Polar Distance 1845.0.			Precession 1845.0.	Secular Variation.	Adopted Proper Motion.	Observations of N.P.D.				Names.	Oeltzen-Argelander Number.
	R.	R.	G.				No. R.	Mean year. R.	G.			
	° ′ ″		″	″	″	″		1800 +				
5071	45 49 11.7		...	— 13.88	— 0.23	...	2	47.7	...	....	....
5072	35 23 9.9		10.2	— 13.89	— 0.16	...	3	45.3	13.6	....	21484
5073	110 27 50.3		...	— 13.90	— 0.36	+ 0.05	3	51.4	...	22 Capricorni η	....
5074	31 9 56.7		...	— 13.91	— 0.16	...	4	48.5	...	....	21488
5075	44 27 2.4		5.2	— 13.92	— 0.22	...	4	45.0	10.1	60 Cygni........	21492
5076	51 20 45.5		...	— 13.92	— 0.25	...	4	48.2	...	....	....
5077	34 49 59.2		56.7	— 13.93	— 0.16	...	4	47.7	12.7	....	21498
5078	46 25 1.9		...	— 13.94	— 0.25	...	3	46.1	...	....	....
5079	43 6 29.0		...	— 13.95	— 0.21	...	3	44.4	...	....	21509
5080	31 10 8.6		...	— 13.95	— 0.16	...	2	48.7	...	....	21517
5081	51 5 58.1		59.9	— 13.96	— 0.24	...	4	49.7	9.7	....	....
5082	44 2 23.1		23.9	— 13.96	— 0.21	...	3	50.1	12.7	....	21519
5083	14 40 30.4		32.1	— 13.96	+ 0.07	— 0.04	4	45.3	12.9	....	21526
5084	45 49 6.1		5.5	— 13.98	— 0.20	...	3	44.4	9.9	....	....
5085	51 57 9.4		10.5	— 14.00	— 0.24	...	18	52.9	11.8	....	....
5086	46 0 6.4		6.2	— 14.00	— 0.22	...	4	49.0	9.9	....	....
5087	107 50 40.0		...	— 14.01	— 0.35	+ 0.05	2	55.7	...	23 Capricorni θ	....
5088	33 32 16.4		18.8	— 14.04	— 0.17	...	3	43.3	13.7	....	....
5089	14 53 5.5		5.1	— 14.04	+ 0.06	...	3	48.8	12.9	....	21560
5090	4 55 5.0		...	— 14.05	+ 0.86	...	9	51.5	...	....	....
5091	33 56 27.1		26.7	— 14.05	— 0.17	...	4	45.2	11.8	....	21562
5092	113 46 1.5		...	— 14.06	— 0.37	...	2	53.8	...	....	....
5093	48 59 54.1		...	— 14.06	— 0.22	...	3	45.1	...	....	....
5094	48 58 56.8		57.1	— 14.06	— 0.22	+ 0.04	3	45.1	10.8	....	....
5095	40 15 46.8		49.1	— 14.08	— 0.19	...	3	44.7	10.7	....	21569
5096	44 16 58.9		58.7	— 14.08	— 0.19	...	4	49.0	12.7	....	21572
5097	33 41 12.3		15.9	— 14.11	— 0.15	...	3	47.7	13.6	....	21589
5098	44 33 58.8		57.7	— 14.12	— 0.21	...	2	45.2	12.7	....	21590
5099	37 19 47.2		46.6	— 14.12	— 0.17	...	3	42.3	11.7	....	21595
5100	23 54 6.2		7.7	— 14.13	— 0.09	...	3	48.4	9.7	....	21600
5101	36 16 13.8		14.2	— 14.13	— 0.17	...	3	46.4	12.7	....	21599
5102	46 41 17.6		17.5	— 14.14	— 0.23	...	11	48.5	6.7	62 Cygni ξ....	....
5103	35 23 4.3		3.3	— 14.15	— 0.19	...	4	46.2	9.8	....	21603
5104	40 8 44.1		46.1	— 14.15	— 0.19	...	3	46.4	10.7	....	21607
5105	40 21 23.9		25.8	— 14.18	— 0.21	...	3	47.4	10.7	....	21631

Ordinal Number.		Magnitude.	Estimates of Magnitude.	Mean Right Ascension 1845.0.			Precession 1845.0.	Secular Variation	Adopted Proper Motion.	Observations of R.A.		
R.	G.	R.		R.		G.				No. R.	Mean year. R.	G.
				h. m. s.		s.	s.	s.	s.		1800 +	
5106	...	5.4	27	20 59 57.29		...	+ 2.331	+ 0.002	+ 0.339	28	50.3	...
5107	...	6.3	24	20 59 58.76		...	+ 2.332	+ 0.002	+ 0.345	19	53.0	...
5108	3392	9.2	7	21 0 11.27		11.60	+ 1.646	− 0.004	......	4	46.0	13.7
5109	3393	8.0	6	21 0 21.52		21.16	+ 1.723	− 0.003	......	4	47.2	13.7
5110	3391	7.3	6	21 0 25.34		24.99	+ 2.051	0.000	......	4	44.4	10.8
5111	...	8.1	10	21 0 51.76		...	+ 2.338	+ 0.002	......	8	53.5	...
5112	...	4.8	9	21 1 8.77		...	+ 3.270	− 0.012	......	8	48.2	...
5113	3394	5.0	7	21 1 15.85		15.87	+ 2.061	+ 0.001	......	5	44.3	8.8
5114	3395	7.8	5	21 1 42.61		42.45	+ 1.919	0.000	......	3	44.0	11.7
5115	3396	7.2	5	21 1 53.33		52.97	+ 2.061	+ 0.001	......	4	44.4	10.8
5116	3397	8.1	5	21 1 56.07		56.03	+ 1.798	− 0.003	......	5	46.7	12.7
5117	...	7.0	1	21 2 ...		...	......	......	......	...	...	...
5118	...	7.7	27	21 2 2.48		...	+ 2.340	+ 0.002	......	19	53.4	...
5119	...	8.0	6	21 2 2.81		...	+ 0.364	− 0.040	......	3	49.3	...
5120	3398	7.5	8	21 2 25.88		25.72	+ 1.920	0.000	......	4	43.8	11.7
5121	3399	7.5	6	21 2 38.17		38.23	+ 1.918	0.000	......	3	44.5	11.7
5122	...	6.9	5	21 2 41.38		...	+ 1.291	− 0.018	......	3	52.0	...
5123	3400	8.1	5	21 2 42.89		42.61	+ 1.766	− 0.003	......	3	44.7	9.8
5124	3403	7.6	6	21 2 45.76		44.64	+ 0.403	− 0.051	......	4	45.1	9.7
5125	3401	7.5	8	21 3 1.91		1.46	+ 1.501	− 0.006	......	4	45.7	11.9
5126	...	9.0	6	21 3 54.90		...	+ 1.302	− 0.018	......	3	50.4	...
5127	3404	8.7	4	21 4 14.44		14.57	+ 1.292	− 0.011	......	3	46.4	11.9
5128	3405	7.8	7	21 4 53.28		51.65	+ 1.668	− 0.003	......	4	47.7	13.7
5129	3406	7.9	9	21 4 57.72		57.53	+ 1.747	− 0.003	......	7	47.6	8.7
5130	...	7.1	5	21 5 6.08		...	+ 2.078	0.000	......	3	44.8	...
5131	...	8.2	7	21 5 7.16		...	+ 1.839	− 0.003	......	4	50.2	...
5132	...	6.2	4	21 5 8.25		...	+ 2.077	0.000	......	4	47.0	...
5133	3407	10.0	4	21 5 17.27		17.45	+ 1.748	− 0.003	......	2	48.7	13.7
5134	3409	5.7	5	21 5 25.60		26.20	+ 0.419	− 0.049	......	3	47.0	9.9
5135	...	7.2	5	21 5 27.61		...	+ 2.281	+ 0.002	......	3	48.1	...
5136	3408	6.1	5	21 5 28.22		28.34	+ 1.849	0.000	+ 0.012	3	47.7	11.9
5137	...	8.1	4	21 5 36.85		...	+ 2.280	+ 0.002	......	4	51.3	...
5138	...	8.6	3	21 5 38.01		...	+ 1.315	− 0.014	......	2	45.2	...
5139	3410	6.6	5	21 6 9.40		9.26	+ 1.291	− 0.011	......	3	45.2	11.9
5140	...	3.6	3	21 6 20.48		...	+ 2.548	+ 0.002	− 0.003	68	46.3	...

Ordinal Number. R.	Mean North Polar Distance 1845.0. R.	Mean North Polar Distance 1845.0. G.	Precession 1845.0.	Secular Variation.	Adopted Proper Motion.	Observations of N.P.D. No. R.	Mean year. R. (1800+)	Mean year. G. (1800+)	Names.	Oeltzen-Argelander Number.
5106	52 0 33.1	...	− 14.18	− 0.24	− 3.22	20	53.0	...	61 Cygni (1st)	......
5107	52 0 36.8	...	− 14.18	− 0.24	− 3.00	18	53.2	...	61 Cygni (2d)	......
5108	33 33 5.5	4.9	− 14.19	− 0.15	...	3	48.0	13.7	....	21537
5109	35 1 49.2	49.9	− 14.20	− 0.16	...	3	47.1	13.7	....	21541
5110	42 48 51.0	50.5	− 14.21	− 0.21	...	3	43.8	10.8	....	21545
5111	52 4 51.5	...	+ 14.24	− 0.24	...	4	52.7	...	....	......
5112	101 59 44.7	...	− 14.25	− 0.34	...	5	48.8	...	13 Aquarii ν...	......
5113	42 58 20.3	20.7	− 14.26	− 0.21	...	16	47.4	8.8	63 Cygni f2....	21564
5114	39 11 42.5	44.6	− 14.29	− 0.20	...	4	45.0	11.7	....	......
5115	42 53 19.6	18.6	− 14.30	− 0.21	...	3	43.8	10.8	....	21683
5116	36 24 15.5	15.2	− 14.30	− 0.18	...	3	47.1	12.7	....	21685
5117	113 6 17.6	...	− 14.31	− 0.36	...	2	53.8	...	....	......
5118	52 5 40.7	...	− 14.31	− 0.24	...	14	53.7	...	....	......
5119	19 6 12.6	...	− 14.31	− 0.03	...	4	48.2	...	....	21694
5120	39 7 2.8	7.4	− 14.33	− 0.19	...	5	47.1	11.7	....	......
5121	39 2 22.9	24.1	− 14.34	− 0.18	...	3	45.3	11.7	....	......
5122	27 41 58.9	...	− 14.34	− 0.13	...	3	52.0	...	....	21709
5123	35 37 7.9	6.7	− 14.35	− 0.18	...	3	46.1	9.8	....	21710
5124	19 18 19.5	17.8	− 14.35	− 0.03	...	5	45.0	9.7	....	21716
5125	30 44 5.4	8.1	− 14.36	− 0.13	...	4	46.7	11.9	....	21721
5126	27 43 42.3	...	− 14.42	− 0.12	...	3	51.7	...	....	21740
5127	27 33 16.0	14.2	− 14.44	− 0.12	...	3	45.3	11.9	....	21753
5128	33 25 31.8	32.0	− 14.47	− 0.14	...	4	46.2	13.7	....	......
5129	34 56 12.9	13.6	− 14.49	− 0.19	...	5	44.5	8.7	....	21772
5130	42 58 31.2	...	− 14.49	− 0.21	...	3	45.2	...	....	21777
5131	36 53 12.1	..	− 14.50	− 0.18	...	3	51.1	...	....	21779
5132	42 56 19.1	...	− 14.50	− 0.21	...	4	45.3	...	....	21780
5133	34 54 59.6	66.2	− 14.51	− 0.18	...	2	50.2	13.7	....	......
5134	19 11 22.1	17.3	− 14.51	− 0.03	...	5	43.1	9.9	....	21791
5135	49 26 48.6	...	− 14.51	− 0.23	...	3	48.0	...	....	......
5136	37 4 4.6	3.7	− 14.51	− 0.18	...	4	44.2	11.9	....	21790
5137	49 23 20.9	...	− 14.52	− 0.23	...	3	51.2	...	....	......
5138	27 43 0.7	...	− 14.52	− 0.13	...	3	48.2	...	....	21796
5139	27 20 9.6	9.3	− 14.55	− 0.10	...	4	45.2	11.9	....	21807
5140	60 24 21.3	...	− 14.56	− 0.25	+ 0.07	4	52.8	...	64 Cygni ζ	......

Ordinal Number.		Magnitude.	Estimates of Magnitude.	Mean Right Ascension 1845.0.			Precession 1845.0.	Secular Variation	Adopted Proper Motion.	Observations of R.A.		
R.	G.	R.	R.	R.		G.				No.	Mean year.	
										R.	R.	G.
				h. m. s.		s.	s.	s.	s.		1800 +	
5141	...	9.1	4	21 6 25.56		...	+ 1.333	− 0.014	......	2	48.2	...
5142	...	9.5	4	21 6 32.38		...	+ 1.311	− 0.014	......	3	50.1	...
5143	...	8.5	5	21 6 43.49		...	+ 0.419	− 0.056	......	3	49.3	...
5144	3411	7.0	5	21 6 52.01		51.66	+ 1.848	− 0.001	......	4	46.0	10.7
5145	...	5.4	4	21 7 9.69		...	+ 3.329	− 0.014	+ 0.005	8	49.3	...
5146	3414	7.7	5	21 7 18.11		17.87	+ 1.103	− 0.020	......	3	47.5	12.7
5147	3412	7.6	6	21 7 25.97		25.58	+ 2.210	+ 0.002	......	4	48.2	9.7
5148	...	8.1	7	21 7 29.38		...	+ 2.276	+ 0.002	......	3	51.1	...
5149	3413	7.5	3	21 7 29.52		28.88	+ 1.848	− 0.001	......	2	49.2	10.7
5150	...	8.3	4	21 7 42.48		...	+ 1.847	− 0.001	......	2	50.2	...
5151	3415	5.4	4	21 7 51.37		51.24	+ 1.530	− 0.006	......	4	49.5	9.4
5152	...	7.0	6	21 7 53.36		...	+ 1.066	− 0.026	......	3	51.1	...
5153	...	7.1	8	21 8 22.23		...	+ 2.293	+ 0.003	+ 0.019	5	50.3	...
5154	3419	5.9	4	21 8 28.99		28.46	− 1.032	− 0.169	......	3	50.7	7.8
5155	...	9.9	5	21 8 46.51		...	+ 2.278	+ 0.002	......	2	49.2	...
5156	3416	6.4	6	21 8 50.39		49.97	+ 1.531	− 0.006	......	4	46.2	9.9
5157	...	8.4	6	21 8 59.14		...	+ 2.281	+ 0.002	......	4	48.5	...
5158	...	9.7	5	21 9 4.16		...	+ 2.270	+ 0.002	......	3	48.0	...
5159	...	10.0	5	21 9 19.23		...	+ 2.283	+ 0.003	......	3	53.4	...
5160	...	9.3	5	21 9 30.92		...	+ 2.274	+ 0.002	......	2	49.2	...
5161	3417	6.6	8	21 9 33.28		32.87	+ 2.273	+ 0.002	......	6	44.8	11.7
5162	...	9.1	4	21 10 1.57		...	+ 1.354	− 0.013	......	2	46.7	...
5163	3418	7.8	4	21 10 8.92		8.31	+ 2.279	+ 0.002	......	3	47.8	11.8
5164	3422	7.2	5	21 10 9.09		8.54	+ 0.565	− 0.020	......	3	46.7	9.8
5165	...	8.1	7	21 10 12.37		...	+ 2.286	+ 0.003	......	5	47.8	...
5166	3426	6.8	7	21 10 18.62		17.42	− 0.202	− 0.093	......	3	47.4	9.7
5167	3420	6.0	6	21 10 33.21		32.82	+ 2.212	+ 0.001	......	5	46.7	11.8
5168	3421	8.6	5	21 10 51.29		50.76	+ 2.259	+ 0.002	......	3	44.5	11.8
5169	3423	4.3	7	21 11 19.77		19.67	+ 2.350	+ 0.003	+ 0.003	9	47.8	6.7
5170	3425	8.1	5	21 11 22.71		22.37	+ 1.928	+ 0.001	......	4	45.2	10.9
5171	3424	6.4	5	21 11 31.55		31.42	+ 2.262	+ 0.002	......	3	45.4	11.7
5172	...	9.3	8	21 11 32.05		...	+ 1.927	+ 0.001	......	5	49.5	...
5173	...	7.7	7	21 11 32.65		...	+ 2.341	+ 0.003	......	4	51.3	...
5174	...	4.0	1	21 11 32.81		...	+ 2.460	+ 0.003	......	3	55.7	...
5175	...	9.0	6	21 11 37.37		...	+ 1.930	+ 0.001	......	3	51.4	...

Ordinal Number.	Mean North Polar Distance 1845.0.		Precession 1845.0.	Secular Variation.	Adopted Proper Motion.	Observations of N.P.D.			Names.	Oeltzen-Argelander Number.
R.	R.	G.				No. R.	Mean year. R.	G.		
	° ′ ″	″	″	″	″		1800 +			
5141	27 52 9.8	...	− 14.57	− 0.13	...	4	48.7	...	....	21819
5142	27 33 29.0	...	− 14.57	− 0.13	...	3	48.4	...	....	21824
5143	19 14 55.0	...	− 14.59	− 0.04	...	3	46.1	...	....	21832
5144	36 53 18.1	16.7	− 14.60	− 0.18	...	3	43.3	10.7	....	21835
5145	105 48 44.1	...	− 14.62	− 0.33	− 0.03	2	51.6	...	29 Capricorni.	....
5146	24 56 49.4	50.5	− 14.62	− 0.09	...	3	45.8	12.7	....	....
5147	46 45 48.0	48.3	− 14.63	− 0.21	...	4	45.2	9.7	....	....
5148	49 0 8.0	...	− 14.63	− 0.23	...	4	51.7	...	....	....
5149	36 48 20.8	19.7	− 14.63	− 0.18	...	3	44.7	10.7	....	21854
5150	36 44 18.6	...	− 14.65	− 0.18	...	3	46.1	...	....	21863
5151	30 38 57.4	58.1	− 14.66	− 0.15	...	4	43.0	9.4	....	21873
5152	24 28 32.8	...	− 14.66	− 0.10	...	4	46.7	...	....	....
5153	49 29 38.2	...	− 14.69	− 0.23	− 0.01	6	51.4	...	....	....
5154	12 30 14.1	14.4	− 14.70	+ 0.09	− 0.03	5	44.9	7.8	77 Draconis ...	....
5155	48 55 27.0	...	− 14.71	− 0.23	...	3	48.1	...	....	....
5156	30 32 25.2	23.6	− 14.71	− 0.13	...	5	46.7	9.9	....	21894
5157	48 59 44.3	...	− 14.72	− 0.23	...	3	47.4	...	....	....
5158	48 36 6.1	...	− 14.73	− 0.23	...	2	48.3	...	....	....
5159	49 2 42.0	...	− 14.74	− 0.23	...	2	50.2	...	....	....
5160	48 44 56.2	...	− 14.76	− 0.23	...	3	49.7	...	....	....
5161	48 37 18.6	23.4	− 14.76	− 0.22	...	4	44.2	11.7	....	....
5162	27 45 9.2	...	− 14.79	− 0.13	...	3	47.8	...	....	21922
5163	48 46 46.1	46.3	− 14.79	− 0.22	...	3	45.4	11.8	....	....
5164	19 48 44.6	43.7	− 14.79	− 0.04	...	3	43.4	9.8	....	21937
5165	49 0 48.6	...	− 14.80	− 0.23	...	4	47.7	...	....	....
5166	15 24 30.0	30.0	− 14.80	+ 0.03	...	5	47.2	9.7	....	....
5167	46 24 25.9	26.8	− 14.82	− 0.21	...	5	46.9	11.8	....	....
5168	47 57 53.4	56.1	− 14.84	− 0.23	...	4	46.2	11.8	....	....
5169	51 15 9.5	9.7	− 14.86	− 0.23	...	5	47.9	6.7	67 Cygni σ....	....
5170	38 9 51.3	53.4	− 14.87	− 0.19	...	4	46.2	10.9	....	21963
5171	47 57 48.4	50.8	− 14.88	− 0.23	...	5	45.7	11.7	....	....
5172	38 6 41.4	...	− 14.88	− 0.18	...	4	46.7	...	....	21967
5173	50 54 7.1	...	− 14.88	− 0.23	...	4	51.2	...	....	....
5174	55 45 4.1	...	− 14.88	− 0.24	...	9	53.7	...	66 Cygni υ....	....
5175	38 9 51.5	...	− 14.88	− 0.18	...	4	46.7	...	....	21971

Ordinal Number.		Magnitude.	Estimates of Magnitudes.	Mean Right Ascension 1845.0.			Precession 1845.0.	Secular Variation	Adopted Proper Motion.	Observations of R.A.		
R.	G.	R.	R.	R.		G.				No. R.	Mean year. R.	G.
				h. m. s.		s.	s.	s.	s.		1800 +	
5176	...	7.0	5	21 11 37.94		...	+ 1.224	− 0.020	......	3	47.8	...
5177	3433	7.8	4	21 12 26.94		26.22	− 1.139	− 0.180	......	3	47.7	9.9
5178	3428	6.0	4	21 12 36.17		36.27	+ 1.789	− 0.001	+ 0.009	3	45.4	8.7
5179	3427	5.3	5	21 12 40.62		40.61	+ 2.230	+ 0.003	......	3	45.4	8.8
5180	3430	7.5	4	21 12 50.60		50.47	+ 1.937	+ 0.001	......	4	46.9	10.9
5181	...	7.0	3	21 12 55.20		...	+ 2.346	+ 0.003	......	3	51.4	...
5182	3429	6.3	4	21 12 55.98		56.02	+ 2.313	+ 0.003	......	4	47.3	11.8
5183	...	6.5	6	21 13 3.31		...	+ 1.648	− 0.004	......	3	47.4	...
5184	...	7.3	7	21 13 20.56		...	− 0.407	− 0.117	......	3	48.7	...
5185	...	5.1	3	21 13 36.58		...	+ 3.349	− 0.015	......	5	49.3	...
5186	3431	8.7	6	21 14 6.53		6.11	+ 2.053	+ 0.002	......	3	45.4	10.7
5187	3432	6.1	7	21 14 8.93		8.66	+ 2.057	+ 0.002	......	5	45.1	10.7
5188	...	8.1	4	21 14 15.73		...	+ 2.068	+ 0.002	......	2	48.2	...
5189	...	7.1	7	21 14 21.45		...	+ 1.951	0.000	......	4	46.4	...
5190	3434	6.8	7	21 14 41.92		41.60	+ 1.923	0.000	......	3	46.4	11.7
5191	3437	2.8	3	21 14 52.44		52.30	+ 1.416	− 0.009	+ 0.021	19	43.7	6.9
5192	3446	6.9	4	21 14 57.42		56.26	− 1.199	− 0.194	......	3	49.4	9.8
5193	3435	8.1	6	21 14 57.55		57.34	+ 2.067	+ 0.002	......	4	47.7	10.7
5194	...	5.6	5	21 14 58.28		...	+ 1.661	− 0.003	......	2	46.3	...
5195	3436	7.8	6	21 14 59.27		59.11	+ 1.929	+ 0.002	......	4	46.7	11.7
5196	...	8.2	5	21 14 59.74		...	+ 1.929	+ 0.002	......	3	54.7	...
5197	3440	7.9	4	21 15 40.27		39.46	+ 1.775	0.000	......	3	47.8	9.7
5198	3438	6.8	7	21 15 44.44		44.09	+ 2.158	+ 0.002	......	5	45.3	11.8
5199	3439	7.8	4	21 15 53.76		53.37	+ 2.266	+ 0.003	......	3	45.8	10.9
5200	3442	4.9	4	21 16 8.73		8.72	+ 1.255	− 0.015	......	5	46.0	8.8
5201	...	7.3	4	21 16 13.43		...	+ 1.554	− 0.006	......	2	48.2	...
5202	...	6.8	5	21 16 24.96		...	+ 1.552	− 0.006	.....	2	49.3	...
5203	3445	7.4	4	21 16 29.45		28.73	+ 1.779	+ 0.001	......	3	45.8	9.7
5204	...	6.1	6	21 16 34.44		...	+ 1.549	− 0.006	......	4	46.7	...
5205	3441	5.6	5	21 16 37.51		37.24	+ 2.074	+ 0.003	......	4	47.9	10.8
5206	3443	7.0	6	21 16 46.85		46.57	+ 2.330	+ 0.003	......	4	48.7	11.8
5207	...	7.6	6	21 16 47.73		...	+ 1.281	− 0.014	......	4	53.2	...
5208	3444	7.3	6	21 16 48.02		48.01	+ 2.336	+ 0.003	......	3	46.7	11.8
5209	...	9.4	7	21 16 49.14		...	+ 2.337	+ 0.003	......	4	51.2	...
5210	3448	8.3	2	21 16 52.06		51.57	+ 1.437	− 0.006	......	2	48.3	12.7

Ordinal Number.	Mean North Polar Distance 1845.0.			Precession 1845.0.	Secular Variation.	Adopted Proper Motion.	Observations of N.P.D.			Names.	Oeltzen-Argelander Number.
							No.	Mean year.			
R.	R.		G.				R.	R.	G.		
	° ′ ″		″	″	″	″		1800 +			
5176	25 53 38.7		...	− 14.88	− 0.11	...	3	46.7	...	....	21973
5177	11 58 30.3		29.1	−− 14.93	+ 0.11	...	3	45.5	9.9	....	21996
5178	34 51 6.0		6.0	− 14.94	− 0.17	...	4	44.7	8.7	....	....
5179	46 42 14.9		14.3	− 14.94	− 0.20	...	3	45.1	8.8	68 Cygni A....	....
5180	38 10 20.6		20.9	− 14.95	− 0.17	...	4	46.5	10.9	....	22004
5181	50 54 8.0		...	− 14.96	− 0.23	...	4	51.7	...	....	....
5182	49 36 38.0		39.5	− 14.96	− 0.22	...	3	46.0	11.8	....	....
5183	32 2 16.5		...	− 14.96	− 0.16	...	5	49.3	...	....	22012
5184	14 20 2.5		...	− 14.98	+ 0.04	...	4	48.8	...	....	....
5185	107 29 28.0		...	− 15.00	− 0.32	− 0.02	2	50.7	...	32 Capricorni ι	....
5186	41 2 21.2		26.3	− 15.03	− 0.20	...	4	51.0	10.7	....	....
5187	41 8 35.6		36.6	− 15.03	− 0.20	...	3	44.1	10.7	....	22045
5188	41 25 46.8		...	− 15.03	− 0.20	...	3	49.5	...	....	22046
5189	38 19 45.8		...	− 15.04	− 0.18	...	4	46.3	...	....	22048
5190	37 35 46.2		45.7	− 15.06	− 0.17	...	4	47.7	11.7	....	....
5191	28 4 11.8		13.2	− 15.07	− 0.13	− 0.01	6	43.9	6.9	5 Cephei α	22062
5192	11 40 11.0		10.7	− 15.08	+ 0.11	...	3	43.4	9.8	....	22071
5193	41 18 11.5		12.9	− 15.08	− 0.20	...	3	45.7	10.7	....	22065
5194	32 1 49.9		...	− 15.08	− 0.16	...	4	49.2	...	....	22066
5195	37 40 42.6		45.8	− 15.08	− 0.18	...	4	48.5	11.7	....	....
5196	37 40 45.9		...	− 15.08	− 0.18	...	3	46.5	...	....	....
5197	34 9 43.5		46.0	− 15.11	− 0.14	...	3	45.3	9.7	....	....
5198	43 55 42.4		42.9	− 15.12	− 0.19	...	3	45.3	11.8	....	22088
5199	47 30 47.7		49.7	− 15.13	− 0.21	...	5	47.0	10.9	....	....
5200	25 47 2.8		2.7	− 15.14	− 0.12	...	4	48.2	8.8	6 Cephei.......	22098
5201	30 1 33.8		...	− 15.15	− 0.15	...	3	46.4	...	....	22100
5202	29 58 11.6		...	− 15.16	− 0.15	...	3	47.2	...	....	22116
5203	34 6 58.7		62.4	− 15.16	− 0.16	...	3	43.8	9.7	....	....
5204	29 54 2.6		...	− 15.17	− 0.15	...	3	47.4	...	....	22127
5205	41 16 22.9		27.7	− 15.17	− 0.19	...	4	42.9	10.8	....	22128
5206	49 43 37.6		38.3	− 15.18	− 0.21	...	5	46.3	11.8	....	....
5207	26 1 37.4		...	− 15.18	− 0.11	...	3	53.0	...	....	22153
5208	49 57 48.6		47.5	− 15.18	− 0.21	...	3	47.7	11.8	....	....
5209	50 0 23.4		...	− 15.18	− 0.22	...	4	46.7	...	....	....
5210	28 7 52.3		53.5	− 15.18	− 0.11	...	3	47.8	12.7	....	22156

Magnitude.	Estimates of Magnitude.	Mean Right Ascension 1845.0		Precession 1845.0	Secular Variation	Adopted Proper Motion.
R.		R.	G.			
		h. m. s.	s.	s.	s.	s.
7.1	5	21 17 6.68	6.19	+ 2.073	+ 0.003	....
6.0	4	21 17 17.80	18.72	− 0.521	− 0.132	+ 0.063
8.8	5	21 17 18.55	...	+ 1.559	− 0.006	......
7.3	5	21 17 30.26	...	+ 1.567	− 0.006	......
7.7	5	21 17 30.52	30.52	+ 2.079	+ 0.003	......
7.0	8	21 17 33.68	33.92	+ 2.234	+ 0.003	......
4.5	1	21 17 48.62	...	+ 3.441	− 0.018	− 0.002
7.6	5	21 18 34.83	...	− 1.917	− 0.310	......
6.7	•2	21 18 46.75	46.15	+ 2.002	+ 0.002	......
8.2	6	21 18 50.41	50.47	+ 2.246	+ 0.003	......
7.2	6	21 19 7.72	...	+ 1.334	− 0.012	+ 0.007
8.1	5	21 19 12.29	11.97	+ 2.182	+ 0.003	......
9.0	4	21 19 13.86	14.03	+ 2.243	+ 0.003	......
9.0	4	21 19 19.30	19.24	+ 2.245	+ 0.003	......
8.2	6	21 19 22.94	22.61	+ 2.088	+ 0.003	......
7.6	5	21 19 25.65	...	+ 2.291	+ 0.004	......
6.7	6	21 19 30.75	30.60	+ 2.091	+ 0.003	......
6.3	6	21 19 32.30	...	− 2.029	− 0.368	......
5.7	5	21 19 38.35	37.31	+ 2.177	+ 0.003	......
8.6	7	21 19 59.28	...	+ 2.091	+ 0.003	......
8.1	5	21 20 11.77	11.69	+ 2.249	+ 0.003	......
8.1	6	21 20 30.14	30.47	+ 2.286	+ 0.003	......
7.6	6	21 20 41.25	41.15	+ 1.966	+ 0.002	......
8.2	7	21 21 1.97	1.61	+ 2.100	+ 0.003	......
7.5	5	21 21 6.03	5.96	+ 2.285	+ 0.003	......
8.0	4	21 21 11.31	11.33	+ 2.239	+ 0.003	......
7.5	6	21 21 22.02	22.13	+ 1.975	+ 0.002	......
6.0	4	21 21 38.43	38.40	+ 1.970	+ 0.002	......
7.2	3	21 21 49.20	...	+ 2.196	+ 0.004	+ 0.005
8.6	4	21 22 4.61	4.27	+ 2.294	+ 0.004	......
7.0	7	21 22 13.23	...	+ 2.194	+ 0.004	......
7.2	5	21 22 58.90	54.74	− 1.577	− 0.249	.....
6.2	6	21 23 8.29	8.27	+ 1.659	− 0.003	+ 0.015
6.8	5	21 23 17.00	16.77	+ 2.247	+ 0.003	......
7.2	5	21 23 19.58	...	+ 0.774	− 0.038	....

| Ordinal Number. | Mean North Polar Distance 1845.0. | | Precession 1845.0. | Secular Variation. | Adopted Proper Motion. | Observations of N.P.D. | | | Names. | Oeltzen-Argelander Number. |
R.	R.	G.				No. R.	Mean year R.	G.		
	° ′ ″	″	″	″	″		1800 +			
5211	41 10 8.8	7.8	− 15.20	− 0.19	...	4	46.2	10.8	....	22146
5212	13 38 28.5	28.6	− 15.21	+ 0.05	...	4	43.8	9.8	....	22153
5213	29 57 36.4	...	− 15.21	− 0.15	...	4	51.8	...	....	22152
5214	30 4 40.6	...	− 15.22	− 0.15	...	3	49.7	...	....	22157
5215	41 16 58.7	58.2	− 15.22	− 0.18	...	3	50.8	13.7	....	22156
5216	46 8 37.6	35.8	− 15.23	− 0.22	...	3	43.7	13.7	....	....
5217	113 4 45.1	...	− 15.24	− 0.33	− 0.02	1	53.7	...	34 Capricorni ζ	....
5218	9 50 46.1	...	− 15.29	+ 0.19	...	4	49.3	...	....	....
5219	39 0 26.2	26.7	− 15.30	− 0.20	...	3	45.1	9.9	....	....
5220	46 22 25.5	26.2	− 15.30	− 0.22	...	3	46.1	13.7	....	....
5221	26 26 17.0	...	− 15.31	− 0.13	− 0.13	3	48.1	...	....	22205
5222	44 10 33.0	32.7	− 15.32	− 0.21	...	3	50.1	11.8	....	22206
5223	46 12 52.3	62.8	− 15.32	− 0.21	...	2	50.2	13.8	....	....
5224	46 16 13.4	12.6	− 15.32	− 0.21	...	2	50.2	13.8	....	....
5225	41 16 24.4	23.9	− 15.33	− 0.19	...	3	45.7	12.7	....	22214
5226	47 52 56.1	...	− 15.33	− 0.21	...	3	46.7	...	....	....
5227	41 20 34.7	35.8	− 15.34	− 0.20	...	5	47.0	12.7	....	....
5228	9 25 19.1	...	− 15.34	+ 0.19	...	3	48.1	...	....	....
5229	43 57 18.0	17.4	− 15.35	− 0.22	− 0.05	3	43.4	11.8	....	22224
5230	41 16 21.7	...	− 15.37	− 0.20	...	3	49.8	...	....	22233
5231	46 16 23.5	22.4	− 15.38	− 0.22	...	2	48.8	13.7	....	....
5232	47 32 53.6	54.4	− 15.39	− 0.21	...	3	45.8	10.8	....	....
5233	37 48 28.0	27.6	− 15.40	− 0.17	...	3	44.7	12.8	....	22256
5234	41 23 24.0	24.2	− 15.42	− 0.19	...	4	46.5	12.7	....	22268
5235	47 26 21.3	21.6	− 15.43	− 0.21	...	5	44.2	10.8	....	....
5236	45 47 12.8	11.3	− 15.43	− 0.20	...	3	47.1	12.8	....	....
5237	37 55 20.4	21.5	− 15.44	− 0.18	...	5	46.0	12.8	....	22276
5238	37 46 22.0	23.2	− 15.45	− 0.18	...	4	43.3	12.8	....	22285
5239	44 15 21.5	...	− 15.46	− 0.20	+ 0.05	4	50.0	...	....	....
5240	47 35 39.8	41.2	− 15.47	− 0.21	...	3	45.1	10.9	....	....
5241	44 6 42.5	...	− 15.48	− 0.20	...	4	47.2	...	....	22296
5242	10 18 52.8	55.8	− 15.52	+ 0.17	...	3	44.4	9.7	....	....
5243	30 55 22.2	23.4	− 15.54	− 0.15	...	5	47.9	9.7	....	....
5244	45 45 9.5	10.4	− 15.54	− 0.20	...	4	46.2	11.9	....	....
5245	20 11 45.2	...	− 15.55	− 0.07	...	4	44.2	...	....	22321

Magnitude.	Estimates of Magnitude.	Mean Right Ascension 1845.0. R.	G.	Precession 1845.0.	Secular Variation	Adopted Proper Motion.
		h. m. s.	s.	s.	s.	s.
7.4	5	21 23 22.84	22.76	+ 2.264	+ 0.004	......
3.2	3	21 23 23.74	...	+ 3.162	− 0.009	− 0.001
7.8	7	21 23 40.01	39.72	+ 1.833	0.000	......
6.9	5	21 23 42.27	42.04	− 0.419	− 0.126	......
5.5	7	21 23 43.96	43.83	+ 2.202	+ 0.004	......
6.8	4	21 23 44.43	45.50	− 0.280	− 0.114	......
6.9	6	21 23 53.66	...	+ 2.206	+ 0.004	......
6.5	5	21 24 0.37	0.09	+ 1.879	0.000	......
7.6	6	21 24 12.08	...	+ 2.330	+ 0.004	......
7.7	7	21 24 33.23	...	+ 2.327	+ 0.004	......
7.0	4	21 24 35.21	34.96	+ 2.255	+ 0.004	......
9.1	7	21 24 41.01	...	+ 2.326	+ 0.004	......
7.6	6	21 24 43.95	43.37	+ 1.988	+ 0.003	......
5.7	3	21 24 45.81	45.86	+ 1.177	− 0.018	......
8.2	6	21 24 46.81	...	+ 2.207	+ 0.004	......
7.9	3	21 24 51.77	...	+ 1.257	− 0.020	......
6.9	3	21 24 53.70	53.15	− 0.121	− 0.097	......
7.4	6	21 25 5.01	...	− 2.431	− 0.402	......
6.0	7	21 25 10.93	10.31	+ 1.989	+ 0.003	......
7.9	4	21 25 16.68	...	+ 2.278	+ 0.004	......
8.1	5	21 25 17.91	...	+ 2.282	+ 0.004	......
7.4	7	21 25 31.98	...	+ 1.638	− 0.004	......
7.6	6	21 25 36.48	36.17	+ 2.319	+ 0.005	......
9.2	4	21 25 43.62	43.87	+ 2.274	+ 0.004	......
7.0	6	21 25 44.06	43.18	− 4.360	− 0.812	......
9.1	5	21 25 50.10	49.81	+ 2.278	+ 0.004	......
6.4	6	21 26 3.27	2.99	+ 2.023	+ 0.003	......
6.6	6	21 26 15.14	14.93	+ 2.008	+ 0.003	......
8.2	4	21 26 34.20	34.35	+ 1.560	− 0.006	......
6.7	5	21 26 34.14	...	+ 1.703	− 0.002	+ 0.028
8.0	3	21 26 35.90	...	+ 0.806	− 0.037	......
3.3	3	21 26 38.31	37.92	+ 0.806	− 0.037	......
8.3	4	21 26 38.62	...	+ 1.565	− 0.006	......
6.1	4	21 26 41.85	...	+ 2.157	+ 0.004	......
6.4	5	21 26 43.86	43.78	+ 1.647	− 0.003	......

Ordinal Number.	Mean North Polar Distance 1845.0.		Precession 1845.0.	Secular Variation.	Adopted Proper Motion.	Observations of N.P.D.			Names.	Oeltzen-Argelander Number.
						No.	Mean year.			
R.	R.	G.				R.	R.	G.		
	o ′ ″	″	″	″	″		1800 +			
5246	46 20 16.2	17.4	— 15.55	— 0.20	...	4	45.5	13.7	....	......
5247	96 15 0.4	...	— 15.56	— 0.29	...	11	48.8	...	22 Aquarii β .	......
5248	34 17 3.3	2.4	— 15.57	— 0.17	...	5	48.9	9.8	....	22330
5249	13 34 38.3	38.0	— 15.57	+ 0.04	...	3	45.4	12.9	....	22335
5250	44 8 27.6	26.7	— 15.57	— 0.19	— 0.11	5	45.7	8.7	71 Cygni g	22332
5251	14 7 13.4	18.2	— 15.57	+ 0.04	...	4	47.0	12.9	....	......
5252	44 15 3.8	...	— 15.58	— 0.20	...	5	47.0	...	....	22336
5253	35 15 31.0	29.9	— 15.59	— 0.18	...	5	48.9	9.9	....	......
5254	48 37 53.5	...	— 15.60	— 0.21	...	4	51.3	...	....	......
5255	48 28 2.6	...	— 15.62	— 0.21	...	4	51.7	...	....	......
5256	45 48 14.7	15.4	— 15.62	— 0.20	...	3	44.2	11.9	....	......
5257	48 24 29.3	...	— 15.63	— 0.21	...	4	53.5	...	....	......
5258	37 44 41.8	42.3	— 15.63	— 0.19	...	3	46.4	11.8	....	22359
5259	23 51 59.5	59.1	— 15.63	— 0.10	+ 0.03	4	47.7	8.8	7 Cephei	......
5260	44 8 38.5	...	— 15.63	— 0.20	...	5	45.3	...	....	22361
5261	24 46 41.1	...	— 15.63	— 0.11	...	3	47.3	...	....	......
5262	14 42 4.1	5.0	— 15.63	+ 0.03	...	3	43.3	12.8	....	......
5263	8 38 46.0	...	— 15.64	+ 0.22	...	3	51.1	...	....	......
5264	37 43 19.9	19.9	— 15.65	— 0.17	...	4	44.7	11.8	....	22370
5265	46 36 31.5	...	— 15.65	— 0.21	...	2	51.7	...	....	......
5266	46 39 27.7	...	— 15.66	— 0.21	...	2	51.2	...	....	......
5267	30 18 2.8	...	— 15.67	— 0.15	...	3	51.4	...	....	22375
5268	47 58 49.9	51.6	— 15.67	— 0.19	...	3	45.3	12.7	....	......
5269	46 19 22.4	21.8	— 15.68	— 0.20	...	3	47.1	13.7	....	......
5270	6 24 4.9	5.3	— 15.68	+ 0.39	...	3	47.3	7.8	....	......
5271	46 26 54.5	59.5	— 15.69	— 0.21	...	3	52.2	13.7	....	......
5272	38 29 18.4	22.3	— 15.70	— 0.17	...	4	47.2	10.8	....	......
5273	38 3 43.8	45.3	— 15.71	— 0.17	...	4	48.0	10.7	....	22397
5274	28 47 51.7	56.2	— 15.72	— 0.11	...	2	48.3	12.9	....	22407
5275	31 15 57.1	...	— 15.72	— 0.15	— 0.10	3	48.2	...	....	22406
5276	20 7 11.2	...	— 15.73	— 0.06	...	2	41.3	...	8 Cephei β (1st)	......
5277	20 7 8.7	9.2	— 15.73	— 0.06	...	21	47.8	6.8	8 Cephei β (2d)	22413
5278	28 50 40.9	...	— 15.73	— 0.14	...	2	51.7	...	....	22410
5279	42 14 19.9	...	— 15.73	— 0.19	...	3	47.8	...	....	22411
5280	30 13 21.6	22.7	— 15.73	— 0.15	...	5	47.1	8.7	....	......

Ordinal Number.		Magnitude.	Estimates of Magnitude.	Mean Right Ascension 1845.0.		Precession 1845.0.	Secular Variation	Adopted Proper Motion.	Observations of R.A.		
R.	G.	R.		R.	G.				No. R.	Mean year R.	G.
				h. m. s.	s.	s.	s.	s.		1800 +	
5281	3492	7.6	5	21 26 58.25	58.20	+ 1.804	0.000	......	3	47.5	13.8
5282	3490	8.5	6	21 27 4.14	3.94	+ 2.009	+ 0.003	......	3	44.4	10.7
5283	3491	9.0	3	21 27 5.93	5.13	+ 2.006	+ 0.003	......	3	44.2	10.7
5284	...	6.5	5	21 27 29.68	...	+ 2.240	+ 0.005	......	3	48.7	...
5285	3494	7.9	4	21 27 49.55	49.36	+ 1.808	0.000	......	3	49.5	13.8
5286	3497	7.3	6	21 27 52.58	52.67	+ 1.701	− 0.023	......	3	47.8	12.9
5287	3496	8.0	5	21 28 5.08	5.07	+ 1.983	+ 0.003	......	2	45.3	14.8
5288	3495	4.1	4	21 28 9.27	9.31	+ 2.250	+ 0.004	......	6	46.3	6.9
5289	...	4.7	1	21 28 23.62	...	+ 3.372	− 0.017	− 0.002	1	53.7	...
5290	...	8.7	11	21 28 27.44	...	−12.094	− 3.955	......	12	53.1	...
5291	...	7.8	4	21 28 31.88	...	+ 2.241	+ 0.004	......	2	51.3	...
5292	3498	7.6	3	21 28 42.64	42.12	+ 2.412	+ 0.004	......	3	47.4	10.9
5293	3503	6.9	3	21 28 58.16	57.55	+ 0.803	− 0.040	......	3	48.1	9.8
5294	3502	8.4	5	21 28 59.63	59.49	+ 1.075	− 0.023	......	2	49.2	12.9
5295	3508	7.6	5	21 29 3.55	3.96	− 0.145	− 0.106	......	2	51.3	8.7
5296	...	8.0	6	21 29 4.49	...	+ 1.786	− 0.001	......	3	48.9	...
5297	3500	6.1	2	21 29 7.10	7.16	+ 2.060	+ 0.004	......	3	46.7	8.8
5298	3499	6.8	4	21 29 9.93	9.73	+ 2.307	+ 0.005	......	4	47.7	9.9
5299	3511	5.5	5	21 29 11.30	13.64	− 1.495	− 0.268	+ 0.119	4	51.8	9.7
5300	...	7.7	6	21 29 16.31	...	+ 2.211	+ 0.004	......	4	53.7	...
5301	3548	.7.5	62	21 29 20.20	17.44	− 9.860	− 2.826	......	70	50.9	7.8
5302	...	5.3	1	21 29 29.76	...	+ 3.193	− 0.010	+ 0.004	3	45.2	...
5303	3505	7.8	3	21 29 49.84	49.83	+ 1.593	− 0.003	......	2	47.3	13.9
5304	3506	8.8	4	21 30 15.04	14.98	+ 2.293	+ 0.005	......	2	50.8	13.7
5305	3504	8.4	3	21 30 17.19	16.62	+ 2.417	+ 0.005	......	3	48.1	10.9
5306	3507	8.2	5	21 30 18.62	19.35	+ 2.296	+ 0.005	......	4	48.5	13.7
5307	3519	6.9	4	21 30 25.42	25.66	− 0.518	− 0.151	......	3	50.4	12.8
5308	...	8.0	5	21 30 34.52	...	− 0.094	− 0.105	......	2	49.8	...
5309	3509	6.0	6	21 30 44.40	44.16	+ 2.397	+ 0.005	......	4	48.0	8.9
5310	3510	8.7	9	21 30 58.99	58.86	+ 1.834	0.000	......	6	47.2	13.8
5311	3516	6.8	4	21 31 13.88	13.62	+ 1.252	− 0.014	......	3	48.2	12.7
5312	3513	9.0	5	21 31 17.04	15.29	+ 1.836	0.000	......	3	51.3	13.9
5313	3517	6.9	6	21 31 26.77	26.03	+ 1.250	− 0.017	......	4	47.5	12.7
5314	...	3.7	A	21 31 29.88	...	+ 3.322	− 0.015	+ 0.013	2	46.7	...
5315	...	8.6	4	21 31 30.72	...	+ 1.957	+ 0.001	......	2	51.2	...

Ordinal Number.	Mean North Polar Distance 1845.0.		Precession 1845.0.	Secular Variation.	Adopted Proper Motion.	Observations of N.P.D.			Names.	Oeltzen-Argelander Number.
						No.	Mean year.			
R.	R.	G.				R.	R.	G.		
	° ′ ″	″	″	″	″		1800 +			
5281	33 10 49.5	52.0	− 15.75	− 0.16	...	2	51.2	13.8	....	22424
5282	37 55 59.8	59.4	− 15.75	− 0.16	...	3	5..4	10.7	....	22429
5283	37 51 0.0	56.8	− 15.75	− 0.16	...	3	48.1	10.7	....	22430
5284	44 49 53.8	...	− 15.77	− 0.20	...	2	50.3	...	....	22441
5285	33 8 47.1	46.3	+ 15.79	− 0.14	...	3	52.7	13.8	....	22447
5286	22 23 23.7	25.0	− 15.80	− 0.10	...	3	44.5	12.9	....	....
5287	37 5 47.1	46.2	− 15.81	− 0.17	...	3	51.8	14.8	....	22452
5288	45 5 27.8	28.6	− 15.81	− 0.19	+ 0.09	3	46.1	6.9	73 Cygni ρ	22453
5289	110 9 26.8	...	− 15.83	− 0.30	...	1	53.7	...	39 Capricorni ε	....
5290	3 5 56.1	...	− 15.83	+ 1.13	...	4	49.6	...	....	....
5291	44 41 33.0	...	− 15.83	− 0.20	...	2	47.8	...	....	22459
5292	51 15 10.6	13.6	− 15.84	− 0.20	...	2	46.3	10.9	....	
5293	19 51 42.1	41.6	− 15.86	− 0.08	...	4	48.2	9.8	....	22470
5294	22 18 28.8	25.2	− 15.86	− 0.09	...	3	51.4	12.9	....	....
5295	14 16 43.6	41.5	− 15.86	+ 0.02	+ 0.03	4	45.9	8.7	....	22482
5296	32 29 32.4	...	− 15.86	− 0.16	...	3	47.1	...	....	....
5297	38 59 25.7	26.4	− 15.86	− 0.18	...	3	45.0	8.8	....	....
5298	46 59 11.0	11.6	− 15.86	− 0.19	...	3	45.8	9.9	....	....
5299	10 9 10.4	11.4	− 15.87	+ 0.13	...	7	50.7	9.7	....	22490
5300	43 35 59.4	...	− 15.87	− 0.20	...	4	51.2	...	....	....
5301	3 36 55.3	56.4	− 15.87	+ 0.90	...	24	49.4	7.8	....	....
5302	98 32 47.2	...	− 15.88	− 0.28	+ 0.04	1	46.8	...	23 Aquarii ξ...	....
5303	28 53 20.9	22.0	− 15.90	− 0.13	...	3	44.8	13.9	....	22509
5304	46 15 53.7	53.3	− 15.92	− 0.18	...	3	44.8	13.7	....	....
5305	51 12 45.7	45.2	− 15.92	− 0.19	...	3	47.2	10.9	....	....
5306	46 22 34.4	35.5	− 15.92	− 0.17	...	3	43.3	13.7	....	....
5307	12 44 54.8	55.5	− 15.93	+ 0.06	...	4	43.4	12.8	....	22537
5308	14 22 36.7	...	− 15.94	+ 0.01	...	3	51.7	...	....	22545
5309	50 16 48.5	50.6	− 15.95	− 0.20	...	3	44.4	8.9	74 Cygni........	....
5310	33 13 28.9	30.9	− 15.96	− 0.15	...	3	49.4	13.8	....	22550
5311	23 57 48.2	49.1	− 15.97	− 0.09	...	3	45.4	12.7	....	....
5312	33 13 21.6	29.9	− 15.98	− 0.16	...	3	50.3	13.9	....	22552
5313	23 55 7.6	8.8	− 15.99	− 0.11	...	3	47.1	12.7	....	....
5314	107 21 33.8	...	− 15.99	− 0.29	+ 0.03	4	50.8	...	40 Capricorni γ	....
5315	35 52 37.2	...	− 15.99	− 0.17	...	3	53.1	...	....	22557

Ordinal Number.		Magnitude.	Estimates of Magnitude.	Mean Right Ascension 1845.0.			Precession 1845.0.	Secular Variation	Adopted Proper Motion.	Observations of R.A.		
R.	G.	R.	R.	R.		G.				No.	Mean year.	
											R.	G.
				h. m. s.		s.	s.	s.	s.		1800 +	
5316	3512	6.8	3	21 31 31.37		31.52	+ 2.426	+ 0.005	+ 0.016	3	47.1	10.9
5317	3514	6.4	5	21 31 31.60		31.42	+ 2.291	+ 0.005	......	3	44.2	11.8
5318	...	8.6	3	21 31 36.95		...	+ 2.390	+ 0.005	......	3	51.1	...
5319	3515	7.1	6	21 31 50.61		50.57	+ 2.385	+ 0.005	......	4	48.2	11.8
5320	...	8.2	6	21 31 51.99		...	+ 1.964	+ 0.002	......	2	51.8	...
5321	3520	7.7	4	21 31 53.57		53.48	+ 2.014	+ 0.004	......	3	47.1	14.8
5322	3522	8.5	3	21 31 59.90		59.63	+ 2.014	+ 0.004	......	2	49.3	14.8
5323	...	8.2	4	21 32 2.66		...	+ 1.837	0.000	......	2	51.2	...
5324	3518	8.4	3	21 32 6.48		6.39	+ 2.389	+ 0.005	......	2	47.8	11.8
5325	3521	8.1	6	21 32 13.03		12.98	+ 2.424	+ 0.006	......	4	49.7	13.7
5326	...	9.4	6	21 32 22.41		...	+ 1.842	0.000	......	4	54.0	...
5327	3523	5.6	4	21 32 29.37		29.12	+ 1.992	+ 0.004	......	4	47.3	9.9
5328	3527	7.0	3	21 32 32.05		32.15	+ 1.132	− 0.020	......	2	48.8	12.9
5329	...	9.3	3	21 32 36.15		...	+ 1.922	+ 0.002	......	2	52.2	...
5330	...	8.7	3	21 32 37.03		...	+ 1.922	+ 0.002	......	3	53.7	...
5331	3526	8.2	8	21 32 54.59		54.52	+ 1.844	+ 0.002	......	4	48.5	13.8
5332	3524	6.9	5	21 32 55.21		55.09	+ 2.146	+ 0.005	......	3	44.2	10.7
5333	3525	8.0	3	21 32 56.20		56.18	+ 2.141	+ 0.005	......	3	44.7	10.7
5334	3528	7.0	3	21 33 2.94		2.65	+ 1.591	− 0.004	......	3	50.8	11.9
5335	...	7.5	4	21 33 19.20		...	+ 2.375	+ 0.006	......	3	51.5	...
5336	3530	7.2	4	21 33 22.86		22.80	+ 2.016	+ 0.004	......	3	48.8	14.8
5337	3529	7.2	5	21 33 35.50		35.43	+ 2.429	+ 0.006	......	3	47.5	13.7
5338	3531	8.5	5	21 33 39.37		38.90	+ 2.307	+ 0.005	......	4	48.7	11.8
5339	3535	5.3	4	21 33 45.55		45.49	+ 1.610	− 0.004	......	3	50.4	11.2
5340	...	7.5	6	21 33 45.83		...	+ 1.929	+ 0.001	......	2	52.3	...
5341	3532	6.7	4	21 33 54.71		54.44	+ 2.309	+ 0.006	......	4	47.5	11.8
5342	3533	7.3	4	21 33 56.66		56.24	+ 2.064	+ 0.004	......	3	51.1	9.8
5343	3538	8.7	5	21 34 0.51		0.45	+ 1.152	− 0.017	......	2	50.2	12.8
5344	3534	5.4	4	21 34 6.33		6.35	+ 2.340	+ 0.006	......	4	48.8	8.9
5345	...	8.4	6	21 34 8.37		...	+ 1.856	+ 0.002	......	4	53.9	...
5346	3536	6.0	4	21 34 9.15		9.09	+ 1.856	+ 0.002	......	3	47.7	11.3
5347	...	8.4	6	21 34 10.42		...	+ 1.856	+ 0.002	......	4	53.5	...
5348	3539	8.7	5	21 34 33.61		33.82	+ 2.030	+ 0.004	......	2	48.2	14.8
5349	3537	7.2	5	21 34 35.71		35.56	+ 2.159	+ 0.005	......	4	46.8	10.8
5350	3540	8.4	5	21 34 38.39		38.39	+ 1.860	+ 0.002	......	3	50.2	13.8

Ordinal Number.	Mean North Polar Distance 1845.0.		Precession 1845.0.	Secular Variation.	Adopted Proper Motion.	Observations of N.P.D.			Names.	Oeltzen-Argelander Number.
	R.	G.				No. R.	Mean year. R.	G.		
	o ′ ″	″	″	″	″		1800 +			
5316	51 22 41.3	42.6	− 16.00	− 0.21	...	3	46.1	10.9	....	......
5317	45 59 50.3	48.8	− 16.00	− 0.20	...	4	45.2	11.8	....	......
5318	49 51 5.6	...	− 16.00	− 0.21	...	2	49.3	...	....	......
5319	49 36 43.3	41.5	− 16.01	− 0.21	...	4	46.5	11.8	....	......
5320	36 3 25.4	...	− 16.01	− 0.17	...	4	52.2	...	....	22561
5321	37 19 2.0	3.2	− 16.01	− 0.17	...	3	47.8	14.8	....	22562
5322	37 17 47.8	51.3	− 16.02	− 0.17	...	2	52.3	14.8	....	22569
5323	33 6 38.4	...	− 16.02	− 0.16	...	3	51.0	...	....	22571
5324	49 43 54.5	57.0	− 16.03	− 0.21	...	2	46.2	11.8	....	......
5325	51 11 11.6	12.4	− 16.03	− 0.21	...	3	50.8	13.7	....	......
5326	33 7 48.9	...	− 16.04	− 0.16	...	2	53.8	...	....	22584
5327	36 39 15.6	13.6	− 16.04	− 0.17	...	4	46.8	9.9	....	......
5328	22 28 30.8	33.0	− 16.04	− 0.08	...	3	46.5	12.9	....	22592
5329	34 55 55.6	...	− 16.04	− 0.17	...	2	52.3	...	....	22593
5330	34 55 13.0	...	− 16.04	− 0.17	...	1	51.8	...	....	22594
5331	33 8 11.3	12.7	− 16.06	− 0.14	...	5	49.5	13.8	....	22604
5332	40 54 6.3	6.6	− 16.06	− 0.19	...	3	45.7	10.7	....	....
5333	40 44 10.0	8.0	− 16.06	− 0.19	...	3	46.8	10.7	....	......
5334	28 23 50.8	55.2	− 16.07	− 0.14	...	3	42.8	11.9	....	22610
5335	48 58 19.6	...	− 16.08	− 0.20	...	3	53.4	...	....	......
5336	37 7 7.2	7.2	− 16.09	− 0.17	...	4	45.5	14.8	....	......
5337	51 11 7.2	8.8	− 16.10	− 0.21	...	4	46.3	13.7	....	......
5338	46 15 29.9	29.4	− 16.11	− 0.20	...	3	46.4	11.8	....	......
5339	28 36 58.1	58.7	− 16.11	− 0.14	...	4	44.0	11.2	9 Cephei.......	22626
5340	34 54 26.7	...	− 16.11	− 0.16	...	4	51.7	...	....	22625
5341	46 16 4.7	4.7	− 16.12	− 0.20	...	4	44.3	11.8	....	......
5342	38 20 14.0	21.4	− 16.12	− 0.18	...	3	44.1	9.8	....	22634
5343	22 30 42.1	43.2	− 16.12	− 0.09	...	3	50.4	12.8	....	22637
5344	47 25 39.1	39.6	− 16.13	− 0.20	− 0.03	4	44.2	8.9	75 Cygni.......	......
5345	33 12 19.0	...	− 16.13	− 0.16	...	2	50.2	...	....	22641
5346	33 12 37.0	37.7	− 16.13	− 0.16	...	5	46.8	11.3	....	22646
5347	33 12 43.9	...	− 16.13	− 0.16	...	2	50.3	...	....	22648
5348	37 18 8.1	9.1	− 16.15	− 0.17	...	3	50.1	14.8	....	......
5349	41 1 6.7	8.1	− 16.15	− 0.18	...	3	46.1	10.8	....	......
5350	33 13 1.0	59.4	− 16.15	− 0.16	...	1	46.8	13.8	....	22669

Ordinal Number.		Magnitude.	Estimates of Magnitude.	Mean Right Ascension 1845.0.		Precession 1845.0.	Secular Variation	Adopted Proper Motion.	Observations of R.A.		
									No.	Mean year.	
R.	G.	R.		R.	G.				R.	R.	G.
				h. m. s.	s.	s.	s.	s.		1800 +	
5351	3542	8.9	3	21 34 45.07	45.44	+ 1.650	− 0.003	......	2	49.2	14.9
5352	...	7.7	5	21 34 48.93	...	+ 2.009	+ 0.001	......	3	49.4	...
5353	3541	7.9	5	21 35 0.26	0.36	+ 2.435	+ 0.005	......	3	50.7	13.7
5354	3543	5.8	3	21 35 20.47	20.26	+ 2.406	+ 0.005	......	5	44.9	10.3
5355	3545	7.7	6	21 35 32.95	33.11	+ 1.862	+ 0.002	......	3	48.1	13.8
5356	...	9.0	2	21 35 ...	...	+ 1.862	+ 0.002	......	...	...	...
5357	3544	6.1	2	21 35 35.52	35.21	+ 1.979	+ 0.004	......	3	45.4	12.7
5358	...	7.8	6	21 35 50.82	...	+ 2.365	+ 0.005	......	3	47.1	...
5359	3546	7.2	6	21 35 55.40	55.25	+ 2.438	+ 0.005	......	4	49.2	13.7
5360	3550	6.7	6	21 35 58.09	57.66	+ 1.759	+ 0.001	......	3	51.1	12.8
5361	3551	9.0	5	21 35 59.98	60.37	+ 1.664	− 0.001	......	2	51.2	14.9
5362	3547	6.0	7	21 36 9.03	8.82	+ 2.403	+ 0.005	+ 0.004	4	47.0	10.7
5363	...	7.8	3	21 36 16.89	...	+ 2.385	+ 0.005	......	3	51.1	...
5364	3549	7.7	6	21 36 19.29	18.76	+ 2.404	+ 0.005	......	3	48.3	10.4
5365	3552	7.5	2	21 36 25.42	25.24	+ 2.371	+ 0.006	......	2	51.2	10.9
5366	...	3.3	1	21 36 34.37	...	+ 2.944	− 0.002	+ 0.003	64	46.2	...
5367	3553	4.3	3	21 36 35.72	35.45	+ 2.121	+ 0.005	......	4	46.6	6.8
5368	...	8.6	4	21 36 37.92	...	+ 2.437	+ 0.005	......	2	52.2	...
5369	3554	6.7	4	21 36 41.38	40.91	+ 2.083	+ 0.005	......	4	47.3	9.9
5370	3555	5.9	4	21 36 52.86	52.92	+ 2.404	+ 0.006	......	2	50.8	12.9
5371	...	8.0	5	21 36 55.59	...	+ 0.249	− 0.084	......	4	54.0	...
5372	3558	7.1	5	21 36 58.96	59.28	+ 0.851	− 0.034	+ 0.020	3	51.7	12.9
5373	3556	5.4	3	21 37 0.42	0.38	+ 2.175	+ 0.006	......	4	49.0	10.8
5374	...	7.5	3	21 37 20.38	...	+ 2.053	+ 0.004	......	3	49.1	...
5375	3560	8.2	4	21 37 29.91	29.14	+ 0.844	− 0.034	......	3	52.5	12.9
5376	3557	6.8	6	21 37 33.61	33.42	+ 1.870	+ 0.003	......	3	49.5	13.9
5377	...	9 0	4	21 37 44.75	...	+ 2.442	+ 0.006	......	2	50.7	...
5378	3559	6.9	3	21 37 53.30	52.93	+ 2.086	+ 0.005	......	2	50.2	9.9
5379	3561	5.8	4	21 38 5.75	5.53	+ 1.800	+ 0.001	......	3	48.5	12.7
5380	...	8.8	3	21 38 10.98	...	+ 2.264	+ 0.005	......	2	49.2	...
5381	3562	8.4	4	21 38 28.32	28.42	+ 2.447	+ 0.006	......	3	50.7	13.7
5382	...	3.7	6	21 38 28.77	...	+ 3.304	− 0.015	+ 0.014	11	50.6	...
5383	3563	6.7	6	21 38 33.34	33.26	+ 2.264	+ 0.006	......	3	45.1	10.7
5384	...	7.1	5	21 38 43.28	...	+ 1.552	− 0.009	......	2	49.3	...
5385	...	4.5	7	21 38 45.96	...	+ 1.830	+ 0.001	......	4	51.2	...

Ordinal Number.	Mean North Polar Distance 1845.0.			Precession 1845.0.	Secular Variation.	Adopted Proper Motion.	Observations of N.P.D.				Names.	Oeltzen-Argelander Number.
R.	R.		G.				No. R.	Mean year R.	G.			
	° ′ ″		″	″	″	″		1800 +				
5351	29 8 38.3		39.2	− 16.15	− 0.10	...	2	52.7	14.9		....	22673
5352	36 43 56.5		...	− 16.15	− 0.17	...	3	45.8	...		....	......
5353	51 13 44.2		45.4	− 16.17	− 0.21	...	2	45.4	13.7		....	......
5354	49 53 46.8		47.1	− 16.19	− 0.20	+ 0.04	3	44.7	10.3		76 Cygni........	......
5355	33 7 13.3		13.6	− 16.20	− 0.15	...	4	48.0	13.8		....	22687
5356	33 7 6.8		...	− 16.20	− 0.15	...	3	46.1	...		....	......
5357	35 49 52.7		51.5	− 16.20	− 0.17	...	4	43.7	12.7		....	......
5358	48 8 7.5		...	− 16.21	− 0.21	...	3	45.7	...		....	......
5359	51 10 46.5		46.4	− 16.22	− 0.21	...	3	46.8	13.7		....	......
5360	30 57 5.6		6.9	− 16.22	− 0.13	...	3	46.4	12.8		....	22695
5361	29 11 56.4		56.7	− 16.23	− 0.13	...	3	50.1	14.9		....	22696
5362	49 37 41.9		43.5	− 16.24	− 0.21	...	3	44.8	10.7		77 Cygni........	......
5363	48 53 5.1		...	− 16.24	− 0.21	...	3	48.8	...		....	......
5364	49 39 29.4		31.1	− 16.24	− 0.21	...	3	44.2	10.4		....	......
5365	48 15 52.7		54.0	− 16.25	− 0.21	...	4	48.3	10.9		....	......
5366	80 49 57.6		...	− 16.25	− 0.25	...	2	46.8	...		8 Pegasi ε	......
5367	39 30 56.2		58.2	− 16.26	− 0.18	...	5	43.1	6.8		80 Cygni π¹...	......
5368	51 7 8.0		...	− 16.26	− 0.21	...	3	53.4	...		....	......
5369	38 24 51.9		51.5	− 16.26	− 0.17	...	3	44.2	9.9		....	22716
5370	49 33 4.8		4.9	− 16.28	− 0.21	− 0.02	3	44.4	12.9		....	......
5371	15 28 46.7		...	− 16.28	− 0.02	...	4	52.3	...		....	22727
5372	19 23 28.0		24.1	− 16.28	− 0.08	...	4	46.4	12.9		....	22729
5373	41 6 21.9		23.4	− 16.28	− 0.19	...	3	45.5	10.8		....	22726
5374	37 27 23.9		...	− 16.29	− 0.17	...	4	50.5	...		....	22737
5375	19 16 43.0		43.1	− 16.30	− 0.08	...	3	48.1	12.9		....	22741
5376	32 58 15.9		15.3	− 16.30	− 0.14	...	4	47.2	13.9		....	22742
5377	51 4 26.7		...	− 16.31	− 0.21	...	2	50.7	...		....	......
5378	38 18 4.4		5.6	− 16.32	− 0.17	...	3	44.7	9.9		....	......
5379	31 26 14.3		14.8	− 16.33	− 0.14	...	3	44.1	12.7		....	22759
5380	43 52 36.3		...	− 16.33	− 0.19	...	3	48.1	...		....	22760
5381	51 10 2.0		0.9	− 16.35	− 0.20	...	2	46.8	13.7		....	......
5382	106 49 38.5		...	− 16.35	− 0.28	+ 0.28	10	51.0	...		49 Capricorni δ	......
5383	43 50 55.3		56.4	− 16.35	− 0.18	...	5	44.6	10.7		....	22770
5384	26 59 4.7		...	− 16.36	− 0.13	...	3	48.1	...		....	22777
5385	31 55 45.3		...	− 16.36	− 0.15	...	4	48.3	...		μ Cephei	22778

Magnitude.	Estimates of Magnitude.	Mean Right Ascension 1845.0.		Precession 1845.0.	Secular Variation	Adopted Proper Motion.	Observations of R.A.		
R.		R.	G.				No.	Mean year.	
							R.	R.	G.
		h. m. s.	s.	s.	s.	s.		1800 +	
4.4	6	21 39 37.71	37.49	+ 0.887	− 0.037	+ 0.028	5	48.5	7.5
6.2	6	21 39 45.25	45.18	+ 2.102	+ 0.005	.....	3	46.1	9.8
6.5	7	21 40 7.43	7.50	+ 2.372	+ 0.006	......	5	46.1	8.9
9.5	3	21 40 11.65	...	+ 1.641	− 0.005	......	2	49.2	...
6.4	5	21 40 37.51	...	+ 1.649	− 0.005	......	3	48.7	...
4.7	4	21 40 58.67	58.42	+ 1.728	0.000	......	3	45.4	8.1
4.9	9	21 41 4.30	3.96	+ 2.206	+ 0.006	......	10	49.0	6.9
7.2	5	21 41 5.38	5.17	+ 2.116	+ 0.005	......	3	44.7	9.9
5.3	5	21 41 9.32	9.78	+ 0.780	− 0.043	− 0.016	5	44.0	8.3
7.4	6	21 41 24.08	...	+ 1.664	− 0.005	......	3	47.4	...
7.8	6	21 41 35.31	34.73	+ 2.355	+ 0.006	......	3	44.7	11.8
8.6	5	21 41 39.09	...	+ 1.735	− 0.001	......	3	50.4	...
7.2	8	21 41 53.86	53.71	+ 2.473	+ 0.006	......	6	44.9	10.9
8.5	5	21 42 5.22	...	+ 0.827	− 0.049	......	3	53.8	...
8.1	6	21 42 12.15	11.85	+ 2.471	+ 0.006	......	4	46.3	10.9
5.5	6	21 42 51.02	51.21	+ 1.767	0.000	......	4	44.8	8.8
7.6	4	21 42 51.61	...	+ 2.427	+ 0.006	......	3	50.0	...
8.1	5	21 42 56.94	56.73	+ 2.046	+ 0.005	......	4	50.3	13.8
8.2	5	21 42 59.13	...	+ 2.433	+ 0.006	......	2	53.3	...
8.8	5	21 43 5.08	4.91	+ 2.477	+ 0.006	......	3	47.4	10.9
8.3	8	21 43 13.29	...	+ 2.431	+ 0.006	......	7	51.0	...
6.6	5	21 43 20.92	20.50	+ 2.208	+ 0.006	......	5	45.8	10.7
6.1	4	21 43 22.08	...	+ 2.431	+ 0.006	......	3	49.1	...
7.2	4	21 43 23.84	...	+ 0.833	− 0.049	......	3	53.8	...
8.4	4	21 43 34.00	...	+ 2.183	+ 0.006	......	3	50.3	...
8.0	3	21 43 34.73	34.16	+ 2.183	+ 0.006	......	3	47.8	9.7
8.1	4	21 43 50.83	...	+ 2.366	+ 0.006	......	4	48.8	...
7.4	4	21 44 2.48	2.00	+ 2.471	+ 0.006	......	3	46.7	10.9
7.0	4	21 44 3.16	2.68	+ 2.369	+ 0.006	......	3	44.8	11.8
8.1	6	21 44 4.85	4.41	+ 2.075	+ 0.006	......	4	49.3	13.7
9.1	3	21 44 5.39	...	+ 0.846	− 0.042	......	3	52.2	...
8.4	5	21 44 6.23	6.29	+ 2.054	+ 0.006	......	3	48.8	13.8
8.0	3	21 44 7.90	...	+ 2.436	+ 0.006	......	2	51.2	...
8.2	3	21 44 9.51	8.90	− 2.393	− 0.451	......	3	51.4	7.7
8.8	4	21 44 11.08	10.63	+ 2.062	+ 0.006	.....	3	51.0	13.7

Ordinal Number.	Mean North Polar Distance 1845.0.			Precession 1845.0.	Secular Variation.	Adopted Proper Motion.	Observations of N.P.D.			Names.	Oeltzen-Argelander Number.
	R.	R.	G.				No. R.	Mean year. R.	Mean year. G.		
	° ′ ″		″	″	′	′		1800 +			
5386	19 24 6.7		6.6	— 16.41	— 0.07	— 0.08	13	49.7	7.5	11 Cephei......	......
5387	38 26 41.8		41.6	— 16.42	— 0.18	...	4	44.0	9.8	....	......
5388	47 39 12.1		13.4	— 16.44	— 0.20	...	3	45.8	8.9	....	......
5389	28 11 17.5		...	— 16.44	— 0.14	...	3	51.5	...	....	......
5390	28 15 9.5		...	— 16.46	— 0.14	...	3	47.2	...	....	22847
5391	29 35 34.8		35.4	— 16.48	— 0.15	...	4	43.3	8.1	10 Cephei ν ...	......
5392	41 24 21.5		21.9	— 16.48	— 0.17	...	4	43.2	6.9	81 Cygni π² ...	22854
5393	38 35 25.5		28.0	— 16.48	— 0.16	...	4	46.0	9.9	....	......
5394	18 23 23.6		24.7	— 16.49	— 0.06	...	4	43.8	8.3	78 Draconis ...	......
5395	28 24 23.8		...	— 16.50	— 0.14	...	4	47.8	...	....	22864
5396	46 42 17.5		17.2	— 16.50	— 0.19	...	4	48.0	11.8	....	......
5397	29 37 24.1		...	— 16.51	— 0.14	...	2	50.2	...	....	......
5398	51 45 41.1		43.9	— 16.52	— 0.20	...	3	45.8	10.9	....	......
5399	18 38 57.4		...	— 16.53	— 0.07	...	2	53.8	...	....	......
5400	51 38 8.6		10.8	— 16.54	— 0.20	...	4	48.7	10.9	....	......
5401	30 1 31.4		31.0	— 16.57	— 0.14	...	7	45.0	8.8	12 Cephei......	22892
5402	49 30 6.1		...	— 16.57	— 0.20	...	2	48.8	...	....	......
5403	36 19 57.3		60.7	— 16.58	— 0.17	...	3	47.8	13.8	....	22895
5404	49 41 22.9		...	— 16.58	— 0.20	...	2	49.8	...	....	......
5405	51 43 9.9		14.0	— 16.58	— 0.19	...	3	47.2	10.9	....	......
5406	49 37 21.5		...	— 16.59	— 0.20	...	4	51.7	...	....	......
5407	41 2 35.9		36.3	— 16.60	— 0.19	...	4	46.0	10.7	....	......
5408	49 34 19.3		...	— 16.60	— 0.20	...	3	48.8	...	....	......
5409	18 33 0.8		...	— 16.60	— 0.07	...	2	53.8	...	....	......
5410	40 12 31.6		...	— 16.61	— 0.18	...	3	45.0	...	....	......
5411	40 12 20.4		21.0	— 16.61	— 0.18	...	3	45.4	9.7	....	22912
5412	46 45 21.6		...	— 16.62	— 0.19	...	2	43.2	...	....	......
5413	51 16 47.6		49.8	— 16.63	— 0.20	...	3	46.4	10.9	....	......
5414	46 49 55.1		53.1	— 16.63	— 0.19	...	4	46.0	11.8	....	......
5415	36 53 54.9		54.9	— 16.63	— 0.16	...	2	51.7	13.7	....	22920
5416	18 21 22.0		...	— 16.63	— 0.07	...	2	54.4	...	....	......
5417	36 20 21.0		24.6	— 16.63	— 0.15	...	3	51.4	13.8	....	22922
5418	49 39 35.2		...	— 16.63	— 0.20	...	3	50.3	...	....	......
5419	7 47 6.7		7.2	— 16.63	+ 0.21	...	2	48.8	7.7	....	......
5420	36 31 25.8		29.5	— 16.63	— 0.17	...	3	49.7	13.7	....	22925

Ordinal Number.		Magnitude.	Estimates of Magnitude.	Mean Right Ascension 1845.0.		Precession 1845.0.	Secular Variation	Adopted Proper Motion.	Observations of R.A.		
R.	G.	R.		R.	G.				No. R.	Mean year R.	G.
				h. m. s.	s.	s.	s.	s.		1800 +	
5421	3590	6.3	4	21 44 16.04	16.34	+ 1.081	− 0.026	+ 0.016	4	50.4	8.9
5422	3588	6.8	4	21 44 20.71	20.19	+ 1.509	− 0.007	......	3	45.1	11.9
5423	3586	6.4	5	21 44 32.99	32.93	+ 2.117	+ 0.006	......	3	46.1	9.9
5424	3585	7.6	4	21 44 36.78	36.55	+ 2.226	+ 0.006	......	3	48.8	11.8
5425	3587	9.0	4	21 44 37.28	37.26	+ 2.063	+ 0.006	......	2	49.7	13.7
5426	3584	6.2	5	21 44 40.52	40.32	+ 2.471	+ 0.006	......	4	47.7	10.9
5427	...	6.1	4	21 44 46.78	...	+ 1.753	0.000	......	2	49.2	...
5428	...	5.2	5	21 44 50.45	...	+ 3.259	− 0.013	+ 0.021	9	51.7	...
5429	3589	7.7	3	21 44 53.70	53.93	+ 2.223	+ 0.006	......	4	47.5	11.5
5430	3591	7.0	2	21 45 32.28	31.60	+ 1.402	− 0.009	......	3	46.4	9.7
5431	3594	7.4	5	21 45 49.90	49.84	+ 1.520	− 0.009	......	3	49.2	11.9
5432	...	7.6	6	21 46 3.04	...	+ 2.381	+ 0.007	......	4	45.3	...
5433	3592	6.8	5	21 46 4.02	3.90	+ 2.259	+ 0.006	......	4	47.5	11.8
5434	3593	8.0	4	21 46 13.11	13.42	+ 2.257	+ 0.006	......	3	49.4	11.7
5435	...	8.4	2	21 46 21.98	...	+ 2.382	+ 0.007	......	2	52.8	...
5436	3596	8.0	7	21 46 26.06	25.91	+ 1.749	0.000	......	4	49.8	12.9
5437	3595	7.4	4	21 46 45.32	44.92	+ 2.435	+ 0.006	......	2	51.8	10.7
5438	3598	7.2	6	21 46 46.24	55.46	+ 2.019	+ 0.005	......	4	46.4	12.7
5439	3599	6.4	6	21 46 46.56	56.30	+ 2.019	+ 0.005	......	4	48.5	12.7
5440	...	7.4	5	21 46 48.02	...	− 0.244	− 0.136	......	4	51.4	...
5441	3600	6.8	6	21 47 5.47	5.34	+ 2.063	+ 0.006	......	3	45.5	12.8
5442	3601	7.1	5	21 47 11.58	11.14	+ 2.051	+ 0.006	.....	3	47.8	12.8
5443	...	7.5	3	21 47 17.64	...	+ 1.739	− 0.001	......	2	49.2	...
5444	...	11.0	1	21 47 ...	...	+ 0.949	......	......	...	...	...
5445	3603	7.7	4	21 47 25.44	25.19	+ 1.572	− 0.003	......	3	49.7	11.9
5446	3604	8.3	5	21 47 25.45	23.92	+ 1.420	− 0.009	......	3	50.4	9.7
5447	3608	7.0	3	21 47 44.52	44.55	+ 1.503	− 0.009	......	3	45.4	14.8
5448	3607	7.0	4	21 47 45.57	45.02	+ 1.563	− 0.003	......	3	47.1	14.8
5449	3602	7.7	15	21 47 49.87	48.80	+ 0.949	− 0.034	......	8	49.7	12.7
5450	3606	6.5	6	21 47 53.89	53.54	+ 2.011	+ 0.005	......	5	45.8	8.7
5451	3605	6.5	5	21 47 54.14	54.13	+ 2.094	+ 0.006	......	4	47.6	13.7
5452	...	8.4	5	21 48 1.94	...	+ 0.925	− 0.037	......	3	53.7	...
5453	3609	6.9	6	21 48 10.81	10.55	+ 1.703	0.000	......	5	48.9	13.9
5454	...	9.2	6	21 48 59.94	...	+ 1.722	− 0.002	......	4	54.0	...
5455	3615	8.5	6	21 49 10.87	10.01	+ 0.954	− 0.031	......	3	48.8	12.7

Ordinal Number.	Mean North Polar Distance 1845.0.			Precession 1845.0.	Secular Variation.	Adopted Proper Motion.	Observations of N.P.D.			Names.	Oeltzen-Argelander Number.
							No.	Mean year.			
R.	R.		G.				R.	R.	G.		
	° ′ ″		″	″	″	″		1800 +			
5421	20 34	2.5	1.2	— 16.64	— 0.08	...	3	44.1	8.9	....	22931
5422	25 33	0.8	1.7	— 16.64	— 0.11	...	3	44.4	11.9	....	....
5423	38 1	29.3	29.4	— 16.65	— 0.17	...	4	44.8	9.9	....	....
5424	41 24	51.6	50.7	— 16.65	— 0.17	...	3	45.1	11.8	....	....
5425	36 28	53.8	55.9	— 16.65	— 0.14	...	3	47.8	13.7	....	22938
5426	51 11	13.8	15.5	— 16.66	— 0.20	...	4	47.2	10.9	....	....
5427	29 26	52.3	...	— 16.66	— 0.14	+ 0.09	3	43.1	...	....	22941
5428	104 16	42.9	...	— 16.66	— 0.26	— 0.02	2	50.7	...	51 Capricorni μ	....
5429	41 17	6.1	6.1	— 16.66	— 0.17	...	4	45.8	11.5	....	....
5430	23 55	38.7	38.2	— 16.70	— 0.10	...	3	42.4	9.7	....	22954
5431	25 29	19.3	23.3	— 16.71	— 0.10	...	3	45.1	11.9	....	....
5432	46 56	34.5	...	— 16.73	— 0.19	...	3	47.4	...	....	....
5433	42 17	20.9	21.5	— 16.73	— 0.18	...	4	45.3	11.8	....	22970
5434	42 10	39.0	38.1	— 16.73	— 0.18	...	2	44.3	11.7	....	22973
5435	46 57	15.2	...	— 16.74	— 0.19	...	2	43.3	...	....	....
5436	29 6	33.8	35.9	— 16.74	— 0.12	...	4	45.5	12.9	....	22980
5437	49 7	24.0	25.3	— 16.76	— 0.19	...	3	45.8	10.7	....	....
5438	34 56	7.8	7.6	— 16.76	— 0.16	...	3	44.1	12.7	....	....
5439	34 55	47.7	50.1	— 16.76	— 0.16	...	3	44.2	12.7	....	....
5440	12 29	15.3	...	— 16.76	+ 0.02	...	2	47.8	...	....	22994
5441	36 2	44.1	42.8	— 16.78	— 0.17	...	3	43.1	12.8	....	23000
5442	35 41	17.9	17.6	— 16.78	— 0.16	...	3	45.0	12.8	....	....
5443	28 47	3.2	...	— 16.78	— 0.13	...	2	44.8	...	....	23002
5444	18 58	6.9	...	— 16.78	— 0.07	...	3	52.7	...	....	....
5445	26 0	21.7	22.7	— 16.79	— 0.11	...	3°	47.4	11.9	....	23008
5446	23 53	16.2	16.0	— 16.79	— 0.10	...	4	49.3	9.7	....	23005
5447	24 58	25.8	26.5	— 16.81	— 0.11	...	3	47.8	14.8	....	23011
5448	25 49	39.7	36.5	— 16.81	— 0.11	...	3	47.1	14.8	....	23012
5449	18 57	44.0	47.3	— 16.81	— 0.06	...	12	51.9	12.7	....	....
5450	34 31	0.8	10.9	— 16.82	— 0.16	...	5	45.3	8.7	....	23016
5451	36 43	55.0	53.9	— 16.82	— 0.17	+ 0.02	3	45.1	13.7	....	23015
5452	18 44	43.6	...	— 16.82	— 0.07	...	2	53.8	...	....	....
5453	28 1	0.5	2.0	— 16.83	— 0.13	...	4	46.0	13.9	....	....
5454	28 8	37.7	...	— 16.89	— 0.13	...	3	48.5	...	....	....
5455	18 50	39.2	41.0	— 16.88	— 0.08	...	3	50.4	12.7	....	23052

Ordinal Number.		Magnitude.	Estimates of Magnitude.	Mean Right Ascension 1845.0.			Precession 1845.0.	Secular Variation	Adopted Proper Motion.	Observations of R.A.		
R.	G.	R.	R.	R.		G.				No.	Mean year.	
										R.	R.	G.
				h. m. s.		s.	s.	s.	s.		1800 +	
5456	3610	7.5	6	21 49 13.59		13.35	+ 2.303	+ 0.008	......	5	49.1	9.8
5457	3612	6.9	5	21 49 21.25		20.98	+ 1.720	0.000	......	3	44.4	13.9
5458	3613	7.7	11	21 49 26.14		25.82	+ 1.721	0.000	......	9	48.3	13.9
5459	3611	6.7	6	21 49 29.28		28.76	+ 2.107	+ 0.006	......	4	43.9	13.7
5460	3616	8.5	6	21 49 40.49		40.29	+ 1.785	+ 0.002	......	3	50.1	12.9
5461	...	5.8	4	21 49 40.81		...	+ 2.007	+ 0.006	− 0.001	4	47.5	...
5462	...	7.2	6	21 49 41.17		...	+ 1.342	− 0.020	......	3	51.4	...
5463	3614	8.4	4	21 49 44.30		44.13	+ 2.100	+ 0.006	......	2	48.7	13.7
5464	3620	8.2	5	21 49 53.15		53.08	+ 0.996	− 0.031	......	3	50.4	12.7
5465	...	7.5	2	21 49 55.97		...	+ 2.157	+ 0.006	......	3	51.4	...
5466	...	7.2	2	21 50 2.34		...	+ 0.892	− 0.038	......	2	48.7	...
5467	...	7.6	5	21 50 2.52		...	+ 3.241	− 0.012	......	8	47.7	...
5468	3617	6.4	2	21 50 2.90		2.65	+ 2.134	+ 0.007	......	3	44.7	11.8
5469	...	7.1	2	21 50 3.94		...	+ 1.204	− 0.020	......	2	50.2	...
5470	3618	8.5	3	21 50 14.64		14.15	+ 2.308	+ 0.008	......	4	50.2	11.8
5471	3619	8.1	4	21 50 26.08		25.66	+ 2.308	+ 0.008	......	3	46.1	11.0
5472	3621	6.1	3	21 50 42.27		42.17	+ 1.791	+ 0.002	......	3	45.5	12.8
5473	3625	6.9	3	21 50 45.71		45.38	+ 0.964	− 0.031	......	3	47.5	12.7
5474	3622	8.3	4	21 50 54.12		54.18	+ 2.133	+ 0.007	......	2	48.7	13.8
5475	3631	6.7	3	21 50 56.26		56.45	+ 0.740	− 0.050	......	2	50.8	8.8
5476	...	6.6	5	21 51 1.44		...	+ 2.335	+ 0.008	......	3	49.7	...
5477	3629	7.3	4	21 51 14.83		14.84	+ 1.544	− 0.003	......	3	51.1	14.8
5478	3624	8.9	6	21 51 15.14		15.39	+ 2.134	+ 0.008	......	3	51.3	13.8
5479	3623	7.9	6	21 51 22.78		22.66	+ 2.418	+ 0.008	......	4	46.2	10.9
5480	...	8.5	2	21 51 23.59		...	+ 1.549	− 0.003	......	3	53.8	...
5481	...	6.1	3	21 51 27.02		...	+ 1.574	− 0.003	......	2	51.2	...
5482	3626	7.4	2	21 51 30.69		30.76	+ 2.230	+ 0.008	......	2	46.7	10.7
5483	...	6.9	4	21 51 33.80		...	+ 1.885	+ 0.003	......	4	52.3	...
5484	3627	8.0	4	21 51 36.38		36.43	+ 2.316	+ 0.008	......	3	50.1	11.0
5485	3628	7.7	6	21 51 44.69		44.40	+ 2.422	+ 0.008	......	3	47.4	10.8
5486	...	8.2	2	21 51 47.11		...	+ 1.890	+ 0.003	......	2	52.3	...
5487	3630	7.7	4	21 51 54.59		54.15	+ 2.420	+ 0.008	......	3	49.3	10.9
5488	3632	8.5	4	21 52 5.72		5.38	+ 2.232	+ 0.009	......	2	48.8	10.7
5489	3633	4.7	3	21 52 16.90		17.07	+ 1.689	− 0.001	+ 0.013	5	45.2	9.9
5490	3634	7.6	4	21 52 34.75		34.94	+ 1.820	+ 0.002	......	2	48.2	12.9

Ordinal Number.	Mean North Polar Distance 1845.0.		Precession 1845.0.	Secular Variation.	Adopted Proper Motion.	Observations of N.P.D.			Names.	Oeltzen-Argelander Number.
R.	R.	G.				No. R.	Mean year. R.	G.		
	° ′ ″	″	″	″	″		1800 +			
5456	43 16 54.4	53.4	— 16.88	— 0.18	...	3	43.7	9.8	....	....
5457	28 7 0.4	4.2	— 16.89	— 0.14	...	4	44.8	13.9	....	....
5458	28 7 52.2	53.0	— 16.89	— 0.14	...	4	45.8	13.9	....	....
5459	36 48 3.1	4.5	— 16.89	— 0.16	...	4	46.3	13.7	....	23064
5460	29 15 2.2	3.7	— 16.89	— 0.14	...	3	50.4	12.9	....	....
5461	34 7 18.2	...	— 16.90	— 0.16	+ 0.05	5	46.1	...	13 Cephei......	23071
5462	22 37 23.2	...	— 16.90	— 0.10	...	4	51.8	...	....	23072
5463	36 33 20.4	20.5	— 16.90	— 0.15	...	3	47.8	13.7	....	23073
5464	19 7 16.2	18.0	— 16.90	— 0.08	...	4	51.8	12.7	....	23079
5465	38 12 18.8	...	— 16.90	— 0.16	...	3	51.4	...	....	....
5466	18 14 28.8	...	— 16.91	— 0.07	...	2	48.2	...	....	....
5467	103 24 14.8	...	— 16.91	— 0.25	— 0.05	4	46.8	...	....	....
5468	37 29 26.7	26.9	— 16.91	— 0.16	...	4	45.2	11.8	....	23080
5469	21 2 6.3	...	— 16.91	— 0.09	...	2	50.3	...	....	....
5470	43 15 56.0	55.0	— 16.92	— 0.17	...	2	46.8	11.8	....	23084
5471	43 14 2.2	0.2	— 16.93	— 0.17	...	2	46.8	11.0	....	23089
5472	29 11 32.9	33.3	— 16.95	— 0.14	...	3	44.3	12.3	....	23095
5473	18 44 31.5	32.3	— 16.95	— 0.07	...	3	44.8	12.7	....	23096
5474	37 18 38.0	41.2	— 16.95	— 0.16	...	2	50.8	13.3	....	23098
5475	17 1 50.2	53.9	— 16.96	— 0.06	...	3	42.8	8.3	79 Draconis A	23103
5476	44 8 37.4	...	— 16.96	— 0.18	...	4	49.2	...	....	....
5477	25 0 37.8	38.2	— 16.97	— 0.11	...	3	46.7	14.3	....	23115
5478	37 16 30.3	28.3	— 16.97	— 0.16	...	3	52.4	13.3	....	23112
5479	47 31 5.1	6.0	— 16.97	— 0.18	...	4	45.8	10.9	....	....
5480	25 3 57.5	...	— 16.97	— 0.12	...	1	53.8	...	....	23117
5481	25 24 51.4	...	— 16.97	— 0.12	...	3	51.5	...	....	23121
5482	40 14 50.9	51.5	— 16.98	— 0.16	...	2	44.7	10.7	....	23124
5483	30 56 25.7	...	— 16.98	— 0.15	...	3	52.5	...	....	23127
5484	43 18 51.7	50.7	— 16.98	— 0.17	...	3	45.8	11.0	....	23130
5485	47 35 15.9	16.5	— 16.99	— 0.18	...	4	49.8	10.8	....	....
5486	31 6 2.4	...	— 16.99	— 0.15	...	2	53.3	...	....	23138
5487	47 29 54.9	57.4	— 17.00	— 0.18	...	2	44.8	10.9	....	....
5488	40 10 32.5	33.2	— 17.01	— 0.16	...	3	47.4	10.7	....	23143
5489	27 6 40.5	40.7	— 17.02	— 0.12	...	4	44.5	9.9	....	....
5490	29 26 33.4	33.0	— 17.03	— 0.13	...	3	48.8	12.9	....	23151

Ordinal Number.		Magnitude.	Estimates of Magnitude.	Mean Right Ascension 1845.0.		Precession 1845.0.	Secular Variation	Adopted Proper Motion.	Observations of R.A.		
R.	G.	R.	R.	R.	G.				No. R.	Mean year. R.	G.
				h. m. s.	s.	s.	s.	s.		1800 +	
5491	...	8.0	1	21 52 43.55	...	+ 3.243	− 0.012	......	2	55.7	...
5492	3635	7.5	5	21 52 50.36	50.34	+ 1.569	− 0.003	......	4	47.5	14.8
5493	3636	7.2	9	21 53 2.11	1.42	+ 1.542	− 0.004	......	5	49.9	14.8
5494	3637	6.2	5	21 53 13.45	13.43	+ 1.534	− 0.005	......	3	46.8	14.9
5495	3639	6.4	4	21 53 25.90	26.02	+ 1.538	− 0.005	......	3	49.1	14.9
5496	...	8.5	2	21 53 30.38	...	+ 2.512	+ 0.008	......	2	52.3	...
5497	3638	7.6	6	21 53 46.29	46.16	+ 2.283	+ 0.009	......	3	45.4	11.8
5498	3648	6.9	5	21 53 46.81	46.03	− 0.469	− 0.175	......	2	51.3	12.7
5499	...	6.7	3	21 54 11.71	...	+ 1.999	+ 0.006	+ 0.019	2	47.7	...
5500	3642	7.4	6	21 54 16.26	15.78	+ 1.816	+ 0.002	......	2	49.2	12.8
5501	3644	5.9	4	21 54 19.69	19.70	+ 1.762	+ 0.001	......	3	44.4	14.9
5502	...	9.6	3	21 54 19.77	...	+ 2.419	+ 0.008	......	2	53.7	...
5503	...	7.4	4	21 54 22.46	...	+ 2.510	+ 0.008	......	3	52.1	...
5504	3641	8.9	5	21 54 23.41	23.07	+ 2.134	+ 0.007	......	3	51.0	13.7
5505	3640	7.8	5	21 54 27.93	27.67	+ 2.288	+ 0.009	......	3	45.4	11.8
5506	3643	7.8	7	21 54 30.24	30.12	+ 2.134	+ 0.008	......	3	51.1	13.7
5507	...	7.1	3	21 54 35.08	...	+ 2.517	+ 0.008	......	2	52.2	...
5508	3645	7.7	1	21 54 37.36	37.07	+ 2.130	+ 0.008	......	2	49.3	13.9
5509	3646	8.7	3	21 54 48.01	48.69	+ 1.763	+ 0.003	......	2	51.3	14.9
5510	...	6.0	1	21 55 7.12	...	+ 3.158	− 0.009	+ 0.003	4	45.0	...
5511	...	8.9	5	21 55 13.21	...	+ 2.421	+ 0.008	......	3	51.7	...
5512	...	8.7	1	21 55 14.59	...	+ 2.517	+ 0.008	......	1	52.6	...
5513	3649	9.4	5	21 55 23.51	23.03	+ 2.138	+ 0.009	......	3	51.7	13.7
5514	3650	7.7	8	21 55 49.21	49.57	+ 2.414	+ 0.009	......	5	46.2	10.7
5515	...	6.8	6	21 55 53.32	...	+ 1.613	− 0.009	......	4	50.8	...
5516	3651	8.7	3	21 55 57.96	58.02	+ 2.148	+ 0.009	......	2	48.7	13.7
5517	3654	6.9	8	21 56 1.23	1.63	+ 1.789	+ 0.006	......	4	49.2	14.9
5518	3652	5.9	5	21 56 10.19	10.09	+ 2.186	+ 0.009	......	4	47.7	8.8
5519	3660	6.3	2	21 56 19.82	19.64	+ 0.634	− 0.059	......	2	49.9	12.8
5520	...	7.9	4	21 56 22.95	...	+ 2.518	+ 0.008	......	3	51.1	...
5521	3653	7.2	3	21 56 22.88	22.61	+ 2.450	+ 0.008	......	4	47.3	10.9
5522	3667	6.4	3	21 56 32.61	31.88	− 0.657	− 0.206	......	3	51.5	12.7
5523	3656	8.0	3	21 56 39.10	39.05	+ 1.843	+ 0.006	......	2	48.7	12.9
5524	3655	6.3	5	21 56 41.74	41.44	+ 2.411	+ 0.009	......	7	49.6	11.9
5525	...	7.3	3	21 56 45.07	...	+ 2.482	+ 0.008	......	2	47.2	...

Ordinal Number.	Mean North Polar Distance 1845.0.		Precession 1845.0.	Secular Variation.	Adopted Proper Motion	Observations of N.P.D.			Names.	Oeltzen Argelander Number.
R.	R.	G.				No. R.	Mean year. R.	Mean year. G.		
	° ′ ″	″	″	″	″		1800 +			
5491	103 45 52.2	...	− 17.04	− 0.25	...	1	46.8	...	....	......
5492	25 8 38.6	40.8	− 17.04	− 0.11	...	3	44.4	14.8	....	23159
5493	24 42 43.4	46.0	− 17.05	− 0.11	...	6	43.6	14.8	....	......
5494	24 34 57.0	56.9	− 17.06	− 0.10	...	3	44.4	14.9	....	......
5495	24 35 59.8	62.3	− 17.07	− 0.10	...	3	43.8	14.9	....	......
5496	51 30 31.0	...	− 17.08	− 0.20	...	2	53.3	...	....	......
5497	41 37 3.9	3.3	− 17.09	− 0.17	...	3	44.0	11.8	....	23181
5498	11 10 58.9	62.6	− 17.09	+ 0.04	...	3	47.6	12.7	....	23189
5499	33 4 56.9	...	− 17.11	− 0.15	− 0.02	4	48.0	...	....	23204
5500	29 4 41.8	42.2	− 17.11	− 0.13	...	4	48.8	12.8	....	23207
5501	28 2 38.4	39.4	− 17.12	− 0.13	...	5	45.6	14.9	....	23212
5502	46 56 25.3	...	− 17.12	− 0.18	...	1	53.8	...	....	......
5503	51 13 0.1	...	− 17.12	− 0.19	...	2	52.8	...	....	......
5504	36 40 6.8	7.0	− 17.12	− 0.16	...	2	48.7	13.7	....	23213
5505	41 41 25.9	28.0	− 17.12	− 0.17	...	4	47.8	11.8	....	23215
5506	36 38 2.8	1.8	− 17.12	− 0.16	...	4	47.3	13.7	....	23218
5507	51 29 49.6	...	− 17.13	− 0.20	...	2	52.3	...	....	......
5508	35 43 22.1	20.3	− 17.13	− 0.16	...	2	51.3	13.9	....	......
5509	27 58 55.7	58.8	− 17.14	− 0.14	...	2	44.3	14.9	....	23228
5510	97 16 8.0	...	− 17.15	− 0.24	...	2	48.2	...	30 Aquarii.....	......
5511	46 51 16.9	...	− 17.16	− 0.18	...	3	52.7	...	....	......
5512	51 29 ...	...	......	...	...	...	...	...	....	......
5513	36 35 4.6	4.8	− 17.16	− 0.15	...	2	52.3	13.7	....	......
5514	46 24 13.6	6.8	− 17.18	− 0.17	...	4	47.5	10.7	....	......
5515	25 18 38.3	...	− 17.18	− 0.12	...	3	43.4	...	....	23260
5516	36 45 2.2	0.0	− 17.19	− 0.15	...	2	49.8	13.7	....	23261
5517	28 15 23.9	24.8	− 17.19	− 0.12	...	6	48.5	14.9	....	23266
5518	37 51 48.6	49.1	− 17.20	− 0.16	...	3	46.3	8.8	....	......
5519	15 44 43.5	43.4	− 17.20	− 0.05	...	4	42.7	12.8	....	23273
5520	51 11 1.7	...	− 17.21	− 0.19	...	2	51.3	...	....	......
5521	47 55 54.7	57.5	− 17.21	− 0.18	...	3	45.9	10.9	....	......
5522	10 25 49.6	50.0	− 17.22	+ 0.05	...	4	47.7	12.7	....	23278
5523	29 11 23.1	22.1	− 17.22	− 0.13	...	3	47.1	12.9	....	......
5524	46 5 44.6	44.5	− 17.22	− 0.17	...	5	43.9	11.9	....	......
5525	49 20 25.5	...	− 17.22	− 0.18	...	2	45.2	...	....	......

Magnitude.	Estimates of Magnitude.	Mean Right Ascension 1845.0.		Precession 1845.0.	Secular Variation	Adopted Proper Motion.
R.	R.	R.	G.			
		h. m. s.	s.	s.	s.	s.
5.7	1	21 56 48.92	...	+ 3.090	− 0.006	......
5.8	6	21 56 52.28	51.94	+ 2.006	+ 0.007	......
7.5	6	21 56 53.28	52.57	+ 2.005	+ 0.007	......
8.8	6	21 56 57.46	56.91	+ 1.581	− 0.003	......
5.0	3	21 57 0.47	0.68	+ 0.909	− 0.039	......
8.6	7	21 57 7.82	7.84	+ 2.413	+ 0.009	......
7.7	5	21 57 33.76	33.34	+ 2.413	+ 0.009	......
7.6	3	21 57 35.79	35.19	+ 2.416	+ 0.009	......
7.6	3	21 57 48.87	48.83	+ 2.130	+ 0.008	......
3.0	A	21 57 49.29	...	+ 3.083	− 0.006	− 0.003
6.8	5	21 57 49.59	49.41	+ 2.423	+ 0.009	......
7.9	6	21 58 2.84	2.72	+ 1.609	− 0.003	......
4.7	5	21 58 3.66	...	+ 3.247	− 0.013	− 0.001
6.6	4	21 58 40.89	40.52	+ 1.601	− 0.003	......
6.5	3	21 58 48.35	47.89	+ 2.360	+ 0.009	......
6.3	5	21 58 51.01	50.82	+ 1.945	+ 0.006	......
6.3	4	21 59 7.46	7.79	+ 2.373	+ 0.009	......
6.6	5	21 59 9.94	9.55	+ 1.945	+ 0.006	......
7.9	4	21 59 13.76	...	+ 1.947	+ 0.005	......
4.7	4	21 59 14.42	13.96	+ 1.786	+ 0.003	......
7.0	6	21 59 17.80	...	+ 1.700	0.000	......
7.3	5	21 59 18.42	18.84	+ 2.242	+ 0.009	......
5.2	3	21 59 18.43	18.15	+ 1.700	0.000	+ 0.037
7.8	5	21 59 23.90	...	+ 1.945	+ 0.005	......
6.9	6	21 59 34.41	34.01	+ 2.414	+ 0.009	......
7.4	3	21 59 35.73	...	+ 2.433	+ 0.008	......
8.2	3	21 59 39.67	39.36	+ 2.430	− 0.009	......
5.6	9	21 59 45.77	45.47	+ 2.418	+ 0.009	......
6.5	5	21 59 46.89	47.10	+ 2.340	+ 0.009	......
8.3	5	21 59 49.19	...	+ 1.881	+ 0.005	......
7.8	3	21 59 50.91	50.65	+ 1.883	+ 0.006	......
6.7	5	21 59 56.25	55.99	+ 2.413	+ 0.009	......
8.5	4	21 59 58.60	58.32	+ 1.647	− 0.002	......
8.8	5	22 0 0.55	59.26	+ 1.637	− 0.002	......
4.8	6	22 0 17.97	17.47	+ 1.814	+ 0.003	......

Ordinal Number.	Mean North Polar Distance 1845.0.			Precession 1845.0.	Secular Variation.	Adopted Proper Motion.	Observations of N.P.D.			Names.	Oeltzen-Argelander Number.
							No.	Mean year.			
R.	R.		G.				R.	R.	G.		
	° ′ ″		″	″	″	″		1800 +			
5526	91 39 15.3		...	− 17.23	− 0.23	...	2	56.8	...	32 Aquarii......	......
5527	32 44 46.2		45.8	− 17.23	− 0.15	...	5	44.3	9.1	14 Cephei......	23285
5528	32 41 50.4		51.1	− 17.23	− 0.15	...	5	46.7	9.8	....	23286
5529	24 39 47.3		49.9	− 17.24	− 0.12	...	3	50.8	13.8	....	......
5530	17 33 26.7		28.3	− 17.24	− 0.07	+ 0.19	6	45.9	7.8	16 Cephei......	23292
5531	46 5 27.7		33.3	− 17.24	− 0.17	...	3	51.4	11.8	....	......
5532	46 1 23.2		23.3	− 17.26	− 0.17	...	3	44.7	11.9	....	......
5533	46 9 28.6		27.7	− 17.26	− 0.17	...	3	43.8	11.9	....	......
5534	35 52 7.2		7.6	− 17.27	− 0.15	...	3	47.1	14.4	....	23306
5535	91 4 15.3		...	− 17.27	− 0.27	+ 0.02	4	49.8	...	34 Aquarii α...	......
5536	46 24 14.3		15.9	− 17.27	− 0.17	...	4	47.0	10.7	....	......
5537	24 54 37.0		37.8	− 17.28	− 0.12	...	3	51.4	13.8	....	......
5538	104 37 9.1		...	− 17.28	− 0.24	+ 0.07	9	51.3	...	33 Aquarii ι...	......
5539	24 41 8.1		12.8	− 17.31	− 0.12	...	3	45.8	13.7	....	......
5540	43 31 5.0		6.7	− 17.32	− 0.17	...	3	45.1	10.9	....	23331
5541	30 56 7.8		8.8	− 17.32	− 0.14	...	5	44.4	9.9	15 Cephei......	23334
5542	44 0 21.7		21.6	− 17.33	− 0.17	...	3	46.8	14.9	....	23343
5543	30 53 1.0		1.4	− 17.33	− 0.14	...	4	44.5	9.9	....	23346
5544	30 55 13.2		...	− 17.34	− 0.14	...	4	47.6	...	....	23355
5545	27 37 59.5		60.4	− 17.34	− 0.14	...	6	46.1	9.9	18 Cephei......	23356
5546	26 7 32.7		...	− 17.34	− 0.13	...	5	48.0	...	17 Cephei ξ (1st)	23357
5547	39 2 59.4		60.3	− 17.34	− 0.16	...	3	49.4	14.9	....	......
5548	26 7 33.4		33.9	− 17.34	− 0.13	− 0.08	3	48.2	6.8	17 Cephei ξ (2d)	23358
5549	30 50 22.6		...	− 17.34	− 0.14	...	4	46.7	...	....	23360
5550	45 38 23.3		22.9	− 17.35	− 0.17	...	4	48.6	11.8	....	......
5551	46 27 53.0		...	− 17.35	− 0.18	...	2	46.8	...	....	......
5552	46 17 51.0		54.1	− 17.36	− 0.18	...	3	47.8	11.9	....	......
5553	45 44 15.8		17.1	− 17.36	− 0.18	...	3	49.1	11.8	....	......
5554	42 31 17.4		16.7	− 17.36	− 0.17	...	4	50.8	14.9	....	23367
5555	29 23 32.1		...	− 17.36	− 0.13	...	3	51.1	...	....	......
5556	29 24 52.9		54.3	− 17.36	− 0.13	...	4	49.3	12.9	....	......
5557	45 30 14.6		15.0	− 17.37	− 0.18	...	3	47.2	11.8	....	......
5558	25 9 50.9		52.0	− 17.37	− 0.12	...	2	51.8	13.9	....	23374
5559	25 0 44.4		49.6	− 17.37	− 0.12	...	3	52.5	13.8	....	......
5560	27 58 10.4		10.6	− 17.38	− 0.13	− 0.04	3	43.7	9.2	20 Cephei......	23389

Ordinal Number.		Magnitude.	Estimates of Magnitude.	Mean Right Ascension 1845.0.			Precession 1845.0.	Secular Variation	Adopted Proper Motion.	Observations of R.A.		
R.	G.	R.		R.	G.					No. R.	Mean year. R.	G.
				h. m. s.	s.		s.	s.	s.		1800 +	
5561	3686	5.1	5	22 0 22.32	21.96		+ 1.841	+ 0.003	......	4	48.3	9.8
5562	3688	8.2	8	22 0 29.89	30.03		+ 1.649	− 0.002	......	5	51.3	13.8
5563	...	9.1	4	22 0 45.48	...		+ 1.839	+ 0.003	......	3	53.4	...
5564	3687	6.9	7	22 0 49.62	49.80		+ 2.248	+ 0.009	......	4	49.2	14.9
5565	3689	7.8	6	22 1 6.89	8.59		+ 2.210	+ 0.009	......	4	44.8	12.7
5566	...	8.4	4	22 1 32.92	...		+ 2.011	+ 0.006	......	3	49.8	...
5567	3690	6.2	8	22 1 41.70	41.57		+ 2.209	+ 0.009	......	5	46.5	12.7
5568	3691	6.4	5	22 1 56.53	56.54		+ 2.012	+ 0.007	......	4	44.3	8.8
5569	...	8.3	5	22 2 2.42	...		+ 2.103	+ 0.007	......	3	52.1	...
5570	3693	7.9	4	22 2 30.30	30.04		+ 2.104	+ 0.008	......	3	47.2	12.8
5571	3692	6.8	4	22 2 33.50	33.19		+ 2.363	+ 0.009	......	3	44.8	10.7
5572	3695	9.0	5	22 3 1.46	1.07		+ 1.922	+ 0.006	......	2	48.3	7.7
5573	...	8.1	5	22 3 9.72	...		+ 1.901	+ 0.005	......	3	48.1	...
5574	3694	6.9	6	22 3 20.56	20.29		+ 2.474	+ 0.009	......	3	44.1	10.9
5575	...	7.1	4	22 3 21.36	...		+ 2.006	+ 0.008	+ 0.017	3	48.7	...
5576	3696	8.5	4	22 3 22.98	22.91		+ 1.927	+ 0.006	......	2	48.7	12.9
5577	...	7.2	3	22 3 23.42	...		+ 2.006	+ 0.008	......	2	50.3	...
5578	3707	7.2	2	22 3 28.59	30.49		− 1.634	− 0.398	......	3	47.8	7.8
5579	3697	7.8	5	22 3 29.75	29.54		+ 1.920	+ 0.006	......	4	50.2	12.9
5580	3709	7.4	2	22 3 34.92	36.63		− 1.630	− 0.397	......	2	48.8	7.8
5581	...	7.5	5	22 3 44.06	...		+ 2.027	+ 0.008	+ 0.018	4	48.6	...
5582	3698	7.5	5	22 3 44.61	44.64		+ 1.933	+ 0.006	......	3	51.4	12.9
5583	3701	7.3	5	22 3 50.51	50.77		+ 1.134	− 0.023	......	4	46.3	13.9
5584	...	8.0	5	22 3 54.93	...		+ 1.775	+ 0.003	......	2	49.8	...
5585	3702	7.0	4	22 4 16.04	16.00		+ 1.125	− 0.023	......	3	48.1	13.9
5586	3699	7.6	5	22 4 24.85	24.89		+ 2.374	+ 0.010	......	3	44.8	10.7
5587	...	8.5	4	22 4 33.38	...		+ 2.296	+ 0.010	......	3	53.5	...
5588	3700	6.2	5	22 4 37.44	37.32		+ 2.484	+ 0.009	......	6	48.7	10.9
5589	...	7.7	4	22 4 40.20	...		+ 2.540	+ 0.008	......	4	51.8	...
5590	3704	6.9	4	22 5 6.24	5.70		+ 1.790	+ 0.004	......	3	47.4	9.8
5591	3703	5.7	6	22 5 8.93	8.14		+ 2.303	+ 0.010	......	3	44.5	9.2
5592	3711	7.4	5	22 5 17.03	16.25		+ 0.835	− 0.051	......	2	46.9	12.7
5593	3705	8.1	5	22 5 22.80	22.50		+ 2.263	+ 0.010	......	3	47.5	11.4
5594	3706	3.9	4	22 5 29.01	28.75		+ 2.067	+ 0.009	......	5	45.0	6.9
5595	3708	7.4	6	22 5 46.53	46.20		+ 2.262	+ 0.010	......	4	48.0	11.6

Ordinal Number. R.	Mean North Polar Distance 1845.0. R.	G.	Precession 1845.0.	Secular Variation.	Adopted Proper Motion.	Observations of N.P.D. No. R.	Mean year. R. 1800 +	G.	Names.	Oeltzen-Argelander Number.
5561	28 28 22.9	24.5	− 17.38	− 0.13	...	4	46.3	9.8	19 Cephei......	23390
5562	25 6 28.3	26.5	− 17.39	− 0.12	...	3	51.8	13.8	....	23401
5563	28 29 30.1	...	− 17.40	− 0.13	...	3	44.2	...	....	23420
5564	38 56 53.5	55.8	− 17.40	− 0.15	...	3	46.4	14.9	....	23424
5565	37 36 35.6	23.3	− 17.42	− 0.15	...	3	49.5	12.7	....	23438
5566	31 56 15.0	...	− 17.44	− 0.14	...	2	44.3	...	....	23448
5567	37 26 54.9	52.1	− 17.44	− 0.15	...	3	45.1	12.7	....	23452
5568	31 54 51.2	51.7	− 17.45	− 0.14	+ 0.04	3	44.5	8.8	....	23459
5569	34 14 53.2	...	− 17.46	− 0.15	...	3	51.1	...	....	23462
5570	34 10 46.5	45.7	− 17.48	− 0.15	...	2	49.8	12.8	....	23480
5571	42 49 25.3	23.9	− 17.48	− 0.17	...	3	44.7	10.7	....	23481
5572	29 38 5.1	5.3	− 17.50	− 0.13	...	4	50.0	7.7	....	23496
5573	29 10 5.9	...	− 17.50	− 0.13	...	2	46.3	...	....	......
5574	47 34 21.7	23.3	− 17.51	− 0.18	...	3	43.5	10.9	....	......
5575	31 27 53.7	...	− 17.51	− 0.14	− 0.01	3	47.8	...	....	23515
5576	29 40 35.2	35.5	− 17.51	− 0.13	...	2	49.3	12.9	....	23516
5577	31 28 10.3	...	− 17.51	− 0.14	...	3	47.8	...	....	23517
5578	7 52 42.1	40.4	− 17.52	+ 0.12	...	6	44.0	7.8	....	......
5579	29 30 34.1	33.8	− 17.52	− 0.13	...	3	48.5	12.9	....	23519
5580	7 52 38.9	40.3	− 17.52	+ 0.12	...	5	42.7	7.8	....	......
5581	31 54 25.8	...	− 17.53	− 0.14	− 0.08	3	46.8	...	....	23527
5582	29 44 12.8	11.4	− 17.53	− 0.13	...	3	49.1	12.9	....	23529
5583	18 31 52.2	51.1	− 17.53	− 0.08	...	4	42.9	13.9	....	23538
5584	26 36 16.0	...	− 17.54	− 0.12	...	3	51.7	...	....	......
5585	18 23 16.1	14.0	− 17.55	− 0.08	...	3	43.7	13.9	....	23553
5586	42 50 48.9	48.8	− 17.56	− 0.16	...	3	44.4	10.7	....	23557
5587	39 57 28.4	...	− 17.56	− 0.16	...	3	44.1	...	....	23563
5588	47 43 48.1	49.3	− 17.57	− 0.17	...	5	45.5	10.9	....	......
5589	50 35 35.4	...	− 17.57	− 0.18	...	3	51.5	...	....	......
5590	26 38 19.1	20.0	− 17.59	− 0.13	...	4	45.3	9.8	....	23590
5591	39 56 26.5	28.5	− 17.59	− 0.16	...	4	45.2	9.2	....	23591
5592	16 1 30.4	30.2	− 17.60	− 0.07	...	3	47.8	12.7	....	23605
5593	38 27 0.6	0.9	− 17.60	− 0.15	...	3	46.1	11.4	....	23606
5594	32 33 41.0	41.2	− 17.60	− 0.14	...	5	43.2	6.9	21 Cephei ζ ...	23609
5595	38 20 0.5	59.1	− 17.62	− 0.15	...	4	43.3	11.6	....	23620

Magnitude.	Estimates of Magnitude.	Mean Right Ascension 1845.0.		Precession 1845.0	Secular Variation	Adopted Proper Motion.
R.	R.	R.	G.			
		h. m. s.	s.	s.	s.	s.
7.1	2	22 5 55.50	...	+ 2.325	+ 0.010	......
8.5	3	22 5 57.03	56.78	+ 2.175	+ 0.009	......
7.1	3	22 6 8.31	...	+ 2.386	+ 0.010	......
8.8	5	22 6 11.18	...	+ 1.844	+ 0.004	......
7.6	2	22 6 13.30	...	+ 1.840	+ 0.004	......
5.5	5	22 6 13.47	13.25	+ 2.123	+ 0.009	+ 0.023
5.2	5	22 6 15.20	15.40	+ 2.025	+ 0.009	......
7.3	5	22 6 34.58	...	+ 2.015	+ 0.008	......
6.5	5	22 6 36.41	35.71	+ 2.041	+ 0.009	......
8.0	4	22 6 40.30	40.23	+ 2.186	+ 0.009	......
5.0	6	22 6 48.87	48.26	+ 1.167	− 0.024	+ 0.003
7.7	5	22 6 51.18	...	+ 2.002	+ 0.008	......
9.2	5	22 6 52.65	...	+ 2.190	+ 0.009	......
5.6	5	22 6 54.68	...	+ 1.974	+ 0.008	......
6.1	4	22 7 5.98	5.76	+ 1.391	− 0.012	......
6.5	4	22 7 12.11	11.84	+ 1.198	− 0.022	......
5.0	2	22 7 13.90	13.65	+ 2.560	+ 0.009	......
7.5	6	22 7 17.24	...	+ 1.845	+ 0.003	......
6.0	6	22 7 27.11	26.75	+ 2.447	+ 0.009	......
5.7	5	22 7 33.07	...	+ 1.858	+ 0.005	− 0.006
7.9	4	22 7 34.41	34.37	+ 2.185	+ 0.009	......
7.3	5	22 7 39.19	...	+ 2.548	+ 0.009	......
8.2	2	22 7 40.75	40.43	+ 2.181	+ 0.009	......
8.0	5	22 7 41.77	...	+ 2.271	+ 0.010	......
7.5	6	22 7 47.31	46.86	+ 2.276	+ 0.009	......
7.4	4	22 7 50.46	50.13	+ 2.043	+ 0.008	......
8.6	2	22 8 5.71	...	+ 2.267	+ 0.010	......
6.0	5	22 8 14.13	13.77	+ 2.502	+ 0.010	......
7.3	3	22 8 29.49	29.09	+ 2.277	+ 0.009	......
9.1	4	22 8 39.03	38.89	+ 2.189	+ 0.009	......
4.9	5	22 8 39.00	...	+ 3.164	− 0.010	+ 0.006
9.4	6	22 8 41.62	...	+ 2.190	+ 0.009	......
6.3	5	22 8 57.37	...	+ 1.879	+ 0.006	− 0.005
3.9	3	22 9 20.02	20.04	+ 2.140	+ 0.010	+ 0.055
7.0	4	22 9 36.89	36.67	+ 2.465	+ 0.010	......

Ordinal Number.	Mean North Polar Distance 1845.0.		Precession 1845.0.	Secular Variation.	Adopted Proper Motion.	Observations of N.P.D.				Names.	Oeltzen Argelander Number.
R.	R.	G.				No. R.	Mean year R.	G.			
	° ′ ″	″	″	″	″		1800 +				
5596	40 34 2.6	...	− 17.62	− 0.16	...	3	52.1	...	....	23630
5597	35 29 43.8	43.5	− 17.62	− 0.14	...	2	50.3	13.7	....	....
5598	42 57 54.5	...	− 17.63	− 0.17	...	3	45.8	...	....	23637
5599	27 27 58.1	...	− 17.63	− 0.12	...	2	50.8	...	....	....
5600	27 21 50.5	...	− 17.63	− 0.12	...	2	51.8	...	....	....
5601	33 55 48.6	48.7	− 17.63	− 0.14	− 0.16	3	43.7	12.8	....	....
5602	31 20 55.4	55.3	− 17.64	− 0.14	...	3	47.4	8.7	22 Cephei λ...	....
5603	31 2 34.6	...	− 17.65	− 0.14	...	3	51.8	...	....	....
5604	31 40 59.3	62.6	− 17.65	− 0.14	...	4	48.8	12.9	....	23654
5605	35 39 59.9	59.3	− 17.65	− 0.14	...	4	48.8	13.7	....	....
5606	18 25 18.5	18.8	− 17.66	− 0.08	...	3	43.8	7.9	24 Cephei......	23664
5607	30 40 28.0	...	− 17.66	− 0.14	...	3	48.5	...	....	....
5608	35 44 4.2	...	− 17.66	− 0.15	...	3	54.1	...	....	....
5609	30 0 22.7	...	− 17.66	− 0.14	...	4	49.3	...	....	23668
5610	20 37 56.9	57.4	− 17.67	− 0.10	...	3	48.5	9.7	....	23671
5611	18 39 5.9	4.2	− 17.67	− 0.08	...	3	43.1	8.9	....	23674
5612	51 3 8.4	9.0	− 17.68	− 0.18	...	2	49.8	9.9	....	....
5613	27 16 46.3	...	− 17.68	− 0.12	...	3	52.5	...	....	....
5614	45 19 35.5	34.8	− 17.68	− 0.16	...	3	46.5	11.8	....	....
5615	27 28 26.5	...	− 17.69	− 0.13	− 0.04	3	46.5	...	....	23687
5616	35 27 10.0	8.3	− 17.69	− 0.15	...	3	48.5	13.7	....	....
5617	50 16 58.3	...	− 17.69	− 0.18	...	3	54.1	...	....	....
5618	35 17 45.9	45.2	− 17.69	− 0.15	...	3	48.5	13.8	....	....
5619	38 12 8.1	...	− 17.69	− 0.15	...	2	53.9	...	....	....
5620	38 22 29.3	29.5	− 17.70	− 0.15	...	4	46.8	11.5	....	....
5621	31 28 6.0	7.1	− 17.70	− 0.14	...	4	44.7	12.8	....	23696
5622	37 59 49.2	...	− 17.71	− 0.15	...	2	50.3	...	....	....
5623	47 48 47.2	47.7	− 17.72	− 0.17	...	3	45.1	10.9	....	....
5624	38 15 16.9	16.0	− 17.72	− 0.15	...	3	44.7	11.8	....	....
5625	35 19 5.4	5.0	− 17.73	− 0.15	...	3	45.8	13.8	....	....
5626	98 33 11.0	...	− 17.73	− 0.21	+ 0.03	7	49.9	...	43 Aquarii θ...	....
5627	35 19 43.6	...	− 17.73	− 0.15	...	2	54.3	...	....	....
5628	27 36 20.6	...	− 17.74	− 0.13	− 0.07	3	47.8	...	....	23721
5629	33 43 40.1	41.4	− 17.76	− 0.14	− 0.02	4	46.2	7.0	23 Cephei ε ...	23742
5630	45 40 53.2	53.8	− 17.77	− 0.16	...	3	45.5	10.8	....	....

Magnitude.	Estimates of Magnitude.	Mean Right Ascension 1845.0.		Precession 1845.0.	Secular Variation	Adopted Proper Motion.
R.	R.	R.	G.			
		h. m. s.	s.	s.	s.	s.
7.2	5	22 9 43.41	43.49	+ 2.067	+ 0.009	......
9.0	2	22 10 ...	...	+ 1.108	− 0.029	......
5.9	3	22 10 3.42	...	+ 1.108	− 0.029	+ 0.008
9.2	4	22 10 34.64	...	+ 1.252	− 0.025	......
7.9	6	22 10 45.90	45.38	+ 1.216	− 0.023	......
6.1	6	22 10 51.25	50.96	+ 2.148	+ 0.010	......
6.8	5	22 10 52.09	49.54	+ 0.667	− 0.060	......
7.9	5	22 11 1.09	...	+ 2.468	+ 0.010	......
8.5	3	22 11 10.85	10.59	+ 2.083	+ 0.009	......
7.4	4	22 11 42.28	42.07	+ 2.369	+ 0.012	......
7.7	9	22 12 11.25	10.90	+ 2.536	+ 0.010	......
9.0	3	22 12 18.06	18.17	+ 2.221	+ 0.012	......
6.7	3	22 12 39.09	38.46	+ 1.755	+ 0.003	......
7.0	7	22 12 39.23	38.83	+ 2.301	+ 0.012	......
7.9	4	22 13 6.17	5.62	+ 2.303	+ 0.012	......
8.7	2	22 13 6.53	...	+ 2.098	+ 0.010	......
5.6	6	22 13 9.58	9.18	+ 1.938	+ 0.009	......
3.7	3	22 13 38.97	...	+ 3.093	− 0.006	+ 0.007
7.7	5	22 13 39.13	38.86	+ 2.435	+ 0.011	......
8.6	6	22 13 53.19	...	+ 2.390	+ 0.013	......
9.1	4	22 13 54.69	54.78	+ 2.381	+ 0.011	......
7.1	5	22 13 56.04	...	+ 2.204	+ 0.011	......
6.6	1	22 14 4.12	...	+ 2.063	+ 0.012	......
5.6	4	22 14 25.38	25.25	+ 2.184	+ 0.012	......
9.2	4	22 14 31.05	30.75	+ 2.382	+ 0.011	......
8.7	3	22 14 31.55	...	+ 2.382	+ 0.011	......
4.7	10	22 14 37.85	37.60	+ 2.461	+ 0.011	......
8.4	4	22 14 39.76	39.49	+ 2.282	+ 0.012	......
10.0	4	22 14 48.08	...	+ 2.395	+ 0.013	......
9.0	6	22 14 48.92	48.91	+ 2.239	+ 0.012	......
6.3	8	22 15 13.42	12.98	+ 2.552	+ 0.011	......
8.4	5	22 15 17.47	17.08	+ 2.221	+ 0.012	......
7.4	5	22 15 25.97	25.93	+ 2.521	+ 0.011	......
8.6	5	22 16 12.47	11.74	+ 0.979	− 0.037	......
7.3	5	22 16 24.79	...	+ 1.747	0.000	......

Ordinal Number.	Mean North Polar Distance 1845.0.			Precession 1845.0.	Secular Variation.	Adopted Proper Motion.	Observations of N.P.D.			Names.	Oeltzen-Argelander Number.
R.	R.		G.				No.	Mean year.			
							R.	R.	G.		
	° ′ ″		″	″	″	″		1800 +			
5631	31 39 14.0		14.1	− 17.77	− 0.14	...	3	46.7	12.8	....	....
5632	17 27 15.2		...	− 17.79	− 0.07	...	2	51.8	...	....	......
5633	17 27 44.6		...	− 17.79	− 0.07	...	2	47.3	...	....	......
5634	18 40 23.1		...	− 17.81	− 0.08	...	2	48.8	...	....	23773
5635	18 18 18.4		21.2	− 17.82	− 0.07	...	3	47.4	12.7	....	23776
5636	33 33 5.4		6.7	− 17.82	− 0.14	...	3	44.1	12.8	....	23777
5637	14 18 30.3		28.9	− 17.82	− 0.03	...	3	46.4	10.9	....	23781
5638	45 29 34.1		...	− 17.82	− 0.16	...	4	46.1	...	....	23782
5639	31 45 49.5		46.9	− 17.83	− 0.14	...	4	47.8	12.8	....	......
5640	40 56 35.1		30.3	− 17.85	− 0.15	...	4	48.3	11.9	....	23815
5641	48 37 53.6		54.9	− 17.87	− 0.17	...	4	49.3	11.8	....	......
5642	35 29 34.1		35.4	− 17.38	− 0.14	...	3	50.4	13.8	....	......
5643	24 38 44.8		44.9	− 17.89	− 0.11	...	5	44.4	9.8	....	......
5644	38 7 8.0		9.7	− 17.89	− 0.15	...	5	42.6	10.9	....	23837
5645	38 6 6.5		10.3	− 17.91	− 0.15	...	3	43.7	10.9	....	23854
5646	31 42 57.5		...	− 17.91	− 0.14	...	2	46.3	...	....	23855
5647	27 58 18.5		18.6	− 17.92	− 0.13	+ 0.02	4	45.2	8.8	25 Cephei......	23857
5648	92 9 59.0		...	− 17.93	− 0.20	− 0.02	6	52.0	...	48 Aquarii γ...	......
5649	43 18 16.6		14.4	− 17.94	− 0.16	...	3	43.8	10.7	....	23869
5650	41 16 28.7		...	− 17.95	− 0.16	...	3	51.8	...	....	23879
5651	40 54 41.6		46.3	− 17.95	− 0.16	...	3	47.8	11.8	....	23883
5652	34 34 29.4		...	− 17.95	− 0.14	...	3	49.4	...	....	23887
5653	30 37 45.8		...	− 17.95	− 0.13	...	3	47.2	...	....	23894
5654	33 51 36.7		37.4	− 17.97	− 0.14	− 0.01	7	47.2	8.7	....	......
5655	40 47 48.2		50.4	− 17.97	− 0.16	...	2	46.8	11.8	....	23905
5656	40 48 24.1		...	− 17.97	− 0.16	...	2	46.3	...	....	23908
5657	44 14 32.8		31.9	− 17.97	− 0.16	...	5	48.0	7.5	2 Lacertæ......	23912
5658	36 57 48.5		47.2	− 17.97	− 0.14	...	3	46.8	14.8	....	......
5659	41 16 5.8		...	− 17.98	− 0.15	...	3	52.4	...	....	......
5660	35 28 56.1		55.0	− 17.98	− 0.14	...	3	51.5	13.8	....	......
5661	48 42 5.8		5.8	− 17.99	− 0.16	...	4	46.3	11.8	....	......
5662	34 47 37.7		37.3	− 18.00	− 0.14	...	4	44.6	12.7	....	23933
5663	47 2 2.5		2.6	− 18.00	− 0.16	...	4	45.7	10.9	....	......
5664	15 37 33.8		33.6	− 18.03	− 0.05	...	3	50.5	13.9	....	......
5665	23 48 58.4		...	− 18.04	− 0.11	...	4	51.3	...	....	......

Magnitude.	Estimates of Magnitude.	Mean Right Ascension 1845.0.		Precession 1845.0.	Secular Variation	Adopted Proper Motion.
R.	R.	R.	G.			
		h. m. s.	s.	s.	s.	s.
6.9	4	22 16 26.00	25.64	+ 0.778	− 0.051	......
8.2	4	22 16 47.49	47.48	+ 2.559	+ 0.011	......
7.5	5	22 16 56.14	56.00	+ 0.865	− 0.051	......
7.4	5	22 17 8.65	7.65	+ 1.772	+ 0.004	......
8.3	6	22 17 9.58	9.62	+ 2.258	+ 0.012	......
7.6	5	22 17 9.64	...	+ 1.772	+ 0.004	......
6.4	4	22 17 17.61	17.33	+ 2.195	+ 0.012	......
6.5	5	22 17 18.30	18.02	+ 2.237	+ 0.013	......
7.1	5	22 17 27.75	27.59	+ 2.370	+ 0.012	......
4.2	6	22 17 28.40	28.19	+ 2.344	+ 0.013	....
7.5	4	22 17 39.59	39.55	+ 0.863	− 0.049	......
8.7	4	22 17 49.12	48.86	+ 2.264	+ 0.012	......
4.3	4	22 18 14.42	14.33	+ 2.416	+ 0.012	......
7.8	6	22 18 30.03	29.76	+ 2.497	+ 0.011	......
7.5	5	22 18 32.75	...	+ 2.568	+ 0.012	......
8.5	4	22 18 39.08	38.00	+ 0.631	− 0.069	......
6.2	6	22 18 51.79	51.71	+ 2.378	+ 0.013	+ 0.006
9.2	8	22 19 0.15	59.81	+ 2.275	+ 0.012	......
7.7	8	22 19 9.94	10.12	+ 2.401	+ 0.013	......
8.9	5	22 19 42.82	42.14	+ 0.902	− 0.046	......
7.6	7	22 19 45.04	44.68	+ 2.318	+ 0.012	......
7.5	7	22 19 52.84	52.80	+ 2.315	+ 0.012	......
8.9	5	22 19 56.81	57.01	+ 2.320	+ 0.012	......
7.3	4	22 20 5.85	5.18	+ 1.073	− 0.029	......
8.8	5	22 20 14.93	14.85	+ 2.321	+ 0.012	......
7.7	5	22 20 25.59	25.45	+ 2.315	+ 0.012	......
7.0	4	22 20 36.09	35.27	+ 1.989	+ 0.010	+ 0.001
8.0	4	22 20 37.06	...	+ 2.425	+ 0.013	......
7.8	6	22 20 49.10	...	+ 2.579	+ 0.012	......
5.0	1	22 20 50.97	...	+ 3.078	− 0.005	+ 0.009
7.1	5	22 21 31.22	30.94	+ 2.390	+ 0.013	......
8.1	2	22 21 39.61	39.75	+ 1.614	+ 0.003	......
7.3	5	22 21 41.82	41.48	+ 2.389	+ 0.013	......
8.4	4	22 21 51.51	51.03	+ 1.126	− 0.029	......
5.9	3	22 22 .6.40	6.52	+ 1.918	+ 0.009	− 0.003

Ordinal Number.	Mean North Polar Distance 1845.0.		Precession 1845.0.	Secular Variation.	Adopted Proper Motion.	Observations of N.P.D.			Names.	Oeltzen-Argelander Number.
						No.	Mean year.			
R.	R.	G.				R.	R.	G.		
	° ′ ″	″	″	″	″		1800 +			
5666	14 17 28.1	27.0	− 18.04	− 0.04	...	4	46.3	12.9	....	23957
5667	48 43 22.1	22.2	− 18.05	− 0.16	...	4	47.5	11.9	....	......
5668	14 45 59.9	61.3	− 18.06	− 0.05	...	5	45.0	13.8	....	......
5669	24 4 32.2	33.2	− 18.07	− 0.11	...	7	49.5	9.7	....	23985
5670	35 32 58.7	58.1	− 18.07	− 0.14	...	4	46.3	13.9	....	23983
5671	24 4 31.5	...	− 18.07	− 0.11	...	2	52.3	...	....	......
5672	33 29 53.5	52.9	− 18.07	− 0.14	...	4	45.7	9.9	....	......
5673	34 49 10.3	10.6	− 18.07	− 0.14	...	4	44.5	12.7	....	23986
5674	39 35 13.5	15.3	− 18.08	− 0.15	...	3	45.7	10.7	....	23989
5675	38 32 45.4	47.4	− 18.08	− 0.15	+ 0.21	6	47.4	6.8	3 Lacertæ β...	23991
5676	14 39 22.8	22.0	− 18.09	− 0.05	...	3	44.8	13.8	....	24000
5677	35 34 36.5	37.8	− 18.09	− 0.14	...	4	46.7	13.8	....	24005
5678	41 18 29.1	29.4	− 18.11	− 0.15	...	5	46.2	7.8	4 Lacertæ......	24018
5679	45 0 2.0	2.7	− 18.11	− 0.16	...	3	47.8	11.9	....	24024
5680	48 45 12.5	...	− 18.12	− 0.16	...	4	47.6	...	....	......
5681	13 12 18.7	15.4	− 18.12	− 0.02	...	2	48.3	12.7	....	24036
5682	39 31 50.0	52.5	− 18.13	− 0.15	...	3	45.1	10.7	....	24041
5683	35 39 40.4	34.8	− 18.13	− 0.14	...	2	51.4	13.9	....	24045
5684	40 23 3.8	5.0	− 18.14	− 0.15	...	3	45.8	15.8	....	24049
5685	14 38 44.9	47.2	− 18.17	− 0.06	...	3	52.5	13.7	....	24059
5686	36 58 14.6	15.1	+ 18.17	− 0.14	...	3	45.4	14.8	....	......
5687	36 50 33.6	33.4	− 18.18	− 0.14	...	3	45.2	14.8	....	......
5688	37 0 19.3	20.2	− 18.18	− 0.14	...	3	48.1	14.9	....	......
5689	15 46 52.2	52.2	− 18.18	− 0.06	...	3	43.8	14.4	....	......
5690	36 57 47.6	49.0	− 18.19	− 0.14	...	3	48.1	14.9	....	......
5691	36 41 2.0	1.2	− 18.20	− 0.14	...	4	46.8	14.8	....	......
5692	27 27 32.8	32.4	− 18.20	− 0.12	− 0.04	5	43.9	9.7	....	24085
5693	41 4 34.4	...	− 18.20	− 0.15	...	3	51.4	...	....	24084
5694	48 46 28.4	...	− 18.21	− 0.16	...	4	45.6	...	....	......
5695	90 48 37.6	...	− 18.21	− 0.19	− 0.03	1	53.9	...	55 Aquarii ζ (1st)	......
5696	39 17 45.6	50.1	− 18.23	− 0.14	...	4	43.8	10.9	....	24107
5697	20 53 36.9	37.8	− 18.24	− 0.10	...	2	50.3	13.8	....	......
5698	39 12 49.2	50.2	− 18.24	− 0.14	...	5	46.0	10.9	....	24118
5699	15 56 17.8	18.5	− 18.24	− 0.05	...	4	45.8	13.5	....	24125
5700	25 39 25.6	26.9	− 18.25	− 0.09	...	4	44.2	8.7	26 Cephei......	24133

Ordinal Number.		Magnitude.	Estimates of Magnitude.	Mean Right Ascension 1845.0.		Precession 1845.0.	Secular Variation	Adopted Proper Motion.	Observations of R.A.		
R.	G.	R.	R.	R.	G.				No. R.	Mean year. R.	G.
				h. m. s.	s.	s.	s.	s.		1800 +	
5701	3782	7.6	5	22 22 11.61	11.40	+ 2.398	+ 0.013	......	3	48.8	10.9
5702	...	5.3	6	22 22 26.40	...	+ 3.182	− 0.011	− 0.004	14	51.5	...
5703	3788	7.6	5	22 22 29.85	29.65	+ 1.140	− 0.029	......	3	49.4	13.9
5704	3785	9.0	5	22 22 41.32	41.49	+ 2.419	+ 0.014	......	3	51.4	15.8
5705	...	7.5	4	22 22 49.25	...	− 1.930	− 0.568	......	3	51.5	...
5706	3786	7.4	5	22 22 49.86	49.66	+ 2.398	+ 0.014	......	3	45.1	10.9
5707	3787	4.2	6	22 23 4.76	4.47	+ 2.483	+ 0.013	......	8	48.5	7.2
5708	...	8.2	5	22 23 6.18	...	+ 2.482	+ 0.013	......	3	51.4	...
5709	3790	7.3	4	22 23 15.23	15.51	+ 2.095	+ 0.014	......	3	45.4	12.9
5710	3795	8.9	4	22 23 17.42	16.56	+ 0.969	− 0.040	......	2	51.4	13.7
5711	3796	7.0	7	22 23 17.77	17.60	+ 0.764	− 0.063	......	4	51.4	12.7
5712	3789	6.5	4	22 23 18.76	18.48	+ 2.331	+ 0.014	......	4	46.9	10.7
5713	...	8.4	4	22 23 21.03	...	+ 2.380	+ 0.014	......	2	52.8	...
5714	...	7.9	4	22 23 21.98	...	+ 2.377	+ 0.014	......	2	52.8	...
5715	...	7.0	6	22 23 24.55	...	+ 2.207	+ 0.014	......	4	52.5	...
5716	3791	3.7	9	22 23 25.46	25.19	+ 2.207	+ 0.014	+ 0.002	5	45.2	7.1
5717	3793	6.7	3	22 23 41.86	41.80	+ 2.381	+ 0.014	......	2	49.3	10.8
5718	3792	4.7	3	22 23 48.31	48.28	+ 2.574	+ 0.012	......	3	46.4	7.8
5719	3794	7.7	4	22 24 5.59	6.43	+ 2.615	+ 0.011	......	3	51.2	14.9
5720	...	7.8	7	22 24 27.11	...	+ 2.251	+ 0.014	......	4	54.0	...
5721	3797	8.2	5	22 24 33.04	33.00	+ 2.432	+ 0.014	......	2	49.3	15.8
5722	3798	8.1	4	22 24 45.84	45.89	+ 2.437	+ 0.014	......	3	48.5	15.8
5723	3820	5.5	4I	22 24 46.66	45.87	− 3.529	− 1.122	+ 0.048	37	50.2	7.5
5724	3799	3.9	5	22 24 54.87	54.70	+ 2.439	+ 0.014	+ 0.015	5	45.4	7.8
5725	3802	7.0	6	22 25 3.79	3.59	+ 2.633	+ 0.014	......	3	47.8	13.6
5726	3800	7.9	5	22 25 5.97	5.98	+ 2.434	+ 0.014	......	3	51.4	15.9
5727	3805	7.3	4	22 25 17.15	16.23	+ 1.624	+ 0.003	......	2	46.9	13.3
5728	3801	8.7	5	22 25 17.36	16.82	+ 2.633	+ 0.011	......	3	47.5	11.8
5729	3824	6.8	4I	22 25 18.72	17.87	− 3.658	− 1.183	+ 0.031	41	50.6	7.9
5730	3809	6.0	7	22 25 28.93	29.08	+ 0.550	− 0.088	− 0.009	4	50.4	8.7
5731	3803	7.9	3	22 25 33.12	33.39	+ 2.623	+ 0.011	......	2	49.3	14.9
5732	3804	6.2	5	22 25 35.72	35.46	+ 2.637	+ 0.011	......	3	45.4	11.8
5733	3806	7.3	6	22 25 43.73	43.76	+ 1.650	+ 0.003	......	2	50.2	13.3
5734	3814	6.5	3	22 26 5.68	3.61	+ 0.077	− 0.152	. ...	2	52.4	9.7
5735	3807	6.1	6	22 26 10.37	10.11	+ 2.357	+ 0.014	......	4	47.0	11.9

Ordinal Number.	Mean North Polar Distance 1845.0.			Precession 1845.0.	Secular Variation.	Adopted Proper Motion.	Observations of N.P.D.				Names.	Oeltzen-Argelander Number.
							No.	Mean year.				
R.	R.		G.				R.	R.	G.			
	° ′ ″		″	″	″	″		1800 +				
5701	39 29	2.1	3.4	— 18.26	— 0.14	...	4	44.1	10.9		....	24135
5702	101 28	10.9	...	— 18.27	— 0.19	— 0.05	6	51.7	...		57 Aquarii σ...	......
5703	15 57	39.1	36.2	— 18.27	— 0.06	...	4	45.3	13.9		....	24151
5704	40 14	52.1	51.6	— 18.27	— 0.14	...	2	46.8	15.8		....	......
5705	6 16	36.7	...	— 18.28	+ 0.12	...	3	51.5	...		....	......
5706	39 17	0.9	2.4	— 18.28	— 0.13	...	3	44.8	10.9		....	24160
5707	43 5	5.7	5.7	— 18.29	— 0.15	— 0.01	4	44.1	7.2		5 Lacertæ......	24167
5708	43 1	42.9	...	— 18.29	— 0.15	...	3	48.5	...		....	24169
5709	29 20	12.7	15.3	— 18.29	— 0.12	...	3	44.8	12.9		....	......
5710	14 36	43.2	43.6	— 18.29	— 0.04	...	2	49.8	13.7		....	24177
5711	13 21	21.5	19.3	— 18.29	— 0.04	...	4	47.3	12.7		....	......
5712	36 32	47.2	45.5	— 18.30	— 0.14	...	3	43.4	10.7		....	......
5713	38 24	14.5	...	— 18.30	— 0.14	...	3	48.8	...		....	24176
5714	38 18	4.1	...	— 18.30	— 0.14	...	2	49.2	...		....	......
5715	32 23	16.3	...	— 18.30	— 0.13	...	7	46.6	...		27 Cephei δ (1st)	24179
5716	32 22	37.2	37.1	— 18.30	— 0.13	...	9	48.7	7.7		27 Cephei δ (2d)	24180
5717	38 22	36.8	39.0	— 18.31	— 0.14	...	4	47.8	10.8		....	24188
5718	47 40	9.2	11.8	— 18.31	— 0.15	...	4	45.4	7.8		6 Lacertæ......	......
5719	50 4	22.8	26.6	— 18.32	— 0.15	...	2	51.3	14.9		....	......
5720	33 34	4.2	...	— 18.34	— 0.13	...	4	52.3	...		....	24222
5721	40 16	20.1	20.9	— 18.34	— 0.14	...	3	50.5	15.8		....	24225
5722	40 25	47.5	48.2	— 18.35	— 0.14	...	3	47.8	15.8		....	24231
5723	4 40	31.3	31.5	— 18.35	+ 0.21	— 0.05	19	49.3	7.5		*2 2. Cepha.*	......
5724	40 30	46.4	47.8	— 18.36	— 0.14	...	4	46.1	7.8		7 Lacertæ α...	24233
5725	29 10	14.8	15.4	— 18.37	— 0.12	...	5	47.2	13.6		....	......
5726	40 12	0.9	1.3	— 18.37	— 0.14	...	4	50.8	15.9		....	24238
5727	20 21	31.6	31.2	— 18.37	— 0.10	...	3	46.7	13.3		....	24245
5728	50 59	48.9	48.1	— 18.37	— 0.15	...	3	48.1	11.8		....	......
5729	4 33	39.9	38.8	— 18.37	+ 0.22	...	10	48.3	7.9		....	......
5730	12 0	16.4	14.1	— 18.38	— 0.04	+ 0.02	6	44.0	8.7		28 Cephei......	......
5731	50 10	46.5	46.3	— 18.38	— 0.15	...	2	49.9	14.9		....	......
5732	51 0	57.8	56.7	— 18.38	— 0.15	...	3	46.1	11.8		....	......
5733	20 37	22.3	22.1	— 18.39	— 0.10	...	4	49.3	13.3		....	24258
5734	10 5	28.2	28.6	— 18.40	0.00	...	4	45.3	9.7		....	......
5735	36 45	37.1	35.6	— 18.40	— 0.14	...	4	45.3	11.9		....	24267

Ordinal Number.		Magnitude.	Estimates of Magnitude.	Mean Right Ascension 1845.0.		Precession 1845.0.	Secular Variation	Adopted Proper Motion.	Observations of R.A.		
R.	G.	R.		R.	G.				No.	Mean year.	
									R.	R.	G.
				h. m. s.	s.	s.	s.	s.		1800 +	
5736	3813	7.3	3	22 26 12.04	11.99	+ 1.022	− 0.037	......	2	51.3	13.8
5737	3808	8.6	4	22 26 31.67	31.63	+ 2.644	+ 0.011	......	3	51.4	11.5
5738	3811	8.1	6	22 26 42.38	42.54	+ 2.449	+ 0.014	......	4	51.3	15.8
5739	3810	6.5	6	22 26 45.48	45.87	+ 2.626	+ 0.011	......	3	46.1	14.9
5740	3812	7.0	6	22 27 3.35	3.12	+ 2.528	+ 0.014	......	4	45.0	10.9
5741	3821	7.8	6	22 27 19.84	19.15	+ 0.830	− 0.051	......	3	51.9	12.7
5742	...	4.2	3	22 27 23.44	...	+ 3.078	− 0.005	+ 0.003	10	47.9	...
5743	...	8.6	4	22 27 36.18	...	+ 2.632	+ 0.012	......	2	51.8	...
5744	3815	7.3	5	22 27 40.43	40.86	+ 2.631	+ 0.011	......	3	46.8	14.9
5745	3816	5.7	5	22 27 40.54	40.19	+ 2.298	+ 0.015	+ 0.005	3	44.7	9.9
5746	3818	9.0	5	22 27 57.22	57.14	+ 2.460	+ 0.014	......	4	48.1	12.8
5747	3819	8.0	5	22 28 0.20	0.08	+ 2.370	+ 0.014	......	4	47.8	11.9
5748	3817	8.4	2	22 28 0.56	0.71	+ 2.633	+ 0.011	......	2	51.3	15.0
5749	3823	6.4	7	22 28 19.98	20.24	+ 2.132	+ 0.015	......	3	45.0	14.8
5750	3831	5.6	8	22 28 27.13	27.52	+ 0.618	− 0.080	......	5	49.6	8.8
5751	3826	6.1	5	22 28 33.46	33.48	+ 1.709	+ 0.004	+ 0.025	3	49.2	13.5
5752	3822	7.5	8	22 28 34.33	34.06	+ 2.653	+ 0.011	......	6	48.7	10.7
5753	3827	6.3	5	22 28 54.17	54.47	+ 1.680	+ 0.003	+ 0.030	3	48.5	12.9
5754	3828	8.6	6	22 28 55.52	55.29	+ 1.701	+ 0.003	......	2	52.3	12.9
5755	...	6.6	7	22 28 58.92	...	+ 2.654	+ 0.011	− 0.001	5	53.4	...
5756	3825	6.1	3	22 28 59.04	58.87	+ 2.654	+ 0.011	......	2	46.8	10.4
5757	...	7.2	6	22 29 18.29	...	+ 2.660	+ 0.012	......	2	47.3	...
5758	3830	7.9	3	22 29 26.85	26.86	+ 2.402	+ 0.014	......	2	48.4	14.5
5759	3829	6.2	5	22 29 27.74	27.48	+ 2.472	+ 0.015	......	5	46.2	8.9
5760	...	7.2	18	22 29 31.63	...	− 2.054	− 0.670	......	16	52.8	...
5761	3834	5.7	5	22 29 31.72	31.63	+ 1.092	− 0.034	......	2	46.3	13.8
5762	3832	8.6	6	22 29 38.20	37.66	+ 2.303	+ 0.015	......	4	48.7	13.9
5763	3833	7.7	4	22 29 42.04	42.30	+ 2.307	+ 0.015	......	3	49.1	13.9
5764	...	6.0	1	22 29 43.65	...	+ 3.115	− 0.007	− 0.007	2	40.9	...
5765	3835	7.8	6	22 30 33.62	32.98	+ 2.457	+ 0.015	......	3	47.5	11.9
5766	3836	7.8	5	22 30 36.12	35.83	+ 2.380	+ 0.015	......	3	49.1	11.9
5767	3840	9.0	6	22 30 41.92	41.86	+ 1.700	+ 0.004	......	3	51.1	12.9
5768	3837	8.0	4	22 30 51.80	51.51	+ 2.445	+ 0.015	......	2	48.4	11.9
5769	...	8.6	4	22 30 52.15	...	+ 2.461	+ 0.015	......	3	52.0	...
5770	3838	8.8	6	22 30 52.64	52.43	+ 2.316	+ 0.015	......	3	50.5	13.9

| Ordinal Number. | Mean North Polar Distance 1845.0. | | | Precession 1845.0. | Secular Variation. | Adopted Proper Motion. | Observations of N.P.D. | | | Names. | Oeltzen-Argelander Number. |
	R.	R.	G.				No. R.	Mean year. R.	G.		
	° ′ ″		″	″	″	″		1800 +			
5736	14 33 32.0		32.3	− 18.40	− 0.05	...	4	49.0	13.8	....	24272
5737	51 13 19.8		20.5	− 18.41	− 0.15	...	3	48.2	11.5	....	......
5738	40 26 26.3		26.3	− 18.42	− 0.14	...	3	46.8	15.8	....	24282
5739	49 58 43.0		44.9	− 18.42	− 0.15	...	4	46.8	14.9	....	......
5740	44 13 57.5		57.7	− 18.43	− 0.14	...	3	44.8	10.9	....	24290
5741	13 12 45.2		45.1	− 18.44	− 0.05	...	5	50.6	12.7	....	24297
5742	90 54 53.2		...	− 18.44	− 0.18	+ 0.06	2	49.8	...	62 Aquarii η...	......
5743	50 8 5.9		...	− 18.45	− 0.15	...	3	52.8	...	....	......
5744	50 1 26.3		26.6	− 18.45	− 0.15	...	3	47.4	14.9	....	......
5745	34 10 32.5		32.7	− 18.45	− 0.13	...	4	45.1	9.9	....	24303
5746	40 34 58.2		58.3	− 18.46	− 0.14	...	2	49.9	12.8	....	24314
5747	36 42 50.4		48.1	− 18.46	− 0.13	...	3	45.1	11.9	....	24315
5748	50 3 59.1		61.1	− 18.46	− 0.15	...	2	51.8	15.0	....	......
5749	29 1 17.6		20.0	− 18.47	− 0.12	...	4	46.5	14.8	....	24319
5750	11 58 17.2		17.7	− 18.48	− 0.03	+ 0.03	6	44.1	8.8	29 Cephei ρ...	......
5751	20 53 17.4		20.9	− 18.48	− 0.09	...	3	44.5	13.5	....	24326
5752	51 12 54.1		54.2	− 18.48	− 0.15	...	4	43.1	10.7	....	......
5753	20 25 34.8		35.4	− 18.49	− 0.09	...	4	47.5	12.9	....	24334
5754	20 42 55.2		52.8	− 18.49	− 0.09	...	3	51.1	12.9	....	24335
5755	51 10 20.8		...	− 18.49	− 0.15	+ 0.27	3	47.5	...	8 Lacertæ (1st)	......
5756	51 9 59.4		60.9	− 18.49	− 0.15	...	3	47.4	10.4	8 Lacertæ (2d)	......
5757	51 27 47.7		...	− 18.50	− 0.15	...	4	48.9	...	....	......
5758	37 35 57.7		58.7	− 18.51	− 0.14	...	2	47.3	14.5	....	......
5759	40 43 50.0		51.2	− 18.51	− 0.14	...	4	46.3	8.9	....	24357
5760	5 43 51.5		...	− 18.51	+ 0.11	...	4	51.4	...	....	......
5761	14 34 20.7		20.1	− 18.51	− 0.06	...	4	45.7	13.8	v. Tho. Capha	24365
5762	33 48 18.9		21.3	− 18.51	− 0.13	...	3	51.1	13.9	....	......
5763	33 56 17.8		16.5	− 18.52	− 0.13	...	3	46.4	13.9	....	......
5764	95 1 34.0		...	− 18.52	− 0.17	+ 0.11	3	54.5	...	63 Aquarii κ...	......
5765	39 41 29.9		31.3	− 18.55	− 0.13	...	4	43.5	11.9	....	24386
5766	36 22 45.0		43.2	− 18.55	− 0.13	...	4	43.4	11.9	....	24389
5767	20 20 27.9		27.1	− 18.56	− 0.10	...	3	43.8	12.9	....	......
5768	39 31 1.3		59.6	− 18.56	− 0.13	...	2	45.3	11.9	....	24396
5769	39 47 15.0		...	− 18.56	− 0.14	...	2	45.3	...	....	24397
5770	33 53 49.6		50.7	− 18.56	− 0.13	...	4	50.4	13.9	....	......

Ordinal Number.		Magnitude.	Estimates of Magnitude.	Mean Right Ascension 1845.0.			Precession 1845.0.	Secular Variation	Adopted Proper Motion.	Observations of R.A.		
R.	G.	R.	R.	R.		G.				No. R.	Mean year. R.	G.
				h. m. s.		s.	s.	s.	s.		1800 +	
5771	3839	4·9	6	22 31	0.96	1.27	+ 2.451	+ 0.015	......	3	44.8	9·9
5772	3842	7.3	6	22 31	11.84	11.63	+ 1.723	+ 0.004	......	3	50.8	12.9
5773	3841	6.4	5	22 31	35.66	35.44	+ 2.578	+ 0.014	......	4	48.2	10.9
5774	3846	5.2	5	22 31	56.06	55.95	+ 1.447	− 0.010	+ 0.043	3	49.4	9.8
5775	3843	7.1	7	22 31	59.82	58.71	+ 2.595	+ 0.014	......	4	50.7	15.7
5776	...	7.6	18	22 32	3.37	...	− 7.508	− 3.451	......	18	51.9	...
5777	...	7.7	4	22 32	9.44	...	+ 1.524	− 0.018	......	3	51.5	...
5778	3845	6.9	6	22 32	11.15	10.13	+ 2.090	+ 0.014	......	3	50.7	9.8
5779	...	8.3	4	22 32	15.52	...	+ 1.522	− 0.018	......	3	54.7	...
5780	3844	5.8	4	22 32	18.92	18.77	+ 2.676	+ 0.012	......	3	48.4	10.8
5781	3847	5.2	4	22 32	32.82	32.72	+ 2.332	+ 0.014	......	3	48.4	13.8
5782	3848	6.9	5	22 33	5.50	4.59	+ 2.473	+ 0.015	......	2	48.2	11.8
5783	3850	5.2	3	22 33	9.81	9.35	+ 2.109	+ 0.016	......	2	47.7	9.5
5784	3849	7.3	5	22 33	11.91	11.69	+ 2.648	+ 0.013	......	3	47.8	10.1
5785	...	9.1	5	22 33	21.46	...	+ 2.107	+ 0.013	......	3	51.7	...
5786	3852	8.0	4	22 33	39.86	39.61	+ 2.467	+ 0.015	......	3	48.1	14.8
5787	3851	4.6	4	22 33	43.52	43.50	+ 2.604	+ 0.014	+ 0.010	5	45.2	7.1
5788	...	4.7	2	22 33	43.97	...	+ 2.983	0.000	+ 0.001	53	45.8	...
5789	3853	7.1	4	22 33	52.59	52.48	+ 2.470	+ 0.015	......	5	49.3	13.6
5790	3857	6.3	7	22 33	52.70	51.93	+ 1.293	− 0.020	......	4	51.5	12.7
5791	3854	6.2	5	22 34	0.82	0.91	+ 2.419	+ 0.014	......	3	47.7	13.8
5792	3855	7.1	5	22 34	24.68	24.47	+ 2.596	+ 0.014	......	4	48.8	10.9
5793	3856	5.7	3	22 34	32.82	32.77	+ 2.670	+ 0.012	......	2	46.4	9.9
5794	3859	7.0	6	22 34	37.36	37.14	+ 2.470	+ 0.015	......	3	48.8	11.9
5795	3858	5.9	5	22 34	41.06	40.47	+ 2.651	+ 0.013	......	3	48.8	11.9
5796	...	8.3	4	22 34	51.95	...	+ 2.506	+ 0.015	......	2	49.8	...
5797	3860	8.1	4	22 34	58.35	58.37	+ 2.490	+ 0.015	......	2	49.3	11.8
5798	3861	8.0	6	22 35	30.24	30.00	+ 2.566	+ 0.014	......	3	49.8	11.8
5799	3862	6.3	5	22 36	1.21	1.31	+ 2.432	+ 0.017	......	3	46.8	13.8
5800	3863	9.1	6	22 36	8.48	8.47	+ 2.374	+ 0.017	......	4	50.8	12.8
5801	3864	6.6	10	22 36	23.64	23.31	+ 2.570	+ 0.014	......	6	49.5	11.8
5802	3865	7.7	4	22 36	34.60	34.22	+ 2.416	+ 0.017	......	3	47.8	13.9
5803	3866	7.4	6	22 36	44.46	43.64	+ 2.591	+ 0.014	......	3	49.4	10.8
5804	3870	7.3	5	22 36	49.97	50.19	+ 2.094	+ 0.017	......	2	48.8	12.9
5805	3868	8.9	7	22 36	50.27	50.07	+ 2.491	+ 0.014	......	4	47.5	14.8

Ordinal Number.	Mean North Polar Distance 1845.0.			Precession 1845.0.	Secular Variation.	Adopted Proper Motion.	Observations of N.P.D.				Names.	Oeltzen-Argelander Number.
							No.	Mean year.				
R.	R.		G.				R.	R.		G.		
	° ′ ″		″	″	″	″		1800 +				
5771	39 15 12.7		14.1	— 18.57	— 0.14	+ 0.11	5	45.2		9.9	9 Lacertæ......	......
5772	20 33 34.8		35.9	— 18.57	— 0.10	...	4	47.8		12.9	....	24406
5773	45 37 15.4		17.4	— 18.58	— 0.14	...	4	45.5		10.9	....	......
5774	17 9 39.3		38.3	— 18.59	— 0.08	...	4	45.6		9.8	31 Cephei	24429
5775	46 29 36.6		38.4	— 18.60	— 0.14	...	4	47.3		15.7	....	......
5776	2 42 29.0		...	— 18.60	+ 0.41	...	6	51.4		...	....	......
5777	17 55 29.0		...	— 18.60	— 0.08	...	4	51.8		...	....	......
5778	27 2 7.8		10.0	— 18.60	— 0.11	...	4	47.8		9.8	....	24437
5779	17 56 0.0		...	— 18.60	— 0.08	...	3	52.1		...	....	24443
5780	51 45 18.2		18.2	— 18.61	— 0.15	...	3	46.4		10.8	10 Lacertæ	......
5781	34 0 30.2		30.1	— 18.61	— 0.12	...	4	44.8		13.8	....	......
5782	39 39 11.0		12.3	— 18.63	— 0.13	...	3	46.5		11.8	....	24463
5783	27 13 13.5		13.2	— 18.63	— 0.11	+ 0.03	5	44.9		9.5	30 Cephei......	24467
5784	49 29 34.3		32.3	— 18.63	— 0.14	...	4	47.3		10.1	....	......
5785	27 7 24.8		...	— 18.64	— 0.11	...	2	45.8		...	....	24478
5786	39 12 16.3		17.1	— 18.65	— 0.13	...	3	44.8		14.8	....	24486
5787	46 31 53.1		53.1	— 18.65	— 0.14	— 0.02	4	44.8		7.1	11 Lacertæ	......
5788	79 58 33.6		...	— 18.65	— 0.16	...	15	50.2		...	42 Pegasi ζ....	......
5789	39 15 35.4		40.2	— 18.65	— 0.13	...	3	43.8		13.6	....	24494
5790	15 26 3.3		4.3	— 18.65	— 0.07	...	6	43.9		12.7	....	......
5791	36 57 39.1		38.7	— 18.66	— 0.12	...	3	44.4		13.8	....	......
5792	45 48 0.1		1.9	— 18.67	— 0.14	...	3	45.1		10.0	....	......
5793	50 34 57.5		59.5	— 18.67	— 0.14	...	4	47.8		9.0	12 Lacertæ	......
5794	39 2 58.6		61.2	— 18.67	— 0.13	...	3	45.5		11.9	....	24513
5795	49 15 42.8		46.1	— 18.68	— 0.14	...	4	47.3		11.9	....	......
5796	40 42 58.4		...	— 18.68	— 0.13	...	4	46.7		...	....	24522
5797	39 52 46.8		47.2	— 18.69	— 0.13	...	4	47.3		11.8	....	......
5798	43 44 31.6		32.4	— 18.71	— 0.14	...	4	49.3		11.8	....	24537
5799	36 54 4.9		3.7	— 18.73	— 0.13	...	3	43.7		13.8	....	......
5800	34 30 1.6		1.6	— 18.73	— 0.12	...	3	46.2		12.8	....	24554
5801	43 38 31.2		30.8	— 18.74	— 0.14	...	5	48.2		11.3	....	24559
5802	36 3 15.2		12.1	— 18.74	— 0.12	...	3	46.5		13.9	....	......
5803	44 47 4.3		4.2	— 18.75	— 0.14	...	4	46.8		10.8	....	......
5804	25 56 18.6		19.0	— 18.75	— 0.10	...	4	48.6		12.9	....	24569
5805	39 19 50.1		53.1	— 18.75	— 0.13	...	4	50.9		14.3	....	24568

Magnitude. R.	Estimates of Magnitude.	Mean Right Ascension 1845.0. R.	G.	Precession 1845.0.	Secular Variation	Adopted Proper Motion.
		h. m. s.	s.	s.	s.	s.
7.2	6	22 36 50.89	50.60	+ 2.617	+ 0.014	......
6.9	5	22 37 2.53	1.81	+ 2.379	+ 0.017	......
6.1	7	22 37 5.92	5.83	+ 2.692	+ 0.013	......
5.6	6	22 37 11.28	11.08	+ 2.659	+ 0.014	......
6.8	4	22 37 38.65	...	+ 2.083	+ 0.014	......
6.7	4	22 37 42.25	42.13	+ 2.192	+ 0.017	......
7.5	7	22 37 47.66	47.15	+ 2.498	+ 0.017	......
6.4	4	22 37 52.38	52.19	+ 2.698	+ 0.013	......
7.8	5	22 38 7.35	7.47	+ 2.451	+ 0.017	......
8.2	4	22 38 12.11	...	+ 2.475	+ 0.018	......
6.7	4	22 38 22.11	22.17	+ 2.480	+ 0.017	......
7.0	4	22 38 35.67	...	+ 2.622	+ 0.015	......
7.9	4	22 38 40.63	39.50	+ 1.500	− 0.003	......
8.5	6	22 38 51.62	51.41	+ 2.504	+ 0.017	......
7.0	5	22 38 57.46	56.89	+ 0.278	− 0.143	......
6.7	7	22 38 58.10	58.14	+ 2.348	+ 0.019	......
8.5	6	22 38 58.39	57.98	+ 2.435	+ 0.017	......
7.7	6	22 39 3.18	3.35	+ 2.509	+ 0.017	......
5.8	7	22 39 13.28	...	+ 3.242	− 0.016	− 0.006
5.6	5	22 39 18.29	17.67	+ 2.629	+ 0.015	......
6.5	9	22 39 34.88	34.56	+ 2.604	+ 0.015	......
7.8	3	22 39 56.64	56.37	+ 2.359	+ 0.020	......
8.5	3	22 40 0.12	...	+ 2.359	+ 0.020	......
7.3	4	22 40 8.52	8.32	+ 2.440	+ 0.018	......
7.5	6	22 40 27.49	26.49	+ 1.524	0.000	......
7.7	4	22 40 31.42	30.65	+ 2.118	+ 0.020	......
7.9	6	22 40 37.34	37.23	+ 2.610	+ 0.014	......
8.0	5	22 40 49.08	48.71	+ 2.448	+ 0.017	......
6.5	5	22 41 14.69	14.24	+ 2.359	+ 0.020	......
7.4	5	22 41 19.52	...	+ 1.006	− 0.056	......
5.0	2	22 41 22.88	...	+ 3.185	− 0.012	− 0.004
7.2	6	22 41 39.99	39.27	+ 1.533	0.000	......
7.0	7	22 42 17.02	16.92	+ 2.148	+ 0.017	......
6.2	5	22 42 22.27	22.05	+ 2.467	+ 0.017	......
7.1	6	22 42 35.68	35.10	+ 0.652	− 0.083	......

Ordinal Number. R.	Mean North Polar Distance 1845.0. R.	G.	Precession 1845.0.	Secular Variation.	Adopted Proper Motion.	Observations of N.P.D. No. R.	Mean year. R. 1800 +	G.	Names.	Oeltzen-Argelander Number.
5806	46 16 49.9	50.7	− 18.75	− 0.14	...	3	44.2	10.5	....	......
5807	34 24 17.9	18.1	− 18.75	− 0.12	...	4	45.3	12.8	....	24576
5808	51 20 43.5	43.2	− 18.75	− 0.14	...	4	46.3	14.4	....	......
5809	48 59 32.0	34.4	− 18.76	− 0.14	− 0.02	5	46.6	8.8	13 Lacertæ	......
5810	25 28 30.5	...	− 18.77	− 0.11	...	5	51.3	...	....	24584
5811	28 8 27.1	28.7	− 18.78	− 0.11	...	4	47.3	12.9	....	24588
5812	39 21 56.9	63.6	− 18.78	− 0.12	...	5	48.0	14.8	....	24591
5813	51 36 40.1	39.1	− 18.78	− 0.14	...	3	49.8	12.9	....	......
5814	37 3 20.8	19.1	− 18.79	− 0.12	...	3	49.1	13.9	....	24597
5815	38 11 20.5	...	− 18.79	− 0.13	...	3	53.1	...	....	......
5816	38 17 47.2	47.6	− 18.79	− 0.12	...	4	46.8	13.8	....	......
5817	46 3 39.4	...	− 18.80	− 0.14	...	3	45.4	...	....	......
5818	16 28 47.3	45.6	− 18.80	− 0.05	...	4	46.0	10.7	....	......
5819	39 19 29.3	31.9	− 18.81	− 0.12	...	4	50.1	14.8	....	24612
5820	9 25 6.5	7.8	− 18.81	− 0.01	...	3	45.5	7.9	....	......
5821	32 39 39.0	33.8	− 18.81	− 0.11	...	4	47.8	9.9	....	......
5822	36 5 39.8	38.9	− 18.81	− 0.11	...	5	51.0	13.9	....	24621
5823	39 29 25.9	27.1	− 18.81	− 0.12	...	4	46.5	14.8	....	24622
5824	110 25 13.1	...	− 18.82	− 0.16	+ 0.20	2	54.4	...	68 Aquarii g^2 .	......
5825	46 16 10.5	12.8	− 18.83	− 0.13	...	8	49.3	11.0	....	......
5826	44 35 55.3	55.1	− 18.84	− 0.13	...	6	46.8	10.1	....	24635
5827	32 44 26.6	23.2	− 18.85	− 0.12	...	3	47.2	9.9	....	......
5828	32 44 42.8	...	− 18.85	− 0.12	...	2	48.4	...	....	......
5829	35 56 34.7	35.0	− 18.85	− 0.12	...	3	46.1	13.9	....	24646
5830	16 23 13.2	14.0	− 18.86	− 0.07	...	4	48.3	10.5	....	24655
5831	25 31 13.5	15.5	− 18.86	− 0.10	...	3	48.9	12.8	....	24656
5832	44 36 29.9	28.3	− 18.87	− 0.14	...	4	46.1	10.8	....	24658
5833	36 3 52.0	49.6	− 18.87	− 0.12	...	3	46.8	13.4	....	......
5834	32 20 1.1	1.2	− 18.88	− 0.12	...	4	46.3	8.9	....	24677
5835	12 17 46.4	...	− 18.88	− 0.06	...	4	51.1	...	....	......
5836	104 24 30.9	...	− 18.88	− 0.16	+ 0.02	2	51.8	...	71 Aquarii τ^2 .	......
5837	16 15 41.9	41.0	− 18.89	− 0.07	...	6	45.3	10.4	....	24693
5838	25 45 19.7	19.1	− 18.91	− 0.09	...	4	48.1	12.8	....	24704
5839	36 24 11.5	11.2	− 18.91	− 0.12	...	4	43.5	11.9	....	......
5840	10 22 45.4	44.6	− 18.92	− 0.02	...	4	45.5	13.3	....	24719

Magnitude.	Estimates of Magnitude.	Mean Right Ascension 1845.0.		Precession 1845.0.	Secular Variation	Adopted Proper Motion.
		R.	G.			
	.	h. m. s.	s.	s.	s.	s.
7.0	6	22 42 41.44	41.26	+ 2.540	+ 0.017	......
6.2	3	22 42 54.37	54.26	+ 2.236	+ 0.020	......
7.9	5	22 42 56.57	...	+ 2.697	+ 0.014	......
8.0	7	22 43 15.85	...	+ 2.687	+ 0.015	......
7.8	3	22 43 22.58	22.17	+ 2.466	+ 0.018	......
6.1	6	22 43 22.90	22.72	+ 2.687	+ 0.014	......
5.6	5	22 43 23.43	22.47	+ 2.442	+ 0.019	......
6.4	4	22 43 31.86	31.86	+ 2.551	+ 0.017	......
7.6	6	22 43 44.54	43.89	+ 2.002	+ 0.017	......
6.9	3	22 43 45.47	...	+ 2.002	+ 0.017	......
8.4	6	22 43 45.82	...	+ 2.688	+ 0.015	......
7.8	5	22 43 56.11	56.23	+ 2.648	+ 0.017	......
7.1	4	22 44 6.67	...	+ 2.105	+ 0.017	......
7.3	7	22 44 9.64	...	+ 2.673	+ 0.015	......
3.6	7	22 44 10.51	10.65	+ 2.122	+ 0.020	......
4.6	5	22 44 31.54	...	+ 3.134	− 0.008	− 0.006
8.5	2	22 44 37.97	...	+ 2.702	+ 0.014	......
8.0	5	22 44 45.61	...	+ 2.703	+ 0.014	......
7.2	3	22 44 48.07	...	+ 2.701	+ 0.014	......
7.0	4	22 45 1.23	0.93	+ 2.626	+ 0.017	......
4.8	8	22 45 3.25	3.30	+ 2.677	+ 0.015	+ 0.015
6.8	4	22 45 16.67	...	+ 2.015	+ 0.017	......
7.6	3	22 45 17.03	17.16	+ 2.718	+ 0.014	......
5.8	6	22 45 20.47	19.60	+ 2.302	+ 0.021	......
8.5	7	22 45 29.24	29.26	+ 2.665	+ 0.016	......
6.9	5	22 45 35.30	35.55	+ 2.263	+ 0.021	......
7.4	4	22 45 57.91	57.97	+ 2.566	+ 0.019	......
6.6	5	22 45 58.23	58.12	+ 2.635	+ 0.017	......
6.4	5	22 46 7.04	6.85	+ 2.723	+ 0.014	......
6.5	5	22 46 10.54	10.12	+ 2.573	+ 0.019	......
8.1	4	22 46 19.98	19.79	+ 2.722	+ 0.014	......
4.2	4	22 46 25.20	...	+ 3.196	− 0.013	− 0.007
8.5	5	22 46 27.90	27.91	+ 2.723	+ 0.014	......
5.6	5	22 46 44.66	44.78	+ 2.665	+ 0.016	......
8.4	3	22 47 0.93	0.70	+ 2.609	+ 0.017	......

Ordinal Number.	Mean North Polar Distance 1845.0.		Precession 1845.0.	Secular Variation.	Adopted Proper Motion.	Observations of N.P.D.			Names.	Oeltzen-Argelander Number.
						No.	Mean year.			
R.	R.	G.				R.	R.	G.		
	° ′ ″	″	″	″	″		1800 +			
5841	39 50 9.2	2.9	− 18.92	− 0.12	...	4	47.8	11.8	....	24720
5842	27 52 41.4	38.0	− 18.92	− 0.09	...	4	47.1	12.9	....	24729
5843	49 46 4.9	...	− 18.93	− 0.13	...	3	53.4	...	....	....
5844	48 53 41.5	...	− 18.94	− 0.13	...	3	49.1	...	....	....
5845	35 58 19.3	16.1	− 18.94	− 0.11	...	3	47.9	13.9	....	....
5846	48 51 57.6	58.0	− 18.94	− 0.13	...	4	46.3	8.8	14 Lacertæ	....
5847	34 55 5.4	6.1	− 18.94	− 0.12	...	5	46.8	9.4	....	....
5848	40 8 34.0	33.0	− 18.95	− 0.12	...	3	45.2	15.9	....	....
5849	22 15 5.7	10.0	− 18.95	− 0.09	...	3	46.5	12.8	....	24747
5850	22 15 3.7	...	− 18.95	− 0.09	...	2	50.8	...	....	....
5851	48 48 43.5	...	− 18.95	− 0.13	...	3	47.8	...	....	....
5852	45 52 53.8	54.9	− 18.85	− 0.12	...	3	49.5	13.8	....	....
5853	24 15 58.5	...	− 18.96	− 0.10	...	4	49.8	...	....	24755
5854	47 34 53.4	...	− 18.97	− 0.13	...	5	45.8	...	....	....
5855	24 36 50.0	50.2	− 18.97	− 0.10	+ 0.14	5	44.4	6.8	32 Cephei ι....	....
5856	98 24 9.7	...	− 18.98	− 0.15	− 0.03	6	48.9	...	73 Aquarii λ...	....
5857	49 30 41.7	...	− 18.98	− 0.13	...	2	51.9	...	..:..............	....
5858	49 29 13.0	...	− 18.99	− 0.13	...	2	50.9	...	....	....
5859	49 30 29.2	...	− 18.99	− 0.13	...	2	50.8	...	....	....
5860	44 5 8.3	5.5	− 18.99	− 0.11	...	5	47.4	10.8	....	24775
5861	47 30 37.2	37.5	− 19.00	− 0.13	...	10	49.4	7.9	15 Lacertæ	....
5862	24 4 58.7	...	− 19.00	− 0.10	...	3	49.2	...	....	24783
5863	50 33 21.8	24.6	− 19.00	− 0.13	...	2	44.8	11.9	....	....
5864	29 7 36.8	36.2	− 19.00	− 0.10	...	4	45.7	9.8	....	24788
5865	46 32 5.9	8.0	− 19.00	− 0.12	...	4	49.9	14.8	....	....
5866	27 50 50.5	49.8	− 19.01	− 0.10	...	3	44.5	12.9	....	24797
5867	40 7 1.9	1.2	− 19.01	− 0.11	...	3	48.1	15.9	....	24805
5868	44 16 25.8	24.8	− 19.01	− 0.12	...	4	46.3	10.8	....	24806
5869	50 39 17.4	18.5	− 19.02	− 0.13	...	4	47.3	11.9	....	....
5870	40 24 37.1	36.5	− 19.02	− 0.11	...	3	45.5	11.8	....	24810
5871	50 29 16.2	18.1	− 19.03	− 0.13	...	3	49.9	11.9	....	....
5872	106 38 37.2	...	− 19.03	− 0.15	...	5	53.5	...	76 Aquarii δ...	....
5873	50 33 17.3	19.8	− 19.03	− 0.13	...	3	51.2	11.9	....	....
5874	46 4 25.2	26.2	− 19.04	− 0.12	...	3	45.5	13.8	....	....
5875	42 15 0.1	0.1	− 19.04	− 0.11	...	2	50.9	11.8	....	24841

Magnitude.	Estimates of Magnitude.	Mean Right Ascension 1845.0.		Precession 1845.0.	Secular Variation	Adopted Proper Motion.
R.		R.	G.			
		h. m. s.	s.	s.	s.	s.
6.1	6	22 47 1.16	0.62	+ 2.724	+ 0.014	......
7.3	4	22 47 3.19	...	+ 2.076	+ 0.018	......
7.1	5	22 47 14.87	...	+ 2.079	+ 0.018	......
7.8	4	22 47 17.39	...	+ 2.143	+ 0.018	......
6.8	5	22 47 40.86	40.23	+ 0.822	− 0.066	......
√ 5.1	6	22 47 55.02	54.45	− 0.002	− 0.217	+ 0.006
8.0	6	22 48 16.34	16.07	+ 2.602	+ 0.019	......
8.7	5	22 48 43.91	43.44	+ 2.431	+ 0.021	......
6.6	3	22 48 48.74	48.62	+ 2.682	+ 0.016	......
8.0	6	22 48 48.89	48.76	+ 2.551	+ 0.020	......
1.3	A	22 49 4.38	...	+ 3.309	− 0.023	+ 0.022
6.0	7	22 49 19.65	19.37	+ 2.720	+ 0.015	......
8.5	10	22 49 25.98	26.26	+ 2.703	+ 0.015	......
8.5	6	22 49 34.21	34.04	+ 2.593	+ 0.020	......
5.4	7	22 49 39.01	38.99	+ 2.607	+ 0.019	......
7.2	5	22 49 41.76	41.50	+ 2.440	+ 0.022	......
5.5	4	22 50 14.25	13.98	+ 2.627	+ 0.019	......
6.6	9	22 50 23.15	23.18	+ 2.708	+ 0.016	......
7.4	7	22 50 27.53	27.31	+ 2.752	+ 0.014	......
7.1	3	22 50 31.80	31.21	+ 2.753	+ 0.014	......
7.4	7	22 50 39.79	39.41	+ 2.404	+ 0.023	......
8.1	5	22 50 56.99	...	+ 1.848	+ 0.008	......
7.4	6	22 51 22.99	...	+ 1.856	+ 0.008	......
7.8	4	22 51 33.39	34.02	+ 0.965	− 0.057	......
8.3	5	22 51 47.57	47.31	+ 2.619	+ 0.019	......
7.3	5	22 51 48.64	48.45	+ 2.605	+ 0.019	......
6.5	6	22 52 28.37	28.66	+ 2.576	+ 0.020	......
7.1	6	22 52 29.58	29.33	+ 2.583	+ 0.020	......
7.8	3	22 52 34.67	34.47	+ 2.333	+ 0.024	......
8.1	2	22 52 40.35	40.38	+ 2.699	+ 0.017	......
9.1	5	22 52 40.84	...	+ 2.495	+ 0.022	......
6.5	1	22 52 40.99	...	+ 3.074	− 0.004	+ 0.005
6.7	6	22 52 49.09	48.76	+ 2.427	+ 0.024	......
6.3	5	22 52 57.96	57.59	+ 1.862	+ 0.016	......
6.8	6	22 53 34.08	33.82	+ 2.694	+ 0.017	......

Ordinal Number.	Mean North Polar Distance 1845.0.			Precession 1845.0.	Secular Variation.	Adopted Proper Motion.	Observations of N.P.D.			Names.	Oeltzen-Argelander Number.
R.	R.		G.				No. R.	Mean year. R.	G.		
	° ′ ″		″	″	″	″		1800 +			
5876	50 26 52.8		56.8	— 19.04	— 0.12	...	3	46.9	11.9	....	......
5877	22 49 55.4		...	— 19.04	— 0.09	...	3	51.5	...	....	24844
5878	22 50 9.0		...	— 19.05	— 0.09	...	3	51.5	...	....	24850
5879	24 12 49.0		...	— 19.05	— 0.10	...	4	50.8	...	....	......
5880	10 27 15.5		15.3	— 19.06	— 0.02	...	5	47.6	12.7	....	......
5881	7 40 9.0		8.5	— 19.07	0.00	— 0.05	6	44.0	7.7	3.4 Aqrb̶	......
5882	41 21 3.8		3.6	— 19.08	— 0.11	...	3	44.5	13.9	....	24872
5883	32 36 53.9		54.6	— 19.10	— 0.10	...	2	48.4	12.8	....	......
5884	46 31 1.6		1.3	— 19.10	— 0.12	...	4	44.8	14.8	....	......
5885	38 12 8.9		9.1	— 19.10	— 0.11	...	3	49.8	13.8	....	24878
5886	120 26 31.5		...	— 19.10	— 0.15	+ 0.18	8	52.9	...	24 Pisc. Austr. α	......
5887	49 13 19.0		21.2	— 19.11	— 0.12	...	5	47.2	9.2	16 Lacertæ	......
5888	47 48 51.9		54.4	— 19.11	— 0.11	...	3	50.5	14.9	....	......
5889	40 17 6.8		9.2	— 19.12	— 0.11	...	3	50.5	15.3	....	24892
5890	41 5 35.1		33.7	— 19.12	— 0.11	...	5	45.6	13.3	....	24895
5891	32 37 51.3		51.2	— 19.12	— 0.10	...	3	43.5	12.8	....	24898
5892	42 8 35.0		34.5	— 19.13	— 0.11	...	3	44.1	11.8	....	24912
5893	47 48 53.5		55.5	— 19.13	— 0.12	...	4	45.5	14.9	....	......
5894	51 26 19.5		19.6	— 19.14	— 0.12	...	4	48.3	14.9	....	......
5895	51 31 6.9		8.6	— 19.14	— 0.12	...	3	46.8	14.9	....	......
5896	30 51 56.7		56.6	— 19.14	— 0.10	...	5	47.8	9.9	....	......
5897	17 59 4.8		...	— 19.15	— 0.08	...	3	48.6	...	....	......
5898	17 59 24.2		...	— 19.16	— 0.08	...	3	46.9	...	....	......
5899	10 35 15.3		14.2	— 19.16	— 0.01	...	3	49.5	15.8	....	......
5900	40 58 32.9		33.7	— 19.17	— 0.11	...	3	50.2	13.9	....	24951
5901	40 7 49.0		47.5	— 19.17	— 0.11	...	3	45.1	11.9	....	24953
5902	38 10 34.7		35.8	— 19.19	— 0.10	...	3	45.8	13.8	....	......
5903	38 31 33.8		33.7	— 19.19	— 0.10	...	4	47.4	14.8	....	......
5904	27 45 7.8		8.2	— 19.19	— 0.09	...	4	48.3	15.9	....	24969
5905	46 11 52.1		49.8	— 19.20	— 0.12	...	4	49.8	11.9	....	......
5906	33 57 36.5		...	— 19.20	— 0.11	...	3	52.1	...	....	24972
5907	90 38 44.8		...	— 19.20	— 0.13	— 0.02	3	57.8	...	3 Piscium	......
5908	31 0 53.5		53.6	— 19.20	— 0.10	...	4	46.8	9.9	....	......
5909	17 41 39.9		39.6	— 19.21	— 0.08	...	5	46.4	16.4	....	24978
5910	45 27 20.8		21.1	— 19.22	— 0.11	...	3	46.2	11.8	....	......

Ordinal Number.		Magnitude.	Estimates of Magnitude.	Mean Right Ascension 1845.0.			Precession 1845.0.	Secular Variation	Adopted Proper Motion.	Observations of R.A.		
R.	G.	R.	R.	R.		G.				No. R.	Mean year. R.	G.
				h. m. s.		s.	s.	s.	s.		1800 +	
5911	...	6.0	2	22 53	34.08	...	+ 2.501	+ 0.022	......	2	51.3	...
5912	3948	8.3	6	22 53	50.66	50.32	+ 2.630	+ 0.019	......	3	47.5	13.9
5913	3949	7.5	3	22 53	55.60	55.44	+ 2.614	+ 0.020	......	3	48.9	15.9
5914	3950	8.6	4	22 54	3.82	3.90	+ 2.541	+ 0.023	......	2	49.3	14.9
5915	3951	7.8	5	22 54	12.31	12.46	+ 2.712	+ 0.017	......	2	48.3	14.8
5916	...	7.9	5	22 54	27.02	...	+ 1.917	+ 0.012	......	2	51.3	...
5917	3953	9.0	4	22 54	29.12	29.07	+ 2.548	+ 0.023	......	2	48.8	14.9
5918	3952	7.6	3	22 54	32.80	32.54	+ 2.698	+ 0.017	......	2	47.3	11.8
5919	3954	3.3	4	22 54	47.99	47.73	+ 2.738	+ 0.016	......	6	46.4	6.8
5920	3955	8.4	5	22 54	48.40	48.34	+ 2.716	+ 0.017	......	3	50.7	11.9
5921	...	6.2	4	22 54	58.43	...	+ 2.509	+ 0.024	......	3	48.8	...
5922	3956	7.3	6	22 54	59.55	59.71	+ 2.624	+ 0.020	......	4	47.5	15.9
5923	3957	6.4	3	22 55	8.02	7.90	+ 2.713	+ 0.017	......	2	50.2	11.9
5924	3960	7.2	6	22 55	23.62	23.45	+ 2.357	+ 0.026	......	3	49.5	13.6
5925	3959	7.2	4	22 55	19.08	18.93	+ 2.441	+ 0.023	......	2	48.3	12.8
5926	3970	4.7	5	22 55	24.69	24.96	− 0.201	− 0.292	+ 0.069	5.	51.3	7.7
5927	3958	5.2	5	22 55	28.81	28.45	+ 2.737	+ 0.017	+ 0.005	3	44.8	9.4
5928	3962	7.9	5	22 55	36.85	36.89	+ 2.579	+ 0.022	......	2	49.8	13.8
5929	3961	6.8	4	22 55	40.58	40.61	+ 2.722	+ 0.017	......	4	48.8	14.8
5930	...	4.8	2	22 55	59.41	...	+ 3.051	− 0.002	......	7	47.9	...
5931	3964	7.1	5	22 56	0.66	0.39	+ 2.456	+ 0.023	......	2	50.3	12.9
5932	3963	7.9	5	22 56	1.01	1.18	+ 2.591	+ 0.022	......	3	50.4	14.9
5933	3965	7.2	4	22 56	4.07	4.25	+ 2.556	+ 0.023	......	3	48.2	14.9
5934	3966	7.6	5	22 56	11.84	11.82	+ 2.464	+ 0.023	......	2	51.3	12.9
5935	...	7.6	5	22 56	15.39	...	+ 2.466	+ 0.025	......	3	52.5	...
5936	3967	8.2	3	22 56	16.05	15.75	+ 2.338	+ 0.026	......	2	51.4	11.0
5937	3973	7.0	3	22 56	23.87	23.95	+ 1.092	− 0.049	......	2	51.4	15.8
5938	3968	6.9	5	22 56	28.14	27.74	+ 2.367	+ 0.026	......	2	51.4	13.6
5939	3969	8.0	3	22 56	41.62	41.76	+ 2.596	+ 0.023	......	3	51.8	14.9
5940	3971	6.6	4	22 57	0.05	59.81	+ 2.451	+ 0.025	......	5	51.2	12.8
5941	...	2.0	Λ	22 57	2.59	...	+ 2.977	+ 0.004	+ 0.003	53	44.3	...
5942	...	7.7	2	22 57	13.62	...	+ 2.762	+ 0.016	+ 0.007	2	52.9	...
5943	3972	4.6	4	22 57	14.19	14.55	+ 2.651	+ 0.021	+ 0.023	5	47.1	9.9
5944	3975	4.9	5	22 57	39.84	39.49	+ 2.249	+ 0.026	......	3	44.8	10.8
5945	3974	8.6	6	22 57	42.67	42.42	+ 2.475	+ 0.023	......	3	51.9	12.9

| Ordinal Number. R. | Mean North Polar Distance 1845.0. | | Precession 1845.0. | Adopted Proper Motion. | Secular Variation. | Observations of N.P.D. | | | Names. | Oeltzen-Argelander Number. |
	R.	G.				No. R.	Mean year. R.	G.		
	° ′ ″	″	″	″	″		1800 +			
5911	33 53 6.5	...	— 19.22	— 0.10	...	4	48.6	...	....	24991
5912	40 52 29.2	27.8	— 19.23	— 0.10	...	3	49.8	13.9	....	....
5913	39 48 58.2	59.8	— 19.23	— 0.10	...	2	50.4	15.9	....	24995
5914	35 37 14.0	16.1	— 19.23	— 0.09	...	2	50.9	14.9	....	....
5915	46 37 58.3	59.5	— 19.23	— 0.11	...	4	49.3	14.8	....	....
5916	18 6 55.1	...	— 19.24	— 0.08	...	4	49.4	...	....	25004
5917	35 51 8.9	8.0	— 19.24	— 0.09	...	2	51.4	14.9	....	....
5918	45 19 20.9	21.1	— 19.24	— 0.11	...	3	47.2	11.3	....	....
5919	48 30 20.9	18.9	— 19.25	— 0.11	...	3	44.8	6.8	1 Andromedæ o	....
5920	46 42 13.4	15.0	— 19.25	— 0.11	...	3	42.5	11.9	....	....
5921	33 43 34.5	...	— 19.25	— 0.10	— 0.02	3	49.5	...	....	25012
5922	39 58 57.3	57.9	— 19.25	— 0.10	...	3	46.5	15.9	....	....
5923	46 15 31.2	30.6	— 19.26	— 0.11	...	3	46.4	11.9	....	....
5924	27 32 24.3	24.7	— 19.27	— 0.09	...	4	46.3	13.6	....	25027
5925	30 38 7.1	8.0	— 19.27	— 0.10	...	4	48.3	9.9	....	....
5926	6 29 1.8	1.8	— 19.27	+ 0.01	...	3	43.4	7.7	..36.αδΜ..	....
5927	48 4 29.1	28.1	— 19.27	— 0.11	...	4	46.5	9.4	2 Andromedæ	....
5928	37 1 27.2	28.6	— 19.27	— 0.10	...	3	49.8	13.8	....	....
5929	46 46 26.7	26.4	— 19.28	— 0.11	...	3	47.5	14.8	....	....
5930	87 0 44.3	...	— 19.28	— 0.12	+ 0.02	2	55.7	...	4 Piscium β...	....
5931	30 58 47.8	47.9	— 19.28	— 0.10	...	3	46.1	12.9	....	....
5932	37 35 13.9	13.3	— 19.28	— 0.10	...	4	49.0	14.9	....	25037
5933	35 35 50.0	50.0	— 19.28	— 0.09	...	4	49.3	14.9	....	....
5934	31 13 42.2	39.1	— 19.28	— 0.10	...	3	47.9	12.9	....	....
5935	31 16 33.7	...	— 19.29	— 0.10	...	2	48.9	...	....	....
5936	26 37 19.7	21.0	— 19.29	— 0.09	...	2	43.8	12.0	....	....
5937	10 29 22.5	22.4	— 19.29	— 0.04	...	4	45.3	15.8	....	25051
5938	27 29 33.2	34.8	— 19.29	— 0.09	...	4	47.8	13.6	....	25052
5939	37 31 52.8	51.2	— 19.30	— 0.10	...	3	46.5	14.9	....	25055
5940	30 23 17.5	18.3	— 19.30	— 0.10	...	3	45.4	12.8	....	....
5941	75 37 38.8	...	— 19.31	— 0.12	+ 0.02	15	45.5	...	54 Pegasi α ...	....
5942	49 33 36.0	...	— 19.31	— 0.11	+ 0.06	3	49.5	...	....	....
5943	40 47 21.7	24.7	— 19.31	— 0.10	— 0.12	3	45.1	9.9	3 Andromedæ	25070
5944	23 37 33.2	33.4	— 19.32	— 0.09	— 0.03	4	45.8	10.8	....	25081
5945	31 6 28.4	28.4	— 19.32	— 0.10	...	3	52.2	12.9	....	....

Magnitude.	Estimates of Magnitude.	Mean Right Ascension 1845.0.		Precession 1845.0.	Secular Variation	Adopted Proper Motion.
R.		R.	G.			
		h. m. s.	s.	s.	s.	s.
7.5	4	22 57 43.80	...	+ 2.759	+ 0.016	......
9.5	4	22 57 44.42	...	+ 2.450	+ 0.026	......
7.9	5	22 57 49.63	49.69	+ 2.380	+ 0.026	......
6.8	6	22 58 18.37	18.35	+ 2.390	+ 0.026	......
7.0	4	22 58 32.94	33.49	+ 1.073	− 0.053	......
7.0	2	22 58 35.90	35.58	+ 2.368	+ 0.029	......
7.9	4	22 58 39.98	39.94	+ 2.740	+ 0.017	......
9.8	4	22 58 57.67	...	+ 1.793	− 0.002	......
8.0	5	22 59 30.42	...	+ 2.708	+ 0.020	......
7.7	6	22 59 34.19	33.96	+ 1.798	+ 0.017	......
8.7	4	22 59 34.40	...	+ 2.708	+ 0.020	......
7.7	6	22 59 44.70	44.21	+ 2.374	+ 0.029	......
7.6	3	22 59 51.95	45.91	+ 2.407	+ 0.028	......
5.0	3	23 0 4.71	4.33	+ 2.504	+ 0.026	+ 0.004
7.2	2	23 0 9.50	...	+ 2.668	+ 0.022	......
6.8	4	23 0 13.16	12.85	+ 2.722	+ 0.020	......
6.6	7	23 0 19.00	18.72	+ 2.630	+ 0.023	......
8.0	6	23 0 32.10	31.77	+ 2.793	+ 0.017	......
5.8	7	23 0 34.83	34.92	+ 2.721	+ 0.020	......
6.2	3	23 0 38.72	38.54	+ 2.503	+ 0.028	......
6.1	3	23 0 43.77	43.80	+ 2.684	+ 0.021	+ 0.018
5.5	1	23 0 45.66	...	+ 3.062	− 0.002	+ 0.011
6.6	5	23 1 3.82	3.51	+ 2.745	+ 0.019	......
8.5	5	23 1 5.62	...	+ 2.790	+ 0.016	......
7.5	7	23 1 29.38	29.66	+ 2.803	+ 0.016	......
7.1	6	23 1 29.42	28.99	+ 1.832	− 0.019	......
6.2	6	23 1 29.45	29.65	+ 2.413	+ 0.029	......
7.4	4	23 1 39.65	...	+ 2.806	+ 0.015	......
6.4	2	23 1 40.94	40.91	+ 2.398	+ 0.029	......
8.0	4	23 1 58.16	...	+ 2.794	+ 0.016	......
6.6	6	23 2 16.66	16.44	+ 2.689	+ 0.022	......
7.0	4	23 2 35.24	35.21	+ 2.805	+ 0.016	......
7.1	4	23 2 35.34	...	+ 2.445	+ 0.027	......
7.2	4	23 2 35.43	...	+ 2.447	+ 0.027	......
4.6	5	23 2 58.92	58.80	+ 1.879	+ 0.020	......

Ordinal Number. R.	Mean North Polar Distance 1845.0. R.	G.	Precession 1845.0.	Secular Variation.	Adopted Proper Motion	Observations of N.P.D. No. R.	Mean year. R. (1800 +)	G.	Names.	Oeltzen-Argelander Number.
	° ′ ″	″	″	″	″					
5946	49 23 58.1	...	— 19.32	— 0.11	...	2	49.3	...	....	....
5947	30 19 47.9	...	— 19.32	— 0.10	...	3	46.8	...	....	....
5948	27 26 16.7	16.8	— 19.33	— 0.09	...	3	50.5	16.0	....	25086
5949	27 35 46.4	47.3	— 19.33	— 0.09	...	4	46.8	15.9	....	25098
5950	10 3 10.9	12.4	— 19.34	— 0.04	...	5	48.8	15.9	....	....
5951	26 44 40.6	40.0	— 19.34	— 0.09	...	2	49.4	10.9	....	25110
5952	46 56 59.8	61.6	— 19.34	— 0.11	...	3	51.2	14.8	....	....
5953	15 23 35.8	...	— 19.35	— 0.06	...	2	51.8	...	....	....
5954	43 54 45.8	...	— 19.36	— 0.10	...	3	49.8	...	....	25128
5955	15 19 7.4	6.6	— 19.36	— 0.06	...	4	51.1	13.8	....	....
5956	43 53 38.9	...	— 19.36	— 0.10	...	2	47.4	...	....	25131
5957	26 32 27.7	29.7	— 19.36	— 0.09	...	4	46.4	10.9	....	25136
5958	27 37 25.8	27.0	— 19.36	— 0.09	...	3	45.6	15.9	....	25138
5959	31 25 0.9	2.9	— 19.37	— 0.09	...	4	44.6	9.8	1 Cassiopeiæ ..	....
5960	40 38 41.1	...	— 19.37	— 0.10	...	3	51.5	...	....	25146
5961	44 46 8.7	7.9	— 19.37	— 0.10	...	3	46.5	11.9	....	25149
5962	38 1 15.9	15.9	— 19.37	— 0.09	...	3	45.5	11.8	....	25153
5963	51 2 33.4	32.3	— 19.38	— 0.09	...	3	50.1	13.9	....	....
5964	44 26 55.0	54.8	— 19.38	— 0.10	...	4	45.6	9.9	4 Andromedæ.	25156
5965	31 6 35.9	35.9	— 19.38	— 0.09	...	4	47.0	12.8	....	....
5966	41 32 51.6	52.5	— 19.38	— 0.10	— 0.13	4	47.2	8.8	5 Andromedæ.	25162
5967	88 42 53.9	...	— 19.38	— 0.11	— 0.15	3	54.5	...	5 Piscium A...	....
5968	46 16 34.9	33.8	— 19.39	— 0.10	...	4	47.3	11.9	....	....
5969	50 31 3.4	...	— 19.39	— 0.10	...	3	54.1	...	....	....
5970	51 40 11.7	12.4	— 19.40	— 0.10	...	5	50.1	13.9	....	....
5971	15 15 22.7	24.5	— 19.40	— 0.06	...	4	45.6	13.8	....	25180
5972	27 12 17.8	17.5	— 19.40	— 0.08	...	4	45.8	15.0	....	....
5973	51 55 23.7	...	— 19.41	— 0.11	...	2	48.4	...	....	....
5974	26 36 56.1	56.9	— 19.41	— 0.09	...	4	44.9	10.8	....	25182
5975	50 42 17.1	...	— 19.41	— 0.10	...	3	53.1	...	....	....
5976	41 11 19.1	19.0	— 19.42	— 0.09	...	3	45.8	11.8	....	25189
5977	51 22 11.5	12.8	— 19.43	— 0.09	...	4	51.8	13.9	....	....
5978	27 55 47.4	...	— 19.43	— 0.09	...	3	49.5	...	....	25202
5979	28 1 23.9	...	— 19.43	— 0.09	...	3	50.2	...	....	25203
5980	15 27 0.2	0.6	— 19.44	— 0.06	...	4	46.6	10.4	33 Cephei π...	25213

Magnitude.	Estimates of Magnitude.	Mean Right Ascension 1845.0.			Precession 1845.0.	Secular Variation	Adopted Proper Motion.
R.	R.	R.		G.			
		h. m. s.		s.	s.	s.	s.
5.6	3	23 3 7.48		7.23	+ 2.534	+ 0.028	+ 0.006
8.3	6	23 3 13.08		12.97	+ 2.430	+ 0.029	......
8.4	5	23 3 13.65		12.80	+ 2.536	+ 0.028	......
5.8	7	23 3 18.19		18.05	+ 2.768	+ 0.018	— 0.018
7.0	5	23 3 26.56		...	+ 2.575	+ 0.026	......
7.5	5	23 3 49.56		49.34	+ 2.770	+ 0.018	......
6.4	5	23 3 49.71		49.24	+ 2.328	+ 0.031	......
7.4	3	23 3 56.40		56.36	+ 2.788	+ 0.017	......
8.3	5	23 4 4.86		4.51	+ 1.275	— 0.026	......
7.5	7	23 4 12.31		12.12	+ 2.654	+ 0.023	......
9.0	6	23 4 15.25		...	+ 2.653	+ 0.024	......
7.5	6	23 4 18.06		18.39	+ 1.294	— 0.026	..... .
7.1	4	23 4 22.73		22.56	+ 2.688	+ 0.023	..... .
7.6	6	23 5 22.71		22.55	+ 2.675	+ 0.023	......
4.6	7	23 5 27.77		27.47	+ 2.713	+ 0.022	+ 0.008
9.8	5	23 5 27.97		...	+ 2.813	+ 0.017	......
7.2	4	23 5 45.65		45.62	+ 2.795	+ 0.018	......
7.5	4	23 5 46.55		46.16	+ 2.815	+ 0.018	......
5.6	3	23 5 50.63		...	+ 2.601	+ 0.027	+ 0.201
8.8	3	23 6 11.61		...	+ 2.757	+ 0.020	......
4.8	8	23 6 17.61		...	+ 3.107	— 0.006	+ 0.001
7.4	6	23 6 35.29		...	+ 0.943	— 0.081	......
7.8	6	23 6 49.53		...	+ 2.372	+ 0.029	......
8.2	4	23 6 55.90		55.45	+ 2.760	+ 0.020	......
8.4	5	23 7 7.49		10.53	+ 2.789	+ 0.019	......
6.1	3	23 7 10.45		10.32	+ 2.709	+ 0.023	......
7.3	9	23 7 10.61		10.48	+ 2.787	+ 0.019	......
8.2	5	23 7 48.52		48.55	+ 2.794	+ 0.020	......
7.6	4	23 7 50.21		50.17	+ 2.761	+ 0.020	......
9.1	5	23 7 56.62		...	+ 1.263	— 0.044	......
8.8	6	23 8 24.52		24.21	+ 2.002	+ 0.030	......
4.2	7	23 9 7.87		...	+ 3.057	— 0.002	+ 0.047
6.5	3	23 9 7.89		6.39	+ 2.083	+ 0.031	......
7.5	4	23 9 13.53		...	+ 2.724	+ 0.024	......
7.5	4	23 9 20.11		...	+ 2.723	+ 0.024	....

Ordinal Number.	Mean North Polar Distance 1845.0.		Precession 1845.0.	Secular Variation.	Adopted Proper Motion.	Observations of N.P.D.			Names.	Oeltzen-Argelander Number.
R.	R.	G.				No. R.	Mean year. R.	G.		
	° ′ ″	″	″	″	″		1800 +			
5981	31 30 26.2	26.3	− 19.44	− 0.09	...	4	43.8	9.8	2 Cassiopeiæ...	25219
5982	27 6 31.3	31.4	− 19.44	− 0.08	...	3	45.5	15.0	....	25221
5983	31 33 6.4	7.2	− 19.44	− 0.09	...	2	46.8	9.8	....	25223
5984	47 17 14.7	13.5	− 19.44	− 0.10	+ 0.14	6	49.5	10.9	6 Andromedæ.	......
5985	33 23 26.7	...	− 19.45	− 0.09	...	4	51.8	...	....	......
5986	47 11 1.5	0.3	− 19.45	− 0.10	...	3	48.2	10.8	....	......
5987	23 35 56.5	56.8	− 19.45	− 0.08	...	4	46.5	10.8	....	25234
5988	48 57 52.2	54.5	− 19.45	− 0.09	...	3	51.2	11.9	....	......
5989	10 12 8.1	9.1	− 19.45	− 0.02	...	3	48.5	15.8	....	25244
5990	37 46 57.0	56.1	− 19.46	− 0.07	...	4	45.4	12.5	....	......
5991	37 48 50.7	...	− 19.46	− 0.09	...	3	52.5	...	....	......
5992	10 16 8.2	8.4	− 19.46	− 0.02	...	3	46.5	15.8	....	25250
5993	40 4 12.7	13.9	− 19.46	− 0.09	...	3	44.5	14.1	....	25249
5994	38 36 40.5	42.1	− 19.48	− 0.09	...	4	46.8	11.8	....	......
5995	41 26 22.7	24.3	− 19.48	− 0.09	− 0.09	4	42.3	7.8	7 Andromedæ.	25270
5996	50 50 13.2	...	− 19.48	− 0.10	...	3	47.6	...	....	......
5997	48 46 45.0	44.0	− 19.49	− 0.10	...	3	45.2	11.9	....	......
5998	50 50 22.5	21.8	− 19.49	− 0.10	...	3	49.2	12.3	....	......
5999	33 41 11.4	...	− 19.49	− 0.09	− 0.28	5	49.2	...	....	......
6000	44 47 16.0	...	− 19.50	− 0.09	...	3	51.2	...	....	......
6001	96 53 0.6	...	− 19.51	− 0.10	+ 0.19	10	52.7	...	90 Aquarii φ..	......
6002	8 15 29.3	...	− 19.51	− 0.03	...	5	51.2	...	....	......
6003	23 45 59.4	...	− 19.52	− 0.08	...	3	47.1	...	....	......
6004	44 43 7.8	8.6	− 19.52	− 0.09	...	4	47.8	13.9	....	......
6005	47 22 0.3	2.0	− 19.52	− 0.09	...	3	47.2	11.9	....	......
6006	40 13 30.2	30.7	− 19.53	− 0.09	...	3	43.8	12.9	....	25309
6007	47 8 29.6	57.5	− 19.53	− 0.09	...	5	46.4	11.9	....	......
6008	47 31 44.0	44.5	− 19.54	− 0.09	...	4	47.5	11.9	....	......
6009	44 19 7.2	6.5	− 19.54	− 0.09	...	3	44.8	11.9	....	......
6010	9 29 22.7	...	− 19.54	− 0.04	...	3	52.5	...	....	......
6011	15 36 28.3	31.7	− 19.54	− 0.06	...	4	47.3	13.8	....	......
6012	87 33 50.3	...	− 19.56	− 0.10	+ 0.01	8	48.7	...	6 Piscium γ...	......
6013	16 36 47.2	48.3	− 19.56	− 0.06	...	5	44.7	5.8	....	......
6014	40 21 25.1	...	− 19.56	− 0.09	...	3	44.2	...	....	25348
6015	40 10 22.7	...	− 19.56	− 0.09	...	3	46.5	...	....	25352

Magnitude.	Estimates of Magnitude.	Mean Right Ascension 1845.0.		Precession 1845.0.	Secular Variation	Adopted Proper Motion.
R.		R.	G.			
		h. m. s.	s.	s.	s.	s.
7.5	4	23 9 21.34	...	+ 1.098	− 0.063	......
5.5	5	23 9 39.49	38.83	+ 2.692	+ 0.026	......
6.0	6	23 9 40.64	40.29	+ 2.268	+ 0.036	......
6.1	3	23 10 0.13	59.85	+ 2.787	+ 0.021	......
7.8	3	23 10 18.46	...	+ 2.727	+ 0.024	......
7.9	2	23 10 32.58	...	+ 2.806	+ 0.020	......
5.2	3	23 10 34.52	34.18	+ 2.750	+ 0.023	......
6.8	3	23 10 40.42	40.33	+ 2.788	+ 0.021	......
5.7	3	23 10 53.75	...	+ 3.122	− 0.008	− 0.002
6.3	5	23 11 2.88	2.95	+ 2.824	+ 0.019	......
8.1	5	23 11 12.25	12.57	+ 1.695	+ 0.003	......
6.4	3	23 11 45.03	44.63	+ 2.797	+ 0.021	......
7.7	4	23 11 45.45	45.51	+ 2.764	+ 0.023	......
6.5	5	23 11 52.73	51.05	+ 2.066	+ 0.031	......
8.6	6	23 11 56.27	55.76	+ 2.709	+ 0.026	......
7.4	4	23 12 16.90	16.94	+ 2.175	+ 0.037	......
5.0	5	23 12 17.07	17.15	+ 2.411	+ 0.037	+ 0.019
5.6	5	23 12 17.45	17.06	+ 2.765	+ 0.023	+ 0.003
7.6	5	23 12 19.99	19.71	+ 2.851	+ 0.017	......
6.2	5	23 12 25.88	25.61	+ 2.769	+ 0.023	+ 0.019
6.2	7	23 12 30.50	30.35	+ 2.829	+ 0.019	+ 0.009
7.8	6	23 12 34.32	...	+ 0.697	− 0.141	......
7.5	3	23 12 38.97	38.78	+ 2.832	+ 0.019	......
4.7	A	23 12 58.40	...	+ 2.955	+ 0.009	......
6.8	5	23 13 13.77	13.98	+ 2.595	+ 0.033	......
8.8	4	23 13 18.18	...	+ 2.719	+ 0.027	......
7.4	5	23 13 23.51	...	+ 2.812	+ 0.020	......
6.1	5	23 13 24.77	...	+ 2.817	+ 0.020	......
8.6	5	23 13 26.43	26.21	+ 2.644	+ 0.031	......
6.2	4	23 13 29.39	...	+ 2.582	+ 0.034	......
6.7	6	23 13 31.48	31.05	+ 2.614	+ 0.032	......
8.6	5	23 13 39.34	39.62	+ 2.650	+ 0.031	......
6.3	2	23 13 49.86	...	+ 2.580	+ 0.034	......
8.6	2	23 13 56.81	56.78	+ 2.601	+ 0.033	......
7.2	3	23 14 7.63	...	+ 2.820	+ 0.021	......

Ordinal Number.	Mean North Polar Distance 1845.0.			Precession 1845.0.	Secular Variation.	Adopted Proper Motion.	Observations of N.P.D.			Names.	Oeltzen-Argelander Number.
							No.	Mean year.			
R.	R.		G.				R.	R.	G.		
	° ′ ″		″	″	″	″		1800 +			
6016	8 27	6.6	...	— 19.56	— 0.03	...	5	51.2	...	....	......
6017	37 37	17.2	17.8	— 19.57	— 0.08	+ 0.28	5	47.2	11.8	....	......
6018	19 57	24.6	24.5	— 19.57	— 0.07	...	7	45.6	9.9	....	25361
6019	45 40	43.1	41.1	— 19.58	— 0.09	...	4	44.6	12.8	....	......
6020	40 1	9.3	...	— 19.58	— 0.09	...	4	46.3	...	....	25375
6021	47 17	28.1	...	— 19.59	— 0.09	...	3	46.1	...	....	......
6022	41 49	51.2	51.9	— 19.59	— 0.09	...	4	42.3	8.3	8 Andromedæ.	25381
6023	45 21	24.4	23.3	— 19.59	— 0.09	...	5	46.8	12.3	....	......
6024	100 27	25.3	...	— 19.59	— 0.10	— 0.01	3	52.1	...	95 Aquarii ψ^3.	......
6025	49 4	19.9	19.1	— 19.60	— 0.09	...	4	44.8	10.5	9 Andromedæ.	......
6026	11 36	46.7	46.5	— 19.60	— 0.04	...	2	47.3	13.8	....	25395
6027	45 42	34.8	34.4	— 19.61	— 0.09	...	4	45.4	12.8	....	......
6028	42 21	2.6	1.4	— 19.61	— 0.08	...	3	44.5	11.9	....	25405
6029	15 32	50.9	51.5	— 19.62	— 0.07	...	3	44.5	13.8	....	......
6030	37 36	49.6	50.2	— 19.62	— 0.09	...	5	49.1	11.8	....	25414
6031	17 9	27.6	25.8	— 19.62	— 0.06	...	3	47.9	11.0	....	25420
6032	22 44	9.9	10.3	— 19.62	— 0.07	— 0.02	14	51.8	7.1	34 Cephei o ...	25418
6033	42 13	25.7	28.7	— 19.62	— 0.08	— 0.03	4	47.9	9.5	11 Andromedæ	25417
6034	51 33	26.2	25.3	— 19.62	— 0.08	...	3	48.9	11.9	....	......
6035	42 28	4.5	4.0	— 19.62	— 0.08	— 0.04	6	46.3	11.9	....	25422
6036	48 46	10.3	10.0	— 19.62	— 0.08	— 0.05	5	48.0	10.8	10 Andromedæ	......
6037	6 36	11.7	...	— 19.63	— 0.02	...	4	51.4	...	....	......
6038	49 5	34.1	32.7	— 19.63	— 0.08	...	3	46.5	10.5	....	......
6039	67 6	24.7	...	— 19.63	— 0.09	...	2	55.8	...	62 Pegasi τ ...	......
6040	29 41	52.7	54.1	— 19.63	— 0.07	...	3	51.8	14.8	....	25437
6041	37 35	6.6	...	— 19.64	— 0.07	...	2	52.9	...	....	25440
6042	46 16	0.9	...	— 19.64	— 0.08	...	2	50.9	...	....	......
6043	46 43	50.1	...	— 19.64	— 0.08	...	2	47.4	...	....	......
6044	39 19	53.2	53.8	— 19.64	— 0.07	...	3	50.2	14.9	....	......
6045	28 52	39.2	...	— 19.64	— 0.07	+ 0.06	2	49.9	...	....	25444
6046	30 34	23.1	21.6	— 19.64	— 0.07	...	3	44.8	10.9	....	......
6047	32 34	13.7	15.5	— 19.64	— 0.07	...	2	52.8	14.9	....	25446
6048	28 38	6.5	...	— 19.64	— 0.07	— 0.04	2	48.9	...	....	25451
6049	29 39	13.8	15.3	— 19.65	— 0.07	...	1	49.9	14.8	....	25452
6050	46 45	34.3	...	— 19.65	— 0.08	...	3	52.5	...	....	......

Magnitude.	Estimates of Magnitude.	Mean Right Ascension 1845.0.		Precession 1845.0.	Secular Variation	Adopted Proper Motion.
R.	R.	R.	G.			
		h. m. s.	s.	s.	s.	s.
7.3	4	23 14 18.02	...	+ 2.618	+ 0.033	......
7.4	6	23 14 22.67	...	+ 1.307	− 0.052	......
7.5	4	23 14 31.38	29.00	+ 1.814	+ 0.029	......
8.0	3	23 14 36.74	36.58	+ 2.708	+ 0.029	......
7.3	4	23 14 48.67	...	+ 2.780	+ 0.024	......
8.7	8	23 15 19.78	19.49	+ 2.723	+ 0.029	......
7.8	7	23 15 35.88	35.63	+ 2.724	+ 0.029	......
5.1	3	23 15 39.35	38.77	+ 2.638	+ 0.033	......
8.9	3	23 15 42.90	...	+ 2.726	+ 0.028	......
6.7	3	23 16 30.61	30.19	+ 2.733	+ 0.029	......
6.4	4	23 16 43.78	43.70	+ 2.854	+ 0.020	......
6.9	5	23 17 6.30	5.86	+ 2.692	+ 0.031	......
6.8	6	23 17 8.74	8.57	+ 2.860	+ 0.020	......
8.6	2	23 17 9.70	9.39	+ 2.724	+ 0.029	......
6.9	5	23 17 10.05	9.68	+ 2.549	+ 0.037	......
8.2	5	23 17 23.53	...	+ 2.619	+ 0.034	......
7.7	4	23 17 48.55	48.48	+ 2.730	+ 0.029	......
7.4	4	23 17 50.37	50.13	+ 2.717	+ 0.029	......
4.6	5	23 17 58.57	58.27	+ 2.622	+ 0.036	+ 0.003
6.9	6	23 18 24.52	24.55	+ 2.760	+ 0.028	......
7.0	4	23 18 33.47	...	+ 2.757	+ 0.028	......
8.3	7	23 18 47.98	47.84	+ 2.760	+ 0.028	......
7.8	4	23 18 55.35	55.86	+ 2.647	+ 0.034	......
5.7	2	23 18 59.31	...	+ 3.068	− 0.002	+ 0.005
8.8	10	23 19 0.78	...	+ 0.233	− 0.290	......
7.2	7	23 19 8.47	8.20	+ 2.763	+ 0.028	......
6.9	4	23 19 24.14	24.27	+ 2.658	+ 0.034	......
6.1	7	23 19 40.01	39.80	+ 2.859	+ 0.020	+ 0.007
9.0	4	23 19 41.82	41.79	+ 2.747	+ 0.029	......
6.9	5	23 19 47.49	46.96	+ 2.435	+ 0.045	......
8.7	4	23 19 58.23	57.55	+ 2.750	+ 0.029	......
8.5	4	23 20 12.54	12.84	+ 2.526	+ 0.043	......
6.9	4	23 20 31.32	31.33	+ 2.584	+ 0.040	......
5.4	3	23 20 45.29	43.98	+ 2.461	+ 0.046	......
7.7	5	23 20 52.58	...	+ 2.694	+ 0.034	......

Ordinal Number.	Mean North Polar Distance 1845.0		Precession 1845.0.	Secular Variation.	Adopted Proper Motion.	Observations of N.P.D.			Names.	Oeltzen-Argelander Number.
R.	R.	G.				No. R.	Mean year. R.	G.		
	° ′ ″	″	″	″	″		1800 +			
6051	30 22 36.9	...	— 19.65	— 0.07	...	2	44.8	...	....	25458
6052	8 31 32.2	...	— 19.65	— 0.03	...	4	51.1	...	....	....
6053	11 50 52.1	57.9	— 19.66	— 0.04	...	3	45.5	13.8	....	25467
6054	36 1 58.7	56.9	— 19.66	— 0.07	...	2	52.8	13.9	....	....
6055	42 3 15.2	...	— 19.66	— 0.08	...	2	42.3	...	....	25477
6056	36 44 30.7	30.7	— 19.68	— 0.07	...	3	51.2	11.8	....	....
6057	36 37 35.9	35.5	— 19.68	— 0.07	...	4	46.3	11.9	....	....
6058	30 42 57.2	56.8	— 19.68	— 0.07	...	7	45.4	10.9	....	25495
6059	36 50 37.1	...	— 19.68	— 0.07	...	1	53.9	...	....	....
6060	36 49 11.2	6.6	— 19.69	— 0.07	...	4	45.3	11.8	....	....
6061	49 14 13.8	14.5	— 19.70	— 0.07	...	3	44.8	11.9	....	....
6062	33 18 53.3	54.3	— 19.70	— 0.07	...	5	47.9	9.9	....	....
6063	49 44 14.6	14.3	— 19.71	— 0.07	...	4	46.8	11.9	....	....
6064	35 39 55.5	56.0	— 19.71	— 0.07	...	3	50.8	14.0	....	....
6065	25 30 21.6	21.4	— 19.71	— 0.07	...	4	45.6	12.8	....	25534
6066	29 15 44.6	...	— 19.71	— 0.07	...	3	49.9	...	....	25537
6067	35 45 55.0	53.1	— 19.71	— 0.07	...	4	45.1	13.6	....	....
6068	34 44 42.3	42.3	— 19.71	— 0.07	...	4	45.8	10.2	....	25543
6069	28 34 4.0	4.0	— 19.72	— 0.07	...	6	45.2	7.9	4 Cassiopeiæ ..	25549
6070	37 52 16.4	16.9	— 19.72	— 0.07	...	4	44.1	11.8	....	25559
6071	37 29 21.9	...	— 19.72	— 0.07	...	3	47.9	...	....	25564
6072	37 40 24.5	22.7	— 19.72	— 0.07	...	4	48.3	11.3	....	25567
6073	29 25 0.9	1.9	— 19.73	— 0.07	...	3	45.2	14.8	....	25568
6074	89 35 32.5	...	— 19.73	— 0.08	+ 0.12	4	54.1	...	8 Piscium κ ...	....
6075	4 47 36.7	...	— 19.73	0.00	...	3	52.5	...	....	....
6076	37 41 3.9	1.6	— 19.73	— 0.07	...	4	46.9	11.8	....	25573
6077	29 45 53.8	54.3	— 19.73	— 0.07	...	3	45.8	14.8	....	....
6078	47 56 26.0	27.2	— 19.74	— 0.07	— 0.03	4	46.6	8.8	13 Andromedæ	....
6079	35 52 42.0	41.4	— 19.74	— 0.07	...	3	49.2	14.0	....	....
6080	20 10 5.1	6.9	— 19.75	— 0.06	...	4	44.8	12.8	....	25589
6081	35 59 13.9	13.8	— 19.74	— 0.07	...	3	47.2	13.9	....	....
6082	22 59 9.0	11.7	— 19.74	— 0.06	...	3	44.2	13.8	....	25600
6083	25 13 41.8	40.4	— 19.75	— 0.06	...	3	47.1	12.9	....	....
6084	20 29 33.8	33.4	— 19.76	— 0.06	+ 0.01	6	46.1	9.5	....	25609
6085	31 9 25.3	...	— 19.76	— 0.07	...	4	50.1	...	....	25612

Magnitude.	Estimates of Magnitude.	Mean Right Ascension 1845.0.		Precession 1845.0.	Secular Variation	Adopted Proper Motion.
R.	R.	R.	G.			
		h. m. s.	s.	s.	s.	s.
7.5	5	23 21 33.30	32.42	+ 2.326	+ 0.043	......
7.4	6	23 21 36.63	36.51	+ 2.776	+ 0.029	......
7.1	6	23 22 2.41	2.15	+ 2.845	+ 0.023	......
8.2	6	23 22 23.60	23.55	+ 2.866	+ 0.023	......
7.5	7	23 22 44.37	44.16	+ 2.728	+ 0.034	......
8.2	4	23 22 45.79	45.16	+ 2.849	+ 0.023	......
5.2	4	23 22 53.72	53.72	+ 2.729	+ 0.034	......
6.7	4	23 22 54.61	54.59	+ 2.300	+ 0.049	......
8.2	3	23 23 12.04	11.87	+ 2.870	+ 0.023	......
6.9	5	23 23 35.69	...	+ 2.645	+ 0.041	......
5.8	7	23 23 40.77	40.68	+ 2.903	+ 0.019	+ 0.026
8.4	4	23 23 42.44	42.41	+ 2.738	+ 0.034	......
7.3	4	23 23 58.96	...	+ 2.806	+ 0.038	......
7.1	13	23 24 6.84	...	+ 0.384	− 0.252	......
7.0	7	23 24 21.66	21.51	+ 2.876	+ 0.023	......
8.6	5	23 24 31.24	31.33	+ 2.857	+ 0.025	......
9.7	2	23 24 32.13	31.81	+ 2.878	+ 0.022	......
9.2	5	23 24 46.81	...	+ 2.517	+ 0.049	......
7.5	4	23 24 49.18	48.40	+ 2.182	+ 0.051	......
8.7	2	23 24 52.76	...	+ 2.473	+ 0.051	......
6.5	5	23 25 15.06	14.33	+ 2.639	+ 0.040	......
7.0	4	23 25 16.17	16.02	+ 2.804	+ 0.029	......
7.8	10	23 25 41.15	...	+ 0.719	− 0.188	......
7.1	5	23 25 47.58	46.34	+ 2.211	+ 0.051	......
7.0	5	23 25 56.39	...	+ 2.491	+ 0.052	......
7.3	4	23 25 59.90	...	+ 2.771	+ 0.034	......
6.7	6	23 26 20.84	20.98	+ 2.869	+ 0.026	......
6.8	3	23 26 26.78	26.59	+ 2.888	+ 0.023	......
8.6	5	23 26 48.59	48.34	+ 2.812	+ 0.031	......
7.9	2	23 27 1.53	2.13	+ 2.428	+ 0.054	......
5.7	4	23 27 3.32	3.06	+ 2.913	+ 0.020	......
7.5	16	23 27 7.38	...	+ 0.527	− 0.207	......
8.4	4	23 27 21.84	22.03	+ 2.874	+ 0.026	......
5.6	35	23 27 48.20	47.15	+ 0.052	− 0.475	+ 0.084
8.5	3	23 27 54.72	54.67	+ 2.835	+ 0.029	......

Ordinal Number.	Mean North Polar Distance 1845.0.		Precession 1845.0.	Secular Variation.	Adopted Proper Motion.	Observations of N.P.D.			Names.	Oeltzen-Argelander Number.
R.	R.	G.				No. R.	Mean year. R.	G.		
	° ′ ″	″	″	″	″		1800 +			
6086	16 44 4.1	5.5	— 19.77	— 0.04	...	4	45.3	9.9	....	25628 ?
6087	37 11 12.6	13.5	— 19.77	— 0.07	...	3	45.4	12.9	....	....
6088	44 23 16.0	15.8	— 19.78	— 0.07	...	5	48.2	11.9	....	....
6089	46 54 46.5	47.2	— 19.78	— 0.07	...	4	49.8	11.8	....	....
6090	32 18 19.7	19.4	— 19.79	— 0.06	...	4	45.8	10.8	....	....
6091	44 23 25.4	27.3	— 19.79	— 0.07	...	4	48.9	11.9	....	....
6092	32 18 18.5	18.8	— 19.79	— 0.06	— 0.02	4	43.8	9.8	....	....
6093	15 37 42.8	38.7	— 19.79	— 0.05	...	3	43.9	11.0	....	25663
6094	46 52 38.7	40.5	— 19.80	— 0.06	...	3	46.2	11.8	....	....
6095	26 27 43.2	...	— 19.80	— 0.06	...	4	43.1	...	....	....
6096	51 36 52.1	51.7	— 19.80	— 0.07	+ 0.05	4	43.1	9.8	14 Andromedæ	....
6097	32 26 20.0	19.5	— 19.80	— 0.06	...	3	47.1	10.9	....	....
6098	38 26 32.8	...	— 19.81	— 0.06	...	4	51.3	...	....	....
6099	4 26 9.4	...	— 19.81	— 0.01	...	6	52.0	...	....	....
6100	46 46 52.5	58.8	— 19.81	— 0.06	...	4	46.8	11.9	....	....
6101	44 4 11.9	11.7	— 19.81	— 0.06	...	3	50.5	13.8	....	25705
6102	47 1 55.1	53.9	— 19.81	— 0.06	...	3	49.9	11.9	....	....
6103	20 18 14.2	...	— 19.82	— 0.05	...	3	49.9	...	....	25711
6104	12 57 39.7	38.7	— 19.82	— 0.04	...	3	44.5	12.8	....	25712
6105	18 52 15.2	...	— 19.82	— 0.05	...	2	50.4	...	....	....
6106	25 6 59.2	58.4	— 19.83	— 0.06	...	4	45.3	9.9	....	25720
6107	37 10 6.7	7.5	— 19.83	— 0.06	...	3	47.1	12.9	....	....
6108	4 50 43.4	...	— 19.83	— 0.01	...	3	51.5	...	....	....
6109	13 2 10.9	10.3	— 19.83	— 0.03	...	4	45.4	12.8	....	25738
6110	18 51 15.1	...	— 19.84	— 0.05	+ 0.03	3	47.5	...	....	....
6111	33 26 47.5	...	— 19.84	— 0.06	...	2	53.3	...	....	....
6112	44 10 22.4	22.3	— 19.84	— 0.06	...	4	46.3	13.6	....	25747
6113	46 57 7.1	9.2	— 19.84	— 0.06	...	3	45.2	11.9	....	....
6114	36 47 16.8	17.4	— 19.85	— 0.06	...	2	50.8	11.3	....	....
6115	16 37 49.1	48.6	— 19.85	— 0.05	...	4	45.3	14.9	....	25762
6116	50 37 3.2	2.9	— 19.85	— 0.06	...	3	47.5	9.0	15 Andromedæ	....
6117	4 17 50.2	...	— 19.85	— 0.01	...	5	51.2	...	....	....
6118	43 59 45.1	44.5	— 19.85	— 0.05	...	2	51.4	13.3	....	25770
6119	3 32 52.8	53.1	— 19.86	0.00	— 0.01	31	49.5	7.7	3.g.阆f.⋀	....
6120	38 27 40.8	42.5	— 19.86	— 0.05	...	2	49.8	12.9	....	....

Magnitude. R.	Estimates of Magnitude. R.	Mean Right Ascension 1845.0. R.	G.	Precession 1845.0	Secular Variation.	Adopted Proper Motion.
		h. m. s.	s.	s.	s.	s.
6.8	4	23 28 1.98	1.60	+ 2.837	+ 0.029	......
8.2	5	23 28 7.28	6.81	+ 2.823	+ 0.031	......
7.2	5	23 28 12.64	11.73	+ 2.642	+ 0.046	......
7.0	3	23 28 17.49	...	+ 2.847	+ 0.029	......
5.5	6	23 28 17.91	17.25	+ 2.541	+ 0.054	......
7.5	5	23 29 18.08	...	+ 2.907	+ 0.023	......
8.6	5	23 29 30.00	30.29	+ 2.848	+ 0.030	......
7.4	3	23 29 30.62	30.02	+ 2.653	+ 0.051	......
7.4	20	23 29 35.24	...	+ 0.909	− 0.133	......
6.8	2	23 29 37.10	...	+ 3.114	− 0.009	+ 0.010
8.9	6	23 29 38.59	39.16	+ 2.490	+ 0.054	......
5.9	7	23 29 58.44	58.26	+ 2.904	+ 0.023	......
4.1	5	23 29 59.58	59.68	+ 2.892	+ 0.025	+ 0.017
7.2	3	23 30 27.31	26.40	+ 2.878	+ 0.026	......
7.1	6	23 30 29.15	28.94	+ 2.914	+ 0.023	......
3.9	4	23 30 32.90	32.64	+ 2.914	+ 0.023	......
6.9	7	23 31 3.15	3.09	+ 2.803	+ 0.037	......
7.0	3	23 31 33.55	...	+ 2.863	+ 0.031	......
5.3	7	23 31 38.71	38.64	+ 2.876	+ 0.029	......
9.2	5	23 31 50.48	51.38	+ 2.542	+ 0.060	......
7.8	6	23 31 53.74	53.33	+ 2.810	+ 0.040	......
4.5	4	23 31 58.82	...	+ 3.056	+ 0.001	+ 0.025
8.9	5	23 32 0.30	0.16	+ 2.538	+ 0.054	......
7.9	5	23 32 1.23	1.05	+ 2.921	+ 0.023	......
7.6	5	23 32 13.90	13.54	+ 2.810	+ 0.037	......
6.6	7	23 32 34.05	33.77	+ 2.497	+ 0.063	......
7.0	6	23 32 38.18	37.98	+ 2.759	+ 0.043	......
6.2	7	23 32 38.62	38.20	+ 2.545	+ 0.063	......
3.8	4	23 32 47.28	46.94	+ 2.920	+ 0.023	+ 0.004
9.0	4	23 32 50.91	50.28	+ 2.761	+ 0.043	......
3.2	1	23 33 2.00	1.64	+ 2.403	+ 0.070	− 0.020
7.0	2	23 33 7.43	...	+ 3.105	− 0.008	+ 0.009
7.4	4	23 33 14.62	14.24	+ 2.493	+ 0.066	......
7.1	8	23 33 25.47	25.34	+ 2.936	+ 0.023	......
6.5	5	23 33 53.83	53.62	+ 2.897	+ 0.026	......

Ordinal Number.	Mean North Polar Distance 1845.0.		Precession 1845.0.	Secular Variation.	Adopted Proper Motion.	Observations of N.P.D.			Names.	Oelzen-Argelander Number.
R.	R.	G.				No. R.	Mean year R.	Mean year G.		
	° ′ ″	″	″	″	″		1800 +			
6121	38 33 59.3	60.4	− 19.86	− 0.05	...	3	44.2	12.9	....	....
6122	36 50 27.8	27.2	− 19.86	− 0.05	...	3	52.2	11.3	....	25780
6123	23 21 54.6	54.7	− 19.86	− 0.05	...	4	48.3	9.3	....	25781
6124	39 35 34.7	...	− 19.86	− 0.06	...	3	53.2	...	....	25785
6125	19 12 52.3	52.3	− 19.86	− 0.05	− 0.01	5	44.6	10.0	....	....
6126	47 32 52.1	...	− 19.87	− 0.06	...	4	44.5	...	....	....
6127	38 34 19.6	18.0	− 19.87	− 0.05	...	2	48.4	12.9	....	....
6128	23 0 28.4	28.7	− 19.87	− 0.05	...	4	46.8	9.8	....	25813
6129	4 40 40.1	...	− 19.87	− 0.02	...	12	52.0	...	....	....
6130	103 55 6.6	...	− 19.88	− 0.06	− 0.02	2	51.8	...	....	....
6131	16 56 16.2	13.8	− 19.88	− 0.04	...	3	49.2	14.8	....	25816
6132	46 25 39.2	41.0	− 19.88	− 0.05	...	4	45.6	8 8	....	....
6133	44 22 51.6	52.2	− 19.88	− 0.05	+ 0.43	5	47.6	6.7	16 Androm. λ .	25831
6134	41 51 21.3	17.6	− 19.89	− 0.05	...	3	46.5	11.9	....	....
6135	47 46 46.0	43.9	− 19.89	− 0.05	...	3	47.8	11.9	....	....
6136	47 35 21.3	21.4	− 19.89	− 0.05	− 0.02	4	42.1	6.8	17 Androm. ι .	....
6137	32 12 11.6	12.0	− 19.89	− 0.04	...	4	45.3	10.8	....	....
6138	38 35 43.5	...	− 19.90	− 0.05	...	3	47.8	...	....	....
6139	40 23 11.1	11.4	− 19.90	− 0.05	...	4	45.6	9.0	18 Andromedæ	25864
6140	17 13 15.6	15.3	− 19.90	− 0.04	...	2	49.9	14.8	....	25869
6141	32 6 26.9	26.2	− 19.90	− 0.04	...	3	47.8	10.9	....	....
6142	85 12 47.0	...	− 19.90	− 0.05	+ 0.45	7	47.1	...	17 Piscium ι...	....
6143	17 0 43.0	43.9	− 19.91	− 0.04	...	2	49.4	14.8	....	25874
6144	47 31 31.9	31.0	− 19.91	− 0.05	...	3	49.8	11.9	....	....
6145	31 53 19.2	18.4	− 19.91	− 0.04	...	4	50.1	10.9	....	....
6146	15 33 57.9	58.6	− 19.91	− 0.04	...	5	48.9	15.9	....	....
6147	27 7 59.5	49.2	− 19.91	− 0.04	...	5	47.4	12.8	....	25886
6148	16 51 22.0	24.1	− 19.91	− 0.04	...	3	48.5	15.0	....	25887
6149	46 31 25.4	25.5	− 19.91	− 0.05	− 0.01	4	43.8	7.2	19 Androm. κ .	....
6150	27 6 31.7	28.1	− 19.91	− 0.04	...	2	51.9	12.8	....	25892
6151	13 13 58.2	57.2	− 19.92	− 0.04	− 0.15	19	48.2	6.8	35 Cephei γ...	25893
6152	102 32 23.6	...	− 19.92	− 0.05	− 0.04	2	53.3	...	....	....
6153	15 6 22.7	18.6	− 19.92	− 0.04	...	3	51.5	13.9	....	....
6154	49 0 29.9	32.6	− 19.92	− 0.05	...	3	47.9	11.8	....	....
6155	41 20 45.7	44.2	− 19.93	− 0.05	...	3	44.5	11.8	....	25917

Magnitude.	Estimates of Magnitude.	Mean Right Ascension 1845.0.		Precession 1845.0.	Secular Variation	Adopted Proper Motion.
R.		R.	G.			
		h. m. s.	s.	s.	s.	s.
8.4	5	23 34 2.87	3.13	+ 2.939	+ 0.023	......
5.3	1	23 34 8.29	...	+ 3.068	− 0.001	− 0.011
7.3	4	23 34 33.18	33.12	+ 2.528	+ 0.069	......
6.9	5	23 34 36.21	35.74	+ 2.928	+ 0.025	......
6.3	5	23 34 37.75	37.67	+ 2.927	+ 0.025	......
6.6	3	23 35 3.97	3.46	+ 2.777	+ 0.046	......
8.3	6	23 35 17.98	18.06	+ 2.592	+ 0.066	......
6.7	4	23 35 33.91	...	+ 2.886	+ 0.033	......
7.1	6	23 36 51.54	51.36	+ 2.882	+ 0.034	......
7.6	4	23 36 53.87	...	+ 2.993	+ 0.027	......
7.7	5	23 36 57.76	57.29	+ 2.881	+ 0.037	......
7.6	5	23 37 2.07	...	+ 2.934	+ 0.027	......
7.2	7	23 37 4.67	4.13	+ 2.946	+ 0.023	......
7.7	6	23 37 10.63	10.32	+ 2.884	+ 0.037	......
6.2	5	23 37 16.45	16.05	+ 2.881	+ 0.037	......
7.4	6	23 37 19.51	...	+ 2.914	+ 0.031	......
7.7	12	23 37 51.64	...	+ 1.703	− 0.083	......
4.8	5	23 38 22.11	21.88	+ 2.942	+ 0.027	......
7.3	4	23 38 26.37	...	+ 2.921	+ 0.043	......
8.0	1	23 38 34.69	...	+ 2.922	+ 0.043	......
7.8	4	23 39 1.65	...	+ 2.900	+ 0.037	......
7.7	2	23 39 15.75	...	+ 2.948	+ 0.027	......
7.8	6	23 39 17.73	...	+ 2.904	+ 0.037	......
4.8	5	23 39 30.38	29.99	+ 2.881	+ 0.040	+ 0.006
6.4	6	23 39 52.15	51.92	+ 2.949	+ 0.027	......
8.1	5	23 39 54.15	...	+ 2.952	+ 0.027	......
6.2	1	23 39 58.44	...	+ 3.077	− 0.003	+ 0.007
8.3	6	23 40 24.01	24.01	+ 2.973	+ 0.020	......
5.0	4	23 40 32.21	31.99	+ 2.803	+ 0.056	+ 0.006
7.6	7	23 40 37.48	37.15	+ 2.849	+ 0.049	......
7.9	7	23 40 49.85	49.74	+ 2.972	+ 0.023	......
8.1	6	23 40 55.39	...	+ 2.913	+ 0.037	......
9.4	7	23 41 10.12	...	+ 2.845	+ 0.051	......
6.5	5	23 41 10.85	10.46	+ 2.845	+ 0.051	......
5.7	6	23 41 19.06	18.83	− 2.871	+ 0.046	......

| Ordinal Number. | Mean North Polar Distance 1845.0. | | Precession 1845.0. | Secular Variation. | Adopted Proper Motion. | Observations of N.P.D. | | | Names. | Oelzen-Argelander Number. |
R.	R.	G.				No. R.	Mean year. 1800 + R.	G.		
	o ' "	"	"	"	"					
6156	49 4 30.5	32.7	— 19.93	— 0.05	...	2	48.9	13.8	....	....
6157	89 4 22.7	...	— 19.93	— 0.05	+ 0.17	5	51.4	...	18 Piscium λ..	....
6158	15 16 28.3	25.4	— 19.93	— 0.03	...	3	43.5	13.9	....	....
6159	46 6 9.7	9.5	— 19.93	— 0.05	...	4	45.3	11.9	....	....
6160	45 52 0.0	0.9	— 19.93	— 0.05	...	4	46.4	10.1	....	....
6161	26 20 38.0	37.0	— 19.94	— 0.04	...	4	45.8	9.9	....	....
6162	16 43 49.4	52.4	— 19.94	— 0.03	...	4	49.9	12.9	....	25952
6163	37 42 25.5	...	— 19.94	— 0.04	...	3	43.2	...	....	....
6164	35 39 11.7	10.4	— 19.95	— 0.04	...	5	45.2	10.5	....	....
6165	44 28 47.6	...	— 19.95	— 0.04	...	4	45.4	...	....	....
6166	35 22 8.7	6.6	— 19.95	— 0.04	...	4	42.6	10.9	....	....
6167	44 35 39.7	...	— 19.95	— 0.04	...	4	46.1	...	....	....
6168	47 6 51.6	51.6	— 19.95	— 0.04	...	4	46.3	11.8	....	....
6169	35 28 2.2	0.6	— 19.95	— 0.04	...	3	44.1	10.9	....	....
6170	35 3 37.5	36.2	— 19.95	— 0.04	...	3	43.5	12.0	....	....
6171	40 16 18.2	...	— 19.95	— 0.04	...	4	52.3	...	....	....
6172	5 23 27.2	...	— 19.95	— 0.02	...	3	50.9	...	....	....
6173	44 26 23.9	23.8	— 19.96	— 0.04	+ 0.01	6	45.2	6.8	20 Androm. ψ	....
6174	40 11 52.4	...	— 19.96	— 0.04	...	5	51.6	...	....	26002
6175	40 4 23.6	...	— 19.96	— 0.04	...	2	53.4	...	....	26006
6176	35 42 28.3	...	— 19.97	— 0.04	...	3	45.2	...	....	26011
6177	44 38 34.7	...	— 19.97	— 0.04	...	2	49.4	...	....	....
6178	35 59 57.7	...	— 19.97	— 0.04	...	3	44.8	...	....	26015
6179	32 12 40.5	40.5	— 19.97	— 0.04	— 0.06	5	43.2	7.4	5 Cassiopeiæ τ	26024
6180	44 1 41.4	41.7	— 19.97	— 0.04	...	4	44.1	11.8	....	....
6181	44 50 33.3	...	— 19.97	— 0.04	...	4	50.9	...	....	....
6182	93 37 24.8	...	— 19.97	— 0.04	— 0.02	2	53.3	...	20 Piscium	....
6183	49 45 8.7	10.6	— 19.98	— 0.04	...	3	44.5	13.3	....	....
6184	23 3 15.4	15.4	— 19.98	— 0.03	— 0.01	6	45.5	8.5	_[signature]_	26034
6185	27 2 37.4	37.1	— 19.98	— 0.03	...	4	47.6	12.3	....	....
6186	48 40 2.2	0.7	— 19.98	— 0.03	...	4	49.9	11.9	....	....
6187	35 12 43.8	...	— 19.98	— 0.04	...	3	49.2	...	....	26042
6188	25 58 15.1	...	— 19.98	— 0.03	...	4	46.3	...	....	26049
6189	25 59 3.6	3.3	— 19.98	— 0.03	...	4	43.8	10.8	....	26050
6190	28 38 49.4	47.7	— 19.99	— 0.03	...	5	46.2	9.5	6 Cassiopeiæ ..	26051

Magnitude.	Estimates of Magnitudes.	Mean Right Ascension 1845.0.		Precession 1845.0.	Secular Variation	Adopted Proper Motion.
R.	R.	R.	G.			
		h. m. s.	s.	s.	s.	s.
6.4	6	23 41 19.56	...	+ 2.888	+ 0.043	......
6.2	5	23 41 36.46	36.11	+ 2.898	+ 0.042	......
8.1	5	23 41 51.05	...	+ 2.920	+ 0.037	......
7.9	6	23 42 20.32	20.27	+ 2.882	+ 0.046	......
6.3	5	23 42 39.10	39.58	+ 2.946	+ 0.033	+ 0.028
7.9	5	23 42 45.94	...	+ 2.978	+ 0.025	......
6.9	5	23 42 52.39	52.94	+ 2.875	+ 0.049	......
7.2	6	23 42 58.01	57.85	+ 2.937	+ 0.037	......
7.6	8	23 43 11.55	11.53	+ 2.987	+ 0.020	......
6.6	6	23 43 26.53	26.51	+ 2.880	+ 0.051	......
7.4	4	23 43 46.63	46.38	+ 2.987	+ 0.023	......
6.7	7	23 44 35.68	...	+ 2.689	+ 0.095	......
6.3	4	23 44 55.03	52.04	+ 2.749	+ 0.089	......
7.2	5	23 45 12.08	12.13	+ 2.996	+ 0.020	......
9.0	7	23 45 23.26	...	+ 2.706	+ 0.088	......
6.4	6	23 45 25.54	25.08	+ 2.924	+ 0.046	......
9.8	3	23 45 30.18	...	+ 2.762	+ 0.081	......
6.6	7	23 45 48.73	48.91	+ 2.969	+ 0.033	+ 0.013
7.3	8	23 46 4.90	...	+ 2.992	+ 0.027	......
6.6	6	23 46 9.57	9.31	+ 2.930	+ 0.046	......
6.8	6	23 46 14.21	13.79	+ 3.006	+ 0.022	......
8.6	7	23 46 23.84	23.69	+ 2.993	+ 0.026	......
4.3	5	23 46 39.98	39.75	+ 2.952	+ 0.041	......
8.3	5	23 47 3.13	2.89	+ 2.971	+ 0.035	......
6.6	5	23 47 21.14	21.75	+ 2.820	+ 0.084	+ 0.027
6.4	6	23 47 44.95	44.50	+ 2.979	+ 0.034	......
6.4	4	23 47 45.46	45.26	+ 2.995	+ 0.029	.....
6.6	6	23 47 49.10	...	+ 2.963	+ 0.041	+ 0.003
7.0	6	23 47 49.16	49.09	+ 2.998	+ 0.029	......
6.9	6	23 47 59.48	59.27	+ 2.994	+ 0.029	......
8.3	5	23 48 40.77	40.63	+ 3.011	+ 0.023	
8.0	5	23 48 43.42	43.18	+ 2.983	+ 0.034	
7.7	5	23 48 46.47	46.98	+ 2.852	+ 0.083	
7.5	5	23 49 8.45	7.89	+ 3.005	+ 0.029	
6.6	4	23 49 8.50	...	+ 2.980	+ 0.041	

Ordinal Number.	Mean North Polar Distance 1845.0.			Precession 1845.0.	Secular Variation.	Adopted Proper Motion.	Observations of N.P.D.			Names.	Oeltzen-Argelander Number.
R.	R.		G.				No.	Mean year.			
							R.	R.	G.		
	° ′ ″		″	″	″	″		1800 +			
6191	30 52 58.7		...	— 19.99	— 0.03	— 0.02	3	47.8	...	....	......
6192	31 53 52.3		51.0	— 19.99	— 0.03	+ 0.02	4	45.4	10.0	....	26056
6193	35 12 10.0		...	— 19.99	— 0.03	...	4	47.3	...	....	26060
6194	28 38 50.3		50.4	— 19.99	— 0.03	...	4	45.4	9.8	....	26068
6195	39 14 20.3		21.5	— 19.99	— 0.03	...	4	45.8	8.8	....	......
6196	47 26 31.0		...	— 20.00	— 0.03	...	5	51.7	...	....	......
6197	27 7 4.8		4.6	— 20.00	— 0.03	...	5	48.8	12.8	....	26080
6198	36 39 42.8		39.0	— 20.00	— 0.03	...	4	47.3	12.C	....	......
6199	49 41 53.8		54.2	— 20.00	— 0.03	...	4	47.3	13.8	....	......
6200	26 52 37.0		37.4	— 20.00	— 0.03	...	5	46.2	12.8	....	26092
6201	48 46 44.0		43.4	— 20.00	— 0.03	...	3	44.8	11.9	....	......
6202	13 15 32.3		...	— 20.01	— 0.03	+ 0.10	5	49.3	...	....	26112
6203	15 19 12.1		13.7	— 20.01	— 0.03	...	4	44.3	12.9	....	......
6204	49 31 0.5		1.9	— 20.01	— 0.03	...	4	47.1	13.8	....	......
6205	13 10 41.8		...	— 20.01	— 0.03	...	3	52.2	...	....	26126
6206	30 9 27.1		27.9	— 20.01	— 0.03	...	5	43.9	10.9	....	......
6207	15 20 56.0		...	— 20.01	— 0.03	...	3	52.2	...	....	......
6208	39 20 21.9		25.4	— 20.02	— 0.03	...	5	46.6	8.3	....	26134
6209	46 18 23.0		...	— 20.02	— 0.03	...	4	51.4	...	....	......
6210	30 0 32.7		32.2	— 20.02	— 0.02	...	4	49.1	10.9	....	26145
6211	51 34 51.1		48.9	— 20.02	— 0.02	...	3	47.2	13.9	....	......
6212	45 59 40.7		40.5	— 20.02	— 0.02	...	4	48.4	11.8	....	......
6213	33 21 46.6		46.9	— 20.02	— 0.02	...	5	44.8	8.9	7 Cassiopeiæ ρ	26155
6214	37 21 51.1		50.2	— 20.02	— 0.02	...	3	46.5	12.8	....	......
6215	16 27 8.6		8.8	— 20.02	— 0.02	...	7	48.0	9 5	....	26168
6216	38 7 40.5		41.2	— 20.03	— 0.02	...	4	45.5	9.9	....	26178
6217	43 30 23.9		23.0	— 20.03	— 0.02	...	3	43.8	12.0	....	......
6218	33 27 1.9		...	— 20.03	— 0.02	— 0.05	4	47.3	...	....	26181
6219	44 30 14.2		12.7	— 20.03	— 0.02	...	4	49.8	14.1	....	26182
6220	42 38 23.8		20.5	— 20.03	— 0.02	...	3	46.5	11.9	....	26184
6221	48 20 37.5		38.3	— 20.03	— 0.02	...	4	49.9	13.8	....	......
6222	37 9 0.3		0.3	— 20.03	— 0.02	...	3	47.8	12.8	....	26197
6223	16 43 29.9		31.3	— 20.03	— 0.02	...	3	49.6	14.8	....	26199
6224	44 14 44.4		43.7	— 20.03	— 0.02	...	3	47.5	11.8	....	26201
6225	35 1 20.6		...	— 20.03	— 0.02	...	4	47.3	...	....	......

Mean Right Ascension 1845.0.		Precession 1845.0.	Secular Variation	Adopted Proper Motion.
R.	G.			
h. m. s.	s.	s.	s.	s.
23 49 12.94	12.86	+ 3.014	+ 0.026	....
23 49 17.73	16.59	+ 2.606	+ 0.155	+ 0.010
23 49 21.31	21.24	+ 2.982	+ 0.040	......
23 49 32.19	31.94	+ 3.004	+ 0.031	......
23 49 33.94	...	+ 2.964	+ 0.048	......
23 49 52.78	52.11	+ 2.877	+ 0.083	......
23 50 17.57	17.60	+ 3.004	+ 0.033	......
23 50 30.42	30.16	+ 3.027	+ 0.023	......
23 50 33.46	...	+ 3.003	+ 0.035	......
23 50 35.51	35.38	+ 3.014	+ 0.029	......
23 50 43.33	...	+ 3.004	+ 0.035	......
23 50 44.39	...	+ 3.074	− 0.003	− 0.008
23 50 51.42	51.08	+ 3.001	+ 0.037	......
23 50 51.56	52.02	+ 2.898	+ 0.083	......
23 50 54.69	54.57	+ 3.016	+ 0.029	......
23 50 59.16	58.87	+ 3.001	+ 0.037	......
23 51 0.30	0.31	+ 3.029	+ 0.023	......
23 51 9.77	9.76	+ 3.021	+ 0.026	......
23 51 10.36	10.32	+ 2.997	+ 0.040	......
23 51 11.54	11.57	+ 3.003	+ 0.034	......
23 51 12.28	12.04	+ 2.955	+ 0.060	......
23 51 21.28	...	+ 3.065	+ 0.003	+ 0.010
23 51 21.74	21.74	+ 3.004	+ 0.037	......
23 51 23.46	23.13	+ 3.011	+ 0.031	......
23 51 30.44	29.84	+ 3.012	+ 0.031	......
23 51 37.29	...	+ 2.990	+ 0.045	
23 52 7.58	7.56	+ 3.034	+ 0.023	
23 52 24.78	22.14	+ 2.462	+ 0.251	
23 52 41.17	...	+ 3.000	+ 0.048	
23 52 50.00	49.87	+ 3.029	+ 0.026	
23 52 51.72	...	+ 2.994	+ 0.052	+ 0.011
23 53 3.35	3.90	+ 2.979	+ 0.060	.....
23 53 14.85	...	+ 2.969	+ 0.071	......
23 53 23.54	...	+ 3.001	+ 0.049	
23 53 25.46	...	+ 3.026	+ 0.034	......

Ordinal Number. R.	Mean North Polar Distance 1845.0.		Precession 1845.0.	Secular Variation.	Adopted Proper Motion.	Observations of N.P.D.			Names.	Oeltzen-Argelander Number.
	R.	G.				No. R.	Mean year. R.	Mean year. G.		
	o ' "	"	"	"	"		1800 +			
6226	48 12 15.7	15.5	− 20.03	− 0.02	...	3	48.9	13.8	....	....
6227	7 40 18.0	20.8	− 20.03	− 0.02	...	4	48.4	7.9	....	....
6228	35 9 22.6	23.2	− 20.03	− 0.02	...	5	43.8	8.8	....	....
6229	42 34 54.3	54.0	− 20.03	− 0.02	...	3	51.2	11.9	....	26207
6230	29 50 12.1	...	− 20.04	− 0.02	...	3	44.9	...	....	26208
6231	16 59 47.1	47.5	− 20.04	− 0.02	...	3	49.2	14.8	....	26217
6232	40 25 32.8	38.6	− 20.04	− 0.02	− 0.09	3	44.9	10.8	....	26229
6233	51 53 54.0	52.4	− 20.04	− 0.02	...	3	53.2	13.9	....	....
6234	39 28 26.5	...	− 20.04	− 0.02	...	2	53.8	...	R Cassiopeiæ..	....
6235	44 33 15.1	16.3	− 20.04	− 0.02	...	4	51.3	13.9	....	26234
6236	39 22 20.8	...	− 20.04	− 0.02	...	2	53.4	...	....	....
6237	94 24 57.5	...	− 20.04	− 0.02	+ 0.12	6	52.3	...	27 Piscium	....
6238	37 28 32.1	31.3	− 20.04	− 0.02	...	3	46.5	12.8	....	26239
6239	17 12 18.8	17.6	− 20.04	− 0.02	...	2	52.4	14.9	....	26240
6240	44 26 58.2	59.0	− 20.04	− 0.02	...	3	47.2	14.0	....	26242
6241	37 11 26.7	22.1	− 20.04	− 0.02	...	2	46.8	12.8	....	26244
6242	51 45 1.5	58.4	− 20.04	− 0.02	...	2	48.4	13.9	....	....
6243	46 17 55.2	55.5	− 20.04	− 0.02	...	3	54.2	13.8	....	....
6244	35 6 28.0	27.5	− 20.04	− 0.02	− 0.03	4	41.1	8.8	8 Cassiopeiæ σ	26247
6245	37 36 36.6	34.3	− 20.04	− 0.02	...	3	52.8	12.8	....	26248
6246	24 2 52.8	52.5	− 20.04	− 0.02	...	2	51.3	14.9	....	26249
6247	83 59 41.4	...	− 20.04	− 0.02	+ 0.13	8	45.6	...	28 Piscium ω..	....
6248	37 17 56.6	55.9	− 20.04	− 0.01	...	4	47.8	12.9	....	26252
6249	40 20 0.7	58.8	− 20.04	− 0.01	...	3	46.8	10.8	....	26254
6250	40 21 17.0	18.2	− 20.04	− 0.01	...	3	49.2	10.9	....	26258
6251	33 11 27.1	...	− 20.04	− 0.01	...	3	51.5	...	....	26259
6252	52 0 11.7	12.4	− 20.04	− 0.01	...	2	49.3	11.9	....	....
6253	4 9 24.1	23.4	− 20.04	− 0.01	...	18	48.9	7.9	*[handwritten] Cephei*	....
6254	31 18 9.4	...	− 20.04	− 0.01	...	2	47.5	...	....	....
6255	45 36 35.8	36.4	− 20.04	− 0.01	...	2	45.4	15.9	....	....
6256	28 41 7.3	...	− 20.04	− 0.01	...	3	52.6	...	....	26279
6257	24 0 56.2	58.2	− 20.04	− 0.01	...	3	47.1	14.9	....	26282
6258	21 17 14.8	...	− 20.04	− 0.01	...	3	51.1	...	....	26286
6259	30 30 28.0	...	− 20.04	− 0.01	...	3	51.8	...	....	26287
6260	40 52 51.7	...	− 20.04	− 0.01	...	2	48.9	...	....	26289

Magnitude.	Estimates of Magnitude.	Mean Right Ascension 1845.0.		Precession 1845.0.	Secular Variation	Adopted Proper Motion.
R.	R.	R.	G.			
		h. m. s.	s.	s.	s.	s.
7.3	4	23 53 29.63	29.09	+ 3.004	+ 0.049	......
7.0	7	23 53 39.51	39.83	+ 3.035	+ 0.029	......
5.1	3	23 53 44.54	44.17	+ 3.006	+ 0.049	......
6.4	5	23 53 47.51	47.17	+ 2.954	+ 0.089	......
6.1	3	23 53 49.32	48.98	+ 3.038	+ 0.026	......
5.3	2	23 53 52.72	...	+ 3.073	− 0.002	......
4.8	2	23 54 0.66	...	+ 3.074	− 0.004	+ 0.002
7.5	5	23 54 12.31	12.06	+ 3.038	+ 0.029	......
8.3	3	23 54 18.29	18.21	+ 3.032	+ 0.031	......
6.3	3	23 54 24.34	23.98	+ 3.104	+ 0.049	......
7.4	3	23 54 27.62	27.48	+ 3.032	+ 0.034	......
7.7	4	23 54 31.67	31.91	+ 2.998	+ 0.066	......
6.2	2	23 54 42.17	...	+ 3.003	+ 0.062	......
7.9	4	23 54 44.68	...	+ 3.004	+ 0.062	......
8.0	1	23 54 47.31	47.26	+ 3.043	+ 0.026	......
8.1	5	23 54 49.00	...	+ 2.619	+ 0.314	......
7.7	5	23 54 54.75	...	+ 2.855	+ 0.188	− 0.006
7.1	3	23 55 12.28	11.96	+ 3.045	+ 0.026	......
7.5	5	23 55 30.25	30.61	+ 2.988	+ 0.086	......
8.2	4	23 55 32.49	32.22	+ 3.036	+ 0.037	......
7.5	3	23 55 35.87	...	+ 3.048	+ 0.026	......
8.2	3	23 55 42.40	41.86	+ 3.003	+ 0.074	......
7.0	4	23 55 46.21	46.08	+ 3.043	+ 0.031	......
7.6	5	23 55 47.39	46.95	+ 3.049	+ 0.026	......
7.8	5	23 55 50.36	50.16	+ 3.010	+ 0.069	......
6.5	6	23 55 55.32	55.44	+ 3.017	+ 0.063	......
9.1	3	23 56 3.64	...	+ 3.044	+ 0.035	......
7.6	4	23 56 13.00	12.63	+ 3.045	+ 0.034	......
7.5	5	23 56 13.95	13.87	+ 3.045	+ 0.034	......
5.7	3	23 56 16.96	16.41	+ 3.033	+ 0.051	......
8.4	7	23 56 21.65	21.46	+ 3.051	+ 0.026	......
6.3	5	23 56 39.92	39.64	+ 3.053	+ 0.026	......
5.8	5	23 56 41.80	41.78	+ 3.026	+ 0.066	......
7.3	2	23 56 44.41	44.02	+ 3.019	+ 0.077	......
6.9	5	23 56 57.09	...	+ 3.042	+ 0.046	......

Ordinal Number.	Mean North Polar Distance 1845.0.		Precession 1845.0.	Secular Variation.	Adopted Proper Motion.	Observations of N.P.D.			Names.	Oeltzen-Argelander Number.
						No.	Mean year.			
R.	R.	G.				R.	R.	G.		
	° ′ ″	″	″	″	″		1800 +			
6261	30 1 26.1	25.9	— 20.04	— 0.01	...	3	45.5	10.9	....	....
6262	46 11 11.8	12.5	— 20.04	— 0.01	...	2	51.4	13.8	....	....
6263	29 38 25.3	25.0	— 20.04	— 0.01	...	3	44.5	9.1	....	26297
6264	17 15 4.1	3.9	— 20.04	— 0.01	...	3	44.1	14.8	....	26299
6265	48 29 45.7	44.1	— 20.04	— 0.01	...	4	45.8	9.9	....	....
6266	93 53 26.6	...	— 20.05	— 0.01	...	1	53.7	...	29 Piscium	....
6267	96 52 32.7	...	— 20.05	— 0.01	+ 0.04	2	52.8	...	30 Piscium	....
6268	46 19 49.3	49.7	— 20.05	— 0.01	...	3	47.6	13.8	....	....
6269	41 5 29.4	27.1	— 20.05	— 0.01	...	3	51.2	12.9	....	....
6270	30 9 34.2	32.8	— 20.05	— 0.01	...	4	48.1	10.6	....	26313
6271	40 21 48.3	49.5	— 20.05	— 0.01	...	2	44.8	10.9	....	26315
6272	23 41 56.9	56.6	— 20.05	— 0.01	...	3	52.5	15.0	....	....
6273	24 45 51.5	...	— 20.05	— 0.01	— 0.01	2	47.9	...	....	26321
6274	24 45 45.5	...	— 20.05	— 0.01	...	2	50.9	...	....	26322
6275	47 56 30.4	30.4	— 20.05	— 0.01	...	2	49.8	11.9	....	....
6276	3 49 52.2	...	— 20.05	— 0.01	...	3	52.2	...	....	....
6277	7 53 23.6	...	— 20.05	— 0.01	— 0.02	3	48.9	...	....	....
6278	48 6 53.7	54.0	— 20.05	— 0.01	...	3	46.5	11.9	....	....
6279	17 41 19.7	22.5	— 20.05	— 0.01	...	2	44.8	14.8	....	26335
6280	37 33 1.1	0.4	— 20.05	— 0.01	...	3	48.9	12.8	....	....
6281	48 30 32.6	...	— 20.05	— 0.01	...	2	53.4	...	....	....
6282	20 33 26.0	25.9	— 20.05	— 0.01	...	2	47.4	15.8	....	....
6283	42 25 32.9	32.7	— 20.05	— 0.01	...	3	46.6	13.9	....	26343
6284	48 50 23.1	24.4	— 20.05	— 0.01	...	2	52.3	11.9	....	....
6285	21 59 10.2	9.7	— 20.05	— 0.01	...	3	45.3	15.9	....	26345
6286	24 9 2.5	2.1	— 20.05	— 0.01	...	4	48.4	14.7	....	26346
6287	41 10 9.2	...	— 20.05	— 0.01	...	3	54.2	..	....	....
6288	40 52 28.8	28.1	— 20.05	— 0.01	...	4	51.1	12.9	....	....
6289	40 59 34.2	32.6	— 20.05	— 0.01	...	3	47.2	13.0	....	....
6290	28 34 32.6	31.6	— 20.05	0.00	...	3	43.9	8.8	9 Cassiopeiæ ..	....
6291	48 16 33.3	36.2	— 20.05	0.00	...	5	53.1	11.9	....	....
6292	48 46 10.7	10.4	— 20.05	0.00	...	3	44.9	12.0	....	....
6293	23 41 51.9	53.8	— 20.05	0.00	...	4	46.8	14.9	....	....
6294	20 22 41.0	41.9	— 20.05	0.00	...	3	51.8	15.8	....	....
6295	32 19 50.7	...	— 20.05	0.00	+ 0.03	3	49.2	...	....	....

Ordinal Number.		Magnitude.	Estimates of Magnitude.	Mean Right Ascension 1845.0.			Precession 1845.0.	Secular Variation	Adopted Proper Motion.	Observations of R.A.		
R.	G.	R.	R.	R.		G.				No.	Mean year.	
										R.	R.	G.
				h. m. s.		s.	s.	s.	s.		1800 +	
6296	...	7.9	3	23 57	0.18	...	+ 3.049	+ 0.036	......	2	51.3	...
6297	4222	5.5	4	23 57	7.73	7.45	+ 3.041	+ 0.051	......	4	48.0	10.9
6298	4223	6.8	4	23 57	12.88	12.64	+ 3.054	+ 0.029	......	3	47.8	15.9
6299	4225	7.1	3	23 57	19.81	19.32	+ 3.031	+ 0.069	......	2	48.8	15.9
6300	4224	8.4	4	23 57	20.42	20.19	+ 3.053	+ 0.031	......	2	51.3	13.9
6301	...	5.1	6	23 57	24.08	...	+ 3.072	− 0.003	+ 0.002	10	52.4	...
6302	4226	7.3	2	23 57	24.97	25.19	+ 3.053	+ 0.031	......	2	49.4	12.9
6303	...	7.7	3	23 57	31.89	...	+ 3.053	+ 0.036	......	3	50.1	...
6304	4227	7.4	4	23 57	36.54	36.11	+ 3.052	+ 0.037	......	2	51.9	12.8
6305	4228	8.3	4	23 57	43.19	42.97	+ 3.057	+ 0.026	......	2	51.8	13.8
6306	4229	8.0	4	23 57	58.84	59.10	+ 3.057	+ 0.034	......	3	45.6	12.9
6307	4230	8.2	4	23 58	0.20	0.32	+ 3.059	+ 0.029	......	3	50.7	13.9
6308	4231	8.7	3	23 58	4.91	4.69	+ 3.056	+ 0.046	......	2	51.9	12.8
6309	...	6.3	4	23 58	11.23	...	+ 3.053	+ 0.047	......	2	48.9	...
6310	4232	8.1	5	23 58	18.96	19.00	+ 3.046	+ 0.071	......	3	51.8	15.8
6311	4233	5.6	5	23 58	25.60	25.01	+ 3.052	+ 0.060	......	3	44.9	9.4
6312	...	8.2	5	23 58	37.14	...	+ 3.049	+ 0.078	......	3	49.6	...
6313	4234	7.9	4	23 59	6.85	6.66	+ 3.054	+ 0.091	......	3	51.9	14.8
6314	...	8.5	7	23 59	7.18	...	+ 2.996	+ 0.399	......	4	53.9	...
6315	4235	8.0	6	23 59	24.62	25.07	+ 3.062	+ 0.074	......	3	49.3	15.9
6316	4236	7.3	7	23 59	38.20	38.00	+ 3.068	+ 0.023	......	4	48.3	11.9
6317	4237	6.8	2	23 59	39.24	39.17	+ 3.068	+ 0.023	......	3	47.5	11.9

Ordinal Number.	Mean North Polar Distance 1845.0.		Precession 1845.0.	Secular Variation.	Adopted Proper Motion.	Observations of N.P.D.			Names.	Oeltzen-Argelander Number.
	R.	G.				No. R.	Mean year R.	Mean year G.		
	° ′ ″	″	″	″	″		1800 +			
6296	39 40 57.7	...	— 20.05	0.00	...	2	43.4	...	....	......
6297	29 32 57.0	58.7	— 20.05	0.00	...	4	43.1	10.9	....	26369
6298	45 37 59.1	59.3	— 20.05	0.00	...	2	51.8	15.9	....	......
6299	21 58 45.0	45.6	— 20.05	0.00	...	3	44.5	15.9	....	26371
6300	42 23 6.1	6.5	— 20.05	0.00	...	2	52.4	13.9	....	26372
6301	96 34 29.0	...	— 20.05	0.00	— 0.03	2	52.9	...	33 Piscium	......
6302	41 5 27.1	24.6	— 20.05	0.00	...	3	52.2	12.9	....	......
6303	40 20 32.6	...	— 20.05	0.00	...	3	47.1	...	....	......
6304	37 41 28.8	29.0	— 20.05	0.00	...	3	45.9	12.8	....	......
6305	46 23 38.8	37.1	— 20.05	0.00	...	3	52.5	13.8	....	......
6306	41 14 27.6	26.6	— 20.05	0.00	...	2	45.4	12.5	....	......
6307	46 7 24.5	22.8	— 20.05	0.00	...	3	47.9	13.5	....	......
6308	37 35 10.0	9.7	— 20.05	0.00	...	2	52.4	12.8	....	......
6309	32 25 40.4	...	— 20.05	0.00	— 0.01	3	48.2	...	....	......
6310	22 13 36.4	34.3	— 20.05	0.00	...	3	50.9	15.8	....	......
6311	26 40 0.8	0.4	— 20.05	0.00	...	4	46.0	9.4	10 Cassiopeiæ.	26386
6312	20 41 37.5	...	— 20.05	0.00	...	2	49.4	...	....	......
6313	17 39 7.6	10.1	— 20.05	0.00	...	3	45.6	14.3	....	26408
6314	4 4 30.1	...	— 20.05	0.00	...	6	52.6	...	....	......
6315	21 47 0.0	58.6	— 20.05	0.00	...	4	46.3	15.7	....	......
6316	50 47 2.1	3.8	— 20.05	0.00	...	3	46.5	11.9	....	......
6317	50 42 50.9	51.3	— 20.05	0.00	...	4	49.1	11.9	....	......